D1484438

The Widow Barnaby by Franc

IN THREE VOLUMES

Frances Milton Trollope was born on March 10th, 1779 at Stapleton in Bristol.

The mother of the world famed Anthony Trollope, and his brother Thomas Adolphus Trollope, she was a late entrant to the ranks of authors being fifty when she embarked upon this new career, and even then more by necessity for income than by design.

Her first book, in 1832, Domestic Manners of the Americans, gained her immediate notice. Although it was a one sided view of the failings of Americans, it was also witty and acerbic.

But much of the attention she received was for her strong novels of social protest. Jonathan Jefferson Whitlaw, published in 1836, was the first anti-slavery novel, and was a great influence on the American writer Harriet Beecher Stowe and her more famous Uncle Tom's Cabin in 1852. Michael Armstrong: Factory Boy began publication in 1840 and was the first industrial novel to be published in Britain.

These were followed by three volumes of The Vicar of Wrexhill, which examined the corruption in the Church of England and evangelical circles.

However her greatest work is more often considered to be the Widow Barnaby trilogy (published between 1839–1843).

In later years Frances Milton Trollope continued to write novels and books on wide, varied and miscellaneous subjects, writing in all in excess of a quite incredible 100 volumes.

Frances Milton Trollope died on October 6th, 1863.

Index of Contents
VOLUME I

CHAPTER I - INTRODUCTION TO THE FAMILY OF THE FUTURE MRS. BARNABY—FINANCIAL DIFFICULTIES—MATERNAL LOVE—PREPARATIONS FOR A FETE
CHAPTER II - A SISTERLY VISIT, AND A CHEERFUL RECEPTION—THE RETREAT OF A RURAL HEIRESS—INTERESTING CONVERSATION—AN UNSATISFACTORY LETTER
CHAPTER III - GRAPHIC DESCRIPTION OF THE MOST INTERESTING OF THE SILVERTON LOCALITIES—A RENCONTRE NOT UNEXPECTED—A SUCCESSFUL MANOEUVRE
CHAPTER IV - A WEDDING, AND ITS CONSEQUENCES—A TRANSFER OF PROPERTY—MISS MARTHA RECEIVES A PROPOSAL OF MARRIAGE—ANOTHER EXPEDITION TO COMPTON BASETT
CHAPTER V - A VISIT FROM THE HEIRESS—MISS AGNES WILLOUGHBY IS SENT TO SCHOOL
CHAPTER VI - WEDDED HAPPINESS—DEATH OF MRS. COMPTON—THE EX-CURATE BROUGHT INTO A PEACEFUL HARBOUR—HE FALLS SICK, AND HIS SISTER AND GRANDCHILD ARE SUMMONED
CHAPTER VII - THE ELEGANCE OF MRS. BARNABY DISPLAYED—ITS EFFECT ON HER AUNT BETSY—INTERVIEW BETWEEN THE BROTHER AND SISTER
CHAPTER VIII - SOLITARY MEDITATION AND IMPORTANT RESOLUTIONS—AGNES WILLOUGHBY ARRIVES AT SILVERTON—HER GRANDFATHER GIVES HER HIS BLESSING, AND DIES—MISS COMPTON MAKES A SUDDEN RETREAT

CHAPTER IX - MR. BARNABY PAYS A VISIT TO COMPTON BASETT, AND RECEIVES FROM THE HEIRESS A FORMAL CONGÉ—AGNES IS SENT BACK TO SCHOOL, AND REMAINS THERE TILL CALLED HOME BY THE NEWS OF HIS DEATH

CHAPTER X - THE WIDOW BARNABY ENTERS ACTIVELY ON HER NEW EXISTENCE—HER WEALTH—HER HAPPY PROSPECTS—MRS. WILMOT VISITS MISS COMPTON, AND OBTAINS LEAVE TO INTRODUCE AGNES WILLOUGHBY

CHAPTER XI - AN IMPORTANT CORRESPONDENCE, AND AN IMPORTANT INTERVIEW

CHAPTER XII - CHOOSING A LADY'S-MAID—A HAPPY MEETING UNHAPPILY BROKEN IN UPON—MISS COMPTON UTTERS A LONG FAREWELL TO AGNES

CHAPTER XIII - MRS. BARNABY SETS FORTH ON HER TRAVELS—THE READER TAKES LEAVE OF MISS COMPTON—MRS. BARNABY ENJOYS HER JOURNEY, AND ARRIVES SAFELY AT EXETER

CHAPTER XIV - HOW TO CHOOSE LODGINGS—REASONS FOR LAYING ASIDE WIDOW'S WEEDS—LADY-LIKE ACCOMPLISHMENTS—AFFECTIONATE FORETHOUGHT—CHARMING SENSIBILITY—GENEROUS INTENTIONS—A CLEVER LETTER, BUT ONE UPON WHICH DOCTORS MAY DISAGREE

CHAPTER XV - THE ENTRÉE OF MRS. BARNABY IN MRS. PETERS'S DRAWING-ROOM—FAMILY CONSULTATIONS— ARRANGEMENTS FOR MISS WILLOUGHBY'S DRESS FOR SOME TIME TO COME

CHAPTER XVI - MRS. PETERS BECOMES UNEASY, BUT CONTRIVES TO ATTAIN HER OBJECT—A PLEASANT WALK DISCOVERED TO BE A GOOD MEANS OF MAKING A PARTY OF YOUNG PEOPLE ACQUAINTED WITH EACH OTHER—MRS. PETERS SHEWS MUCH PROMPTITUDE AND EXPERIENCE IN TAKING LODGINGS —SHE ALSO DISCOVERS THE BEST MODE OF LIONIZING A LADY WHO IS TOO BEAUTIFUL—ANOTHER COUNTRY WALK IMPROVES THE INTIMACY BETWEEN THE YOUNG LADIES.

CHAPTER XVII - MRS. BARNABY TAKES POSSESSION OF HER LODGINGS, AND SETS ABOUT MAKING HERSELF COMFORTABLE—SHE OPENS HER PLANS A LITTLE TO AGNES, AND GIVES HER SOME EXCELLENT ADVICE—THE COMFORT OF A MIDSUMMER FIRE—THE APARTMENT OF AGNES SET IN ORDER—A LECTURE ON USEFULNESS—VIRTUOUS INDIGNATION

CHAPTER XVIII - CONDITIONS OF AN AGREEMENT BETWEEN MRS. PETERS AND HER DAUGHTERS —MRS. BARNABY BEGINS HER FASHIONABLE CAREER UNDER THE PROTECTION OF MISS ELIZABETH —SHE REHEARSES A BALL IN HER HEART AS SHE EXAMINES THE ROOM—THE LIBRARY.

VOLUME II

CHAPTER I - DIFFICULTIES ATTENDING A YOUNG LADY'S APPEARANCE AT A BALL—A WET SUNDAY—DIFFERENCE OF TASTE

CHAPTER II - THE BALL

CHAPTER III - MELANCHOLY MEDITATIONS—AN EVENTFUL WALK—A PLEASANT BREAKFAST—A COMFORTABLE CONVERSATION IN A CLOSET

CHAPTER IV - A TETE-A-TETE IN A DRAWING-ROOM—AUTOBIOGRAPHY—A REMARKABLE DISCOVERY CONCERNING THE DUKE OF WELLINGTON

CHAPTER V - A YOUNG LADY'S PLOT—A CONSULTATION, AND THE HAPPY RESULT OF IT—A TERRIBLE INTERRUPTION, AND A DANGEROUS EXPEDITION—CONFIDENTIAL INTERCOURSE

CHAPTER VI - THE READER IS LET INTO A SECRET, AND THE YOUNG LADY'S PLOT PROVED TO BE OF NO AVAIL—A JUDICIOUS MODE OF OBTAINING INFORMATION—A HAPPY AND VERY WELL-TIMED MEETING.

CHAPTER VII - TRANSIENT HAPPINESS—AN ACCIDENT, LEADING TO THE DISCOVERY OF AN UNKNOWN TALENT IN MISS WILLOUGHBY, AND UNEXPECTED APPRECIATION OF IT IN COLONEL HUBERT—SOME REFLECTIONS ON THE PECULIARITIES OF THE FEMALE MIND.

CHAPTER VIII - SOME FARTHER PARTICULARS RESPECTING THE STATE OF MRS. BARNABY'S HEART—TENDER DOUBTS AND FEARS, ON THE PART OF THE MAJOR, ALL SET TO REST BY THE GENTLE KINDNESS OF THE WIDOW—SOME ACCOUNT OF MRS. PETERS'S CONCERT, AND OF THE TERRIBLE EVENTS WHICH FOLLOWED IT.

CHAPTER IX - MAJOR ALLEN PAYS A VISIT AT BATH PRODUCTIVE OF IMPORTANT RESULTS—SYMPATHY BETWEEN HIMSELF AND THE WIDOW BARNABY—EXCHANGE IS NO ROBBERY—VALEDICTORY COMPLIMENTS.

CHAPTER X - A DISAGREEABLE BREAKFAST-TABLE—MR. STEPHENSON GIVES HIS FRIEND COLONEL HUBERT WARNING TO DEPART—A PROPOSAL, AND ITS CONSEQUENCES.

CHAPTER XI - MRS. BARNABY FEELS CONSCIOUS OF IMPROVEMENT, AND REJOICES AT IT—HOPES FOR THE FUTURE—A CONVERSATION IN WHICH MUCH GENEROUS SINCERITY IS DISPLAYED—A LETTER INTENDED TO BE EXPLANATORY, BUT FAILING TO BE SO

CHAPTER XII - A LUCKY ESCAPE—A MELANCHOLY PARTING—MRS. BARNABY SETTLES HERSELF AT CHELTENHAM —HER FIRST SORTIE—BOARDING-HOUSE BREAKFAST—A NEW ACQUAINTANCE—A MEDICAL CONVERSATION

CHAPTER XIII - THE ACQUAINTANCE RIPENS INTO FRIENDSHIP—USEFUL INFORMATION OF ALL SORTS—AN EXCELLENT METHOD OF TALKING FRENCH, ATTENDED WITH LITTLE LABOUR AND CERTAIN SUCCESS—A COLLECTOR—A SALE-ROOM—A PEER OF THE REALM

CHAPTER XIV - A CHELTENHAM BALL—AN INTRODUCTION—A CONQUEST

CHAPTER XV - NEW HOPES BEGET A NEW STYLE OF EXISTENCE—A PARTY—AGNES HAS SOME SUCCESS, WHICH MRS. BARNABY DOES NOT QUITE APPROVE—LORD MUCKLEBURY ENTERS INTO EPISTOLARY CORRESPONDENCE WITH THE WIDOW, BY WHICH HER HOPES ARE RAISED TO THE HIGHEST PITCH—BUT LORD MUCKLEBURY LEAVES CHELTENHAM

VOLUME III

CHAPTER I - MRS. BARNABY LOSES HER SENSES, AND RECOVERS THEM—SHE TAKES A DESPERATE RESOLUTION—MISS MORRISON PROVES HERSELF A FRIEND IN NEED—AGNES FINDS CONSOLATION IN SORROW

CHAPTER II - MRS. BARNABY EFFECTS HER RETREAT FROM CHELTENHAM—SHE CARRIES WITH HER A LETTER—ITS EFFECT—AN AMIABLE ATTORNEY—SPECIMENS OF A NOBLE STYLE OF LETTER-WRITING— CONSOLATION

CHAPTER III - A BOLD MEASURE—A TOUR DE FORCE ON THE PART OF MRS. BARNABY, AND OF SAVOIR FAIRE ON THAT OF LORD MUCKLEBURY—SIGHT-SEEING—THE WIDOW RESOLVES UPON ANOTHER JOURNEY

CHAPTER IV - AN ADVENTURE—ANOTHER LETTER FROM MISS MORRISON PRODUCTIVE OF A POWERFUL EFFECT UPON HER BROTHER—HE FORSAKES HIS CLIENT AND HIS FRIEND—AGNES IS LEFT ALONE, AND EMPLOYS SOME OF HER LEISURE IN WRITING A LETTER TO MISS COMPTON

CHAPTER V - AGNES RECEIVES AN UNEXPECTED VISITER, AND AN IMPORTANT COMMUNICATION —SHE ALSO RECEIVES A LETTER FROM CHELTENHAM, AND FROM HER AUNT BARNABY

CHAPTER VI - AGNES RECEIVES ANOTHER UNEXPECTED VISIT—MRS. BARNABY RETURNS TO HER LODGINGS AND CATCHES THE VISITER THERE

CHAPTER VII - AGNES ELOPES WITH HER AUNT BETSY

CHAPTER VIII - AGNES APPEARS LIKELY TO PROFIT BY THE CHANGE OF AUNTS

CHAPTER IX - BRINGS US BACK, AS IT OUGHT, TO MRS. BARNABY

CHAPTER X - GIVES SOME ACCOUNT OF COLONEL HUBERT'S RETURN TO CHELTENHAM

CHAPTER XI - AGNES APPEARS AT CLIFTON IN A NEW CHARACTER

CHAPTER XII - A PARTY—A MEETING—GOOD SOMETIMES PRODUCTIVE OF EVIL

CHAPTER XIII - DEMONSTRATING THE HEAVY SORROW WHICH MAY BE PRODUCED BY A YOUNG LADY'S HAVING A LARGER FORTUNE THAN HER LOVER EXPECTED

CHAPTER XIV - RETURNS TO MRS. BARNABY, AND RELATES SOME OF THE MOST INTERESTING AND INSTRUCTIVE SCENES OF HER LIFE, TOGETHER WITH SEVERAL CIRCUMSTANCES RELATIVE TO ONE DEARER TO HER THAN HERSELF

CHAPTER XV - AGNES GROWS MISERABLE—AN EXPLANATORY CONVERSATION WITH COLONEL HUBERT LEAVES HER MORE IN THE DARK THAN EVER—A LETTER ARRIVES FROM FREDERIC STEPHENSON

CHAPTER XVI - A DISCOVERY SCENE—PRODUCTIVE OF MANY NEW RELATIONS, AND VARIOUS OTHER CONSEQUENCES

CHAPTER XVII - GREAT CONTENTMENT

CHAPTER XVIII - A RETROSPECT AND CONCLUSION

VOLUME I

CHAPTER I

INTRODUCTION TO THE FAMILY OF THE FUTURE MRS. BARNABY—FINANCIAL DIFFICULTIES
—MATERNAL LOVE—PREPARATIONS FOR A FETE

Miss Martha Compton, and Miss Sophia Compton, were, some five-and-twenty years ago, the leading beauties of the pretty town of Silverton in Devonshire.

The elder of these ladies is the person I propose to present to my readers as the heroine of my story; but, ere she is placed before them in the station assigned her in my title-page, it will be necessary to give some slight sketch of her early youth, and also such brief notice of her family as may suffice to make the subsequent events of her life, and the persons connected with them, more clearly understood.

The Reverend Josiah Compton, the father of my heroine and her sister, was an exceedingly worthy man, though more distinguished for the imperturbable tranquillity of his temper, than either for the brilliance of his talents or the profundity of his learning. He was the son of a small landed proprietor at no great distance from Silverton, who farmed his own long-descended patrimony of three hundred acres with skilful and unwearied industry, and whose chief ambition in life had been to see his only son Josiah privileged to assume the prefix of reverend before his name. After three trials, and two failures, this blessing was at last accorded, and his son ordained, by the help of a very good-natured examining chaplain of the then Bishop of Exeter.

This rustic, laborious, and very happy Squire lived to see his son installed Curate of Silverton, and blessed with the hand of the dashing Miss Martha Wisett, who, if her pedigree was not of such respectable antiquity as that of her bridegroom, had the glory of being accounted the handsomest girl at the Silverton balls; and if her race could not count themselves among the landed gentry, she enjoyed all the consideration that a fortune of one thousand pounds could give, to atone for any mortification which the accident of having a ci-devant tallow-chandler for her parent might possibly occasion.

But, notwithstanding all the pride and pleasure which the Squire took in the prosperity of this successful son, the old man could never be prevailed upon by all Mrs. Josiah's admirable reasonings on the rights of primogeniture, to do otherwise than divide his three hundred acres of freehold in equal portions between the Reverend Josiah Compton his son, and Elizabeth Compton, spinster, his daughter.

It is highly probable, that had this daughter been handsome, or even healthy, the proud old yeoman might have been tempted to reduce her portion to the charge of a couple of thousand pounds or so upon the estate; but she was sickly, deformed, and motherless; and the tenderness of the father's heart conquered the desire which might otherwise have been strong within him, to keep together the fields which for so many generations had given credit and independence to his race. To leave his poor little Betsy in any degree dependent upon her fine sister-in-law, was, in short, beyond his strength; so the home croft, and the long fourteen, the three linny crofts, the five worthies, and the ten-acre clover bit, together with the farm-house and all its plenishing, and one half of the live and dead farming stock, were bequeathed to Elizabeth Compton and her heirs for ever—not perhaps without some hope, on the part of her good father, that her heirs would be those of her reverend brother, also; and so he died, with as easy a conscience as ever rocked a father to sleep.

But Mrs. Josiah Compton, when she became Mrs. Compton, with just one half of the property she anticipated, waxed exceeding wroth; and though her firm persuasion, that "the hideous little crook-back could not live for ever," greatly tended to console and soothe her, it was not without very constant reflections on the necessity of keeping on good terms with her, lest she might make as "unnatural a will as her father did before her," that she was enabled to resist the temptation of abusing her openly every time they met; a temptation increased, perhaps, by the consciousness that Miss Betsy held her and all her race in the most sovereign contempt.

Betsy Compton was an odd little body, with some vigour of mind, and frame too, notwithstanding her deformity; and as the defects in her constitution shewed themselves more in her inability to endure fatigue, than in any pain or positive suffering, she was likely to enjoy her comfortable independence considerably longer, and considerably more, than her sister thought it at all reasonable in Providence to permit.

The little lady arranged her affairs, and settled her future manner of life, within a very few weeks after her father's death, and that without consulting brother, sister, or any one else; yet it may be doubted if she could have done it better had she called all the parish to counsel.

She first selected the two pleasantest rooms in the house for her bed-room and sitting-room, and then skilfully marked out the warmest and prettiest corner of the garden, overlooking some of her own rich pastures, with the fine old grey tower of Silverton in the distance, as the place of her bower, her flower-garden, and her little apiary. She then let the remainder of her house, and the whole of her well-conditioned dairy-farm, for three hundred pounds a-year, with as much waiting upon as she might require, as much cream, butter, milk, and eggs, as she should use, and as much fruit and vegetables as her tenants could spare—together with half a day's labour every week for her tiny flower-garden.

She had no difficulty in finding a tenant upon these terms; the son of a wealthy farmer in the neighbourhood had a bride ready as soon as he could find a farm-house to put her into, and a sufficient dairy upon which to display her well-learned science. Miss Betsy's homestead was the very thing for them. The bride's portion was five hundred pounds for the purchase of the late Squire Compton's furniture and the half of his fine stock of cows, &c. &c. the which was paid down in Bank of England notes within ten minutes after the lease was signed, and being carefully put into the funds by Miss Betsy, became, as she said to herself (but to nobody else), a sort of nest egg, which, as she should only draw out the interest to lay it in again in the shape of principal, would go on increasing till she might happen to want it; so that, upon the whole, the style and scale of her expenses being taken into consideration, it would have been difficult to find any lady, of any rank, more really and truly independent than Miss Betsy.

She felt this, and enjoyed it greatly. Now and then, indeed, as she remembered her old father, and his thoughtful care for her, her sharp black eyes would twinkle through a tear; but there was more softness than sorrow in this; and a more contented, or, in truth, a more happy spinster might have been sought in vain, far and near, notwithstanding her humped back.

Far different was the case of those who inherited the other moiety of the estate called Compton Basett. The reverend Josiah, indeed, was himself too gentle and kind-hearted to feel anger against his father, or a single particle of ill-will towards his sister; yet was he as far from sharing her peace and contentment as his disappointed and vituperative wife. How, indeed, can any man hope to find peace and contentment, even though he has passed the rubicon of ordination, and has been happy enough to marry the favourite flirt of ten successive regiments, if he be never permitted to close his eyes in sleep till he has been scolded for an hour, and never suffered to wake at any signal, save the larum of his lady's tongue.

It was in vain that day and night he continued submissively to reiterate the phrases, "to be sure, my dear," ... "certainly," ... "there is no doubt of it," ... "he ought not to have done so, my love," ... "you are quite right, my dear," ... and the like. All this, and a great deal more, submission and kindness was in vain; Mrs. Compton's complainings ceased not, and, what was harder still, she always contrived by some ingenious mode of reasoning to prove that all the mischief which had happened was wholly and solely her husband's fault.

Mean while the two little girls sent to bless this union of masculine softness and feminine hardness, grew on and prospered, as far as animal health went, just as much as if their father were not taking to smoking and hot toddy as a consolation for all his sorrows, or their mother to a system of visiting and gossiping, which left her no time, had she possessed the talent, to do more for their advantage than take care that they had enough to eat. They were very fine on Sundays, or whenever their ma' expected company; and not too dirty at other times to pass muster at the day-school, at which they were destined to receive all the education which fate intended for them.

Miss Betsy, little as she admired her sister-in-law, and dearly as she loved her sunny garden in summer and her snug chimney-corner in winter, now and then left both to pass a few hours in Silverton; for she loved her brother, despite the weakness of character which appeared to her keen faculties to be something very nearly approaching fatuity; and being as well aware as the prettiest young lady in the town could be, that she was herself totally unfit to be married, she looked to his children with the interest with which human beings are apt to consider those who must become the possessors of all they leave behind.

For many years Miss Betsy looked forward with hope for one of two greatly desired events. That most coveted was the death of her sister-in-law; the other, and for many years the most probable, was the birth of a male heir to her brother.

But time wore away, and both were abandoned. Had it been otherwise, had Miss Betsy seen a male Compton ready to unite in his own person all the acquired and inherited honours of his twaddling father, and all the daily increasing hoard that she was herself accumulating, her temper of mind would probably have been very different. As it was, she looked upon the little girls as much more belonging to their mother than to their father; and the steady thriftiness, which, had it been pursued for the sake of a nephew, would have had some mixture of generous devotion in it, now that its result could only benefit nieces, by no means very dearly loved, seemed to threaten the danger of her becoming saving for mere saving's sake.

There was, however, in the heart of Miss Betsy much to render such an incrustation of character difficult; but there was also much to displease her in those who alone could claim her kindness on the plea of kindred; so that the most acute observer might have been at a loss to say what tone her vexed temper might finally take towards them.

Nevertheless, the two young sisters, at the respective ages of fifteen and seventeen, were as forward and handsome girls as ever drew the attention of a country town. They were equally handsome, perhaps, though very unlike. Martha was tall, dark-eyed, fresh-coloured, bold-spirited, and believed in her heart that she was to be called "my lady," and to drive in a coach and four. Sophia, the younger girl, was less tall and less bright-coloured; her hair was light, and her eyes, though their lashes were black, were of the softest grey. Her chief beauty, however, consisted in a complexion of great delicacy, and a mouth and teeth that could hardly be looked at without pleasure, even by cross Miss Betsy herself.

Miss Martha Compton was a young lady endowed with a vast variety of brilliant talents. She could dance every night, and very nearly all night long, though she had only learned for six weeks; she could make pasteboard card-boxes and screens, work satin-stitch, and (like most other clever young ladies bred in a country town abounding with officers) quote the oft profaned lyrics of Tom Moore.

The reputation of her sister for talents rested on a basis much less extended; it would indeed have been a false concord to talk of her talents, for she had but one in the world. Untaught, and unconscious of the power nature had bestowed, she sang with the sweet shrillness of the lark, and had science been set to work upon her for six months, Silverton might have boasted one of the finest native voices in the kingdom.

Mrs. Compton was proud of both her daughters, and however difficult it might be to procure shoes and gloves out of an income of somewhat less than four hundred pounds a-year, the winter balls of Silverton never opened till the Miss Comptons were ready to stand up.

Had she been a little less brutally cross to her poor husband, Mrs. Compton would really at this time have been almost interesting from the persevering industry and ingenuity with which she converted the relics of her own maiden finery into fashionable dancing-dresses for her girls. And on the whole the Miss Comptons were astonishingly well-dressed; for, besides the above-mentioned hoards, every article of the family consumption was made to contribute to the elegance of their appearance. Brown sugar was substituted for white at the morning and the evening meal; the butcher's bills were kept down wonderfully by feeding the family upon tripe twice a-week ... the home-brewed was lowered till the saving in malt for one year bought two glazed calico slips, four pair of long white gloves, and a bunch of carnations for Martha and of lilies for Sophia. Nothing, in short, was over-looked or forgotten that could be made to distil one drop of its value towards decorating the beauties of Silverton.

Few subjects have furnished more various or more beautiful images for the poet's pen than maternal fondness. From the heart-stirring fury of the dauntless lioness when her young ones are threatened, down to the patient hen red-breast as she sits abroad, lonely, fasting, and apart from all the joys of birdhood, awaiting the coming life of her loved nestlings ... in short, from one extremity of animal creation to the other, volumes of tender anecdotes have been collected illustrative of this charming feature of female nature; and yet much still remains to be said of it. Where is the author who has devoted his power of looking into the human heart, to the task of describing the restless activity, the fond watchfulness, the unwearied industry of a proud, poor, tender mother, when labouring to dress her daughters for a ball? Who has told of the turnings, the dyings, the ironings, the darnings, that have gone to make misses of ten pounds a-year pin-money look as smart as the squanderer of five hundred? Yet such things are: the light of morning never steals into the eyes of mortals to spur them on again to deeds of greatness after nightly rest, without awaking many hundred mothers whose principal business in life is to stitch, flounce, pucker, and embroider for their daughters!... All this is very beautiful!... I speak not of the stitching, flouncing, puckering, and embroidering ... but of the devotion of the maternal hearts dedicated to it.... All this is very beautiful!... yet never has gifted hand been found to bring forth in delicate penciling, traits such as these with half the study that has been often bestowed on the painting a cobweb. This is unjust.

Great, however, as were Mrs. Compton's exertions for the establishment of her daughters by the ways and means above described, her maternal efforts were not confined to these: for their sakes she on one occasion armed herself for an enterprise which, notwithstanding the resolute tone of her character, cost her some struggles. This desperate undertaking, which was nothing less than the penetrating to the rarely-invaded retreat of Miss Betsy, for the purpose of asking her to give the girls a little money, was occasioned by a great event in the annals of Silverton.

The officers of the — regiment, a detachment of which had been quartered there for a twelvemonth, gallantly determined to give the neighbouring families a fête before they left the town, in return for the hospitalities they had received. I am writing of the year 1813, a period when the palmy days of country quarters still existed, and many may still remember the tender sensibilities excited by a departing regiment, and the gay hopes generated by an arriving one. Either of these events were well-calculated to chase the composure of spirits arising from the unbroken routine of ordinary existence, and it may easily be imagined that, upon an occasion where the effects of both were brought to act upon the hearts and souls of a set of provincial fair ones at the same moment, the emotions produced must have been of no ordinary nature.

Such was the case at the fête given by the first battalion of the — regiment on their leaving Silverton; for, as it chanced that they were to be replaced by the second battalion of the same corps, the compliment intended for the neighbourhood was so arranged as to be shared by the officers who were about to be introduced to it; and thus an immense mass of joys and sorrows, regrets and hopes, tears and smiles, all came into action at once; and volumes might be filled in the most interesting manner, solely in describing the states of mind produced in the most charming portion of the inhabitants of twenty-seven of the principal houses of Silverton and its vicinity.

"It was so quite unlike any other party that ever was given," as Mrs. Compton well observed, in talking over the matter with her daughters, "that it was downright impossible not to make some difference in the way of preparing for it."

"Different!... I believe it is different!" exclaimed Miss Martha; "it is the first ball we ever showed ourselves at by daylight, and I should like to know how we, that always lead everything, are to present ourselves in broad sunshine with dyed pink muslin and tarnished silver?"

"You can't and you shan't," replied her affectionate mother, "if I sell the silver spoons and buy plated ones instead.... I will not have my girls disgraced in the face of two regiments at once. But, upon my life, girls, money is not to be had for the asking; for truth it is, and no lie, that there is not above twenty pounds in the bank to last till Michaelmas, and the butcher has not been paid these five months. But don't look glum, Martha!... Shall I tell you what I have made up my mind to do?"

"Carry a plate round the mess-room, mamma, when they are all assembled, perhaps," replied the lively young lady, "and if you asked for aid for the sake of our bright eyes, it is likely enough you might get something; but if it is not that, what is it, mother?"

"Why, I will walk over to Compton Basett, Martha, and ask the ram's-horn, your aunt, for five pounds outright, and tell her into the bargain what it is for, and, stingy and skinflint as she is, I can't say that I shall be much surprised if she gives it; for she is as proud as she's ugly; and it won't be difficult to make her see, this time, that I am asking more for credit's sake than for pleasure."

"Go, mother, by all means," replied the young lady with a sneer, that seemed to indicate despair of any aid from Miss Betsy. "All I know is, that she never gave me anything since I was born but a bible and prayer-book, and it don't strike me as very likely she'll begin now. Set off, however, by all manner of means, and if you come back empty-handed, I'll tell you what my scheme shall be."

"Tell me now, Martha," said the mother. "It's no joke, I can tell you, striding over the hill this broiling day. I don't want to go for nothing, I promise you. Tell us your scheme, girl, at once."

"Why, if I was you, mother, I would go to Smith's shop, and tell him confidentially that I wanted a little more credit, and that everything would be sure to be settled at Christmas."

"That won't do, Martha Compton. Your father has given him a bill already for thirty pounds, due in November, and it is a chance if it gets honoured, I promise you. Smith knows too much about our money matters to be caught napping."

"Well then, set off, mother! I'd offer to go with you, only I know that Captain Tate will be sure to be walking on the Hatherton Road, and I shouldn't wonder yet if he was to come out with a proposal."

"Oh! never mind me, child, I can go alone, and that's what you can't do, my dear.... You must take Sophy with you, mind that, and don't get talked of just as the new set are coming in."

"Nay, for that matter, Sophy will be as likely to meet Willoughby as I shall be to meet Tate, so there is no fear I should have to go alone."

"Well!... take care of yourselves, and don't let the sun get to tan your necks, mind that."

Having given these parting injunctions, Mrs. Compton set forth upon her expedition, the result of which shall be given in the next chapter.

CHAPTER II

A SISTERLY VISIT, AND A CHEERFUL RECEPTION—THE RETREAT OF A RURAL HEIRESS—INTERESTING CONVERSATION—AN UNSATISFACTORY LETTER

Mrs. Compton said no more than the truth, when she declared that it was no joke to walk from Silverton to Compton Basett in the dog-days. A long shadeless hill was to be mounted, several pastures, beautifully open to the sun, with all their various stiles, were to be conquered, and finally a rough stony lane, that might have crippled the hoof of a jackass, was to be painfully threaded before she could find herself at Miss Betsy's door. Yet all this she undertook, and all this she performed, strengthened by the noble energy of maternal love.

On reaching at length the comfortable, well-conditioned abode of her husband's rural ancestors, she so far suspended her steadfast purpose as to permit herself to drop into a deliciously cool woodbine-covered seat in the porch, and there indulged the greatly-needed luxuries of panting and fanning herself at her ease for a few minutes, before she set to work on the stony heart of the spinster.

Just as she was beginning to think that it was time her rest should end, and her important labour begin, a curly-headed little girl, of some eight or nine years old, came from the house, and very civilly asked her "What she pleased to want?"

"I want to see Miss Betsy ... can't you go to her, my little girl, and tell her that her sister, Mrs. Compton, is come to pay her a visit?"

"Yes, ma'am," replied the child, "there she is, you can see her, if you please to look this way ... there ... at the end of the long walk, where you see the bit of grass-plat and the two elm trees. Miss Betsy always sits in her bower in a sun-shiny morning watching the bees."

"Well!... trot away to tell her Mrs. Compton is coming, and then she won't be surprised, you know."

The child did as she was bid, tripping lightly along a well-kept gravel walk which led to the grass-plat, while Mrs. Compton followed with sedater step behind.

How the announcement of her arrival was received by the little spinster she could not judge, though she was at no great distance when it was made; but her messenger having entered beneath the flowery shelter of Miss Betsy's bower, both parties were effectually concealed from her sight, and despite the profound contempt she constantly expressed for the "little fright," she paused at some paces from the entrance, to await the child's return.

The interval was not long; but though her little envoy speedily reappeared, she brought no message, and silently pointing to the bower, ran back towards the house.

Mrs. Compton looked after her, as if she had rather she would have remained; but she called her courage (of which she had usually a very sufficient stock) to aid her in meeting "the ugly little body's queer ways," and marched forward to the encounter.

A few steps brought her to the front of Miss Betsy's bower, and there she saw the still happy heiress seated on a bench, which, though it might upon occasion hold two persons, had nevertheless very much the comfortable air of an arm-chair, with a last year's new novel on a little table before her (a subscription to a library at Exeter being one of her very few expensive indulgences).

Miss Betsy's dress was always as precisely neat and nice as that of a quaker; and on the present occasion no bonnet concealed the regular plaiting of her snow-white muslin cap, which, closely fitting round her pale but intelligent features, was so peculiarly becoming, that her visitor muttered in her heart, "She can dress herself up, nasty crooked little thing, and we shall soon see if she has generosity enough to make her nieces look half as smart."

"Good morning to you, sister Betsy," it was thus she began the difficult colloquy that she was come to hold. "You look charming well to-day, with your beautiful cap, and your pretty arbour, and your book, and your arm-chair, and all so very snug and comfortable.... Ah, goodness me! nobody knows but those who have tried, what a much finer thing it is to be single than married!"

"Did you come all the way from Silverton, Mrs. Compton, to tell me that?" said the lady of the bower, pointing to a stool that stood at the entrance.

"Why no, sister Betsy, I can't say I did," replied Mrs. Compton, seating herself. "I am come upon an errand not over agreeable, I assure you—neither more nor less than to talk of your poor brother's troubles and difficulties; and what is worst of all, I don't feel over sure that you will care anything about it."

"And what makes you think that, Mrs. Compton?" said Miss Betsy in a sort of cheerful, clear voice, that certainly did not evince any painful acuteness of sympathy.

"How can I think that you care much about him, or any of us, sister Betsy, since 'tis months and months that you have never come near us?... I am sure we often talk of you, and wish you would be a little more sociable."

"That is exceedingly obliging, Mrs. Compton," replied Miss Betsy in the same cheering, happy tone of voice, "and I should be very wrong not to oblige you, if I could fancy that my doing so could be of any real use or service. But to tell you the truth, I suspect that my poor brother likes to have a better dinner when I am at table than when I am not; and if all's true that gossips tell about his butcher's bill, that can be neither right nor convenient; ... and as for you, Mrs. Compton, and the young ladies, I greatly doubt if my frequent appearance among you would contribute much to your intimacy with the officers."

"You talk very strangely, sister Betsy.... I am sure I was not thinking of the officers at all, but only of how glad we always were to see you."

"That is very kind, indeed!" replied the provoking spinster in the same happy voice; "and I assure you that I do believe my brother likes to see me very much, and what is more remarkable still, I have more than once fancied that my niece Sophy looked rather pleased when I came in."

"And so did Martha, I am sure, ... and so did I, sister Betsy; you can't deny that: ... then why don't you come to see us oftener?"

"For no reason in the world," replied Miss Betsy gaily, "but because I like to stay at home better."

"So much the worse for us, ... so much the worse for us, sister Betsy.... If you had been to see us, you must have found out what I am now come to tell you, and that is, that poor dear Josiah is in very great difficulty indeed; and though we generally, I must say, bear all our hardships remarkably well, yet just at this time it comes upon us with unbearable severity."

"Does it indeed, Mrs. Compton?... But you have never yet turned your head to look at my bees; ... for my part, I can sit and watch them by the hour together, if my book is not too interesting: ... careful little fellows! It is but just three o'clock," (standing up as she spoke to look out upon a sundial that glittered in the middle of the grass-plat,) "but just past three, and they are beginning to come home with their work already."

Mrs. Compton felt what the French call desoutée, but she recovered herself, and returned to the charge.

"You are a happy woman, sister Betsy," said she, "with nothing to care about but your books and your bees!"

"I am very happy indeed!" replied the maiden, in an accent that well befitted the words; "and so are my bees too, for it is beautiful weather, and one can almost see the flowers grow, they come on so finely."

"But I want to talk to you, sister Betsy, about our troubles.... You don't know how I slave and fag to make our poor girls look like somebody.... No Saturday night ever comes that I do not sit up till past midnight striving to make their things decent for Sunday!"

"Do you indeed, Mrs. Compton?... I was told that they wore pink bows in their bonnets last Sunday, and green the Sunday before; ... but I did not know that you sat up to change them."

"Change them!... God bless you!... I wish that was all I have got to do.... Why, I had to wash those pink ribbons, and then dip them in saucer pink, and then rub them very nearly dry, till my poor arms almost came off, and then iron them, and then sew in the wire ribbon again, and then make them up.... I'll leave you to judge how much sleep I was likely to get; for I could not have the bonnets till after the girls came home from the evening parade, where they had been with Mrs. Colonel Williamson—they never go to parade without one of the regimental ladies as a chaperon."

"But why don't the young ladies rub their ribbons a little themselves?" asked Miss Betsy.

"Oh! that would not answer at all, sister Betsy. Why, that very Saturday night they were at a musical party at Colonel Williamson's, and Sophy was the principal lady singer. She and that elegant young Willoughby always sing together, and the best judges in Silverton say it is as fine as anything in London."

"Well, that's very nice indeed, Mrs. Compton, ... and I don't suppose she could well rub her ribbons while she was singing."

As she said this, Miss Betsy's eye returned, as if drawn by some strong attraction (as had been often the case before since the conversation began) to the volume that lay open on the little table before her. Mrs. Compton became desperate, and rising from her stool, approached the table, and boldly closed the book.

"Upon my word, you must hear what I have got to say, sister Betsy, and leave alone reading for a minute or so, while I talk to you of what concerns the honour of your family."

"The honour of the family?..." said the spinster in an accent of some alarm, employing herself, however, in finding her place again, and then putting a mark in it. "I hope you have got nothing very bad to tell me about the young ladies, Mrs. Compton?"

"Nothing in the world but good, sister Betsy, if you will but lend us a helping hand, once and away.... You seem to know all the news, and therefore I dare say you have heard that the first battalion of the — are to go to Plymouth on the seventeenth, and that the second battalion are to march into Silverton on the same day; so the colonels have agreed that a fête, a public breakfast and dancing to the band, in tents, in a field behind the Spread Eagle, shall be given by the officers of the first battalion on the sixteenth, and that all or nearly all the officers of the second battalion shall have leave to come forward one day's march to join it, and be introduced to all the neighbourhood. Now, just fancy our girls being invited to such a party as this, and not having a dress in the world that they can go in.... Just tell me what you think of this, sister Betsy?"

"Not having had much experience in such matters, Mrs. Compton, I really am quite at a loss to guess what it is that young ladies are likely to do in such a case."

"Don't you think it would be very natural, sister Betsy, to turn towards some kind, generous, rich relation, and ask their help out of such a strait?... don't you think this would be natural and right, sister Betsy?"

"Yes, very natural and right indeed, Mrs. Compton."

"Thank God!... then all our troubles are at an end!... Dear, blessed, sister Betsy!... ten pounds, ten pounds will be quite enough for us all, and buy a pair of new black stockings for Josiah into the bargain, in case he should like to go."

Miss Betsy made no reply, but drawing the table a little towards her, opened her book, and began to read.

"It's a long walk I have to go, sister," resumed Mrs. Compton, "and I shall be particularly glad to get home; ... so, will you have the kindness to give me the money at once?"

"Ma'am?..." said Miss Betsy, looking up with a most innocent expression of countenance.

"Whatever sum you may be pleased to grant us, sister Betsy, I beg and entreat you to give me directly."

"So I would, Mrs. Compton, without a moment's delay," replied Miss Betsy, with the most cheerful good-humour, "only I don't intend to give you any money at all."

"Oh! isn't that treachery?... isn't that cruelty?" exclaimed the agitated matron, wringing her hands. "Did not you say, sister Betsy, that it would be the most natural and right thing in the world to ask one's rich relations in such a moment as this?"

"But I never said it would be right to ask me, Mrs. Compton."

"But you meant it, if you did not say it, and that I'm sure you can't deny, ... and isn't it hard-hearted to disappoint me now?"

"It is a great deal more hard-hearted in you, Mrs. Compton, to take upon you to say that I am rich. I am a poor crooked ram's-horn of a body, as you know well enough, and I want the comfort and the consolation of all the little countrified indulgences that my good father provided for me by his will. You were a beauty, Mrs. Compton, and your daughters are beauties, and it must be a great blessing to be a beauty; but when God denied me this, he gave me a kind-hearted father, who took care that if I could not have lovers, I should have wherewithal to do tolerably well without them; and I am not going to fly in the face of Providence, or of my father either, in order to dress you and your daughters up to please the officers. So now, Mrs. Compton, I think you had better go home again."

"And is this the way you treat your poor brother's children, Miss Betsy?... your own flesh and blood!... and they, poor girls, sitting at home in the midst of their faded, worn-out trumpery, and thinking what a disgrace they shall be to the name of Compton in the eyes of all the country, if their aunt Betsy won't come forward to help them!"

"Stop a minute, Mrs. Compton, and I will help them in the best manner I can. But I must go into my own room first, and you may sit here the while."

"Will you give me a draught of milk; sister Betsy?" said the again sanguine visitor, "my mouth is perfectly parched."

The same little girl who had acted as her usher was again within call, and Miss Betsy summoned her by name.

"Go to your mother, Sally, and desire her to spare me a pennyworth of fresh milk; and here, my dear, is the money to pay for it. Don't drop it, Sally."

"Dear me, sister Betsy, I don't want to put you to the expense of a penny for me; ... I thought that you had milk allowed you in your rent."

"And so I have, as much as I can use. But you are not me, Mrs. Compton; and I make a great point of being just and exact in all ways.... And now I will go for what I promised you."

In about ten minutes the little lady returned with something in her hand that looked like a sealed letter.

"Please to give this to my nieces, Mrs. Compton, with my good wishes for their well doing and happiness; and now, if you please, I will wish you good morning, for I am rather tired of talking. Don't open that letter, but give it sealed to your daughters. Good morning, Mrs. Compton."

Miss Betsy then carefully took up the empty cup which her visitor had drained, and returned to the house, leaving her sister-in-law to set off upon her homeward walk in a condition painfully balancing between hope and fear; nevertheless she obeyed the command she had received, and delivered the letter unopened into the hands of her daughter Martha.

That young lady tore it asunder by the vehemence of her haste to obtain information as to what it might contain, but Miss Sophia, who was of a more gentle nature, quietly took the dissevered parts, and having carefully placed them side by side upon the table, read as follows:

"NIECE MARTHA AND NIECE SOPHIA,

"Your mother tells me that you are greatly troubled in your minds as to what dresses you shall appear in at a fête, or entertainment, about to be given by some officers. She tells me that your dresses are all very dirty, wherefore I hereby strongly advise you never on any account to put them on again till such time as they shall be made clean; for it is by no means an idle proverb which says, 'Cleanliness is next to godliness.' Your mother spoke also of some articles which, as she said, it would be necessary for you to put on upon this occasion, all of which you possessed, but in a state greatly faded—which means, as I take it, that they have lost their colour by exposure to the sun; observing, (what is indeed very obviously true,) that as this fête or entertainment is to be given by daylight, the loss of colour in these articles would, if seen at such a time, become particularly conspicuous. It is therefore her opinion, and it is in some sort mine also, that the wearing such faded apparel would be exposing yourselves to the unpleasant observations of your richer, cleaner, and smarter neighbours. For which reason my opinion is, (and I shall be very glad if it prove useful to you,) that you avoid such a disagreeable adventure, by staying at home.

"I am your aunt,

"ELIZABETH COMPTON."

The effect likely to be produced by such a communication as this, upon ladies in the situation of Mrs. Compton and her daughters, must be too easily divined to require any description; but the resolution taken in consequence of it by Miss Martha, being rather more out of the common way, shall be related in a chapter dedicated to the subject.

GRAPHIC DESCRIPTION OF THE MOST INTERESTING OF THE SILVERTON LOCALITIES—A RENCONTRE NOT UNEXPECTED—A SUCCESSFUL MANOEUVRE

After uttering a few of those expressions which, by a very remarkable sort of superstition, most nations of the civilized world hold to be a relief under vexation, Miss Martha Compton resumed the bonnet and parasol which she had but recently laid aside, and without consulting either mother or sister, who were occupied in a reperusal of Miss Betsy's epistle, she sallied forth, and deliberately took her way in a direction leading towards the barracks, which were situated close by the turnpike that marked the entrance to the town.

Let it not be supposed, however, that the young lady had any intention of entering within the boundary of that region, whose very name is redolent to all provincial female hearts as much of terror as of joy; she had no such desperate measure in her thoughts. Nor was there need she should; for between the curate's dwelling and the barrack-yard there was a three-cornered open space, planted with lime trees, displaying on one side some of the handsomest shops in the town, among which were the pastry-cook's and the circulating library, (both loved resorts of idle men,) and beneath the trees a well-trodden, a very well-trodden walk, rarely or never without some lounging red coat to enliven its shade. When it is added, that in this open space the band played morning and evening, all the world will be aware that if not the centre, it was decidedly the heart of Silverton, for to and from it the stream of human life was ever flowing, and all its tenderest affections were nourished there.

Being by necessity obliged to pass along this walk, or the pavement which skirted the road beside it, Miss Martha Compton had no occasion whatever to enter the barrack-yard, or even to approach its enclosure, in order to ensure meeting, within the space of any given hour before mess-time, any officer she might wish to see.

There was at this particular epoch much of constancy in the feelings of the fair Martha; for though she had parted from Captain Tate only three-quarters of an hour before, it was Captain Tate, and Captain Tate only, that she now wished to see. Nor did she long wish in vain. When her tall person, straight ankles, and flashing eyes first entered upon the "High Street Parade," Captain Tate was swallowing the fourth spoonful of a raspberry ice; but, ere she had reached the middle of it, he was by her side.

"Oh! Captain Tate!" she exclaimed, with heightened colour and brightened eyes, ... "I did not expect to see you again this morning.... I thought for certain you would be riding with the colonel, or the major, or some of them."

"Ah! Miss Martha!... You don't know what it is to be ordered from quarters where ... you don't know what it is to be torn heart and soul and body asunder, as I shall be in a few days, ... or you would not fancy one should be riding out of town, as long as one had the power of staying in it!"

"Oh dear!... you won't mind it, I'm sure ... you will like Plymouth quite as well ... or perhaps better than you do Silverton: ... we shall all remember you longer than you will remember us."

"Do not say so!... do not say so!... beautiful Martha!—you cannot think it."

"I'm sure I do," responded the young lady, with a very distinct sigh.

It was exceedingly wrong in Captain Tate (yet all his family and intimate friends declared that he was as worthy a fellow as ever lived)—it was exceedingly wrong in him to offer his arm to Miss Martha the moment he heard this sigh; for in fact he was engaged to be married to his cousin, and the marriage ceremony was only deferred till he should be gazetted as a major; yet he scrupled not, as I have related, to offer his arm, saying in a very soft, and even tender accent,—

"I know it is not the etiquette of dear, quiet little Silverton, for the officers to offer their arms to the young ladies; but just at the last ... at such a moment as this, not even the Lord Mayor of the town himself could think it wrong."

This reasoning seemed quite satisfactory, for Miss Martha's arm was immediately placed within his.

"It is very true, as you say, Captain Tate; the last time does make a difference. But it will be very dull work for you going to Smith's shop with me; ... and I must go there, because mamma has sent me."

"Dull!... Oh! Miss Martha, do you really think that any place can be dull to me where you are?"

"How do I know, Captain Tate?... How can any girl know how much, or how little."

"Good heaven!... we are at the shop already!" said the Captain, interrupting her.... "How such dear moments fly!"

Miss Martha answered not with her lips, but had no scruple to let her fine large eyes reply with very intelligible meaning, even though at that very moment she had reached the front of the counter, and that Mr. Smith himself stood before her, begging to know her commands. Her arm, too, still confidingly hung upon that of the stylish-looking young officer; and there certainly was both in her attitude and manner something that spoke of an interest and intimacy between them of no common kind.

A few more muttered words were exchanged between them before the draper's necessary question met any attention whatever, yet in general the Miss Comptons were particularly civil to Mr. Smith, and at length, when she turned to answer him, she stopped short before she had well pronounced the words "mull muslin," saying with an air of laughing embarrassment, and withdrawing her arm,—

"Upon my word and honour, you must go, Captain Tate.... I can no more buy anything while you stand talking to me than I can fly."

"Did not you promise me?" said the Captain reproachfully, and not knowing what in the world to do with himself till it was time to dress.

"Yes, I know I did," she replied; "but the truth is," ... and she pressed both her hands upon her heart, and shook her head ... "the thing is impossible.... You must leave me, indeed!... we shall meet to-night at the Major's, you know ... farewell!..." and she stretched out her hand to him with a smile full of tender meaning.

The Captain looked rather puzzled, but fervently pressed her hand, and saying "Au revoir then!" left the shop. The young lady looked after him for a moment, and then, turning to Mr. Smith with a look, a sigh, and a smile not at all likely to be misunderstood, said,—

"I suppose, Mr. Smith, you have heard the news about me?... There never was such a place for gossip as Silverton."

Mr. Smith smilingly protested he had heard nothing whatever about her, but added, with very satisfactory significance, that he rather thought he could guess what the news was, and begged very respectfully to wish her joy of it.

"You are very kind, Mr. Smith; I am sure it is the last thing I expected ... so much above me in every way.... And now, Mr. Smith, I want to speak to you about the things that must be bought. I am sure you are too neighbourly and too kind to put difficulties in my way. It is a very different thing now, you know, as to what I buy; and I am sure you will let me have quite on my own account, and nothing at all to do with papa, a few things that I want very much at the present moment."

Miss Martha looked so handsome, and the whole affair seemed so clear and satisfactory, that Mr. Smith, careful tradesman as he was, could not resist her appeal, and declared he should be happy to serve her with whatever articles she might choose to purchase.

Her dark eyes sparkled with the triumph of success; she had often felt her own powers of management swelling within her bosom when she witnessed the helpless despondency of her father, or listened to the profitless grumbling of her mother, upon every new pecuniary pressure that beset them; and it is not wonderful if she now believed more firmly than ever, that much suffering and embarrassment might very often be spared, or greatly alleviated, by the judicious exercise of such powers as she felt conscious of possessing.

As a proof that her judgment was in some measure commensurate with her skill, she determined not to abuse the present opportunity by contracting a debt which it would be quite impossible for her father to pay; so, notwithstanding all the tempting finery with which the confiding Mr. Smith spread the counter, she restrained her purchases to such articles as it might really have endangered all their schemes of future conquest to have been without, and then took her leave, amidst blushes and smiles, and with many assurances to the gently-facetious shopkeeper, that let her be where she would, she should never forget his obliging civility.

It was a moment of great triumph for Martha when Mr. Smith's man arrived, and the huge and carefully packed parcel was brought up to the chamber where Mrs. Compton and her daughters sat at work.

"What in the world is this?" exclaimed the mother, seizing upon it. "Is it possible that her letter was only a joke, and that the little fright has actually sent you some dresses at last?"

"It is much more likely, I fancy, that I have coaxed Mr. Smith into giving us a little more credit. It can all be paid off by a little and a little at a time, you know; and at any rate, here are some very pretty dresses for the fête, besides about three pounds' worth of things that we really could not do without any longer."

"And do you really mean, Martha, that you have got Smith to send in all these beautiful things on credit?"

"I do indeed, mamma."

"Was there ever such a girl!... Only look, Sophy, at this lovely muslin! Why, it will wash, and make up again with different trimmings as good as new for a dozen regiments to come!... Oh! you dear clever creature, what a treasure you are!... I wish to God I had trusted all to you from the first, and not tired myself to death by walking over to that stingy little monster ... but, tired or not, we must cut these dear sweet dresses out at once. Nancy Baker must come in and make the bodies, and we must set to, girls, and run the seams ... and a pleasure it will be too, God knows!... I have worked at turning and twisting old gowns into new ones till I have hated the sight of an ironing box and a needle; but this is another guess sort of a business, and I shall set about it with a right good will, I promise you."

And so she did, and the dresses went on prosperously, as well as everything else connected with the officers' fête; and when the wished-for, but dreaded day arrived, in which so many farewell sighs were to be sighed, and so many last looks looked, and so many scrutinizing glances given, as to what might be hoped for from the flirtations of the ensuing year, the sun shone so brightly as evidently to take part with the new-comers, permitting not one single cloud to sympathise with those who were about to depart.

Of all the beauties assembled at this hybrid festival, none appeared to greater advantage than the Misses Compton. Their dresses were neither dirty nor faded, but exceedingly well calculated to set off their charms as favourably as their mother herself could have desired. Captain Tate, after dancing his last dance with Martha, pointed her out with some feeling of triumph to one of the new arrivals as the girl upon whom he had bestowed the largest share of his regimental gallantries; but he was far from imagining, as he did so, how very much better she had contrived to manage the flirtation than himself. She had made it the means of clothing herself and sister from top to toe, while to him it had been very costly in gloves, ices, eau de cologne, and dancing-pumps.

CHAPTER IV

A WEDDING, AND ITS CONSEQUENCES—A TRANSFER OF PROPERTY—MISS MARTHA RECEIVES A PROPOSAL OF MARRIAGE—ANOTHER EXPEDITION TO COMPTON BASETT

The regimental gala which had been looked forward to with so much interest, though very gay and very agreeable, did not perhaps produce all the results expected by the soft hearts and bright eyes of Silverton, for only one wedding was achieved in consequence of it. This one made a very hasty and imprudent bride of Sophia Compton. Her charming voice, joined to her pretty person, was too enchanting for the enthusiastic Lieutenant Willoughby to leave behind him; and just as the full moon rose upon the tents of the revellers, he drew her gently into the deep shadow of that appropriated to the sutlers, and there swore a very solemn oath that it was quite impossible he should continue to exist, if she refused to elope with him that evening.

Upon the whole, Miss Sophia was by no means sorry to hear this, but could not help expressing a modest wish that he would be so obliging as to change the plan of operations, and instead of eloping with her, would just speak to papa, and so be married in a proper way.

For a considerable time, longer indeed than it was possible to remain in the shadow of the sutler's tent, the young gentleman declared this to be impossible; because, in that case, his own relations must be informed of the affair, and he knew perfectly well that if this happened, effectual measures would be taken to prevent his ever possessing his adorable Sophia at all. These arguments were repeated, and dwelt upon with very convincing energy, for the space of one whole quadrille, during which the tender pair sat ensconced behind a fanciful erection, on the front of which was traced, in letters formed of laurel leaves, the words, "TO THE LADIES." Nor was his pretty listener insensible to their force, or the probable truth of the "misery" they predicted; it was, therefore, all things considered, much to the credit of Miss Sophy that she persevered in her refusal of accepting him on the terms he offered.

Lieutenant Willoughby was by no means a wicked young man, but it was his nature to covet particularly whatever it was least convenient to obtain; and it was, I believe, of him that a youthful anecdote has been recorded which sets this disposition in a striking point of view. Upon occasion of some dainty, but pernicious delicacy, being forbidden, or some frolic tending too strongly to mischief being stopped, he is said to have exclaimed, "It is a very, very shocking thing, mamma, that everything that is nice is called wrong, and everything that is nasty is called right." This was said when he was seven years old, but at twenty-two he was very nearly of the same unfortunate opinion, and invariably valued everything in proportion to the conviction he felt that he should be opposed in his pursuit of it.

When, therefore, Miss Sophia persisted in her declaration that she would not run away with him, Lieutenant Willoughby became perfectly desperate in his determination to obtain her; and having a sort of natural instinct which convinced him that no proposal of marriage would be ill-received by Mrs. Compton, he wrung the hand of his Sophy, implored her not to dance with anybody else, and then having sought and found her mother amidst the group of matrons who sat apart admiring their respective daughters, he drew her aside, and told his tale of love.

This, as he expected, was by no means unkindly received; and when Mrs. Compton, having recovered from her first ecstasy, began to hint at income and settlement, the impassioned young gentleman contrived to puzzle her so completely, by stating the certainty of his being disinherited if his marriage were immediately known, and the handsome fortune it was possible he might have if it were kept profoundly secret, that he sent her home as vehemently determined to let him marry her daughter, without saying a word to his family about the matter, as he could possibly have desired.

The result of this may be easily divined. Nothing approved by Mrs. Compton was ever effectually opposed by Mr. Compton; so Miss Sophia was married to Lieutenant Willoughby within ten days of the regimental ball, and within one year afterwards a female infant, called Agnes Willoughby, was placed in the care of the Curate of Silverton and his wife; her young mother being dead, and her broken-spirited father about to set off for the West Indies, having found his father implacable, his well-married sisters indignant, and nothing left him whereon to found a hope of escape from his difficulties except thus giving up his little girl to her grandfather, and exchanging his commission in the gay — regiment for one in a corps about to embark for a service very likely to settle all his embarrassments by consigning him to an early tomb.

Meanwhile the Curate of Silverton was becoming every day more involved in debt; and his dashing eldest daughter, though handsomer than ever, painfully conscious that among all the successive legions of lovers whose conspicuous adorations had made her the most envied of her sex, there was not one who offered any rational probability of becoming her husband.

The first of these misfortunes was the most embarrassing, and so imperiously demanded a remedy, that the poor Curate at length consented to find it in the sale of his moiety of his paternal acres. It is certain that his nightly potations of hot toddy had very considerably impaired his powers of caring for anything; nevertheless, it was not without a pang that he permitted his wife to insert an advertisement in the county paper, proclaiming the sale by auction of certain crofts and meadows, barns and byres, making part and parcel of a capital dairy-farm, known by the name of Compton Basett.

When the day of sale arrived, several competitors appeared who bid pretty briskly for the lot; for the land, particularly thirty acres of it, known by the name of "the butcher's close," was some of the best in the county; but the successful candidate, who, it was pretty evident from the first, was determined that it should be knocked down to no one else, was farmer Wright, Miss Betsy's prosperous and well-deserving tenant. This, though the purchase was a large one for a mere farmer, (amounting to six thousand five hundred and twenty-five pounds,) did not greatly surprise the neighbourhood, for the Wrights were known to be a prudent, thrifty, and industrious race. It is possible they might have been more surprised had they known that it was Miss Betsy herself, and not her tenant, who was the purchaser. But so it was. The twenty-five years which had elapsed since the death of her father had enabled this careful little lady to accumulate, by means of her rent, her five hundred pounds and its compound interest, and the profits of her well-managed apiary, a much larger sum than it required to become the possessor of her brother's share of Compton Basett; and when she had finished the affair, and leased out the whole property (the butcher's close included) to her friend and tenant farmer Wright, for the annual rent of six hundred pounds (now including two chickens per week for her own use), she still remained possessed of four thousand pounds sterling, safely lodged in the funds; a property which went on very rapidly increasing, as her scale of expense never varied, and rarely exceeded ten pounds per annum beyond the profits of her bees, and her stipulated accommodation from the farm. But, in spite of this strict economy, Miss Betsy was no bad neighbour to the poor, and in a small and very quiet way did more towards keeping dirt and cold out of their dwellings, than many who spent three times as much upon them, and made ten times as much fuss about it.

It was not, however, till many years later, that the fact of her being the possessor of the whole of the Compton Basett estate, became known to any one but farmer Wright; and as to the amount of her half-yearly increasing property in the funds, she had no confidant but her broker. This mystery, this profound secrecy, in the silent rolling up of her wealth, was perhaps the principal source of her enjoyment from it. It amused her infinitely to observe, that while the bad management and improvidence of her brother and his wife were the theme of eternal gossipings, her own thrift seemed permitted to go quietly on, without eliciting any observation at all. Her judicious and regularly administered little charities, assisted in producing this desired effect, much more than she had the least idea of; for the praises of Miss Betsy's goodness and kindness proceeded from many who had profited more from her judgment, and her well-timed friendly loans, than from her donations; and the gratitude for such services was much more freely and generally expressed, than if the favours conferred had been merely those of ordinary alms-giving. It was therefore very generally reported in Silverton that Miss Betsy Compton gave away all her income in charity, which was the reason why she never did anything to help her embarrassed relations. These erroneous reports were productive of at least one advantage to the family of the Curate of Silverton, for it effectually prevented their having any expectations from her beyond a vague and uncertain hope, that if she did not bequeath her farm-house and acres to a hospital, the property might be left to them. But not even the croaking ill-will of Mrs. Compton could now anticipate a very early date for this possible bequest; for, pale and delicate-looking as she ever continued, nobody had ever heard of Miss Betsy's having a doctor's bill to pay; and as she was just seven years younger than her brother the Curate, who, moreover, was thought to be dropsical, there appeared wofully little chance that her death would ever benefit her disappointed sister-in-law at all. A very considerable portion of the purchase-money of the estate had dwindled away ... the little Agnes Willoughby had attained the age of eleven years, and Mr. Compton had become so ill as to have been forced to resign his curacy, when Mr. Barnaby, the celebrated surgeon and apothecary of Silverton, who for the last ten years had admired Miss Martha Compton more than any lady he had ever looked upon, suddenly took courage, and asked her point-blank to become his wife.

Had he done this some few years before, his fate would have been told in the brief monosyllable no, uttered probably with as much indignation as any sound compounded of two letters could express; but since that time the fair Martha had seen so many colonels, majors, captains, ... ay, and lieutenants too, march into the town, and then march out again, without whispering anything more profitable in her ear than an assurance of her being an angel, that the case was greatly altered; and after the meditation of a moment, she answered very modestly, ... "You must speak to my mother, Mr. Barnaby."

Perfectly satisfied by the reply, Mr. Barnaby did speak to her mother; but the young lady took care to speak to her first, and after a long and very confidential conversation, it was determined between them that the offer of the gentleman should be accepted, that fifty pounds out of the few remaining hundreds should be spent upon her wedding-garments, and that whenever it pleased God to take poor Mr. Compton, his widow and little grand-daughter should be received into Mr. Barnaby's family.

It has not been recorded with any degree of certainty, whether these last arrangements were mentioned to the enamoured Galen, when the important interview which decided the fate of Miss Martha took place; but whether they were or not, the marriage ceremony followed with as little delay as possible.

Two circumstances occurred previous to the ceremony which must be mentioned, as being calculated to open the character of my heroine to the reader. No sooner was this important affair decided upon, than Miss Martha told her mamma, that it was her intention to walk over to Compton Basett, and inform Miss Betsy of the news herself.

"And what do you expect to get by that, Martha?" said the old lady. "I have not forgot yet my walk to Compton Basett just before poor dear Sophy's marriage, nor the trick the little monster played me, making me bring home her vile hypocritical letter as carefully as if it had been a bank-note for a hundred pounds.... You must go without me, if go you will, for I have taken my last walk to Compton Basett, I promise you."

"I don't want you to trouble yourself about it in any way, mother," replied Miss Martha. "I'll make Agnes walk with me; and whether I get anything out of the little porcupine or not, the walk can do us no great harm."

"'Tis not so hot as when I went, that's certain," said Mrs. Compton, becoming better reconciled to the expedition. "She has never seen Agnes since the poor little thing was thought to be dying in the measles, just five years ago; and then, you know, she did hire a nurse, and send in oranges and jellies, and all that sort of trumpery; ... and who can say but her heart may soften towards her again, when she sees what a sweet pretty creature she is grown?"

"I can't say I have much faith in good looks doing much towards drawing her purse-strings. She has seen poor Sophy and me often enough, and I can't say that we ever found our beauty did us any good with her, neither is it that upon which I reckon now. But telling her of a wedding is not begging, you know, ... and I don't think it impossible but what such a prudent, business-like wedding as mine, may be more to her taste than poor Sophy's, where there was nothing but a few fine-sounding names to look to ... and much good they did her, poor thing!"

"Well, set off, Martha, whenever you like. There is no need to make little Agnes look smart, even if I had the means to do it, for it's quite as well that she should be reminded of the wants of the poor child by the desolate condition of her old straw-bonnet.... When do you think you shall go?"

"This afternoon; I'm sure of not seeing Barnaby again till tea-time, for he has got to go as far as Pemberton, so we may start as soon as dinner is over."

Miss Martha Compton and her young companion set off accordingly about three o'clock, and pursued their way, chiefly in silence, to Miss Betsy's abode; for Agnes rarely spoke to her aunt, except when she was spoken to, and Miss Martha was meditating profoundly the whole way upon the probability of obtaining Mr. Barnaby's consent to the re-furnishing his drawing-room. It was the month of April, the air deliciously sweet and mild, and birds singing on every tree; so that although the leaves were not yet fully out, they found Miss Betsy sitting as usual in her bower, and enjoying as keenly the busy hum about her bee-hives, as ever Miss Martha did the bustling animation produced by the murmurings of a dozen red-coats.

Miss Betsy was at this time about fifty years of age, and though the defect in her shape was certainly not lessened by age, she was altogether an exceedingly nice-looking little old lady; and her cap was as neat and becoming, and her complexion very nearly as delicate, as at the time of Mrs. Compton's visit just twelve years before.

She fixed her eyes for a moment upon Martha as she approached the bower, but appeared not to know her; the little girl following close behind, was for a minute or two invisible; but the instant she caught sight of her, she rose from her seat, and stepping quickly forward, took the child by her hand, drew her in, and placed her on the bench by her side.

Little Agnes, who knew she was come to see her aunt, felt assured by this notice that she was in her presence, and, moreover, that she was a very kind person; so, when the old lady, after examining her features very attentively, said, "You are little Agnes, are you not?" she replied without hesitation or timidity, "Yes, I am; and you are good aunt Betsy, that used to give me the oranges."

"Do you remember that, my child?... 'tis a long while, almost half your little life. Take off your bonnet, Agnes, and let me see your face."

Agnes obeyed, the "desolate" straw-bonnet was laid aside, and Miss Betsy gazed upon one of the fairest and most delicate little faces that the soft beams of an April sun ever fell upon.

The pale recluse kept her keen eyes fixed upon the little girl for many minutes without pronouncing a word; at length she said, but apparently speaking only to herself,—

"It is just such a face as I wanted her to have.... Her father was a gentleman.... She will never have red cheeks, that is quite certain."

"How d'ye do, aunt Betsy?..." said Miss Martha, in a very clear and distinct voice; probably thinking that she had remained long enough in the background.

"Very well, I thank you," was the reply; "and who are you?"

"Dear me, aunt, you must say that for fun, ... for it is hardly likely you should know Agnes, that was almost a baby the last time you ever saw her, and forget me, that was quite grown up at that same time."

"Oh!... then you are Miss Martha, the great beauty, are you? You look very old indeed, Miss Martha, considering that you can't be very much past thirty, and that I suppose is the reason I did not know you. How is your poor father, Miss Martha?"

"He's very bad, aunt Betsy; but I hope the news I am come to tell you will be a comfort to him, and please you too."

"And what news can that be, Miss Martha?"

"I am going to be married, aunt Betsy, to a person that is extremely well off, and able to set me above all poverty and difficulties for ever; ... and the only thing against it is, that papa cannot afford to give me any money at all for my wedding clothes, which is a dreadful disgrace to the name of Compton; and to tell you the truth at once, for I am a frank, honest-hearted girl, that never hides anything, I am come over here on purpose to ask you to give me a few pounds, just to prevent my having to ask my husband for a shift."

"If you have no shift, Miss Martha, while you are wearing such a gay bonnet as that, I think any man must be a great fool for taking you. However, that is his affair, and not mine. I cannot afford to buy your wedding-clothes, Miss Martha; nor do I intend ever to give you any money at all for any purpose whatever, either now, or at any future period; so, if you are wise, as well as frank, you will never ask me again. If you marry a gentleman, and have children who shall behave according to my notions of honour, honesty, and propriety, it is possible that the little I may leave will be divided among them, and any others whom I may think have an equal claim upon me. But I heartily hope you will have none, for I feel certain I should not like them; and I would rather that the poor little trifle I may have left when I die, should go to some one I did like."

Miss Martha's heart swelled with rage, yet, remote as Miss Betsy's contingent benefits were likely to be, they had still influence sufficient to prevent her breaking out into open violence, and she sat silent, though with burning cheeks and a beating heart. The address she had just listened to was certainly not of the most agreeable style and tone, but it may be some apology for Miss Betsy's severity to state, that the scene which had taken place in Mr. Smith's shop rather more than twelve years before, in which a certain Captain Tate took an important, though unconscious, part, was accurately well-known to the little spinster, Mrs. Wright (the wife of her tenant) having witnessed the whole of it.

When she had finished her speech to Miss Martha, which was spoken in her usual gay tone of voice, Miss Betsy turned again towards Agnes, who was then standing at the entrance of the bower, earnestly watching the bees.

"They are pretty, curious creatures, are they not, Agnes?" said she. "I hope some day or other you will be as active and industrious. Do you love to work, my little girl?"

"I love to play better," replied Agnes.

"Ay ... that's because you are such a young thing. And who are your playfellows, Agnes?"

"I have not got any playfellows but myself," was the reply.

"And where do you play?"

"In grandpapa's garden, behind the house."

"And what do you play at?"

"Oh! so many things. I play at making flower-beds in the summer, and at snow-balls in the winter; and I know a blackbird, and ever so many robin-redbreasts, and they know me, and I...."

"Do you know how to read, Agnes?"

"A little," ... replied the child, blushing deeply.

"Come here, then, and read a page of my book to me."

Poor Agnes obeyed the summons, and submissively placing herself by the side of her aunt, took the book in her hands and began to read. But it was so very lame and imperfect a performance, that Miss Betsy wanted either the cruelty or the patience to let it proceed; and taking the volume away, she said, in a graver tone than was usual with her, "Nobody seems to have given themselves much trouble about teaching you, my little girl; ... but I dare say you will read better by and bye.... Are you hungry, Agnes?... do you wish for something to eat after your walk?"

Delighted at being thus relieved from exposing her ignorance, the little girl replied gaily—

"I am very hungry indeed, ma'am."

"Then sit here to rest for a few minutes, and I will see what I can get for you;" and so saying, Miss Betsy rose, and walked briskly away towards the house.

"Old brute!..." exclaimed Miss Martha, as soon as she was quite beyond hearing.... "There's a hump for you!... Isn't she a beauty, Agnes?"

"A beauty, aunt Martha?... No, I don't think she is a beauty, though I like the look of her face too; ... but she certainly is not a beauty, for she is not the least bit like you, and you are a beauty, you know."

"And who told you that, child?"

"Oh! I have heard grandmamma and you talk about it very often.... and I heard Mr. Barnaby say, when he came in yesterday, 'How are you, my beauty?' ... and besides, I see you are a beauty myself."

"And pray, Agnes," replied her aunt, laughing with great good-humour, "how do you know a beauty when you see one?"

"Why, don't I see every time I walk by Mr. Gibbs's shop, his beauties in the window, with their rosy cheeks, and their black eyes, and their quantity of fine ringlets? and you are exactly the very image of one of Mr. Gibbs's beauties, aunt Martha."

Miss Martha remembered that there was one very pretty face in the window of the village perruquier, and doubted not that the little Agnes's observation had reference to that one; it was therefore with one of her most amiable smiles that she replied,—

"You little goose!... how can I be like a painted wax image?"

But the protestations and exclamations by which the simile might have been proved good, were broken off by the approach of a maid-servant from the house, who said that Miss Betsy was waiting for them.

They found the neat little lady in her pretty sitting-room, with a lily-white cloth spread on a table near the open window, and a home-made loaf, a little bowl of native cream, and a decanter of bright spring-water, with a couple of tumblers near it.

Simple as this repast was, it was well relished by both the nieces, though decidedly served in honour of only one. However, no positive objection being made to Miss Martha's taking her share of it, she spared neither the loaf nor the cream; and remembering her mother's account of her penny repast, felt something like triumph as she ate, to think how much more she had contrived to get out of her churlish relative.

But this was all she got ... excepting, indeed, that she felt some consolation for her disappointment in having to tell her mother, on her return, that if she had children, (and of course she should, as everybody else had,) they were to have their share of all the old maid might leave.

"Ugly old hypocrite!... it won't be much, take my word for it," replied Mrs. Compton.... "She likes all the beggars in the parish a vast deal better than she does her own flesh and blood.... Don't talk any more of her, Martha.... I should be glad if I was never to hear her name mentioned again!"

CHAPTER V

A VISIT FROM THE HEIRESS—MISS AGNES WILLOUGHBY IS SENT TO SCHOOL

In about a month after this visit, and less than a week before the day fixed upon for the happiness of Mr. Barnaby, Miss Betsy Compton very unexpectedly made a visit to her brother. She found him a good deal altered, but she found him also with his toddy and pipe, both objects of such hatred and disgust to her anchoritish spirit, that all the kind feelings which might have been awakened by his failing health, were chased by looking upon what caused it.

To see her feeble-minded brother was not, however, the only or the principal object of her visit to Silverton; and she permitted not many minutes to be wasted in mutual questionings that meant very little, before she let him understand what was.

"I am come to speak to you, brother," she said, "about little Agnes. I should like to know in what manner you intend to educate her?"

"Mrs. Compton manages all that, sister Betsy," replied the invalid; "and, at any rate, I am sure I have no money to teach her anything."

"But it is a sin, brother, to let the child run wild about the garden as you would a magpie.... Do you know that she can't read?"

"No, sister Betsy, I know nothing at all about it, I tell you.... How can I help it? Am I in a condition to teach anybody to read?"

"There are others more to blame than you are, brother, no doubt; ... but let it be who's fault it will, it must not go on so. I suppose you will make no objection to my sending her to school?"

"Oh dear, no! not I; ... but you had better ask Mrs. Compton about it."

"Very well.... But I have your consent, have I not?"

"Dear me, yes, sister Betsy.... Why do you tease me so, making me take the pipe out of my mouth every minute?"

Miss Betsy left the little smoke-dried back parlour appropriated to the master of the house, and made her way to the front room up stairs called the drawing-room, which had been reserved, since time out of mind, for the use of the ladies of the family and their visitors. There she found, as she expected, Mrs. Compton and her daughter amidst an ocean of needle-work, all having reference, more or less, to the ceremony which was to be performed on the following Thursday.

"So, Mrs. Compton," was her salutation to the old lady, and a nod of the head to the young one. "I have been speaking to my brother," continued Miss Betsy, "concerning the education of little Agnes, and he has given his consent to my putting her to school."

"His consent!..." exclaimed Mrs. Compton; "and, pray, is she not my grandchild too?... I think I have as good a right to take care of the child as he has."

"She has a right," replied the spinster, "to expect from both of you a great deal more care than she has found; and were I you, Mrs. Compton, I would take some trouble to conceal from all my friends and acquaintance the fact that, at eleven years of age, my grandchild was unable to read."

"And that's a fact that I can have no need to hide, Miss Betsy, for it's no fact at all—I've seen Martha teaching her scores of times."

"Then have her in, Mrs. Compton, and let us make the trial. If I have said what is not true, I will beg your pardon."

"Lor, mamma!" said Miss Martha, colouring a little, "what good is there in contradicting aunt Betsy, if she wants to send Agnes to school? I am sure it is the best thing that can be done for her, now I am going to be married.... And Mr. Barnaby asked me the other day, if you did not mean to send her to school."

"I don't want to keep her from school, God knows, poor little thing, or from anything else that could do her good.... Only Miss Betsy speaks so sharp.... But I can assure you, sister, we should have put her to the best of schools long and long ago, only that, Heaven knows, we had not the means to do it; and thankful shall I be if you are come at last to think that there may be as much charity in helping your own blood relations, as in giving away your substance to strangers and beggars."

"You are right, Mrs. Compton, as far as relates to sending Agnes to school ... that will certainly be a charity. When can the child be got ready?"

"As soon as ever you shall be pleased to give us the means, sister Betsy."

"Do you mean, Mrs. Compton, that she has not got clothes to go in?"

"I do indeed, sister Betsy."

"Let me see what she has got, and then I shall know what she wants."

"That is easily told, aunt, without your troubling yourself to look over a few ragged frocks and the like. She wants just everything, aunt Betsy," said the bride expectant, brave in anticipated independence, and rather inclined to plague the old lady by drawing as largely as might be on her reluctant funds, now they were opened, even though the profit would not be her own.

"If she really does want everything, Martha Compton, while you are dressed as you now are, very cruel injustice has been done her," replied the aunt. "Your sister had no portion given her, either of the patrimony of her father, or the thousand pounds brought by her mother; and as her marriage with a man who had not a sixpence was permitted, this child of hers has an equal right with yourself to share in the property of your parents."

"The property of their parents!... Why bless me, Betsy Compton, how you do talk!... as if you did not know that all the property they ever had, is as good as gone. Has not farmer Wright got the estate? And has not the butcher, and the baker, and the shoemaker, and all the rest of them, got what it sold for, as well as my thousand pounds among them, long ago?"

"Then you are now on the very verge of ruin, Mrs. Compton?" said the spinster gravely.

"Yes, sister Betsy, we are," replied the matron reproachfully. "And I can't but say," she continued, "that a lone woman like you, without any expenses whatever but your own meat and drink, which everybody says is next to nothing,—I can't but say that you might have helped us a little before now, and no harm done."

"That is your opinion of the case, Mrs. Compton: mine is wholly different. I think harm is done whenever power of any kind is exerted in vain. I have no power to help you.... Were all I have, poured out upon you, while I lodged myself in the parish workhouse, my conviction is, that I should only be enabling you to commit more follies, and, in my judgment, more sins."

"Well, well, Miss Betsy, it is of no use talking to you—I know that of old; and to tell you the truth, when I do come to beggary, I had rather beg of anybody else than of you. I hear far and near of your charity to others, but I can't say that I ever saw any great symptom of it myself."

"Let me see what clothes little Agnes has got, Mrs. Compton, if you please. Our time will be more profitably employed in seeing what I may be able to do for her, than in discoursing of what I am not able to do for you. Miss Martha then, I suppose, may be able to bring her things in."

"Why, as far as the quantity goes, they won't be very difficult to carry. But I don't see much use in overhauling all the poor child's trumpery ... unless it is just to make you laugh at our poverty, ma'am."

The spinster answered this with a look which shewed plainly enough that, however little beauty her pale face could boast, it was by no means deficient in expression. Miss Martha hastened out of the room to do her errand without saying another word.

I will not give the catalogue of poor Agnes's wardrobe, but only observe that it was considerably worse than Miss Betsy expected; she made, however, no observation upon it; but having examined it apparently with very little attention, she took leave of the mother and daughter, saying she would call again in a day or two, and took with her (no permission asked) a greatly faded, but recently fitted frock, which abduction mother and daughter remonstrated against, loudly declaring it was her best dress, except the old white muslin worked with coloured worsteds, and that she would have nothing upon earth to wear.

"It shall not be kept long," was the reply; and the little lady departed, enduring for a moment the atmosphere of her brother's parlour as she passed, in order to tell him, as she thought herself in duty bound to do, that she should get some decent clothes made for the child, and call again as soon as they were ready to take her to school.

The poor gentleman seemed greatly pleased at this, and said, "Thank you, Betsy," with more animation than he had been heard to impart to any words for many years.

It was just three days after Miss Martha Compton had become Mrs. Barnaby, that the same post-chaise drove up to the door that had carried her away from it on an excursion of eight-and-forty hours to Exeter, which the gallant bridegroom had stolen a holiday to give her; but upon this occasion it was hired neither by bride nor bridegroom, but by the little crooked spinster, who was come, according to her promise, to take Agnes to school.

Mrs. Compton was just setting out to pay her first morning visit to the bride, and therefore submitted to the hasty departure of the little girl with less grumbling than she might have done, if less agreeably engaged.

"You must bid your grandpapa good-b'ye, Agnes," said Miss Betsy, as they passed the door of his parlour, and accordingly they all entered together.

"God bless you, my poor little girl!" said the old man after kissing her forehead, "and keep your aunt Betsy's favour if you can, ... for I don't think I can do much more to help anybody.... God bless you, Agnes!"

"Dear me, Mr. Compton!... you need not bring tears in the child's eyes by speaking that way.... I am sure she has never wanted friends since her poor dear mother died; and there's no like she should either, with such an aunt as Martha, married to such a man as Mr. Barnaby.... I suppose she is not to be kept from her family, sister Betsy, but that we shall see her in the holidays. I am sure I don't know where she is likely to see things so elegant as at her aunt Barnaby's.... Such a drawing-room!... and a man in livery, at least a boy, ... and everything else conformable.... I suppose this is to be her home, Miss Betsy, still?"

"I am glad you have mentioned this, Mrs. Compton," replied her sister-in-law, "because now, in the presence of my brother, I may explain my intentions at once. Whatever you may think of my little means, either you or your wife, or your daughter, brother Josiah, I am not rich enough in my own opinion to make it prudent for me to saddle myself with the permanent charge of this poor child. Moreover, to do so, I must altogether change the quiet manner of life that I have so long enjoyed, and I am not conscious of being bound by any tie sufficiently strong to make this painful sacrifice a duty. Something I think I ought to do for this child, and I am willing to do it. I conceive that it will be more easily in my power to spare something from my little property to obtain a respectable education for her, than either in your's, brother, or even in that of her newly-married aunt Barnaby; for doubtless it would not be agreeable for her to begin her wedded life by throwing a burden upon her husband. But, on the other hand, it will certainly be much more within the power of her aunt Barnaby to give her a comfortable and advantageous home afterwards, than in mine. I will therefore now take charge of her for five years, during which time she shall be supplied with board, lodging, clothes, and instruction, at my expense; or, in case I should die, at that of my executors. After this period I shall restore her to you, brother, or to her grandmother, if both or either of you shall be alive, or if not, to her aunt Barnaby; and when I die she shall have a share, with such others as I may think have a claim upon me, of the small matter I may leave behind. But this of course must be lessened by the expenses I am now contracting for her."

"And are we never to see her for five years, sister Betsy?" said Mrs. Compton very dolorously.

"To tell you the truth, Mrs. Compton, I think the coming home to you twice a-year, for the holidays, could be no advantage to her education, and the expense of such repeated journeyings would be very inconvenient to me. I have therefore arranged with the persons who are to take charge of her that she is to pass the vacations with them. I shall, however, make a point of seeing her myself more than once in the course of the time, and will undertake that she shall come to Silverton twice during these five years, for a few days each time.... And now, I think, there is no more to say; so come, my little girl, for it is not right to keep the driver and the horses any longer waiting."

The adieux between the parties were now hastily exchanged, little Agnes mounted the post-chaise, aunt Betsy followed, and they drove off, though in what direction they were to go, after leaving the Silverton turnpike, no one had ever thought of inquiring.

Poor Mrs. Compton stood for some moments silently gazing after the post-chaise, and on re-entering her drawing-room, felt a sensation that greatly resembled desolation from the unwonted stillness that reigned there. She was instantly cheered, however, by recollecting the very agreeable visit she was going to pay; and only pausing to put on her new wedding bonnet and shawl, set off for Mr. Barnaby's, saying to the maid, whom she passed as she descended, "I should like, Sally, to have seen what sort of things she has got for the poor child."

"If they was as neat and as nice as the little trunk as was strapped on in the front, and that's where they was packed, no doubt,... there wouldn't be no need to complain of them," was the reply. And now, leaving Agnes to aunt Betsy and her fate, I must return to the duty I have assigned myself, and follow the fortunes of Mrs. Barnaby.

CHAPTER VI

WEDDED HAPPINESS—DEATH OF MRS. COMPTON—THE EX-CURATE BROUGHT INTO A PEACEFUL HARBOUR—HE FALLS SICK, AND HIS SISTER AND GRANDCHILD ARE SUMMONED

The first five or six months of Mrs. Barnaby's married life were so happy as not only to make her forget all her former disappointments, but almost to persuade her that it was very nearly as good a thing to marry a middle-aged country apothecary, with a good house and a good income, as a beautiful young officer with neither.

Since her adventure with Mr. Smith, the draper, milliner, mercer, and haberdasher of Silverton par excellence, Mrs. Barnaby's genius for making bargains had been sadly damped; not but that she had in some degree saved her credit with that important and much-provoked personage by condescending to wear the willow before his eyes; she even went so far as to say to him, with a twinkling of lids that passed for having tears in her own,—

"No young lady was ever so used before, I believe.... I am sure, Mr. Smith, you saw enough yourself to be certain that I was engaged to Captain Tate,... yet the moment he found a girl with a little money he sent back all my letters...!"

Perhaps Mr. Smith believed the lady ... perhaps he did not; but at any rate he gave her no encouragement to recommence operations upon his confiding nature; on the contrary, he ceased not to send in his little account very constantly once every three months, steadfastly refusing to give credit for any articles, however needful. After the sale of the Compton Basett property the bill was paid, but no farther accommodation in that quarter ever obtained; indeed the facility of selling out of the funds a hundred pounds a time as it was wanted, superseded the necessity of pressing for it, and in a little way Miss Martha and Mr. Smith had continued to deal most amicably, but always with a certain degree of mutual shyness.

How delightfully different was the case now!... Mrs. Barnaby had only to send her maid or her man (boy) to the redundant storehouse of Mr. Smith, and all that her heart best loved was sent for her inspection and choice, without the slightest doubt or scruple.

Mr. Barnaby was proud of his wife; for if not quite as slender and delicate, she really looked very nearly as handsome as ever, a slight soupçon of rouge refreshing the brilliancy of her eyes, and concealing the incipient fading of her cheeks; while the total absence of mauvaise honte (an advantage which may be considered as the natural consequence of a twelve years' reign as the belle of a well-officered county town,) enabled her to preside at his own supper parties, and fill the place of honour as bride at those of his neighbours, with an easy sprightliness of manner that he felt to be truly fascinating. In short, Mr. Barnaby was excessively fond of his lady, and as he was known to have made much more money than he had spent, as no bill had ever been sent to him without immediate payment following, and as Mrs. Barnaby's nature expanded itself in this enlarged sphere of action, and led her to disburse five times as much as Mr. Barnaby had ever expended without her, all the tradesmen in the town were excessively fond of her too. Wherever she went she was greeted with a smile; and instead of being obliged to stand in every shop, waiting till some one happened to be at leisure to ask her what she wanted to buy, her feathers and her frills were no sooner discovered to be approaching the counter, than as many right arms as were in presence thrust forward a seat towards her, while the well-pleased master himself invariably started forth to receive her commands.

Any bride might have found matter for rejoicing in such a change, but few could have felt it so keenly as Mrs. Barnaby. She was by nature both proud and ambitious, and her personal vanity, though sufficiently strong within her to form rather a conspicuous feature in her character, was, in truth, only a sort of petted imp, that acted as an agent to assist in forwarding the hopes and wishes which her pride and ambition formed.

This pride and ambition, however, were very essentially different from the qualities known by these names among minds of a loftier nature. The ambition, for instance, instead of being "that last infirmity of noble mind" for which Milton seems to plead so feelingly, was, in truth, the first vice of a very mean one. Mrs. Barnaby burned with ambition to find herself in a situation that might authorize her giving herself the airs of a great lady; and her pride would have found all the gratification it sought, could she have been sure that her house and her dress would be daily cited among her acquaintance as more costly than their own.

Mrs. Barnaby had moreover un esprit intriguant in the most comprehensive sense of the phrase, for she would far rather have obtained any object she aimed at by means of her own manoeuvring, than by any simple concurrence of circumstances whatever; and this was perhaps the reason why, at the first moment the proposals of Mr. Barnaby, whom she had (comparatively speaking) used no tricks to captivate, produced a less pleasurable effect upon her mind, than a similar overture from any one of the innumerable military men whom she had so strenuously laboured to win, would have done. However, she was for this very reason happier than many other brides, for, in fact, she became daily more sensible of the substantial advantages she had obtained; and, on the whole, daily better pleased with her complaisant husband.

As her temper, though quietly and steadily selfish, was neither sour nor violent, this state of connubial happiness might have continued long, had not some untoward accidents occurred to disturb it.

The first of these was the sudden and dangerous illness of Mrs. Compton, which was of a nature to render it perfectly impossible for Mr. and Mrs. Barnaby to continue their delightful little parties at home and abroad. The dying lady ceased not to implore her daughter not to leave her, in accents so piteous, that Mr. Barnaby himself, notwithstanding his tender care for his lady's health, was the first to declare that she must remain with her. This heavy burden, however, did not inconvenience her long, for the seizure terminated in the death of the old lady about a week after its commencement.

But even this, though acknowledged to be "certainly a blessing, and a happy release," could not restore the bride to the triumphant state of existence the illness of her mother had interrupted; for, in the first place, her deep mourning was by no means becoming to her, and she was perfectly aware of it; and her white satin, and her silver fringe, would be sure to turn yellow before she could wear them again. Besides, what was worse than all, a young attorney of Silverton married the daughter of a neighbouring clergyman, who, of course, was immediately installed in all a bride's honours, to the inexpressible mortification of Mrs. Barnaby.

The annoyance which followed these vexations was, however, far more serious: the resources of poor Mr. Compton were completely exhausted; he had drawn out his last hundred from the funds, and actually remained possessed of no property whatever, except the nearly expired lease, and the worn-out furniture of the house in which he lived.

Mrs. Barnaby listened to the feeble old man's statement of his desperate position with dismay; she knew just enough of his affairs to be aware that it was very likely to be true, though with mistaken tenderness her mother had always refrained from representing their embarrassments to her daughter, as being of the hopeless extent which they really were.

What, then, was to be done? The choice lay between two measures only, both deeply wounding to her pride. In the one case she must leave the old man to be arrested in his bed for the price of the food which for a few months longer perhaps he might still get on credit ... in the other she must undergo the humiliation of informing her husband that all the gay external appearances she and her mother had so laboriously presented to the public eye, were in reality but so much cheatery and delusion; and that, if he would not take compassion on her father's destitute condition, the poor old man must either die in the county prison or the parish workhouse.

The alternative offered more of doubt than of choice, and it might have been long ere she decided, had she not cleverly recollected that, if she decided upon leaving him to get on as he could for a few weeks longer, she must at last submit to her husband's knowing the real state of the case; she therefore resolutely determined that he should know it at once.

The time she chose to make the disclosure was the hour when men are generally supposed to be in the most amiable frame of mind possible, namely, when hunger, but not appetite, has been satisfied, and digestion not fully begun; that is to say, Mr. Barnaby was enjoying his walnuts and his wine.

"My dear Barnaby!..." she began, "I have some very disagreeable intelligence to communicate to you, which has reached me only to-day, and which has distressed me more than I can express."

"Good heaven!... What can you mean, my dear love?... For God's sake do not weep, my beautiful Martha, but tell me what it is, and trust to me for consolation."

"And that indeed I must do, dearest Barnaby!... for who else have I now to look to?... My poor father ... I had no idea of it till this morning ... my poor father is...."

"Dying, perhaps, my poor love!... Alas! Martha dearest, I have long known that his case was perfectly hopeless, and I had hoped that you had been aware of this also; but really, my love, his state of health is such as ought in a great degree to reconcile you to his loss.... I am sure he must suffer a great deal at times."

Mrs. Barnaby's first impulse was to reply that what she had to tell was a great deal worse than that; but this would have been the truth, and a sort of habitual, or it might indeed be called natural cautiousness, led her always to pause before she uttered anything that she had no motive for saying, excepting merely that it was true; and she generally found, upon reconsideration, that there was hardly anything which might not, according to her tactics, be improved by a leetle dressing up. So, in reply to this affectionate remonstrance from her husband, Mrs. Barnaby answered with a sob:—

"No, my dear Barnaby!... I have no reason to doubt but that Providence will spare my sole remaining parent for some short time longer, if only to prove to him that his happy daughter has the will as well as the means to supply to him the exemplary wife he has lost! But, alas! dear Barnaby, who in this world can we expect to find perfect? My poor dear mother, in her great anxiety to spare his age and weakness the suffering such intelligence must occasion, most unwisely concealed from him and from me the failure of the merchant in whose hands he had deposited the sum for which he sold his patrimonial estate.... His object in selling it was to increase his income, principally indeed for my poor mother's sake, and now the entire sum is lost to us for ever!"

"God bless me!... This is a sad stroke indeed, my dear! What is the name of this merchant?... I hope, at least, that we may get some dividend out of him."

"I really do not know his name, but I know that it is a New York merchant, and so I fear there is little or no chance of our ever recovering a penny."

"Why, really, in that case, I will not flatter you with much hope on the subject. And what has the poor old gentleman got to live upon, my dear Martha?"

"Nothing, Barnaby!... absolutely nothing: and unless your tender affection should induce you to permit his spending the little remnant of his days under our roof, I fear a prison will soon enclose him!"

A violent burst of weeping appeared to follow this avowal; and Mr. Barnaby, who was really a very kind-hearted man, hastened to console her by declaring that he was heartily glad he had a home to offer him.... "So, dry up your tears, my dear girl, and let me see you look gay and happy again," said he; "and depend upon it, we shall be able to make papa very comfortable here."

The disagreeable business was over, and therefore Mrs. Barnaby did look gay and happy again. Moreover, she gave her husband a kiss, and said in a very consolatory accent, "The poor old man need not be in our way much, my dear Barnaby; ... I have been thinking that the little room behind the laundry may be made very comfortable for him without any expense at all; I shall only just have to...."

"No, no, Martha," interrupted the worthy Galen, "there is no need of packing the poor gentleman into that dismal little place.... Let him have the room over the dining-room; the south is always the best aspect for the old; and, besides, there is a closet that will serve to keep his pipes and tobacco, and his phials and his pill-boxes, out of sight."

"You are most ex-cess-ively kind, my dear Barnaby," replied his lady; "but did not you tell me that you meant to offer the Thompsons a bed when the bachelors' ball is given?... And I am sure you would not like to put them anywhere but in the south room."

"I did say so, my dear, and I am sure I meant it at the time; but a bed for the ball-night is of so little consequence to them, and a warm, comfortable room, for your father is so important, that, do you know, it would seem to me quite silly to bring the two into comparison."

"Well!... I am sure I can't thank you enough, and I will go the first thing to-morrow to tell my father of your kindness."

"I must pass by his house to-night, my dear, in my way to the Kellys', and I will just step in and tell him how we have settled it."

It was impossible even for Mrs. Barnaby to find at the moment any plausible reason for objecting to this good-natured proposal; but, in truth, it was far from agreeable to her. Her poor father was quite ignorant of the elegant turn she had given to the disagreeable fact of his having spent his last shilling, and she was by no means desirous that her kind-hearted husband should enter upon any discussion of his "misfortunes" with him. But a moment's reflection sufficed to bring her ready wit into play again; and then she said, in addition to the applause she had already uttered,—"By the by, my dear Barnaby, I am not quite sure that I can let you enjoy this pleasure without my sharing it with you. I know it will make my dear father so very happy!"

"Well, then, Martha, put on your bonnet and cloak, and come along; ... it will be better you should go too, or I might linger with him too long to explain matters, and I really have no time to lose."

The kindness thus manifested by the worthy Barnaby was not evanescent; it led him to see that the money produced by the sale of the little remnant of poor Mr. Compton's property, was immediately disposed of in the payment of such trifling debts as, despite his long waning credit, he had been able to contract; and for the two years and eight months that he continued struggling with advancing age and increasing disease, his attention to him was unremitting.

During the whole of that time Miss Betsy Compton never saw him. All hope, and indeed all urgent want of assistance from her well-guarded purse having ended, Mrs. Barnaby's anger and hatred towards the spinster, flourished unchecked by any motives of interest; and Miss Betsy was not a person to present herself uninvited at the house of a rich apothecary, who had the privilege of calling her aunt. She had indeed from time to time taken care to inform herself of the condition of her brother, and finding that he wanted for nothing, but was, on the contrary, very carefully nursed and attended, she settled the matter very easily with her conscience; and with the exception of the pension, and other little expenses of Agnes, her income, yearly increasing, continued to roll up for no other purpose, as it should seem, than merely to afford her the satisfaction of knowing that she was about ten times as rich as anybody (excepting, perhaps, farmer Wright,) believed her to be.

When, however, the last hours of the old man were approaching, he told Mr. Barnaby that he should like to see both his sister and his grandchild; and ten minutes had not passed after he said so, before an express was galloping towards Compton Basett with a civil gentleman-like letter from the apothecary to Miss Betsy, informing her of the condition of her brother, and expressing the hospitable wish that she and the little Agnes would be pleased to make his house their home as long as the poor gentleman remained alive.

Miss Betsy had some strong prejudices, but she had strong discernment too; and few old maids whose personal knowledge of the world had been as contracted as hers, would have so instantly comprehended the good sense and the good feeling of the author of this short note as she did. Her answer was brief, but not so brief as to prevent the friendly feeling with which she wrote it from being perceptible; and ere they met, this stranger aunt, and nephew, were exceedingly well-disposed to be civil to each other.

Miss Betsy's arrangements were soon made. She wrote to the person to whose care she had intrusted Agnes, desiring her immediately to send her under proper protection to Silverton, and having done this, she set off in farmer Wright's chaise-cart to pay her first visit to her married niece, and her last to her dying brother.

CHAPTER VII

THE ELEGANCE OF MRS. BARNABY DISPLAYED—ITS EFFECT ON HER AUNT BETSY—INTERVIEW BETWEEN THE BROTHER AND SISTER

Agnes Willoughby had never been in Silverton from the day that her aunt Betsy first took her from her grandfather's house. Had Mrs. Compton lived, she would probably have battled for the performance of Miss Betsy's promise, that the little girl should sometimes visit them; but though it is probable Mrs. Barnaby might occasionally have thought of her niece with some degree of interest and curiosity, the feeling was not strong enough to induce her to open a correspondence with Miss Betsy; still it was certainly not without something like pleasure that she found she was again to see her.

Miss Betsy arrived late in the evening of the day on which the summons reached her; and, being shewn into Mrs. Barnaby's smart drawing-room, was received with much stateliness by that lady, who derived considerable consolation, under the disagreeable necessity of welcoming a person she detested, from the opportunity it afforded her of displaying the enormous increase of wealth and importance that had fallen upon her since they last met.

Poor Miss Betsy really felt sad at the thoughts of the errand upon which she was come; nevertheless she could not, without some difficulty, suppress her inclination to smile at the full-blown dignity of Mrs. Barnaby. Fond as this lady was of parading her grandeur on all occasions, she had never, even among the dear friends whom she most especially desired to inspire with envy, felt so strong an inclination to shew off her magnificence as on the present. The covers were removed from the chairs and sofas; the eclipse produced by the dim grey drugget, when stretched across the radiance of the many-coloured carpet, was over; five golden-leaved annuals, the glory of her library, were spread at well-graduated distances upon her round table; her work-box, bright in its rose-coloured lining, her smart embossed letter-case, her chimney ornaments, her picture frames, her foot-stools, all were uncovered, all were studiously shown forth to meet the careless eye of Miss Betsy; while the proud owner of all these very fine things, notwithstanding the gloomy state of her mansion, was herself a walking museum of lace and trinkets.... Nor were her manners less superb than her habiliments.

"I am sorry, Miss Compton," she said.... "I may call you Miss Compton now, as my marriage put an end to the possibility of any confusion.... I am sorry that your first introduction to my humble abode should have been made under circumstances so melancholy. Dismal as of necessity everything must look now, I can assure you that this unpretending little room is the scene of much domestic comfort."

This was unblushingly said, though the cold, stiff-looking apartment was never entered but upon solemn occasions, when the whole house was turned inside out for the reception of company. Miss Betsy, or rather Miss Compton, (as, in compliance with Mrs. Barnaby's hint, we will in future call her,) looked round upon the spotless carpet, and upon all the comfortless precision of the apartment, and replied,—

"If this is your common living room, niece Martha, you are certainly much improved in neatness; and seeing it so prim, it is quite needless to ask if you have any children."

This reply was bitter every way; for, first, it spoke plainly enough the spinster's disbelief in the domestic elegance of her niece; and secondly, it alluded to her being childless, a subject of very considerable mortification to Mrs. Barnaby.

How far this sort of ambush warfare might have proceeded it is impossible to say, as it would have been difficult to place together any two people who more cordially disliked each other; but before Mrs. Barnaby had time to seek for words bearing as sharp a sting as those she had received, her husband entered. He waited not for the pompous introduction his wife was preparing, but walking up to his guest addressed her respectfully but mournfully, saying he feared it was necessary to press an early interview with her brother, if she wished that he should be sensible of her kindness in coming to him.

Miss Compton immediately rose, and uttering a short, strong phrase expressive of gratitude for his kindness to the dying man, said she was ready to attend him. She found her brother quite sensible, but very weak, and evidently approaching his last hour; he thanked her for coming to him, warmly expressed his gratitude to Mr. Barnaby, and then murmured something about wishing to see little Agnes before he died.

"She will be here to-morrow, brother," replied Miss Compton, "and in time, I trust, to receive your blessing."

"Thank you, thank you, sister Betsy; ... but tell me, tell me before you go, ... have you sold father's poor dear fields as I have done? That is all I have got to be very sorry for.... I ought never to have done that, sister Betsy."

Mr. Barnaby had left the room as soon as he had placed Miss Compton in a chair by the sick man's bed, and none but an old woman who acted as his nurse remained in it.

"You may go, nurse, if you please, for a little while; I will watch by my brother," said Miss Compton. The woman obeyed, and they were left alone. The old man followed the nurse with his eyes as she retreated, and when she closed the door said,—

"I am glad we are alone once more, dear sister, for you are the only one I could open my heart to.... I don't believe I have been a very wicked man, sister Betsy, though I am afraid I never did much good to anybody, nor to myself neither; but the one thing that lies heavy at my heart, is having sold away my poor father's patrimony.... I can't help thinking, Betsy, that I see him every now and then at the bottom of my bed, with his old hat, and his spud, and his brown gaiters ... and ... I never told anybody; ... but he seems always just going to repeat the last words he ever said to me, which were spoken just like as I am now speaking to you, Betsy, with his last breath; ... and he said, 'Josiah, my son, I could not die with a safe conscience if I left my poor weakly Betsy without sufficient to keep her in the same quiet comfort as she has been used to. But it would grieve me, Josiah....' Oh! how plain I hear his voice at this minute!—'it would grieve me, Josiah,' he said, 'if I thought the acres would be parted for ever ... they have been above four hundred years belonging to us from father to son; and once Compton Basett was a name that stood for a thousand acres instead of three hundred;' ... and then ... don't be angry, sister Betsy," said the sick man, pressing her hand which he held, "but he said, 'I don't think Betsy very likely to marry; and if she don't, Josiah, why, then, all that is left of Compton Basett will be joined together again for your descendants,' ... and yet, after this I sold my portion, Betsy, ... and I do fear his poor spirit is troubled for it—I do indeed ... and it is that which hangs so heavy upon my mind."

"And if that be all, Josiah, you may close your eyes, and go to join our dear father in peace. He struggled with and conquered his strongest feeling, his just and honourable pride, for my sake; and for his, as well as for the same feeling, which is very strong within my own breast also, I have lived poorly, though not hardly, Josiah, and have added penny to penny till I was able to make Compton Basett as respectable a patrimony as he left it. It was not farmer Wright who bought the land, brother—it was I."

The old man's emotion at hearing this was stronger than any he had shewn for many years. He raised his sister's hand to his lips, and kissed it fervently. "Bless you, Betsy!... bless you, my own dear sister!"... he said in a voice that trembled as much from feeling as from weakness, and for several minutes afterwards he lay perfectly silent and motionless.

Miss Compton watched him with an anxious eye, and not without a flutter at her heart lest she should suddenly find this stillness to be that of death. But it was not so; on the contrary, his voice appeared considerably stronger than it had done since their interview began, when he again spoke, and said,—

"I see him now, sister Betsy, as plainly as I see the two posts at the bottom of my bed, and he stands exactly in the middle between them; he has got no hat on, but his smooth white hair is round his face just as it used to be, and he looks so smiling and so happy.... Do not think I am frightened at seeing him, Betsy; quite the contrary.... I feel so peaceful ... so very peaceful...."

"Then try to sleep, dear brother!" said Miss Compton, who felt that his pulse fluttered, and, aware that his senses were wandering, feared that the energy with which he spoke might hasten the last hour, and so rob his grandchild of his blessing.

"I will sleep," he replied, more composedly, "as soon as you have told me one thing. Who will have the Compton Basett estate, Betsy, when you are dead?"

"Agnes Willoughby," replied the spinster, solemnly.

"That is right.... Now go away, Betsy, ... it is quite right ... go away now, and let me sleep."

She watched him for a moment, and seeing his eyes close, and hearing a gentle, regular breathing that convinced her he was indeed asleep, she crept noiselessly from his bedside; then having summoned the nurse, and re-established her beside the fire, retired to the solitude of her own room.

CHAPTER VIII

SOLITARY MEDITATION AND IMPORTANT RESOLUTIONS—AGNES WILLOUGHBY ARRIVES AT SILVERTON—HER GRANDFATHER GIVES HER HIS BLESSING, AND DIES—MISS COMPTON MAKES A SUDDEN RETREAT

When Miss Compton reached her room, she found a tiny morsel of fire just lighted in a tiny grate; and as the season was November, the hour nine P. M., and the candle she carried in her hand not of the brightest description, the scene was altogether gloomy enough. But not even to save herself from something greatly worse, would she at that moment have exchanged its solitude for the society of Mrs. Barnaby, although she had been sure of finding her in the best-lighted room, and seated beside the brightest fire that ever blazed. So, wrapping around her the stout camlet cloak by the aid of which she had braved the severity of many years' wintry walks to church, she sat down in the front of the little fire, and gave herself up to the reflections that crowded upon her mind.

Elizabeth Compton did not believe in the doctrine of ghosts; her mind was of a strong and healthy fibre, which was rarely sufficiently wrought upon by passing events to lose its power of clear perception and unimpassioned judgment; but the scene she had just passed through, had considerably shaken her philosophy. Five-and-thirty years had passed since Josiah and Elizabeth shared the paternal roof together. They were then very tender friends, for he was affectionate and sweet-tempered; and she, though nearly seventeen, was as young in appearance, and as much in need of his thoughtful care of her, as if she had been many years younger. But this union was totally and for ever destroyed when Josiah married; from the first hour they met, the two sisters-in-law conceived an aversion for each other which every succeeding interview appeared to strengthen; and this so effectually separated the brother from the sister, that they had never met again with that peculiar species of sympathy which can only be felt by children of the same parents, till now, that the sister came expressly to see the brother die.

This reunion had softened and had opened both their hearts: Josiah confessed to his dear sister Betsy that his conscience reproached him for having made away with his patrimony ... a fact which he had never hinted to any other human being ... and she owned to him that she was secretly possessed of landed property worth above six hundred a-year, and also—which was a confidence, if possible, more sacred still—that Agnes Willoughby would inherit it.

It would be hardly doing justice to the good sense of Miss Betsy to state, that this rational and proper destination of her property had never been finally decided upon by her till the moment she answered her brother's question on the subject; and still less correctly true would it be to say, that the dying man's delirious fancy respecting the presence of their father was the reason that she answered that appeal in the manner she did; yet still there might be some slight mixture of truth in both. Miss Compton was constantly in the habit of telling herself that she had not decided to whom she would leave her property; but it is no less true, that the only person she ever thought of as within the possibility of becoming her heir, was Agnes. It is certain also, as I have stated above, that Miss Compton did not believe that departed spirits ever revisited the earth; nevertheless, the dying declaration of Josiah, that he saw the figure of his father, did produce a spasm at her heart, which found great relief by her pronouncing the words, "Agnes Willoughby."

And now that she was quietly alone, and perfectly restored to her sober senses, she began to reconsider all that she had spoken, and to pass judgment upon herself for the having yielded in some degree to the weakness of a visionary imagination.

The result, however, of this self-examination was not exactly what she herself expected. At first she was disposed to exclaim mentally, "I have been foolish—I have been weak;" ... but as she gazed abstractedly on her little fire, and thought—thought—thought of all the chain of events (each so little in itself, yet all so linked together as to produce an important whole,) by which she, the sickly, crooked, little Betsy Compton, had become the proprietor of the long preserved patrimony of her ancestors, ... and also, when she remembered the infinite chances which had existed against either of her portionless, uneducated nieces, forming such a marriage as might produce a child of gentle blood to be her successor,—when she thought of all this, and that, notwithstanding the lieutenant's poverty, the name of Willoughby could disgrace none to which it might be joined, she could not but feel that all things had been managed for her better than she could have managed them for herself.

"And if," thought she, "I was influenced, by hearing my poor father so accurately described, to bind myself at once by a promise to make little Agnes my heir, how do I know but that Providence intended it should be so?"

"Is my freedom of action then gone for ever?" she continued, carrying on her mental soliloquy. The idea was painful to her, and her head sunk upon her breast as she brooded upon it.

"Not so!" she muttered to herself, after some minutes' cogitation. "I am not pledged to this, nor shall it be so. If indeed some emanation from my father's mind has made itself felt by his children this night, it ought not to make a timid slave of me, but rather rouse my courage and my strength to do something more than mere justice to the race that seems so strangely intrusted to my care. And so I will!... if the girl be such a one as may repay the trouble; ... if not, I will shew that I have still some freedom left."

Miss Compton had never seen Agnes Willoughby from the time she first took her from Silverton. Deeply shocked at the profound ignorance in which she found the poor little girl when she visited Compton Basett, she had set herself very earnestly to discover where she could immediately place her, with the best chance of her recovering the time she had so negligently been permitted to lose, and by good luck heard of a clergyman's family in which young ladies were received for a stipend of fifty pounds a-year, and treated more like the children of affectionate parents than the pupils of mercenary teachers. The good spinster heard all this, and was well pleased by the description; yet would she not trust to it, but breaking through all her habits, she put herself into a post-chaise and drove to the rectory of Empton, a distance of at least twenty miles from the town of Silverton. Here she found everything she wished to find; a small, regular establishment, a lady-like and very intelligent woman, with an accomplished young person, (her only child,) fully capable of undertaking the education of a gentleman's daughter; while the venerable father of the family and of the parish, by his gentle manners and exemplary character, ensured exactly the sort of respectability in the home she sought for the little Agnes, which she considered as its most essential feature.

The preliminaries were speedily arranged, and as soon as a neat and sufficient wardrobe was ready for her use, her final separation from her improvident grandmother took place in the manner that has been related.

When Miss Compton left the little girl in the charge of Mrs. Wilmot, she had certainly no idea of her remaining there above three years without visiting or being seen by any of her family; but Mrs. Wilmot, in her subsequent letters, so strongly urged the advantage of not disturbing studies so late begun, and now proceeding so satisfactorily, that our reasonable aunt Betsy willingly submitted to her remaining quietly where she was; an arrangement rendered the more desirable by the death of her grandmother, and the breaking up of the establishment which had been her only home.

The seeing her again after this long absence was now an event of very momentous importance to Miss Compton. Should she in any way resemble either her grandmother or her aunt Barnaby, the little spinster felt that the promise so solemnly given would become a sore pain and grief to her, for rather a thousand times would she have bequeathed her carefully collected wealth to the county hospital, than have bestowed it to swell the vulgar ostentation of a Mrs. Barnaby. The power of choice, however, she felt was no longer left her. She had pledged her word, and that under circumstances of no common solemnity, that Agnes Willoughby should be her heir.

The poor little lady, as these anxious ruminations harassed her mind, became positively faint and sick as the idea occurred to her, that the eyes of little Agnes had formerly sparkled with somewhat of the brightness she thought so very hateful in her well-rouged aunt; and at length, having sat till her candle was nearly burnt out, and her fire too, she arose in order to return to the fine drawing-room, and bid her entertainers good night; but she stood with clasped hands for one moment upon the hearthstone before she quitted it, and muttered half aloud, ... "I have said that Agnes Willoughby shall be my heir, ... and so she shall; ... she shall (be she a gorgon or a second Martha) inherit the Compton Basett acres, restored, improved, and worth at least one fourth more than when my poor father ... Heaven give his spirit rest!... divided them between his children. But for my snug twelve thousand pounds sterling vested in the three per cents, and my little mortgage of eighteen hundred more for which I so regularly get my five per cent., that at least is my own, and that shall never, never go to enrich any one who inherits the red cheeks and bright black eyes of Miss Martha Wisett.... No!... not if I am driven to choose an heir for it from the Foundling Hospital!"

Somewhat comforted in spirit by this magnanimous resolve, Miss Compton found her way to the drawing-room, and would have been fully confirmed in the wisdom of it, had any doubt remained, by the style and tone of Mrs. Barnaby, whom she found sitting there in solitary state, her husband being professionally engaged in the town, and her own anxiety for her dying father quite satisfied by being told that he was asleep.

"And where have you been hiding yourself, aunt Betsy, since you left papa?" said the full-dressed lady, warmed into good humour by the consciousness of her own elegance, and the delightful contrast between a married woman, sitting in her own handsome drawing-room, (looking as she had just ascertained that she herself did look by a long solitary study of her image in the glass,) and a poor crooked little old maid like her visitor. "I have been expecting to see you for this hour past. I hope Barnaby will be in soon, and then we will go to supper. Barnaby always eats a hot supper, and so I eat it with him for company, ... and I hope you feel disposed to join us after your cold drive."

"I never eat any supper at all, Mrs. Barnaby."

"No, really?... I thought farm-house people always did, though not exactly such a supper as Barnaby's, perhaps, for he always will have something nice and delicate; and so, as it pleases him, I have taken to the same sort of thing myself ... veal cutlets and mashed potatoes, ... or half a chicken grilled perhaps, with now and then a glass of raspberry cream, or a mince pie, as the season may be, all which I take to be very light and wholesome; and indeed Barnaby thinks so too, or else I am sure he would not let me touch it.... You can't think, aunt Betsy, what a fuss he makes about me.... To be sure, he is a perfect model of a husband."

"God grant she may be the colour of a tallow-candle, and her eyes as pale and lustreless as those of a dead whiting!" mentally ejaculated the whimsical spinster; but in reply to her niece she said nothing. After sitting, however, for about ten minutes in the most profound silence, she rose and said,—

"I should like to have a bed-candle, if you please, ma'am. I need not wait to see the doctor. If he thinks there is any alteration in my brother, he will be kind enough to let me know."

The lady of the mansion condescendingly rang the bell, which her livery-boy answered with promptness, for he was exceedingly well drilled, Mrs. Barnaby having little else to do than to keep him and her two maids in proper order; ... the desired candle was brought, and Miss Compton having satisfied herself that her brother still slept, retired to rest.

The following day was an important one to her race; ... the last male of the Compton Basett family expired, and the young girl to whom its small but ancient patrimony was to descend, appeared for the first time before Miss Compton in the character of her heiress.

It was about mid-day when the post-chaise which conveyed Agnes arrived at Mr. Barnaby's door. Had the person expected been a judge in whose hands the life and death of the spinster freeholder was placed, her heart could hardly have beat with more anxiety to catch a sight of his countenance, and to read her fate in it, than it now did to discover whether her aspect were that of a vulgar beauty or a gentlewoman.

Miss Compton was sitting in the presence of Mrs. Barnaby when the carriage stopped at the door, and had been for some hours keenly suffering from the disgust which continually increased upon her, at pretty nearly every word her companion uttered. "If she be like this creature," thought she, as she rose from her seat with nervous emotion, "if she be like her in any way ... I will keep my promise when I die, but I will never see her more."

Nothing but her dread of encountering this hated resemblance prevented her from going down stairs to meet the important little girl; but, after a moment's fidgetting, and taking a step or two towards the door, she came back and reseated herself. The suspense did not last long; the door was opened, and "Muss Willerby" announced.

A short, round, little creature, who though nearly fourteen, did not look more than twelve, with cheeks as red as roses, and large dark-grey eyes, a great deal brighter than ever her aunt's or grandmother's had been, entered, and timidly stopped short in her approach to her two aunts, as if purposely to be looked at and examined.

She was looked at and examined, and judgment was passed upon her by both; differing very widely, however, as was natural enough, but in which (a circumstance much less natural, considering the qualifications for judging possessed by the two ladies,) the younger shewed considerably more discernment than the elder. Mrs. Barnaby thought her—and she was right—exceedingly like what she remembered her very pretty mother at the same age, just as round and as rosy, but with a strong mixture of the Willoughby countenance, which was very decidedly "Patrician" both in contour and expression.

But poor Miss Compton saw nothing of all this ... she saw only that she was short, fat, fresh-coloured, and bright-eyed!... This dreaded spectacle was a death-blow to all her hopes, the hated confirmation of all her fears. It was in vain that when the poor child spoke, her voice proved as sweet as a voice could be,—in vain that her natural curls fell round her neck as soon as her bonnet was taken off in rich chestnut clusters—in vain that the smile with which she answered Mrs. Barnaby's question, "Do you remember me, Agnes?" displayed teeth as white and as regular as a row of pearls,—all these things were but so many items against her in the opinion of Miss Compton, for did they not altogether constitute a brilliant specimen of vulgar beauty? Had Agnes been tall, pale, and slight made, with precisely the same features, her aunt Betsy would have willingly devoted the whole of her remaining life to her, would have ungrudgingly expended every farthing of her income for her comfort and advantage, and would only have abstained from expending the principal too, because she might leave it to her untouched at her death. But now, now that she saw her, as she fancied, so very nearly approaching in appearance to everything she most disliked, all the long-indulged habits of frugality that had enabled her (as she at this moment delighted to remember) to accumulate a fortune over which she still had entire control, seemed to rise, before her, and press round her very heart, as the only means left of atoning to herself for the promise she had been led to make.

"I will see the eyes of my father's son closed," thought she, "and then I will leave the beauties to manage together as well as they can till mine are closed too, ... and by that time, perhaps, the rents of the lands that I must no longer consider as my own, and my interest and my mortgages, may have grown into something rich enough to make them and theirs wish that they had other claims upon Elizabeth Compton besides being her nearest of kin."

These thoughts passed rapidly, but their impression was deep and lasting. Miss Compton sat in very stern and melancholy silence, such as perhaps did not ill befit the occasion that had brought them all together; but Mrs. Barnaby, whose habitual propensity to make herself comfortable, prevented her from sacrificing either her curiosity or her love of talking to ceremony, ceased not to question Agnes as to the people she had been with, the manner in which she had lived, and the amount of what she had learned.

On the first subject she received nothing in return but unbounded, unqualified expressions of praise and affection, such as might either be taken for the unmeaning hyperbole of a silly speaker, or the warm out-pouring of well-deserved affection and gratitude, so Miss Compton classed all that Agnes said respecting the family of the Wilmots under the former head: her record of their manner of living produced exactly the same result; and on the important chapter of her improvements, the genuine modesty of the little girl did her great disservice; for when, in answer to Mrs. Barnaby's questions.... "Do you understand French?... Can you dance?... Can you play?... Can you draw?" she invariably answered, "A little," Miss Compton failed not to make a mental note upon it, which, if spoken, would have been, "Little enough, I dare say."

This examination had lasted about half an hour, when Mr. Barnaby entered, and, addressing them all, said, "Poor Mr. Compton has woke up, and appears quite collected, but, from his pulse, I do not think he can last long.... Is this Miss Willoughby, Martha?... I am sorry that your first visit, my dear, should be so sad a one; ... but you had better all come now, and take leave of him."

The three ladies rose immediately, and without speaking followed Mr. Barnaby to the bedside of the dying man. He was evidently sinking fast, but knew them all, and expressed pleasure at the sight of

Agnes. "Dear child!" he said, looking earnestly at her, "I am glad she is come to take my blessing.... God bless you, Agnes!... She is very like.... God bless you, Agnes!... God bless you all!"

Mr. Barnaby took his wife by the arm and led her away; she took her weeping niece with her, but Miss Compton shook her head when invited by Mr. Barnaby to follow them, and in a very few minutes completed the duty to perform which she had left her solitude, for with her own hands she closed her brother's eyes, and then stole to her room, from which she speedily dispatched an order for a post-chaise to come immediately to the door.

The conduct and manners of Mr. Barnaby had pleased the difficult little lady greatly, and she would willingly have shaken hands with him before leaving his house; but to do this she must have re-entered the drawing-room, and again seen Mrs. Barnaby and Agnes, a penance which she felt quite unequal to perform; so, leaving a civil message for him with the maid, she went down stairs with as little noise as possible as soon as the chaise was announced, and immediately drove off to Compton Basett.

CHAPTER IX

MR. BARNABY PAYS A VISIT TO COMPTON BASETT, AND RECEIVES FROM THE HEIRESS A FORMAL CONGÉ—AGNES IS SENT BACK TO SCHOOL, AND REMAINS THERE TILL CALLED HOME BY THE NEWS OF HIS DEATH

Some surprise and great indignation were expressed by Mrs. Barnaby on hearing that Miss Compton had departed without the civility of taking leave. She resented greatly the rudeness to herself, but, as she justly said, the meaning of it was much more important to Agnes than to her.

"What is to become of her, Mr. Barnaby, I should like to know?..." said the angry lady. "Agnes says that Mrs. Wilmot expects her back directly, and who is to pay the expense of sending her, I wonder?"

Mr. Barnaby assured her in reply that there would be no difficulty about that, adding, that they should doubtless hear from Miss Compton as soon as she had recovered the painful effect of the scenes at which she had so lately been present.

Days passed away, however, the funeral was over, and everything in the family of Mr. Barnaby restored to its usual routine, yet still they heard nothing of Miss Compton.

"I see clearly how it is," said the shrewd lady of the mansion. "Aunt Betsy means to throw the whole burden of poor dear little Agnes upon us, ... and what in the world are we to do with her, Barnaby?"

"I cannot think she has any such intention, Martha. After the excellent education she has been giving her for the last three or four years, it is hardly likely that she would suddenly give her up, when it is impossible but she must have been delighted with her. But, at any rate, make yourself easy, my dear Martha; if she abandons her, we will not; we have no children of our own, and I think the best thing we can do is to adopt this dear girl.... She is really the sweetest little creature I ever saw in my life. I can assure you, that when her education is finished, I, for one, should be delighted to have her live with us.... What say you to it, Martha?"

"I am sure you are goodness itself, my dear Barnaby; and if the crabbed, crooked old maid would just promise at once to leave her the little she may have left after all her ostentatious charities, I should make no objection whatever to our adopting Agnes. She is just like poor Sophy, and it certainly is a pleasure to look at her."

"Well, then, don't fret yourself any more about aunt Betsy. I will call upon her one of these days when I happen to be going Compton Basett way, and find out, if I can, what she means to do about sending her back to Mrs. Wilmot. It would be a pity not to finish her education, for it is easy to see that she has had great justice done her."

It was not, however, till some word from Agnes gave him to understand that she was herself very anxious about going on with her studies, and desirous of letting Mrs. Wilmot know what was become of her, that he made or met an opportunity of conversing with Miss Compton. He found her reading a novel in her chimney corner, and dressed in deep, but very homely mourning. She received him civilly, nay, there was even something of kindness in her manner when she reverted to the time she had passed in his house, and thanked him for the hospitality he had shewn her. He soon perceived, however, that the name of Agnes produced no feeling of interest; but that, on the contrary, when he mentioned her, the expression of the old lady's face changed from very pleasing serenity to peevish discomfort; so he wisely determined to make what he had to say a matter of business, and immediately entered upon it accordingly.

"My principal reason, Miss Compton, for troubling you with a visit," said he, "is to learn what are your wishes and intentions respecting Miss Willoughby. Is it your purpose to send her back to Mrs. Wilmot?"

"I have already been at a great and very inconvenient expense, Mr. Barnaby, for the education of Agnes Willoughby; but as I have no intention whatever of straitening my poor little income any further by incurring cost on her account, I am glad that what I have done has been of the nature most likely to make her independent of me and of you too, Mr. Barnaby, in future. When I first placed her with Mrs. Wilmot I agreed to keep her there for five years, seventeen months of which are still unexpired. To this engagement I am willing to adhere; and though I can't say I think her a very bright girl, but rather perhaps a little inclining towards the contrary, yet still I imagine that when she knows she has her own bread to get, she may be induced to exert herself sufficiently during the next year and five months to enable her to take the place of governess to very young children, or perhaps that of teacher in a second or third rate school. That's my notion about her, Mr. Barnaby; and now, if you please, I never wish to hear any more upon the subject."

Greatly displeased by the manner in which Miss Compton spoke of his young favourite, Mr. Barnaby rose, and very drily wished her good morning; adding, however, that no farther delay should take place in sending Miss Willoughby back to resume her studies.

He was then bowing off, but the little lady stopped him, saying, "As I have been the means of sending the child to such a distance from her nearest relation, I mean your wife, sir, it is but just that I should pay such travelling expenses as are consequent upon it. Here, sir, is a ten-pound-note that I have carefully set apart for this purpose; have the kindness to dispense it for her as may seem most convenient. And now, sir, farewell! I wish not again to have my humble retreat disturbed by any persons so much above me in all worldly advantages as you and your elegant wife, and having performed what I thought to be my duty by the little Willoughby, I beg to have nothing farther to do with her. I dare say your lady will grow exceedingly fond of her, for it seems to me that they are vastly alike, and if that happens; there will be no danger of the young girl's wanting anything that a poor little sickly and deformed old body like me could do for her. Good morning, Mr. Barnaby."

Mr. Barnaby silently received the ten pounds, which he thought he had no right to refuse; and having patiently waited till Miss Compton had concluded her speech, he returned her "good morning," and took his leave.

The worthy apothecary's account of his visit produced considerable sensation. Agnes indeed received it in silence, but the offensive brightness of her eyes was dimmed for a moment or two by a few involuntary tears. Her young heart was disappointed; for not only had the strong liking conceived by the Wilmot family for her aunt Betsy led her to believe that she must unquestionably like her too, but she gratefully remembered her former gentle, quiet kindness to herself; and (worse still), on being brought back amongst her relatives, she had, contrary to what is usual in such cases, conceived the greatest predilection for the only one among them who did not like her at all.

But it was not in silence that Mrs. Barnaby received her husband's statement of the capricious old lady's firmly pronounced resolve of never having anything more to do with Agnes Willoughby. All the old familiar epithets of abuse came forth again as fresh and vigorous as if but newly coined; and though these were mixed up with language which it was by no means agreeable to hear, her judicious husband suffered her to run on without opposition till she was fairly out of breath, and then closed the conversation by putting a bed-candle into her hand, and saying,

"Now let us all go to bed, my dear, ... and I dare say you will have much pleasure in proving to your peevish relative that, as long as you live, Agnes will want no other aunt to take care of her."

The good seed sown with these words brought forth fruit abundantly. Mrs. Barnaby could not do enough in her own estimation to prove to the whole town of Silverton the contrast between Miss Compton and herself—the difference between a bad aunt and a good one.

Fortunately for the well-being of Agnes at this important period of her existence, she had inspired a strong feeling of affectionate interest in a more rational being than Mrs. Barnaby; her well-judging husband thought they should do better service to the young girl by sending her back to Mrs. Wilmot with as little delay as possible, than by keeping her with them for the purpose of proving to all the world that they were the fondest and most generous uncle and aunt that ever a dependant niece was blest with, and she was sent back to Empton accordingly.

In order to do justice to the kindness of Mr. Barnaby's adoption of the desolate girl, it must be remembered that neither he nor his wife had any knowledge of the scene which passed between Miss Compton and her brother before his death, neither had they the least idea that the old lady possessed anything beyond her original moiety of the Compton Basett estate; and they both believed her to be so capricious as to render it very probable (although it was remembered she had once talked of leaving it to those who had claims on her) that some of the poor of her parish might eventually become her heirs,—an idea which the unaccountable dislike she appeared to have taken to Agnes greatly tended to confirm.

Once during the time that remained for her continuance with the Wilmots, Agnes paid a fortnight's visit to the abode she was now taught to consider as her home: the next time she entered it, (a few weeks only before the period fixed for the termination of her studies,) she was summoned thither by the very sudden death of her excellent and valuable friend Mr. Barnaby. This event produced an entire and even violent change in her prospects and manner of life, as well as in those of her aunt; and it is from this epoch that the narrative promised by the title of "The Widow Barnaby" actually commences, the foregoing pages being only a necessary prologue to the appearance of my heroine in that character.

CHAPTER X

THE WIDOW BARNABY ENTERS ACTIVELY ON HER NEW EXISTENCE—HER WEALTH—HER HAPPY PROSPECTS—MRS. WILMOT VISITS MISS COMPTON, AND OBTAINS LEAVE TO INTRODUCE AGNES WILLOUGHBY

Mrs. Barnaby was really very sorry for the death of her husband, and wept, with little or no effort, several times during the dismal week that preceded his interment; but she was not a woman to indulge long in so very unprofitable a weakness; and accordingly, as soon as the funeral was over, and the will read, by which he left her sole executrix and sole legatee of all he possessed, she very rationally began to meditate upon her position, and upon the best mode of enjoying the many good things which had fallen to her share.

She certainly felt both proud and happy as she thought of her independence and her wealth. Of the first she unquestionably had as much as it was possible for woman to possess, for no human being existed who had any right whatever to control her. Of the second, her judgment would have been more correct had she better understood the value of money. Though it is hardly possible any day should pass without adding something to the knowledge of all civilized beings on this subject, it is nevertheless certain that there are two modes of education which lead the mind in after life into very erroneous estimates respecting it. The one is being brought up to spend exactly as much money as you please, and the other having it deeply impressed on your mind that you are to spend none at all. In the first case, it is long before the most complete reverse of fortune can make the ci-devant rich man understand how a little money can be eked out, so as to perform the office of a great deal; and in the last, the change from having no money to having some will often, if it come suddenly, so puzzle all foregone conclusions, as to leave the possessor wonderfully little power to manage it discreetly.

The latter case was pretty nearly that of Mrs. Barnaby: when she learned that her dear lost husband had left her uncontrolled mistress of property to the amount of three hundred and seventy-two pounds per annum, besides the house and furniture, the shop and all it contained, she really felt as if her power in this life were colossal, and that she might roam the world either for conquest or amusement, or sustain in Silverton the style of a retired duchess, as might suit her fancy best.

Never yet had this lady's temper been so amiably placid, or so caressingly kind, as during the first month of her widowhood. She gave Agnes to understand that she wished to be considered as her mother, and trusted that they should find in each other all the happiness and affection which that tenderest of ties was so well calculated to produce.

"It will not be my fault, Agnes," she said, "if such be not the case. Thanks be to heaven, and my dear lost Barnaby, I have wealth enough to consult both your pleasure and advantage in my future mode of life; and be assured, my dear, that however much my own widowed feelings might lead me to prefer the tranquil consolations of retirement, I shall consider it my duty to live more for you than for myself; and I will indeed hasten, in spite of my feelings, to lay aside these sad weeds, that I may be able, with as little delay as possible, to give you such an introduction to the world as my niece has a right to expect."

Agnes was at a loss what to reply; she had still all the frank straight-forwardness of a child who has been educated by unaffected, sensible people, and yet she knew that she must not on this occasion say quite what she thought, which would probably have been,—

"Pray, don't fancy that I want you to throw aside your widow's weeds for me, aunt.... I don't believe you are one half as sorry for uncle Barnaby's death as I am".... But fortunately there was no mixture of bêtise in her frankness; and though it might have been beyond her power to express any great satisfaction at being thus addressed, she had no difficulty in saying,—"You are very kind to me, aunt," for this was true.

Notwithstanding this youthful frankness of mind, however, Agnes had by this time lost in a great measure that very childish look which distinguished her at the time her appearance so little pleased the fastidious taste of Miss Compton. She was still indeed in very good health, which was indicated by a colour as fresh, and almost as delicate too, as that of the wild rose; but her rapid growth during the last two years had quite destroyed the offensive "roundness," and her tall, well-made person, gave as hopeful a promise as could be wished for of womanly grace and beauty. The fair face was already the very perfection of loveliness; and had the secretly proud Miss Compton seen her as she walked in her deep heavy mourning beside her wide-spreading aunt to church, on the Sunday when that lady first restored herself to the public eye, she might perchance have thought, that not only was she worthy to inherit Compton Basett and all its accumulated rents, but any other glory and honour that this little earth of ours could bestow.

A feeling of strong mutual affection between the parties, led both the Wilmot family and Agnes to petition earnestly that the few weeks which remained of the stipulated (and already paid for) five years, might be completed; and Mrs. Barnaby, though it was really somewhat against her inclination, consented.

But though she had not desired this renewed absence of her niece, the notable widow determined to put it to profit, and set about a final arrangement of all her concerns with an activity that proved good Mr. Barnaby quite right in not having troubled her with any assistant executor.

She soon contrived to learn who it was who wished to succeed her "dear Barnaby," and managed matters so admirably well as to make the eager young man pay for the house, furniture, shop, &c. &c., about half as much again as they were worth, cleverly contriving, moreover, to retain possession for three months.

This important business being settled, she set herself earnestly and deliberately to consider what, when these three months should be expired, she should do with her freedom, her money, herself, and her niece. In deciding upon this question, she called none to counsel, for she had sense enough to avow to herself that she should pay not the slightest attention to any opinion but her own. In silence and in solitude, therefore, she pondered upon the future; and, to assist her speculations, she drew forth from the recesses of an old-fashioned bureau sundry documents and memoranda relative to the property bequeathed to her by her husband.

It was evident that her income would now somewhat exceed four hundred a-year, and this appeared to her amply sufficient to assist the schemes already working in her head for future aggrandizement, but by no means equal to what she felt her beauty and her talents gave her a right to hope for.

"It is, however, a handsome income," thought she, "and such a one as, with my person, may, and must, if properly made use of, lead to all I wish!"...

Mrs. Barnaby had once heard it said by a clever man, that human wishes might oftener be achieved, did mortals better know how to set about obtaining them.

"First," said the oracle, "let him be sure to find out what his wishes really are. This ascertained, let him, in the second place, employ all his acuteness to discover what is required for their fulfilment. Thirdly, let him examine himself and his position, in order to decide how much he, or it, can contribute towards this. Fourthly, let him subtract the sum of the capabilities he possesses from the total of means required. Fifthly, let him learn by, with, and in his heart of hearts, what it is that constitutes the remainder; and sixthly, and lastly, let him gird up the loins of his resolution, and start forth DETERMINED to acquire them. Whoso doeth this, shall seldom fail."

In the course of her visitings, military friendships and all included, Mrs. Barnaby, even in the small arena of Silverton, had heard several wise things in her day; but none of them ever produced such lasting effect as the words I have just quoted. They touched some chord within her that vibrated, ... not indeed with such a thrill as they might have made to ring along the nerves of a fine creature new to life, and emulous of all things good and great, but with a little sharp twitch, just at that point of the brain where self-love expands itself into a mesh of ways and means, instinct with will, to catch all it can that may be brought home to glut the craving for enjoyment; and so pregnant did they seem to her of the only wisdom that she wished to master, that her memory seized upon them with extraordinary energy, nor ever after relinquished its hold.

Little, however, could it profit her at the time she heard it; but she kept it, "like an ape in the corner of his jaw, first mouthed, to be last swallowed."

It was upon these words that she now pondered. Her two elbows set on the open bureau, her legs stretched under it, her lips resting upon the knuckles of her clasped hands, and her eyes fixed in deep abstraction on the row of pigeonholes before her, she entered upon a sort of self-catechism which ran thus:—

Q. What is it that I most wish for on earth?

A. A rich and fashionable husband.

Q. What is required to obtain this?

A. Beauty, fortune, talents, and a free entrance into good society.

Q. Do I possess any of these?... and which?

A. I possess beauty, fortune, and talents.

Q. What remains wanting?

A. A free entrance into good society.

"TRUE!" she exclaimed aloud, "it is that I want, and it is that I must procure."

Notwithstanding her sanguine estimate of herself, the widow, when she arrived at this point, was fain to confess that she did not exactly know how this necessary addition to her ways and means was to be acquired. Beyond the town of Silverton, and a thinly inhabited circuit of a mile or two round it, she had not a personal acquaintance in the world. This was a very perplexing consideration for a lady determined upon finding her way into the first circles, but its effect was rather to strengthen than relax her energies.

There was, however, one person, and she truly believed one only in the wide world, who might, at her first setting out upon her progress, be useful to her. This was a sister of Mr. Barnaby's, married to a clothier, whose manufactory was at Frome, but whose residence was happily at Clifton near Bristol. She had never seen this lady, or any of her family, all intercourse between the brother and sister having of late years consisted in letters, not very frequent, and the occasional interchange of presents,—a jar of turtle being now and then forwarded by mail from Bristol, and dainty quarters of Exmoor mutton, and tin pots of clouted cream, returned from Silverton.

Nevertheless Mrs. Peters was her sister-in-law just as much as if they had lived next door to each other for the last five years; and she had, of course, a right to all the kindness and hospitality so near a connexion demands.

A clothier's wife, to be sure, was not exactly the sort of person she would have chosen, had choice been left her; but it was better than nothing, infinitely better; ... "and besides," as the logical widow's head went on to reason, "she may introduce me to people above herself.... At a public place, too, like Clifton, it must be so easy! And then every new acquaintance I make will serve to lead on to another.... I am not so shy but I can turn all accidents to account; and I am not such a fool as to stand at one end of a room, when I ought to be at the other...."

Mrs. Barnaby never quoted Shakspeare, or she would probably have added here,—

"Why, then the world's mine oyster, which I with wit will open," for it was with some such thought that her soliloquy ended.

Day by day the absence of Agnes wore away, and day after day saw some business preparatory to departure dispatched. Sometimes the hours were winged by her having to pull about all the finery in her possession, and dividing it into portions, some to be abandoned for ever, some to be enveloped with reverend care in cotton and silver paper for her future use, and some to be given to the favoured Agnes.

While such cares occupied her hands, her thoughts naturally enough hurried forward to the time when she should lay aside her weeds. This was a dress so hatefully unbecoming in her estimation, that she firmly believed the inventor of it must have been actuated by some feeling akin to that which instituted the horrible Hindoo rite of which she had heard, whereby living wives were sacrificed to their departed husbands.

"Only!" she cried, bursting out into involuntary thanksgiving, "ours, thank God! is not for ever!"

To appear for the first time in the fashionable world in this frightful disguise, was quite out of the question; and consequently she could not make her purposed visit to Clifton till the time was arrived for throwing them off, and till ... to use her own words, "lilacs and greys were possible".... Yet there were other considerations that had weight with her too.

"His sister, however, shall just see me in my widow's weeds," thought she; "it may touch her heart perhaps, and must make her feel how very nearly we are related; ... but before any living soul out of the family can come near me, I will take care to look ... what I really am!... Six months!... it must, I suppose, be six months first!... Dreadful bore!"

The first half of this probationary term was to be passed at Silverton,—that was already wearing fast away,—and for the latter part of it she determined to take lodgings in Exeter.

"Yes ... it shall be Exeter!" she exclaimed, and then added, with a perfect quiver of delight, "Oh! what a difference now from what it was formerly!... How well I remember the time when a journey to Exeter appeared to me the very gayest thing in the world!... and now I should no more think of staying there than a queen would think of passing her life in her bed-room!"

The more she meditated on the future, indeed, the more enamoured did she become of it, till at length, her affairs being very nearly all brought to a satisfactory conclusion, a restless sort of impatience seized upon her; and nearly a fortnight before the time fixed for the return of Agnes she wrote a very peremptory letter of recall, but altogether omitted to point out either the mode of conveyance, or the protection she deemed necessary for her during the journey.

Perhaps Mrs. Wilmot was not sorry for this, as it afforded her an excuse for remaining herself to the last possible moment with a pupil who had found the way to create almost a maternal interest in her heart, and moreover gave her an opportunity of seeking an interview with the singular but interesting recluse who five years before had placed in her hands the endearing, though ignorant little girl, whose education had proved a task so unusually pleasing.

The principal reason, however, for Mrs. Wilmot's wishing to pay Miss Compton a visit, arose from the description Agnes had given of her conduct towards her, and of the system of non-intercourse which it was so evidently the little lady's intention to maintain.

Without having uttered a word resembling fault-finding or complaint, Agnes had somehow or other made the Wilmots feel that, though aunt Betsy certainly did not like her, she liked aunt Betsy a great deal better than she did aunt Barnaby; and this, added to the favourable impression Miss Compton had herself left upon their minds, made the good Mrs. Wilmot exceedingly anxious that she should not remain ignorant of the treasure she possessed in her young relation.

The delay of a few days before Mrs. Wilmot could take her pupil home, was inevitable; and when they arrived Mrs. Barnaby had bustled her affairs into such a state of forwardness, that, though she received them without any great appearance of melancholy or ill-humour, she hinted pretty plainly that Agnes came too late to be of much use to her in packing.

Mrs. Wilmot made a very sufficient apology for the delay, and then took leave, saying that she should remain in Silverton that night, and drive out the next morning to pay her compliments to Miss Compton. The bare mention of the spinster's name at once converted the widow's civility into rudeness; she offered her guest neither refreshment nor accommodation of any kind; and poor Agnes had the pain of seeing her dearest friend depart to pass the night at an inn, when she would have gladly stood by to watch her slumbers all night, might she have offered her own bed for her use.

On the following morning Mrs. Wilmot paid her purposed visit to Miss Compton, and found her, in dress, occupation, and mode of life, so precisely what she has been described before, that not a word need be added on the subject. Greatly different, however, was the welcome she accorded that lady to what we have formerly seen her bestow upon her relatives. She greeted her, indeed, with a smile so cordial, and a tone of voice so pleasantly expressive of the satisfaction her visit gave, that it was only when the object of it was brought forward, that Mrs. Wilmot, too, discovered that Miss Compton could be a very cross little old lady when she chose it.

"I shall quite long, my dear madam, to hear your opinion of my pupil," said Mrs. Wilmot, "for I cannot but flatter myself that you will be delighted with her."

"Then ask me nothing about her, ma'am, if you please," replied the recluse.

"But it is near two years, Miss Compton, since you saw her, and she is wonderfully improved in that time," said Mrs. Wilmot.... "Yet I own I should have thought that even then, two years ago, when you did see her, that you must have found her a very charming girl, full of sweetness and intelligence, and with a face...."

"We had better say no more about her, if you please, Mrs. Wilmot," tartly interrupted the recluse.... "I dare say you made the best you could of her, and it is no fault of yours that old Wisett's great grand-daughter should be a Wisett; ... but I hate the very sight of her, as I do, and have done, and ever shall do, that of all their kin and kind ... so it is no good to talk of it...."

"The sight of her!..." reiterated the astonished Mrs. Wilmot. "Why, my dear Miss Compton, she is reckoned by every one that sees her to be one of the loveliest creatures that nature ever formed.... If her timid, artless manners, do not please you, it is unfortunate; but that you should not think her beautiful, is impossible."

"I beg your pardon, ma'am ... I should not care a straw for the manners of a child, for I know that time and care might change them, ... but it is her person that I can't endure; ... there is no disputing about taste, you know. I should not have thought, indeed, that she was quite the style for you to admire so violently; ... but, of course, that is nothing to me.... I know that the look of her eyes, and the colour of her cheeks, is exactly what I think the most detestable; ... there is no right or wrong in the matter ... it is all fancy, and the sight of her makes me sick.... Pray, ma'am, say no more about her."

There was but one way in which Mrs. Wilmot could comprehend this extraordinary antipathy to what was so little calculated to inspire it, and this was by supposing that Miss Compton's personal deformity rendered the sight of beauty painful to her; an interpretation, indeed, as far as possible from the truth, for the little spinster was peculiarly sensible to beauty of form and expression wherever she found it; but it was the only explanation that suggested itself; and with mingled feelings of pity and contempt, Mrs. Wilmot replied,—"There may be no right or wrong, Miss Compton, in a judgment passed on external appearance only, for it may, as you observe, be purely a matter of taste; but surely it must be otherwise of an aversion conceived against a near relative whose amiable disposition, faultless conduct, and brilliant talents, justly entitle her to the love, esteem, and admiration of the whole world.... This is not merely a matter of taste, and in this there may be much wrong."

Miss Compton appeared struck by these words, but after pondering a moment upon them, replied,—"And how can I tell, Mrs. Wilmot, but that your judgment of this child's character and disposition may be as much distorted by unreasonable partiality, as your opinion of her vulgar-looking person?"

A new light here broke in upon the mind of Mrs. Wilmot; she remembered the remarkable plumpness of the little Agnes before she made that sudden start in her growth which, in the course of two important years, had converted a clumsy-looking child into a tall, slight, elegantly made girl; and with greatly increased earnestness of manner she answered,—

"I only ask you to see her once, Miss Compton.... I have no wish whatever that your judgment should be influenced by mine with respect either to the person or the mind of Agnes Willoughby; but I greatly wish that your own opinion of her should be formed upon what she now is, and not upon what she has been. I am sure you must feel that this is reasonable.... Will you then promise me that you will see her?"

"I will," ... replied Miss Compton. "The request is reasonable, and I promise to comply with it. Yet it can only be on one condition, Mrs. Wilmot."

"And what is that, Miss Compton?"

"That I may see her without her horrid aunt Barnaby."

Mrs. Wilmot smiled involuntarily, but answered gravely, "Of course, Miss Compton, that must be as you please.... Rather than you should fail to see my pretty Agnes, I will remain another day from home on purpose to bring her to you myself. Will you receive us if we come over to you at this hour to-morrow morning?"

"I will," ... again replied the recluse; "and whatever may be the result of the interview, I shall hold myself indebted to the kind feelings which have led you to insist upon it."

"Thank you, thank you!" said Mrs. Wilmot, rising to take her leave. "To-morrow, then, you will see me again, with my young charge."

CHAPTER XI

AN IMPORTANT CORRESPONDENCE, AND AN IMPORTANT INTERVIEW

On returning to her solitary quarters at the King's Head, Mrs. Wilmot called for pen, ink, and paper, and wrote the following note to her young pupil.

"MY DEAR AGNES,

"I am just returned from a visit to Compton Basett, where I was very kindly received by your aunt. She wishes to see you before you leave the neighbourhood, and I have promised to take you to her to-morrow morning; I will therefore call at eleven o'clock, when I hope I shall find you ready to accompany me. With compliments to Mrs. Barnaby, believe me, dear Agnes,

"Affectionately yours,

"MARY WILMOT."

To this epistle she speedily received the following answer.

"MRS. BARNABY presents her compliments to Mrs. Wilmot, and begs to know if there is any reason why she should not join the party to Compton Basett to-morrow morning? If not, she requests Mrs. Wilmot's permission to accompany her in the drive, as the doing so will be a considerable convenience; Mrs. Barnaby wishing to pay her duty to her aunt before she leaves the country."

To return a negative to this request was disagreeable: being absolutely necessary, however, it was done without delay; but it was with burning cheeks and flashing eyes that Mrs. Barnaby read the following civil refusal.

"MRS. WILMOT regrets extremely that she is under the necessity of declining the company of Mrs. Barnaby to-morrow morning, but Miss Compton expressly desired that Agnes should be brought to her alone."

To this Mrs. Barnaby replied,—

"As Mrs. Wilmot has been pleased to take upon herself the office of go between, she is requested to inform Miss Betsy Compton, that the aunt who has adopted Agnes Willoughby, intends to bestow too much personal care upon her, to permit her paying any visits in which she cannot accompany her."

The vexed and discomfited Mrs. Wilmot returned to Compton Basett with these two notes in her hand instead of the pretty Agnes, and her mortification was very greatly increased by perceiving that the disappointment of the old lady fully equalled her own. This obvious sympathy of feeling led to a more confidential intercourse than had ever before taken place between the solitary heiress and any other person whatever; so contrary, indeed, was this species of frank communication to her habits, that it was produced rather by the necessity of giving vent to her angry feelings, than for the gratification of confessing any other.

In reply to her first indignant burst of resentment, Mrs. Wilmot said,—

"I lament the consequences of this ill-timed impertinence, for my poor pupil's sake, more than it is easy for me to explain to you, Miss Compton.... Do me the justice to believe that I am not in the habit of interfering in the family concerns of my pupils, and then you will be better able to appreciate the motives and feelings which still lead me to urge you not to withdraw your protection and kindness from Agnes Willoughby."

"I do believe that your motives are excellent; and I can believe, too, that if your pupil deserve half you have said of her, the protection and kindness even of such a being as myself might be more beneficial to her than being left at the mercy of this hateful, vulgar-minded woman.... But what would you have me do, Mrs. Wilmot?... You would not ask me to leave my flowers, my bees, my books, and my peaceful home, to keep watch over Mrs. Barnaby, and see that she does not succeed in making this poor girl as detestable as herself?... You would not expect me to do this, would you?"

"No, Miss Compton; no one, I think, would willingly impose such a task upon you as that of watching Mrs. Barnaby. But I see no objection to your watching Agnes."

"And how is the one to be done without the other? It is quite natural that the child of one of Miss Martha Wisett's daughters, should live with the other of them. My relationship to this girl is remote in comparison to hers."

"Miss Compton," replied Mrs. Wilmot, "I fear that my acquaintance with you hardly justifies the pertinacity with which I feel disposed to urge this point; but, indeed, it is of vital importance to one that I very dearly love, and one whom you would dearly love too, would you permit yourself to know her."

"Do not apologise to me for the interest you take in her," returned the old lady in a tone rather more encouraging.... "There is more need, perhaps, that I should apologise for the want of it ... and ... to say truth," she added after a considerable pause, "I have no objection to explain my motives to you, ... though it has never fallen in my way before to meet any one to whom I wished to do this. My life has been an odd one; ... though surrounded by human beings with whom I have lived on the most friendly terms, I have passed my existence, as to anything like companionship, entirely alone. I have never been dull, for I have read incessantly, and altogether I think it likely that I have been happier than most people. But in the bosom of this unrepining solitude it is likely enough that I have nursed opinions into passions, and distastes into hatred. Thus, Mrs. Wilmot, the reasonable opinion that I set out with, for instance, when inheriting my father's long-descended acres, that it was my duty in all things to sustain as much as in me lay the old claim to gentle blood which attached to my race, (injured, perhaps, in some degree, by this division of its patrimony in my favour,) even this reasonable opinion, Mrs. Wilmot, has by degrees grown, perhaps, into unreasonable strength; for I would rather, madam, press age and ugliness remarkable as my own to my heart, as the acknowledged descendant of that race, than a vulgar, coarse-minded, coarse-looking thing, though she were as buxom as Martha Wisett when my poor silly brother married her."

The latter part of this speech was uttered with great rapidity, and an appearance of considerable excitement; but this quickly subsided, and the little spinster became as pale and composed as usual, while she listened to Mrs. Wilmot's quiet accents in reply.

"There is nothing to surprise me in this, Miss Compton; the feeling is a very natural one. But the more strongly it is expressed, the more strongly must I wonder at your permitting the sole descendant of your ancient race to be left at the mercy of a Mrs. Barnaby."

Not all the eloquence in the world could have gone so far towards obtaining the object Mrs. Wilmot had in view as this concluding phrase.

"You are right!... excellent woman!... You are right, and I deserve to see my father's acres peopled by a race of Barnaby's.... I will save her!..."

But here the poor old lady stopped. A sudden panic seized her, and she sat for several minutes positively trembling at the idea that she might unadvisedly take some step which should involve her in the horrible necessity of being encumbered for the rest of her life with a companion whose looks or manner might remind her of a Martha Wisett, or a Mrs. Barnaby.

"I dare not do it!" she exclaimed at last. "Do not ask it ... do not force me; ... or, at any rate, contrive to let me see her first, in a shop, or in the street, or any way.... I can decide on nothing till I have seen her!"

"I would do anything within my power to arrange this for you," replied Mrs. Wilmot; "but I cannot delay my return beyond to-morrow; nor do I believe that my agency would render this more easy. Why should you not at once call on both your nieces, Miss Compton? There would be no difficulty in this, and it would give you the best possible opportunity of judging both of the appearance and manners of Agnes."

"Both my nieces!... no difficulty!... You understand little or nothing of my feelings.... But go home, go home, Mrs. Wilmot. Do your own duty, which is a plain one, ... and leave me to find out mine, if I can."

"You will not, then, abandon the idea of seeing this poor girl, Miss Compton?"

"No, I will not," was the reply, pronounced almost solemnly.

"Then, farewell! my dear madam; I can ask no more than this, except, indeed, your forgiveness for having asked thus much so perseveringly."

"I thank you for it, Mrs. Wilmot.... I believe you are a very good woman, and I will endeavour to act, if God will give me grace, as I think you would approve, if you could read all the feelings of my heart. Farewell!"

And so they parted; the active, useful matron to receive the eager welcome of her expecting family, and the solitary recluse to the examination of her own thoughts, which were alternately both sweet and bitter, sometimes cheering her with a vision of domestic happiness and endearment to soothe her declining age, and sometimes making her shudder as she fancied her tranquil existence invaded and destroyed by the presence of one whom she might strive in vain to love.

CHAPTER XII

CHOOSING A LADY'S-MAID—A HAPPY MEETING UNHAPPILY BROKEN IN UPON—MISS COMPTON UTTERS A LONG FAREWELL TO AGNES

Mrs. Wilmot did not leave Silverton without taking an affectionate leave of Agnes, and when this was over, the poor girl felt herself wholly, and for ever, consigned to the authority and companionship of Mrs. Barnaby. It would be difficult to trace out the cause of the sharp pang which this conviction brought with it; but it was strong enough at that moment to rob the future of all the bright tints through which eyes of sixteen are apt to look at it. She cherished, certainly, a deep feeling of gratitude for the kindness that afforded her a home; but, unhappily, she cherished also a feeling equally strong, that it was less easy to repay the obligation with affection than with gratitude.

Not a syllable had been said to her by Mrs. Wilmot respecting the interview she was still likely to have with her aunt Compton; for she had promised this secrecy to the nervous and uncertain old lady, who, while trembling with anxious impatience to see this important niece, shrunk before the difficulties she foresaw in finding such an opportunity as she sought, for she still resolutely persevered in her determination not to see Mrs. Barnaby with her; ... but yet, when finally she did contrive to come within sight of the poor girl, it was exactly under the circumstances she so earnestly wished to avoid.

Mrs. Barnaby, in her often meditated estimate of revenue and expenses, had arrived at the conclusion that she ought not to travel without a maid, but that the said maid must be hired at the lowest rate of wages possible. The necessity for this addition to her suite did not arise from any idle wish for personal attendance, to which she had never been much accustomed, but from the conviction that there was something in the sound of "my maid" which might be of advantage to her on many occasions.

The finding out and engaging a girl that might enact the character of lady's-maid showily and cheaply, was the most important thing still left to be done before they quitted Silverton. The first qualification was a tall person, that might set off to advantage such articles of the widow's cast-off finery as might be unnecessary for Agnes; the next, a willingness to accept low wages.

While meditating on the subject, it occurred to Mrs. Barnaby that one of the girls she had seen walking in procession to church with the charity-school, was greatly taller than all the rest, and, in fact, so remarkably long and lanky, that she felt convinced she might, if skilfully dressed up, pass extremely well for a stylish lady's-maid.

Delighted at the idea, she immediately summoned Agnes to walk with her to the school-house, which was situated outside the town, about a mile, on the road leading to Compton Basett. On reaching the building, her knock was answered by the schoolmistress herself, who civilly asked her commands.

"I must come in, Mrs. Sims, before I can tell you," was the reply, and it was quite true; for, as Mrs. Barnaby knew not the name of her intended Abigail, the only mode of entering upon her business, must be by pointing out the girl whose length of limb had attracted her. But no sooner had she passed the threshold than she perceived the long and slender object of her search immediately opposite to her, in the act of taking down a work-basket from the top of a high commode; which manoeuvre, as it placed her on tip-toe, and obliged her to stretch out her longitude to the very utmost, displayed her to the eyes of Mrs. Barnaby to the greatest possible advantage, and convinced her very satisfactorily that her judgment had not erred.

"That is the girl I wanted to speak about," she said, pointing to the lizard-like figure opposite to her. "What is her name, Mrs. Sims?"

"This one, ma'am, as is fetching my basket?" interrogated Mrs. Sims in her turn.

"Yes, that one ... that tall girl.... What is her name?"

"Betty Jacks, ma'am, is her name."

"Jacks?" repeated Mrs. Barnaby, a little disconcerted; "Jacks!... that won't do.... I can never call her Jacks; but for that matter, I could give her another name easy enough, to be sure.... And what is she good for?... what can she do?"

"Not over much of anything, ma'am. She was put late to me. But she can read, and iron a little, and can do plain work well enough when she chooses it."

"When she chooses it!... and she'll be sure to choose it, I suppose, when she goes to service. I want a girl to wait upon me, and to sew for me when she has nothing else to do, and I think this one will do for me very well."

"I ask your pardon, ma'am," replied Mrs. Sims, "but if I might make so bold, I would just say that for a notable, tidy, good girl, Sally Wilkins there, that one at the end of the form, is far before Betty Jacks in being likely to suit."

"What!... that little thing? Why, she is a baby, Mrs. Sims."

"She is eleven months older than Betty Jacks, ma'am, and greatly beyond her in every way."

"But I don't like the look of such a little thing. The other would do for what I want much better. Come here, Betty Jacks. Should you like to go out to service with a lady who would take care that you should always be well dressed, and let you travel about with her, and see a great deal of the world?"

"Yes, my lady," replied the young maypole, grinning from ear to ear, and shewing thereby a very fine set of teeth.

"Well, then, Betty Jacks, I think we shall suit each other very well. But I shan't call you Betty though, nor Jacks either ... mind that. You won't care about it, I suppose, if I find out some pretty, genteel-sounding name for you, will you?"

"No, my lady!" responded the delighted girl.

"Very well; ... and I will give you three pounds a year wages, and good clothes enough to make you look a deal better than ever you did before. What do you say to it?"

"I'll be glad to come, and thankye, too, my lady, if father will let me."

"Who is her father, Mrs. Sims?"

"Joe Jacks the carpenter, ma'am."

"I don't suppose he is likely to make much objection to her getting such a place as mine, is he?"

"That is what I can't pretend to say, ma'am," replied the schoolmistress very gravely.... "I don't think Betty over steady myself, but of course it is no business of mine, and it will be far best that you should see Joe Jacks yourself, ma'am, and hear what he says about it."

"To be sure; ... and where can I see him?"

"He'll be certain to be here to-morrow morning, ma'am, for he'll come to be paid for the bench he made for me; and if so be you would take the trouble to call again just about one, when Betty will be going home with him for the half holiday they always haves of a Saturday, why then, ma'am, you'd be quite sure to see him, and hear what he'd got to say."

"Very well, then, that will do, and we shall certainly walk over again to-morrow, if the weather is anything like fine.—Good morning to you, Mrs. Sims!... Mind what I have said to you, Betty; this is a fine chance for you, and so you must tell your father. Come along, Agnes."

It so chanced that within half an hour of their departure Miss Compton also paid a visit to the school. Mrs. Sims was one of the persons whom she had saved from severe, and probably lasting penury, by one of those judicious loans, which, never being made without good and sufficient knowledge of the party accommodated, were sure to be repaid, and enabled her to perform a most essential benefit without any pecuniary loss whatever.

There were no excursions which gave the old lady so much pleasure as those which enabled her to contemplate the good effects of this rational species of benevolence, and farmer Wright never failed to offer her a place in his chaise-cart whenever his business took him near any of the numerous cottages where this agreeable spectacle might greet her. On the present occasion he set her down at the door of the school-house, while he called upon a miller at no great distance; and Mrs. Sims, who was somewhat disturbed in mind by the visit and schemes of Mrs. Barnaby, no sooner saw her enter than she led her through the throng of young stitchers and spellers to the tidy little parlour behind.

"Well, now, Miss Compton, you are kindly welcome," she said; "and I wish with all my heart you had been here but a bit ago, for who should we have here, ma'am, but your own niece, Mrs. Barnaby."

Miss Compton knit her brows with an involuntary frown.

"And that sweet, pretty creature, Miss Willoughby, comed with her.... She is a beauty, to be sure, if ever there was one."

"What did they come for, Mrs. Sims?" inquired Miss Compton with sudden animation.

"Why, that is just what I want to tell you, ma'am, and to ask your advice about. She come here—Mrs. Barnaby I mean—to look after that saucy Betty Jacks, by way of taking her to be her servant, and travelling about with her; and, upon my word, Miss Compton, she might just as well take my cat there, for any good or use she's likely to be of: and besides that, ma'am, I have no ways a good opinion of the child,—for child she is, though she's such a monster in tallness;—she does not speak the truth, Miss Compton, and that's what I can't abide, and I don't think she'll do me any credit in any way; ... but yet I'm afraid it would be doing a bad action if I was to stand in the girl's light, and prevent her going, by telling all the ill I think of her, when they comes again to-morrow to settle about it."

Mrs. Sims ceased, and certainly expected a decided opinion from Miss Compton on the subject, for that lady had kept her eyes fixed upon her, and appeared to be listening with very profound attention; but the only reply was, "And do you think the girl will come with her?"

"Come with who, ma'am?"

"With Mrs. Barnaby, to be sure."

"Oh no, ma'am! she won't come with her.... She will go home, as usual, to-night, and is to come back to meet the ladies here, a little after noon to-morrow, with her father."

"But Agnes ... Miss Willoughby I mean, ... are you sure she will come back with her aunt to-morrow?"

"I am sure I can't say, ma'am, ... but I think she will; for I well remember Mrs. Barnaby said with her grand way, ... 'We will walk over to-morrow if the weather be anyways fine.'"

Miss Compton now seemed sunk in profound meditation, of which Mrs. Sims fully hoped to reap the fruits; but once more she was disappointed, for when Miss Compton again spoke, it was only to say,—

"I want to see Agnes Willoughby, Mrs. Sims, and I do not want to see Mrs. Barnaby. Do you think you could manage this for me, if I come here again to-morrow?"

"I am sure, ma'am," replied Mrs. Sims, looking a little surprised and a little puzzled—"I am sure there is nothing that I am not in duty bound to do for you, if done it can be; and if you will be pleased to say how the thing shall be managed, I will do my part with a right good will to make everything go as you wish."

This was a very obliging reply, but it shewed Miss Compton that she must trust to her own ingenuity for discovering the ways and means for putting her design in practice. After thinking about it a little, and looking round upon the locale, she said,—

"I will tell you how it must be. I will be here to-morrow before the time you have named to them, and you shall place me in this room. When Mrs. Barnaby is engaged in talking to the girl and her father, take Agnes by the hand and lead her in to me, saying, if you will, that you have something you wish her to see, ... which will be no more than the truth. If Mrs. Barnaby happens to hear this, and offers to follow, then, as you value my friendship, close the door and lock it,—never mind what she thinks of it.... I will take care her anger shall do you no harm."

"Oh dear, ma'am! I'm not the least afraid of Mrs. Barnaby's anger, ... nor do I expect she will take any notice. She seems so very hot upon having that great awkward hoyden, Betty Jacks, that I don't think, when she is engaged with the father about it, she will be likely to take much heed of Miss Agnes and me. But at any rate, Miss Compton, I'll take good care, ma'am, that she shan't come a-near you. And now, ma'am, will you be so good as to tell me if you think I shall be doing a sin letting this idle hussy set off travelling with her?"

"No sin at all, Mrs. Sims," replied Miss Compton with decision. "Let the girl be what she may, depend upon it she is quite ..." but here she stopped; adding a minute after, "Do go, Mrs. Sims, and see if farmer Wright's cart is come back."

A few minutes more brought the humble vehicle to the door, when the heiress climbed to her accustomed place in it, and gave herself up to meditation so unusually earnest, as not only to defeat all the good farmer's respectful attempts at conversation, but to occupy her for one whole hour after her return, and that so completely as to prevent her from opening her half-read volume, though that volume was Walter Scott's.

Thoughts and schemes were working and arranging themselves in her head, which were, in truth, important enough to demand some leisure for their operations. This "beauty if ever there was one," this poor motherless and father-forgotten Agnes, this inevitable heiress of the Compton acres, ought she, because she had found her short and fat two years before, to abandon her to the vulgar patronage of the hateful Mrs. Barnaby? A blush of shame and repentance mantled her pale cheek as this question presented itself, and she acknowledged to her own heart the sin and folly of the prejudice which had led her to turn away from the only being connected with her, to whom she could be useful. She remembered, too, in this hour of self-examination and reproach, that the father of this ill-treated girl was a gentleman; and that she ought, therefore, to have been kindly fostered by the last of the Comptons as a representative more worthy to revive their antiquated claims to patrician rank, than could have been reasonably expected from any descendant of her brother Josiah.

These thoughts having been sufficiently dwelt upon, examined, and acknowledged to be just, the arrangement of her future conduct was next to be considered; and, notwithstanding the singularly secluded life she had led, the little lady was far from being ignorant of the entire change it would be her duty to make in the whole manner of her existence, should she decide upon taking Agnes Willoughby from Mrs. Barnaby, and becoming herself her sole guardian and protectress.

Could she bear this?... and could she afford it? The little, weak-looking, but wirey frame of the spinster, had a spirit within it of no inconsiderable firmness; and the first of these questions was soon answered by a mentally ejaculated "I WILL," which, in sincerity and intensity of purpose, was well worth the best vow ever breathed before the altar. For the solution of the other, the old lady turned to her account books, and found the leading items in the column of receipts to be as follows:—

£.

By annual rent from the Compton Basett farm	600
By interest on 12,000l. in the 3 per cent.	360
By interest on 1,800l. lent on mortgage at 5 per cent.	90
By interest on 6,000l. lent on mortgage at 4 per cent.	240
By interest on 2,500l. lent on mortgage at 5 per cent.	125
	£1415

Of this income, (the last item of which, however, had been entered only three weeks before, being the result of the latest appropriation of her savings,) Miss Compton spent not one single farthing, nor had done so since the payment in advance of three hundred and fifty pounds to Mrs. Wilmot for the education and dress of Agnes. In fact, the profits arising from the honey she sold, fully furnished all the cash she wanted; as her stipulated supplies from the farm amounted very nearly to all that her ascetic table required.... She used neither tea nor wine, milk supplying their place.... She had neither rent, taxes, nor servants, to pay; and her toilet, though neat to admiration, cost less than any lady would believe possible, who had not studied the enduring nature of stout and simple habiliments, when worn as Miss Compton wore them.

Such being the facts, it might be imagined that a schedule like the above would have appeared to such a possessor of such an income a sufficient guarantee against any possible pecuniary embarrassment from inviting one young girl to share it with her. But Miss Compton, as she sat in her secluded bower, had for years been looking out upon the fashionable world through the powerful though somewhat distorting lunette d'approche furnished by modern novels; and if she had acquired no other information thereby, she at least had learned to estimate with some tolerable degree of justness the difference between the expense of living in the world, and out of it.

"If I do adopt her, and make her wholly mine," thought she, "it shall not be for the purpose of forming her into a rich country-town miss.... She shall be introduced into the world, ... she shall improve whatever talents Nature may have given her by lessons from the best masters; ... her dress shall be that of a well-born woman of good fortune, and she shall be waited upon as a gentlewoman ought to be. Can I do all this, and keep her a carriage besides, for fourteen hundred a-year?... No!..." was uttered aloud by the deeply meditative old lady. "What then was she to decide upon? Should she wait for two more years before she declared her intentions, and by aid of the farther sum thus saved enable herself to reach the point she aimed at?" Something that she took for prudence very nearly answered "YES," but was checked by a burst of contrary feeling that again found vent in words,—"And while I am saving hundreds of pounds, may she not be acquiring thousands of vulgar habits that may again quench all my hopes?... No; it shall be done at once." So at length she laid her head on her pillow resolved to take her heiress immediately under her own protection ... (provided always that the examination which was to take place on the morrow should not prove that the Wisett style of beauty was unbearably predominant,) and that having arranged with her honest tenant some fair equivalent for her profitable apiary, her lodgings, and her present allowances, she should take her at once to London, devote one year to the completion of her education, and leave it to fate and fortune to decide what manner of life they should afterwards pursue.

For a little rustic old woman who had never in her life travelled beyond the county town of her native shire, this plan was by no means ill concocted, and must, I think, display very satisfactorily to all unprejudiced eyes the great advantages to be derived from a long and diligent course of novel-reading, as, without it, Miss Compton would, most assuredly, never have discovered that fourteen hundred a-year was insufficient to supply the expenses of herself and her young niece.

But, alas!... All this wisdom was destined to be blighted in the bud.

Miss Compton was true to her appointment, and so was Mrs. Barnaby; the fair Agnes, too, failed not to make her appearance; and moreover the critical eyes of the old lady failed not to discover, at the very first glance, that no trace of Wisett vulgarity was there to lessen the effect of her exceeding loveliness. But all this was of no avail ... for the matter went in this wise.

The first who arrived of the parties expected by Mrs. Sims, was Joe Jacks the carpenter. His daughter Betty had given him such an account of the proposal made to her, as caused him to be exceedingly anxious for its acceptance; and he now came rather before the appointed time, in order to hint pretty plainly to Mrs. Sims that he should take it very ill, if she did not give a good word to help his troublesome Betty off his hands.

Then came Miss Compton, who walked straight through the school-room, and ensconced herself in the little parlour behind it, and in about ten minutes afterwards the stately Mrs. Barnaby and her graceful companion arrived also.

Mrs. Sims was by no means deficient in her manner of managing the little intrigue intrusted to her; she waited very quietly till she perceived Mrs. Barnaby completely occupied in making the carpenter understand, that if she engaged to find shoes, shifts, and flannel petticoats for his daughter, as well as all her finery, the wages could not be more than two pounds.... And then she laid a gentle hand on Agnes, who, not being particularly interested in the discussion, suffered herself to be abducted without resistance, and in the next moment found herself in the presence of Miss Compton.

The young girl knew her in a moment, for she had made a deep impression on her memory, both by her kindness at one period, and her capricious want of it at another. But far different was the effect of memory in the old lady; for not only was she unable to recognize in the figure before her the Agnes of her recollection, or rather of her fancy, but it was not immediately that she could be made to believe in the identity.

"You do not mean to tell me, Mrs. Sims, that this young lady is Agnes Willoughby?" said she, rising up, and really trembling from agitation.

"Dear me, yes, Miss Compton, to be sure it is."

"Do you not know me, dear aunt?" said Agnes, approaching her, and timidly holding out her hand.

"Your aunt?... am I really your aunt?... Is it possible that you are my poor brother's grandchild?"

"I am Agnes Willoughby," replied the young girl, puzzled and almost frightened by the doubts and the agitation she witnessed.

"If you are!" exclaimed Miss Compton, suddenly embracing her, "I am a more guilty creature than I ever thought to be!"

At this moment, and while the arms of the diminutive spinster were still twined round the person of Agnes, who had just decided in her own mind that her great-aunt was the most unintelligible person in the world, the door of the little parlour opened with a jerk that shewed it yielded to no weak hand, and the full-blown person of the widow Barnaby stood before them. Her eyes and her rouge were as bright as ever, and her sober cap and sable draperies vainly, as it should seem, endeavoured to soften those peculiarities of the Wisett aspect against which Miss Compton had sworn eternal hatred, for never had she appeared more detestable; her usual bravura manner indeed was somewhat exaggerated by her indignation at the concealment which had been attempted, and which had been adroitly pointed out to her by the sharp-witted Betty Jacks.

"Soh!... you thought I should not find you out, I suppose!" she exclaimed, as she shut the door behind her.

"God give me patience!" cried the irritated recluse, suddenly disengaging herself from Agnes. "This is strange persecution, Mrs. Barnaby," and as she spoke she endeavoured to effect her retreat. But this could not be done in a straight direction, inasmuch as it required a considerable circuit safely to weather either side of the expansive widow; and before Miss Compton reached the door, that lady had so established herself before it as to render her leaving the room without permission absolutely impossible.

The time had been, when the hope of "getting something out of the little hunch-back," would have enabled Mrs. Barnaby to put a very strong restraint upon any feeling likely to offend her, but this was over. She thought her turn was come now, and considered her own revenues and her own position as so immeasurably superior to those of the little "old woman clothed in grey" who stood shaking before her, that her pride would never have forgiven her avarice had it led her to neglect this favourable opportunity of displaying some of the contempt and scorn which she had felt she had heretofore received from her.

"Upon my word, Miss Compton," she began, "I do really wonder you are not ashamed of yourself, to come visiting this vulgar body Mrs. Sims, instead of profiting by the notice of your own relations, which might do you honour. And your dress, Miss Compton!... What must my niece, Miss Willoughby, think, at seeing the sister of her own grandfather going about in such a horrid, coarse, miserable stuff gown as that? We all know how you have been squandering your little property upon the beggars you get to flatter you, but that is no reason for behaving as you do towards me. My excellent husband has left me in circumstances of such affluence as might enable me to assist you by the gift of some of my own clothes, if you conducted yourself as you ought to do."

This harangue would probably have been cut short, had Miss Compton retained breath enough to articulate; but astonishment and indignation almost choked her; instead of speaking, she stood still and panted, till Agnes, inexpressibly shocked and terrified, moved a chair towards her, and entreated her to sit down. Her only reply, however, was rudely pushing Agnes and her chair aside, and then, with a sort of desperate effort, exclaiming,—

"Woman!... Let me pass!"

"Oh! yes—you may pass and welcome," said Mrs. Barnaby, standing aside.—"You have behaved to me from first to last more like a fiend than an aunt, and I certainly shall not break my heart if I never set my eyes on you again. Come, Agnes, my love, I have concluded my business in this musty-smelling place, and now let us be gone.... Don't stand fawning upon her.... I promise you it will be all in vain.... You will get nothing by it, my dear."

Distressed beyond measure at this painful scene, and not well knowing how to express the strong feeling which drew her to the side of Miss Compton, Agnes stood timidly uncertain what she ought to do, when Mrs. Barnaby's authoritative voice again uttered, "Come, my dear Agnes, I am impatient to take you away from what I consider so very disgraceful a meeting."

Thus painfully obliged to decide upon either taking leave of her older relative, or of departing without it, Agnes turned again towards Miss Compton, and silently bending down, offered to kiss her cheek. But the angry old lady started away from her, saying,—"None of that, if you please!—No fawning upon me. You are her 'dear love,' and her 'dear Agnes,' ... and none such shall ever be graced or disgraced by me!" And thus saying, she walked past the tittering Mrs. Barnaby, and out of the house; preferring the chance of toiling two miles to reach her home, rather than endure another moment passed under the same roof with her.

CHAPTER XIII

MRS. BARNABY SETS FORTH ON HER TRAVELS—THE READER TAKES LEAVE OF MISS COMPTON —MRS. BARNABY ENJOYS HER JOURNEY, AND ARRIVES SAFELY AT EXETER

Within a week after this unfortunate interview, all Mrs. Barnaby's earthly possessions, excepting her money, were deposited in the waggon that travelled between Silverton and Exeter; and the day afterwards herself, her niece, and her maid, whom she had surnamed Jerningham, (the two former in the coach, and the latter on the top of it,) set forth on their way to that fair and ancient city of the west.

Before we follow them thither, we must stop for a moment to bid a long adieu to poor Miss Compton. Unfortunately for her temper, as well as her limbs, farmer Wright did not over-take her till within a few yards of their home; and the agitation and fatigue, both equally unusual to her, so completely overpowered her strength and spirits, that having taken to her bed as soon as she reached her room, she remained in it for above a fortnight, being really feverish and unwell, but believing herself very much worse than she really was. During the whole of this time, and indeed for several months afterwards, she never attempted to separate the innocent image of Agnes from the offensive one of Mrs. Barnaby. The caress which the poor girl had offered with such true tenderness and sympathy, was the only distinct idea respecting her that remained on the mind of Miss Compton; and this suggested no feeling but that of indignation, from the conviction that Mrs. Barnaby's "dear love," not a whit less detestable, was only more artful than herself; or that, not yet being in possession of the wealth of which her hateful protectress boasted, she deemed it prudent to aim at obtaining whatever she herself might have to bestow.

Notwithstanding all these disagreeable imaginings, however, the old lady gradually recovered both her health and her usual tranquil equality of spirits, sometimes even persuading herself that she was very glad she had not been seduced, by the appearance of Agnes, to sacrifice her own comfort for the advantage of an artful girl, who was, after all, quite as much the grand-daughter of a Wisett as of a Compton.

Never during the prosperous years that Mrs. Barnaby had been the mistress of her comfortable house at Silverton, (excepting, perhaps, for the delightful interval while she was treated throughout the town as a bride,) did she feel half so grand or so happy a personage as now that she had no house at all. There was an elegance and freedom, which she never felt conscious of before, in thus setting off upon her travels with what she believed to be an ample purse, of which she was the uncontrolled mistress, a beautiful niece to chaperone, and a lady's-maid to wait upon her; and had Agnes, who sat opposite to her, been less earnestly occupied in recalling all the circumstances of her last strange interview with her aunt Compton, she must have observed and been greatly puzzled by the series of (perhaps) involuntary grimaces which accompanied Mrs. Barnaby's mental review of her own situation.

"A rich and handsome widow!... Could fate have possibly placed her in any situation she should have liked so well?" This was the question she silently asked herself, and cordially did her heart answer "No."

As these thoughts worked in her mind her dark, well-marked eyebrows raised themselves, her eyes flashed, and her lips curled into a triumphant smile.

The person who occupied the transverse corner to herself was a handsome young man, who had joined the Silverton coach, from the mansion of a gentleman in the neighbourhood, to which, however, he was himself quite a stranger; and having in vain tried to get sight of the features concealed by the long crape veil beside him, he took to watching those no way concealed by the short crape veil opposite.

"Mother and daughter, of course," thought he. "A young specimen, without rouge or moustache, would not be amiss."

Mrs. Barnaby perceived he was looking at her, and settled her features into dignified but not austere harmony.

"It is very pleasant travelling this morning, ma'am," said the young man.

"As pleasant as a stage-coach can be, I imagine; ... but I am so little accustomed to the sort of thing that I am not a very good judge. Do you know, sir, where the coach stops for dinner?"

"I cannot say I do; I never travelled this road before."

"Then you are not a resident in the neighbourhood?"

"No, ma'am, quite a bird of passage. It is the first time I have ever been in Devonshire. It seems to be a beautiful county indeed."

"Very!"... Mrs. Barnaby heartily hoped that no comparisons would follow, as it was not at all her intention to confess, either on the present or any future occasion, that she had never seen any other; and she therefore rather abruptly changed the conversation by adding, "Do you know, sir, whether there are many outside passengers?... I hope my maid will not be annoyed in any way.... It is the first time I ever put her outside a coach!"

"Poor woman!" thought the young man—"lost her husband, and her money with him, I suppose. I must contrive to look at this tall, slender girl, though."

But Agnes seemed little disposed to give him any opportunity of doing so, for she continued to keep her eyes fixed on the scene without, thus very nearly turning her back on her curious neighbour.

Mrs. Barnaby's first act of active chaperonship was a very obliging one; she perceived the young man's object, and not having the slightest inclination to conceal the beauty of Agnes, which she held to be one of the many advantages with which she was herself surrounded, she said,—

"My dear Agnes, do look at that pretty cottage; it is a perfect picture of rural felicity!"

Agnes obeyed the words, and followed with her eyes the finger that pointed through the opposite window, thus indulging her neighbour with a full view of her exquisite profile. The effect was by no means what Mrs. Barnaby expected; the young man looked, and instead of being led by what he saw into talkative civility, he became very respectfully silent. But respectful silence was not an offering to which Mrs. Barnaby in the most brilliant season of her beauty had ever been accustomed; it puzzled her, till a thought struck her which is worth recording, because it very greatly influenced her conduct and feelings for a long time afterwards. This gentleman, whose attentions for the journey she greatly wished to conciliate, had addressed her in the easy style by which "fast" young men are apt to believe they can propitiate the favour of every woman somewhat under fifty years of age, and somewhat, too, beneath themselves in condition. Our traveller had no fear of blundering when he settled that Mrs. Barnaby belonged to this class; but the instant he caught a glimpse of the countenance of Agnes, he became equally sure that she at least belonged to a higher one. It was not wonderful that poor Miss Compton doubted, when she looked at her, the possibility of her being a descendant of the buxom Martha Wisett, for, excepting something in the form and soft lustre of her dark-brown eyes, her features bore no resemblance to her mother, or her mother's family, but a most decided one to that of her father, who, though a very foolish, hot-headed lieutenant, when we made his acquaintance, was descended from a race of aristocratic ancestors, rather remarkable for their noble and regular cast of features, which appeared indeed to be their least alienable birthright.

The traveller, though a young man, had lived sufficiently in the world to have learned at least the alphabet of character as written on the countenances of those he met, and he spelt gentlewoman so plainly on that of Agnes, that he felt no more right to address her without introduction than he would have done had the stage-coach been an opera-box.

"That's very odd," ... thought Mrs. Barnaby. "She certainly is a most beautiful creature ... quite as handsome as I was even in poor dear Tate's days, and yet the moment he got a sight of her, his pleasant, gay manner, changed all at once, and he now looks as glum as a boy at school.... Though she is my niece, she is not like me; that's certain, ... and who knows but that many men may still prefer my style to hers?... As to this one, at least, it is impossible to doubt it, and it will be great folly in me to set out with a fancy that my face and figure, especially when I get back to dress again, will not stand a comparison with hers. For some years, at any rate, in justice to myself, I will keep this in mind; and not take it for granted that every glance directed towards us is for the child, and not for the woman."

This agreeable idea seemed all that was wanting to make the journey perfectly delicious, and not even the continued reserve of the young man could affect in any great degree the charming harmony of her spirits. We hear much of the beautiful freshness of hope in young hearts just about to make their first trial of the joys of life; but it is quite a mistake to suppose that any such feeling can equal the fearless, confident, triumphant mastery and command of future enjoyment, which dilates the heart, in the case of such an out-coming widow as Mrs. Barnaby.

The Silverton coach set its passengers down at Street's hotel, in the Church-yard; and my heroine, who now for the first time in her life found herself at an inn, with the power of ordering what she chose, determined to enjoy the two-fold gratification of passing for a lady of great fashion and fortune, and of taking especial care of her creature-comforts into the bargain.

"Do you want rooms, ma'am?" said the head of a waiter, suddenly placing itself among the insides.

"Yes, young man, I want the best rooms in the house.... Where is my maid?—Let her be ready to attend me as soon as I get out. We have nothing with us but three trunks, one square box, one hat-box, two carpet-bags, and my dressing-case. Let everything be conveyed to my apartments. Now open the door, and let me get out.... Follow me, Agnes.... You will come, if you please, without delay, young man, to receive my orders respecting refreshments."

Two lighted candles were snatched up as they passed the bar, and Mrs. Barnaby proceeded up the stairs in state, the waiter and his candles before, Agnes and "my maid" behind.

"This room is extremely dark and disagreeable.... Pray, send the master of the house to me; I wish to give my orders to him."

"My master is not at home, ma'am."

"Not at home?... Extremely negligent, I must say. Perhaps it will be better for me to proceed to some other hotel, where I may be able to see the head of the establishment. I have not been accustomed to be treated with anything like neglect ... people of my condition, indeed, seldom are."

"If you will be pleased, my lady, to give your orders to me," said the waiter very respectfully, "you shall find nothing wanting that belongs to a first-rate house."

"Then, pray, send my maid to me.... Oh! there you are, Jerningham."

"Yes, ma'am," answered the gawky soubrette, tucking back the veil with which Mrs. Barnaby had adorned one of her own bonnets, and staring at the draperied windows, and all the other fine things which met her eyes.

"You will see, Jerningham, that my sleeping apartment is endurable."

Now Betty Jacks, though careless and idle, was by no means a stupid girl; but she was but fifteen years old, and her experiences not having hitherto been upon a very extended scale, she found herself at a loss to understand what her new mistress meant, about nine times out of every ten that she spoke to her. On receiving the order above mentioned, she meditated for an instant upon what an "endurable sleeping apartment" might be; but the sagacity which failed to discover this, sufficed to suggest the advantage of not confessing her ignorance; and she answered boldly, "Yes, sure, ma'am."

"Go, then," said the lady, languidly throwing her person upon a sofa; and then turning to the waiter, who still remained with the door in his hand, she pronounced with impressive emphasis,—

"Let there be tea, sugar, and cream brought, with buttered toast, and muffins also, if it be possible.... Agnes, my love, I am afraid there is hardly room for you on the sofa; but sit down, dear, and try to make yourself comfortable on a chair."

The two ladies were now left to themselves, Betty Jacks joyfully accompanying the smart young waiter to the regions below. "And who may be your missus, my dear?" he said, giving her an encouraging chuck under the chin; "she can't have much to do, I'm thinking, with any of the county families, for they bean't much given to stage-coaches, and never without their own gentlemen to guard 'em.... Is she a real grand lady, or only a strutting make-believe?"

Betty, thinking it much more for her own credit to serve a real grand lady than a make-believe, readily answered.

"To be sure, she is a real grand lady, Mr. Imperdence.... We comes up along from Silverton, and she's one of the finest ladies in the town."

"In the town," repeated the knowing waiter significantly.... "I understand.... Well, she shall have some tea; .... And now, my girl, you had better go and do what she bid you."

"Well now, if I hav'n't downright forgot already!" said the unblushing Betty. "Will you tell me what it was then?"

"How old are you, my dear?" was the unsatisfactory reply.

"And pray what's that to you?... But come now, do tell me, willy', what was it missus told me to do?"

"To go see after her bed, my dear, and all that, and unpack her nightcap, I suppose."

"Well, then, give me a candle,—that's a good man.... But where is her bed, though?"

"You bean't quite hatched yet, my gay maypole, but you'll do well enough some of these day.... Here, Susan! shew this young waiting-maid a bed-room for two ladies—and one for yourself too, I suppose, my dear. I shouldn't wonder, Susan, if it was possible the grand lady up stairs may pay less than a duchess; but take my word for it she'll blow you sky high, if you don't serve her as if you thought she was one."

"How did she come?" snappishly inquired the chamber-maid.

"By the Royal Regulator," answered the waiter. "But inside, Susan, inside, you know, and with her lady's-maid here to wait upon her; so mind what you're about, I tell you."

"Come this way, young woman, if you please," said the experienced official, who was not to be bullied out of a first-floor room by the report of duchess-like airs, or the sight of a lanky child for a waiting-maid. So Betty was made to mount to a proper stage-coach elevation.

Mrs. Barnaby, however, got her tea, and her toast, and her muffins, greatly to her satisfaction, even though the master of the establishment knew nothing about it; and though she did make Agnes's slender arm pay for the second flight of stairs, in order to prove how very little used she was to such fatigue, she was, on the whole, well pleased with her room when she reached it, well pleased with her bed, well pleased with her breakfast, and ready to set off as soon as it was over to look out for lodgings and adventures.

CHAPTER XIV

HOW TO CHOOSE LODGINGS—REASONS FOR LAYING ASIDE WIDOW'S WEEDS—LADY-LIKE ACCOMPLISHMENTS—AFFECTIONATE FORETHOUGHT—CHARMING SENSIBILITY—GENEROUS INTENTIONS—A CLEVER LETTER, BUT ONE UPON WHICH DOCTORS MAY DISAGREE

Of lodgings Mrs. Barnaby saw enough to offer a most satisfactory selection, and heartily to weary Agnes, who followed her up and down innumerable stairs, and stood behind her, during what seemed endless colloquies with a multitude of respectable-looking landladies, long after she had flattered herself that her aunt must have been suited to her heart's desire by what she had already seen. Of adventures the quiet streets of Exeter were not likely to produce many; but the widow had the satisfaction of observing that lounging gentlemen were abundant, a cavalry officer still visible now and then, and that hardly one man in ten of any class passed her without staring her full in the face.

At length, after having walked about till she was sufficiently tired herself, and till poor Agnes looked extremely pale, she entered a pastry-cook's shop for the purpose of eating buns, and of taking into deliberate consideration whether she should secure apartments in the Crescent, which were particularly comfortable, or some she had seen in the High Street, which were particularly gay.

Mrs. Barnaby often spoke aloud to herself while appearing to address her niece, and so she did now.

"That's a monstrous pretty drawing-room, certainly; and if I was sure that I should be able to get any company to come and see me, I'd stick to the Crescent.... But it's likely enough that I shall find nobody to know, and in that case it would be most horribly dull.... But if we did not get a soul from Monday morning to Saturday night, we could never be dull in the High Street. Such lots of country gentlemen!... And they always look about them more than any other men." And then, suddenly addressing her niece in good earnest, she added,—

"Don't you think so, Agnes?"

"I don't know, ma'am," replied Agnes, in an accent that would have delighted her aunt Compton, and which might have offended some sort of aunts; but it only amused her aunt Barnaby, who laughed heartily, and said, for the benefit of the young woman who presided at the counter, as well as for that of her niece,—

"Yes, my dear, that's quite right; that's the way we all begin.... And you will know all, how, and about it, too, long and long before you will own it."

Agnes suddenly thought of Empton parsonage, its pretty lawn, its flowers, its books, and its gentle intellectual inmates, and involuntarily she closed her eyes for a moment and sighed profoundly; but the reverie was not permitted to last long, for Mrs. Barnaby, having finished her laugh and her bun, rose from her chair, saying,—

"Come along, child!... The High Street will suit us best, won't it, Agnes?"

"You must best know what you best like, aunt," replied the poor girl almost in a whisper, "but the Crescent seemed to me very quiet and agreeable."

"Quiet!... Yes, I should think so!... And if that's your fancy, it is rather lucky that it's my business to choose, and not yours. And it's my business to pay too.... It's just sixpence," she added with a laugh, and pulling out her purse. "One bun for the young lady, and five for me. Come along, Agnes ... and do throw back that thick crape veil, child.... Your bonnet will look as well again!"

Another half hour settled the situation of their lodgings in Exeter. Smart Mrs. Tompkin's first-floor in the High Street, with a bed in the garret for Jerningham, was secured for three months; at the end of which time Mrs. Barnaby was secretly determined as nearly as possible to lay aside her mourning, and come forth with the apple blossoms, dazzling in freshness, and couleur de rose. The bargain for the lodgings, however, was not concluded without some little difficulty, for Mrs. Tompkins, who owned that she considered herself as the most respectable lodging-house keeper in Exeter, did not receive this second and conclusive visit from the elegant widow with as much apparent satisfaction as was expected.

"Here I am again, Mrs. Tompkins!" said the lively lady in crape and bombasin. "I can see no lodgings I like as well as yours, after all."

"Well.... I don't know, ma'am, about that," replied the cautious Mrs. Tompkins; "but, to say the truth, I'm not over and above fond of lady lodgers ... they give a deal more trouble than gentlemen, and I've always been used to have the officers as long as there were any to be had; and even now, with only three cavalry companies in the barracks, it's a rare chance to find me without them."

"But as you do happen to be without them now, Mrs. Tompkins, and as your bill is up, I suppose your lodgings are to let, and I am willing to take them."

"And may I beg the favour of your name, ma'am?" said the respectable landlady, stiffly.

"Barnaby!" answered the widow, with an emphasis that gave much dignity to the name. "I am the widow of a gentleman of large fortune in the neighbourhood of Silverton, and finding the scene of my lost happiness too oppressive to my spirits, I am come to Exeter with my niece, and only one lady's-maid to wait upon us both, that I may quietly pass a few months in comparative retirement before I join my family and friends in the country, as their rank and fortune naturally lead them into more gaiety than I should at present like to share. I am not much accustomed to be called upon thus to give an account of myself; but this is my name, and this is my station; and if neither happens to satisfy you, I must seek lodgings elsewhere."

"I beg your pardon, ma'am, I'm sure," replied Mrs. Tompkins, considerably awed by this imposing statement, "but in our line it is quite necessary, and real ladies, as I dare say you are, are always served the better for being known. At what inn is your lady's-maid and your luggage put up, ma'am?"

"At Street's hotel, Mrs. Tompkins; and if we agree about the apartments, I shall go there, pay my bill, and return directly. You have flies here, I think, have you not?... I have no carriage with me."

"Yes, ma'am, we have flies, and none better; but if it's only for the luggage, a porter would do better, and 'tis but a step to walk."

The bargain was then concluded, the ladies returned to the hotel, and after a short struggle in the heart of the widow between economy, and her rather particular love of a comfortable dinner, she decided upon an early broiled chicken and mushrooms before her removal, in preference to a doubtful sort of mutton chop after it. But at seven o'clock the two ladies were seated at tea in the drawing-room, the lady's-maid having been initiated by the factotum of the house into all the mysteries of the neighbouring "shop for everything," and performing her first act of confidential service very much to the satisfaction of her mistress, who could not wonder that a city like Exeter should be dearer than such a little out-of-the-way place as Silverton.

Mrs. Barnaby knew not a single soul in Exeter, and she lay in bed on the following morning for a full hour later than usual, ruminating on the possibilities of making acquaintance with somebody who might serve as a wedge by which she might effect an entry into the society to be found there. Once seen and known, she felt confident that no difficulty would remain, but the first step was not an easy one.

She doubted not, indeed, that she might easily enough have obtained some introductions from among her acquaintance at Silverton, but it was no part of her plans to make her entrée into the beau monde, even of Exeter, as the widow of an apothecary. "No!" thought she, as she turned herself by a vigorous movement from one side of the bed to the other, "I will carve out my own fortune without any Silverton introductions whatever! I know that I have a head of my own, as well as a face, and when once I have got rid of this nasty gown and that hideous cap, we shall see what can be done."

Walking up and down the High Street, however, which formed nearly her only occupation during all the hours of light, was, she soon found, the only gaiety she could hope for, and it proved a source of mingled joy and woe. To see so many smart people, and so many beautiful bonnets, was an enchantment that made her feel as if she had got to the gates of Paradise; but the impossibility of speaking to the smart people, or wearing the beautiful bonnets, soon turned all the pleasure into bitterness, and she became immeasurably impatient to cure at least one of these miseries, by throwing aside her hated weeds. To do this, soon became, as she said, necessary to her existence; and her landlady at last turned out to be a perfect treasure, from the sympathy and assistance she afforded her in the accomplishment of her wishes.

Mrs. Tompkins had speedily discovered both that her lodger really had money, and that the gentleman of large fortune whom she had lost was the apothecary of Silverton. The respect obtained by the first quite obliterated, in Mrs. Tompkins' eyes, any contempt that might have been generated by the falsehoods which the second brought to light, and on the whole nothing could be more friendly than their intercourse.

"There can be no use, Mrs. Tompkins," said the doleful widow, "do you think there can ... in my going on wearing this dismal dress, that almost breaks my heart every time I look at myself?... It is very nearly six months now since my dear Mr. Barnaby died, and I believe people of fashion never wear first mourning longer."

Mr. Barnaby, however, had been alive and well exactly three months after the period named by his widow as that of his death; and that, too, Mrs. Tompkins knew as well as she did; but Mrs. Tompkins' sister was a milliner, and family affection being stronger within her than any abstract love of propriety, she decidedly voted for laying aside the weeds immediately, there being "no yearthly good," as she well observed, "in any woman's going on breaking her heart by looking at herself in the glass." So the sister was sent for, and after a long consultation in the widow's bed-room, it was decided that the following Sunday should send her to the cathedral in a black satin dress, with lavender-coloured bonnet, fichu, gloves, reticule, and so forth.

Considering the complete dependence of Agnes, and the great aptitude of such a disposition as that of Mrs. Barnaby to keep this ever in her mind, she certainly felt a greater degree of embarrassment at the idea of communicating this resolution to her than might have been expected. Her friends might fairly have drawn an inference considerably in her favour from this, ... namely, that she was ashamed of it. But however respectable its cause, the feeling was not strong enough to offer any effectual impediment to her purpose, and she came forth from the council-chamber where this great measure had been decided on, wishing, for the moment at least, that Agnes was at the bottom of the sea, but firm in her determination to announce to her the important resolution she had taken, without a moment's further delay.

"I don't know how it is, my dear Agnes," said she, after seating herself, and looking steadfastly at her niece for a minute or two; "but though I don't dislike to see you in deep mourning, the sight of it on myself makes me perfectly wretched.... Why should I go on making my poor heart ache, for no reason upon earth that I know of, but because, when people happen to be where they are known by everybody, it is customary to wear a certain dress for a certain number of days and weeks; but, thank Heaven! Agnes, there is not a single soul in all Exeter that knows me, and I really think there is something very like a rebellion against Providence in refusing to take advantage of this lucky circumstance, which doubtless the mercy of Heaven has arranged on purpose, so as to enable me to spare myself without impropriety. It is easy enough, Agnes, for ordinary-minded women, to wear, for a whole year together, a dress that must remind them every instant of the most dreadful loss a woman can sustain!—it is easy enough for others, but it will not do for me!... And in justice to myself, and indeed to you too, Agnes, I am determined to make the effort at once, and discard a garb that breaks my poor heart every time I cast my eyes on any part of it. You must, of course, perceive that it is not for myself alone, my dear child, that I make this effort to restore the health and spirits with which nature has hitherto so bountifully blessed me; ... it is indeed chiefly for you, Agnes!... it is for your sake, my dear, that I am determined, as far as in me lies, to stop the sorrow that is eating into my very vitals.... But never be unjust to me, Agnes!... Whenever you see me shaking off the gloom of my widowed condition, remember it is solely owing to my love for you.... Remember this with gratitude, Agnes, and, for the sake of truth, let others know it too, whenever you have an opportunity of alluding to it."

And now again did young Agnes doubt her power of answering with propriety. The principle of truth was strong within her, and to have expressed either sympathy or gratitude would have been an outrage to this principle, which would have made her hate herself ... she could not, she would not do it; and in reply to her aunt's harangue, who seemed to wait for her answer, she only said,

"The dress of a widow is indeed very sad to look upon; no one can doubt that, aunt Barnaby."

"Good Heaven!... then you also suffer from the sight of it, my poor child!... Poor dear Agnes! I ought to have thought of this before; ... but I will wound your young heart no longer. This week shall end a suffering so heavy, and so unnecessary for us both, and I trust you will never forget what you owe me. And yet, my dear, though I hope and believe I shall be sustained, and find myself capable of making this effort respecting my own dress, there is a tender weakness still struggling at my heart, Agnes, which would make it very painful to me were I immediately to see you change yours. Do you feel any repugnance, my dear girl, to wearing that deep mourning for your poor uncle for some months longer?"

Agnes now felt no difficulty whatever in answering as she was expected to do, and very eagerly replied, "Oh! dear no, aunt ... none in the least."

"I rejoice," said the widow, solemnly, "to perceive in you, young as you are, Agnes, feelings so perfectly what they ought to be; ... you would spare me suffering from sadness too profound, yet would you, my child, in all things not injurious to me, desire to testify your deep respect for the invaluable being we have lost. This is exactly what I would wish to see, and I trust you will ever retain a disposition so calculated to make me love you. But look not so sad, my love!... I really must invent some occupation to cheer and amuse you, Agnes.... Let me see ... what say you, dearest, to running some edging for me on a tulle border for my tour de bonnet?"

The widow faithfully kept her kind promise to Agnes, and never again (excepting for a short interval that will be mentioned hereafter) did she run the risk of grieving any heart by the sight of deep mourning for her lost Barnaby, for though she restrained herself for some time longer within the sober dignity of black satins and silks as the material of her robes, there was no colour of the rainbow that did not by degrees find its way amidst her trimmings and decorations. During this period all the hours not devoted to the displaying her recovered finery in church or street, were employed in converting cheap muslin into rich embroidery, and labouring to make squares of Scotch cambric assume the appearance of genuine batiste, rich with the delicate labours of Moravian needles.

It was a great happiness for Agnes that satin-stitch had never ranked as a necessary branch of female education at Empton Rectory; had she been able to embroider muslin, her existence would have been dreadful, for, beyond all question, few of her waking hours would have been employed upon anything else; one of Mrs. Barnaby's favourite axioms being, that "there is NOTHING which makes so prodigious a difference in a lady's dress, as her wearing a great profusion of good work!"... So a great profusion of good work she was quite determined to wear, and deep was her indignation at the culpable negligence of Mrs. Wilmot, upon finding that an accomplishment "so particularly lady-like, and so very useful," had been utterly neglected.

To invent an occupation for herself during the hours thus employed by her aunt, soon became the subject of all Agnes's meditations. She knew that it must be something that should not annoy or inconvenience Mrs. Barnaby in the slightest degree, and it was this knowledge, perhaps, which made her too discreet to ask for the hire of a pianoforte, for which, nevertheless, she longed, very much like a hart for the water brook; for the musical propensities of her father and mother had descended to her, and of all the pleasures she had yet tasted, that derived from her study and practice of music had been the greatest. But that her aunt should pay money for no other purpose than for her to amuse herself by making a noise in their only sitting-room, was quite out of the question. So the piano she mentally abandoned for ever; but there were other studies that she had pursued at Empton, which, if permitted to renew, even without the aid of any master, would greatly embellish an existence, which the poor girl often felt to be as heavy a gift as could well have been bestowed upon a mortal. Having at length decided what it was she would ask for, she took courage, hemmed twice, and then said,—

"Should you have any objection, aunt, to my endeavouring by myself to go on with my French and Italian, while you are at work?... I am sometimes afraid that I shall forget all I have learned."

"I am sure I hope not, and it will be very stupid, and very wicked of you, Agnes, if you do. Your teaching is all we ever got out of that hunch-backed Jesabel of an aunt; and you must always recollect, you know, that it is very possible you may have to look to this as your only means of support. I am sure I am excessively fond of you, I may say passionately attached to you, it is quite impossible you can ever deny that; but yet we must neither of us ever forget that it is likely enough I may marry again, and have a family; and in that case, my dear, much as I love you, (and my disposition is uncommonly affectionate,) it will be my bounden duty to think of my husband and children, which would probably make it necessary for you to go out as a governess or teacher at a school."

"I understand that very well, aunt," replied Agnes, greatly comforted by the prospect thus held out, "and that is a great additional reason for my endeavouring to render myself fit to undertake such a situation. I was getting on very well at Empton. Will you be so very kind as to let me try to get on by myself here?"

"Certainly, Agnes.... I shall wish to encourage your laudable endeavours; ... but I must say it was a most abominable shame in that Mrs. Wilmot not to teach you satin-stitch, which, after all, is the only really lady-like way in which a young woman can assist in maintaining herself. Just look at this collar, Agnes; ... the muslin did not cost sixpence ... certainly not more than sixpence, and I'd venture to say that I could not get the fellow of it in any shop in Exeter for two guineas.... It is long before French, or Italian either, will bring such a percentage as that.... Now listen to me, Agnes, before you set-to, upon your stupid books again.... I'll tell you what I am willing to do for you. I hate teaching too much to attempt instructing you myself, but I will pay a woman to come here to give you lessons, if you will tell me truly and sincerely that you shall be able to learn it, and to stick to it. I am so fond of you, Agnes, so particularly fond of you, that I should not at all mind keeping you on, even when I am married, if you will take fairly and honestly to this elegant and lady-like employment, ... for I should never have any difficulty, I dare say, in disposing of what you did, beyond what I might want for myself and children—that is, provided you bring yourself to work in this sort of perfectly elegant style. What d'ye say to it, Agnes?"

"You are very kind, aunt," replied the terrified girl, blushing violently, "but indeed, indeed, I am afraid, that as I have never begun yet, I should find it quite impossible to bring my stubborn fingers to work as yours do. I never was particularly clever in learning to work, I believe, and what you do is so very nice that I could never hope to do anything like it."

"Perhaps you are right, my dear, ... it is not every woman whose fingers can move as mine do," replied Mrs. Barnaby, looking down complacently at the mincing paces of her needle; ... "but your hands are not clumsy, Agnes, rather the contrary, I must say; and I can't but think, child, that if you were to set-to with hearty good will, and practise morning, noon, and night, it is very likely you might learn enough, after a year or two of constant pains-taking, to enable you to give up all your wearisome books at once and for ever. That is worth thinking of twice, I promise you."

"Indeed, indeed, dear aunt, I never should make anything of it!..." exclaimed Agnes eagerly; "I am sure it is one of the things that people must begin early, ... and I don't at all dislike books, ... and I would rather go out to teach, if you please, than work muslin, ... for I am quite, quite sure that I never should do it well, no, not even decently."

"So much the worse for you, child!... At any rate, I have done my duty by offering to have you taught: please to remember that."

"And may I begin then, aunt, with my books?"

"And where are you to get books, Miss Agnes?... It is of no use to expect I can buy them, and that you will find.... I see already that Silverton is no rule for the rest of the world as to expense, and that I shall have quite enough to do with my money without wasting it on trumpery; ... so, pray, don't look to my buying books for you, for most assuredly I shall do no such thing."

"Oh no, aunt!... I do not think of it,—there is not the least occasion for such extravagance; you shall see how well I am provided." And so saying, she ran out of the room, and in a few minutes returned with a small and very neat mahogany box, which in travelling had been carefully covered by a leathern case, and which her aunt had suffered to accompany her unchallenged, because she presumed it to be the treasury of all "her best things;" a species of female property for which the widow had never-failing respect, even when it did not belong to herself, which was perhaps more than could be said respecting any other sort of property whatever.

Agnes brought this box in with difficulty, for though small, it was heavy, and when opened displayed to the somewhat surprised eyes of her aunt a collection of tiny volumes, so neatly fitting their receptacle, as to prove that they must have been made to suit each other.

"This was Mr. Wilmot's present to me, aunt," said Agnes, taking out a volume to exhibit its pretty binding. "Was it not kind of him?"

"It looks very extravagant, I think, for a man whose wife keeps school.... He must have been sadly puzzled to know what to do with his money."

"No, aunt, that was not the reason, for Mr. Wilmot is not extravagant at all; but he told me that aunt Betsy, instead of paying every half year, like other people, insisted upon giving him the five years' stipend for me, as well as the money for my clothes, all at once; and that he had always determined upon laying out the interest this sum had brought in a present for me. I think it was very generous of him."

"And what in the world have you got there, child? All grammars and spelling-books, I suppose; ... but it's the most senseless quantity of school books that ever were got together for one person, I think.... I see no generosity in anything so very silly."

"They are not school books, aunt, I assure you."

"Then what are they, pray? Why do you make such a mystery about it?"

"Oh! it's no mystery; ... but I did not know... I will read you the titles, if you please, aunt. Here are Shakspeare, Milton, Spencer, and Gray; ... these are all my English books."

"And what are these?"

"Racine, Corneille, La Fontaine, and Boileau."

"What useless trash!.... And these?"

"Dante, Tasso, and Petrarch; ... and these six larger volumes are the 'componimenti lirici' of various authors."

"Oh goodness, child!... don't jabber your stupid school jargon to me.... There!... take them all away again; I can't very well see how they are to help you make a governess of yourself: grammars, I should think, and dictionaries, would be more to the purpose for that sort of profitable usefulness."

"And I have got them too, aunt, in my clothes trunk; and if you will but be pleased to let me give my time to it, I am quite sure that I shall get on very well."

"Get on!... get on to what, child?"

"To reading both French and Italian with facility, ... and perhaps to writing both with tolerable correctness."

"Well, ... if it will enable you to get your bread one of these days, I am sure that I don't wish to hinder it,—so go to work as soon as you will,—only pray don't let me hear any more about it, for I quite hate the sort of thing,—though of course, my dear, if I was in your situation, I should know it was my duty to think differently. But those whom Providence has blessed with wealth, have a right to indulge their taste, ... and my taste is altogether that of a lady."

From this time the aching void in the heart, and almost in the intellect of Agnes, seemed supplied. Her aunt, when she did not want her as a walking companion, suffered her to go on reading and scribbling to her heart's content, and the more readily, perhaps, from its giving her the air of being still a child learning lessons, which was exactly the footing on which she wished to keep her, if possible, for another year or two, as she was by no means insensible to the inconvenience of having a grown-up niece, while still in the pride of beauty herself.

In this manner the period allotted for their stay at Exeter wore away; Mrs. Barnaby's wardrobe, embroidery, and all, was quite ready for display; Betty Jacks, alias Jerningham, had learned to look exceedingly like a disreputable young woman, to run of errands, and to iron out tumbled dresses; the bright sun of June had succeeded the lovely temperature of a Devonshire spring, and everything seemed to invite the adventurous widow to a wider field of display. But before she made this onward movement from which she hoped so much, it was necessary to apprize her sister-in-law, Mrs. Peters, of her affectionate intention of passing a few months at Clifton, in order to become acquainted with her and her family. The letter by which this intention was announced, is too characteristic of my heroine to be omitted.

"MY DEAREST SISTER,

"Under the dreadful calamity that has fallen upon me, no idea has suggested the slightest glimpse of comfort to my widowed heart but the hope of becoming acquainted with my lost Barnaby's sister! Beloved Margaret!... So let me call you, for so have I been used to hear you called by HIM!... Beloved Margaret! Let me hope that from you, and your charming family, I shall find the sympathy and affection I so greatly need.

"Your admirable brother ... my lost but never-to-be-forgotten husband ... was as successful as he deserved to be in the profession of which he was the highest ornament, and left an ample fortune,—the whole of which, as you know, he bequeathed to me with a confidence and liberality well befitting the perfect, the matchless love, which united us. But, alas! my sister, Providence denied us a pledge of this tender love, and where then can I so naturally look for the ultimate possessors of his noble fortune as amongst your family? I have one young niece, still almost a child, whom I shall bring with me to Clifton. But though I am passionately attached to her, my sense of justice is too strong to permit my ever suffering her claims to interfere with those more justly founded. When we become better acquainted, my dearest Margaret, you will find that this sense of what is right is the rule and guide of all my actions, and I trust you will feel it to be a proof of this, that my style and manner of living are greatly within my means. In fact, I never cease to remember, dear sister, that, though the widow of my poor Barnaby, I am the daughter of the well-born but most unfortunate clergyman of Silverton, who was obliged to sell his long-descended estate in consequence of the treachery of a friend who ruined him. Thus, while the high blood which flows in my veins teaches me to do what is honourable, the unexpected poverty which fell upon my own family, makes me feel that there is more real dignity in living with economy, than in spending what my confiding husband left at my disposal, and thus putting it out of my power to increase it for the benefit of his natural heirs.

"This will, I hope, explain to you satisfactorily my not travelling with my own carriage, and my having no other retinue than one lady's-maid. Alas!... it is not in pomp or parade that a truly widowed heart can find consolation!

"Let me hear from you, my dear sister, and have the kindness to tell me where you think I had better drive, on arriving at Clifton. With most affectionate love to Mr. Peters, and the blessing of a fond aunt to all your dear children, I remain, dearest Margaret,

"Your ever devoted sister,

"MARTHA BARNABY."

This letter was received by Mrs. Peters at the breakfast-table, round which were assembled three daughters, one son, and her husband. The lady read it through in silence, cast her eyes rapidly over it a second time, and then handed it over to her spouse with an air of some solemnity, though something very like a smile passed across her features at the same moment.

Mr. Peters also read the letter, but not like his lady, in silence.

"Very kind of her indeed!... Poor dear lady!... a true mourner, that's plain enough to be seen.... She must be an excellent good woman, my dear, this widow of poor Barnaby; and I'm heartily glad she is coming among us. Your aunt Barnaby's coming, girls, and I hope you'll all behave so as to make her love you.... Is there any objection, Margaret, to the children's seeing this letter?"

"None at all," replied the lady ... "excepting...."

"Excepting what, my dear?... I am sure it is a letter that would do her honour anywhere, and I should be proud to read it on the exchange.... What do you mean by excepting?"

"It is no matter.... The girls and I can talk about it afterwards, ... and James, I think, will understand it very clearly at once."

"Understand it?... to be sure he will.... I never read a better letter, or one more easily understood, in my life.—Here, James, read it aloud to your sisters."

The young man obeyed, and read it very demurely to the end, though, more than once, his laughing blue eye sent a glance to his mother that satisfied her she was right in her estimate of his acuteness.

"That's an aunt worth having, isn't it?..." said old Peters, standing up, and taking his favourite station on the hearth-rug, with his back to the grate, though no fire was in it.... "Now I hope we shall have no airs and graces, because she comes from a remote part of the country, but that you will one and all do your best to make her see that you are worthy of her favour."

"I will do all I can to shew myself a dutiful and observant nephew.... But don't you think, sir, that 'the lady doth protest too much?'"

"Oh! but she'll keep her word," ... replied his mother, laughing.

"Keep her word?... to be sure she will, poor lady! She is broken-hearted and broken-spirited, as it's easy to see by her letter," observed the worthy Mr. Peters; "and I do hope, wife, that you will be very kind to her."

"And where shall I tell her to drive, Mr. Peters?"

"To the York hotel, my dear, I should think."

"Do you know that I rather fancy she expects we should ask her to come here?"

"No!... Well, that did not strike me. Let me see the letter again.... But it's no matter; whether she does or does not it may be quite as well to do it; ... and she says she likes to save her money, poor thing."

The father and son then set off to walk to Bristol, and Mrs. Peters and her three daughters were left to sit in judgment on the letter, and then to answer it.

"I see what you think, mamma," said the eldest girl, as the door closed after them; "you have no faith in this widowed aunt's lachrymals?"

"Not so much, Mary, as I might have, perhaps, if she said less about her sorrows."

"And her generous intentions in our favour, mamma," ... said the youngest, "perhaps you have no faith in them either."

"Not so much, Lucy," said the lady, repeating her words, "as I might have, perhaps, if she said less about it."

"I hope you are deceived, all of you," said Elizabeth, the second girl, very solemnly; "and I must say I think it is very shocking to put such dreadful constructions upon the conduct of a person you know so little about."

"I am sure I put no constructions," replied Mary, "I only ventured to guess at mamma's."

"And I beg to declare that my sins against this generous new relative have gone no farther," said Lucy.

"Well, well, we shall see, girls," said the lively mother. "Let us all start fair for the loaves and fishes; ... and now, Elizabeth, ring the bell, let the breakfast be removed, and you will see that I shall reply in a very sober and proper way to this pathetic communication."

The letter Mrs. Peters composed and read to her daughters, was approved even by the sober-minded and conscientious Elizabeth; it contained an obliging offer of accommodation at their house in Rodney Place, till Mrs. Barnaby should have found lodgings to suit her, and ended with kind regards from all the family, and "I beg you to believe me your affectionate sister, Margaret Peters."

So far, everything prospered with our widow. This invitation was exactly what she wished, and having answered, accepted, and fixed the day and probable hour at which it was to begin, Mrs. Barnaby once more enjoyed the delight of preparing herself for a journey that was to lead her another step towards the goal she had in view.

CHAPTER XV

THE ENTRÉE OF MRS. BARNABY IN MRS. PETERS'S DRAWING-ROOM—FAMILY CONSULTATIONS— ARRANGEMENTS FOR MISS WILLOUGHBY'S DRESS FOR SOME TIME TO COME

In one respect Mrs. Barnaby was considerably more fortunate than she had ventured to hope, for the "clothier," and the clothier's family, held a much higher station in society than she had anticipated. Mr. Peters had for many years been an active and prosperous manufacturer, neither above his business, nor below enjoying the ample fortune acquired by it; his wife was a lively, agreeable, lady-like woman, formed to be well received by any society that the chances of commerce might have thrown her into, being sufficiently well educated and sufficiently gifted to do credit to the highest, and without any pretensions which might have caused her either to give or receive pain, had the chances been against her, and she had become the wife of a poor instead of a rich manufacturer. The eldest son, who was excellently well calculated to follow the steps of his lucky father, was already married and settled at Frome, with a share of the business of which he was now the most efficient support; the younger son, who was intended for the church, was at present at home for a few months previous to his commencing term-keeping at Oxford; and the three daughters, from appearance, education, and manners, were perfectly well qualified to fill the situation of first-rate belles in the Clifton ball-room. Their house and its furniture, their carriage and establishment, were all equally beyond the widow's expectations, so that, in short, a very agreeable surprise awaited her arrival at Clifton.

It was a lovely evening of the last week in June, that a Bristol hackney-coach deposited Mrs. Barnaby, her niece, her Jerningham, and her trunks, at No. 4, Rodney Place. The ladies of the Peters family had just left the dinner-table, and were awaiting their relative in the drawing-room. Let it not be supposed that the interesting widow made her entrée among them in the dress she had indulged in during her residence at Exeter; she was not so thoughtless; and so well had poor Agnes already learned to know her, that she felt little surprise when she saw her, the day before they left that city, draw forth every melancholy article that she had discarded, and heard her say,—

"My life passes, Agnes, in a constant watchfulness of the feelings of others.... It was for your sake, dear girl, that I so early put off this sad attire, and the fear of wounding the feelings of my dear sister-in-law now induces me to resume it, for a few days at least, that she may feel I come to find my first consolation from her!"

So the next morning Mrs. Barnaby stepped into the stage-coach that was to convey her to Bristol with her lilacs, her greys, and her pink whites, all carefully shrouded from sight in band-boxes, and herself a perfect model of conjugal woe.

"Shew me to my sister!" said the widow, as soon as she had counted all her own packages, and with a cambric handkerchief, without an atom of embroidery, in her hand, her voice ready to falter, her knees to tremble, and her tears to flow, she followed the servant up stairs.

Mrs. Peters came very decorously forward to meet her, but she was, perhaps, hardly prepared for the very long embrace in which her unknown sister held her. Mrs. Peters was a very little woman, and was almost lost to sight in the arms and the draperies of the widow; but when at last she was permitted to emerge, Agnes was cheered and greatly comforted by the pleasing reception she gave her; while the young ladies in their turn (with the exception of the grave and reasonable Elizabeth, perhaps,) submitted rather impatiently to the lingering and sobbing embraces of their new aunt, as they had by no means gazed their fill on the lovely creature she brought with her.

Though there was certainly no reason in the world why the niece of Mrs. Barnaby should not be beautiful, both Mrs. Peters and her daughters gazed on her with something like astonishment. It seemed as if it were strange that they had not heard before of what was so very much out of the common way; and so great was the effect her appearance produced, and so engrossing the attention she drew, that Mrs. Barnaby passed almost uncriticised; and when the ladies of the family met afterwards, a female committee, in Mrs. Peters's dressing-room, and asked each other what they thought of their new relation, no one seemed prepared to say more of her than ... "Oh!... she has been handsome, certainly ... only she rouges, and is a great deal too tall; .... But, did you ever see so beautiful, so elegant a creature, as her niece?" Such, with a few variations, according to the temper of the speaker, was the judgment of all.

Before this judgment was passed upon the new arrivals in the dressing-room, the aunt and niece had also undergone the scrutiny of both father and son, who had joined them at the tea-table.

They, too, had held their secret committee, and freely enough exchanged opinions on the subject.

"Upon my word, James, she is an extremely fine woman, and I really never saw any person conduct herself better upon such an occasion. All strangers, you know, and she, poor soul!... with her heart breaking to think what she has lost!... I really cannot but admire her, and I flatter myself we shall all find means to make her like us too. I hope you agree with me, James, in my notions about her!"

"Oh! dear, yes.... I am sure I do ... a very excellent person—indeed, I have no doubt of it.... But did you ever, sir, see such a creature as her niece? She seemed to me something more like a vision—an emanation—than a reality."

"A what, James?"

"I beg your pardon, my dear sir, but I believe I have lost my senses already. Don't you think, father, I had better set off for Oxford to-morrow morning?"

"Good gracious! no, James.... Why should you go away just as your aunt Barnaby is come, and she having such kind intentions towards you all?"

"Very well, sir," replied the gay-hearted youth; "if such be your pleasure, I will brave the danger, and trust to Providence.... But, good night, father!... I must say one word to my sisters before they go to bed".... And the privileged intruder entered his mother's dressing-room while the party were still discussing the merits of the new-comers.

"Oh! here comes James," exclaimed Lucy, making room for him on the sofa where she was seated. "That's delightful! Come, mamma, sit down again ... let us hear what this accomplished squire of dames says of her.... Do you think now, James, that Kattie M'Gee is the prettiest girl you ever saw?"

"Prettiest?—why, yes, prettiest, as contra-distinguished from most beautiful,—perhaps I do," replied the young man, with an ex-cathedra sort of air; ... "but if you mean to ask who I think the very loveliest creation ever permitted to consecrate the earth by setting her heaven-born feet upon it, I reply Miss Agnes Willoughby!"

"Bravo!... That will do," replied Lucy. "I thought how it would fare with the puir Scottish lassie the moment I beheld this new divinity."

"Poor James! I am really sorry for you this time," said his mother, "for I cannot give you much hope of a cure from the process that has hitherto proved so successful.... I see no chance whatever of a "fairer she" coming to cauterize, by a new flame, the wound inflicted by this marvellous Miss Willoughby."

"They jest at scars who never felt a wound!" exclaimed the young man fervently.... "Mary!... Elizabeth!... have you none of you a feeling of pity for me?... Oh! how I envy you all!... for you can gaze and bask in safety in the beams of this glorious brightness, while I, as my mother says, am doomed to be scorched incurably!"

"If you have any discretion, James, you will run away," said his eldest sister.... "Her generous aunt, you know, has declared that she shall never have any of uncle Barnaby's money; and if you stay you may depend upon it that, while you are making love to the niece, I shall be winning the heart of the aunt, and contrive by my amiable cajoleries to get your share and my own too of all she so nobly means to bestow upon us."

"Nonsense, Mary!... Don't believe her, James!..." cried the worthy matter-of-fact Elizabeth. "If you are really in love with her already, I think it would be a very good scheme indeed for you to marry her, because then Mrs. Barnaby could be doing her duty to you both at once."

"Very true, Elizabeth," ... said the mother; "but you none of you recollect that while you have been regaling yourselves with the charms of the young lady, I have been worn to a thread by listening to the noble sentiments of the old ... old?... mercy on me! the elder one. Pray, offer to set off with them, James, in quest of lodgings as soon as breakfast is over to-morrow, for I foresee that I cannot stand it long.... And now go away all of you, for I am tired to death. Good night!... Good night!"

And now let us see the impression made on the aunt and niece by their reception, for, though separate rooms were prepared for them, Mrs. Barnaby did not permit the weary Agnes to enjoy the supreme luxury of this solitary apartment till she had indulged herself with a little gossip.

Mrs. Peters had herself shewn Mrs. Barnaby to her room, at the door of which she was preparing to utter a final good night, but was not permitted to escape without another sisterly embrace, and being held by the hand for some minutes, while the widow said,—

"You know not how soothing it is to my feelings, dearest Margaret!... you must allow me to call you Margaret ... you know not how soothing, how delightful it is to my feelings to lay my head and poor aching heart to rest under the roof of my dear Barnaby's sister!... Alas! none but those who have suffered as I have done, can fully understand this.... And yet I so much wish you to understand me, dearest sister!... I so long to have my heart appreciated by you!... Step in for one moment, will you?"... And the request was seconded by a gentle pulling, which sufficed to bring the imprisoned Mrs. Peters safely within the door.... "I cannot part with you till I have explained a movement ... a rush of sentiment, I may call it,—that has come upon me since I entered this dear dwelling. The time is come, is fully come, you know, when fashion dictates the laying aside this garb of woe; and as my excellent mother brought me up in all things respectfully to follow the usages of society, I have been struggling to do so in the present instance ... and have actually already furnished myself with a needful change of apparel ... never yet, however, dearest Margaret!"—and here she pressed her handkerchief to her eyes,—"never yet have I had the courage to wear it. But, thank Heaven! I now feel strengthened, and when we meet to-morrow you shall see the influence the sight of you and your dear family has had upon me. And now, good night, my sister!... I will detain you no longer,... but do explain to your charming family, dear Margaret! how this sudden change in my appearance has been wrought.... Good night!... But where is Agnes?... Poor love! she will not sleep, even in your elegant mansion, till she has received my parting kiss. She perfectly dotes upon me!... Will you have the kindness to let her be sent to me?"

In the happiest state of spirits from the conscious skill with which she had managed this instantaneous change of garments ... delighted with the unexpected elegance of the house, and all within it ... with her reception, ... and, above all else, with the recollection of the able manner in which she had propitiated the favour of these important relatives by her letter, the widow rang the bell for her Jerningham, and anxiously awaited her arrival and that of her niece, that she might indulge a little in the happy, boastful vein that swelled her bosom.

"Well, my dear," she broke out, the instant Agnes entered, "I hope you like my brother and sister, and my nieces and my nephew.... Upon my word, Agnes, you are the luckiest girl in the world! What a family for you to be introduced to, on a footing of the greatest intimacy too, and that on your very first introduction into life! They must be exceedingly wealthy ... there can be no doubt of it. I suppose you have seen a great many servants, Jerningham?"

"Oh my!—sure enough, ma'am!... There's the footman, and the boy, and the coachman."

"A coachman!" interrupted Mrs. Barnaby; "they keep a carriage, then?... I really had no idea of it. My dear Barnaby never told me that.... I wonder at it!... And well, Jerningham, how many maids are there?

"Oh lor! ma'am, I hardly can tell, for I was tooked to sit in one room, and there was one, and maybe two maids, as bided in another; that was the kitchen I sem, ma'am, and everything was so elegant, ma'am...."

"I dare say it was, Jerningham, ... and you must be very careful to keep up your own consequence, and mine too, in such a house as this. You understand me, Jerningham: I have already, you remember, given you some hints.... You have not forgotten, I hope?"

"No, that I haven't, ma'am," replied the girl; "and ... I mean to tell 'em ..." but looking at Agnes, she stopped short, as it seemed, because she was there.

"Very well ... that's quite right, ... and I'll give you these gloves of mine. Mend them neatly to-morrow morning, and never be seen to go out without gloves, Jerningham.... And now unpack my night-bag, ... and you had better just open my trunk too. Remember to learn the hour of breakfast, and come to me exactly an hour and a half before. I shall put on my black satin to-morrow, and my lavender trimmings.... You know where to find them all, don't you?"

"Yes, ma'am."

"Very well, forget nothing, and I will give you that cap with the lilac bows that I dirtied-out at Exeter.... Mercy on me, Agnes, how you are yawning!"

"I am very tired, aunt, and I will wish you good night now, if you please."

"What!... without one word of all you have seen? Well, you are a stupid girl, Agnes, and that's the fact.... You find nothing, I suppose, to like or admire in my sister's house, or in those delightful, fashionable-looking young people?"

"Yes, indeed I do, aunt, ... only I think I am too sleepy to do justice to them. They are very agreeable, and I like them very much indeed."

"I am glad to hear it, child, ... and I hope you will do your best to make yourself agreeable to them in return. If you were not such a baby, that young man would make a capital match for you, I dare say. But we must not think about that, I suppose.... And, now you may go; ... but stay one minute. Observe, Agnes, I have explained to my sister all my feelings about my mourning, and you must take care to let the young people understand that you keep on with crape and bombasin some time longer, because you like it best.... And, by the by, I may as well tell you at once, my dear, that as you look so particularly well in deep mourning, and are so fond of wearing it, you had better not think of a change for some time to come. I am sorry to tell you, my dear, that I find everything as I come up the country a vast deal indeed dearer than I expected, and therefore it will be absolutely necessary to save every penny I can. Now the fact is, that my mourning has been taken so much care of, and altogether so little worn, that the best gown is very nearly as good as new, and the worst has still a deal of wear left in it. So, I think the best thing we can do, Agnes, is to have both of them made up to fit you, that is, when your own are quite worn-out; ... and my bonnets too, if I can teach Jerningham to wash the crape nicely in a little small beer, they will come out looking quite like new, ... and they are so becoming to you!... and in this way, you see, my dear, a great many pounds may be saved."

"Thank you, aunt," meekly replied Agnes.

"Well, there's a good girl, go to bed now, and be sure to make the young ladies understand that you go on with crape and bombasin because you like it."

CHAPTER XVI

MRS. PETERS BECOMES UNEASY, BUT CONTRIVES TO ATTAIN HER OBJECT—A PLEASANT WALK DISCOVERED TO BE A GOOD MEANS OF MAKING A PARTY OF YOUNG PEOPLE ACQUAINTED WITH EACH OTHER—MRS. PETERS SHEWS MUCH PROMPTITUDE AND EXPERIENCE IN TAKING LODGINGS —SHE ALSO DISCOVERS THE BEST MODE OF LIONIZING A LADY WHO IS TOO BEAUTIFUL— ANOTHER COUNTRY WALK IMPROVES THE INTIMACY BETWEEN THE YOUNG LADIES

The impressions mutually received overnight, were not greatly changed when the parties met again on the following morning; excepting, indeed, that Mr. Peters was rather surprised at seeing the widow looking so very smart, and so very much handsomer.

The young people could hardly admire Agnes more than they had done before, though they confessed that they were not fully aware of the particular beauty of her hair, or of the perfect symmetry of her person, till they had seen her by daylight; but Mrs. Peters pleaded guilty to disliking her affectionate sister quite as much on Tuesday morning as she had done on Monday night; and as the sun shone brightly she took advantage of this to introduce the subject that was decidedly next her heart.

"You must take care to put this beautiful day to profit, Mrs. Barnaby," said she. "Of course you have heard of our rocks, and our downs, Miss Willoughby? and you could not look at them through a more favourable atmosphere.... We shall have time to take you to our famous windmill, and to shew you some lodgings too, Mrs. Barnaby, for we Bristol people never sacrifice business to pleasure. I thought of you yesterday morning when I saw a bill up at Sion Row ... some of the prettiest lodgings in Clifton, and it will be dangerous to put off looking at them, they are so very likely to be taken."

The good-natured Mr. Peters felt a great inclination to say that there could be no need of hurry in looking out for lodgings, as he should be so very glad to keep the ladies where they were; but, though the most perfect harmony (real harmony) and good feeling existed between Mr. Peters and his wife, a very salutary understanding also existed, that whenever she said anything that he did not quite comprehend, which not unfrequently happened, he was neither to contradict nor observe upon it till the matter had been inquired into between them when they were tête-à-tête, upon which occasions he always found her as ready to hear as to render reasons, and it was rare indeed that the conference broke up without their being of the same mind.

In conformity to this excellent rule, the good man suffered this lodging-hunting expedition to be arranged without offering any objection, and set off on his daily walk to the Bristol exchange, with no other observation than that he should leave James to escort them, as he did not think he should find him a very gay companion if he took him away.

The ladies then immediately dispersed to bonnet and cloak themselves, and in a few minutes the whole party, amounting to seven, all turned out upon the broad flagstones of Rodney Place, and dividing into three couples, with James hanging on upon that of which Agnes was one, proceeded, headed by Mrs. Barnaby and Mrs. Peters, towards Sion Row.

Before they reached it, however, James called a council with his eldest sister and Miss Willoughby, upon the necessity of so very large a party all going to look for lodgings.

"Would it not be better, Mary," said the young man, "for us to take Miss Willoughby to the down? The others can follow if they like it, you know, and we shall be sure to meet them coming back."

"Very well, then, tell mamma so, will you?" replied the young lady, turning off in the direction indicated.

The message caused the elder ladies to stop; Mrs. Peters looked very much as if she did not like her share in the division, but, after a moment's hesitation, she good-humouredly nodded assent, and walked on, Elizabeth, (who in her heart believed Mrs. Barnaby was the kindest person in the world, because she said so,) joining the elder ladies, and the four others striking off towards the beautiful rising ground on the right.

There is a sort of free-masonry among young people which is never brought into action till the elders are out of the way, and it was probably for this reason that Agnes felt better acquainted with her companions, before they had pursued their walk for half an hour, than all the talk of the preceding evening, or that of the breakfast-table, had enabled her to become. Something, too, might have been effected in the way of familiarity by an accident arising from the nature of the scenery upon which they paused to gaze. On reaching the windmill, and looking down upon the course of the Avon, winding its snake-like path at their feet, with the woods of Leigh, rich in their midsummer foliage, feathering down on one side, and rocks of limestone, bright in their veins of red and grey, freshly opened by the quarrying, rising beautifully bold on the other, Agnes stood wrapt in ecstasy. All she had yet seen of Nature had been the flowery meads and blooming apple orchards of the least romantic part of Devonshire; and though there was beauty enough in this to awaken that love of landscape which is always one of the strongest feelings in a finely-organized mind, she was quite unprepared for the sort of emotion the scene she now beheld occasioned her. She pressed forward before her companions, and, utterly unmindful of danger, leaned over the verge of the giddy precipice, till young Peters, really alarmed, seized her by the arm and drew her back again. Tears were in her eyes, and her face was as pale as marble.

"My dear Miss Willoughby!" said Mary, kindly, "the precipice has made you giddy, ... I do believe, if James had not seized you, that you would have fallen!"

"Oh! no, no," replied Agnes, shaking her head, while a bright flush instantly chased the paleness, "I do assure you I was not in any danger at all ... only I never saw anything so beautiful before."

"Let us sit down," said Lucy. "There is no dampness whatever. It is almost the first day of real summer, and the air is delicious. Is it not beautiful here, Agnes?"

A look of gratitude, and almost of affection, was the answer; and as the little party sat together, inhaling that most delicious of essences which the sun draws forth when herbs and flowers are what he shines upon, with a lovely landscape around, and each other's fair young faces and blithe voices beside them, was it wonderful that the recent date of their acquaintance should be forgotten, or that they laughed, and chatted, and looked about, and enjoyed themselves, with as much gaiety and as little restraint as if they had known each other for years.

They were all very happy, and a full hour passed unheeded as they amused themselves, sometimes with idle talk, sometimes with listening to the reverberating thunder that arose from the blasting of the rocks below them, and sometimes by sitting silent for a whole minute together, pulling up handfuls of the fragrant thyme with which their couch was strewed. They were all very happy, but none of the party had any notion of the happiness of Agnes. It was the first moment of real positive enjoyment she had tasted since she left Empton, and a feeling like renewed life seemed to seize upon her senses. Without reasoning about it, she had felt, during the last few months, as if it were her fate to be unhappy, and that all she had to do was to submit; but, to her equal delight and astonishment, she now found that nobody ever was so much mistaken, for that she was one of the most particularly happy people in the world, wanting nothing but sun, sweet air, and a lovely landscape, to make her forget that such a thing as sorrow existed; and the only thought that threw a shadow upon the brightness of her spirit, was that which suggested that she must have been very wicked to have doubted for a moment the goodness of God, who had formed this beautiful world on purpose to make people happy.

But, though every moment of such an hour as this seems to leave its own sweet and lasting impression on the memory, the whole is soon gone; and when Mary, with the wisdom called for by being the eldest of the party, jumped up, exclaiming that they had quite forgotten their appointment to meet her mother on the down, Agnes roused herself with a sigh, as if she had passed through a momentary trance.

They met the rest of their party, however, though the order of the meeting was changed, for it was our young set who encountered the others on their return, after a ramble of half a mile or so towards the turnpike, which it is probable had not been enlivened by any such raptures as those felt by Agnes.

The two parties now joined, and the conversation was general, not very lively perhaps, but by no means devoid of interest to Agnes, who had fallen so heartily in love with St. Vincent's rocks, as to make her hear of being fixed for some time in their neighbourhood with the greatest delight.

"Well, ma'am, have you seen any lodgings that you liked?" said the eldest Miss Peters to Mrs. Barnaby.

"Yes, my dear Mary, I have, indeed," replied the widow; "thanks to your dear kind mamma, who has really been indefatigable. Clifton seems exceedingly full, I think, and I am not sorry for it, for my poor dear Agnes really wants a little change to rouse her spirits.... That mourning habit that she so delights in, is, I am sorry to say, but too just a type of her disposition."

The brother and sisters, who had so lately shared in the gay hilarity of Agnes's laughter, exchanged glances, but said nothing, while she herself blushing, and half laughing again at the same recollection, changed the subject by saying.—

"And have you taken lodgings, aunt?"

"Yes, my dear, I have ... small but very delightful lodgings in Sion Row ... the very Row, Agnes, that you heard my dear sister mention this morning as so desirable!... and which we quite despaired of getting at first, for there appeared to be all sorts of difficulties. But," turning to Mrs. Peters, "you seem to understand all these things, Margaret, so admirably well! You made the good woman do exactly what you pleased.... So clever,... and so like your poor dear brother!..."

"My poor dear brother must have been wonderfully changed if he ever shewed himself half so self-willed!" thought the conscious Mrs. Peters, who had certainly used something like bribery and corruption to remove all difficulties in procuring for her sister-in-law apartments, which must by agreement be entered upon the following day.

"But you have got them, aunt, at last?... I am so glad of it!... for I think Clifton the most beautiful place I ever saw in my life."

"Falling in love with the young man, that is quite clear," thought the active-minded widow.

A fresh return of happiness awaited Agnes on re-entering the house. Lucy threw her wraps aside and sat down to the pianoforte: she played prettily, and sang, too, well enough to delight the thirsty ears of Agnes, who had never heard a note, excepting at the cathedral at Exeter, since she had left her school. The evident pleasure which her performance gave to her young auditor, encouraged the good-natured Lucy to proceed, and, excepting during an interval occupied by eating sandwiches for luncheon, she continued to play and sing till three o'clock.

Though by no means one of those performers who like to keep the instrument wholly to themselves, it never occurred to her to ask Agnes to play. There was something so childishly eager in the delight with which she listened, that Lucy fancied it was the novelty of the thing that so captivated her attention; and with something of that feeling, perhaps, against which her father had warned them all, and which leads young ladies at Clifton to fancy that young ladies in Devonshire must be greatly behind-hand in all things, she somehow or other took it for granted that it was very unlikely Agnes Willoughby should have learned to play or sing.

When the time-piece on the chimney struck three, there seemed to be a general movement among the Peters family, indicative of another sortie.

"I suppose you walk again, mother?" said the young man.

"I suppose so, James. I dare say Mrs. Barnaby will like to go to the library and put her name down at the rooms."

"Oh yes!... I shall, indeed, ... for poor Agnes's sake!..."

"Very well; that is all quite right.... You and I are smart enough, Mrs. Barnaby, but I suppose the girls will choose to change their walking bonnets for bonnets for the walk, and we must wait for them. Here are all the annuals, I believe, ... and I am deep in this review."

So saying, Mrs. Peters threw aside her shawl, seated herself in a low bee-hive that just fitted her little person, and "happified" herself with a biting article in the Quarterly.

Mrs. Barnaby smilingly turned to the piles of pretty books that decorated the loo-table; but hardly had the young ladies disappeared, and Mrs. Peters occupied herself, than she rose, and silently glided out of the room.

Agnes had no better bonnet to put on than the one she had already displayed, but she ran up stairs with the other girls, because one of them had put out a hand inviting her to do so, and it was therefore to one of their rooms she went, instead of her own: another step this, and a very considerable one too, towards intimacy between young ladies; for few things produce a more genial flow of talk than the being surrounded by a variety of objects in which all parties take a common interest.

Had Mrs. Barnaby been upon this occasion a little less humble-minded in her estimate of her own charms, it would have been better for her; but, unfortunately, a restless spirit within whispered to her that she was not quite beautiful enough for the "walk," and the "library," and the "rooms," and it was to refresh her rouge a little, that she followed the young ladies up stairs.

Now her rouge had been decidedly sufficient before, and moreover, after she had touched up her bloom to the point she deemed to be the most advantageous, it struck her that her lavender and black bonnet and plumes looked sombre, and would be rendered infinitely more becoming by introducing among the blonde beneath a few bright blossoms of various colours; so that, when she re-entered the drawing-room, she looked precisely like a clever caricature of what she had been when she left it,—the likeness not lost, but all that touched upon the ridiculous or outré brought out and exaggerated.

Mrs. Peters looked up as she entered, and gave her one steady glance, then rose from her chair and rang the bell.

The young people were all seated in array, waiting for the widow's re-appearance as a signal to depart, and all rose together as she entered; but they had yet longer to wait, for Mrs. Peters, after ringing the bell, quietly reseated herself, and prepared to resume her book, saying,—

"Upon second thoughts, dear friends, I think we shall do better if we order the carriage, and take Mrs. Barnaby and Miss Willoughby to Bristol. The library and all that will be within five minutes' walk of their lodgings, and as they leave us to-morrow, it will be making better use of our time to go to Bristol to-day." At this moment a servant entered, and the determined little lady, without waiting to hear any opinions on her proposal, desired to know if the coachman was in the house.

"Yes, ma'am," was the reply.

"Then tell him to bring the carriage round as quickly as he can.... You may give Miss Willoughby another song, Lucy, in the interval. I want you, Mary, in my room for a moment."... And Mrs. Peters left the room, followed by her eldest daughter.

"Have I puzzled you, Mary?" said she, laughing, and closing the door of the dressing-room as soon as they had entered it.... "Don't think me whimsical, child, but upon my word I cannot undertake to parade that painted and plumaged giantess through Clifton. I will sacrifice myself for a two hours' purgatory, and listen with the patience of a martyr to the record of her graces, her virtues, and her dignity, but it must be in the close carriage. I always prefer performing my penances in private. Elizabeth evidently believes in her, and I really think admires her beauty into the bargain; so she had better go with us, for I presume, Mary, you have no wish to be of the party?"

"Oh yes, I will certainly go, if Agnes does.... But, mamma, I hope you won't take a fancy against our being a great deal with Miss Willoughby. I will agree in all you may choose to say against this overwhelming aunt Barnaby, but it would grieve me to be rude to her charming niece. She is, I do assure you, the very sweetest creature I ever made acquaintance with."

"It is evident that you have taken a great fancy for her, ... and, upon the whole, it is a fancy that does you honour, for it clearly proves you to be exempt from the littleness of fearing a rival.... There is not a single girl in the neighbourhood that can be compared to her in beauty—I am quite ready to acknowledge that; ... but you must excuse me, Mary, if I doubt the possibility of my sympathizing with you in your general and unqualified admiration of a young lady brought up by my portentous sister Barnaby."

"But Agnes Willoughby was not brought up by her, mamma ... quite the contrary.... You laugh, mamma, but I do assure you...."

"I laugh at your 'quite the contrary,' which means, I suppose, that she has been brought down by her; and you will be brought down too, my dear, if you suffer yourself to be identified with her and her rouge in public."

"Identified with Mrs. Barnaby?... I am quite sure that I do not like her at all better than you do; and I will make myself into a porcupine, and set up my quills at her whenever she comes near me, if you wish it; but then, on your side, you must promise" ... and the young lady took her mother's hand very coaxingly ... "you must promise to take the trouble of talking a little to Agnes ... will you?"

"Yes, I will, if I have an opportunity; ... and I am sure, if she is good for anything, I pity her.... Now, then, let us go down again, and you shall see how well I will behave."

Before they reached the drawing-room, however, Mary Peters had conceived a project of her own. She knew what sort of a drive it would be when her mother was "behaving well" to a person she disliked, and she instantly addressed a whispered request to Agnes that she would stay at home, and chat, instead of going to Bristol.

"If I may!..." replied Agnes, colouring with pleasure at the proposal; but the yoke upon her young neck was far from being as easy a one as that by which Mrs. Peters guided her daughters, and she felt so much doubt of obtaining permission if she asked it herself, that she added, "Will you ask for me?"

"Mrs. Barnaby," said her courageous friend, "you must do without your niece during your drive, if you please, for she is going to look over my portfolios."

"You are excessively kind, my dear Mary!" replied the benign Mrs. Barnaby, too well satisfied at displaying herself in her beloved sister's carriage to care three straws what became of her niece the while. "I am sure Agnes can never be sufficiently grateful for all your kindness."

The delighted Agnes instantly disembarrassed herself of all out-of-door appurtenances, and Lucy, without saying a word about it, quietly did the same. The carriage was announced, the radiant widow stalked forth, Mrs. Peters took Elizabeth by the arm, and followed her, shaking her head reproachfully at Lucy as she passed her, and the young man escorted them down stairs; but having placed them in the carriage, he declined following them, saying,—

"I dare say my father will be glad of the drive home, for it is quite hot to-day.—You will be sure to find him at the Exchange Coffee-house if you get there by half-past four.... A pleasant ride!... Good morning!" and the next moment he joined the happy trio in the drawing-room.

"And what shall we do with ourselves?" said he. "Would Miss Willoughby like to promenade among the beaux and belles? Or will she let us keep her all to ourselves, and take another delightful country walk with us? Which do you vote for, Miss Willoughby."

"For the country walk, decidedly," she replied.

"Then let us go down by the zig-zag, and walk under the rocks," said Lucy; and in another minute they were en route for that singular and (despite the vile colour of the water) most beautiful river-path.

The enjoyment of this second ramble was not less to Agnes than that of the first, for, if the newness of the scenery was past, the newness of her companions was past too; and she suffered herself to talk, with all the open freedom of youth and innocence, of her past life, upon which Mary, with very friendly skill, contrived to question her; for she was greatly bent upon discovering the source and cause of the widely different tone of mind which her acuteness had discovered between Mrs. Barnaby and her protegée. This walk fully sufficed to explain it; for though Agnes would have shrunk into impenetrable reserve had she been questioned about her aunt Barnaby, she opened her heart joyfully to all inquiries respecting Empton, and the beloved Wilmots; nor was she averse, when asked if Mrs. Barnaby had placed her with these very delightful people, to expatiate upon the eccentric character of her half-known aunt Betsy. On the contrary, this was a subject upon which she loved to dwell, because it puzzled her. The one single visit she had made to Miss Compton in her bower, with the simple but delicious repast which followed it ... the old lady's marked kindness to herself, her mysteriously rude manner to her aunt Martha, ... the beauty of her bower, the prettiness of her little parlour, had all left a sort of vague and romantic impression upon her mind, which no subsequent interviews had tended to render more intelligible. And all this she told, and with it the fact that it was this same dear, strange, variable aunt Compton, who had placed her in the care of Mrs. Wilmot.

"Miss Compton of Compton Basett," repeated Mary; "that is a mighty pretty aristocratic designation. Your aunt Betsy is an old spinster of large fortune, I presume?"

"Why, no, I don't believe she is; indeed, my aunt Barnaby says she is very poor, but that she might have been a great deal richer had she not given so much of her property to the poor; ... but I wish I knew something more of her.... I cannot help thinking that, with all her oddities, I should like her very much. There is one thing very strange about her," she added musingly, "she is quite deformed, quite crooked, and yet I think she is one of the most agreeable-looking persons I ever saw in my life."

"She has a handsome face, perhaps?" said Lucy.

"No, I believe not. She is very pale, and her face is small, and there is nothing very particular in her features; but yet, somehow or other, I love dearly to look at her."

"The force of contrast, perhaps?" whispered James to his eldest sister.

"No doubt of it," she replied.

And thus they walked and talked, till it was quite time to turn back, and though their pace was somewhat accelerated, it was as much as they could do to get home in time to dress for their six o'clock dinner.

But the walk was not only agreeable, but profitable to Agnes, for at the end of it Miss Peters felt fully prepared to give a reason for her confidence relative to the cause of the dissimilarity between Mrs. Barnaby and her niece.

CHAPTER XVII

MRS. BARNABY TAKES POSSESSION OF HER LODGINGS, AND SETS ABOUT MAKING HERSELF COMFORTABLE—SHE OPENS HER PLANS A LITTLE TO AGNES, AND GIVES HER SOME EXCELLENT ADVICE—THE COMFORT OF A MIDSUMMER FIRE—THE APARTMENT OF AGNES SET IN ORDER—A LECTURE ON USEFULNESS—VIRTUOUS INDIGNATION

The following morning Mrs. Peters took care, without being particularly rude, that a movement of some activity "to speed the parting guest," should be perceptible in her household. Mr. Peters took a very kind leave of both ladies at breakfast, and expressed a very friendly wish of being useful to them as long as they should remain at Clifton; but his judicious lady, who generally knew, without any discourtesy, how to make him perceive that his first impressions were somewhat less acute than her own, had pointed out to him a few peculiarities in Mrs. Barnaby, which he certainly did not approve. The principal of these, perhaps, was that of her rouging, which for some time he steadfastly refused to believe, declaring that her complexion was the most beautiful he ever saw; but when, his examination being sharpened, he could withhold his belief no longer, he ingenuously confessed he did not like it, and allowed that, though he thought it would be great folly to lose the fine fortune she had promised them on that account, he certainly thought he should feel more comfortable when the rouge pots were all gone into lodgings, because they were articles he did not wish to put in the way of his girls.

As soon as Mr. Peters had taken his leave, the footman was very audibly instructed to order a porter to come for Mrs. Barnaby's luggage; "And let it be before the hall dinner, Stephen, that William may be able to walk beside the things, and see that none of them are dropped by the way."

And then Mrs. Barnaby was very kindly asked if she would not like to send her maid to see that a fire was lighted in the drawing-room, and that anything she wanted for dinner might be ordered in?... And then the thoughtful Mrs. Peters proposed, after Betty Jacks had been gone about an hour, that James should go to the lodgings, and that they should not set off themselves till he came back and gave notice that everything was ready and comfortable.

In short, Mrs. Barnaby, her niece, her maid, and all their travelling baggage, were safely deposited at No. 1, Sion Row, before the clock struck three.

The widow looked about her when she first got into her own drawing-room very much as if she did not know how she got there. She was puzzled and mystified by the tactics of Mrs. Peters. Delighted beyond all bounds of moderation in finding the family so infinitely higher in station than she had anticipated, her first idea, on perceiving what a land of milk and honey she had fallen into, was to exert all her fascinating talents to enable her to stay there as long as possible. But the conviction that this scheme would not take, came upon her, she hardly knew how. She had not the slightest inclination to persuade herself that the "dear Margaret" was otherwise than civil to her, yet she felt as if she was to be kept in order, and neither go, nor stay, except as she might receive permission; but, finally, she contrived to heal the wound her vanity had thus received by believing that Mrs. Peters's high fashion, and superior knowledge of life, naturally rendered her manners unlike any she had hitherto been acquainted with, and consequently that she might occasionally mistake her meaning.

Upon the whole, however, she began her Clifton campaign in very good spirits. The Peterses must be extremely useful acquaintance, and might be safely boasted of anywhere as dear and near relations. This was very different from arriving, as she had done, at Exeter, without a chance of making a single acquaintance besides her dress-maker. Moreover, she had got through the difficulty of throwing off her weeds admirably; she had managed matters so that the dress of Agnes should be perfectly respectable, and yet cost her nothing for a twelvemonth; she had just received a quarter's income without any deduction, and, to crown all, "she never was in better looks in her life."

Short, then, was the interval of discomfort that kept her inactive on first entering her lodgings. "It was not quite such a drawing-room as that of Mrs. Peters, to be sure, but it was the most fashionable part of Clifton; and with her management, and admirable ways of contriving things, she should soon make it extremely lady-like."

"Well, now then we must set to work, Agnes," she said, drawing off her gloves. "Come, Jerningham, you must not stand looking out of the window, child; there is an immense deal to do before we can be comfortable. And the first thing will be to get all the trunks up, those that came by the waggon, and those that came with us."

"Then I'm sure, ma'am," replied the waiting-maid, "I don't know where you'll find room to put 'em."

"They must all be brought in here, Jerningham, to begin; and when I have got all my own things unpacked, we must see how we shall be off about drawers, and closets, and pegs, and all that; and then the empty trunks and boxes must be carried into your garret, Jerningham, or into that little room inside mine, that I mean to give up to Agnes."

"To me, aunt?... How very kind!" exclaimed her niece, delighted beyond measure at the idea of some place, no matter what, where she might be alone.

"Yes, my dear.... You have not seen the rooms yet; come with me, Agnes, while Jerningham goes down about the trunks, and I will shew you our apartments."

"But what am I to do then, ma'am, about the trunks?" said Betty Jacks in a fit of despair; "I'm sure I can't carry 'em up any how."

"Then ask the people of the house to help you."

"Why, there's only the old lady and one maid, ma'am, and I'm sure they can't and they won't."

Mrs. Barnaby meditated for a moment, and then drew out her purse. "Here is sixpence, Jerningham: go to the next public-house, and hire a man to bring up my boxes. It is immensely expensive, Agnes, this moving about, and we really must be very careful!... Of course, my dear, you do not want any dinner after the Rodney Place luncheon? I took care to take a couple of glasses of wine on purpose; and you should remember, my dear, that I have every earthly thing to pay for you, and never neglect an opportunity of sparing me when you can. After we have done our unpacking we can dress, and go out to the pastry-cook's—there is hardly anything I like better than cakes—and you can have a biscuit, you know, if you should want anything before tea."

The majestic lady then led the way to their "apartments," which consisted of a small bed-room behind the drawing-room, and a very small closet, with a little camp-bed behind that.

"Here, my dear, is the room I intend for you. It is, I believe, generally used for a servant, but I have been at the expense of hiring a garret for Jerningham on purpose that you might have the comfort of this. In fact, that bed of mine is not larger than I like for myself, and the drawers, and all that, are not at all more than I shall want; so remember, if you please, not to let any single article of yours, great or small, be ever seen in my room; I shall be puzzled enough, I am sure, as it is, to find room for my own things. You have a great advantage over me there, Agnes; ... that fancy of yours for keeping yourself in deep mourning makes it so easy for you to find space enough for everything."

"Oh yes!" replied Agnes joyfully, "everything shall be put into the closet. What very pleasant lodgings these are, aunt ... so much better than those at Exeter! It is such a nice closet this, and I am so much obliged to you for giving it up to me!"

"I shall be always ready to make sacrifices for you, Agnes, so long as you continue to behave well. Here come some of the boxes ... now then, you must kneel down and help to unpack them."

It was a long and a wearisome task that unpacking, and often did Agnes, as the sun shone in upon them while they performed it, think of her pleasant walks with her new friends, and long to breathe again the air that blew upon her as she stood on the top of St. Vincent's rocks.

Mrs. Barnaby, on the contrary, was wholly present to the work before her; and though she waxed weary and warm before it was completed, her spirits never flagged, but appeared to revive within her at every fresh deposit of finery that she came upon, and again and again did she call upon Agnes and Jerningham to admire the skill with which she had stowed them.

At length the work was done, and every disposable corner of her room filled; under the bed, over the bed, in the drawers, and upon the drawers, not an inch remained unoccupied by some of the widow's personalities.

It was by this time so late that the cake scheme was given up, and the drawing-room being restored to order, the two ladies sat down to tea. It was then that Mrs. Barnaby's genius displayed itself in sketching plan's for the future: she had learned from Mrs. Peters and the simple-minded Elizabeth, during their drive to and from Bristol, all particulars respecting the Clifton balls, and moreover that the Peters family seldom failed to attend them.

"This will be quite enough to set us going respectably: people that come in their own carriage, must have influence. I trust that those stupid humdrums, the Wilmots, gave you some dancing lessons, Agnes?"

"Yes, aunt."

"You are always so short in your answers, you never tell me anything. Do you think you could get through a quadrille without blundering?"

"Yes, I hope so, aunt."

"Remember, if you can't, I shall be most dreadfully angry, for it would destroy all my plans entirely.—I mean, Agnes, that you shall dance as much as possible;—nothing extends one's acquaintance among young men so much. I am not quite sure myself about dancing. I don't think I shall do it here, on account of dear Margaret ... perhaps she might think it too soon. I shall probably take to cards; that's not a bad way of making acquaintance either; but in all things remember that you play into my hands, and whenever you have a new partner remember that you always say to him, 'You must give me leave to introduce you to my aunt'.... Do you hear me, Agnes?"

"Yes, aunt," replied the poor girl with an involuntary sigh.

"What a poor, stupid creature you are, to be sure!" returned Mrs. Barnaby in a tone of much displeasure. "What in the world can you sigh for now, just at the very moment that I am talking to you of balls and dancing? I wish to Heaven you were a little more like what I was at your age, Agnes! Be so good as to tell me what you are sighing for?"

"I don't know, aunt; I believe I am tired."

"Tired?... and of what, I should like to know? Come, come, let us have no fine lady airs, if you please; and don't look as if you were going to cry, whatever you do. There is nothing on earth I dislike so much as gloom. I am of a very cheerful, happy temper myself, and it's perfect misery to me to see anybody look melancholy.... I declare, Agnes, I am as hungry as a hound!... I don't like to ring for Jerningham again, she looked so horridly cross; and I wish, my dear, you would just toast this round of bread for me. Mrs. Peters was quite right about the fire ... it is such a comfort! and coals are so cheap here.... Let me stir it up a little ... there, now its as bright as a furnace; you can just kneel down in the middle here upon the rug."

Agnes obeyed, and after some minutes' assiduous application to the labour imposed, she presented the toasted bread, her own fair face scarcely less changed in tint by the operation.

"Gracious me, child! what a fright you have made of yourself!... you should have held the other hand up before your face.... You are but a clumsy person, I am afraid, at most things, as well as at satin-stitch. Will you have some more tea, my dear?..." draining, as was her habit, the last drop into her own cup before she asked the question, and then extending her hand to that genial source of hospitality, the tepid urn.

"No more, thank you, aunt.... I will go now, if you please, and take all my things out of your way ... and I shall make my closet so comfortable!..."

"I dare say you will. But stay a moment, Agnes: if you find you have more room than you want, do put my two best bonnet-boxes somewhere or other among your things, so that I can get at them ... so that Jerningham can get at them, I mean, easily."

"I will, if I can, aunt, but I am afraid there will hardly be room for my chair. However, you shall come and see, if you please, yourself, and then you will be the best judge; but I will go first, and get everything in order."

"Very well, then, Agnes, you may tell Jerningham to separate everything like mourning from my things, and give it all to you. And you must contrive, my dear, to cut and make up everything to fit yourself, for I really can be at no expense about it. It is perfectly incredible how money goes in this part of the country, so different from our dear Silverton!... However, I will not grumble about it, for I consider it quite my duty to bring you out into the world, and I knew well enough before I set out, that it could not be done for nothing. But it is a sort of self-devotion I shall never complain of, if you do but turn out well."

Agnes was standing while this affectionate speech was spoken, and having quietly waited for its conclusion, again uttered her gentle "thank you, aunt," and retired to arrange the longed-for paradise of her little closet.

Darkness overtook her before she had fully completed her task; but, perhaps, she wilfully lingered over it, for it kept her alone, and permitted her bright and innocent spirit to indulge itself by recalling all the delight she had felt in looking down upon the bold and beautiful scenery of the Avon, and she blessed Heaven for the fund of happiness she was now conscious existed within her, since the power of looking out upon Nature seemed sufficient to produce a joy great enough to make her forget aunt Barnaby, and everything else that gave her pain. A part, too, of her hours of light, was spent in opening more than one of her dear little volumes to seek for some remembered description of scenery which she thought would be more intelligible to her now than heretofore; and as Spencer happened to fall into her hands, it was no great wonder if his flowery meads and forests drear, tempted her onwards till she almost lost herself among them.

At length, however, she had done all that she thought she could do towards giving a closet the appearance of a room; and having stowed her tiny looking-glass out of the way, and placed pens, ink, and a book or two, on the rickety little table in its stead, she looked round in the dusky twilight with infinite satisfaction, and thought, that were she quite sure of taking a long country walk about three times a week with the Peterses, she should be very, very happy, let everything else go on as it might.

Having come to this satisfactory conclusion, (for a walk three times a week was an indulgence she might reasonably hope for,) she cast one fond look round upon her dark but dear solitude, and then went to rejoin her aunt in the drawing-room, and announce its state of perfection to her. She found her seated at the open window.

"What have you been about, Agnes, all this time?" she said. "It is lucky that my cheerful, happy temper, does not make solitude as dreadful to me as it is to most people, or I should be badly off, living with you. You are but a stupid, moping sort of a body, my dear, I must say, or you would have guessed that there was more to see at the front of the house than at the back of it. I declare I never saw such a delightful window as this in my life. You would never believe what a mall there has been here from the moment I took my place till just now, that it's got almost dark; ... and even now, Agnes, if you will come here," ... she added in a whisper, ... "but don't speak ... you may see one couple left, and lovers they are, I'll be bound for them.... Here, stand here by me."

"No, thank you, aunt," said Agnes, retreating; "I don't want to see them, and I think it is more comfortable by the fire."

"You don't choose to spoil sport, I suppose; ... but don't be such a fool, and pretend to be wiser than your betters. Come here, I say; you shall take one peep, I am determined."

And as this determination was enforced by a tolerably strong pull, Agnes yielded, and found herself, greatly against her inclination, standing at the open window, with her head obligingly thrust out of it by her resolute aunt.

The lamps were by this time lighted, and at that moment a remarkably tall, gentleman-like looking personage passed beneath one that stood almost immediately below the window, receiving its full glare upon his features. Beside him was a lady, and a young one, slight, tall, and elegant-looking, who more than leaned upon his arm, for her head almost reclined upon his shoulder; and, as they passed, Agnes saw his hand raised to her face, and he seemed to be playing with her ringlets.

Agnes forcibly withdrew her head, while Mrs. Barnaby threw herself half out of the window for a minute, then drew back, laughing heartily, and shut down the sash.

"That's capital!..." she cried; "they fancied themselves so very snug. But wasn't he a fine figure of a man, Agnes? I never saw a finer fellow in my life. He's taller than Tate by half a head, I am sure. But you're right about the fire too, for the wind comes over that down uncommonly cold. I shall go to work for an hour, and then have a little bread and cheese and a pint of beer."

Mrs. Barnaby suited the action to the word, and unlocked her work-box, in which she found ready to her hand good store of work prepared for her beloved needle.

"Now, only see, Agnes, what a thing it would have been for you, if you had learned to work satin-stitch!" she said, "Here am I, happy and amused, and before I go to bed I dare say I shall have done a good inch of this beautiful collar.... And only look at yourself! What earthly use are you of to anybody?... I wonder you are not ashamed to sit idle in that way, while you see me hard at work."

"May I get a book, aunt?"

"Books, books, books!... If there is one thing more completely full of idleness than another, it is reading,—just spelling along one line after another.... And what comes of it? Now, here's a leaf done already, and wait a minute and you'll see a whole bunch of grapes done in spotting. There is some sense in that: but poring over a lot of rubbishly words is an absolute sin, for it is wasting the time that Heaven gives us, and doing no good to our fellow-creatures."

"And the grapes!" thought Agnes, but she said nothing.

"Why don't you answer when I speak to you, child?... Did that stupid Mrs. Wilmot never tell you to speak when you were spoken to?... What a different creature you would have been if I had had the placing you, instead of that crooked, frumpish old maid!... But I am sadly afraid it is too late now to hope that you will ever be good for much."

"I should be very glad to try to make myself competent for the situation of a governess, aunt, as you once mentioned to me," replied Agnes.

"Oh! by the by, I want to speak to you about that. You are not to say one word on that subject here, remember, nor indeed anywhere, till at such time as I shall give you leave. It will be cruelly hard for me to have the monstrous expense of maintaining you, exactly as if you were my own child, and not have the credit of it. And, besides I don't feel quite sure that I shall send you out as a governess ... it must depend upon circumstances. Perhaps I shall get you married, and that might suit me just as well. All you have to do is to keep yourself always ready to go out at a minute's warning, if I say the word; but you need mention it to nobody, and particularly not to my relations here."

"Very well, aunt.... I will say nothing about it. But in order to be ready when you say the word, I think I ought to study a good deal, and I am willing to do it if you will give me leave."

"How you do plague me, child, about your learning! Push the candles this way, can't you, and snuff them, when you see me straining my poor eyes with this fine work.... And do you know, miss, I think it's very likely those books you are so mighty fond of are nothing in the world but trumpery story-books, for I don't believe you'd hanker after them so, if they were really in the teaching line. For, after all, Agnes, if I must speak the truth, I don't believe you ever did pay attention to any single thing that could be really useful in the way of governessing. Now, music, for instance, nobody ever heard you say a word about that; and you ought to sing too, if you wer'n't more stupid than anything ever was, for both your father and mother sang like angels."

"I can sing a little, aunt," said Agnes.

"There, now, ... isn't it as plain as possible that you take no pleasure in it?... though everybody said your poor dear mother could have made her fortune by singing. But you care for nothing but books, books, books!... and what profit, I should like to know, will ever come of that?"

"But I do care very much indeed for music, aunt," said Agnes eagerly, "only I did not talk about it, because I thought it might not be convenient for you to have an instrument for me. But I believe I could learn to get my bread by music, if I had a pianoforte to study with."

"Grant me patience!... And you really want me to go and get you a pianoforte, which is just the most expensive thing in the world?... And that after I had so kindly opened my heart to you about my fears of not having money enough!... I do think that passes anything I ever heard in my life!"

"Indeed, aunt, I never would have said a word about it if...."

"If?... if what, I should like to know? Heaven knows it is seldom I lose my temper about anything, but it is almost too much to hear you ask me to my face to ruin myself in that way, ... and you without a chance of ever having a penny to repay me!"

"Pray forget it, aunt!... Indeed I do not wish to be an expense to you, and will very gladly try to labour for my own living, if you will let me."

"Mighty fine, to be sure!... Much you're good for, ar'n't you?... I wish you'd get along to bed. My temper is too good to bear malice, and I shall forget all about it to-morrow, perhaps; but I can't abide to look at you to-night after such a speech as that ... there's the truth; ... so get to bed, that's a good girl, as fast as you can.... There are some things too much even for an angel to bear!"

Agnes crept to her little bed, and soon cried herself to sleep.

CHAPTER XVIII

CONDITIONS OF AN AGREEMENT BETWEEN MRS. PETERS AND HER DAUGHTERS—MRS. BARNABY BEGINS HER FASHIONABLE CAREER UNDER THE PROTECTION OF MISS ELIZABETH—SHE REHEARSES A BALL IN HER HEART AS SHE EXAMINES THE ROOM—THE LIBRARY.

Mrs. Barnaby was quite right in thinking that the Peters family would be very useful acquaintance; for prodigiously as Mrs. Peters disliked her sister-in-law, she no sooner ceased to be galled by her unwelcome presence in her house, than she recovered her good-humour, and felt as much aware as any reasonable person could desire, of the claim her brother's widow really had upon her and her family. These excellent dispositions were assiduously fostered by her daughters, to whose wishes she never turned a deaf ear. She found the eldest and the youngest very seriously interested in Agnes, and earnest in their desire to see more of her; while Elizabeth persevered in her belief that poor Mrs. Barnaby was one of the very best-hearted women in the world, and very much to be pitied, because nobody seemed to like her ... though she did mean to divide her fortune so generously amongst them.

"I hope, mamma," said the eldest Miss Peters, when the ladies of the family were sitting round the drawing-room fire after dinner, "I hope that you will overcome your terror of Mrs. Barnaby and her rouge sufficiently before Tuesday night to permit her joining our party in the ball-room, for I would not forsake that sweet Agnes upon such an occasion for more than I will say."

"Why, I do feel my spirits revive, Mary, considerably, since I have felt quite certain that none of my dear sister's amiable feelings were likely to involve me in the necessity of enduring her presence in my house for evermore. You may fancy you exaggerate, perhaps, when you talk of my terrors; ... but no such thing, believe me. It was terror she inspired, and nothing short of it."

"And Agnes, mamma?... what did she inspire?" said Mary.

"Pity and admiration," replied her mother.

"Very well, then," returned the petted girl, kissing her, "we shall not quarrel this time; but I was half afraid of it. It would, in truth, have been very foolish, and very unlike you, mamma, who understand the sort of thing better than most people, I believe, if we had lost the great pleasure of being kind to Miss Willoughby, and behaved extremely ill to uncle Barnaby's widow into the bargain, solely because you don't like tall massive ladies, with large black eyes, who wear rouge, and talk fine; ... for you must confess, if you will be quite honest and speak the truth, that Mrs. Peters is rather too well-established a person at Clifton, to fear losing caste by being seen with a Mrs. Barnaby, even had the association not been redeemed by the matchless elegance of her beautiful niece."

"Did any one ever hear a mamma better scolded?" said Mrs. Peters, turning to the younger girls.

"Mary is quite right, mamma," said Lucy. "Depend upon it we should have broken into open rebellion, had you persevered in threatening to cut the Barnaby connexion."

"Indeed I must say," added Elizabeth, "that I have thought you very severe upon our poor aunt, mamma. Think of her kindness!"

"Our aunt!" sighed Mrs. Peters. "Is it absolutely necessary, beloveds! that she should be addressed in public by that tender title?"

"Not absolutely, perhaps," replied Mary, laughing; "and I dare say Elizabeth will make a bargain with you, mamma, never to call her aunt again, provided you promise never to forget that she is our aunt, though we may not call her so."

"And what must I do, young ladies, to prove my eternal recollection of this agreeable tact?"

"You must be very civil to Agnes, and let them both join our party at tea, and at all the balls, and never object to our calling upon the Barnaby, for the sake of getting at the Willoughby, and ... now don't start, and turn restive, mamma, ... you must ask them whenever we have an evening party here with young people, that might be likely to give Agnes pleasure."

"And must I embrace Mrs. Barnaby every time she comes into my presence, and every time she leaves it?"

"No, ... unless you have done something so very outrageously rude before, as to render such a penitentiary amende necessary."

"Come here, Mary," said the gay mother, "and let me box your ears immediately."

The young lady placed herself very obediently on the foot-stool at Mrs. Peters's feet, who having patted each pretty cheek, said, "Now tell me, Mary, if you can, what it is that has thus fascinated your affections, hoodwinked your judgment, perverted your taste, and extinguished your pride?"

"If you will let me turn your questions my own way, mother," replied the daughter, "I will answer them all. My affection is fascinated, or, I would rather say, won, by the most remarkable combination of beauty, grace, talent, gentleness, and utter unconsciousness of it all, that it has ever been my hap to meet with. And, instead of being hoodwinked, my judgment, my power of judging, seem newly roused and awakened by having so very fine a subject on which to exercise themselves. I never before felt, as I did when listening to Agnes as she innocently answered my prying questions concerning her past life, the enormous difference there might be between one human mind and another. It was like opening the pages of some holy book, and learning thence what truth, innocence, and sweet temper could make of us. If admiring the uncommon loveliness of this sweet girl with something of the enthusiasm with which one contemplates a choice picture, be perversion of taste, I plead guilty, for it is with difficulty that I keep my eyes away from her; ... and for my pride, mamma, ... if any feeling of the kind ever so poisoned my heart as to make me turn from what was good, in the fear that it might lead me into contact with what was ungenteel, be thankful with me, that this sweet 'light from heaven' has crossed my path, and enabled me to see the error of my ways."

Mary spoke with great animation, and her mother listened to her till tears dimmed her laughing blue eyes.

"You are not a missish miss, Mary, that is certain," said she, kissing her, "and assuredly I thank Heaven for that. This pretty creature does indeed seem by your account to be a pearl of price; but, par malheur, she has got into the shell of the very vilest, great, big, coarse, hateful oyster, that ever was fished up!... Fear nothing more, however, from me.... You are dear good girls for feeling as you do about this pretty Agnes, and I give you carte blanche to do what you will with her and for her."

The consequence of this was an early call made on the following morning at Mrs. Barnaby's lodgings by the three Misses Peters. There were not many subjects on which the aunt and niece thought or felt in common; but it would be difficult to say which of the two was most pleased when their visiters were announced.

"We are come—that is, Lucy and I—to make you take a prodigious long walk with us, Agnes," said Miss Peters; "and Elizabeth, who is not quite so stout a pedestrian as we are, is come with us, to offer her services to you, Mrs. Barnaby, for a home circuit, if you like to make one. And pray do not forget that Tuesday is the ball night, and that we shall expect you to go, and join our party in the room."

"Dearest Mary!... dearest Elizabeth!... dearest Lucy! How good of you all! Agnes, put on your bonnet, my dear, instantly, and never forget the kindness of these dear girls.... I shall, indeed, be thankful to you, Elizabeth, if you will put me in the way of getting a few trifles that will be necessary for Tuesday.... Are your balls large?... Are there plenty of gentlemen?..." &c. &c.

And where was Agnes's heavy sense of sadness now? The birds, whose cheerful songs seemed to call her out, were not more light of heart than herself, as she followed her friends down the stairs, and sprung through the door to meet the fresh breeze from the down with a foot almost as elastic as their own glad wings. We must leave the young ladies to pursue their way, being joined at no great distance from the door by James Peters, through a long and delightful ramble that took them along "the wall," that forms the garde fou to the most beautiful point of Durdham Down, and so on amidst fields and villas that appeared to Agnes, like so many palaces in fairy-land; and while thus they charm away the morning, we must follow Mrs. Barnaby and the good-natured Elizabeth through their much more important progress among the fashionable resorts of the Clifton beau monde.

"And about tickets, my dear Elizabeth?" said the widow, as she offered her substantial arm to her slight companion; "what is it the fashion to do? To subscribe for the season, or pay at the door?"

"You may do either, Mrs. Barnaby; but if you wish your arrival to be known, I believe you had better put your name on the book."

"You are quite right, my dear. Where is the place to do this? Cannot you take me at once?"

"Yes, I could take you certainly, for it is almost close by; but perhaps papa had better save you the trouble, Mrs. Barnaby?"

"By no means, my dear. His time is more valuable than mine. Let us go at once: I shall like it best."

Elizabeth, though a little frightened, led the way; and as Mrs. Barnaby entered the establishment that at its very threshold seemed to her redolent of wax-lights, fiddles, and fine clothes, such a delightful flutter of spirits came upon her, as drove from her memory the last fifteen or sixteen years of her life, and made her feel as if she were still one of the lightest and loveliest nymphs in the world. She insisted upon seeing the ball-room, and paced up and down its ample extent with a step that seemed with difficulty restrained from dancing; she examined the arrangement for the music, looked up with exultation at the chandeliers, and triumphed in anticipation at their favourable influence upon rouge, eyes, feathers, and flowers. Had there been any other man present beside the waiter, she would hardly have restrained her desire to make a tour de waltz; and, as it was, she could not help turning to the quiet young man, and saying with a condescending smile, "The company must look very well in this room, sir?"

As they passed in their way out through the room in which the subscription-books were kept, they met a gentleman, whose apparent age wavered between thirty-five and forty, tall, stout, gaily dressed, fully moustached, and with an eye that looked as if accustomed to active service in reconnoitring all things. He took off his hat, and bowed profoundly to Miss Peters, bestowing at the same time a very satisfactory stare on the widow.

"Who is that, my dear?" said the well-pleased lady.

"That is Major Allen," replied Elizabeth.

"Upon my word, he is a very fine, fashionable-looking man. Is he intimate with your family?"

"Oh no!... We only know him from meeting him sometimes at parties, and always at the balls."

"Is he a man of fortune?"

"I am sure I don't know. He has got a smart horse and groom, and goes a great deal into company."

"Then of course he cannot be a poor man, my dear. Is he a dancer?"

"No.... I believe he always plays cards."

"And where shall we go now, dearest?... I want you to take me, Elizabeth, to all the smartest shops you know."

"Some of the best shops are at Bristol, but we have a very good milliner here."

"Then let us go there, dear.... And did not your mamma say something about a library?"

"Yes, there's the library, and almost everybody goes there almost every morning."

"Then there of course I shall go. I consider it as so completely a duty, my dear Elizabeth, to do all these sort of things for the sake of my niece. My fortune is a very good one, and the doing as other people of fortune do, must be an advantage to poor dear Agnes as long as she is with me; ... but I don't scruple to say to you, my dear, that the fortune I received from your dear uncle, will return to his family in case I die without children.... And a truly widowed heart, my dear girl, does not easily match itself again. But the more you know of me, Elizabeth, the more you will find that I have many notions peculiar to myself. Many people, if they were mistress of my fortune, would spend three times as much as I do; but I always say to myself, 'Poor dear Mr. Barnaby, though he loved me better than anything else on earth, loved his own dear sister and her children next best; and therefore, as he left all to me ... and a very fine fortune he made, I assure you ... I hold myself in duty bound, as I spend a great deal of money with one hand upon my own niece, to save a great deal with the other for his.'"

"I am sure you seem to be very kind and good to everybody," replied the grateful young lady.

"That is what I would wish to be, my dear, for it is only so that we can do our duty.... Not that I would ever pledge myself never to marry again, my dear Elizabeth. I don't at all approve people making promises that it may be the will of Heaven they should break afterwards; and those people are not the most likely to keep a resolution, who vow and swear about it. But I hope you will never think me stingy, my dear, nor let anybody else think me so, for not spending above a third of my income, or perhaps not quite so much; for, now you know my motives, you must feel that it would be very ungenerous, particularly in your family, to blame me for it."

"It would indeed, Mrs. Barnaby, and it is what I am sure that I, for one, should never think of doing.... But this is the milliner's.... Shall we go in?"

"Oh yes!... A very pretty shop, indeed; quite in good style. What a sweet turban!... If it was not for the reasons that I tell you, I should certainly be tempted, Elizabeth. Pray, ma'am, what is the price of this scarlet turban?"

"Four guineas and a half, ma'am, with the bird, and two guineas without it."

"It is a perfect gem! Pray, ma'am, do you ever make up ladies' own materials?"

"No, ma'am, never," replied the decisive artiste.

"Do you never fasten in feathers?... I should not mind paying for it, as I see your style is quite first-rate."

"For our customers, ma'am, and whenever the feathers or the coiffure have been furnished in the first instance by ourselves."

"You are a customer, Elizabeth, are you not?"

"Mamma is," replied the young lady. "You know Mrs. Peters of Rodney Place, Mrs. Duval?"

"Oh yes!... I beg your pardon, Miss Peters. Is this lady a friend of yours?"

"Mrs. Peters is my sister-in-law, Mrs. Duval, and I hope that will induce you to treat me as if I had already been a customer. I should like to have some feathers, that I mean to wear at the ball on Tuesday, fastened into my toque, like these in this blue one here. Will you do this for me?"

"Yes, ma'am, certainly, if you will favour us with your name on our books."

"That's very obliging, and I will send my own maid with it as soon as I get home."

"Is there anything else I can have the pleasure of shewing you, ladies?"

"I want some long white gloves, if you please, and something light and elegant in the way of a scarf."

The modiste was instantly on the alert, and the counter became as a sea of many-coloured waves.

"Coloured scarves are sometimes worn in slight mourning, I believe, are they not?"

"Oh yes! ma'am, always."

"What do you say to this one, Elizabeth?" said the widow, selecting one of a brilliant geranium tint.

"For yourself, Mrs. Barnaby?"

"Yes, my dear.... My dress will be black satin, you know."

"I should think white would look better," said Elizabeth, recollecting her mother's aversion to fine colours, and recollecting also the recent weeds of her widowed aunt.

"Well, ... perhaps it might. Let me see some white, if you please."

"Perhaps you would like blonde, ma'am?" said the milliner, opening a box, and displaying some tempting specimens.

"Beautiful indeed!... very!... What is the price of this one?"

"A mere trifle, ma'am.... Give me leave to begin your account with this."

"Well, I really think I must.... I know they clean as good as new."

"What is Agnes to wear?" inquired Elizabeth.

"There is one of my troubles, my dear; she will wear nothing but the deepest mourning. Between you and me, Elizabeth, I suspect it is some feeling about her poor mother, or else for her father, who has never been heard of for years, but whom we all suppose to have died abroad,—I suspect it is some feeling of this sort that makes her so very obstinate about it. But she can't bear to have it talked of, so don't say a word to her on the subject, or she will be out of sorts for a week, and will think it very cruel of me to have named it to you. I perfectly dote upon that girl, Elizabeth, ... though, to be sure, I have my trials with her! But we have all our trials, Elizabeth!... and, thank Heaven! I have a happy temper, and bear mine, I believe, as well as most people. But about that strange whim that Agnes has, of always wearing crape and bombasin, you may as well just mention it to your mamma and sisters, to prevent their taking any notice of it to her; for if they did, you may depend upon it she would not go to the ball at all.... Oh! you have no idea of the obstinacy of that darling girl!... These gloves will do at last, I think.... Your gloves are all so remarkably small, Mrs. Duval!... And that's all for this morning."

"Where shall I send them, ma'am, and to what name?"

"To Mrs. Barnaby, No. 1, Sion Row."

"Thank you, ma'am.... They shall be sent immediately."

"Now then, Elizabeth, for the library," said the widow with an expressive flourish of the hand.

And to the library they went, which to Mrs. Barnaby's great satisfaction was full of smart people, and, amongst others, she had to make her way past the moustached Major Allen, in order to reach the table on which the subscription-book was laid.

"I beg your pardon, madam, a thousand times!" said the Major; "I am afraid I trod on your foot!"

"Don't mention it!... it is of no consequence in the world! The shop is so full, it is almost impossible to avoid it."

The Major in return for this civil speech again fixed his broad, wide, open eyes upon the widow, and she had again the satisfaction of believing that he thought her particularly handsome.

Miss Peters found many of her acquaintance among the crowd, with whom she conversed, while Mrs. Barnaby seated herself at the table, and turned over page after page of autographs with the air of a person deeply interested by the hope of finding the names of friends and acquaintance among them, whereas it would have been a circumstance little short of a miracle had she found there that of any individual whom she had ever seen in her life; but she performed her part admirably, smiling from time to time, as if delighted at an unexpected recognition. Meanwhile many an eye, as she well knew, was fixed upon her, for her appearance was in truth sufficiently striking. She was tall, considerably above the average height, and large, though not to corpulency; in short, her figure was what many people, like Mr. Peters, would call that of a fine woman; and many others, like Mrs. Peters, would declare to be large, ungainly, and vulgar. Her features were decidedly handsome, her eyes and teeth fine, and her nose high and well-formed; but all this was exaggerated into great coarseness by the quantity of rouge she wore, and the redundance of harsh-looking, coal-black ringlets which depended heavily down each side of her large face, so as still to give a striking resemblance, as Agnes, it may be remembered, discovered several years before, to the wax heads in a hair-dresser's shop. This sort of face and figure, which were of themselves likely enough to draw attention, were rendered still more conspicuous by her dress, which, though, like herself, really handsome, was rendered unpleasing by its glaring purpose of producing effect. A bonnet of bright lavender satin, extravagantly large, and fearfully thrown back, displayed a vast quantity of blonde quilling, fully planted with flowers of every hue, while a prodigious plume of drooping feathers tossed themselves to and fro with every motion of her head, and occasionally reposed themselves on her shoulder. Her dress was of black silk, but ingeniously relieved by the introduction of as many settings off, of the same colour with her bonnet, as it was well possible to contrive; so that, although in mourning, her general appearance was exceedingly shewy and gay.

"Who is your friend, Elizabeth?" said a young lady, who seemed to have the privilege of questioning freely.

"It is Mrs. Barnaby," replied Miss Peters in a whisper.

"And who is Mrs. Barnaby, my dear?.... She has quite the air of a personage."

"She is the widow of mamma's brother, Mr. Barnaby of Silverton."

"Silverton?... That's the name of her place, is it?... She is a lady of large fortune, I presume?"

"Yes, she is, Miss Maddox," replied Elizabeth, somewhat scandalized by the freedom of these inquiries; "but I really wish you would not speak so loud, for she must hear you."

"Oh no!... You see she is very busy looking for her friends. Good morning, Major!" said the same fair lady, turning to Major Allen, who stood close beside her, listening to all her inquiries and to the answers they received. "Are we to have a good ball on Tuesday?"

"If all the world can be made to know that Miss Maddox will be there, all the world will assuredly be there to meet her," replied the gentleman.

"Then I commission you to spread the tidings far and near. I wonder if there will be many strangers?"

"Some of the Stephenson and Hubert party, I hear—that is, Colonel Hubert and young Frederick Stephenson—they are the only ones left. The bridal party set off from the Mall this morning at eleven o'clock. Lady Stephenson looked more beautiful than ever."

"Lady Stephenson?.... Oh! Emily Hubert.... Yes, she is very handsome; and her brother is vastly like her."

"Do you think so?... He is so thin and weather-beaten ... so very like an old soldier."

"I don't like him the worse for that," replied the lady. "He looks as if he had seen service, and were the better for it. He is decidedly the handsomest man at Clifton."

The Major smiled, and turned on his heel, which brought him exactly vis-à-vis to Miss Elizabeth Peters.

"Your party mean to honour the ball on Tuesday, I hope, Miss Peters?"

"I believe so, Major Allen. It is seldom that we are not some of us there."

"Shall you bring us the accession of any strangers?" inquired the Major.

"Mrs. Barnaby and her niece will be with us, I think."

"I flatter myself that altogether we shall muster strong. Good morning!" and with another sidelong glance at the widow, Major Allen walked out of the shop.

Not a word of all this had been lost upon Mrs. Barnaby. She had thought from the very first that Elizabeth Peters must be selected as her particular friend, and now she was convinced that she would be invaluable in that capacity. It was quite impossible that any one could have answered better to questions than she had done. It was impossible, too, that anything could be more fascinating than the general appearance of Major Allen; and if, upon farther inquiry, it should prove that he was indeed, as he appeared to be, a man of fashion and fortune, the whole world could not offer her a lover she should so passionately desire to captivate!

Such were the meditations of Mrs. Barnaby as she somewhat pensively sat at her drawing-room window, awaiting the return of Agnes to dinner on that day; and such were very frequently her meditations afterwards.

VOLUME II

CHAPTER I

DIFFICULTIES ATTENDING A YOUNG LADY'S APPEARANCE AT A BALL—A WET SUNDAY— DIFFERENCE OF TASTE

Though it was two minutes and a half past the time named for dinner when Agnes made her appearance, she found her aunt's temper very slightly acerbated by the delay, for the delightful recollections of her morning expedition still endured, and she was more inclined to boast than to scold.

"Well, Agnes, I hope at last I have some news that will please you," she said. "What think you of my having subscribed for us both for six weeks?"

"Subscribed for what, aunt? ... to the library?"

"Yes; I have subscribed there, too, for a month ... and we must go every day, rain or shine, to make it answer. But I have done a good deal more than that for you, my dear; I subscribed to the balls entirely for your sake, Agnes: and whatever becomes of you in future life, I trust you will never forget all I have done for you now."

"But I am afraid, aunt, it will cost you a great deal of money to take me with you to the balls; and as I have never been yet, I cannot know anything about it, you know; and I do assure you that I shall not at all mind being left at home."

"And a pretty story that would make, wouldn't it?... I tell you, child, I have paid the money already ... and here are the cutlets; so sit down, and be thankful for all my kindness to you.... Is my beer come, Jerningham?"

Agnes sat down, and began eating her cutlet; but it was thoughtfully, for there were cares that rested heavily upon her heart; and though they were certainly of a minor species, she must be forgiven if at sixteen and a half they were sufficient to perplex her sorely. She had neither shoes nor gloves fit to appear at a ball. She dared not ask for them, she dared not go without them, and she dared not refuse to go at all.

"This certainly is the most beautiful place I ever saw in my life!" said the widow, while renewing her attack upon the dish of cutlets; "such shops!... such a milliner! and, as for the library, its perfectly like going into public! What an advantage it is every morning of one's life to be able to go to such a place as that! Elizabeth Peters seemed to know everybody; and I heard them talking of people of the highest fashion, as some of those we are sure to meet at the ball. What an immense advantage it is for you, Agnes, to be introduced in such a manner at such a place as this!"

"It is indeed a most beautiful place, aunt, and the Peterses are most kind and charming people."

"Then for once in your life, child, you are pleased!... that's a comfort.... And I have got something to shew you, Agnes, such a scarf!... real French blonde: ... its monstrous expensive, I'm afraid; but everybody says that the respectability of a girl depends entirely upon the style of her chaperon. I'm sure I would no more let my poor dear sister's child go out with me, if I was shabbily dressed, than I would fly. I wonder Mrs. Duval does not send home my things; but perhaps she waits for me to send my turban. She's going to put my feathers in for me, Agnes,—quite a favour I assure you; ... but she was so respectful in her manner to Elizabeth Peters. I am sure, if I had had any notion what sort of people they were, I should have made Barnaby leave his business to Mr. Dobbs for a little while, that he might have brought me to see them long ago."

"It is indeed a pleasure to meet with such friends," said Agnes; "and perhaps..."

"Perhaps what, child?"

"If either of the three girls stay away from the ball, perhaps, aunt, you would be so kind as to let me stay away too, and we should pass the evening so delightfully together."

"God give me patience, Agnes, for I'm sure you are enough to drive one wild. Here have I been subscribing to the balls, and actually paying down ready money beforehand for your tickets; and now, ungrateful creature that you are, you tell me you won't go!... I only wish the Peterses could hear you, and then they'd know what you are."

"My only objection to going to the ball, aunt," said Agnes with desperate courage, "is, the fear that you would be obliged to get gloves and shoes for me."

"Gloves and shoes!... why, that's just the advantage of mourning. You'll have my black silk stockings, you know, all except a pair or two of the best,—and with black stockings I don't suppose you would choose to put on white shoes. That would be rather too much in the magpie style, I suppose, wouldn't it?... And for gloves, I don't see how, in such very deep mourning, you would wear anything but black gloves too; and there are two pair of mine that you may have. I could lend you an old pair of my black satin shoes too, only your feet and your hands are so frightfully out of proportion to your height.... I was always reckoned to be most perfectly in proportion, every part of my figure; but your hands and feet are absolutely ridiculous from their smallness: you take after your father in that, and a great misfortune it is, for it will prevent your ever profiting by my shoes or my gloves either, unless you are clever enough to take them in,—and that I don't believe you are—not fingers and all...."

"May I wear long sleeves then, aunt?" said Agnes with considerable animation, from having suddenly conceived a project, by means of which she thought she might render herself and her sables presentable.

"Because you have got no long gloves, I suppose? Why yes, child, I see no objection, in such very deep mourning as yours. It is a strange whim you have taken, Agnes; but it is certainly very convenient."

"And will you give me leave, aunt, to use all the black you have been so kind as to give me?"

"Use it?... use all of it?... Yes; I don't want to have any of it again: the great desire of my life is to be liberal and generous to you in all ways, Agnes. But I don't know what you mean about using it all,—you can't mean all the things at once?"

"No, aunt," replied Agnes, laughing, "I don't mean that; but if I may use the crape that covers nearly the whole of your best gown, I think I could make my own frock look very well, for I would make it the same as one I saw last year at Empton. May I?"

"Yes, if you will, child; but to say the truth, I have no great faith in your mantua-making talents. However, I am glad to see that you have got such a notion in your head; and if it turns out well, I may set you to work for me perhaps one of these days. I have a great deal of taste in that way; but with my fortune it would be ridiculous if I did much beside ornamental work.... There.... Take away, Jerningham, and bring the two cheesecakes.... Agnes, do you wish for one?"

"No, thank you, aunt."

"What an odd girl you are!... You never seem to care about what you eat.... I must say that I am a little more dainty, and know what is nice, and like it too. But poor dear Barnaby spoilt me in that way; and if ever you should be lucky enough to be the idol of a husband, as I was, you will learn to like nice eating too, Agnes ... for it is a thing that grows upon one, I believe. But I dare say at the out-of-the-way place your aunt Betsy put you to, there was no great chance of your being over-indulged that way.... That will do, Jerningham, give me that drop of beer; and now eat up your own dinner as fast as you can, and ask little Kitty to shew you the way to Mrs. Duval's, the milliner; and take with you, very carefully mind, the hat-box that you will find ready tied up on my bed, and bring back with you my new scarf and gloves.... I long to shew you my scarf, Agnes.... You shall not be ashamed of your chaperon,—that's a point I'm resolved upon."

It was Saturday night, and the important ball was to be on the following Tuesday; so Agnes, as soon as the dinner was ended, hastened to set about her work, a general idea of which she had very clearly in her little head, but felt some misgivings about her skill in the detail.

Hardly, however, had she brought forth "her needle and her shears," when her aunt exclaimed,—

"Good gracious, child!... you are not going to set to work now?... Why, it is the pleasantest part of the day, and I mean to take you out to walk with me under the windows where we saw all the smart people last night.—Just look out, and you will see they are beginning to come already. Put on your things, my dear; and put your bonnet a little back, and try to look as smart as you can. You are certainly very pretty, but you are a terrible dowdy in your way of putting on your things. You have nothing jaunty and taking about you, as I used to have at your age, Agnes; and I'm sure I don't know what to do to improve you.... I suspect that your aunt will get more eyes upon her now than you will with all your youth,—and that's a shame.... But I always was famous for putting on my things well."

Agnes retired to her little room; but her quiet bonnet was put on much as usual when she came out from it; and Mrs. Barnaby might have been discouraged at seeing the very undashing appearance of her companion, had she not been conscious that the manner in which she had repaired her own charms, and the general style of her dress and person, were such as might well atone for it.

Nor was she disappointed as to the degree of attention she expected to draw; not a party passed them without giving her a decided stare, and many indulged their curiosity by a very pertinacious look over the shoulder after them.

This was very delightful, but it was not all: ere they had taken half a dozen turns, the widely-roaming eyes of Mrs. Barnaby descried two additional gentlemen, decidedly the most distinguished-looking personages she had seen, approaching from the further end of the walk.

"That tall one is the man we watched last night, Agnes: I should know him amongst a thousand."

Agnes looked up, and felt equally convinced of the fact.

The two gentlemen approached; and Mrs. Barnaby herself could not have wished for a look of more marked examination than the tall individual bestowed upon her as he went by: but satisfactory as this was, and greatly as it occupied her attention, she was aware also that his companion looked with equal attention at Agnes.

"For goodness' sake, Agnes, throw back that abominable veil; it is getting quite dark already, and I'm sure you cannot see."

"I can see very well, thank you, aunt," replied Agnes.

"Fool!..." muttered Mrs. Barnaby; but she would not spoil her features by a frown, and continued to enjoy for three turns more the repeated gaze of the tall gentleman.

The following day being Sunday was one of great importance to strangers about to be initiated into the society of the place; and Mrs. Barnaby had fondly flattered herself that Mrs. Peters, or at least the young ladies, would upon such an occasion have extended their patronage, both to help them to a seat, and to tell them "who was who." But in this she was disappointed: in fact, a compact had been entered into between Mrs. Peters and her son and daughters, by which it was agreed that, on condition of her permitting them to join her party at the balls, she was always to be allowed to go to church in peace. This was so reasonable that even the petted Mary submitted to it without a murmur; and the consequence was that Mrs. Barnaby found herself left to her own devices as to the manner in which she should make the most of the Sabbath-day.

Fortunately for the tranquillity of Mrs. Peters, the landlady of the lodgings, on being questioned, gave it as her opinion that the chapel at the Hot Wells, which was within a very pleasant walk, would be more likely to offer accommodation to strangers than the parish church, that being always crowded by the resident families; so to the chapel at the Hot Wells Mrs. Barnaby resolved to go, and the tea-urn was ordered half an hour earlier than usual, that time enough might be allowed to "get ready."

"Now do make the best of yourself, Agnes, to-day, will you? I am sure those men are not Bristol people.... So different they looked—didn't they?—from all the rest. Of course, you will put on your best crape bonnet, and one of my nicest broad-hemmed white crape collars ... there is one I have quite clean ... I have no doubt in the world we shall see them."

Having finished her breakfast, and reiterated these orders, Mrs. Barnaby turned her attention to her own toilet, and a most elaborate one it was, taking so long a time as to leave scarcely sufficient for the walk; but proving at length so perfectly satisfactory as to make her indifferent to that, or almost any other contretems.

On this occasion she came forth in a new dress of light grey gros-de-Naples, with a gay bonnet of paille de riz, decorated with poppy blossoms both within and without, a "lady-like" profusion of her own embroidery on cuffs, collar, and pocket-handkerchief, her well-oiled ringlets half hiding her large, coarse, handsome face, her eyes set off by a suffusion of carmine, and her whole person redolent of musk.

This was the figure beside which Agnes was doomed to make her first appearance at the crowded chapel of the Hot Wells. Had she thought about herself, the contrast its expansive splendour offered to her own slight figure, her delicate fair face seen but by stealth through her thick veil, and the sad decorum of her sable robe, might have struck her as being favourable; instead of that, however, it was another contrast that occurred to her; for, as she looked at Mrs. Barnaby, she suddenly recollected the general look and air of her aunt Compton, just at the moment when the widow attacked her so violently on the meanness of her apparel during their terrible encounter at the village school, and she could not quite restrain a sigh as she thought how greatly she should have preferred entering a crowded and fashionable chapel with her.

But no sighing could effect the change, and they set forth together, as strangely a matched pair in appearance as can well be imagined. They entered the crowded building just as the Psalms concluded, and were stared at and scrutinised with quite as much attention as was consistent with the solemnity of the place: moreover, seats were after some time offered to them, and there was no reason in the world to believe that they were in any way overlooked. Nevertheless Mrs. Barnaby was disappointed. Neither the tall gentleman nor his companion were there; nor did Major Allen, or any one like him, appear to reward her labour and her skill.

Long and wearisome did the steep up-hill walk back to her lodgings appear after this unpropitious act of devotion, and sadly passed the remainder of the day, for it rained hard ... no strollers, not even an idle endimanché, came to awaken the musical echo she loved to listen to from the pavement under the windows. In short, it was a day of existence lost, save that she found out one or two new defects in Agnes, and ended at last by very nearly convincing herself that it was in some way or other her fault that it rained.

But happily nothing lasts for ever in this world, and Agnes found herself quietly in bed at last.

The next morning rose bright in sunshine, and the widow rose too, and "blessed the useful light," which she determined should see her exactly at the fashionable hour take her way to the library, and the pastry-cook's, or wherever else she was most likely to be seen; but, fortunately for the refacimento upon which Agnes desired to employ herself, this fashionable hour was not early, and her sable draperies had made great progress before her aunt gave notice that she must get ready to go out with her. To have a voice upon any question of this kind had fortunately never yet occurred to Agnes as a thing possible, and once more, like a Bella Donna beside a Hollyhock, she appeared, with all the effect of the strongest contrast, in the gayest part of Clifton.

This day seemed sent by fate to make up for the misfortunes of the last. On entering the library, Mrs. Barnaby immediately placed herself before the authographic volume in which she took such particular interest, and hardly had she done so, when the tall and the short gentlemen entered the shop. Again it was decidedly evident that the tall one fixed his eyes on the widow, and the shorter one on her companion. The widow's heart beat. Never had she forgotten the evident admiration her own face and manner produced on her fellow traveller from Silverton, or the chilling effect that followed the display of the calm features of her delicate niece. She knew that Agnes was younger, and perhaps even handsomer, than herself; but this only tended to confirm her conviction that an animated expression of countenance, and great vivacity of manner, would do more towards turning a young man's head than all the mere beauty in the world.

What would she have given at that moment for some one with whom she might have conversed with laughing gaiety ... to whom she might have displayed her large white teeth ... and on whom she might have turned the flashings of her lustrous eyes!

It was in vain to look to Agnes at such a moment as this, for she well knew that nothing she could utter would elicit any better excuse for laughter than might be found in "Yes, aunt," or "No, aunt." So nothing was to be done but to raise a glass recently purchased to her eye, in order to recognize the unknown passers-by; but in doing this she contrived to make "le petit doigt" show off her rings, and now and then cast such a glance at the strangers as none but a Mrs. Barnaby can give.

After this dumb show had lasted for some minutes, the two gentlemen each threw down the newspaper they had affected to read, and departed. Mrs. Barnaby's interest in the subscription-book departed likewise; and after looking at the backs of one or two volumes that lay scattered about the counter, she, too, left the shop, and proceeded with a dignified and leisurely step along the pavement. The next moment was one of the happiest of her life, for on turning her head to reconnoitre a richly-trimmed mantilla that had passed her, she perceived the same pair of gentlemen at the distance of two paces behind them.

This indeed was an adventure, and to the widow's unspeakable delight it was made more piquant still by what followed. Near the end of the street was the well-frequented shop of a fashionable pastry-cook,—an establishment, by the way, which Mrs. Barnaby had not yet lived long enough to pass with indifference, for the two-fold reason, that it ever recalled the dear rencontres of her youth, when the disbursement of one penny was sure to secure a whole half hour of regimental flirting, and also because her genuine love for cakes and tarts was unextinguishable. There was now again a double reason for entering this inviting museum; for, in the first place, it would prevent the necessity of turning round as soon as they had walked up the street, in order to walk down it again, thereby proving that they had no engagements at all; and, secondly, it would give the two uncommonly handsome men an opportunity of following them in, if they liked it.

And it so happened that they did like it. Happy Mrs. Barnaby!... No sooner had she seated herself beside the counter, with a plate of queen cakes and Bath buns beside her, than the light from the door ceased to pour its unbroken splendour upon her elegant dress, and on looking up, her eye again met the gaze first of the one, and then of the other stranger, as they entered the shop together.

Agnes was standing behind her, with her face rather unmeaningly turned towards the counter, for when a plate with various specimens of pastry delicacies was offered to her by one of the shop-women, she declined to take anything by a silent bow.

The two gentlemen passed her, and established themselves at a little table just beyond, desiring that ices might be brought to them.

"You have ices, have you?" said Mrs. Barnaby, delighted at an opportunity of speaking; ... "bring me one, if you please." And then, trusting to her niece's well known discretion, she turned her chair, so as to front both Agnes and the two gentlemen, and said with great kindness of accent ... "Agnes, love!... will you have an ice?"

"No, thank you, aunt," ... the anticipated reply, followed.

"Then sit down, dearest, will you?... while I take mine."

The younger of the two gentlemen instantly sprang from his chair, and presented it to her. Agnes bowed civilly, but passed on to a bench which flanked the narrow shop on the other side; but Mrs. Barnaby smiled upon him most graciously, and said, bowing low as she sat,—

"Thank you, sir, very much ... you are extremely obliging."

The young man bowed again, reseated himself, and finished his ice in silence, when his companion having done the same, each laid a sixpence on the counter, and walked off.

"Who are those gentlemen, pray?... do you know their names?" said Mrs. Barnaby eagerly to the shop-girl.

"The tall gentleman is Colonel Hubert, ma'am; and the other, young Mr. Stephenson."

"Stephenson," ... musingly repeated the widow,—"Stephenson and Hubert?... I am sure I have heard the names before."

"Sir Edward Stephenson was married on Saturday to Colonel Hubert's sister, ma'am," said the girl, "and it is most likely that you heard of it."

"Oh, to be sure I did!... I remember now all about it.... They said he was the handsomest man in the world—Colonel Hubert I mean ... and so he certainly is ... handsomer certainly than even Major Allen: don't you think so, Agnes?"

"I don't know Major Allen, aunt."

"Not know Major Allen, child?... Oh! I remember ... no more you do, my dear ... come, get up; I have done.... The young man, Agnes," she said, turning to her niece as they left the shop, "seemed, I thought, a good deal struck by you. I wish to goodness, child, you would not always keep that thick veil over your face so.... It is a very handsome veil I know, and certainly makes your mourning look very elegant; but it is only in some particular lights that one can see your face under it at all."

"I don't think that signifies much, aunt, and it makes me feel so much more comfortable."

"Comfortable!... very well, child, poke along, and be comfortable your own way ... but you certainly have a little spice of the mule in you."

The widow was perhaps rather disappointed at seeing no more of the two strangers; they had turned off just beyond the pastry-cook's shop, and were no longer visible; but, while she follows in gentle musings her walk home, we will pursue the two gentlemen who had so captivated her attention.

The only resemblance between them was in the decided air of bon ton that distinguished both; in every other respect they were perfectly dissimilar. Mr. Stephenson, the shorter and younger of the two, had by far the more regular set of features, and was indeed remarkably handsome. Colonel Hubert, his companion, appeared to be at least ten years his senior, and looked bronzed by the effect of various climates. He had perhaps no peculiar beauty of feature except his fine teeth, and the noble expression of his forehead, from which, however, the hair had already somewhat retired, though it still clustered in close brown curls round his well-turned head. But his form and stature were magnificent, and his general appearance so completely that of a soldier and a gentleman, that it was impossible, let him appear where he would, that he should pass unnoticed ... which perhaps to the gentle-minded may be considered as some excuse for Mrs. Barnaby's enthusiastic admiration.

"For Heaven's sake, Hubert!" said the junior to the senior, as they paced onwards, "do give me leave to know a pretty girl when I see one.... In my life I never beheld so beautiful a creature!... Her form, her feet, her movement,—and what a voice!"

"Assuredly," said Colonel Hubert in reply to this tirade, "the sweet variety of tone, and the charming change of her ever musical cadences, must naturally excite your admiration. 'No, thank you, aunt,' ... it was inimitable! You are quite right, Frederick; such words could not be listened to with indifference."

"You are an odious, carping, old, fusty, musty bachelor, and I hate you with all my heart and soul!" exclaimed the young man. "Upon my honour, Hubert, I shudder to think that some ten or a dozen years hence I may be as hard, cold, and insensible as you are now.... Tell me honestly, can you at all recollect what your feelings were at two-and-twenty on seeing such a being as that sable angel from whom you have just dragged me?"

"Perhaps not exactly; and besides, black angels were never the objects of my idolatry. But don't stamp your foot at me, and I will answer you seriously. I do not think that from the blissful time when I was sixteen, up to my present solemn five-and-thirty, I could ever have been tempted to look a second time at any miss under the chaperonship of such a dame as that feather and furbelow lady."

"Then why, in the name of common sense, did you gaze so earnestly at the furbelow lady herself?"

"To answer that truly, Frederick, would involve the confession of a peculiar family weakness."

"A family weakness?... Pray, be confidential; I will promise to be discreet; and, indeed, as my brother has just made, as the newspapers say, a 'lovely bride' of your sister, I have some right to a participation in the family secrets. Come, disclose!... What family reason have you for choosing to gaze upon a great vulgar woman, verging towards forty, and refusing to look at a young creature, as beautiful as a houri, who happens to be in her company?"

"I suspect it is because I am near of kin to my mother's sister.... Did you never hear of the peculiarity that attaches to my respected aunt, Lady Elizabeth Norris? She scruples not to avow that she prefers the society of people who amuse her by their absurdities to every other."

"Oh yes!... I have heard all that from Edward, who has, I can tell you, been occasionally somewhat horrified at what the queer old lady calls her soirées antíthèstiques. But you don't mean to tell me, Hubert, that you ever take the fancy of surrounding yourself with all the greatest quizzes you can find in compliment to your old aunt?"

"Why, no.... I do not go so far as that yet, and perhaps I sometimes wish that she did not either, for occasionally she carries the whim rather too far; yet I believe truly that I am more likely to gaze with attention at a particularly ridiculous-looking woman than at any young nymph under her protection ... or possessing the awful privilege of calling her AUNT!"

"A young nymph!... what a hateful phrase! Elegant, delicate creature!... I swear to you, Colonel Hubert, that you have lowered yourself very materially in my estimation by your want of tact in not immediately perceiving that, although a nepotine connexion unhappily exists between them, by marriage probably, or by the half blood, there must still be something very peculiar in the circumstances which have brought so incongruous a pair together."

"Well, Frederick, you may be right ... and perhaps, my friend, my eyes begin to fail me; for, to tell you the truth, your adorable's crape veil was too thick for me to see anything through it."

"To be sure it was!" cried Stephenson, quite delighted at the amende; "I thought it was impossible you could underrate such a face as that."

"It is a great blessing to have young eyes," rejoined the Colonel, relapsing into his bantering tone.

"What!... At it again, thou crusty old Mars?... Then I leave you."

"Au revoir, my Corydon!..." and so they parted.

CHAPTER II

THE BALL

The evening of the ball, so much dreaded by the niece, and so much longed for by the aunt, arrived at last; and by a chance not over common in the affairs of mortals, while the hopes of the one lady were more than realised, the fears of the other were proved to be altogether groundless. Many favourable accidents, indeed, concurred to lessen the difficulties anticipated by Agnes. In the first place, her almost funeral robes (for which, if the truth be spoken, it must be avowed she had not the slightest partiality,) assumed an appearance, under her tasteful fancy, which surprised even herself; for though, when she set about it, she had a sort of beau ideal of a black crape robe floating in her imagination, her hopes of giving it form and substance by her own ingenuity were not very sanguine. Mrs. Barnaby, either from the depth of her sorrow, or the height of her elegance, had commanded, when she ordered her widow's mourning, that one dress should touch the heart of every beholder by having a basement of sable crape one yard in breadth around it. This doleful dress was costly, and had been rarely worn at Silverton, that it might come forth in greater splendour at Exeter. But at Exeter, as we have seen, the widow's feelings so completely overpowered her, that she could not wear it at all; and thus it came under the fingers of Agnes in very respectable condition. Of these circumambulatory ells of crape, the young artificer contrived to fabricate a dress that was anything but unbecoming. The enormous crape gigots (for those were the days of gigots), which made part of her black treasure, hung from her delicate fair arms like transparent clouds upon the silvery brightness of the moon ... so, at least, would Frederick Stephenson have described it ... while the simple corsage, drawn, à la vierge, rather higher than fashion demanded round her beautiful bust, gave a delicate and sober dignity to her appearance, that even those who would have deemed it "a pity to be so covered up" themselves, could not but allow was exceedingly becoming.

As soon as her labour was ended, she prudently made an experiment of its effect; and then, in "trembling hope" of her aunt's approval, made her appearance before her. Her success here perfectly astonished her.

"Mercy on me, child!—What an elegant dress!—Where on earth did you get it from?"

"From your gown, aunt."

"Oh, to be sure!—I understand. It is not many people that would give away such a dress as that, Agnes—perfectly new, and so extremely elegant. I hope it won't turn your brain, my dear, and that you will never forget who gave it to you. Certainly I never thought you so handsome before; and if you will but study my manner a little, and smile, and show your fine teeth, I do really think I may be able to get a husband for you, which would certainly be more creditable than going out as a governess.... So you can work, Agnes, I see ... and a good thing too, considering your poverty. It does not look amiss upon the whole, I must say; though I don't see any reason for your covering yourself up so; I am sure your neck is white enough to be seen, and it would be odd if it wasn't, considering who your mother was; for both she and I were noted, far and near, for that beauty; but I can't say I ever hid myself up in that way.... And what shoes, child, have you got to wear with it?"

"These, aunt," said Agnes, putting out her little foot incased in leather, with a sole of very respectable thickness.

"Well, upon my word, that's a pity ... it spoils all ... and I don't think you could dance in them if you did get a partner.... What would you say, Agnes, if I bought you a thin pair of prunella pumps on purpose?"

"I should be very much obliged to you, aunt."

"Well, then, for once I must be extravagant, I believe; so, get on your other gown, child, as quick as you can, and your bonnet and shawl, and let us go to the shop round the corner. I did not mean to stir out to-day ... there is wind enough to make one's eyes perfectly blood-shot.... However, the shop's close by.... Only, if you do marry well, I hope you will never forget what you owe me."

Agnes had been too hard at work to take any long walk, though invited to do it; but her friend Mary called upon her both Monday and Tuesday; and having found her way into the closet, seemed to think, as she pulled over Agnes's books, and chatted with her concerning their contents, that they might often enjoy themselves tête-à-tête there.

"Shall you like it, Agnes?" she added, after sketching such a scheme to her.

"I think, Mary, you could make me like anything ... but can I really make you like sitting in this cupboard, instead of your own elegant drawing-room?"

"If you will sit with me here, my new friend," answered Miss Peters with an air of great sincerity.

"Then must I not be wicked if I ever think myself unhappy again ... at least, as long as we stay at Clifton."

"Dear girl!... you should not be so if I could help it.... But I must go ... nine o'clock this evening, remember, and wait for us in the outer room, if you do not find us already there."

These instructions Agnes repeated to her aunt; but that lady's ardent temper induced her to order a fly to be at her door at half-past eight precisely; and when it arrived, she was for at least the fourth time putting the last finishing touch to her blonde, and her feathers, and her ringlets, and her rouge, and therefore it took her not more than five minutes for a last general survey, before she declared herself "ready!" and Jerningham received orders to precede her down the stairs with a candle.

If the former descriptions of the widow's appearance have not been wholly in vain, the reader will easily conceive the increased splendour of her charms when elaborately attired for a ball, without my entering into any minutiæ concerning them. Suffice it to say, that if the corsage of the delicate Agnes might have been deemed by some too high, that of Mrs. Barnaby might have been thought by others too low; and that, taken all together, she looked exceedingly like one of the supplementary dames brought forth to do honour to the banquet scene in Macbeth.

Arriving half an hour before the time appointed, they, of course, did not find the Peters family; nor did this latter party make their appearance before the patience of Mrs. Barnaby had given way, and she had insisted, much to the vexation of Agnes, upon going on to the ball-room without them.

There the atmosphere was already in some degree congenial to her. The lustres were blazing, the orchestra tuning, and a few individuals, as impatient as herself, walking up and down the room, and appearing greatly delighted at having something new to stare at.

This parade was beginning to realize all the worst fears of Agnes, (for the room was filling fast, and Mrs. Barnaby would not hear of sitting down,) when she descried Mrs. Peters, her son, her three daughters, and two other gentlemen, enter the room.

Mrs. Barnaby saw them too, and instantly began to stride towards them; but timidity now made Agnes bold, and she held back, still courageously retaining her aunt's arm, and exclaiming eagerly,—

"Oh, let them come to us, aunt!"

"Nonsense, child!... Don't hold me so, Agnes; it will be exceedingly rude if we do not join them immediately, according to our engagement."

The pain of violently seizing upon Mrs. Peters was, however, spared her by the watchful kindness of Mary, who caught sight of them immediately, and, together with Elizabeth, hastened forward to meet them.

Miss Peters gave a glance of approbation and pleasure at the appearance of Agnes, who did not look the less beautiful, perhaps, from the deep blush that dyed her cheeks as she marked the expression of Mrs. Peters' countenance, as she approached with her eyes fixed upon her aunt. That lady, however, let her have felt what she might at sight of her remarkable-looking sister-in-law, very honourably performed her part of the compact entered into with her daughters, smiling very graciously in return for her affectionate relative's raptures at seeing her, and shewing no symptom of anything she felt on the occasion, excepting immediately retiring to the remotest corner of the room, where she very nearly hid herself behind a pillar.

Mrs. Barnaby of course followed her, with the young ladies, to the seat she had chosen; but her active genius was instantly set to work to discover how she might escape from it, for the feelings produced by such an eclipse were perfectly intolerable.

"I must pretend that I see some person whom I know," thought she, "and so make one of the girls walk across the room with me;" but at the instant she was about to put this project into execution, James Peters came up to the party, and very civilly addressed her. This was something, for the young man was handsome and well-dressed; but better still was what happened next, for she immediately felt at once that she was about to become the heroine of an adventure. Major Allen, whose appearance altogether, including moustaches, favouris, collier grec, embroidered waistcoat, and all, was very nearly as remarkable as her own, entered the room, looked round it, fixed his eyes upon her spangled turban, and very decisively turned off from the throng in order to pay his compliments to the Peters' party, distinguishing her by a bow that spake the profoundest admiration and respect.

Elizabeth was the last of the row, her mother (with Mrs. Barnaby next her) being at the other end of it; and close to Elizabeth the dashing Major placed himself, immediately entering into a whispered conversation with her, which obliged her to turn herself round from the rest, in such a manner that not even Lucy, who came next in order, could overhear much of what passed.... Nevertheless, the widow felt as certain as if she could have followed every word of it, that this earnest conversation was about her.

Nor was she mistaken, for thus it ran:

"Good evening, Miss Elizabeth.... You are just arrived, I presume.... An excellent ball, is it not?... I told you it would be.... What an exceedingly fine woman your aunt is, Miss Peters!... It is your aunt, I think?"

"Yes ... our aunt, certainly ... the widow of my mother's brother, Major Allen."

"Ay.... I understood she was your aunt.... She is a woman of large fortune, I hear?"

"Yes, very large fortune."

"But she is in lodgings, is she not?... She does not seem to have taken the whole house."

"Oh, no ... only quite small lodgings: but she does not spend the third of her income, nor near it."

"Really?... then, I suppose, handsome as she is, that she is a little in the skin-flint line, eh?..." and here the Major shewed his horse-like teeth by a laugh.

"Not that at all, I assure you," replied the young lady, amiably anxious to exonerate her aunt from so vile an aspersion; "indeed, I should say quite the contrary; for she has very generous and noble ideas about money, and the use a widow ought to make of a fortune left by her husband, in case she does not happen to marry again. I am sure I hope people won't be so ill-natured as to say she is stingy because she does not choose to spend all her income;—it will be abominable if they do, because her motives are so very noble."

"I am sure she has a most charming advocate in you.... And what, then, may I ask ... for what is noble should never be concealed ... what can be the reason of economy so unnecessary?"

"She does not think it is unnecessary, Major Allen; for she has an orphan niece who is left quite dependent upon her, and what she is saving will be for her."

"Amiable indeed!... Then her property is only income, I presume? Really that is a pity, considering how remarkably well such a disposition would employ the capital."

"Oh! no, that is not so neither; my uncle Barnaby left everything entirely at her own disposal; only she thinks," ... and here the silly and loquacious Elizabeth stopped short, for the idea suddenly occurred to her that it was not right to talk so much of her aunt's concerns to so slight an acquaintance as Major Allen; and not exactly knowing how to end her sentence, she permitted a sudden thought to strike her, and exclaimed, "I wonder when they will begin dancing?"

But the Major had heard enough.

He resumed the conversation, however, but very discreetly, by saying, "That young lady in mourning is her niece, I suppose? and a beautiful creature she is.... But how comes she to be in such deep mourning, when that of her aunt is so slight?"

Had the simple Elizabeth understood the principle of vicarial mourning upon which these habiliments had been transferred from the widow to her niece, she would doubtless, from the talkative frankness of her nature, have disclosed it; but as her confidential conversation with her new relative had left her ignorant of this, she answered, with rather a confused recollection of Mrs. Barnaby's explanation, "I believe it is because she wears it out of romantic sorrow for her own papa, though he has been dead for years and years."

"Will you ask your brother, Miss Peters, to introduce me to Mrs. Barnaby?"

"Certainly, Major Allen, if you wish it.... James," added the young lady, stretching out her fan to draw his attention from Agnes, with whom he was talking, "James, step here ... Major Allen wishes you to introduce him to Mrs. Barnaby."

The Major rose at the moment, and strengthened the request by adding, "Will you do me that honour, Mr. Peters?"

The young man bowed slightly, and without answering moved to the front of the happy widow, followed by the obsequious Major, and said, "Major Allen wishes to be introduced to you, Mrs. Barnaby.... Major Allen, Mrs. Barnaby."

It was not without an effort that this consummation of her dearest hopes was received with some tolerable appearance of external composure by the lady; but she felt that the moment was an important one, and called up all her energy to support her under it. Perhaps she blushed, but that, for obvious reasons, was not perceptible; but she cast down her eyes upon her fan, and then raised them again to the face of the bending Major with a look that really said a great deal.

The established questions and answers in use on such occasions were going on with great zeal and animation on both sides, when a fresh source of gratification presented itself to the widow in the approach of Mr. Frederick Stephenson to Agnes, in a manner as flatteringly decided as that of the Major to herself; but, being quite a stranger to the Peters family, he was preceded by the master of the ceremonies, who whispered his name and family to Mrs. Peters, asking permission to present him to the young lady in mourning, who appeared to be of her party.

This was of course readily accorded; when the introduction took place, and was followed by a petition from the young man for the honour of dancing with her.

Agnes looked a vast deal more beautiful than he had ever dared to believe possible through her veil as she answered, "I am engaged."

"Then the next?" said Mr. Stephenson eagerly.

Agnes bowed her blushing assent, and the young man continued to stand before her, going through pretty nearly the same process as the Major.

This lasted till the quadrilles began to form, when James Peters claimed her hand for the dance.

Two of the Miss Peters soon followed, when Major Allen said, "As the young ladies are forsaking you, madam, may you not be induced to make a party at whist?"

"I should have no objection whatever, Major," replied Mrs. Barnaby, "provided there was room at a table where they did not play high."

"Of course, if I have the honour of making a table for you, my dear madam, the stakes will be of your own naming.... Will you permit me to go and see what can be done?"

"You are excessively kind.... I shall be greatly obliged."

The active Mars departed instantly, with a step, if not as light, at least as zealous in its speed, as that of Mercury when bent upon one of his most roguish errands, and in a wonderfully short space of time he returned with the intelligence that a table was waiting for her. He then presented his arm, which she took with condescending dignity, and led her off.

"Ah! sure a pair were never seen,
So justly formed to meet by nature!"

exclaimed Mrs. Peters to Lucy, as they walked away; and greatly relieved, she rose and taking her daughter by the arm, joined a party of her friends in a more busy part of the room.

Meanwhile the quadrilles proceeded, and Agnes, notwithstanding the heart-beating shyness inevitably attending a first appearance, did not lose her look of sweet composure, or her graceful ease. James Peters was an attentive and encouraging partner, and she would probably soon have forgotten that this was the first time she had ever danced, except at school, had she not, when the dance was about half over, perceived herself to be an object of more attention to one of the standers-by than any girl, so very new, can be conscious of, without embarrassment. The eyes which thus annoyed her were those of Colonel Hubert. His remarkable height made him conspicuous among the throng, which was rendered more dense than usual by a wish, every moment increasing, to look at the "beautiful girl in deep mourning;" and perhaps her happening to know who he was, made her fancy that it was more embarrassing to be looked at by him than by any one else. The annoyance, however, did not last long, for he disappeared.

Colonel Hubert left the place where he had stood, and the study in which he had certainly found some interest, for the purpose of looking for his friend Stephenson. He found him in the doorway.

"Frederick, I want you," said the Colonel. "Come with me, my good fellow, and I will prove to you that, notwithstanding my age and infirmities, I still retain my faculties sufficiently to find out what is truly and really lovely as ably as yourself. Come on, suffer yourself to be led, and I will show you what I call a beautiful girl."

Stephenson quietly suffered himself to be led captive, and half a dozen paces placed him immediately opposite to Agnes Willoughby.

"Look at that girl," said Colonel Hubert in a whisper, "and tell me what you think of her."

"The angel in black?"

"Yes, Frederick."

"This is glorious, by Heaven!... Why, Hubert, it is my own black angel!"

"You do not mean to tell me that the girl we saw with that horribly vulgar woman, and this epitome of all elegance, are the same?"

"But, upon my soul, I do, sir.... And now what do you say to the advantage of being able to see through a thick veil?"

"I cannot believe it, Stephenson," ... replied Colonel Hubert, again fixing his eyes in an earnest gaze upon Agnes.

"Then die in your unbelief, and much good may it do you. Why, I have been introduced to her, man ... her name is Willoughby, and I am to dance the next quadrille with her."

"If this be so ... peccavi!..." said the Colonel, turning abruptly away.

"I think so," replied his friend following, and relinquishing even the pleasure of looking at Agnes for that of enjoying his triumph over Hubert. "Won't this make a good story?... And don't you think, Colonel, that for a few years longer, at least, it may be as well to postpone the adoption of your lady aunt's system, and when you see two females together, look at both, to ascertain whether one of them may not be the loveliest creature in the universe, before you give up your whole soul to the amiable occupation of quizzing the other?"

"You think this is a very good jest, Frederick ... but to me, I assure you, it seems very much the contrary."

"Because it is so melancholy for a man of five-and-thirty to lose his eye-sight?"

"Because, Stephenson, it is so melancholy to know that such a being as that fair girl is in the hands of a woman whose appearance speaks her to be so utterly vulgar, to say the very least of it."

"Take care, my venerable philosopher, that you do not blunder about the old lady as egregiously as you before did about the young one. When I got the master of the ceremonies to perform for me the precious service of an introduction, I inquired about the party that she and the furbelow aunt were with, and learned that they were among the most respectable resident inhabitants of Clifton."

"I am heartily glad of it, Frederick ... and yet, if their party consisted of the noblest in the land, I should still feel this aunt to be a greater spot upon her beauty than any wart or mole that ever disfigured a fair cheek ... at least, it would, I think, be quite sufficient to keep my heart safe, if I thought this uncommon-looking creature still more beautiful than I do ... which, I confess, would not be easy."

"I wish your heart joy of its security," returned Stephenson. "And now be off, and leave me to my happiness; for see, the set breaks up, and I may follow her to her place, and again present myself.... Come, tell me honestly, do you not envy me?"

"I never dance, you know."

"So much the worse for you, mon cher," and the gay young man turned off, to follow the way that he saw Agnes lead. This was to the quarter where she had left her aunt and Mrs. Peters, but she found neither.

"Don't be frightened," said her good-natured partner; "we shall find my mother in a moment."... And when they did find her, she received Agnes with a smiling welcome, which contrasted pretty strongly with the stately and almost forbidding aspect with which she ever regarded Mrs. Barnaby.

Young Stephenson saw this reception, and saw also the empressement with which the pretty, elegant Mary Peters seemed to cling to her. More than ever persuaded that he was right, and his friend wrong, he suddenly determined on a measure that he thought might ensure a more permanent acquaintance than merely being a partner of a dance; and before presenting himself to claim her hand, he again addressed the master of the ceremonies with a request that he would present him to Mrs. Peters.

That obliging functionary made not the least objection; indeed he knew that there was not a lady in the room, either young or old, who would not thank him for an introduction to Sir Edward Stephenson's handsome brother, himself a Comet in the Blues, and the inheritor of his mother's noble estate in Worcestershire, which made him considerably a richer man than his elder brother. All this was known to everybody, for the beautiful Miss Hubert and her lover Sir Edward had been for a week or two the lions of Clifton; and though they had mixed very little in its society, there was nobody who could be considered as anybody, who would not have been well pleased at making the acquaintance of Frederick Stephenson. The young man, too, knew well how to make the most of the ten minutes that preceded the second dance; and Mrs. Peters smiled to think, as she watched him leading Agnes to join the set, how justly her keeping faith had been rewarded by this introduction of the most desiré partner in the room.

Meanwhile Mrs. Barnaby was led to the card-room by Major Allen; but he led her slowly, and more than once found himself obliged to stop for a minute or two, that she might not be incommoded by pressing too quickly through the crowd. And thus it was they talked, as they gently won their way.

"And what may be the stake Mrs. Barnaby permits herself?" said the Major, bending forward to look into the widow's eyes.

"Very low, I assure you, Major!" replied the lady, with a wave of the head that sent her plumes to brush the hirsute magnificence of his face.

"Shorts and crown points, perhaps," rejoined the Major, agreeably refreshed by the delicate fanning he had received.

"Oh fie! Major ... how can you suspect me of such extravagance?... No, believe me, I know too well how to use the blessings of wealth, to abuse them by playing so high as that ... but I believe gentlemen think that nothing?"

"Why no, my dear madam, I cannot say that men ... that is, men of a certain fashion and fortune, think much of crown points.... For my own part, I detest gambling, though I love whist, and never care how low I play ... though occasionally, when I get into a certain set, I am obliged to give way a little ... but I never exceed five pound points, and twenty on the rubber; and that you know, unless the cards run extravagantly high, cannot amount to anything very alarming ... especially as I play tolerably well, and, in fact, never play so high if I can help it...."

"But, Major," said the lady, stopping short in their progress, "I really am afraid that I must decline playing at your table ... the amount of what I could lose might not perhaps be a great object to me, any more than to you ... but it is a matter of principle with me, and when that is the case I never swerve ... so take me back again, will you, to my sister Peters and my party."

This was said with a sort of clinging helplessness, and delicate timidity, that was very touching.

"Good heavens!" exclaimed the Major with great animation, "how very little you know me!... I would take you, charming Mrs. Barnaby, to the world's end, if you would consent to go with me; ... but think not that I would sit down at one table, though I might sweep from it stakes amounting to thousands, when I could play with you for straws at another!"

Remember, reader, that she to whom this was said had been Miss Martha Compton of Silverton but six short years before, and then judge with what feelings she listened to it. They were such, that for a moment no power of speech was left to her ... but she abandoned her purpose of retreat; and when at length they stood before the table at which two sporting-looking gentlemen were waiting to receive them, she gently seated herself, murmuring at the same time in the Major's ear, "Not higher than half-crowns, if you please."

He pressed her hand as he resigned the arm with which she had favoured him, and as he did so replied, "Depend upon me."

Before the arrangements for playing were finally settled, the friendly Major Allen took the two gentlemen a pace or two apart, and communicated in a few words what brought them back to the table, perfectly contented with the half-crown, and gallantly anxious to have the honour of cutting highest, that they might have the happiness of winning the lady as a partner, if they won nothing else.

But this happiness fell to the Major, as well as most others during the three or four rubbers that followed; for he and his fair partner played with great luck, which helped to produce between them that amicable state of spirits which tends to make every word appear a pleasantry, and every look a charm.

In the midst of this very agreeable game, in the course of which both the eyes and the voice of the widow proclaimed how very greatly she enjoyed it, Colonel Hubert wandered into the room, and having given a glance at one or two other tables as he passed them, stationed himself on a sofa, from whence he commanded a full view of that at which Mrs. Barnaby was engaged. His recent examination of her niece gave him a feeling of interest in this aunt, that nearly superseded the amusement he might otherwise have derived from her appearance and manner. That both were likely to be affected by the intense interest and pleasure she took in her occupation, as well as in the partner who shared it with her, may be easily conceived, when it is stated that not even the entrance of the magnificent Colonel was perceived by her.

Her vivacity, her enjouement, became more striking every moment; her words were full of piquant and agreeable meaning, which her eyes scrupled not to second; while the Major assumed more and more the air and manner of a man enchanted and enamoured beyond the power of concealment. But it was not the spirit of quizzing that sat upon Colonel Hubert's brow as he contemplated this scene; on the contrary, his fine countenance spoke first disgust, and then a degree of melancholy that might have seemed ill befitting the occasion, and in a few minutes he walked away and re-entered the ball-room.

Whether intentionally or not may be doubted; but he soon again found himself opposite to the place which Agnes occupied in the quadrille, and being there, watched her with a degree of attention that seemed equally made up of curiosity and admiration. "It is strange," thought he, "that the most repulsive and the most attractive women I ever remember to have seen, should be so closely linked together."

In a few minutes the quadrille ended, when Mr. Stephenson, who had danced it with the eldest Miss Peters, said to his friend as he passed him, "We are now going to tea, and if you will come with us, I will introduce you."

Colonel Hubert followed almost mechanically, yet not without a feeling somewhat allied to self-reproach at permitting himself to join the party of a Mrs. Barnaby.

This obnoxious individual was, however, nearly or rather wholly forgotten within a very few minutes after the introduction took place. Mrs. Peters's manners were, as we know, particularly lady-like and pleasing, her daughters all pretty-looking, and one of them, at least, singularly animated and agreeable, her son and the other gentlemen of her party perfectly comme il faut, and Agnes ... what was Agnes in the estimation of the fastidious, high-minded, and high-born Colonel Hubert? He would have been totally unable to answer this question satisfactorily himself, nor would it be just that a precise answer to it should be expected from the historian. This interval of conversation and repose lasted rather longer than usual; for the whole party (each for some reason or other of their own) enjoyed it, or at any rate betrayed no wish to bring it to a conclusion. Had Colonel Hubert, indeed, been told that he enjoyed it, he would strenuously and sincerely have denied the statement. He looked at Agnes with wonder and compassion strongly blended,—he listened to the gay and artless tone of her conversation with Mary Peters and young Stephenson, without being able to deny that, whether she had fallen from the stars, or been raised and wholly educated by that terrible incarnation of all he most detested, her vulgar aunt, every word she uttered bore the stamp of well-bred association, right feeling, and bright intelligence ... he allowed all this, and he allowed too that never, through all the varieties of his campaigning life, had he seen in any rank, or in any clime, a loveliness so perfect; yet he almost trembled as he watched the passionate devotion with which his friend gazed at and listened to her.

Colonel Hubert knew the character of Stephenson well; it was generous, ardent, and affectionate in the highest degree; but passionate withal, self-willed, and only amenable to control when it came in the shape of influence exercised by friendship, unmixed with authority of any kind.

He was just three-and-twenty, and had been in possession of a noble property from the day he attained the age of twenty-one. Singularly free from vice of any kind, his friends, in seeing him take the management of his estates into his own hands, had but one fear for him. It was not racing, gambling, debauchery, or extravagance, they dreaded: had he already passed fifty years of sober life exempt from all these, they would scarcely have felt more secure of his being safe from them; but it was in the important affair of marriage that they dreaded his precipitancy. More than once already his distinguished and highly connected family had been terrified by the idea that some irremediable misfortune in this respect was about to fall upon them; and earnestly did they wish that he should speedily form such a connexion as they could approve, and had a right to expect. Unfortunately this wish had been too evident; and the idea of being disposed of in marriage by his brother and sisters had become a bugbear from which the young man shrank with equal indignation and contempt. The marriage of his elder brother with Miss Hubert had naturally led to great intimacy between the families; and of all the acquaintance he had ever made, Colonel Hubert was the one for whom Frederick Stephenson felt the warmest admiration and esteem; and certainly he was more proud of the affectionate partiality that distinguished individual had shewn him than of any other advantage he possessed. Sir Edward Stephenson observed this, and had told his betrothed Emma that he drew the best possible augury from it for his brother's safety. "He is so proud of Montague's friendship," said he, "that it must be a most outrageous love-fit which would make him hazard it by forming a connexion unworthy in any way. So jealously does he deprecate the interference of his own family on this subject, that I have long determined never more to let him see how near it is to my heart ... and I will not even mention the subject to your brother, lest, par impossible, he might ever discover that I had done so; but I wish you, love, would say a word to him before we leave Clifton.... Tell him that Frederick has still a great propensity to fall in love at first sight, and that we shall all bless him everlastingly, if he will prescribe change of air whenever he may happen to see the fit seize him."

The fair Emma promised and kept her word; and such was the theme on which their discourse turned the night before the wedding, when, Sir Edward being engaged with the lawyer, who had just arrived from London with the settlements, the brother and sister took that stroll upon the pavement of Sion Row, which had first exhibited the stately figure of Colonel Hubert to Mrs. Barnaby's admiration. Little did Agnes think, when her head was made to obtrude itself through the window upon that occasion, that her ears caught some words of a conversation destined to prove so important to her future happiness.

That the "falling in love at first sight" had already taken place, Colonel Hubert could not doubt, as he watched his enthusiastic friend's look and manner, while conversing with Agnes, and gravely and sorrowfully did he ponder on the words of his sister in their last tête-à-tête.

"Save him, dearest Montague, if you can," said she, "from any folly of this sort; for I really think Sir Edward would never be happy again if Frederick formed any disgraceful marriage."

"And a disgraceful marriage it would and must be," thought he; "neither her surpassing beauty ... nor her modest elegance either, can make it otherwise."

As if sent by fate to confirm him in this conviction, the widow at this moment approached the party, leaning on the arm of the Major. Having finished her fifth rubber, and pocketed her sixteen half-crowns, Major Allen's two friends pleaded an engagement elsewhere, and Mrs. Barnaby accepted his offered escort to the tea-table.

A look of happiness is very becoming to many faces, it will often indeed lend a charm to features that in sorrow can boast of none; but there are others on which this genial and expansive emotion produces a different effect, and Mrs. Barnaby was one of them. Her eyes did not only sparkle, they perfectly glared with triumph and delight. She shook her curls and her feathers with the vivacity of a Bacchante when tossing her cymbals in the air; and her joyous laugh and her conscious whisper, as each in turn attracted attention from all around, were exactly calculated to produce just such an effect as the luckless Agnes would have lived in silence and solitude for ever to avoid witnessing.

The habile Major descried the party the instant he entered the room, and led the lady directly to it. But the table was fully occupied, and for a moment no one stirred but Agnes, who, pale and positively trembling with distress, stood up, though without saying a word.

Mrs. Peters coloured, and for a second looked doubtful what to do; but when she saw Major Allen address himself with the manner of an old acquaintance to Elizabeth, she rose, and slightly saying, "I am sorry you are too late for tea, Mrs. Barnaby," moved off, followed, of course, by her daughters, and the gentlemen attending on them.

"I dare say we shall find a cup that will do ... never mind us.... Agnes, don't you go, but try that pot, will you, at the bottom of the table; this is as dry as hay."

The Major was immediately on the alert, and seizing on the tea-pot seized the hand of Agnes with it. Neck, cheeks, and brow were crimson in an instant; and as she withdrew her hand from his audacious touch, her eye caught that of Colonel Hubert fixed upon her. Shame, vexation, and something almost approaching to terror, brought tears into that beautiful eye, and for a moment the gallant soldier forgot everything in an ardent longing to seize by the collar and fling from the chamber the man who had thus dared to offend her. But Frederick Stephenson, who also saw the action, quitted the side of his partner, contrary to all the laws of etiquette, and quickly placing himself beside Agnes, bestowed such a glance on the Major as immediately turned the attention of that judicious personage to the tea-pot and Mrs. Barnaby.

"You dance with me now, Miss Willoughby," said young Stephenson, which, as he had enjoyed that honour twice before, he had been too discreet to hint at till the arrival of the widow and the Major had rendered her being immediately occupied so particularly desirable. Agnes perfectly understood his motive, and though her cheeks again tingled as she remembered how impossible it was for her to run effectually from the annoyance that so cruelly beset her, she felt touched and grateful for his kindness; and the smile with which she accepted it, would have sufficed to subdue the heart of Frederick had an atom of it been unsubdued before.

CHAPTER III

MELANCHOLY MEDITATIONS—AN EVENTFUL WALK—A PLEASANT BREAKFAST—A COMFORTABLE CONVERSATION IN A CLOSET

The slumbers of Agnes that night were not heavy, for she waked while the birds were still singing their morning hymn to the sun, which poured its beams full upon her face through her uncurtained window. She turned restlessly upon her little bed, and tried to sleep again; but it would not do; and as she listened to the twittering without, so strong a desire seized her to leave the narrow boundary of her little closet, and breathe the air of heaven, that after the hesitation and struggle of a few moments she yielded, and noiselessly creeping out of bed, and performing the business of her toilet with the greatest caution, ventured to open the door communicating with her aunt's chamber, when she had the great satisfaction of hearing her snore loud enough to mask any sound she might herself make in passing through the room.

In like manner she successfully made her way down stairs and out of the house, and her heart beat with something like pleasure as she felt the sweet morning breeze blow from the downs upon her cheek. She walked towards the beautiful point on which the windmill stands; but, alas! she was no longer happy enough to feel that the landscape it commanded could confer that sort of perfect felicity which she had before thought belonged to it. She sat down again on the same spot where Mary, Lucy, James, and herself had sat before, but with how different a feeling! and yet it wanted one whole day of a week since that time. What new sorrow was it that weighed thus upon her spirits?... The good-humoured liking that her new acquaintance then testified towards her, had since ripened into friendship ... at the ball of the preceding evening she had, in fashionable phrase, met with the most brilliant success ... she had danced every dance, and three of them with the partner that every lady in the room would best have liked to dance with; and yet there was a feeling of depression at her heart greater than she had ever been conscious of before. How was this?... Could Agnes herself tell the cause of it?... Yes, if she had asked herself, she could have answered, and have answered truly, that it was because she now knew that the better, the more estimable, the more amiable the society around her might be, the more earnestly she ought to endeavour to withdraw from it.... This conviction was enough to make her feel sad, and there was no need to seek farther in order to discover other sources of sadness, if any such there were, within her bosom.

And thus she sat, again pulling thyme from the hill-side; but it was no longer so sweet as before, and she threw it from her, like a child who has broken its toy, and just reached the sage conviction that its gaudy colouring was good for nothing. While indulging in this most unsatisfactory fit of musing, the sound of a horse's feet almost close behind startled her; but instead of turning her head to see whom it might be, she started up, and walked onward. The horseman, however, was perhaps more curious than herself, for he immediately rode past her, nor scrupled to turn his head as he did so, to ascertain who the early wanderer might be.

But even before he had done so Agnes knew, by a moment's glance at his figure as he passed her, that it was Colonel Hubert.

He checked his horse, and touched his hat, and for half an instant Agnes thought he was going to speak to her: perhaps he thought so too; but if he did, he changed his mind, for looking about in the distance, as if reconnoitring his position, he pressed the sides of his horse and galloped on, a groom presently following.

Agnes breathed more freely. "Thank God, he did not speak to me!" she exclaimed. "If he had, I should have wanted power to answer him.... Never, no, never can I forget ... were I to see him every day to the end of my life, I should never forget the expression of his face as my aunt Barnaby ... and that dreadful man ... walked up the room towards the tea-table!... no, nor the glance he gave, so full of vexation and regret, when his kind-hearted, sweet-tempered friend, asked me again to dance with him!... Proud, disdainful man! I hope and trust that I never may behold him more!... It is he who first taught me to know and feel how miserable is the future that awaits me!" This soliloquy, partly muttered and partly thought, was here interrupted by her once more hearing the sound of a horse's feet on the turf close behind her.

"He has turned back!" thought she, "though I did not see him pass me. Oh! if he speaks to me, how shall I answer him!"

But again the horseman rode past, and another rapid glance showed her that this time it was not Colonel Hubert, nor did she trouble herself to think whom else it might be; and if she had, the labour would have been thrown away, for in this case, as before, the rider looked back, and displayed to her view the features of Major Allen.

He instantly stopped his horse, and jumped to the ground, then skilfully wheeling the animal round, placed himself between it and the terrified Agnes, and began walking beside her.

Her first impulse was to stand still, and ask him wherefore he thus approached her; but when she turned towards him to speak, the expression of his broad, audacious countenance, struck her with dismay, and she suddenly turned round, and walked rapidly and in silence back towards the windmill, and the buildings beyond it.

"Are you afraid of me, my charming young lady?" said the Major with a chuckle, again wheeling his charger so as to place himself beside Agnes.... "No reason, upon my soul.... How is your adorable aunt?... Tell her I inquired for her, and tell her too, upon the honour of an officer and a gentleman, that I consider her as by far the finest woman I ever saw.... But why do you run on so swiftly, my pretty little fawn? Your charming aunt will thank me, I am sure, for not letting you put yourself in a fever;" and so saying his huge hand grasped the elbow of Agnes, and he held her forcibly back.

A feeling of terror, greater than the occasion called for perhaps, induced Agnes to utter a cry at again feeling this hateful gripe, which seemed as if by magic to bring her relief, for at the same moment Colonel Hubert was on the other side of her. Agnes looked up in his face with an undisguised expression of delight, and on his offering his arm she took it instantly, but without either of them having uttered a word.

There was something in the arrangement of the trio that Major Allen did not appear to approve, for having taken about three steps in advance, he suddenly stopped, and saying in a sort of blustering mutter, "You will be pleased to give my best compliments to your aunt," he sprung upon his horse so heedlessly as to render it probable both lady and gentleman might get a kick from the animal, and making it bound forward, darted off across the down.

Agnes gently withdrew her arm, and said, but in a voice not over steady, "Indeed, sir, I am very much obliged to you!"

"I am glad to have been near you, Miss Willoughby, when that very insolent person addressed you," said Colonel Hubert, but without making any second offer of his arm. And a moment after he added, "Excuse me for telling you that you are imprudent in walking thus early and alone. Though Clifton on this side appears a rural sort of residence, it is not without some of the disagreeable features of a watering-place."

"I have lived always in the country.... I had no idea there was any danger," ... said Agnes, shocked to think how much her own childish imprudence must have strengthened Colonel Hubert's worst opinion of her and her connexions.

"Nor is there, perhaps, any actual danger," replied the Colonel; "but there are many things that may not exactly warrant that name, which nevertheless...."

"Would be very improper for me!... Oh! it was great ignorance—great folly!" interrupted Agnes eagerly; "and never, never again will I put myself in need of such kindness."

"Has your aunt always lived with you in the country?" was a question which Colonel Hubert felt greatly disposed to ask, but, instead of it, he said, turning down from the windmill hill, "You reside at Rodney Place, I believe, and, if I mistake not, this is the way."

"No, sir ... we lodge in Sion Row.... It is here, close by.... Do not let me delay your ride any more.... I am very much obliged to you;" ... and without waiting for an answer, Agnes stepped rapidly down the steep side of the hill, and was half-way towards Sion Row before the Colonel felt quite sure of what he had intended to say in return.

"But it is no matter.... She is gone," thought he, and taking his reins from the hand of his groom, he remounted, and resumed his morning ride.

Mrs. Barnaby had not quitted her bed when Agnes returned; but she was awake, and hearing some one enter the drawing-room, called out, "Who's there?"

"It is I, aunt," said Agnes, opening the door with flushed cheeks and out of breath, partly, perhaps, from the agitation occasioned by her adventure, and partly from the speed with which she had walked from the windmill home.

"And where on earth have you been already, child? Mercy on me, what a colour you have got!... The ball has done you good as well as me, I think. There, get in and take your things off, and then come back and talk to me while I dress myself."

Agnes went into her little room and shut the door. She really was very much afraid of her aunt, and in general obeyed her commands with the prompt obedience of a child who fears to be scolded if he make a moment's delay. But at this moment a feeling stronger than fear kept her within the blessed sanctuary of her solitary closet. She seemed gasping for want of air ... her aunt's room felt close after coming from the fresh breeze of the hill, and it was, therefore, as Agnes thought, that the sitting down alone beside her own open window seemed a luxury for which it was worth while to risk the sharpest reprimand that ever aunt gave.... But why, while she enjoyed it, did big tears chase each other down her cheeks?

Whatever the cause, the effect was salutary. She became composed, she recovered her breath, and her complexion faded to its usual delicate tint, or perhaps to a shade paler; and then she began to think that it was not wise to do anything for which she knew she should be reproached ... if she could help it ... and now she could help it; so she smoothed her chestnut tresses, bathed her eyes in water, and giving one deep sigh at leaving her own side of the door for that which belonged to her aunt, she came forth determined to bear very patiently whatever might be said to her.

Fortunately for Agnes Mrs. Barnaby had just approached that critical moment of her toilet business, when it was her especial will and pleasure to be alone; so, merely saying in a snappish accent, "What in the world have you been about so long?" she added, "Now get along into the drawing-room, and take care that the toast and my muffin are ready for me, and kept hot before the fire;—it's almost too hot for fire, but I must have my breakfast warm and comfortable, and we can let it out afterwards."

Agnes most joyfully obeyed. It was a great relief, and she was meekly thankful for it; but she very nearly forgot the muffins and the toast, for the windows of the room were open, and looked out upon the windmill and the down, a view so pleasant that it was several minutes before she recollected the duties she had to perform. At last, however, she did recollect them, and made such good use of the time that remained, that when her aunt entered bright in carmine and lilac ribbons, everything was as it should be; and she had only to sit and listen to her ecstatic encomiums on the ball, warm each successive piece of muffin at the end of a fork, and answer properly to the ten times repeated question,—

"Hav'n't you got a good aunt, Agnes, to take you to such a ball as that?"

At length, however, the tedious meal was ended, and Mrs. Barnaby busied herself considerably more than usual in setting the little apartment in order. She made Jerningham carefully brush away the crumbs—a ceremony sometimes neglected—set out her own best pink-lined work-box in state, placed the table agreeably at one of the windows, with two or three chairs round it, and then told Agnes, that if she had any of her lesson-book work to do, she might sit in her own room, for she did not want her.

Gladly was the mandate obeyed, and willingly did she aid Betty Jacks in putting her tiny premises in order, for she was not without hope that her friend Mary would pay her a visit there to talk over the events of the evening; an occupation for which, to say the truth, she felt considerably more inclined than for any "lesson-book work" whatever.

Nor was she disappointed ... hardly did she feel ready to receive her before her friend arrived.

"And well, Carina, how fares it with you to-day? Do you not feel almost too big for your little room after all the triumphs of last night?" was the gay address of Miss Peters as she seated herself upon one of Agnes's boxes. But it was not answered in the same tone; nay, there was much of reproof as well as sadness in the accent with which Agnes uttered,—

"Triumphs!... Oh! Mary, what a word!"

"You are the only one, I believe, who would quarrel with it. Did ever a little country girl under seventeen make a more successful début?"

"Did ever country girl of any age have more reason to feel that she never ought to make any début at all?"

"My poor Agnes!..." said Miss Peters more gravely, "it will not do for you to feel so deeply the follies that may, and, I fear, ever will be committed by your aunt and my aunt Barnaby.... It is a sad, vexing business, beyond all doubt, that you should have to go into company with a woman determined to make herself so outrageously absurd; but it is not fair to remember that, and nothing else ... you should at least recollect also that the most distinguished man in the room paid you the compliment of joining your party at tea."

"Paid me the compliment!... Oh! Mary."

"And oh! Agnes, can you pretend to doubt that it was in compliment to you?... And in compliment to whom was it that he danced with you?"

"He never danced with me, Mary," said Agnes, colouring.

"My dear child, what are you talking about? Why, he danced with you three times."

"Oh yes ... Mr. Stephenson ... he is indeed the kindest, most obliging...."

"And the handsomest partner that you ever danced with.... Is it not so?"

"That may easily be, Mary, if by partner you mean a gentleman partner, for I never danced with any till last night; and it is only saying that he is handsomer than your brother and Mr. Osborne, and I think he is."

"And I think so too, therefore on that point we shall not quarrel. But tell me, how did you like the ball altogether?... Did it please you?... Were you amused?... Shall you be longing to go to another?"

"Let me answer your last question first.... I hope never, never, never again to go to a ball with my aunt Barnaby.... But had it not been for the pain, the shame, the agony she caused me, I should have liked it very much indeed ... particularly the tea-time, Mary.... How pleasant it was before she came with that horrid, horrid man! Shall you ever forget the sight as they came up the room towards us?... Oh! how he looked at her!"

Agnes shuddered, and pressed her hands to her eyes, as if to shut out an object that she still saw.

"It was tremendous," replied her friend: "but don't worry yourself by thinking Mr. Stephenson looked at her just then, for he really did not. You know he was sitting at the corner of the table by me, and his back was turned to her, thank heaven!... But I will tell you who did look at her, if Stephenson did not ... that magnificent-looking Colonel stared as if he had seen an apparition; but I did not mind that half so much, nor you either, I suppose.... An old soldier like him must be used to such a variety of quizzes, that nobody, I imagine, can appear so preposterous to him as they might do to his young friend.... By the by, I think he is a very fine-looking man for his age; don't you?"

"Who?" said Agnes innocently.

"Why, Colonel Hubert.... His sister, who is just married to Sir Edward Stephenson, is nearly twenty years younger than he is, they say."

"Twenty years?" said Agnes.

"Yes.... Must it not be strange to see them together as brother and sister?... he must seem so much more like her father."

"Her father!" said Agnes.

"Yes, I should think so. But you do not talk half as much about the ball as I expected, Agnes: I think you were disappointed, and yet I do not know how that could be. You dance beautifully, and seem very fond of it; you had the best partners in the room, danced every dance, and were declared on all sides to be the belle par excellence,... and yet you do not seem to have enjoyed it."

"Oh! I did enjoy it all the time that she was out of the room playing cards; I enjoyed it very, very much indeed ... so much that I am surprised at myself to feel how soon all my painful shyness was forgotten.... But ... after all, Mary, though you call her your aunt Barnaby, as if to comfort me by sharing my sufferings, she is not really your aunt, and still less is she your sole protector ... still less is she the being on whom you depend for your daily bread. Alas! my dear Mary, is there not more cause for surprise in my having enjoyed the ball so much, than in my not having enjoyed it more?"

"My poor Agnes, this is sad indeed," said Mary, all her gaiety vanishing at once, "for it is true. Do not think me indifferent to your most just sorrow.... Would to Heaven I could do anything effectually to alleviate it! But while you are here, at least, endeavour to think more of us, and less of her. Wherever you are known, you will be respected for your own sake; and that is worth all other respect, depend upon it. When you leave us, indeed, I shall be very anxious for you. Tell me, dear Agnes, something more about your aunt Compton. Is it quite impossible that you should be placed under her protection?"

"Oh yes!... She would not hear of it. She paid for my education, and all my other expenses, during five years; and my aunt Barnaby says, that when she undertook to do this, she expressly said that it was all she could ever do for me. They say that she has ruined her little fortune by lavish and indiscriminate charity to the poor, and aunt Barnaby says that she believes she has hardly enough left to keep herself alive. But I sometimes think, Mary, that I could be very happy if she would let me work for her, and help her, and perhaps give lessons in Silverton.... I know some things already well enough, perhaps, to teach in such a remote place as that, when better masters cannot be procured; and I should be so happy in doing this ... if aunt Compton would but let me live with her."

"Then why do you not tell her so, Agnes?"

"Because the last—the only time I have seen her for years, though she kissed and embraced me for a moment, she pushed me from her afterwards, and said I was only more artful than aunt Barnaby, and that I should never be either graced or disgraced by her ... those were her words, I shall never forget them ... and she has the reputation of being immoveably obstinate in her resolves."

"That does not look very promising, I must confess. But wisdom tells us that the possibility of future sorrow should never prevent our enjoying present happiness. Now, I do think, dear Agnes, that just now you may enjoy yourself, if you like us as well as we like you,... for we are all determined to endure aunt Barnaby for your sake, and in return you must resolve to be happy in spite of her for ours. And now adieu!... I want to have some talk with mamma this morning; but I dare say you will hear from me, or see me again, before the end of the day. Farewell!..." And Miss Peters made a quiet exit from the closet and from the house; for she had heard voices in the drawing-room as she came up the stairs, and now heard voices in the drawing-room as she went down; and having business in her head upon which she was exceedingly intent, she was anxious to avoid being seen or heard by Mrs. Barnaby, lest she should be detained.

CHAPTER IV

A TETE-A-TETE IN A DRAWING-ROOM—AUTOBIOGRAPHY—A REMARKABLE DISCOVERY CONCERNING THE DUKE OF WELLINGTON

The voices which alarmed Miss Peters were those of Mrs. Barnaby and Major Allen. The acquaintance between them had gone quite far enough on the preceding evening to justify the gentleman's amiable empressement to inquire for the lady's health; besides, he was somewhat curious to know if the pretty, skittish young creature he had encountered in his morning's ride, had recounted the adventure to her aunt. It was his private opinion that she had not; and if so, he should know what to think of the sudden appearance and protecting demeanour of her tall friend. It was thus he reasoned as he walked towards Sion Row as soon as he had finished his breakfast; and yet, though he had lost so little time, he did not arrive till at least three minutes after the widow had begun to expect him.

"I need not ask my charming Mrs. Barnaby how she rested after her ball ... eyes do not sparkle thus, unless they have been blessed with sleep;" ... and the lady's hand was taken, bowed upon, and the tips of her fingers kissed, before she had quite recovered the soft embarrassment his entrance had occasioned.

"You are very kind to call upon me, Major Allen.... Do sit down.... I live as yet comparatively in great retirement; for during Mr. Barnaby's lifetime we saw an immense deal of company,—that old-fashioned sort of country visiting, you know, that never leaves one's house empty.... I could not stand it when I was left alone ... and that was the reason I left my beautiful place."

"Siverton or Silverton Park, was it not?... I think I have heard of it."

"Yes, Silverton.... And do you know, Major, that the remembrance of all that racket and gaiety was so oppressive to my nerves during the first months of my widowhood, that I threw off everything that reminded me of it ... sold my carriages and horses, let my place, turned off all my servants; and positively, when I set off for this place in order to see my sister Peters and her family, I knew not if I should ever have strength or spirits to enter into general society again."

"Thank God, dearest madam, that you have made the effort!... Though the hardened and war-worn nature of man cannot melt with all the softness of yours, there is yet within us a chord that may be made to vibrate in sympathy when words of true feeling reach it! How well I understood your feelings ... and how difficult it is not to envy, even in death, the being who has left such a remembrance behind!... But we must not dwell on this.... Tell me, dear Mrs. Barnaby, tell,—as to a friend who understands and appreciates you,—do you regret the having left your elegant retirement?... or do you feel, as I trust you do, that Providence has not gifted you so singularly for nothing?... do you feel that your fellow-creatures have a claim upon you, and that it ought not to be in secret and in solitude that the hours of such a being should be spent? Tell me, do you feel this?"

"Alas! Major Allen, there is so much weakness in the heart of a woman, that she is hardly sure for many days together how she ought to feel.... We are all impulse, all soul, all sentiment, ... and our destiny must ever depend upon the friends we meet in our passage through this thorny world!"

"Beautiful idea!... Where is the poet that has more sweetly painted the female heart?... And what a study it offers when such a heart is thrown open to one! Good God! to see a creature so formed for enjoyment,—so beaming with innocent cheerfulness,—so rich in the power of conferring happiness wherever she deigns to smile, ... to see such a being turn weeping and alone from her hospitable halls, and from all the pomp and splendour that others cling to ... what a spectacle! Have you no lingering regret, dearest lady, for having left your charming mansion?"

"Perhaps there are moments ... or rather, I should say, perhaps there have been moments, when something of the kind has crossed me. But if I had not disposed of my place, I should never have seen Clifton.... My spirits wanted the change, and I feel already better in this delightful air. But I confess I do regret having sold my beautiful greys, ... I shall never meet any I like so well again."

"A set, were they?"

"Oh yes."

"Four greys ... and all well matched?"

"Perfectly.... Poor Mr. Barnaby took so much pains about it.... It was his delight to please me.... I ought not to have sold them."

"It was a pity," ... said the kind Major with a sigh.

"Don't talk about it, Major Allen!..." and here one of the widow's most curiously embroidered pocket-handkerchiefs, delightfully scented with musk, was lightly and carefully applied to her eyes.

"Nay," said the Major, venturing gently to withdraw it, "you must not yield to this dangerous softness.... I cannot bear to have those eyes concealed!... it produces the chilling sensation of an eclipse at noon-day.... I shall run away from you if you will not look at me."

"No, do not," ... said the widow, making an effort to smile, which was rewarded by a look of gratitude, and a seemingly involuntary kiss bestowed upon the hand that had withdrawn the envious handkerchief.

"And that pretty little girl, your niece, Mrs. Barnaby," ... said the Major, as if considerately changing the conversation; "how is she this morning?"

"Oh! quite well, poor child, and in my dressing-room, going over her Italian and French lessons before she does them with me."

"Good Heaven!... Is it possible that you devote yourself thus?... Take care, charming Mrs. Barnaby ... take care that you do not permit your affectionate nature to form an attachment to that young person which may destroy all your future prospects in life!... At your age, and with your exquisite beauty, you ought to be looking forward to the renewal of the tender tie that has already made your happiness;... And who is there ... pardon me if I speak boldly ... who is there who would venture to give his whole heart, his soul, his entire existence to one who has no heart to give in return? Think you, Mrs. Barnaby, that it can be in the power of any niece in the world to atone to a woman of your exquisite sensibility for the loss of that ardent affection which can only exist between a husband and wife?... Tell me, do you believe this?"

"It is a question," replied the widow, casting her eyes upon the ground, "that I have never asked myself."

"Then neglect it no longer.... For God's sake—for the sake of your future happiness, which must be so inexpressibly dear to all who know you ... all who appreciate you justly ... for the sake of the young girl herself, do not involve yourself by undertaking the duties of a mother towards one who from her age could never have stood to you in the relation of a child."

"Alas! no," ... said Mrs. Barnaby; "I lost my only babe a few weeks before its father.... Had it lived, it would this spring have been three years old!... You say true ... the age of Agnes must ever prevent my feeling for her as a child of my own.... My poor sister was indeed so much older than myself, that I always rather looked upon her as an aunt, or as a mother, than as my sister."

"Of course you must have done so; and, interesting and inexpressibly touching as it is to witness your beautiful tenderness towards her child, it is impossible not to feel that this tenderness carried too far will inevitably destroy the future happiness of your life. Forgive, I implore you, a frankness that can only proceed from my deep interest in your welfare.... Is this young person entirely dependent upon you?"

"At this moment she is; but she will be provided for at the death of her great-aunt, Mrs. Elizabeth Compton of Compton Basett; ... and to say the truth, Major Allen, as you so kindly interest yourself in what concerns me, I neither do nor ever shall consider myself bound to retain Agnes Willoughby in my family, under any circumstances that should render her being so inconvenient."

"I delight in receiving such an assurance ... dear, excellent Mrs. Barnaby!... What a heart!... what an understanding!... what beauty!... what unequalled sweetness! No wonder the late Mr. Barnaby delighted, as you say, to please you! 'Lives there the man,' as the immortal Byron says—'Lives there the man with soul so dead,' as to be capable of doing otherwise?... But to return to the subject of this poor little girl ... she might be termed pretty, perhaps, in any society but yours.... Tell me, is this Mrs. Compton, of Compton Basett, wealthy?... Is she also a relation of yours?"

"Yes, she is immensely wealthy.... It is a magnificent estate. She is a maiden sister of my father's."

"Then Miss Willoughby will eventually be a great fortune.... How old is your aunt?"

"My aunt is near sixty, I believe, ... but the provision intended for Agnes is only sufficient to maintain her like a gentlewoman. The bulk of the property is settled on me and my heirs."

"I fear you will think me an unseasonable visitor," said the fully-satisfied Major, rising, "and I will go now, lest you should refuse to admit me again."

"Do not go yet," ... said the gentle widow, playfully refusing the hand extended to take leave. "What in the world now have you got to do, that should prevent your bestowing a little more time on me?"

"It would be difficult, Mrs. Barnaby," said the Major with an eloquent look, "to find any occupation sufficiently attractive to take me from you, so long as I dared flatter myself that it was your wish I should remain."

"Well, then ... sit down again, Major Allen ... for do you know, I want you to tell me all about yourself.... Where have you served?—what dangers have you passed through? You have no idea how much interest I should take in listening to the history of your past life."

"My sweet friend!... Never should I have entered upon such a subject unbidden ... yet with such an auditor, how dear will the privilege become of talking of myself!... But you must check me, if I push your gentle patience too far. Tell me when you are weary of me ... or of my little narrative."

"I will, I will ... depend upon it, ... only do not stop till I do, Major."

"Adorable sweetness!... Thus, then, I am to be my own biographer, and to a listener whose opinion would, in my estimation, outweigh that of all the congregated world, if placed in judgment on my actions. It is probable, my charming friend, that my name as Ensign Allen may not be totally unknown to you.... It was while I still held that humble rank, that I was first fortunate enough to distinguish myself. In an affair of some importance in the Peninsula, I turned what might have been a very disastrous defeat into a most complete victory, and was immediately promoted to a company. Shortly after this I chanced to shew the same sort of spirit, which was, I believe, born with me, in a transaction nowise professional, but which, nevertheless, made me favourably mentioned, and certainly contributed to bring me into the rather general notice with which Europe at present honours me.... Yet it was merely an affair with a party of brigands, in which I put seven fellows hors de combat, and thereby enabled that celebrated grandee, the Duke d'Almafonte d'Aragona d'Astrada, to escape, together with his beautiful daughter, and all their jewels. The service might have been, I own, of considerable importance to them, but the gratitude it produced in the minds of both father and daughter, greatly exceeded what was called for ... he offered me ... so widely separated as we now are, there can be no indelicacy in my confiding the circumstance to you, my dear Mrs. Barnaby, but ... the fact is, he offered me his only daughter in marriage, with an immense fortune. But, alas! how capricious is the human will!... my hour, my dear friend, was not yet come.... I felt, beautiful as Isabella d'Almafonte was accounted by all the world, that I could not give her my heart, and I performed the painful duty of refusing her hand. Nothing, however, could be more noble than the subsequent conduct of the duke, ... at the first painful moment he only said ... 'Captain Allen, we must submit' ... of course he said it in Spanish, but it would look like affectation, in such a narrative as this, were I not to translate it ... 'Capitano Alleno, bisogno submittajo nos,' were his words.... I am sure I shall never forget them, for they touched me to the very heart.... I could not speak, my feelings choked me, and I left his palace in silence. Five years had elapsed, and I had perhaps too nearly forgotten the lovely but unfortunate Isabella d'Almafonte, when I received a packet from a notary of Madrid, informing me that her illustrious father was dead, and had gratefully bequeathed me a legacy, amounting in English money to thirty thousand pounds sterling. I was by that time already in possession of the estates of my ancestors, and such a sum might have appeared a very useless bagatelle, had not an accident rendered it at that time of really important convenience."

"Good heaven! how interesting!" exclaimed Mrs. Barnaby. "And what, dear Major, became of the unfortunate Isabella?"

"She took the veil, Mrs. Barnaby, in the convent de Los Ceurores Dolentes, within a few months of her noble father's death.... Before this event she had not the power of disposing of herself as she wished; ... but her excellent father never tortured her by the proposal of any other marriage...."

"Admirable man!" cried Mrs. Barnaby, greatly touched. "Dear Major Allen!" she added, in a voice that seemed to deprecate opposition, "you must, indeed you must, do me an immense favour. When Mrs. Peters took me to Bristol in her coach the other day, I bought myself this album; it has got nothing in it as yet but my own name; now, if you do not wish to break my heart, you must write the name of Isabella d'Almafonte in this first page ... it will be an autograph inexpressibly interesting!"

The Major took the book and the pen that were offered by the two hands of Mrs. Barnaby, and said with a profound sigh,—

"Break your heart!... I should never have broken the heart of any woman, if what she asked had been seconded by such eyes as those!"

A silence of some moments followed, a part of which was employed by the Major in writing the name of Isabella d'Almafonte, and a part in gazing on the downcast lids of the admired eyes opposite to him; but this too trying interval ended at length by the lady's recovering herself enough to say, "And that accident, Major Allen, that made the duke's little legacy convenient to you?... what was it?... Do not have any reserve with one whom you have honoured by the name of friend!"

"Reserve to you!... never!... While you continue to admit me to your presence, all reserve on my part must be impossible. The accident was this, my friend; and I am not sorry to name it, as it gives me an opportunity of alluding to a subject that I would rather you heard mentioned by me than by any other. After the battle of Waterloo—(concerning which, by the by, I should like to tell you an anecdote)—after the battle of Waterloo, I became, in common with nearly all the officers of the army, an idle man; and like too many others, I was tempted to seek a substitute for the excitement produced by the military ardour in which I had lived, by indulging in the pernicious agitations of the gaming-table. It is very likely, that if you speak of me in general society, you will be told that I have played high.... My dear Mrs. Barnaby, this is true. My large fortune gave me, as I foolishly imagined, a sort of right to play high if it amused me; and for a little while, I confess, it did amuse me; ... but I soon found that a gentleman was no match for those who made gambling a profession, and I lost largely,—so largely, indeed, that I must have saddled my acres with a mortgage, had not the legacy of the Duke d'Almafonte d'Aragona d'Estrada reached me just in time to prevent the necessity."

"I rejoice to hear it," replied the widow kindly; "and you have never hazarded so largely since, dear Major, have you?"

"Oh! never.... In fact, I never enter a room now where anything like high play is going on.... I cannot bear even to see it, and I believe I have in this way offended many who still permit themselves this hateful indulgence; offended them, indeed, to such a degree, that they perfectly hate me, and utter the most virulent abuse every time they hear my name mentioned; ... but for this I care little: I know I am right, Mrs. Barnaby, and that what loses their friendship and esteem, may be the means of gaining for me the regard of those, perhaps, on whom my whole happiness may depend during my future life."

The same dangerous sort of silence as before seemed creeping on them; but again the widow had the courage to break it, by recalling to the memory of her musing and greatly pre-occupied companion the anecdote respecting Waterloo which he had promised her.

"Waterloo!" said he, rousing himself.... "Ay, dearest Mrs. Barnaby, I will tell you that, though there are many reasons which render me very averse to speak of it lightly. In the first place, by those who know me not, it might be thought to look like boasting; and, moreover, if I alluded to it in any society capable of the baseness of repeating what I said, it might bring upon me very active, and indeed fatal, proofs of the dislike—I may say hatred—already felt against me in a certain quarter."

"Gracious heaven, Major!... be careful then, I implore you, before whom you speak! There appear to be many strangers here, of whose characters it is impossible to know anything.... If you have enemies, they may be spies expressly sent to watch you."

"I sometimes think so, I assure you.... I catch such singular looks occasionally, as nothing else can account for; and the enemy I allude to is one who has power, as well as will, to punish by evil reports, if he cannot positively crush and ruin, those who interfere with his ambition."

"Is it possible? Thank heaven! at least you can have no doubt of me.... So, tell me, I beseech you to tell me, to whom is it that your alarming words refer?"

The Major drew his chair close to Mrs. Barnaby, took one of her hands between both of his, and having gazed for a moment very earnestly in her face, whispered,—

"The Duke of Wellington!"

"Good God!..." exclaimed the widow, quite in an agony: "the Duke of Wellington! Is the Duke of Wellington your enemy, Major Allen?"

"To the teeth, my fairest! to the teeth!" replied the Major, firmly setting the instruments he mentioned, and muttering through them with an appearance of concentrated rage, the outward demonstration of which was increased by the firmness of the grasp in which he continued to hold her hand.

"But how can this be so?" faltered Mrs. Barnaby.... "So brave a man as you!... one, too, who had distinguished himself so early! How can he be so base?"

"How can he be otherwise, my friend?" replied the Major with increasing agitation, "when" ... and here he lowered his voice still more, whispering almost in her very ear, "it is I—I,—Ferdinand Alexander Allen, who ought by right to be the Duke of Wellington, instead of him who now wears the title!"

"You astonish me more than I am able to express!"

"Of course I do.... Such, however, is the fact. The battle of Waterloo would have been lost,—was lost, positively lost,—till I, disdaining in such a moment to receive orders from one whom I perceived to be incompetent, rushed forward, almost knocking the Duke off his horse as I did so ... sent back the French army like a flock of sheep before an advancing lion ... seized with my own hand on the cocked hat of Napoleon ... drew it from his head, and actually flogged his horse with it till horse and rider together seemed well enough inclined to make the best of their way out of my reach.... God bless you, my dearest lady! the Duke of Wellington had no more to do in gaining the battle of Waterloo than you had.... I now leave you to judge what his feelings towards me are likely to be."

"Full of envy and hatred, beyond all doubt!" solemnly replied Mrs. Barnaby; "and I will not deny, Major Allen, that I think there is great danger in your situation. A person of such influence may do great injury, even to a man of your well-known noble character. But how extraordinary it is that no hint of this has ever transpired."

"I beg your pardon, my dear madam; this is very far from being the case. At your peaceful residence beneath the shades of Silverton Park, it is highly probable that you may have remained ignorant of the fact; but, in truth, the Duke's reputation among the people of England has suffered greatly; though no one, indeed, has yet proposed that his sword should be taken from him. The well-known circumstance of stones having been thrown at his windows ... a fact which probably has never reached you ... is quite sufficient to prove that the people must be aware that what the English army did at Waterloo, was not done under his generalship.... No, no, England knows too well what she owed to that victory so to treat the general who achieved it; and had they not felt doubts as to who that general was, no stones would have been levelled at Apsley House. Many of the common soldiers—fine fellows!—have been bold enough to name me, and it is this that has so enraged the Duke, that there is nothing which he has not taught his emissaries to say against me.... I have been called swindler, black-leg, radical, horse-jockey, and I know not what beside; and I should not wonder, my charming friend, if sooner or later your friendship were put to the proof, by having to listen to similar calumnies against me; but now, you will be able to understand them aright, and know the source from whence they come."

"Well, I never did hear anything so abominable in my life!" said Mrs. Barnaby warmly.... "Not content with taking credit to himself for all that was gained by your extraordinary bravery, he has the baseness to attack your character!... It is too detestable!... and I only hope, that when I get among my own connexions in town, I shall not have the misfortune of meeting him often.... I am certain I should not be able to resist saying something to shew what I thought. Oh! if he were really the brave man that he has been fancied to be, how he must have adored you for your undaunted courage!... And you really took Napoleon's hat off his head?... How excessively brave!... I wish I could have seen it, Major!... I am sure I should have worshipped you.... I do so doat upon bravery!"

"Sweet creature!... That devoted love of courage is one of the loveliest propensities of the female mind. Yes, I am brave—I do not scruple to say so; and the idea that this quality is dear to you, will strengthen it in me four-fold.... But, my dear, my lovely friend! I must bid you adieu. I expect the steward of my property in Yorkshire to-day, and I rather think he must be waiting for me now.... Soften, then, the pain of this parting, by telling me that I may come again!"

"I should be sorry indeed to think this was our last meeting, Major Allen," said the widow gently; "I am seldom out in the morning before the hour at which you called to-day."

"Farewell then!" said he, kissing her hand with an air of mixed tenderness and respect, "farewell!... and remember that all I have breathed into your friendly ear must be sacred; ... but I know it would be so without this injunction; Mrs. Barnaby's majestic beauty conceals not the paltry spirit of a gossip!"

"Indeed you are right!... indeed you are right!... To my feelings the communications of a friend are sweet, solemn pledges of regard, that it would be sacrilege to violate. Farewell, Major!—farewell!"

CHAPTER V

A YOUNG LADY'S PLOT—A CONSULTATION, AND THE HAPPY RESULT OF IT—A TERRIBLE INTERRUPTION, AND A DANGEROUS EXPEDITION—CONFIDENTIAL INTERCOURSE

Mary Peters left Agnes considerably earlier than she had intended, in order to communicate to her mother a project which had entered her head during the short time they spent together. Though the project, however, was formed during their interview, the idea upon which it was founded had repeatedly occurred to her before, short as the time had been that was given for its ripening. This idea was suggested to her by the evident admiration of Mr. Stephenson for her friend; on which she had meditated as they drove from the Mall to Rodney Place, as she brushed and papilloted her nut-brown curls before her glass, and as she strolled the next morning from her own home to that of Agnes; it might plainly have been expressed thus ... Frederick Stephenson is over head and ears in love with Agnes Willoughby.

Such was the idea; but the project was concerning a much more serious matter,—namely, that a marriage between the parties might easily be brought about; and, moreover, that the effecting this would be one of the very best actions to which it could be possible to dedicate her endeavours.

To do Miss Peters justice, she was in general neither a busy body nor a match-maker; but she was deeply touched by the melancholy feeling Agnes had expressed respecting her own position; she felt, too, both the justness of it, and the utter helplessness of the poor girl herself either to change or amend it.

"Nothing but her marrying can do it," thought Mary; "and why should she not marry this young man, who is so evidently smitten with her?... Poor Agnes!... What a change—what a contrast it would be!... And if mamma will help me, I am sure we may bring it about. He is perfectly independent, and violently in love already, ... and she is a creature that appears more beautiful and more fascinating every time one sees her."

It was exactly when her meditations reached this point that she discovered it to be necessary that she should go home directly, and home she accordingly went, luckily finding her mother alone in her dressing-room.

"I am delighted to find you by yourself, mamma," began Mary, "I have a great deal to say to you," and then followed a rapid repetition of all Agnes had just said to her.

"Is it not a dreadful situation, mamma?" she added.

"So dreadful, Mary," replied Mrs. Peters, "that were not the youngest of you about three years older than herself, I really think I should propose taking her as a finishing governess. Poor little thing!... what can we do for her?"

"Now listen, mamma," answered Mary, raising her hand gravely, as if to bespeak both silence and attention, "and do not, I implore you, mar the usefulness of what I am going to say by turning it into jest, ... it is no jest, mother. Mr. Stephenson, the young man we saw last night, is most certainly captivated by the beauty of Agnes in no common degree. I was near enough to her all the evening to see plainly how things were going on; and were she less miserable in her present condition, I might think it a fair subject for a jest, or a bet perhaps on the chances for and against his proposing to her. But as it is,—thinking of her as I do, feeling for her as I do,—I think, mamma, that it is my duty to endeavour, by every means in my power, to turn these chances in her favour. Dearest mother, will you help me?"

"But what means have you, my dear girl?" replied Mrs. Peters gravely. "I believe I share both your admiration and your pity for Agnes as fully as you could desire; but I really see not what there is that we can with propriety do to obtain the object you propose ... though I am quite aware of its value."

"I will ask you to do nothing, my dearest mother, in which you shall find a shadow of impropriety. Would there be any in inviting this young man to your house, should you chance to become better acquainted with him?"

"No; but I think we must take some strangely forward steps to lead to this better acquaintance."

"That will depend altogether upon his degree of inclination for it. Should he prove ritroso, I consent to draw off my forces instantly; but if, as I anticipate, he should push himself upon us as an acquaintance, I want you to promise that you will not on your part defeat his wishes,—nay, a little more perhaps ... I would wish you, dear mother, to feel with me, that it would be right and righteous to promote them."

"I rather think it would, Mary, as you put the case. Agnes Willoughby is by no means lowly born: her father was a gentleman decidedly; and I understood from my brother that the Comptons, though for some centuries, I believe, rather an impoverished race, derive their small property from ancestors of very great antiquity; so there is nothing objectionable on that tender point.... And for herself, pretty creature, she would certainly be an ornament and a grace as head and chieftainess of the most aristocratic establishment in the world; so, as a matter of conscience, I have really no scruples at all; but, as matter of convenance, I can only promise not to check, by any want of civility on my part, whatever advances the gentleman may choose to make. Will this content you, my little plotter?"

"Yes ... pretty well; for I am not without hope that you will warm in the cause, if it goes on at all, and then, perhaps, I shall squeeze an invitation out of you, and so on. And, by the way, mamma, when are we to have our little musical soirée? I believe young De Lacy is not going to stay much longer, and if he goes, what are we to do for our bass?"

"We shall be puzzled, certainly. You may write the cards directly, Mary, if you will."

Mary rose at once to set about it; but on opening a certain drawer in the commode, and examining its contents, she said, "We must send to the library, mamma; there are not half enough cards here,... besides ... I want you to walk with us, and I want Agnes to join the party. May I send her a note desiring her to come to take her luncheon here?"

"I comprehend your tactics, my dear.... Agnes is to walk with us just about three o'clock, when all the world are out and about.... We want invitation cards, and may just as well, when we are out, go to the library for them ourselves.... There we shall be sure of seeing Mr. Stephenson ... he will be very likely to join us ... etc. etc. etc.... Is not that your plan?"

"And if it is, mamma," replied Mary, laughing, "I see not that it contains anything beyond what has been agreed to by our compact."

"Very well, Mademoiselle Talleyrand ... write your note."

This was promptly done, and promptly dispatched, and reached Agnes about two minutes after Major Allen had taken his departure. She was aware of his visit; for Betty Jacks had obligingly opened her closet-door to inform her of it; and she now stood with the welcome note in her hand, meditating on the best manner of forwarding the petition to her aunt, not quite liking to send in the note itself, doubtful of Betty's delivering a message on the subject so as to avoid giving offence, but dreading, beyond all else, the idea of presenting herself before the Major.

"Major Allen is still there, Jerningham, is he not?... I have seen nothing of my aunt."

"No, miss, he is this moment gone ... and a beautiful, sweet man he is, too."

Agnes hesitated no longer, but, with Mary's note in her hand, entered the drawing-room to ask leave to obey the summons it contained. She found Mrs. Barnaby in a state of considerable, but very delightful agitation. The album was open before her, her two elbows rested on the table, and her hands shaded her eyes, which were fixed on the interesting name of Isabella d'Almafonte in a fit of deep abstraction.

Agnes uttered her request, but was obliged to repeat it twice before the faculties of the widow were sufficiently recalled to things present for her to be able to return a coherent answer. When at length, however, she understood what was asked, she granted her permission with quite as much pleasure as Agnes received it. At that moment she could endure nothing but solitude, or Major Allen, and eagerly answered ... "Oh yes, my dear! go, go; I do not want you at all."

A liberated bird is not more quick in reaching the shelter of the desired wood, than was Agnes in making her way from Sion Row to Rodney Place; and so great was her joy at finding herself there, that for the moment she forgot all her sorrows, and talked of the ball as if she had not felt infinitely more pain than pleasure there. As soon as the luncheon was ended, Mrs. Peters and Elizabeth, Mary and Agnes, set off upon their walk, not "over the hills, and far away," as heretofore, but along the well-paved ways that led most certainly to the resorts of their fellow mortals. Lucy and James, having heard that the evening for their music party was fixed at the distance only of one fortnight, declared that it was absolutely necessary to devote the interval to "practice," and therefore they remained at home.

If the plan of Mary Peters was such as her mother had described it, nothing could have been more successful; for even before they reached the library, they met Mr. Stephenson and Colonel Hubert. The moment the former perceived them, he stepped forward, quitting the arm of his friend, who certainly rather relaxed than accelerated his pace, and having paid his compliments with the cordial air of an old acquaintance to Mrs. Peters and Elizabeth, passed them and took his station beside Agnes. Both she and her friend received his eager salutation with smiles: Mary, as we know, had her own motives for this; and Agnes had by no means forgotten how seasonably he had led her off on the preceding evening from her aunt, Major Allen, and the forsaken tea-table. Her bright smile, however, soon faded as she marked the stiff bow by which Colonel Hubert returned Mrs. Peters's civil recognition of him. He too passed the first pair of ladies, and joined himself to the second; but though he bowed to both of them, it seemed that he turned and again took the arm of Stephenson, solely for the purpose of saying to him, "Are you going to give up your walk to the Wells, Frederick?"

"Most decidedly, mon cher," was the cavalier reply.

"Then I must wish you good morning, I believe," said Colonel Hubert, attempting to withdraw his arm.

"No, don't," cried the gay young man good-humouredly, and retaining his arm with some show of violence; "I will not let you go without me: you will find nothing there, depend upon it, to reward you on this occasion for your pertinacity of purpose."

Colonel Hubert yielded himself to this wilfulness, and passively, as it seemed, accompanied the party into the library. Nothing could be more agreeable than the animated conversation of young Stephenson: he talked to all the ladies in turn, contrived to discover a multitude of articles of so interesting a kind, that it was necessary they should examine and talk about them; and finally, bringing forward the book of names, fairly beguiled Mrs. Peters and her daughters into something very like a little gossip concerning some among them.

It was while they were thus employed that Colonel Hubert approached Agnes, who, of course, could take no part in it, and said,... "Are you going to remain long at Clifton, Miss Willoughby?"

Agnes blushed deeply as he drew near, and his simple question was answered in a voice so tremulous, that he pitied the agitation (resulting, as he supposed, from their meeting in the morning) which she evinced; and feeling perhaps that she was not to blame because his headstrong friend was determined to fall in love with her, he spoke again, and in a gentler voice said, "I hope you have forgiven me for the blunt advice I ventured to give you this morning."

"Forgiven!" repeated Agnes, looking up at him, and before her glance fell again it was dimmed by a tear. "I can never forget your kindness!" she added, but so nearly in a whisper, that he instantly became aware that her friends had not been made acquainted with the adventure, and that it was not her wish they should be. He therefore said no more on the subject; but, led by some impulse that seemed not, certainly, to proceed from either unkindness or contempt, he continued to converse with her for several minutes, and long enough indeed to make her very nearly forget the party of friends whose heads continued to be congregated round the librarian's register of the Clifton beau monde.

Frederick Stephenson meanwhile was very ably prosecuting the object he had in view, namely, to establish himself decidedly as an acquaintance of Mrs. Peters; and so perfectly comme il faut in all respects was the tone of herself and her daughters, that he was rapidly forgetting such a being as Mrs. Barnaby existed, and solacing his spirit by the persuasion that the only girl he had ever seen whom he could really love was surrounded by connexions as elegant and agreeable as his exigeante family could possibly require. Nor, to say truth, was his friend greatly behind-hand in the degree of oblivion which he permitted to fall upon his faculties respecting this object of his horror and detestation. It was not very easy, indeed, to remember Mrs. Barnaby, while Agnes, awakened by a question as to what part of England it was in which she had enjoyed the rural liberty of which he had heard her speak, poured forth all her ardent praise on the tranquil beauty of Empton.

"It is not," said she, beguiled, by the attention with which he listened to her, into forgetfulness of the awe he had hitherto inspired,—"it is not so majestic in its beauty as Clifton; we have no mighty rocks at Empton—no winding river that, quietly as it flows, seems to have cut its own path amongst them; but the parsonage is the very perfection of a soft, tranquil, flowery retreat, where neither sorrow nor sin have any business whatever."

"And was Empton parsonage your home, Miss Willoughby?"

"Yes ... for five dear happy years," replied Agnes, in an accent from which all gaiety had fled.

"You were not born at Empton, then?"

"No; I was only educated there; but it was there at least that my heart and mind were born, and I do not believe that I shall ever feel quite at home anywhere else."

"It is rather early for you to say that, is it not?" said Colonel Hubert with a smile more calculated to increase her confidence than to renew her awe.... "May I ask how old you are?"

"I shall be seventeen in August," replied Agnes, blushing at being obliged to confess herself so very young.

"She might be my daughter," thought Colonel Hubert, while a shade of melancholy passed over his countenance which it puzzled Agnes to interpret. But he asked her no more questions; and the conversation seemed languishing, when Frederick Stephenson, beginning to think that it was his turn now to talk to Agnes, and pretty well satisfied, perhaps, that he had made a favourable impression upon the Peters family, left the counter and the subscription-book, and crossed to the place where she had seated herself. Colonel Hubert was still standing by her side, but he instantly made way for his friend; and had he at that moment spoken aloud the thoughts of his heart, he might have been heard to say,—"There is nothing here to justify the rejection of any family ... she is perfect alike in person and in mind ... things must take their course: I will urge his departure no further."

Scarcely, however, had these thoughts made their rapid way across his brain, before his ears were assailed by the sound of a laugh, which he recognised in an instant to be that of Mrs. Barnaby. A flush of heightened colour mounted to his very eyes, and he felt conscience-struck, as if whatever might hereafter happen to Stephenson, he should hold himself responsible for it, because he had mentally given his consent to his remaining where the danger lay. And well might the sound and sight of Mrs. Barnaby overturn all such yielding thoughts. She came more rouged, more ringleted, more bedizened with feathers and flowers, and more loud in voice than ever.... She came, too, accompanied by Major Allen.

No thunder-cloud, sending forth its flashings before it, ever threw a more destructive shadow over the tranquil brightness of a smiling landscape, than did this entrée of the facetious pair over the happy vivacity of the party already in possession of the shop. Mrs. Peters turned very red; Miss Willoughby turned very pale; Mary stopped short in the middle of a sentence, and remained as mute as if she had been shot; even the good-natured Elizabeth looked prim; and the two gentlemen, though in different ways, betrayed an equally strong consciousness of the change that had come over them. Mr. Stephenson put on the hat which he had laid beside him on the counter; and though he drew still nearer to Agnes than before, it was without addressing a word to her. Colonel Hubert immediately passed by them, and left the shop.

This last circumstance was the only one which could at that moment have afforded any relief to Agnes; it at once restored her composure and presence of mind, though it did not quite bring back the happy smiles with which she had been conversing five short minutes before.

"Ah! my sister Peters and the children here!" cried Mrs. Barnaby, flouncing gaily towards them.... "I thought we should meet you.... What beautiful weather, isn't it? How d'ye do, sir? (to Mr. Stephenson). I think you were among our young ladies' partners last night?... Charming ball, wasn't it?... Dear Major Allen, do look at these Bristol stones! ain't they as bright as diamonds?... Well, Agnes, you have had your luncheon, I suppose, with the dear girls, and now you will be ready to go shopping with me. We are going into Bristol, and I will take you with us."

Agnes listened to her doom in silence, and no more thought of appealing from it than the poor criminal who listens to his sentence from the bench; but Mr. Stephenson turned an imploring look on Mrs. Peters, which spoke so well what he wished to express, that, she exerted herself so far as to say, "We had hoped, Mrs. Barnaby, that you meant to have spared Agnes to us for the rest of the day, and we shall be much obliged if you will leave her with us."

"You are always very kind, dear Margaret," returned the widow, "but I really want Agnes just now.... She shall come to you, however, some other time.... Good-b'ye! good-b'ye!—we have no time to lose.... Come, Agnes, let's be off."

A silent look was all the leave-taking that passed between Agnes and her greatly annoyed friends. Mrs. Barnaby took her arm under her own, and as soon as they quitted the shop bestowed the other on Major Allen; she was in high spirits, which found vent in a loud laugh as soon as they had turned the corner.

"What a stuck-up fellow that great tall Colonel is, Major Allen," said she. "Do you know anything of him?... If I am not greatly mistaken, he is as proud as Lucifer."

"I assure you, if he is proud, my dear madam, it must be a pride of the very lowest and vilest kind, merely derived from the paltry considerations of family and fortune; for, entre nous, he is very far from having been a distinguished officer. The Duke of Wellington, indeed, has always been most ridiculously partial to him; but you," lowering his voice, "you are a pretty tolerable judge of what his good opinion is worth."

"Yes, yes, Major.... I shall never be taken in there again.... Why, Agnes, how you drag, child! I shall be tired to death before I get to Bristol if you walk so."

"Will the young lady take my other arm?" said the Major.

"Thank you, dear Major!... You are very kind. Go round, Agnes, and take the Major's arm."

"No, I thank you, aunt; I do not want any arm. I will walk beside you, if you please, without taking hold of you at all."

"Nonsense, child!... That will look too particular, Major," ... said the widow, turning to him; upon which, without waiting further parley, Major Allen dropped the arm he held, and gaily placed himself between the two ladies, saying, "Now then, fair ladies, I have an arm for each."

Agnes felt the greatest possible longing to run away; but whether it would have strengthened into a positive resolution to do so, upon once more feeling the touch of the Major's hand, which upon her retreating he very vigorously extended towards her, it is impossible to say, for at that moment the sound of a rapidly-advancing pair of boots was heard on the pavement behind them, and in the next Mr. Stephenson was at her side. He touched his hat to Mrs. Barnaby, and then addressing Agnes said, "If you are going to walk to Bristol, I hope you will permit me to accompany you, ... for I am going there too."

Agnes very frankly replied, "Thank you!" and without a moment's hesitation accepted the arm he offered.

"I am sure you are very obliging, Mr. Stephenson," said Mrs. Barnaby, "and we shall certainly be able to walk with much greater convenience. I think you two had better go before, and then we can see that you don't run off, you know."

This lively sally was followed by a gay little tittering on the part both of the Major and the lady, as they stood still for Mr. Stephenson and the suffering Agnes to pass them.

The young man seemed to have lost all his vivacity: he spoke very little, and even that little had the air of being uttered because he felt obliged to say something. Poor Agnes was certainly in no humour for conversation, and would have rejoiced in his silence, had it not made her feel that whatever might be the motive for his thus befriending her, he derived no pleasure from it. Ere they had walked a mile, however, an accident occurred which effectually roused him from the dejection that appeared to have fallen upon his spirits. A herd of bullocks met them on the road, one of which, over-driven and irritated by a cur that worried him, darted suddenly from the road up to the path, and made towards them with its horns down, and its tail in the air. On seeing this, the young man seized Agnes in his arms, and sprang with her down the bank into the road. The animal, whose object was rather to leave an enemy behind him, than to do battle with any other, passed on towards the Major and his fair companion, who were at a considerable distance behind, leaving Agnes trembling indeed, and somewhat confused, but quite unhurt, and full of gratitude for the prompt activity that had probably saved her. As soon as she had in some degree recovered her composure, she turned back to ascertain how her aunt had fared, Mr. Stephenson assiduously attending her, and they presently came within sight of a spectacle that, had any mirth been in them, must have drawn it forth.

Major Allen, by no means approving the style in which the animal appeared inclined to charge them, had instantly perceived, as Mr. Stephenson had done before, that the only means of getting effectually out of its way was by jumping down the bank, which at that point was considerably higher than it was a few hundred yards farther on; nevertheless, though neither very light nor very active, he might have achieved the descent well enough had he been alone. But what was he to do with Mrs. Barnaby? She uttered a piercing cry, and threw herself directly upon his bosom, exclaiming, "Save me, Major!—save me!"

In this dilemma the Major proved himself an old soldier. To shake off the lady, he felt (in every sense of the word) was quite impossible; but there was no reason that she should stifle him; and therefore grasping her with great ardour, he half carried, half pushed her towards the little precipice, and skilfully placing himself so that, if they fell, she should fall first, he cried out manfully, "Now spring!" And spring they did, but in such a sort, that the lady measured her length in the dust, a circumstance that greatly broke the Major's fall; for, although he made a considerable effort to roll beyond her, he finally pitched with his knees full upon her, thus lessening his descent very materially.

When the young people reached them, they had both recovered their equilibrium, but not their composure. Major Allen was placed with one knee in the dust, and on the other supporting Mrs. Barnaby, who, with her head reclining on his shoulder, seemed to have a very strong inclination to indulge herself with a fainting fit. Her gay dress was lamentably covered with dust, her feathers broken and hanging distressingly over her eyes, and her whole appearance, as well as that of the hero who supported her, forlorn and dejected in the extreme.

"Are you hurt, aunt?" said Agnes, approaching her.

"Hurt!... am I hurt?... Gracious Heaven! what a question! If my life be spared, I shall consider it little short of a miracle.... Oh! Major Allen," she continued with a burst of sobbing, "where should I have now been ... but for you?..."

"Trampled or tossed, Mrs. Barnaby ... trampled or tossed to death decidedly," replied the Major, not wishing to lessen her sense of obligation, yet restrained by the presence of witnesses from expressing his feelings with all the ardour he might otherwise have shown.

"Most true!—most true!" she replied. "Never shall I be able to express the gratitude I feel!"

"Can you not stand up, aunt?" said Agnes, whose cheeks were crimsoned at the absurdity of the scene. "How will you be able to get home if you cannot stand?"

"God knows, child!... God only knows what is yet to become of me.... Oh! Major, I trust myself wholly to you."

Poor Agnes uttered a sound not much unlike a groan, upon which Stephenson, on whom it fell like a spur, urging him to save her from an exhibition so painfully ridiculous, (for it was quite evident that Mrs. Barnaby was not really hurt,) proposed that he should escort Miss Willoughby with all possible speed back to Clifton, and dispatch thence a carriage to bring Mrs. Barnaby home.

Major Allen, who desired nothing more ardently than to get rid of him, seconded the proposal vehemently.

"You are quite right, sir; it is the only thing to be done," he said; "and if you will hasten to perform this, I will endeavour so to place Mrs. Barnaby as to prevent her suffering any great inconvenience while waiting till the carriage shall arrive."

"Ought I not to remain with my aunt?" said Agnes to Mr. Stephenson, but in a whisper that was heard only by himself.

"In my opinion, you certainly ought not," he replied in the same tone. "Believe me," he added, "I have many reasons for saying so."

Nothing but her earnest desire to do that, whatever it might be, which was the least improper, (for that, as she truly felt, was all that was left her,) could have induced Agnes to propose inflicting so terrible a penance on herself; but strangely as she was obliged to choose her counsellor, there was a grave seriousness in his manner which convinced her he had not answered her lightly; and therefore, as her aunt said not a word to detain her, she set off on her return with as much speed as she could use, saying as she departed, "Depend upon it, aunt, there shall be no delay."

Mr. Stephenson again offered her his arm; but she now declined it, and the young man for some time walked silently by her side, wishing to speak to her, yet honestly doubting his own power of doing so with the composure he desired.

At length, however, the silence became embarrassing, and he broke it by saying, with something of abruptness,—

"Will you forgive me, Miss Willoughby, if I venture to forget for a moment how short a time it is since I have had the happiness of knowing you, ... will you forgive me if I speak to you like a friend?"

"Indeed I will, and be very thankful too," replied Agnes composedly, ... for his manner had taught her to feel assured that she had no cause to fear him.

"You are very kind," he resumed, with some little embarrassment; "but I feel that it is taking an almost unwarrantable liberty; and were it not that this walk offers an opportunity which I think I ought not to lose, I might perhaps endeavour to say what I wish to Mrs. Peters.... I allude to Major Allen, Miss Willoughby! I wish you could lead your aunt to understand that he is not a person fit for your society. Though he is probably a stranger here, he is well known elsewhere as a needy gambler, and, in short, a most unprincipled character in every way."

"Good Heaven!" exclaimed Agnes, "what shall I do?"

"Can you not venture to hint this to your aunt?" said he.

"She would probably be very angry," replied Agnes with spontaneous frankness; "but what is worse than that, she would, I know, insist upon my telling her where I heard it."

"Say that you heard it from me, Miss Willoughby," replied the young man.

New as Agnes was to the world and its ways, she felt that there was something very honourable and frank in this proceeding, and it produced so great a degree of confidence in return, that she answered in a tone of the most unembarrassed friendliness.

"Will you give me leave, Mr. Stephenson, to repeat this to Mrs. Peters and Mary?... They will know so much better than I do what use to make of it."

"Indeed I think you are right," he replied eagerly, "and then the anger that you speak of will not fall on you."

"It will not in that case, I think, fall on any one," said Agnes. "My aunt has fortunately a great respect for Mrs. Peters; and if anybody can have influence over her mind, she may."

Can it be wondered at if, after this, the conversation went on improving in its tone of ease and confidence? It had begun, on the side of the young man, with a very sincere resolution not to suffer his admiration for his lovely companion to betray him into a serious attachment to one so unfortunately connected; but, before they reached Sion Row, he had arrived at so perfect a conviction that he could nowhere find so pure-minded and right-thinking a being to share his fortune, and to bless his future life, that he only refrained from telling her so from a genuine feeling of respect, which perhaps the proudest peeress in the land might have failed to inspire.

"No," thought he, "it is not now, while she is compelled by accident to walk beside me, that I will pour out my heart and all its love before her, but the time shall come...."

Agnes, ere they parted again, appealed to him for his opinion whether she ought to go in the carriage sent to meet her aunt.

"No, indeed, I think not," he replied. "Has she no maid, Miss Willoughby, who could go for her?"

"Oh yes!" exclaimed Agnes, greatly relieved; "I can send Jerningham."

"Sweet creature!" whispered the enamoured Frederick to his heart, "what a delicious task to advise, to guide, to cherish such a being as that!"

His respectful bow at parting, the earnest, silent, lingering look he fixed upon her fair face ere he turned from the door that was opened to receive her, might have said much to a heart on the qui vive to meet his, half way; but Agnes did not observe it; she was looking up towards the windmill, and thinking of her early morning walk and its termination.

CHAPTER VI

THE READER IS LET INTO A SECRET, AND THE YOUNG LADY'S PLOT PROVED TO BE OF NO AVAIL—A JUDICIOUS MODE OF OBTAINING INFORMATION—A HAPPY AND VERY WELL-TIMED MEETING.

"Well, Mary!... I suppose you are wishing yourself joy on the success of your plottings and plannings," said Mrs. Peters to her daughter about ten days after this memorable walk on the Bristol road, for during that interval much had occurred that seemed to promise success to her wishes. In fact, Frederick Stephenson had quietly become a regular visitor at Rodney Place, and the power of Agnes to accept the constant invitations which brought her there likewise increased in exact proportion to the widow's growing delight in the tête-à-tête visits of the Major. The friendly hint of Mr. Stephenson had produced no effect whatever, excepting indeed that it tended greatly to increase the tone of friendly intercourse between the Peters family and himself. He had released Agnes from the task of mentioning the matter at all, and took an early opportunity of confiding to Mrs. Peters his ideas on the subject. She received the communication with the gratitude it really deserved, but confessed that Mrs. Barnaby was a person so every way disagreeable to her, that the task of attempting to guide her would be extremely repugnant to her feelings.

"But Miss Willoughby!..." said Frederick; "it is for her sake that one would wish to keep this odious woman from exposing herself to ruin and disgrace, if possible."

"And for her sake I will do it," answered Mrs. Peters. "She is as deserving of all care as her aunt is unworthy of it."

This reply convinced Mr. Stephenson that Mrs. Peters was one of the most discerning as well as most amiable women in the world, but no other advantage arose from the praiseworthy determination of the "dear Margaret;" for when that lady said to her gravely, at the very first opportunity she could find,—

"Pray, Mrs. Barnaby, do you know anything of that Major Allen's private character?" The answer she received was,—"Yes, Mrs. Peters, a great deal, ... and more, probably, than any other person whatever at Clifton; ... and I know, too, that there are agents—paid, hired agents—employed in circulating the most atrocious lies against him."

"I am not one of them, I assure you, madam," said Mrs. Peters, abruptly leaving her seat, and determined never again to recur to the subject; a comfortable resolution, to which she reconciled her conscience by remembering the evident devotion of Mr. Stephenson to Agnes, the symptoms of which were daily becoming less and less equivocal.

It was within a few hours after this short colloquy with the widow, that Mrs. Peters thus addressed her daughter, "Well, Mary!... I suppose you are wishing yourself joy on the success of your plottings and plannings."

"Why, yes," ... replied Mary; "I think we are getting on pretty well, and unless I greatly mistake, it will be the fault of Agnes, and of no one else, if she suffers much more from being under the protection of our precious aunt Barnaby."

Mrs. Peters and Mary were perfectly right in their premises, but utterly wrong in their conclusion. Mr. Stephenson was indeed passionately in love with Agnes, and had already fully made up his mind to propose to her, so soon as their acquaintance had lasted long enough to render such a step decently permissable, which, according to his calculations, would be in about a fortnight after he had first danced with her. In short, he was determined to find a favourable opportunity, on the evening of Mrs. Peters's promised music party, to declare his passion to her; for he had already learned to know that few occasions offer, in the ordinary intercourse of society, more favourable for a tête-à-tête than a crowded concert-room.

Thus far, therefore, the observations and reasonings of Agnes's watchful friends were perfectly correct. But, alas! they saw only the surface of things. There was an under current running the other way of which they never dreamed, and of which, even had it been laid open to their view, they would neither have been able to comprehend or believe the power. As to the heart of Agnes, by some strange fatality they had never taken it into their consideration at all, or at any rate had conceived it so beyond all doubt inclined the way they wished, that no single word or thought amidst all their deliberations was ever bestowed upon it.... But the heart of Agnes was fixedly, devotedly, and for ever given to another.

No wonder, indeed, that such an idea had never suggested itself to her friends, ... for who could that other be?... Could it be James, her first partner, her first walking companion, and very nearly the first young man she had ever spoken to in her life?... Assuredly not; for had she been asked, she could not have told whether his eyes were blue or black, hardly whether he were short or tall, and certainly not whether she had seen him twenty times, or only twelve, since their first meeting.

Who, then, could it be? There was but one other person whom the accidents of the last important fortnight had thrown constantly in her way; and Mrs. Peters and Mary would as soon have thought that the young Agnes had conceived a passion for the Pope, as for the stately, proud, reserved Colonel Hubert.

Yet "she could an if she would" have told her how far above all other mortals his noble head rose proudly, ... she could have told that on his lofty brow her soul read volumes, ... she could have told that in the colour of his thoughtful eye, the hue of heaven seemed deepened into black by the rich lash that shaded it.... All this she could have told; and, moreover, could have counted, with most faithful arithmetic, not only how many times she had seen him, but how many times his eyes had turned towards her, how many times he had addressed a word to her, how many smiles had been permitted to cheer her heart, how many frowns had chilled her spirit as they passed over his countenance.... Little could any one have guessed all this, but so it was; and Frederick Stephenson, with all his wealth, his comeliness, and kind heart to boot, had no more chance of being accepted as a husband by the poor, dependant Agnes Willoughby than the lowest hind that ploughs the soil by the proudest lady that owns it.

Meanwhile my real heroine, the Widow Barnaby, thought little of Agnes, or any other lady but herself, and less still perhaps of Mr. Stephenson, or any other gentleman but the Major. The affair on the Bristol road, though injurious to her dress, and rather dusty and in some degree disagreeable at the time, had wonderfully forced on the tender intimacy between them. Yet Mrs. Barnaby was not altogether so short-sighted as by-standers might suppose; and though she freely permitted herself the pleasure of being made love to, she determined to be very sure of the Major's rent-roll before she bestowed herself and her fortune upon him; for, notwithstanding her flirting propensities, the tender passion had ever been secondary in her heart to a passion for wealth and finery; and not the best-behaved and most discreet dowager that ever lived, was more firmly determined to take care of herself, and make a good bargain, "if ever she married again," than was our flighty, flirting Widow Barnaby.

She was fully aware that many difficulties lay in the way of her getting the information she wanted. In the first place, she had no acquaintance except the Peterses, who were his declared enemies; and she loved both justice and the Major too well to let his happiness (which was now avowedly dependant upon her accepting his hand) rest on such doubtful testimony.... And secondly, there was considerable caution required in the manner of asking questions so special as those she wished to propose, lest they might reach the ears of her lover; and it was necessary, if the tender affair finally terminated in wedlock, that it should be brought about without any appearance on her side of such sordid views, lest a suspicion might arise on his that her own wealth was not quite so great as she wished him to believe. Respecting settlements, she had already decided upon what she should propose ... she would make over the whole of her fortune unconditionally to him, provided he would make her a settlement of one poor thousand a-year for life in return.

Some days passed away after the Major had actually proposed and been conditionally accepted ... in case a few weeks' longer acquaintance confirmed their affection ... before Mrs. Barnaby had discovered any method by which she might satisfy her anxious curiosity respecting the actual state of Major Allen's affairs. During this time she was willing to allow, even to herself, that her affections were very deeply engaged, but yet she steadfastly adhered to her resolution of not bestowing upon him the blessing of her hand, till she learned from some one besides himself that he was a man of large fortune.

At length, when almost in despair of meeting with any one whom she could trust on such a subject, it occurred to her that Betty Jacks, who had not only continued to grow till she was nearly as tall as her mistress, but had made such proficiency in the ways of the world since she left Silverton, as rendered her exceedingly acute, might make acquaintance with Major Allen's groom, and learn from him what was generally considered to be the amount of his master's income. The idea had hardly struck her before she determined to put it in execution; and having rung the bell, Betty, after the usual interval that it took her to climb from the kitchen, stood before her.

"Come in, Jerningham," said Mrs. Barnaby, "and shut the door. I have something particular that I wish to say to you."

Betty anticipated a scolding, and looked sulky.

"I am very well satisfied with you, Jerningham," resumed the lady, "and I called you up chiefly to say that you may have the cap with the pink ribbons that I put off yesterday morning."

"Thank you, ma'am," said Betty, turning to go.

"Stay a moment, Jerningham: I have something I want to talk to you about."

Betty advanced, and took hold of the back of a chair to support her lengthy person, a habit which she had fallen into from the frequent long confidential communications her lady was accustomed to hold with her.

"Pray, Jerningham, do you know Major Allen's groom?" inquired Mrs. Barnaby in a gentle voice.

"Lor! no, ma'am; how should I come for to know his groom?"

"Nay, my good girl, there would be no harm in it if you did. I have remarked that he is a particularly smart, respectable-looking servant, and I must say I think it would be quite as well if such a good-looking girl as you did make acquaintance with the servant of a gentleman like Major Allen; it would give you a proper protector and companion, Jerningham, in a Sunday evening walk, or anything of that kind; and really it looks as if he did not think you worth noticing, considering how intimate the two families are become."

"Oh! for that, ma'am, I don't believe the young man would have any objection; and I don't mean to say as how I never spoke to him," replied Betty.

"Very well, Jerningham, that is just what I wanted to know; because, if you are sufficiently acquainted to speak, such a sharp clever girl as you are, would find it easy enough to improve the intimacy, and that's what I want you to do, Jerningham. And then I want you, some fine evening, perhaps, after I have had my tea, to let him take a walk with you; and when you are talking of one thing and the other, I want you to find out whether his master is reckoned a rich gentleman or a poor one.... Do you understand, Jerningham?"

Betty Jack's black eyes kindled into very keen intelligence at this question, and she answered with very satisfactory vivacity, "Yes, ma'am, I understands."

"Well, then, set about it as soon as you can; and remember, Jerningham, if he asks any questions about me, that you make him understand my fortune is a great deal larger than it appears to be, which it really is, you know,—only just now I am travelling quietly by way of a change. If you do all this cleverly and well, I will give you my old parasol, which only wants a stitch or two to make it quite fit to use."

"Thankee, ma'am.... I could find him in a minute at the beer-shop, if you like it."

"Well, then, do so, my good girl, and you may say, if you will, that you could take a walk with him this evening."

The arrangement was probably made without great difficulty, for on the following morning Betty was ready with her report. Any detailed account of the interview between the Major's man and the widow's woman would be unnecessary, as the girl's account of it was what principally affected the interests of our widow, and that shall be faithfully given.

Betty Jacks made her appearance in the drawing-room as soon as Agnes had left it after breakfast, with that look of smirking confidence which usually enlivens the countenance of a soubrette when she knows she has something to say worth listening to.

Her anxious mistress instantly saw that the commission had not been in vain.

"Well, Jerningham!" she cried with a deep respiration that was more like panting than sighing, "what news do you bring me?"

"All that is best and honourablest for the Major, ma'am. His man William says that he is a noble gentleman every way, with plenty of money to spend, and plenty of spirit to spend it with; and that happy will the lady be who wins his heart, and comes to the glory and honour of being his wife."

"That is enough, Jerningham," said the happy Mrs. Barnaby.... "You seem to have behaved extremely well, and with a great deal of cleverness; and as I see I may trust to your good sense and prudent behaviour, I will give you leave to go to the play at Bristol, and will give you a gallery ticket any evening that the Major's worthy and faithful servant may like to take you.... Indeed, I should not mind giving him a gallery ticket too, and so you may tell him."

Betty Jacks turned her head to look out of the window, and a furtive sort of smile kindled in her eye for a moment; but she thanked her mistress for her kindness, and then made her exit with great decorum.

It was just two days after this that Mrs. Barnaby yielded to Major Allen's request that she would taste the air of a delicious morning by taking a little turn with him in the Mall. Twice had they enjoyed the sunny length of the pavement, indulging in that sort of tender conversation which their now fully avowed mutual attachment rendered natural, when, in making their third progress, they were met by a gentleman somewhat younger than the Major, but with much his style of dress and whiskered fashion, who, the instant he saw Major Allen, uttered a cry of joy, ran towards him, and caught his hand, which he not only shook affectionately, but even pressed to his heart with an air of the most touching friendship.

"My dearest Maintry!" exclaimed the Major, "what an unexpected pleasure is this!... When did you reach England?... What brings you here?..." Then, suddenly recollecting himself, he turned to Mrs. Barnaby, and entreated her forgiveness for the liberty he had taken in thus stopping her.

"But I well know," he added, "that your generous heart will find an excuse for me in its own warm feelings, when I tell you that Captain Maintry is the oldest friend I have in the world—the oldest and the dearest.... We have served together, Mrs. Barnaby ... we have fought side by side through many a well-contested field ... and since universal peace has sheathed our swords, we have shared each other's hospitality, hunted on each other's grounds, studied nature and mankind together, and, in a word, have lived and loved as brothers, ... and yet we have now been parted for two years. A large property has devolved to him from his mother's family in Westphalia, and the necessity of attending to his farms and his signioral privileges, has separated him thus long from his friend.... You will forgive me, then, my beloved Martha!... Maintry ... from thee I can hide nothing!... you have told me a thousand times that I should never be brought to resign my freedom to mortal woman.... Look here!... and tell me if you can wonder that such vaunting independence can attach to me no longer?"

Nothing could be more kind than Mrs. Barnaby's reply to this, nothing more gracious than Captain Maintry's flattering answer; and the next minute they were all walking on together as if already united by the tenderest ties. Many interesting questions and answers passed between the two gentlemen concerning absent friends of high rank and great distinction, as well as some good-natured friendly questions on the part of Captain Maintry relative to many of the Major's principal tenants in Yorkshire, as honourable to the kind feelings of the inquirer as to the good conduct and respectability of the worthy individuals inquired for.

After all this had lasted most agreeably for some time, Captain Maintry suddenly paused, and said to his friend,—

"My dear Allen, the pleasure of seeing you, and the unexpected introduction to this honoured lady, have together turned my brain, I believe, or I should have told you at once that I have brought letters from Prince Hursteinberg for you which require an immediate answer. I never heard one man speak of another as he does of you, Allen; he declares you are the most noble character he ever met with in any country, and that is no light thing for such a man as the Prince to say. His letter is to ask whether you can spare him a hunting mare of your own breeding, and three couple of those famous pointers for which your principal estate is so celebrated. He made me promise that I would see that you sent off an answer by the first post, for if you cannot oblige him in this, he must apply elsewhere. You know his passion for la chasse, and he must not be disappointed. Come, my dear fellow ... tear yourself away from this attractive lady for one short hour, and then the business will be done."

"Certainly not till I have seen Mrs. Barnaby safely home," replied the Major gravely.

"Then you will be too late for the post.... We have told Mrs. Barnaby that we are brothers ... let her see you treat me as such.... Trust her to my care; I will escort her to her own home while you go for an hour or so to yours. I have left the packet with your faithful William.... By the by, I am glad to see that you still retain that capital good fellow about you.... An honest servant is worth his weight in gold, Mrs. Barnaby.... There, Allen, you see, I am in possession of the lady's arm; so you may be off, and I will join you as soon as I have escorted her to her quarters."

"Most cordially do I congratulate my friend, madam," said Captain Maintry, as soon as Major Allen had taken his leave, "on the happy prospects that have opened before him.... To see you, and not appreciate his felicity, is impossible. Friendship may conquer envy, but it cannot render us blind!... Nor is it Major Allen alone whom I must congratulate; ... permit me to indulge my feelings towards that long-tried and dearly-valued friend, by telling you, Mrs. Barnaby, that you are a very happy woman indeed!... Such worth, such honour, are rarely—alas! too rarely—met with in man. And then he has such a multitude of minor good qualities, as I may call them, such an absence of all ostentation ... nobody would believe from his manner of living that he possessed one of the finest estates in Yorkshire ... yet such is the fact.... His courage, too, is transcendently great, and his temper the sweetest in the world!... Yet this man, Mrs. Barnaby, great and good as he is, has not been able to escape enemies.... You have no idea of the lies that have been put in circulation concerning him by those who envy his reputation, and hate his noble qualities."

"I know it, Captain Maintry, but too well," replied Mrs. Barnaby; ... "but a woman who could be influenced by such idle and malevolent reports, would be unworthy to become his wife; and for myself, I can assure you that, far from its producing the desired effect upon me, such malignity only binds me to him more closely."

"There spoke a heart worthy of him!" fervently exclaimed the Captain.... "And I doubt not, my dearest madam, that these generous feelings will be put to the proof, for ... I blush for my species as I say it ... there are many who, when they hear of his approaching happiness, will put every sort of wickedness in action to prevent it."

This conversation, with a few little amiable sentiments in addition from both parties, brought them to the door of the widow's home, when Captain Maintry resisted her invitation to enter upon the plea that he must devote every moment he could command to his friend, as unhappily he was obliged to return to Bath, on business of the greatest importance, with as little delay as possible.

After this it was quite in vain that even the amiable, soft-hearted Elizabeth,—who had grown exceedingly ashamed, by the by, of her speaking acquaintance with Major Allen,—it was in vain that even she ventured to hint that she believed Major Allen was no longer invited anywhere.... Mrs. Barnaby knew all about it, on better authority than any one else; and she quietly made up her mind to leave Clifton and proceed to Cheltenham as speedily as possible, in order that her marriage, within seven months of her husband's death, might not take place under the immediate observation of his nearest relations.

CHAPTER VII

TRANSIENT HAPPINESS—AN ACCIDENT, LEADING TO THE DISCOVERY OF AN UNKNOWN TALENT IN MISS WILLOUGHBY, AND UNEXPECTED APPRECIATION OF IT IN COLONEL HUBERT—SOME REFLECTIONS ON THE PECULIARITIES OF THE FEMALE MIND.

It must be remembered that all these interesting particulars respecting the affairs of Mrs. Barnaby's heart were perfectly unknown both to Agnes and her friends. It had, indeed, been quite as much as the posthumous affection of Mrs. Peters for her brother could achieve, to endure with some appearance of civility the advances of his widow towards intimacy; but to pursue her with attentions when she seemed desirous of escaping them, was quite beyond her strength and courage; so, rejoicing in the effect without investigating the cause, she permitted her to keep herself within the retirement of her own drawing-room without ever seeking the reason of her so doing.

Treacherous as was this interval of calm, it was productive of most exquisite happiness to poor Agnes while it lasted. Delightful walks, abundance of books, lively conversation, and a thousand flattering marks of kindness from everybody who came near her, formed a wonderful contrast to the vulgar brow-beating of her selfish aunt, and even to the best joys of her solitary closet.

But it was an interval delusive in every way. Mrs. Peters had no suspicion that her brother's widow, within seven months after his death, was on the eve of marriage with a pennyless swindler.

Agnes had no suspicion that she was herself desperately in love with Colonel Hubert, or that Mr. Stephenson was desperately in love with her.

Colonel Hubert began to think, that, as he saw Agnes constantly with the Peters family, and no longer saw Mrs. Barnaby at all, the connexion between them was neither so permanent nor so injurious as he had supposed, and therefore that he would act more prudently by letting matters take their course, than by any further interference; convinced that, if Frederick did choose a wife for himself, instead of permitting his friends to choose for him, he would never find a woman more likely to do him honour than Miss Willoughby. There were, moreover, some other delusions under which he laboured, both as to his own feelings and those of others; but for the present he was destined, like the rest of the party among whom he lived, to remain enveloped in a mist of error and misconception.

Poor Stephenson, more fatally deluded than all of them, guessed not that he was standing on a pinnacle of hope from whence he was soon to be dashed a thousand fathom deep into the whirlpool of despair.... In short, preparations for the music party went on very prosperously, while

"Malignant Fate sat by and smiled"

at all that was to happen before that music party was over.

Mrs. Peters confessed, after a little battling the point with her family, that it would be impossible to avoid sending a card of invitation to Mrs. Barnaby, and sent it was; when, as she said herself, her virtue was rewarded by receiving through Agnes a message in return, expressing much regret that a previous engagement must prevent its being accepted.

On the morning of the day fixed for this party Agnes remained in her closet at least one hour beyond the time at which it was now her daily custom to set off from Rodney Place, some little preparation for her evening appearance requiring her attention. When at length she arrived there she found a note desiring her to sit down, and wait for the return of the ladies, who, after remaining at home till beyond her usual time of coming, had all driven to Bristol to execute sundry errands of importance.

On reading this note, Agnes walked up stairs to the drawing-room, which she found uncarpeted, in preparation for the music of the evening, and a grand pianoforte standing in the middle of it. Now it so happened that, notwithstanding the constant visits of Agnes in Rodney Place, and the general love of music which reigned there, she had never been asked if she could play or sing, and had never by any chance done either. There are some houses, and very pleasant ones, too, in their way, in which music is considered by the family as a sort of property belonging of right to them, en portage with professors indeed, but with which no one else can interfere,—at least within their precincts, without manifest impertinence. The house of Mrs. Peters was one of these. James, who, as we have seen, was an exceedingly amiable young man, never did anything from morning to night, if he could help it, but practise on the violoncello, and sing duets with his sister Lucy. Miss Peters was the only one who shared not in the talent or the monopoly, for Elizabeth played the harp, and Lucy sang and accompanied herself on the piano during by far the greater part of every day. Agnes was delighted by their performance; and though she longed once more to touch the keys herself, and perhaps to hear her own sweet voice again, she had never found courage sufficient to enable her to ask permission to do so.

When, therefore, she found herself perfectly alone, with the tempting instrument before her, and a large collection of music placed beside it, she eagerly applied her hand to try if it were open: it yielded to her touch, and in a moment her hands were running over the keys with that species of ecstasy which a young enthusiast in the science always feels after having been long deprived of the use of an instrument.

Agnes played correctly, and with great taste and feeling, but she could by no means compete with Lucy Peters as an accomplished pianiste; she had enjoyed neither equal practice nor equal instruction. But there was one branch of the "gay science" in which she excelled her far beyond the reach of comparison, for Agnes had a voice but rarely equalled in any country. Of the pre-eminence of her power she was herself profoundly ignorant, and if she preferred hearing her own glorious notes to those of any other voice which had yet reached her, she truly believed it was because there was such a very great pleasure in hearing one's-self sing,—an opinion that had been considerably strengthened by her observations on Lucy.

It was with very great delight, unquestionably, that Agnes now listened to the sounds she made. The size of the room, the absence of the carpet, the excellence and the isolation of the instrument, were all advantages she had not enjoyed before, and her pleasure was almost childish in its ecstasy. She let her rich voice run, like the lark's, into wanton playfulness of ornament, and felt her own power with equal joy and surprise.

But when this first out-pouring of her youthful spirit was over, she more soberly turned to the volumes beside her; and hesitating a moment between the gratification of exploring new regions of harmony with an uncertain step, and that of going through, with all the advantages of her present accessaries, what had so often enchanted her without them, she chose the last; and fixing upon a volume of Handel, which had been the chief source from which the old-fashioned but classic taste of Mr. Wilmot had made her master draw her subjects of study, she more soberly set about indulging herself with one of his best-loved airs. The notes of "Angels ever bright and fair," then swelled gloriously through the unpeopled room, and "Lord, remember David," followed. After this she "changed her hand," and the sparkling music of Comus seemed to make the air glad, as she carolled through its delicious melodies.

Amidst all this luxury of sound, it is not surprising that the knocker or the bell should give signal either of the return of the family, or the approach of some visiter, without the fair minstrel's being aware of it. This in fact occurred, and with a result that, had she been in the secret, would have converted the clear notes of her happy song into inarticulate "suspirations of forced breath."

Colonel Hubert had promised his friend Frederick, when they parted at the breakfast-table, to join him at Rodney Place, as he had often within the last few days done before, for the purpose of joining the party in their usual morning walk. But Frederick had arrived there so early, that he had handed Mrs. Peters and her daughters into their carriage when they set off for Bristol, and then turned from the door in despair of seeing Agnes for some hours.

Having sought his friend Hubert, and missed him, he betook himself to a gallop on the downs by way of beguiling the time till two o'clock, when he intended to make another attempt to meet her, by joining the luncheon party on Mrs. Peters's return. Colonel Hubert, meanwhile, knocked at that lady's door exactly at the moment when the happy performer in the drawing-room was giving full license to her magnificent voice in a passage of which he had never before felt the power and majesty.

Colonel Hubert stopped short in the midst of the message he was leaving; and the butler who opened the door to him, and who by this time knew him as one of the most honoured guests of the mansion, stepped back smiling into the hall,—a sort of invitation for him to enter, which he had no inclination to refuse. He accordingly stepped in, and the door was closed behind him.

"Pray, who is it that is singing?" inquired the Colonel, as soon as the strain ended.

"I think, sir, it must be Miss Willoughby, for I have let in nobody else since the ladies went," replied the man.

"Miss Willoughby!" repeated Colonel Hubert unconsciously; "Miss Willoughby!... Impossible!"

"I think, sir, by the sound," rejoined the servant, "that one of the drawing-room doors must be open; and if you would please to walk up, Colonel, you might hear it quite plain without disturbing her."

If Colonel Hubert had a weakness, it was his unbounded love for music, though even here he had proved his power of conquering inclination when he thought it right to do so. When quite a young man he had been tempted by this passion to give so much time to the study of the violin, as to interfere materially with all other pursuits. A friend, greatly his senior, and possessing his highest esteem, pointed out to him very strongly the probable effect of this upon his future career. The next time the beloved professor arrived to give Colonel Hubert a lesson, he made him a present of his violin, and gave up the pursuit for ever ... but not the love for it ... that Nature had implanted beyond the power of will to eradicate.

In short, this invitation from Mrs. Peters's butler was too tempting to be resisted, and nodding his approval of it to the man, he walked softly up the stairs, and found, as that sagacious person had foreseen, that the door of the back drawing-room was open. Colonel Hubert entered very cautiously, for the folding-doors between the two apartments were partly open also, but he was fortunate enough to glide unseen behind one of its large battants, the rising hinges of which were in such a position as to permit him, without any danger of being discovered, to see as well as hear the unsuspicious Agnes.

Poor girl! could she have been conscious of this, her agitation would have amounted to agony; and yet no imaginable combination of circumstances could have been so favourable to the first, the dearest, the most secret wish of her heart ... which was, that when she lost sight of him, which she must soon do,—as she well believed, for ever,—he might not think her too young, too trifling, too contemptible, ever to recall her to his memory again.

There was, perhaps, no great danger of this before; but now it could neither be hoped nor feared that Colonel Hubert should ever forget what he, during these short moments, heard and saw. There is perhaps no beautiful woman who sings well, who would not appear to greater advantage, if thus furtively looked at and listened to, than when performing, conscious of the observation of all around her. But to Agnes this advantage was in the present instance great indeed, for never before had he seen her beautiful countenance in the full play of bright intelligence and unrestrained enthusiasm, ... and never had he imagined that she could sing at all! She was lovely, radiant, inspired; and Colonel Hubert was in a fair way of forgetting equally that she was the chosen of his friend, the niece of Mrs. Barnaby, and that he was just twenty years her senior, when the house-door was assailed by the footman's authoritative rap, and the moment after the ladies' voices, as they ran up the stairs, effectually awakened him to the realities of his situation.

He now for the first time felt conscious that this situation had been obtained by means not perfectly justifiable, and that an apology was certainly called for, and must be made. He therefore retraced his steps, but with less caution, through the still open door; and meeting Mrs. Peters just as she reached the top of the stairs, said in a voice, perhaps somewhat less steady than usual,—

"Will you forgive me, Mrs. Peters, and plead for my forgiveness elsewhere, when I confess to you that I have stolen up stairs, and hid myself for at least half an hour in your back drawing-room, for the purpose of hearing Miss Willoughby sing?... She is herself quite ignorant of this délit; ... and when you pronounce to her my guilt, I hope, at the same time, you will recommend me to mercy."

"Miss Willoughby singing!" exclaimed Mrs. Peters; "surely you must be mistaken, Colonel Hubert.... Agnes never sang in her life."

"Agnes singing!... Oh no!..." cried Lucy; "that is quite impossible, I assure you."

"And what says the young lady herself?" replied Colonel Hubert, as Agnes came forward to meet her friends.

But she was assailed with such a clamorous chorus of questions, that it was some time before she in the least understood what had happened. To the reiterated.... "Have you really been singing, Agnes?..." "Do you really sing?..." "How is it possible we never found it out?..." and the like; she answered quietly enough, ... "I sing a little, and I have been trying to amuse myself while waiting for you." But when Mrs. Peters laughingly added, "And do you know, my dear, that Colonel Hubert has been listening to you from the back drawing-room all the time?" all semblance of composure vanished. She first coloured violently, and then turned deadly pale; and, totally unable to answer, sat down on the nearest chair instinctively, to prevent herself from falling, but with little or no consciousness of what she was about.

Colonel Hubert watched her with an eye which seemed bent upon reading every secret of the heart that so involuntarily betrayed its own agitation; but what he saw, or thought he saw there, seemed infectious, for he, too, lost all presence of mind; and quickly approaching her with heightened colour, and a voice trembling from irrepressible feeling, he said,—

"Have I offended you?... Forgive me, oh! forgive me!"

There was a world of eloquence in the look with which she met his eyes; innocent, unpractised, unconscious as it was, it raised a tumult in the noble soldier's breast which it cost many a day's hard struggle afterwards to bring to order. But nobody saw it—nobody guessed it. The whole bevy of kind-hearted ladies were filled, from the "crown to the toe," with the hope and belief that Frederick Stephenson and Agnes Willoughby were born for each other, and they explained all the agitation they now witnessed by saying,—

"Did any one ever see so shy a creature!"—"How foolish you are to be frightened about it, Agnes;" and ... "Come, my dear child, get the better of this foolish terror; and if you can sing, let us have the pleasure of hearing you."

"That's right, mamma!" said Lucy laughing; "make her sing one song before we go down to luncheon.... It is not at all fair that Colonel Hubert should be the only person in the secret."

"Sing us a song at once—there's a dear girl!" said Mrs. Peters, seating herself upon a sofa.

"Indeed, indeed, ma'am, I cannot sing!" replied Agnes, clasping her hands as if begging for her life.

"Upon my word, this is a very pretty mystery," said Mary. "The gentleman declares that he has been listening to her singing this half hour, and the lady protests that she cannot sing at all. Permit me, mamma, to examine the parties face to face. If I understand you rightly, Colonel Hubert, you stated positively that you heard Miss Willoughby sing. Will you give me leave to ask you in what sort of manner she sang?"

"In a manner, Miss Peters," replied Colonel Hubert, endeavouring to recover his composure, "that I have seldom or never heard equalled in any country.... She sings most admirably."

"Good, very good," said Mary; "a perfectly clear and decisive evidence. And now, Miss Willoughby, give me leave to question you. If I mistake not, you told us about five minutes ago that you possessed not the power of singing in any manner at all?"

"Not at this moment, Mary, certainly," replied Agnes rallying, and infinitely relieved by perceiving that the overwhelming emotion under which she had very nearly fainted, had neither been understood nor even remarked by any one.

"Then will you promise," said Lucy with tant soit peu of new-born rivalry, "will you promise to sing for us to-night?"

"You do not mean at your concert, do you, Lucy?" replied Agnes, laughing.

"And why not?" said Lucy. "Colonel Hubert declares that you sing admirably."

"Colonel Hubert is very kind to say so," answered Agnes, while rather more than her usual delicate bloom returned to her cheeks; "but he would probably change his opinion were he to hear me sing before a large party."

"I am too hungry to battle the point now, Agnes," said Mrs. Peters, "so let us come down to luncheon; but remember, my dear, if you really can sing, if it be only some easy trifling ballad, I shall not take it well of you if you refuse, for I am sorry to say there is a terrible falling off among our performers. I find three excuses sent since I went out; and I met Miss Roberts just now, our prima donna, after Lucy, who says she is so hoarse that she doubts if she shall be able to sing a note."

This was said as the party descended the stairs, so that Agnes escaped without being obliged to answer; at which she greatly rejoiced, as refusal or acquiescence seemed alike impossible.

Colonel Hubert stopped at the door of the dining-room, wished the party good morning, and persisted in making his retreat, though much urged by Mrs. Peters to join their meal. But he was in no mood for it—he wanted to be alone—he wanted in solitude to question, and, if possible, to understand his own feelings; and with one short look at Agnes he left them, slipped a crown into the hand of the butler who opened the door for him, and set off for a long walk over Durdham Downs, taking, as it happened, exactly the same path as that in which he had met Agnes a fortnight before.

As soon as he was gone, another rather clamorous assault was made on Agnes upon the subject of her having so long kept her power of singing a secret from them all.

"I cannot forgive you for not having at least told me of it," said Mary.

"And what was there to tell, my dearest Mary? You that are used to such playing as that of Elizabeth and Lucy, would have had fair cause to laugh at me, had I volunteered to amuse you in their stead."

"I don't know how that may be," said Lucy; "what Colonel Hubert talked about was your singing. Do you think you can sing as well as me?"

"It is a difficult question to answer, Lucy," replied Agnes with the most ingenuous innocence; "but perhaps I might, one of these days, if I were as well instructed as you are."

"Well, my dear, that is confessing something, at any rate," said Lucy, slightly colouring. "I am sure I should be very happy to have you in a duet with me, only I suppose you have not been taught to take a second."

"Oh yes!... I think I could sing second," replied Agnes with great simplicity; "but I have not been much used to it, because in all our duets Miss Wilmot always took the second part."

"And who is Miss Wilmot, my dear?" said Mrs. Peters.

"The daughter of the clergyman, mamma, where Agnes was educated," replied Mary.

"Here comes Mr. Stephenson," exclaimed Mrs. Peters gaily. "Now, Agnes, you positively must go up stairs again, and let us hear what you can do. I shall be quite delighted for Mr. Stephenson to hear you sing, if you really have a voice, for I have repeatedly heard him speak with delight of his sister, Lady Stephenson's, singing."

"Then I am sure that is a reason for never letting him hear mine," said Agnes, who was beginning to feel very restless, and longing as ardently for the solitude of her closet, in order to take a review of all the events of the morning, as Colonel Hubert for the freedom of the Downs. But the friends around her were much too kind and much too dear for any whims or wishes of her own to interfere with what they desired; and when, upon the entrance of Frederick, they all joined in beseeching her to give them one song, she yielded, and followed meekly and obediently to the pianoforte.

She certainly did not sing now as she had done before; the fervour, the enthusiasm was passed; yet, nevertheless, the astonishment and delight of her auditors were unbounded. Praises and reproaches were blended with the thanks of her female friends, who, forgetting that they had never invited her performance, seemed to think her having so long concealed her talent a positive injury and injustice. But in the raptures of Frederick Stephenson there was no mixture of reproach; he seemed rapt in an ecstasy of admiration and love, the exact amount of which was pretty fairly appreciated by every one who listened to him except herself. A knavish speech sleeps not so surely in a foolish ear, as a passionate rhapsody in one that is indifferent. Our Agnes was by no means dull of apprehension on most occasions; but the incapacity she shewed for understanding the real meaning of nineteen speeches out of every twenty addressed to her by Frederick, was remarkable. It is probable, indeed, that indifference alone would hardly have sufficed to constitute a defence so effectual against all the efforts he made to render his feelings both intelligible and acceptable; pre-occupation of heart and intellect may account for it better. But whatever the cause of this insensibility, it certainly existed, and in such a degree as to render this enforced exhibition, and all the vehement praises that followed it, most exceedingly irksome. A greater proof of this could hardly be given than by her putting a stop to it at last by saying,—

"If you really wish me to sing a song to-night, my dear Mrs. Peters, you must please to let me go now, or I think I shall be so hoarse as to make it impossible."

This little stratagem answered perfectly, and at once brought her near to the solitude for which she was pining.

"Wish you to sing to-night, petite?..." said Mrs. Peters, clapping her little hands with delight ... "I rather think I shall.... I have had the terror of Mrs. Armstrong before my eyes for the last fortnight, and I think, Mary, that we have a novelty here that may save us from the faint praise usually accorded by her connoisseur-ship...."

"I imagine we have, mamma," replied Mary, who was in every way delighted by the discovery of this unknown talent in her favourite. "But Agnes is right; she must really sing no more now.... You have had no walk to-day, Agnes, have you?" kindly adding, "if you like it, I will put on my bonnet again and take a stroll with you."

Agnes blushed when she replied,—"No, I have not time to walk to-day.... I must go home now;" much as she might have done if, instead of intending to take a ramble with her thoughts, she had been about to enjoy a tête-à-tête promenade with the object of them.

"At least we will walk home with you," replied her friend; and accordingly the two eldest girls and Mr. Stephenson accompanied her to Sion Row.

Ungrateful Agnes!... It was with a feeling of joy that made her heart leap that she watched the departure of her kind friends, and of him too who would have shed his blood for her with gladness ... in order that in silence and solitude she might live over again the moments she had passed with Hubert—moments which, in her estimation, outweighed in value whole years of life without him.

Dear and precious was her little closet now. There was nothing within it that ever tempted her aunt to enter; her retreat, therefore, was secure, and deeply did she enjoy the conviction that it was so. It was not Petrarch, it was not Shakspeare, no, nor Spencer's fairy-land, in which, when fancy-free, she used to roam for hours of most sweet forgetfulness, that now chained her to her solitary chair, and kept her wholly unconscious of the narrow walls that hemmed her in. But what a world of new and strange thoughts it was amidst which she soon lost herself!... Possibilities, conjectures, hopes, such as had never before entered her head, arose within her as, with a singular mixture of distinctness of memory and confusion of feeling, she lived again through every instant of the period during which Colonel Hubert had been in her presence, and of that, more thrilling still as she meditated upon it, when she unconsciously had been in his. How anxiously she recalled her attitude, the careless disorder of her hair, and the unmeasured burst of enjoyment to which she had yielded herself!... How every song she had sung passed in review before her!... Her graces, her roulades, her childish trials of what she could effect, all seemed to rise in judgment against her, and her cheeks tingled with the blushes they brought. Yet in the midst of this, perhaps,

... a sense of self-approving power
Mixed with her busy thought ...

and she felt that she was not sorry he had heard her sing.

Then came the glowing picture of the few short moments that followed the discovery ... the look that she had seen fixed upon her ... the voice that trembled as he asked to be forgiven ... his flushed cheek ... the agitation—yes, the agitation of his manner, of the stately Hubert's manner, as he approached, as he stood near, as he looked at, as he spoke to her! It was so; she knew it, she had seen it, she had felt it.... How strange is the constitution of the human mind!... and how mutually dependent are its faculties and feelings on each other!.... The same girl who was so "earthly dull" as to be unable to perceive the undisguised adoration of Frederick Stephenson, was now rapt in a delirium of happiness from having read, what probably no other mortal eye could see, in the involuntary workings of Colonel Hubert's features for a few short instants, while offering an apology which he could hardly avoid making.

We have left the Widow Barnaby too long, and must hasten back to her. There was altogether a strange mixture of worldly wisdom and of female folly in her character, for first one and then the other preponderated, as circumstances occurred. Had a man, richer than she believed the fascinating Major to be, proposed to her even at the very tenderest climax of his courtship, there is no doubt in the world but she would have accepted him, but when all her pecuniary anxieties were lulled into a happy doze by the pleasing statements of Messrs. William and Maintry, her love-making propensities awoke; she was again the Martha Compton of Silverton; and became so exceedingly attached to the Major's society, that neither Mrs. Peters's concert, nor any other engagement in which he did not share, could have compensated for one of those delightful tête-à-tête evenings during which Agnes enjoyed the society of her friends.

When Major Allen saw the invitation card from Rodney Place lying on the table, he said,—

"Do you intend to go, dearest?"

"Have you a card, Major?" was the reply; and when the rejoinder produced a negative, she added,—"Then most assuredly I shall not go;" a degree of fidelity that was very satisfactory to the Major, who began to discover that his newness in the society of Clifton was wearing off, and that he was eyed askance whenever he ventured to appear where gentlemen assembled.

A thousand fond follies, of course, diversified these frequent tête-à-têtes; and upon one occasion the Major in a sudden burst of jealous tenderness declared, that, notwithstanding the many proofs of affection she had granted him, there was one without which he could not be satisfied, as his dreams perpetually tormented him with visions of rivals who succeeded in snatching her from him.

"Oh! Major, what folly!" exclaimed the lady. "Have you not yet learned to read my heart?... But what is there ... foolish as you are ... what is there that I could refuse to you ... that it was not inconsistent with my honour to grant?..."

"Your honour!... Beautiful Juno! know you not that your honour is dearer to me than my own?... What I would ask, my beloved Martha, can attach no disgrace to you, ... but, in fact, I shall not know a moment's ease till you have given me a promise of marriage. I know, my love, that you have relations here who will leave no stone unturned to prevent our union, ... and the idea that they may succeed distracts me!... Will you forgive this weakness, and grant what I implore?"

"You know I will, foolish man!... but I will have your promise in return, or you will think my love less fervent than your own," returned the widow playfully.

To this the Major made no objection; and so, "in merry sport," these promises were signed and exchanged amidst many lover-like jestings on their own folly.

This happened just three days before the eventful concert; and in the interval Major Allen received a letter from his friend Maintry, who was still at Bath, requesting him to join him there in order to give him the advantage of his valuable advice on a matter of great importance. It was, of course, with extreme reluctance that he tore himself away; but it was a sacrifice demanded by friendship, and he would make it, as he told the widow, on condition that she would rescind her refusal to Mrs. Peters, and pass the evening of his absence at her house. She agreed to this, and he left her only in time to enable her to dress for the party.

The being accompanied by her aunt was a considerable drawback to any pleasure Agnes had anticipated from the evening, and the stroke came upon her by surprise, for Mrs. Barnaby did not deem it necessary to stand on such ceremony with her sister as to ask leave to come after having been once invited.

Mrs. Peters looked vexed and disconcerted when she entered; but, perceiving the anxiety with which Agnes was watching to see how she bore it, she recalled her smiles, placed her prodigiously fine sister-in-law on a sofa with two other dowagers, desired Mr. Peters to go and talk to her, and then seizing upon Agnes, led her among the party of amateurs who were indulging in gossip and tea at a snug table in the second drawing-room. She was immediately introduced as a young friend who would prove a great acquisition, and two or three songs in her own old-fashioned style were assigned, pretty nearly without waiting for her consent, to her performance; but with an observation from Mrs. Peters that she could not refuse, because they were the very songs she had sung when Mr. Stephenson was there in the morning.

All this was said and done in a bustle and a hurry, and Agnes carried off captive to the region where the business of the evening was already beginning with the tuning of instruments and the arrangement of desks, before she well knew what she intended to do or say. She would have felt the embarrassment more had her mind been fully present to the scene; but it was not. She knew that Mr. Stephenson and his friend were expected, and no spot of earth had much interest for her at that moment except the doorway.

Her suspense lasted not long, however, for they soon entered together, and then her heart bounded, the colour varied on her cheek, and her whole frame trembled. Mr. Stephenson was by her side in a moment; but she was conscious of this only sufficiently to make her feel a pang because Colonel Hubert had not followed him. Far from approaching her, indeed, he seemed to place himself studiously at a distance, and instantly a deep gloom appeared in the eyes of Agnes to have fallen upon every object.... The lights were dim, every instrument out of tune, and the civilities of Mr. Stephenson so extremely troublesome, that she thought, if they continued, she must certainly leave the room.

The overture began, and she was desired to sit down in the place assigned her; but this, as she found, left her open on one side to the pertinacious whisperings of Mr. Stephenson, and with a movement of irritation quite new to her, she got up again, with her cheeks burning, to ask for a place in the very middle of a row of ladies who could not comply with her request without real difficulty.

As soon as she had reached her new station she raised her eyes, and looked towards the spot where she had seen Colonel Hubert place himself; there he was still, and moreover his eyes were evidently fixed upon her.

"Why will he not speak to me?" mentally exclaimed poor Agnes; ... "or why does he so look at me?"

It would not have been difficult for Colonel Hubert to have given an answer. While they were taking coffee together half an hour before they set off, Frederick Stephenson told his friend that his fate would that night be decided, for he had made up his mind to propose to Miss Willoughby.

Colonel Hubert started.... "Of course, Frederick, you do not decide upon this without being pretty certain what the answer will be," was the reply of Colonel Hubert.

"You know the definition Silvius gives of love," returned Frederick. "It is to be all made of faith and service ... and so am I for Agnes.... Wherefore, as my service is, and shall be perfect, so also shall be my faith, nor will I ever submit myself to the misery of doubting.... Either she is mine at once, or I fly where I can never see her more."

After this, Colonel Hubert very naturally preferred looking on from a distance, to making any approach that might disturb the declared purpose of his friend.

"By-standers see most," ... is an old proverb, and all such speak truly. Frederick, notwithstanding his "perfect service," was not by many a degree so near discovering the true state of Miss Willoughby's feelings as his friend: not, indeed, that Colonel Hubert discovered anything relating to himself, but he saw weariness and distaste in the movement of Agnes's head, and the mournful expression of her face, even before the decisive manoeuvre by which she escaped from him, who was only waiting for an opportunity of confessing himself "to be all made of adoration, duty, and observance."

An indescribable sensation of pleasure tingled through the veins of Colonel Hubert as he observed this, but the next moment his heart reproached him with a bitter pang. "Am I then a traitor to him who has so frankly trusted me?" thought he. "No, by Heaven!... Poor Frederick!... Angel as she is, he well deserves her, for from the very first he has thought of her, and her only; ... while I ... the study of her aunt's absurdities I deemed the more attractive speculation of the two.... Agnes, you are avenged!"

The good-humoured Frederick, mean time, though foiled in his hope of engrossing her, quickly found consolation in listening to Miss Peters, who confided to him all her doubts and fears respecting the possibility of her friend's finding courage to sing before so large an audience.

"For God's sake, do not plague her about it," said he. "Though, to be sure, such a voice as hers would be enough to embellish any concert in the world."

"It is only on mamma's account," replied Mary, "that I am anxious for it; ... she has been so disappointed about Miss Roberts!... I wish, after Lucy's next duet with James, while Elizabeth is accompanying the violoncello, that you would contrive to get near her, where she is trying to keep out of the way, poor thing!... and tell her that my mother wishes to speak to her."

Frederick readily undertook the commission, not ill pleased to be thus confirmed in his belief that she had not run away from him, but for some other reason which he had not before understood. Miss Peters was far from imagining what an effectual means she had hit upon for making her friend Agnes take a place among the performers. She had continued to sit during the long duet, triumphing in the clever management that had placed her out of the way of everybody, and perfectly aware ... though she by no means appeared to watch him steadily ... that Colonel Hubert did not feel at all more gay or happy than herself. But, lo! just at the moment indicated by Mary, the smiling, bowing, handsome Frederick Stephenson contrived civilly and silently to make his way between crowded rows of full-dressed ladies to the place where Agnes fancied herself in such perfect security. He delivered his message, but not without endeavouring to make her understand how superlatively happy the commission had made him.

This was too much.... To sit within the same room that held Colonel Hubert, without his taking the slightest notice of her, and that, too, after all the sweet delusive visions of the morning, was quite dreadful enough, without having to find answers for words she did not hear, and dress her face in smiles, when she was so very much disposed to weep. "I will sing every song they will let me," thought she. "Ill or well, it matters not now.... I will bear anything but being talked to!"

Giving the eager messenger nothing but a silent nod in return for all his trouble, Agnes again rose, and made her way to Mrs. Peters.

It chanced that Mary, Lucy, and one or two other ladies were in consultation with her at a part of the room exactly within sight of Mrs. Barnaby, who, having found her neighbours civilly disposed to answer all her questions, had thus far remained tolerably contented and quiet. But the scene she now witnessed aroused her equally to jealousy and astonishment. Mrs. Peters—who, from the moment she had deposited her on the sofa, had never bestowed a single word upon her, but, on the contrary, kept very carefully out of her way,—had hitherto been supposed by her self-satisfied sister-in-law to be too much occupied in arranging the progress of the musical performance to have any time left to bestow upon her relations; yet now she saw her in the centre of the room, devoting her whole attention to Agnes, evidently presenting her to one or two of the most elegant-looking among her company, and finally taking her by the hand, as if she had been the most important personage present, and leading her with smiles, and an air of the most flattering affection, to the pianoforte.

"Who is that beautiful girl, ma'am?" said one of Mrs. Barnaby's talkative neighbours, thinking, perhaps, that she had a right, in her turn, to question a person who had so freely questioned her.

"What girl, ma'am?" returned Mrs. Barnaby; for use so lessens marvel, that she had become almost unconscious of the uncommon loveliness of her niece; or, at any rate, was too constantly occupied by other concerns to pay much attention to it.

"That young lady in black crape, whom Mrs. Peters has just led to the instrument.... Upon my word, I think she is the most beautiful person I ever saw!"

"Oh!... that's my niece, ma'am; ... and I'm sure I don't know what nonsense my sister Peters has got in her head about her.... I hope she is not going to pretend to play without asking my leave. It is time I should look after her." And so saying the indignant Mrs. Barnaby arose, determined upon sharing the notice at least, if not the favour, bestowed upon her dependant kinswoman. But she was immediately compelled to reseat herself by the universal "Hush!..." that buzzed around her; for at that moment the superb voice of Agnes burst upon the room, and "startled the dull ear" of the least attentive listener in it.

The effect was so wholly unlooked-for, and so great, that the demonstration of it might naturally have been expected to overpower so young a performer; Miss Peters, therefore, the moment the song was over, hastened to her friend, expecting to find her agitated, trembling, and in want of an arm to support her; but instead of this she found Agnes perfectly tranquil ... apparently unconscious of having produced any sensation at all in the company at large, and in fact looking, for the first time since she entered the room, happy and at her ease.

The cause of this could only be found where Miss Peters never thought of looking for it,—namely, in the position and countenance of Colonel Hubert. He had not, indeed, yet spoken much to her; but enough, at least, to convince her that he was not more indifferent than in the morning, and, ... in short, enough to raise her from the miserable state of dejection and annoyance which made her fly with such irritated feelings from the attentions of Frederick, to such a state of joyous hopefulness as made her almost giddily unmindful of every human being around her, save one.

Though Agnes had restlessly left the place whence she had first seen Colonel Hubert ensconce himself in a corner, apparently as far from her as possible, she chose another equally convenient for tormenting herself by watching him, and for perceiving also that nothing, save his own will and pleasure, detained him from her. From this, as we have seen, she was again driven by poor Frederick; and forgetting her shyness and all other minor evils in the misery of being talked to when her heart was breaking, she determined upon singing, solely to get out of his way.

Her false courage, however, faded fast as she approached the instrument. She remembered, with a keenness amounting almost to agony, those songs of the morning that she had since been rehearsing in spirit, in the dear belief that they had charmed away his stately reserve for ever; and she was desperately meditating the best mode of making a precipitate retreat, when, on reaching the spot kept sacred to the performers and their music-desks, she perceived Colonel Hubert in the midst of them, who immediately placed himself at her side, (where, according to rule, he had no business to be,) and asked her in a whisper, if she meant to accompany herself.

The revulsion of feeling produced by this most unexpected address was violent indeed. Her whole being seemed changed in a moment. Her heart beat, her eyes sparkled with recovered happiness, and she literally remembered nothing but that she was going to sing to him again. In answer to his question, she said with a smile that made him very nearly as forgetful of all around as herself, "Do you think I had better do it?... Or shall I ask Elizabeth?"

"No, no; ask no one," he replied.

"And what shall I sing?" again whispered Agnes.

"The last song you sang this morning," was the reply.

Orpheus was never inspired by a more powerful feeling than that which now animated the renovated spirit of Agnes, and she performed as she never had performed before.

The result was a burst of applause, that ought, selon les regles, to have been overpowering to her feelings; yet there she stood, blushing a little certainly, but looking as light-hearted and as happy as the Peri when readmitted into Paradise. Just at this moment, and exactly as Colonel Hubert was offering his arm to lead her back again to a place among the company, Mrs. Barnaby, feathered, rouged, ringleted, and desperately determined to share the honours of the hour, made her way, proud in the consciousness of attracting an hundred eyes, up to the conspicuous place where Agnes stood. She had already taken Colonel Hubert's arm, and for an instant he seemed disposed to attempt leading her off in the contrary direction; but if he really meditated so bold a measure, he was completely foiled, for Mrs. Barnaby, laying her hand on his in a very friendly way, exclaimed in her most fascinating style of vivacity,—

"No, no, Colonel ... you are vastly obliging; but I must take care of my own niece, if you please!... She sings just like her poor mother, my dear Mary," she added, changing her tone to a sentimental whine.... "I assure you it is almost too much for my feelings;" and as she said this she drew the unhappy Agnes away, having thrown her arm round her waist, while she kissed her affectedly on the forehead.

Colonel Hubert hovered about her for a few minutes; but whatever might be the fascinations that attracted him, they were apparently not strong enough to resist another personal attack from Mrs. Barnaby.

"What a crowd!" she exclaimed, suddenly turning towards him. "Do, Colonel, give me your arm, and we will go and eat some ice in the other room;" upon which he suddenly retreated among the throng, and in two minutes had left the house. It is true, that at the moment the widow so audaciously asked for his arm, Frederick Stephenson was just presenting his to Agnes, which it is possible might have added impulse to the velocity of this sudden exit; but whichever was the primary feeling, both together were more than he could bear; and accordingly, like many other conquered heroes, he sought safety in flight.

Of what happened in that room during the rest of the evening, poor Agnes could have given no account; to sing again she assured her friends was quite beyond her power, and she looked so very pale and so very miserable as she said this, that they believed she had really over-exerted herself; and, delighted by the brilliant success of her one song, permitted her to remain unmolested by further solicitations.

Frederick Stephenson also doubted not that the unusual effort she had made before so large a party was one cause of her evident dejection, though he could not but feel that the appearance and manner of her aunt were likely enough to increase this; but, at all events, it was no time to breathe into her ear the tale of love he had prepared for it; so, after asking Miss Peters if he should be likely to find her friend at Rodney Place on the following morning, and receiving from her a cordial ... "Oh! yes, certainly," he also took his leave, more in love than ever; and though mortified by the disappointment this long-expected evening had brought him, as sanguine as ever in his hopes for the morrow.

Mrs. Barnaby was one of the last guests that departed, as, next to the pleasure of being made love to, the gratification of finding herself in a large party, with the power of calling the giver of it her "dear sister," ranked highest in her present estimation. Agnes was anxiously waiting for her signal to depart; but no sooner was she shut up in the fly with her than she heartily wished herself back again, for a torrent of scolding was poured forth upon her as unexpected as it was painful.

"And it is thus, ungrateful viper as you are, that you reward my kindness!... Never have you deigned to tell me that you could sing ... no, you wicked, wicked creature, you leave me to find it out by accident; while your new friends, or rather new strangers, are made your confidants,—while I am to sit by and look like a fool, because I never heard of it before!..."

"It was only because there was a pianoforte there, aunt.... I cannot sing without one."

"Ungrateful wretch!... reproaching me with not spending my last shilling in buying pianofortes! But I will tell you, miss, what your fine singing shall end in.... You shall go upon the stage ... mark my words ... you shall go upon the stage, Miss Willoughby, and sing for your bread. No husband of mine shall ever be taxed to maintain such a mean-spirited, ungrateful, conceited upstart as you are!"

Agnes attempted no farther explanation; and the silent tears these revilings drew, were too well in accordance with her worn-out spirits and sinking heart to be very painful. She only longed for her closet, and the unbroken stillness of night, that she might shed them without fear of interruption.

But this was destined to be a night of disappointments, for even this melancholy enjoyment was denied her.

On arriving at their lodgings, the door was opened by the servant of the house; and when Mrs. Barnaby imperiously demanded, "Where is my maid?... where is Jerningham?" she was told that Jerningham had gone out, and was not yet returned.

Now Jerningham was an especial favourite with her mistress, being a gossip and a sycophant of the first order; and the delinquency of not being come home at very nearly one o'clock in the morning, elicited no expression of anger, but a good deal of alarm.

"Dear me!... what can have become of her?... Poor dear girl, I fear she must have met with some accident!... What o'clock was it when she went out?"... Such questionings lasted till the stairs were mounted, and the lady had entered her bed-room.

But no sooner did she reach the commode and place her candle upon it, than she uttered a tremendous scream, followed by exclamations which speedily explained to Agnes and the servant the misfortune that had befallen her. "I am robbed—I am ruined!... Look here!... look here!... my box broken open, and every farthing of money gone.... All my forks too!... all my spoons, and my cream-jug, and my mustard-pot!... I am ruined—I am robbed!... But you shall be answerable,—the mistress of the house shall be answerable.... You must have let the thieves in ... you must, for the house-door was not broke open."

The girl of the house looked exceedingly terrified, and asked if she had not better call up her mistress.

"To be sure you had, you fool!... Do you think I am going to sleep in a room where thieves have been suffered to enter while I was out?... How do I know but they may be lurking about still, waiting to murder me?"

The worthy widow to whom the house belonged speedily joined the group in nightcap and bedgown, and listened half awake to Mrs. Barnaby's clamorous account of her misfortune.

As soon as she began to understand the statement, which was a good deal encumbered by lamentations and threats, the quiet little old woman, without appearing to take the least offence at the repeated assertion that she must have let the thieves in herself, turned to her servant and said,—

"Is the lady's maid come in, Sally?"

"No, ma'am," said Sally; "she has never come back since she went out with the gentleman's servant as comed to fetch her."

"Then you may depend upon it, ma'am, that 'tis your maid as have robbed you," said the landlady.

"My maid!... What! Jerningham?... Impossible!... She is the best girl in the world—an innocent creature that I had away from school.... 'Tis downright impossible, and I never will believe it."

"Well, ma'am," said the widow, "let it be who it will, it won't be possible to catch 'em to-night; and I would advise you to go to bed, for the poor young lady looks pale and frightened; ... and to-morrow morning, ma'am, I would recommend your asking Mr. Peters what is best to be done."

"And how am I to be sure that there are no thieves in the house now?" cried Mrs. Barnaby.... "Open the door of your closet, Agnes, and look under the beds; ... and you, Mrs. Crocker, you must go into the drawing-room, and down stairs and up stairs, and everywhere, before I lay my poor dear head upon my pillow.... I don't choose to have my throat cut, I promise you.—Good Heavens!... What will Major Allen say?"

"I don't think, ma'am, that we should any of us like to have our throats cut," replied Mrs. Crocker; "and luckily there is no great likelihood of it, I fancy.... Good night, ladies."

And without waiting for any further discussion, the sleepy mistress of the mansion crept back to bed ... her hand-maiden followed her example, and Agnes was left alone to receive upon her devoted head the torrent of lamentations by which the bereaved Mrs. Barnaby gave vent to her sorrows during great part of the night.

On the following morning the widow took Mrs. Crocker's very reasonable advice, and repaired to Rodney Place in time to find Mr. Peters before he set off on his daily walk to Bristol. Agnes, pale, fatigued, and heavy-hearted, accompanied her, and so striking was the change in her appearance from what it had been the day before, that those of the party round the breakfast-table, who best loved her, were much more pleased than pained, when they learned that the cause of her bad night and consequent ill looks, was her aunt's having been robbed of nearly a hundred pounds and a few articles of plate.

They were too judicious, however, to mention their satisfaction, and the sorrows of the widow received from all the party a very suitable measure of condolence. Mr. Peters indeed did much more than condole with her, for he cordially offered his assistance; and it was soon settled, by his advice, that Mrs. Barnaby should immediately accompany him to the mayor, and afterwards proceed according to the instructions of a lawyer to whom he immediately dispatched a note, requesting that he would meet them forthwith before the magistrate. The carriage was then ordered: Agnes, by the advice of all parties, was left at Rodney Place; and Mrs. Barnaby, somewhat comforted, but still in great tribulation, set off in her dear sister's coach (her best consolation) to testify before the mayor of Bristol, not only that she had been robbed, but that there certainly was some reason to suppose her maid Jerningham the thief.

Mr. Peters found his lawyer ready to receive them, who, after hearing the lady's statement, obtained a warrant for the apprehension of Elizabeth Jacks and of William — (surname unknown), groom or valet, or both, to Major Allen, lodging at Gloucester Row, Clifton. The widow had very considerable scruples concerning the implication of this latter individual; but having allowed that she thought he must be the "gentleman's servant" spoken of by Mrs. Crocker's maid as having accompanied Jerningham when she left the house, she was assured that it would be necessary to include him; and she finally consented, on its being made manifest to her that, if he proved innocent, there would be no difficulty whatever in obtaining his release. Mrs. Barnaby was then requested accurately to describe the persons of her maid and her supposed companion, which she did very distinctly, and with the less difficulty, because the persons of both were remarkable.

"There wasn't another man likely to be in her company, was there, ma'am?" said a constable who was in attendance in the office.

"No," replied Mrs. Barnaby confidently, "I don't know any one at all likely to be with her. I am almost sure that she had not any other acquaintance."

"But the man might," observed another official.

"That's true," rejoined the first, "and therefore I strongly suspect that I saw the girl and the man too enter a house on the quay just fit for such sort of company; ... but there was another fellow along with them."

"Then we will charge you with the warrant, Miles," said the magistrate. "If you can succeed in taking them into custody at once, it is highly probable that you may be able to recover the property."

This hint rendered the widow extremely urgent that no time should be lost; and in case the constable should succeed in finding them at the place he had named, she consented to remain in a room attached to the office, that no time might be lost in identifying the parties.

"There will be no harm, I suppose, in taking the other fellow on suspicion, if I find them still together?" said the constable; adding, "I rather think I know something of that t'other chap already." He received authority to do this, and then departed, leaving Mrs. Barnaby, her faithful squire, Mr. Peters, and the lawyer, seated on three stools in a dismal sort of apartment within the office, the lady, at least, being in a state of very nervous expectation. This position was not a pleasant one; but fortunately it did not last long, for in considerably less than an hour they were requested to return into the office, the three prisoners being arrived.

Mr. Peters gave the lady his arm, and they entered by a door exactly facing the spot on which stood the three persons just brought in, with the constable and two attendant officers behind them. The group, as expected, consisted of two men and a girl, which latter was indeed the tall and slender Betty Jacks, and no other; the man at her left hand was William, the Major's civil groom; and he at her right was ... no, it was impossible, ... yet she could not mistake ... it must be, and, in fact, it was that pattern of faithful friendship, Captain Maintry!

Mrs. Barnaby's agitation was now, beyond all suspicion of affectation, very considerable, and his worship obligingly ordered a glass of water and a chair, which having been procured and profited by, he asked her if she knew the prisoners.

"Yes!..." she answered with a long-drawn sigh.

"Can you point them out by name?"

"The girl is my maid Jer ... Betty Jacks ... that man is William, Major Allen's groom ... and that other...."

"You had better stop there," interrupted the self-styled captain, "or you may chance to say more than you know."

"You had better be silent, I promise you," said the magistrate. "Pray, ma'am, do you know that person?... Did you ever see him before?"

"Yes, I have seen him before," replied Mrs. Barnaby, who was pale in spite of her rouge; for the recollection of all the affectionate intimacy she had witnessed between this man and her affianced Major turned her very sick, and it was quite as much as she could do to articulate.

"I should be sorry, ma'am, to trouble you with any unnecessary questions," said the magistrate; "but I must beg you to tell me, if you please, where it is you have seen him, and what he is called?"

"I saw him in the Mall at Clifton, sir," ... replied Mrs. Barnaby.

"And many an honest man besides me may have been seen in the Mall at Clifton," said the soi-disant Captain Maintry laughing.

"And you have never seen him anywhere else, ma'am?"

"No, sir, never."

"Pray, was he then in company with that groom?"

"No," ... replied the widow faltering.

Maintry laughed again.

"You cannot then swear that you suspect him of having robbed you?"

"No, sir."

Here the constable whispered something in the ear of the magistrate, who nodded, and then resumed his examination.

"Did you hear this man's name mentioned, madam, when you saw him in the Mall?"

"Yes, sir, I did."

"That has nothing to do with the present business," interrupted Maintry, "and therefore you have no right to ask it."

"I suspect that you have called yourself in this city by more names than one," replied the magistrate; "and I have a right to discover this if I can.... By what name did you hear him called when you saw him at Clifton, ma'am?"

"I heard him called Captain Maintry."

"Captain indeed!... These fellows are all captains and majors, I think," said the magistrate, making a memorandum of the name. Mrs. Barnaby's heart sunk within her. She remembered the promise of marriage, and that so acutely as almost to make her forget the business that brought her there.

The magistrate and the lawyer, however, were less oblivious, and proceeded in the usual manner to discover whether there were sufficient grounds of suspicion against any of the parties to justify committal. The very first question addressed to Betty Jacks settled the business, for she began crying and sobbing at a piteous rate, and said, "If mistress will forgive me I'll tell her all about it, and a great deal more too; and 'twasn't my fault, nor William's neither, half so much as Joe Purdham's, for he set us on;" and she indicated Joe Purdham with a finger which, as her lengthy arm reached within an inch of his nose, could not be mistaken as to the person to whom it intended to act as index. But had this been insufficient, the search instituted on the persons of the trio would have supplied all the proof wanted. Very nearly all the money was discovered within the lining of Purdham's hat; the pockets of Betty were heavy with forks and spoons, and the cream-jug and mustard-pot, carelessly enveloped each in a pocket-handkerchief, were lodged upon the person of William.

In a word, the parties were satisfactorily identified and committed to prison; the property of Mrs. Barnaby was in a fair way of being restored, and her very disagreeable business at Bristol done and over, leaving nothing but a ride back in her sister's coach to be accomplished.

Mr. Peters offered his arm to lead her out, and with a dash of honest triumph at having so ably managed matters, said, "Well, madam ... I hope you are pleased with the termination of this business?"

What a question for Mrs. Barnaby to answer!... Pleased!... Was she pleased?... Pleased at having every reason in the world to believe that she had given a promise of marriage to the friend and associate of a common thief!... But the spirit of the widow did not forsake her; and, after one little hysterical gasp, she replied by uttering a thousand thanks, and a million assurances that nothing could possibly be more satisfactory.

She was not, however, quite in a condition to meet the questionings which would probably await her at Rodney Place; and as Mr. Peters did not return in the carriage, she ordered the man to set her down at Sion Row. She could not refuse to Mrs. Crocker the satisfaction of knowing that Jerningham was the thief, that Jerningham was committed to prison, and that she was bound over to prosecute; but it was all uttered as briefly as possible, and then she shut herself in her drawing-room to take counsel with herself as to what could be done to get her out of this terrible scrape without confessing either to Mr. Peters or any one else that she had ever got into it.

For the remainder of the day she might easily plead illness and fatigue to excuse her seeing anybody; and as it was not till the day following that she expected the return of the Major, she had still some hours to meditate upon the ways and means of extricating herself.

Towards night she became more tranquil, for she had made up her mind what to do.... She would meet him as fondly as ever, and then so play her game as to oblige him to let her look at the promise she had given. "Once within reach of my hand," thought she, "the danger will be over." This scheme so effectually cheered her spirits, that when Agnes returned home in the evening she had no reason whatever to suspect that her aunt had anything particularly disagreeable upon her mind, ... for she only called her a fool twice, and threatened to send her upon the stage three times.

CHAPTER IX

MAJOR ALLEN PAYS A VISIT AT BATH PRODUCTIVE OF IMPORTANT RESULTS—SYMPATHY BETWEEN HIMSELF AND THE WIDOW BARNABY—EXCHANGE IS NO ROBBERY—VALEDICTORY COMPLIMENTS.

The adventures of Major Allen have no connexion with this narrative, excepting as far as the widow Barnaby is concerned, and therefore with his business at Bath, or anything he did there, we have nothing to do beyond recording about ten minutes' conversation which he chanced to have with one individual of a party with whom he passed the evening after his arrival.

Among the many men of various ages who were accustomed to meet together wherever those who live by their wits were likely to prosper, there was on this occasion one young man who had but recently evinced the bad ambition of belonging to the set. Major Allen had never seen him before; but hearing him named as a famous fine fellow who was likely to do them honour, he scrupled not to converse with perfect freedom before him. The most interesting thing he had to record since the party last met, was the history of his engagement with the widow Barnaby, whom he very complacently described as extremely handsome, passionately in love with him, and possessed of a noble fortune both in money and land.

The Nestor of the party asked him with very friendly anxiety if he had been careful to ascertain what the property really was, as it was no uncommon thing for handsome widows to appear richer than they were.

"Thank you for nothing, most sage conjuror," replied the gay Major; "age has not thinned my flowing hair; but I'm not such a greenhorn neither as to walk blindfold. In the first place, the lady is sister-in-law to old Peters, one of the wealthiest of turtle-eaters, and it was from one of his daughters that I learned the real state of her affairs,—an authority that may be the better depended on, because, though they receive her as a sister, and all that, it is quite evident that they are by no means very fond of her.... In fact, they are rather a stiff-backed generation, whereas my widow is as gay as a lark."

"Is she a Bristol woman?" inquired one of the party.

"No, she is from Devonshire," was the reply. "The name of her place is 'Silverton Park.'"

"Silverton in Devonshire?" said the young stranger. "May I ask the lady's name, sir?"

"Her name is Barnaby," replied Major Allen briskly; "do you happen to know anything about her?"

"The widow Barnaby of Silverton?... Oh! to be sure I do, and a fine woman she is too,—no doubt of it. She is the widow of our apothecary."

"The widow of an apothecary?... No such thing, sir; you mistake altogether," replied the Major. "Do you happen to know such a place as Silverton Park?"

"I never heard of such a park, sir; but I know Silverton well enough," said the young man, "and I know her house, or what was her house, as well as I know my own father's, which is at no great distance from it neither. And I know the shop and the bow-window belonging to it, and a very pretty decent dwelling-house it is."

Major Allen grew fidgety; he wanted to hear more, but did not approve the publicity of the conversation, and contrived at the moment to put a stop to it, but contrived also to make an appointment with his new acquaintance to breakfast together on the following morning; and before their allowance of tea and toast was dispatched, Major Allen was not only fully disenchanted respecting Silverton Park, and the four beautiful greys, but quite au fait of the reputation for running up bills which his charmer had enjoyed previous to her marriage with the worthy apothecary.

It was this latter portion of the discourse which completed the extinction of the Major's passion, and this so entirely, that he permitted himself not to inquire, as he easily might have done, into the actual state of the widow's finances; but, feeling himself on the edge of a very frightful precipice, he ran off in the contrary direction too fast to see if there were any safe mode of descending without a tumble. It may indeed be doubted whether the snug little property actually in possession of his Juno, would have been sufficient for his honourable ambition, even had he been as sure of her having and holding it, as she was herself; for, to say the truth, he rated his own price in the matrimonial market rather highly,—had great faith in the power of his height and fashionable tournure, and confidence unbounded in his large eyes and collier Grec. It is true, indeed, that he had failed more than once, and that too "when the fair cause of all his pain" had given him great reason to believe that she admired him much; nevertheless, his self-approval was in no degree lessened thereby, nor was it likely to be, so long as he could oil and trim his redundant whiskers without discovering a grey hair in them.

In short, what with his well-sustained value for himself, and his much depreciated value for the widow, he left Bath boiling with rage at the deception practised upon him, and arrived at Clifton determined to trust to his skill for obtaining a peaceable restitution of the promise of marriage, without driving his Juno to any measures that might draw upon them the observation of the public, a tribunal before which he was by no means desirous of appearing.

The state of Mrs. Barnaby's mind respecting this same promise of marriage has already been described, wherefore it may be perceived that when Major Allen made his next morning visit at Sion Row, a much greater degree of sympathy existed between himself and the widow than either imagined. It was in the tactics of both, however, to meet without any appearance of diminished tenderness; and when he entered with the smile that had so often gladdened her fond heart, she stretched out a hand to welcome him with such softness of aspect as made the deluded gentleman tremble to think how difficult a task lay before him.

Neither was Mrs. Barnaby's heart at all more at ease. Who could doubt the sincerity of the ardent pressure with which that hand was held?... Who could have thought that while gazing upon her in silence that seemed to indicate feelings too strong for words, he was occupied solely in meditating how best he could get rid of her for ever?

The conversation was preluded by a pretty, well-sustained passage of affectionate inquiries concerning the period of absence, and then the Major ejaculated ... "Yes, my sweet friend!... I have been well in health, ... but it is inconceivable what fancies a man truly in love finds to torment himself!"... Whilst the widow mentally answered him,... "Perhaps you were afraid I might see your friend Maintry stuck up in the pillory, or peeping at me through the county prison windows;" ... but aloud she only said with a smile a little forced,... "What fancies, Major?"

"I am almost afraid to tell you," he replied; "you will think me so weak, so capricious!"

This word capricious sounded pleasantly to the widow's ears ... it seemed to hint at some change—some infidelity that might make her task an easier one than she expected, and assuming an air of gaiety, she said,—

"Nay ... if such be the case, speak out without a shadow of reserve, Major Allen; for I assure you there is nothing in the world I admire so much as sincerity."

"Sincerity!" muttered the half entrapped fortune hunter aside.... "Confound her sincerity!..." and then replied aloud,—"Will you promise, dear friend, to forgive me if I confess to you a fond folly?"

Mrs. Barnaby quaked all over; she felt as if fresh grappling-irons had been thrown over her, and that escape was impossible. "Nay, really," said she, after a moment's reflection; "I think fond follies are too young a joke for us, Major; they may do very well for Agnes, perhaps ... but I think you and I ought to know better by this time.... If I can but make him quarrel with me," thought she, ... "that would be better still!"

"If I can but once more coax her to let me have my way," thought he, ... "the business would be over in a moment!"

"Beauty like yours is of no age!" he exclaimed; "it is immortal as the passion it inspires, and when joined with such a heart and temper as you possess becomes...."

"I do assure you, Major," said the widow, interrupting him rather sharply, "you will do wrong if you reckon much upon my temper ... it never was particularly good, and I can't say I think it grows better."

"Oh! say not so, for this very hour I am going to put it to the test.... I want you to...."

"Pray, Major, do not ask me to do anything particularly obliging; for, to say the truth, I am in no humour for it.... It has occurred to me more than once, Major Allen, since you set off so suddenly, that it is likely enough there may be another lady in the case, and that the promise you got out of me was perhaps for no other purpose in the world but to make fun of me by shewing it to her."

"Hell and furies!" growled the Major inwardly, "she will stick to me like a leech!"

"Oh! dream not of such villany!" he exclaimed; "it was concerning that dear promise that I wished to speak to you, my sweet Martha.... Methinks that promise...."

"I tell you what, Major Allen," cried the widow vehemently, "if you don't let me see that promise this very moment, nothing on earth shall persuade me that you have not given it in jest to some other woman."

"Good Heaven!..." he replied; "what a moment have you chosen for the expression of this cruel suspicion! I was on the very verge of telling you that I deemed such a promise unworthy a love so pure—so perfect as ours; and therefore, if you would indulge my fond desire, you would let each of us receive our promise back again."

The Major was really and truly in a state of the most violent perturbation as he uttered these words, fearing that the fond and jealous widow might suspect the truth, and hold his pledge with a tenacity beyond his power to conquer. He had, however, no sooner spoken, than a smile of irrepressible delight banished the frowns in which she had dressed herself, and she uttered in a voice of the most unaffected satisfaction,... "If you will really do that, Major Allen, I can't suspect any longer, you know, that you have given mine to any one else."

"Assuredly not, most beautiful angel!" cried the delighted lover: "thus, then, let us give back these paper ties, and be bound only by...."

The widow stretched out her hand for the document which he had already taken from his pocket-book; but to yield this, though he had no wish to keep it, was not the object nearest his heart; holding it, therefore, playfully above his head, he said, "Let not one of us, dearest, seem more ready than the other in this act of mutual confidence!... give mine with one hand, as you receive your own with the other."

"Now then!..." said Mrs. Barnaby, eagerly extending both her hands, in order at once to give and take.

"Now then!..." replied the Major joyously, imitating her action; and the next instant each had seized the paper held by the other with an avidity greatly resembling that with which a zealous player pounces upon the king when she has the ace in the hand at "shorts."

"Now, Mrs. Barnaby, I will wish you good morning," said the gentleman, bowing low as he tore the little document to atoms.... "I have been fortunate enough, since I last enjoyed the happiness of seeing you, to discover the exact locality of Silverton Park, and the precise pedigree of your beautiful greys."

The equanimity of the widow was shaken for a moment, but no longer; she, too, had been doing her best to annihilate the precious morsel of paper, and, rising majestically, she scattered the fragments on the ground, saying in a tone at least as triumphant as his own, "And I, Major Allen, or whatever else your name may chance to be, have, since last I had the felicity of seeing you, enjoyed the edifying spectacle of beholding your friend Captain Maintry, alias Purdham, in the hands of justice, for assisting your faithful servant William in breaking open my boxes and robbing me.... Should the circumstance be still unknown to you, I fear you may be disappointed to hear that both my money and plate have been recovered. There may be some fanciful difference between Silverton Park and a snug property at Silverton, ... but I rather suspect that, of the two, I have gained most by our morning's work. Farewell, sir!... If you will take my advice, you will not continue much longer in Clifton.... I may feel myself called upon to hint to the magistrates that it might assist the ends of justice if you were taken up and examined as an accomplice in this affair."

The lady had decidedly the best of it, as ladies always should have; for the crest-fallen Major looked as if he must, had he been poetically inclined, have exclaimed in the words of Comus,—

"She fables not, I feel that I do fear,"...

and without any farther attempt to carry off the palm of victory, he made his way down stairs; and it is now many years since he has been heard of in the vicinity of Clifton.

CHAPTER X

A DISAGREEABLE BREAKFAST-TABLE—MR. STEPHENSON GIVES HIS FRIEND COLONEL HUBERT WARNING TO DEPART—A PROPOSAL, AND ITS CONSEQUENCES.

Mrs. Barnaby and Major Allen were not the only persons to whom that twenty-sixth of April proved an eventful day.

Colonel Hubert and his friend Stephenson met as usual at the breakfast-table, and it would be difficult to say which of them was the most pre-occupied, and the most unfit for ordinary conversation. Stephenson, however, though vexed at not being already the betrothed husband of his lovely Agnes, was full of hopeful anticipation, and his unfitness for conversation arose rather from the fulness of his heart, than the depression of his spirits.

Not so Colonel Hubert: it was hardly possible to suffer from a greater feeling of melancholy dissatisfaction with all things than he did on the morning after Mrs. Peters's concert.

That the despised Agnes, the niece of the hateful Mrs. Barnaby, had risen in his estimation to be considered as the best, the first, the loveliest of created beings, was not the worst misfortune that had fallen upon him.

There was, indeed, a degree of perversity in the case that almost justified his thinking himself the most unfortunate of mortals. After having attained the sober age of thirty-seven years, if not untouched, at least uninjured, by all the reiterated volleys which he had stood from Cupid's quiver, it was certainly rather provoking to find himself falling distractedly in love with a little obscure girl, young enough to be his daughter, and perhaps, from the unhappy circumstance of her dependence upon such a relative as Mrs. Barnaby, the very last person in the world with whom he would have wished to connect himself. This was bad enough; but even this was not all. With the airs of a senior and a Mentor, he had taken upon himself to lecture his friend upon the preposterous absurdity of giving way to such an attachment, thus rendering it almost morally impossible for him under any imaginable circumstances to ask the love of Agnes, even though something in his inmost heart whispered to him that he should not ask in vain. Nor did the catalogue of his embarrassments end here, for he was placed vis-à-vis to his open-hearted friend, who, he was quite certain, would within five minutes begin again the oft-repeated confidential avowal of his love; accompanied, probably, with renewed assurances of his intentions to make proposals, which Colonel Hubert, from what he had seen last night, fancied himself quite sure would never be accepted.

What a wretched, what a hopeless dilemma was he placed in! Was he to see the man he professed to love expose himself to the misery of offering his hand, in defiance of a thousand obstacles, to a woman who, he felt almost sure, would reject him? Or could he interfere to prevent it, at the very moment that his heart told him nothing but the pretensions of Frederick could prevent his proposing to her himself.

Colonel Hubert sat stirring his coffee in moody silence, and dreading to hear Frederick open his lips; but his worst fears as to what he might utter, were soon realized by Stephenson's exclaiming,—

"Well, Hubert!... it is still to do. I was defeated last night, but it shall not be my fault if I go to rest this, without receiving her promise to become my wife. Her aunt is a horror—a monster—anything, everything you may please to call her; but Agnes is an angel, and Agnes must be mine!"

Colonel Hubert looked more gloomy still; but he continued to stir his coffee, and said nothing.

"How can you treat me thus, Hubert?..." said the young man reproachfully. "There is a proud superiority in this affected silence a thousand times more mortifying than anything you could say. Begin again to revile me as heretofore for my base endurance of a Barnaby ... describe the vexation of my brother, the indignation of my sisters!... this would be infinitely more endurable than such contemptuous silence."

"My dear, dear Frederick, I know not what to say," replied the agitated Hubert.... "Had my words the power to make you leave this place within the hour, I would use my last breath to speak them ... for certain am I, Frederick,—I am most surely certain,—that this suit can bring you nothing but misery and disappointment. Let me acknowledge that the young lady herself is worthy of all love, admiration, and reverence; ... I truly think so.... I believe it.... I am sure of it ... but" ... and here Colonel Hubert stopped short, resumed his coffee-cup, and said no more.

"This is intolerable, sir," said the vexed Frederick. "Go on, if you please, say all you have to say, but stop not thus at unshaped insinuations, more injurious, more insulting far, than anything your eloquence could find the power to utter."

"Frederick, you mistake me.... I insinuate nothing.... I believe in my inmost soul that Agnes Willoughby is one of the most faultless beings upon earth.... But this will not prevent your suit to her from being a most unhappy one.... Forget her, Frederick ... travel awhile, my dear friend ... leave her, Stephenson, and your future years will be the happier."

"Colonel Hubert, the difference in our ages is your only excuse for the unnatural counsel you so coldly give. You are no longer a young man, sir.... You no longer are capable of judging for one who is; and I confess to you, that for the present I think our mutual enjoyment would rather be increased than lessened were we to separate. If I remember rightly, you purposed when we came here to stay only till your sister's marriage was over. It is now a fortnight since that event took place, and it is probably solely out of compliment to me that you remain here. If so, let me release you.... In future times I hope we may meet with pleasanter feelings than any we can share at present; and, besides, my stay here,—which which for aught I know may be prolonged for months,—will, under probable circumstances, throw me a good deal into intimacy and intercourse with your detested Mrs. Barnaby, wherein I certainly cannot wish or desire that you should follow me; and therefore ... all things considered, you must hold me excused if I say ... that I should hear of your departure from Clifton with pleasure."

Colonel Hubert rose from his seat and walked about the room. He felt that his heart was softer at that moment than befitted the age with which Frederick reproached him. He was desired to absent himself by one for whose warm-hearted young love he had perhaps neglected the soberer friendships of superior men, and that, too, at a moment when he felt that he more than ever deserved a continuance of that love. Was he not at that instant crushing with Spartan courage a passion within his own breast which he believed ... secretly, silently, unacknowledged even to his own heart, to be returned ... and this terrible sacrifice was made, not because his pride opposed his yielding to it, but because he could not have endured the idea of supplanting Frederick even when it should be acknowledged that no shadow of hope remained for him. And for this it was that he was thus insultingly desired to depart.

Generous Hubert!... A few moments' struggle decided him. He resolved to go, and that immediately. He would not remain to witness the broken spirit of his hot-headed friend after he should have received the refusal which, as he so strongly suspected, awaited him, ... neither would he expose himself to the danger of seeing Agnes afterwards.

Without as yet replying to Frederick, he rang the bell, and desired that post-horses might immediately be ordered for his carriage, and his valet told to prepare his trunks for travelling with as little delay as possible. These directions given, the friends were once more tête-à-tête, and then Colonel Hubert ventured to trust his voice, and answer the harsh language he had received.

"Frederick," he said, "you have spoken as you would not have done had you given yourself a little more time for consideration, ... for you have spoken unkindly and unjustly. I would still prevail on you, if I could, to turn away from this lovely girl without committing yourself by making her an offer of marriage. I would strongly advise this—I would strongly advise your remembering, while it is yet time, the pang it may cost you should anything ... in short, believe me, you would suffer less by leaving Clifton immediately with me, than by remaining under circumstances which I am sure will turn out inimical to your happiness.... Will you be advised, and let us depart together?"

"No, Colonel Hubert, I will not. I have no wish to detain you, ... I have already said this with sufficient frankness; be equally wise on your side, and do not attempt to drag me away in your train."

These were pretty nearly the last words which were exchanged between them; Frederick Stephenson soon left the house to wander about till the hour arrived for making his visit in Rodney Place; and in less than two hours Colonel Hubert was driving rapidly through Bristol on his way to London.

As soon as Mrs. Barnaby and the friendly Mr. Peters were fairly off the premises, and on their road to look after the thief, Mary called a consultation on the miserably jaded looks of poor Agnes; and having her own particular reasons for not choosing that she should look half dead ... inasmuch as she was persuaded the promised visit of Frederick was not intended to be for nothing ... she peremptorily insisted upon her taking sal volatile, bathing her eyes in cold water, and then either lying on the sofa or taking a walk upon the down till luncheon-time, that being the usual hour of Mr. Stephenson's morning visits.

Agnes submitted herself very meekly to all this discipline, save the depositing herself on the sofa, to which she objected vehemently, deciding for the walk on the down as the only thing at all likely to cure her head-ache. It was on their way to this favourite magazine of fresh air that Mr. Stephenson met them. To Agnes the rencontre was an extreme annoyance, for she wanted to be quite quiet, and this was what Frederick Stephenson never permitted her to be. But she could not run away; and so she continued to walk on till, just after passing the turnpike, she discovered that Mary and Elizabeth Peters were considerably in their rear. This tête-à-tête, however, caused her not the slightest embarrassment; and if she was to be talked to, instead of being permitted to sink into the dark but downy depths of meditation, which was now her greatest indulgence, it mattered very little to her who was the talker. She stopped, however, from politeness to her friends, and a sort of natural instinct of bienséance towards herself, saying, "I was not aware, Mr. Stephenson, that we had been walking so fast; I think we had better turn back to them."

"May I entreat you, Miss Willoughby," said the young man, "to remain a few moments longer alone with me.... It is not that you have walked fast, but your friends have walked slowly, for they, at least, I plainly perceive, have read my secret.... And is it possible that you, Agnes, have not read it also?... Is it possible that you have yet to learn how fervently I love you?"

No young girl hears such an avowal as this for the first time without feeling considerable agitation and embarrassment; but many things contributed to increase these feelings tenfold in the case of Agnes ... for first, which is rarely the case, the declaration was wholly unexpected; secondly, it was wholly unwelcome; and, thirdly, it inspired a feeling of acute terror lest, flattering and advantageous as she knew such a proposal to be, it might tempt her friends ... or set on her terrible aunt ... to disturb her with solicitations which, by only hearing them, would profane the sentiment to which she had secretly devoted herself for ever.

Greatly, however, as she wished to answer him at once and definitively, she was unable to articulate a single word.

"Will you not speak to me, Agnes?" resumed Frederick, after a painful pause. "Will you not tell me what I may hope in return for the truest affection that ever warmed the heart of man?... Will you not even look at me?"

Agnes now stood still as if to recover breath. She knew that he had a right to expect an answer from her, and she knew that sooner or later she should be compelled to speak it; so, making an effort as great perhaps in its self-command as many that have led a hero to eternal fame, she said, but without raising her eyes from the ground, "Mr. Stephenson, I am very sorry indeed that you love me, because it is quite, quite impossible I should ever love you in return."

"Good God! Miss Willoughby, ... is it thus you answer me?... Do you know that the words you utter so lightly, so coldly, must, if persisted in, doom me to a life of misery? Can you hear this, Agnes, and feel no touch of pity?"

"Pray do not talk in that way, Mr. Stephenson!... It gives me so very much pain."

"Then you will unsay those cruel words?... You will tell me that time and faithful, constant love may do something for me.... Oh! tell me it shall be so."

"But I cannot tell you so, Mr. Stephenson," said Agnes with the most earnest emphasis. "It would be most wicked to do so because it would be untrue. You are very young and very gay, Mr. Stephenson; and I cannot think that what I have said can vex you long, particularly if you will believe it at once, and talk no more about it. And now I think that we had better walk back to Mary, if you please."

Having said this she turned about, and began to walk rapidly towards Clifton.

"Can this be possible?..." said the young man, greatly agitated; "so young, and seemingly so gentle, and yet so harsh and so determined. Oh! Agnes, why did you not let me guess this end to all my hopes before they had grown so strong? You must have seen my love—my adoration.... You must have known that every earthly hope for me depended upon you!"

"No, no, no," cried Agnes, greatly distressed. "I never knew it—I never guessed it.... How should I guess what was so very unlikely?"

"Unlikely!... Are you laughing at me, Agnes?... Unlikely! Ask your friends—ask Miss Peters if she thought it unlikely."

"I do not believe so strange a thought ever entered her head, Mr. Stephenson; for if it had, I am sure she would have put me on my guard against it."

"On your guard against it, Miss Willoughby! What is there in my situation, fortune, or character, that should render it necessary for your friend to put you on your guard against me?... Surely you use strange language."

"Then do not make me talk any more about it, Mr. Stephenson. It is very likely that I may express myself amiss, for I am so sorry and so vexed that indeed I hardly know what I say; ... but pray forgive me, and do not be unhappy about me any longer."

"Agnes!... you love another!" suddenly exclaimed Frederick, his face becoming crimson.... "There is no other way of accounting for such cold indifference, such hard insensibility."

Agnes coloured as violently in her turn, and bursting into tears, said with great displeasure, "That is what nobody in the world has a right to say to me, and I will never, if I can help it, permit you to say it again."

She now increased her speed, and had nearly reached the Misses Peters, notwithstanding all the beautiful summer flowers they had found by the way's side; saying no more in reply, either to the remonstrances or the passionate pleadings of Mr. Stephenson, when at length he laid his hand upon her arm, and detained her while he said, "Agnes, if you accept my love, and consent to become my wife, I will release you from the power of your aunt, place you in a splendid home, and surround you with friends as pure-minded and as elegant as yourself. Is this nothing?... Answer me then one word, and one word only.... Is your refusal of my hand and my affection final?"

"Yes, sir," said Agnes, still weeping; for his accusation of her having another love, continued to ring in her ears, and make her heart swell almost to bursting.

"Speak not in anger, Agnes!..." said he mildly. "What I have felt for you does not deserve such a return."

"I know it, I know it," replied Agnes, weeping more violently still, "and I am very wrong, as well as very unhappy. Pray, Mr. Stephenson, forgive me," and she held out her hand to him.

He took it, and held it for a moment between both his. "Unhappy, Agnes?..." he said, "why should you be unhappy? Oh! if my love, my devotion, could render you otherwise!... But you will not trust me?... You will not let me pass my life in labouring to make yours happy?"

"Nothing can make me happy, Mr. Stephenson; pray do not talk any more about it, for indeed, indeed, I cannot be your wife."

He abruptly raised her hand to his lips, and then let it fall. "May Heaven bless and make you happy in your own way, whatever that may be!" he cried, and turning from her, reached the verge of the declivity that overhung the river, then plunging down it with very heedless haste, he was out of sight immediately.

This was a catastrophe wholly unexpected by Miss Peters, who now hastened to meet the disconsolate-looking Agnes. "What in the world can you have said to him, my dear, to send him off in that style? I trust that you have not quarrelled."

Most unfeignedly distressed and embarrassed was Agnes at this appeal, and the more so because her friend Mary was not alone.... To her perhaps she might have been able to tell the terrible adventure which had befallen her, but before Elizabeth it was impossible; and, pressing Mary's arm, she said in a whisper, "Ask me no questions, dearest Mary, now, for I cannot answer them ... wait only till we get home."

But to wait in a state of such tormenting uncertainty was beyond the philosophy of Mary, so she suddenly stopped, saying, "Elizabeth! walk on slowly for a few minutes, will you?... I have something that I particularly wish to say to Agnes."... And the good-natured Elizabeth walked on, without ever turning her head to look back at them.

"What has happened?... what has he said to you?... and what have you said to him?" hastily inquired the impatient friend.

"Oh, Mary!... he has made me so very unhappy ... and the whole thing is so extremely strange.... I cannot hide anything from you, Mary, ... but it will kill me should you let my aunt hear of it.... He has made me an offer, Mary!"

"Of course, Agnes, I know he has.... But how does that account for his running off in that strange wild way? and how does it account for your crying and looking so miserable? Why did he run away as if he were afraid to see us, Agnes? and when are you going to see him again?"

"I shall never see him again, Mary," said Agnes gravely.

"Then you have quarrelled!... Good Heaven, what folly! I suppose he said something about your aunt that you fancied was not civil; ... but all things considered, Agnes, ought you not to have forgiven it?"

"Indeed, Mary, he said nothing that was rude about my aunt, and I am sure he did not mean to be uncivil in any way ... though certainly he hurt and offended me very much ... but perhaps he did not intend it."

"Hurt and offended you, Agnes?... Let me beg you to tell me at once what it was he did say to you."

"I will tell you everything but one, and that I own to you I had rather not repeat ... and it does not signify, for that was not the reason he ran off so."

"And what was the reason?"

"A very foolish one indeed, and I am sure you will laugh at it ... it was only because I said I could not marry him."

"You said that, Agnes?... You said you could not marry him?"

"Yes, I did! I do not wish to marry him; indeed, I would not marry him for the world."

"And this is the end of it all!" exclaimed Miss Peters with much vexation. "I have much mistaken you, Agnes.... I thought you were suffering greatly from being dependent on your aunt Barnaby."

"And do you doubt it now, Mary?"

"How can I continue to think this, when you have just refused an offer of marriage from a young man, well born, nobly allied, with a splendid fortune, extremely handsome, and possessed, as I truly believe, of more excellent and amiable qualities than often fall to the share of any mortal. How can I believe after this that you really feel unhappy from the circumstances of your present situation?"

"All that you say is very true, and I cannot deny a word of it; ... but what can one do, Mary, if one does not happen to love a man?... you would not have one marry him, would you?"

"How like a child you talk!... Why should you not love him? with manners so agreeable, such excellent qualities, and a fortune beyond that of many noblemen."

"But you don't suppose I could love him the better for his being rich, do you, Mary?"

"You are a little fool, Agnes, and I know not what to suppose. Perhaps, my dear, you think him too old for you? Perhaps you will not choose to fall in love till you meet an Adonis about your own age?"

"It is you who are talking nonsense now," replied Agnes with some warmth. "So far from his being too old, I think ... that is to say I don't think.... I mean that I suppose everybody would think people a great deal older, might be a great deal.... But this is all nothing to the purpose, Mary.... I would not marry Mr. Stephenson if.... But let us say no more on the subject ... only, for pity's sake, do not let my aunt know anything about it!"

"She shall not hear it from me, Agnes," replied Miss Peters.... "But I cannot understand you,—you have disappointed me.... However, I have no right to be angry, and so, as you say, we will talk no more about it. Come, let us overtake Elizabeth; we must not let her go all the way to Clifton in solitary state."

And so ended the very promising trial at match-making, upon which the pretty Mary Peters had wasted so many useless meditations! It was a useful lesson to her, for she has never been known to interfere in any affair of the kind since.

CHAPTER XI

MRS. BARNABY FEELS CONSCIOUS OF IMPROVEMENT, AND REJOICES AT IT—HOPES FOR THE FUTURE—A CONVERSATION IN WHICH MUCH GENEROUS SINCERITY IS DISPLAYED—A LETTER INTENDED TO BE EXPLANATORY, BUT FAILING TO BE SO

Mrs. Barnaby's first feelings after the Major left her were agreeable enough. She had escaped with little injury from a great danger, and, while believing herself infinitely wiser than before, she was conscious of no reason that should either lower her estimate of herself, or check the ambitious projects with which she had set forth from her native town to push her fortune in the world. But her views were improved and enlarged, her experience was more practical and enlightened, and her judgment, as to those trifling fallacies by which people of great ability are enabled to delude people of little, though in no degree changed as to its morale, was greatly purified and sharpened as to the means to be employed. Thus, by way of example, it may be mentioned that, during the hour of mental examination which followed Major Allen's adieux, Mrs. Barnaby determined never again to mention Silverton Park; and, if at any time led to talk of her favourite greys, that the pastures they fed in, and the roads they traversed, should on no account be particularly specified. Neither her courage nor her hopes were at all lowered by this her first adventure; on the contrary, by setting her to consider from whence arose the blunder, it led her to believe that her danger had been occasioned solely by her own too great humility in not having soared high enough to seek her quarry.

"In making new acquaintance," thus ran her soliloquy—"in making new acquaintance, the rank and station of the party should be too unequivocal to render a repetition of such danger possible.... I was to blame in so totally neglecting the evident admiration of Colonel Hubert, in order to gratify the jealous feelings of Major Allen.... That was a man to whom I might have devoted myself without danger, his family and fortune known to all the world ... and himself so every way calculated to do me honour. But it is too late now!... His feelings have been too deeply wounded.... I cannot forget the glances of jealous anger which I have seen him throw on that unworthy Allen.... But my time must not be wasted in regrets; I must look forward."

And look forward she did with a very bold and dashing vein of speculation, although for the present moment her power of putting any new plans in action was greatly paralyzed by her having been bound over to prosecute Betty Jacks and her accomplices at the next Bristol assizes. Now Bristol and its vicinity had become equally her contempt and aversion. The Major had taught her to consider the trade-won wealth of the Peterses as something derogatory to her dignity; and though she still hoped to make them useful, she had altogether abandoned the notion that they could make her great. During the time that it would be necessary for her to remain at Clifton, however, she determined to maintain as much intimacy with them as "their very stiff manners" would permit, and carefully to avoid anything approaching to another affair of the heart till she should have left their neighbourhood, and the scene of her late failure, behind.

As soon as her spirits had recovered the double shock they had received from the perfidies of Betty Jacks and Major Allen, she remembered with great satisfaction the discovery made of Agnes's singing powers. Though more than eighteen years had passed since her musical father and mother had warbled together for the delight of the Silverton soirées, Mrs. Barnaby had not forgotten the applause their performances used to elicit, nor the repeated assurances of the best informed among their auditors, that the voices of both were of very first-rate quality. The belief that Agnes inherited their powers, now suggested more than one project. In the first place, it would make the parties she was determined to give extremely attractive, and might very probably be sufficient to render her at once the fashion, either at Cheltenham, which she intended should be the scene of her next campaign, or anywhere else where it was her will and pleasure to display it. Nor was this ornamental service the only one to which she thought it possible she might convert the voice of Agnes. She knew that the exploits she contemplated were hazardous, as well as splendid; and that, although success was probable, failure might be possible, in which case she might fall back upon this newly-discovered treasure, and either marry her niece, or put her on the stage, or make her a singing mistress, as she should find most feasible and convenient.

With these notions in her head, she attacked Agnes on the singular concealment of her talent, as well as upon other matters, during breakfast the morning after the unlamented Major's departure, which was in fact the first time they had been alone together, Agnes having passed the whole of the preceding day at Rodney Place.

In answer to her niece's gentle salutation, she said in a tone very far from amiable, though it affected to be so,—

"Yes, yes, good morning, aunt!... that's all very well; ... and now, please to tell me where I shall find another young lady living with a generous relation to whom she owes her daily bread, who, knowing that relation's anxiety about everything concerning her, has chosen to make a secret of the only thing on earth she can do.... Tell me, if you can, where I shall find anything like that?"

"If you mean my singing, aunt, I have told you already why I never said anything about it.... My only reason was, because I did not like to ask you for a piano."

"That's all hypocrisy, Miss Agnes; and let who will be taken in by you, I am not ... and you may just remember that, miss, now and always. You were afraid, perhaps, that I might make you of some use to me. But the scheme won't answer. With the kindest temper in the world, I have plenty of resolution to do just whatever I think right, and that's what I shall do by you. I shall say no more about it in this nasty, vulgar, merchandizing sort of a place; but as soon as we get among ladies and gentlemen that I consider my equals, I shall begin to give regular parties like other people of fashion, and then ... let me hear you refuse to sing when I ask you ... and we shall see what will happen next."

"Indeed, aunt, I believe you are mistaken about my voice," replied Agnes; "I have never had teaching enough to enable me to sing so well as you seem to suppose; and, in fact, I know little or nothing about it, except what dear good Mr. Wilmot used to tell me; and I don't believe he has heard any really good singing for the last twenty years."

"And I was not at Mrs. Peters's the other night, I suppose, Miss Willoughby?... and I did not hear all the praise, and the rapture, and the fuss, didn't I?... What a fool you do seem to take me for, Agnes!... However, I don't mean to quarrel with you.... You know what sacrifices I have made, and not all your bad behaviour shall prevent my making more still for you.... You shall have a master, if I find you want one; and when we get to Cheltenham, you shall be sure to have a pianoforte. Does that please you?"

"I shall be very glad to be able to practice again, aunt, only...."

"Only what, if you please?"

"Why, I mean to say that I should be sorry you should expect to make a great performer of me; ... for I am certain that you will be disappointed."

"Stuff and nonsense!... Don't trouble yourself about my disappointments—I'll take care to get what I want.... And there's another talent, Miss Agnes, which I shall expect to find in you; and I hope you have made a secret of that too, for I never saw much sign of it.... I want you to be very active and clever, and to act as my maid till I get one. Indeed, I'm not sure I shall ever get one again, they seem to be such plagues; and if I find you ain't too great a fool to do what I want, I have a notion that I shall take a tiger instead—it will be much more respectable.... Pray, Agnes, have you any idea about dressing hair?"

"I think I could do it as well for you, aunt, as Jerningham did," replied Agnes with perfect good-humour.

"And that's not quite so well as I want; but I suppose you know that as well as I do, only you choose to shew off your impertinence.... And there's my drawers to keep in order ... dunce as you are, I suppose you can do that; and fifty other little things there will be, now that good-for-nothing baggage is gone, which I promise you I do not intend to do for myself."

Did Agnes repent having sent the enamoured possessor of seven thousand a-year from her in despair, as she listened to this sketch of her future occupations? No, not for a moment. No annoyances that her aunt could threaten, no escape from them that Mr. Stephenson could offer, had the power of mastering in her mind the one prominent idea, which, like the rod of the chosen priest, swallowed up all the rest.

And this engrossing, this cherished, this secretly hoarded idea ... how was it nurtured and sustained? Did the object of it return to occupy every hour of her life by giving her looks, words, and movements to meditate upon? No; Colonel Hubert appeared no more at Clifton; and Agnes, notwithstanding the flashes of fond hope that, like the soft gleaming of the glow-worm, had occasionally brightened the gloom of her prospects, was left to suppose that he had taken his departure in company with his offended friend, and that she should probably never hear of him more. Was he then angry at her refusal? Was the notice he had taken of her for his friend's pleasure rather than his own? Poor Agnes! there was great misery in this thought. They had indeed both left Clifton on the same day, though they had not left it together. But that she knew not.... Colonel Hubert, as we have seen, was already on his way to London when the impetuous Frederick staked all his dearest hopes upon his sanguine, but most mistaken judgment of a young girl's heart; and when the ill-fated experiment was over, he posted with all speed across the country to Southampton, and there embarked to take refuge among the hills and the orchards of Normandy.

The recollection of the manner in which he had driven Colonel Hubert from him, was no slight aggravation of his unhappiness, when he gave himself time to take breath, and to reflect a little. He felt deeply, bitterly, the loss of Agnes, but perhaps he felt more bitterly still the loss of his friend. The first, as he could not help confessing to himself, was the loss of a good he had possessed only in his own fond fancy; the last was that of the most substantial good that man can possess ... a tried, attached, and honourable friend.

For many days, and many nights too, Frederick suffered sorely from the battle that was going on between his pride and his consciousness of having been wrong; but, happily for his repose, his pride at length gave way, and the following letter was written and directed to the United Service Club, whence, sooner or later, he knew it would reach the friend to whom it was addressed.

"Most men, my dear Hubert, would be too angry at the petulance I exhibited during our last interview even to receive an apology for it, ... but you are not one of them; and you will let me tell you, without receiving the confession too triumphantly, that I have never known a moment's peace from that day to this, nor ever shall till you send me your forgiveness as frankly as I ask it. You may do this with the more safety, dear Hubert, because we shall never again quarrel on the same occasion; and so perfectly have I found you to be right in all you said and all you hinted on that fair but unfortunate subject, that henceforward I think I shall be afraid to pronounce upon the colour of a lady's hair, or the tincture of her skin, till I have heard your judgment thereon. Let us, therefore, never talk again either of the terrible Mrs. Barnaby or her beautiful niece; but, forgetting that anything of the kind could breed discord between us, remember only that I am, and ever must be,

"Your most affectionate friend,

"FREDERICK STEPHENSON."

How many times did Colonel Hubert read over this letter before he could satisfy himself that he understood it? This is a question that cannot be answered, because he never did by means of these constantly repeated readings ever arrive at any such conclusion at all. Had Mrs. Barnaby's name been altogether omitted, he might have fancied that his own deep but unacknowledged belief that Miss Willoughby would refuse his friend, had been manifest in the dissuasive words he had spoken, notwithstanding his caution. But this allusion to the widow, who had so repeatedly been the theme of his prophetic warnings, left him at liberty to suppose that Frederick's solitary and repentant rumination upon all he had propounded on that fertile subject, had finally induced him to give up the pursuit, and to leave Clifton without having proposed to her niece.

Anything more destructive to the tranquillity of Colonel Hubert than this doubt can hardly be imagined. He had long persuaded himself, it is true, that it was impossible, under any circumstances, he could ever confess to Agnes what his own feelings were, as his friendship for Stephenson must put it totally out of his power to do so.... The frankness of Frederick's early avowal of his passion to him, and the style and tone of the opposition with which he had met it, must inevitably lay him under such an imputation of dishonour, if he addressed her himself, as he could not bear to think of.... Nevertheless, he felt, or fancied, that he should be much more tranquil and resigned could he have known to a certainty whether Stephenson had proposed to her or not. It was long, however, ere any opportunity of satisfying himself on this point arose. The reconciliation, indeed, between himself and his friend, was perfect, and their letters breathed the same spirit of affectionate confidence as heretofore; but how could Colonel Hubert abuse this confidence by asking a question which could not be answered in any way, without opening afresh the wound that he feared still rankled in the breast of his friend?

It would be selfish and ungenerous in the extreme, and must not be thought of; but this forbearance robbed the high-minded Hubert of the only consolation that his situation left him,—namely, the belief that the young Agnes, notwithstanding the disparity in their years, had been too near loving him to accept the hand of another. Of the two interpretations to which the letter of Frederick was open, this, the most flattering to himself, was the one that faded fastest away from the mind of Colonel Hubert, till he hardly dared remember that he had once believed it possible; and he finally remained with the persuasion that his too tractable friend had yielded to his arguments against the marriage, without ever having put the feelings of Agnes to the test, which he would have given the world to believe had been tried, and been withstood.

CHAPTER XII

A LUCKY ESCAPE—A MELANCHOLY PARTING—MRS. BARNABY SETTLES HERSELF AT CHELTENHAM —HER FIRST SORTIE—BOARDING-HOUSE BREAKFAST—A NEW ACQUAINTANCE—A MEDICAL CONVERSATION

In addition to Mrs. Barnaby's pretty strong confidence in herself and her own devices, she soon learned to think that she was very especially favoured by fortune; for just as she began to find her idle and most unprofitable abode at Clifton intolerably tedious, and that the recovery of her property hardly atoned for the inconvenience of being obliged to prosecute those who had stolen it, she received the welcome intelligence that the trio had escaped by means of the superior ingenuity of Captain Maintry, alias Purdham. The ends of justice being considerably less dear to the widow's heart than the end of the adventures she promised herself at Cheltenham, she welcomed the intelligence most joyfully, and set about her preparations for departure without an hour's delay.

Several very elegant shops at Clifton had so earnestly requested the honour of her name upon their books, that Mrs. Barnaby had found it impossible to refuse; and the consequence was, that when she announced her intended departure, so unexpected an amount of "mere nothings" crowded in upon her, that she would have been very considerably embarrassed, had not the manner of raising money during the last years of her father's life been fresh in her memory, shewing her, as her property was all in the funds, and, happily or unhappily, standing in her own name, that nothing could be more easy than to write to her broker, and order him to sell out a couple of hundreds.

Confidence in one's self,—the feeling that there is a power within us of sufficient strength to reach the goal we have in view,—is in general a useful as well as a pleasant state of mind; but in Mrs. Barnaby it was very likely to prove otherwise. In all her meditations, in all her plottings, in all her reasonings, she saw nothing before her but success; the alternative, and all its possible consequences, never suggested itself to her as possible, and therefore no portion of her clever ingenuity was ever employed, even in speculation, to ward it off.

In a word, then, her bills, which, by the by, were wholly and solely for her own dress, were all paid without difficulty or delay, and the day was fixed for the departure of herself and Agnes by a stage-coach from Bristol to Cheltenham.

Poor Agnes wept bitterly as she received the affectionate farewells of her friends in Rodney Place; and Mary, who really loved her, wept too, though it is possible that the severe disappointment which had attended her matrimonial project for her, had a little dulled the edge of the enthusiasm at first excited by the sweetness and beauty of the poor motherless girl. But, under no circumstances, could the grief of Miss Peters at losing sight of her have been comparable to that felt by Agnes herself. How little had the tyranny of Mrs. Barnaby, and all the irksome désagrémens of her home, occupied her attention during the month she had spent at Clifton! How completely it had all been lost sight of in the society of Mary, and the hospitable kindness of Rodney Place!

"But, Oh! the heavy change!"... That which had been chased by the happy lightness of her young spirit, as a murky cloud is chased by the bright sun of April, now rolled back upon her, looking like a storm that was to last for ever! She knew it, she felt its approach, and, like a frightened fawn, trembled as she gazed around, and saw no shelter near.

"You will write to me, dear Agnes!" said Mary. "I shall think of you very often, and it will be a real pleasure to hear from you."

"And to write to you, Mary, will be by far the greatest pleasure I can possibly have. But how can I ask you to write to me in return?... I am sure my aunt will never let me receive a letter; ... and yet, would it not be worth its weight in gold."

"Don't take up sorrow at interest, Agnes," replied Mary, laughing. "I don't think your dragon will be so fierce as that either.... I can hardly imagine she would refuse to let you correspond with me."

Agnes endeavoured to return her smile, but she blushed and faltered as she said, "I mean, Mary, that she would not pay postage for me."

"Impossible!" cried Miss Peters, indignantly; "you cannot speak seriously.... I know my mother does not believe a word about her very large fortune, any more than she does her very generous intention of leaving it to us. But she says that my uncle must have left something like a respectable income for her; and though we none of us doubt (not even Elizabeth) that she will marry with all possible speed, and when she has found a husband, with all her worldly goods will him endow; still, till this happens, it is hardly likely she will refuse to pay the postage of your letters."

"Perhaps she will not," said Agnes, blushing again for saying what she did not think; "but, at any rate, try the experiment, dearest Mary.... To know that you have thought of me will be comfort inexpressible."

"And suppose Mr. Frederick Stephenson were to ramble back to Clifton, Agnes, ... and suppose he were to ask me which way you are gone ... may I tell him?"

"He never will ask you, Mary...."

"But an' if he should?" persisted Miss Peters.

"Then tell him that it would be a great deal more kind and amiable if he never again talked about me to any one."

Arrived at Cheltenham, Mrs. Barnaby set about the business of finding a domicile with much more confidence and savoir faire than heretofore. A very few inquiries made her decide upon choosing to place herself at a boarding-house; and though the price rather startled her, she not only selected the dearest, but indulged in the expensive luxury of a handsome private sitting-room.

"I know what I am about," thought she; "faint heart never won fair lady, and sparing hand never won gay gentleman."

It was upon the same principle that, within three days after her arrival, she had found a tiger, and got his dress (resplendent with buttons from top to toe) sent home to her private apartments, and likewise that she had determined to enter her name as a subscriber at the pump-room.

The day after all this was completed, was the first upon which she accounted her Cheltenham existence to begin; and having informed herself of the proper hours and fitting costume for each of the various stated times of appearing at the different points of re-union, she desired Agnes carefully to brush the dust from her immortal black crape bonnet, and with her own features sheltered by paille de fantaisie, straw-coloured ribbons, and Brussels lace, she set forth, leaning on the arm of her niece, and followed by her tiger and parasol, to take her first draught at the spring, at eight o'clock in the morning.

Her spirits rose as she approached the fount on perceiving the throng of laughing, gay, and gossiping invalids that bon ton and bile had brought together; and when she held out her hand to receive the glass, she had more the air of a full-grown Bacchante, celebrating the rites of Bacchus, than a votary at the shrine of Hygeia. But no sooner had the health-restoring but nauseous beverage touched her lips, or rather her palate, than, making a horrible grimace, she set down the glass on the marble slab, and pushed it from her with very visible symptoms of disgust. A moment's reflection made her turn her head to see if Agnes was looking at her; ... but no ... Agnes indeed stood at no great distance; but her whole attention seemed captivated by a tall, elegant-looking woman, who, together with an old lady leaning on her arm, appeared like herself to be occupied as spectators of the water-drinking throng.

Satisfied that her strong distaste for the unsavoury draught had not been perceived, Mrs. Barnaby backed out of the crowd, saying, as she took the arm of her niece in her way, "This water must be a very fine medicine, I am sure, for those who want it; but I don't think I shall venture upon any more of it till I have taken medical advice ... it is certainly very powerful, and I think it might do you a vast deal of good, Agnes."

These words being spoken in the widow's audible tone, which she always rather desired than not should make her presence known at some distance ... excepting, indeed, when she was making love ... were very distinctly heard by the ladies above mentioned; and the elder of them, having witnessed Mrs. Barnaby's look of disgust as she sat down her unemptied glass, laughed covertly and quietly, but with much merriment, saying, though rather to herself than her companion, "Good!... very good, indeed!... This will prove an acquisition."

A turn or two up and down the noble walk upon which the pump-room opens was rendered very delightful to the widow by shewing her that even at that early hour many dashing-looking, lace-frocked men, moustached and whiskered "to the top of her bent," might be met sauntering there; and having enjoyed this till her watch told her the boarding-house breakfast hour was arrived, she turned from the fascinating promenade in excellent spirits, and after a few minutes passed at the mirror in arranging her cap and her curls, and refreshing her bloom, entered for the first time the public eating-room, well disposed to enjoy herself in every way.

Having left the Peters family behind her, she no longer thought it necessary to restrain her fancy in the choice of colours; and, excepting occasionally on a provincial stage, it would be difficult to find a costume more brilliant in its various hues than that of our widow as she followed the obsequious waiter to the place assigned her. Agnes came after her, like a tranquil moon-lit night following the meretricious glare of noisy fireworks; the dazzled sight that had been drawn to Mrs. Barnaby as she entered, rested upon Agnes, as if to repose itself, and by the time they both were seated, it was on her fair, delicate face, and mourning garb, that every eye was fixed. The vicarial crape and bombasin which she wore in compliance with the arrangement of her too sensitive aunt, did Agnes at least one service among strangers, for it precluded the idea of any near relationship between her companion and herself; and though no one could see them together without marvelling at the discordant fellowship of two persons so remarkably contrasted in manner and appearance, none explained it by presuming that they were aunt and niece.

The party assembled and assembling at the breakfast-table consisted of fourteen gentlemen and five ladies; the rest of the company inhabiting the extensive and really elegant mansion preferring to breakfast in their own apartments, though there were few who did not condescend to abandon their privacy at dinner. Of the gentlemen now present, about half were of that lemon tint which at the first glance shewed their ostensible reason for being there was the real one. Of the other half it would be less easy to render an account. The five ladies were well dressed; and, two being old, and three young, they may be said for the most part to have been well-looking. Any more accurate description of them generally would but encumber and delay the narrative unnecessarily, as such among them as may come particularly in contact with my heroine or her niece will of necessity be brought into notice.

Our two ladies were of course placed side by side, Mrs. Barnaby being flanked to the right by a staid and sober gentleman of middle age, who happily acted as a wet blanket to the crackling and sparkling vivacity of the widow, obliging her, after one or two abortive attempts at conversation, and such sort of boarding-table agaceries as the participation of coffee and eggs may give room for, either to eat her breakfast in silence, or to exercise her social propensities on the neighbour of Agnes. This was an elderly lady, who, though like Mrs. Barnaby, but just arrived for the season, had, unlike her, been a constant visiter at Cheltenham for the last twelve years; and being an active-minded spinster of tolerably easy means, and completely mistress of them, was as capable of giving all sorts of local information as Mrs. Barnaby was desirous of receiving it. Miss Morrison (such was her name) being now, and having ever been, a lady of great prudence and the most unimpeachable discretion, might probably have taken fright had she chanced, at first meeting with our widow, to see her under full sail in chase of conquest; but luckily this was not apparent at their first interview, and the appearance and manner of Agnes offering something like a guarantee for the respectability of the lady to whose charge she was intrusted, she met Mrs. Barnaby's advances towards making an acquaintance with great civility.

Before many sentences had been exchanged between them, the spinster had the satisfaction of perceiving, that all her minute acquaintance with Cheltenham and its ways gave her an immeasurable superiority over her richly-dressed new acquaintance; while the widow with like facility discovered that all she most particularly desired to know, might be learned from the very respectable-looking individual near whom her good fortune had placed her.

The consequence of this mutual discovery was so brisk an exchange of question and answer as obliged Agnes to lean back in her chair, and eat her breakfast by means of a very distant communication with the table; ... but she was thankful her aunt had fallen upon a quiet though rather singular-looking female of forty, instead of another whiskered Major Allen, and willingly placed herself in the attitude least likely to interrupt their conversation.

"Never been at Cheltenham before?... really!... Well, ma'am, I have little doubt that you will soon declare it shall not be your last visit, though it is your first," said Miss Morrison.

"Indeed, ma'am, I think you will prove right in that opinion," replied Mrs. Barnaby, "for I never saw a place I admired so much. We are just come from Clifton, which is called so beautiful, ... but it is not to be compared to Cheltenham."

"You are just come from Clifton, are you, ma'am?... I understand it is a very beautiful place, but terribly dull, I believe, when compared to this.... If a person knows Cheltenham well, and has a little notion how to take advantage of all that is going on, he may pass months and months here without ever knowing what it is to have an idle hour.... I don't believe there is such another place in the whole world for employing time."

"I am sure that's a blessing," replied Mrs. Barnaby earnestly. "If there is one thing I dread and hate more than another, it is having nothing to do with my time. Idleness is indeed the root of all evil."

"I'm pleased to hear you say so, ma'am," said Miss Morrison, "because it is so exactly my own opinion, and because, too, you will find yourself so particularly well off here as to the avoiding it; and I shall be very happy, I'm sure, if any advice of mine may put you in the way of making the most of the advantages in that line that Cheltenham offers."

"You are exceedingly kind and obliging, ma'am," returned Mrs. Barnaby very graciously; "and I shall be very grateful for any counsel or instruction you can bestow. With my handsome fortune I should consider it quite a crime if I did not put my time to profit in such a place as Cheltenham."

This phrase produced its proper effect; Miss Morrison eyed the speaker not only with increased respect, but increased good-will.

"Indeed, my dear madam, you are quite right," she said; "and by merely paying attention to such information as I shall be able to give you, I will venture to say that you will never have the weight of an idle hour upon your hands while you remain here; for what with the balls, and the music at the libraries, and the regular hours for the walks, and attendance at all the sales, (and I assure you we have sometimes three in a day,) and shopping, and driving between the turnpikes, if you have a carriage, and morning visits, and evening parties, and churches and chapels, if you have a taste for them, and looking over the new names, and the pump-room, and making new acquaintance, and finding out old ones, there is not a day of the week, or an hour in the day, in which one may not be well employed."

"I am sure, ma'am, it is perfectly a pleasure to a person of my active turn of mind to listen to such a description; and it is a greater pleasure still to meet with a lady like yourself, with taste and good sense to value what is valuable, and to find out how and where to enjoy it.... I hope we shall become better acquainted; I have a private drawing-room here where I shall be delighted to see you.... Give me leave to present you with my card."

A gilt-edged and deeply-embossed card, inscribed—

MRS. BARNABY,   The — Hotel and Boarding House.   No. 5.

was here put into Miss Morrison's hand, who received it with an air of great satisfaction, and reiterated assurances that she would by no means fail of paying her compliments.

Unlike many vain persons who receive every civility under the persuasion that it is offered for their own beaux yeux, Miss Morrison had sufficient good sense and experience to understand that any convenience or advantage she might derive from Mrs. Barnaby, or Mrs. Barnaby's private drawing-room, must be repaid by accommodation of some sort or other. All obligations of such kind were, for a variety of excellent reasons, always repaid by Miss Morrison with such treasure as her own lips could coin, aided by her wit and wisdom, without drawing on any other exchequer; and now, having placed her little modest slip of pasteboard, bearing in broad and legible, though manuscript characters,—

by the side of Mrs. Barnaby's buttered roll, she began at once, like an honest old maid as she was, to pay the debt almost before it was incurred.

"I don't know how they do those sort of things at Clifton, Mrs. Barnaby," she said, "but here the medical gentlemen, or at least many of them, always call on the new-comers; and though I hope and trust that neither you nor this pretty young lady,—who, I suppose, is your visiter,—though I hope with all my heart that you won't, either of you, have any occasion in the world for physic or doctors, yet I advise you most certainly to fix on one in your own mind beforehand, and just let him know it. There are not more kind and agreeable acquaintances in the world than gentlemen of the medical profession ... at least, I'm sure it is so here. There are one or two apothecaries in particular,—surgeons, though, I believe they are called,—who certainly are as elegant, conversable gentlemen, as can be met with in London or anywhere, unless, indeed, just in Paris, where I certainly found the apothecaries, like everything else, in a very out-of-the-common-way style of elegance, toutafay par fit, as we say on the Continent. Of course, you have been abroad, Mrs. Barnaby?"

"No, Miss Morrison, I have not," replied the widow, making head against this attack with great skill and courage. "I am obliged to confess that the extreme comfort and elegance of my own home, have absolutely made a prisoner of me hitherto; ... but since I have lost my dear husband I find change absolutely necessary for my health and spirits, and I shall probably soon make the tour of Europe."

"Indeed!... Oh dear! how I envy you!... But you speak all the languages already?"

"Oh! perfectly."

"I'm so glad of that, Mrs. Barnaby, ... for, upon my word, I find it quite out of my power to avoid using a French word every now and then since I came from abroad, and it is so vexing when one is not understood. A lady of your station has, of course, been taught by all sorts of foreigners; but those who can't afford this indulgence never do get the accent without going abroad.... I'm sure you'll find, before you have been a week on the Continent, a most prodigious difference in your accent, though I dare say its very good already. But, a prop po, about the apothecaries and surgeons that I was talking about.... I hope you will give orders at the door that, if Mr. Alexander Pringle calls, and sends in his card, he shall be desired to walk up; and then, you know, just a prop po de nang, you can talk to him about whatever you wish to know; ... and you can say, if you like it, that Miss Morrison particularly mentioned his name.... There is no occasion do too that you should give him any fee; but you may ask him a few questions about the waters cum sa, and you will find him the most agreeable, convenient, and instructive acquaintance do mund."

The breakfast was now so evidently drawing to its close, that the new friends deemed it advisable to leave the table; and Mrs. Barnaby having repeated her invitation, and Miss Morrison having replied to it by kissing her fingers, and uttering "Mercy! Mercy! O revor," they parted ... the widow to give orders, as she passed to her drawing-room, that if Mr. Alexander Pringle called on her, he should be admitted; and the spinster to invent and fabricate, in the secret retirement of her attic retreat, some of those remarkably puzzling articles of dress, the outline of which she had studied during a three weeks' residence in Paris, and which passed current with the majority of her friends and acquaintance for being of genuine Gallic manufacture.

The prediction of Miss Morrison was speedily verified; Mr. Alexander Pringle did call at the hotel to leave his card for Mrs. Barnaby, and, in consequence of the orders given, was immediately admitted to her presence.

She was alone; for Agnes, though unfortunately there was no little dear miserable closet for her, had received the welcome congé, now always expressed by the words, "There, you may go to your lessons, child, if you will," and had withdrawn herself to an out-of-the-way corner in their double-bedded room, where already her desk, and other Empton treasures, had converted about four feet square of her new abode into a home. The sofa, therefore, with the table and its gaudy cover, adorned with the widow's fine work-box, a boarding-house inkstand of bright coloured china, and THE ALBUM (still sacred to the name of Isabella d'Almafonte), had all been set in the places and attitudes she thought most becoming by Mrs. Barnaby herself, and, together with her own magnificent person, formed a very charming picture as the medical gentleman entered the room; ... but it is probable Mr. Alexander Pringle expected rather to find a patient than to be ushered into the presence of a lady in a state of health apparently so perfect.

"Pray, sit down, sir!... Mr. Pringle, I believe?" said Mrs. Barnaby, half rising, and pointing to a chair exactly opposite her place upon the sofa.

Mr. Pringle took the indicated chair; but before he was well seated in it, the idea that some mistake might be the source of this civility occurred to him, and he rose again, made a step forward, and laid his card, specifying his name, profession, and address, on the table immediately before the eyes of the lady.

"Oh yes!" said she, smiling with amiable condescension, "I understand perfectly; ... and should myself, or my young niece, or any of my servants, require medical assistance, Mr. Pringle, this card (placing it carefully in her work-box) will enable us to find it. But, though at present we are all pretty well, I am really very glad to have an opportunity of seeing you, sir.... Miss Morrison ... I believe you know Miss Morrison?... (Mr. Pringle bowed).... Miss Morrison has named you to me in a manner that made me extremely desirous of making your acquaintance.... Gentlemen of your profession, Mr. Pringle, have so much knowledge of the world, that it is a great advantage for a stranger, on first arriving at a new place, to find an opportunity of conversing with them. Will you afford me five minutes while I explain to you my very peculiar situation?"

"Assuredly, madam," replied Mr. Pringle, "I shall be most happy to listen to you."

"Well, then ... without farther apology I will explain myself. My name is Barnaby.... I am a widow of good fortune, and without children ... for I have lost both my little ones!" Here Mrs. Barnaby drew forth one of her embroidered handkerchiefs, as she always did when speaking of her children "which were not;" and this frequently happened, for she had a great dislike to being considered as one unblessed by offspring,—a peculiarity which, together with some others, displaying themselves in the same inventive strain, proved an especial blessing to Agnes, inasmuch as it made her absence often desirable. Having wiped her eyes, and recovered her emotion, she continued: "I have no children; ... but an elder sister ... so much older, indeed, as almost to be considered as my mother, ... died several years ago, leaving an orphan girl to my care. In truth, I am not a great many years older than my niece, and the anxiety of this charge has been sometimes almost too much for me.... However, she is a good girl, and I am most passionately attached to her. Nevertheless she has some peculiarities which give me pain, ... one is, that she will never wear any dress but the deepest mourning, thus consecrating herself, as I may say, to the memory of her departed parents. Now this whim, Mr. Pringle, shews her spirits to be in a state requiring change of scene, and it is on this account that I have left my charming place in Devonshire, in the hope that variety, and a gayer circle than is likely to be found in the immediate neighbourhood of a large mansion in the country, might be of service to her."

"Indeed, ma'am, I think you are quite right," replied Mr. Pringle. "What age is the young lady?"

"Just seventeen ... and I should have no objection whatever to take her into company ... and this is indeed the point on which I most wish for your advice. I came to Cheltenham, sir, fully expecting to find my friends the Gordons ... near relations of the Duke, and persons of first-rate fashion and consequence, who would at once have placed us in the midst of all that is most elegant in the way of society here.... But, by a letter they sent to meet us at Clifton, I find that they are absolutely obliged to pay a visit of some weeks to the Duchess of Bedford, ... and thus I find myself here a perfect stranger, without any means whatever of getting into society."

"A most vexatious contretems, certainly, madam," replied Mr. Pringle; "but there can be no doubt of your obtaining quite as much society as you wish, for Cheltenham is extremely full just now, and a lady in your situation of life can hardly fail of meeting some of your acquaintance.... Of course you will go to the pump-room, Mrs. Barnaby, and look over the subscription-books, and I doubt not you will soon find there are many here whom you know.... Besides, I will myself, if you wish it, take care to make it known that you intend to enter into society ... and probably intend to receive...."

"Indeed, sir, you will oblige me.... On my own account I should certainly never particularly desire to make acquaintance with strangers, but there is nothing I would not be willing to do for this dear girl!... Of course I shall make a point of subscribing to everything, and particularly of taking my poor dear niece to all the balls.... She is really very pretty, and if I can but contrive to get suitable partners for her, I think dancing may be of great service. Are there many of the nobility here at present, Mr. Pringle?"

"Yes, madam, several, and a great deal of good company besides."

"That gives us a better chance of finding old acquaintance certainly.... But there is another point, Mr. Pringle, on which I am anxious to consult you.... My niece is decidedly very bilious, and I feel quite convinced that a glass of the water every morning would be of the most essential benefit to her.... Unfortunately, dear creature, she is quite a spoiled child, and I do not think she will be prevailed on to take what is certainly not very pleasant to the taste, unless ordered to do it by a medical man."

"I must see the young lady, ma'am," replied Mr. Pringle, "before I can venture to prescribe for her in any way."

Mrs. Barnaby internally wished him less scrupulous, but feeling that it would be better he should send in a bill and charge a visit, than that she should lose a daily excuse for visiting the delightful pump-room, and, moreover, feeling more strongly still that, in order to make Agnes swallow the dose instead of herself, it would be good economy to pay for half a dozen visits, she rose from the sofa, and said with a fascinating smile.... "I will bring her to you myself, my dear sir, but I hope you will not disappoint me about prescribing the Cheltenham waters for her. I know her constitution well, and I venture to pledge myself to you, that she is exactly the subject for the Cheltenham treatment.... So bilious, poor girl!... so dreadfully bilious!"

Mrs. Barnaby left the room, and presently returned with Agnes, who was considerably surprised at being told that it was necessary a medical man should see her; for, in the first place, save a heaviness at her heart, she felt quite well; and in the second, she had never before, since she left Empton, perceived any great anxiety on the part of her aunt as to her being well or ill. However, she yielded implicit obedience to the command which bade her leave the letter she was writing to Miss Peters, and meekly followed her imperious protectress to their sitting-room.

Mr. Alexander Pringle was decidedly a clever man, and clever men of his profession are generally skilful in discerning diagnostics of various kinds. He had expected to see a yellow, heavy-eyed girl, looking either as if she were ready to cry with melancholy, or pout from perverseness; instead of which, he saw a lovely, graceful creature, with a step elastic with youth and health, and an eye whose clear, intelligent glance, said as plainly as an eye could speak, "What would you with me?... I have no need of you."

He immediately perceived that the amiable child-bereaved widow had quite misunderstood the young lady's case.... It might be, perhaps, from her too tender affection; but, let the cause be what it would, it was not to solve any professional doubts that he took her delicate hand to feel the "healthful music" of her pulse. Nevertheless, Mr. Pringle, who had seven promising children, knew better than to reject the proffered custom of a rich widow who had none; so, looking at his beautiful patient with much gravity, he said,—

"There is little or nothing, madam, to alarm you. The young lady is rather pale, but I am inclined to believe that it rather proceeds from the naturally delicate tint of her complexion than from illness. It will be proper, however, that I should see her again, and, mean time, I would strongly recommend her taking about one-third of a glass of water daily. If more be found necessary, the dose must be increased; but I am inclined to hope that this will prove sufficient, with the help of a few table-spoonfuls of a mixture ... by no means disagreeable, my dear young lady ... which I will not fail to send in." And so saying, Mr. Pringle rose to take leave, but was somewhat puzzled by Agnes saying, with a half smile in which there was something that looked very much as if she were quizzing him,—

"You must excuse me, sir, if I decline taking any medicine whatever till I feel myself in some degree out of health."

Mr. Pringle, who was very near laughing himself, answered with great good-humour,... "Well then, Mrs. Barnaby, I suppose we must do without it, ... and I don't think there will be much danger either." He then took his departure, leaving Mrs. Barnaby quite determined that Agnes should drink the water, but not very sorry that she was to have no physic to pay for ... whilst Agnes was altogether at a loss to guess what this new vagary of her aunt might mean.

"What made you think I was ill, aunt?" said she.

"Ill?... Who told you, child, that I thought you ill?... I don't think any such thing, ... but I did not choose you should drink the waters till I had the opinion of the first medical man in the place about it. There is no expense, no sacrifice, Agnes, that I am not ready to make for you."

"But I don't mean to drink the waters at all, thank you, aunt," replied Agnes.

"Don't mean, miss?... you don't mean?... And perhaps you don't mean to eat any dinner to-day? and perhaps you don't mean to sleep in my apartment to-night?... Perhaps you may prefer walking the streets all night?... Pretty language, indeed, from you to me!... And now you may take yourself off again, and, as you like to stick to your lessons, you may just go and write for a copy, 'I must do as I'm bid.'"

Agnes quitted the room in silence, and Mrs. Barnaby prepared to receive her new friend, Miss Morrison, who she doubted not would call before the hour she had named as the fashionable time for repairing to the public library; nor was she at all displeased by this abrupt departure, as, for obvious reasons, it was extremely inconvenient for her to have Agnes present when she felt inclined to enter upon a little autobiography. But, while anticipating this agreeable occupation, she recalled, as she set herself to work upon one of her beautiful collars, the scrape she had got into respecting her park, and firmly resolved not even to mention a paddock to Miss Morrison by name, whatever other flights of fancy she might indulge in.

"This has been no idle day with me as yet," thought she, as she proceeded with her elegant "satin-stitch".... "I have got well stared at, though only in my close straw-bonnet, at the pump-room,—have made a capital new acquaintance, and,"—remembering with a self-approving smile all she had said to Mr. Pringle,—"I know I have not been sowing seed on barren ground.... I have not forgotten how glad my poor dear Barnaby was to get hold of something new.... He will repeat it every word, I'll answer for him."

CHAPTER XIII

THE ACQUAINTANCE RIPENS INTO FRIENDSHIP—USEFUL INFORMATION OF ALL SORTS—AN EXCELLENT METHOD OF TALKING FRENCH, ATTENDED WITH LITTLE LABOUR AND CERTAIN SUCCESS—A COLLECTOR—A SALE-ROOM—A PEER OF THE REALM

The visit of Miss Morrison, which quickly followed, was long and confidential. Mrs. Barnaby very condescendingly explained to her all the peculiar circumstances of her position, which rendered her the most valuable friend in the world, and also the most eligible match extant for a man of rank and fortune; but all these latter particulars were communicated under the seal of secrecy, never, upon any account, to be alluded to or mentioned to any one; and in return for all this, Miss Morrison gave the widow a catalogue raisonnée of the most marriageable men at present in Cheltenham, together with the best accounts of their rent-rolls and expectancies that it had been in the power of pertinacious questionings to elicit. But it would be superfluous to narrate this part of the conversation at length, as the person and affairs of many a goodly gentleman were canvassed therein, who, as they never became of much importance to Mrs. Barnaby, can be of none to those occupied by the study of her character and adventures. There were other points, however, canvassed in this interview, which were productive of immediate results; and one of these was the great importance of attending the sales by auction, which, sometimes preluded by soft music, and always animated as they went on by the most elegant conversation, occupied the beau monde of Cheltenham for many hours of every day.

"Your descriptions are delightful, Miss Morrison!" exclaimed the animated widow. "I could almost fancy myself there already, ... and go I will constantly, you may depend upon that; ... and I want to consult you about another thing, Miss Morrison.... There's my niece, you know—the little girl you saw at breakfast ... do you think it would be quite the thing to make her leave her books and lessons, and all that, to waste her time at the sales?... And besides, baby as she is, she gets more staring at than I think at all good for her."

"Jay non doot paw," replied Miss Morrison, "for she is divinely handsome, say toon bow tay par fit, as they say at Paris; and my belief is, that if you wish to be the fashion at Cheltenham, the best thing you can do is to let her be seen every day, and all day long. That face and figure must take, say clare."

Mrs. Barnaby fell into a reverie that lasted some minutes. That she did wish to be the fashion at Cheltenham was certain, but the beauty of Agnes was not exactly the means by which she would best like to obtain her wish. She had hoped to depend solely on her own beauty and her own talents, but she was not insensible to the manifest advantage of having two strings to her bow; and as the ambition, which made her determine to be great, was quite as powerful as the vanity which made her determine to be beautiful, the scheme of making Agnes a partner in her projects of fascination and conquest was at least worthy of consideration.

"I must think about it, Miss Morrison," she replied; "there is no occasion to decide this minute."

"Poing do too," said Miss Morrison; "I always like myself to walk round a thing, as I call it, before I decide to take it. Besides, my dear madam, a great deal depends upon knowing what is your principal object.... Bo coo depong de sell aw.... If you intend to be at all the parties, to be marked with a buzz every time you enter the pump-room, the ball-room, or the sales, I would say, dress up that young lady in the most elegant and attractive style possible, and you will be sure to succeed ... paw le mowyndra doot de sell aw.... But if, on the other hand, your purpose is to marry yourself, set o tra shews, and you must act altogether in a different way."

"I understand you, my dear Miss Morrison, perfectly," replied the widow, greatly struck by the sound sense and clear perception of her new friend; "and I will endeavour, with the most perfect frankness, to make you understand all my plans, for I feel sure that you deserve my full confidence, and that nobody can be more capable of giving me good advice.... The truth is, Miss Morrison, that I do wish to marry again. My fortune, indeed, is ample enough to afford me every luxury I can wish for; ... but a widowed heart, my dear Miss Morrison ... a widowed heart is a heavy load to bear, where the temper, like mine, is full of the softest sensibility and all the tenderest affections.... Therefore, as I said, it is my wish to marry again; but God forbid I should be weak and wicked enough to do so in any way unbecoming my station in society,—a station to which I have every right, as well from birth as fortune. No attachment, however strong, will ever induce me to forget what I owe to my family and to the world; and unless circumstances shall enable me rather to raise than debase myself in society, I will never, whatever my feelings may be, permit myself to marry at all."

"Crowyee moy vous avay raisong share dam!" exclaimed Miss Morrison.

"Such being the case," resumed the widow, "it appears to me evident, that the first object to be attended to is the getting into good society; and if, in order to obtain this, I find it necessary to bring forward Agnes Willoughby, it must certainly be done ... especially as her singing is much more remarkable, I believe, than even the beauty of her person."

"Et he po-se-ble?" said Miss Morrison, joyfully. "Then, in that case, share a me, there is nothing in the whole world, of any sort or kind, that can prevent your being sought out and invited to every fashionable house in the place. An ugly girl, that sings well, may easily get herself asked wherever she chooses to go; but a beautiful one, aveck ung talong samblabel, may not only go herself, but carry with her as many of her friends as she pleases."

"Really!..." said Mrs. Barnaby, thoughtfully. "This is a great advantage; ... and you feel sure, Miss Morrison, that if I do make up my mind to bring her forward, this will be the case?"

"O we," replied her friend confidently, "set ung fay certaing ... there is no doubt about it; and if you will, I am ready to make you a bet of five guineas, play or pay, that if you contrive to make her be seen and heard once, you will have your table covered with visiting cards before the end of the week ... nong douty paw."

"Well!... we must consider about it, Miss Morrison; ... but I should like, I think, to go first to some of these crowded places that you talk about without her, just to see ... that is, if you would be kind enough to go with me."

"Most certainly I will," replied Miss Morrison, "aveck leplu grang plesire.... Suppose we go to the sale-rooms this morning? There is a vast variety of most useful and beautiful things to be sold to-day, and as they always go for nothing, you had better bid a little. It is thought stylish."

"And must certainly draw attention," said Mrs. Barnaby, with vivacity.

"You are quite right ... say sa, ... and it is just about time to get ready.... All our gentlemen will be there, you may be sure; and perhaps, you know, some one of them may join us, which is a great advantage, ... for nothing makes women look so much like nobody as having no man near them.... As to marriage, I don't think of it for myself ... jay pre mong party; ... but I confess I do hate to be anywhere without the chance of a man's coming to speak to one ... mays, eel foh meytra mong shappo ... o reyvoyr!"

Mrs. Barnaby now found herself at last obliged to confess she did not understand her.

"Of course I know French perfectly," she said; "but as I have never been in the country, and not much in the habit of speaking it, even at home, I cannot always follow you.... I would give a great deal, Miss Morrison, to speak the language as beautifully as you do!"

"It is a great assistance in society, certainly," replied Miss Morrison, very modestly; "but I do assure you that it is quite impossible for anybody in the world to speak it as I do without being in the country, and taking the same incessant pains as I did. As to learning it from books, it is all nonsense to think of it ... how in the world is one to get the accent and pronunciation?... But I must say that I believe few people ever learned so much in so short a time as I did. I invented a method for myself, without which I should never have been able to speak as I do. I never was without my pencil and paper in my hand, and I wrote down almost every word I heard, in such a manner as that I was always able to read it myself, without asking anybody. The English of it all I got easily afterwards, for almost everybody understands me when I read my notes according to my own spelling, especially English people; and these translations I wrote down over against my French, which I call making both a grammar and dictionary entirely of my own invention, ... and I have often been complimented upon it, I assure you."

"And I'm sure you well deserve it. I never heard anything so clever in my life," replied Mrs. Barnaby. "But how soon shall we begin our walk?"

"Now directly, if you please.... I will go and put on my hat ... that was what I said to you in French.... Eel foh meytra mong shappo."

Mrs. Barnaby then repaired to her toilet; and having done her very utmost to make herself as conspicuously splendid and beautiful as possible, turned to Agnes, who was still writing in her dark corner, and said,... "You had better finish what you are about, Agnes, and I hope it is something that will improve you.... I am going out with Miss Morrison on business ... and if the evening is fine, I will take you a walk somewhere or other."

Agnes again blessed their rencontre with this valuable new friend, and saw the satin and feathers of her aunt disappear with a feeling of great thankfulness that she was spared the necessity of attending them.

On leaving Mrs. Barnaby, Mr. Alexander Pringle paid a visit to his good friend and patient Lady Elizabeth Norris, (the aunt of Colonel Hubert,) who, as usual, was passing a few weeks of the season at Cheltenham, as much for the sake of refreshing her spirits by the variety of its company, as for the advantage of taking a daily glass of water at its spring. The worthy apothecary was as useful by the information and gossippings he furnished on the former subject, as by his instructions on the latter, and was invariably called in, the day after her ladyship's arrival, however perfect the state of her health might be; and given moreover to understand that a repetition of a professional visit would be expected at least three times a week during her stay.

He now found the old lady sitting alone; for Sir Edward and Lady Stephenson, who were her guests, were engaged in one of their favourite morning expeditions, exploring the beautiful environs of the town, a pleasure which they enjoyed as uninterruptedly as the most sentimental newly-married pair could desire, as, by a strange but very general spirit of economy, few of the wealthy and luxurious visitants of Cheltenham indulge themselves in the expense of a turnpike.

"Soh! Pringle ... you are come at last, are you?" said Lady Elizabeth.... "I have been expecting you this hour ... the Stephensons' are off and away again to the world's end, in search of wild flowers and conjugal romance, leaving me to my own devices—a privilege worth little or nothing, unless you can add something new to my list here for next Wednesday."

"Perhaps I may be able to assist your ladyship," returned her Esculapius; "that is, provided Lady Stephenson knows nothing about it, for I fear she has not yet forgiven my introduction of Mr. Myrtle and the two Misses Tonkins."

"Stuff and nonsense!... What does it signify, now she is married and out of the way, what animals I get into my menagerie?... But I don't think, Pringle, that you are half such a clever truffle-dog as you used to be.... What a time it is since you have told me of anything new!"

"Upon my word, my lady, it is not my fault," replied the apothecary, laughing; "I never see or hear anything abroad without treasuring it in my memory for your ladyship's service; and I am now come expressly to mention a new arrival at the —, which appears to promise well."

"I rejoice.... Is it male or female?"

"Female, my lady, and there are two."

"Of the same species, and the same race?"

"Decidedly not; but the contrast produces a very pleasant effect; and, moreover, though infinitely amusing, they are quite comme il faut. I understand the elder lady is sister to Mrs. Peters of Clifton."

Mr. Pringle then proceeded to describe his visit to Mrs. Barnaby, and did justice to the florid style of her beauty, dress, and conversation. But when he came to speak of the young girl who was vouée au noir, and of her aunt's pertinacious resolution that she should take the waters and be treated as an invalid, notwithstanding the very excellent state of her health, the old lady rubbed her hands together, and exultingly exclaimed, "Good!... admirable!... You are a very fine fellow, Pringle, and have hit this off well. Why, man, I saw your delightful widow this morning at the Pump, rouge, ringlets, and all;... I saw her taste the waters and turn sick; and now, because she must have a reason for shewing herself at the Pump, she is going to make the poor girl drink for her.... Capital creature!... I understand it all ... poor little girl!... And so the widow wants acquaintance, does she?...

I offer myself, my drawing-room shall be open to her, Pringle.... And now, how can I manage to get introduced to her?"

"You will not find that very difficult, Lady Elizabeth, depend upon it.... I will undertake to promise for this Mrs. Barnaby, that she will be visible wherever men and women congregate. At the ball, for instance, to-morrow night; does your ladyship intend to be there?"

"Certainly.... And if she be there, I will manage the matter of introduction, with or without intervention, and so obtain this full-blown peony for my shew on Wednesday next."

Whilst fate and Mr. Pringle were thus labouring in one quarter of the town to bring Mrs. Barnaby into notice, she was herself not idle in another in her exertions to produce the same effect. The sale-room, to which the experienced Miss Morrison led her, was already full when they entered it; but the little difficulty which preceded their obtaining seats was rather favourable to them than otherwise; for, as if on purpose to display the sagacity of that lady's prognostications, two of the gentlemen who had made part of their company at breakfast, not only made room for them, but appeared well disposed to enter into conversation, and to offer every attention they could desire.

"Mr. Griffiths, if I mistake not," said Miss Morrison, bowing to one of them; "I hope you have been quite well, sir, since we met last year.... Give me leave to introduce, Mr. Griffiths, Mrs. Barnaby."

"I am happy to make your acquaintance," said the gentleman, bowing low. "Your young friend whom I saw with you this morning is not here ... is she?"

"No, sir," replied Mrs. Barnaby, in the most amiable tone imaginable; "the dear girl is pursuing her morning studies at home."

"Introduce me, Griffiths," whispered his companion.

"Mr. Patterson, Mrs. Barnaby; Mr. Patterson, Miss Morrison," and a very social degree of intimacy appeared to be immediately established.

"Oh! what a lovely vase!" exclaimed Mrs. Barnaby. "What an elegant set of candle-sticks!" cried Miss Morrison, as the auctioneer brought forward the articles to be bid for, which being followed by a variety of interesting observations on nearly all the people, and nearly all the goods displayed before them, afforded Mrs. Barnaby such an opportunity of being energetic and animated, that more than one eye-glass was turned towards her, producing that reciprocity of cause and effect which it is so interesting to trace; for the more the gentlemen and ladies looked at her, the more Mrs. Barnaby talked and laughed, and the more Mrs. Barnaby talked and laughed, the more the gentlemen and ladies looked at her. Flattered, fluttered, and delighted beyond measure, the eyes of the widow wandered to every quarter of the room; and for some time every quarter of the room appeared equally interesting to her; but at length her attention was attracted by the almost fixed stare of an individual who stood in the midst of a knot of gentlemen at some distance, but nearly opposite to the place she occupied.

"Can you tell me, sir, who that tall, stout gentleman is in the green frock-coat, with lace and tassels?... That one who is looking this way with an eye-glass."

"The gentleman with red hair?" returned Mr. Patterson, to whom the question was addressed.

"Yes, that one, rather sandy, but a very fine-looking man."

"That is Lord Mucklebury, Mrs. Barnaby.... He is a great amateur of beauty; and upon my word he seems exceedingly taken with some fair object or other in this part of the room."

The sight of land after a long voyage is delightful ... rest is delightful after labour, food after fasting; but it may be doubted if either of these joys could bear comparison with the emotion that now swelled the bosom of Mrs. Barnaby. This was the first time, to the best of her knowledge and belief, that she had ever been looked at by a lord at all ... and what a look it was!... No passing glance, no slight unmeaning regard, directed first to one and then to another beauty, but a long, steady, direct, and unshrinking stare, such as might have made many women leave the room, but which caused the heart of Mrs. Barnaby to palpitate with a degree of ecstasy which she had never felt before—no, not even when the most admired officer of a new battalion first fixed his looks upon her in former days, and advanced in the eyes of all the girls to ask her to dance; ... for no Lord anything had ever done so; and thus, the fulness of her new-born joy, while it had the vigorous maturity of ripened age, glowed also with the early brightness of youth. It might indeed have been said of Mrs. Barnaby at that moment, that, "like Mrs. Malaprop and the orange-tree, she bore blossom and fruit at once."

One proof of the youthful freshness of her emotion was the very naïve manner in which it was betrayed. She could not sit still ... her eyes rose and fell ... her head turned and twisted ... her reticule opened and shut ... and the happy man who set all this going must have had much less experience than my Lord Mucklebury, if he had not immediately perceived the effect of himself and his eye-glass.

Could Mrs. Barnaby have known at that moment the influence produced by the presence of Miss Morrison, she would have wished her a thousand fathoms deep in the ocean; for certain it is, that nothing but her well-known little quizzical air of unquestionable Cheltenham respectability, prevented the noble lord from crossing the room, and amusing himself, without the ceremony of an introduction, in conversing with the sensitive lady, whose bright eyes and bright rouge had drawn his attention to her. As it was, however, he thought he had better not, and contented himself by turning to his ever-useful friend Captain Singleton, and saying in a tone, the familiarity of which failed not to make up for its imperiousness, "Singleton!... go and find out who that great woman is in the green satin and pink feathers ... there's a good fellow."

Mrs. Barnaby did not hear the words, but she saw the mission as plainly as my Lord Mucklebury saw her, and her heart thereupon began to beat so violently, that she had no breath left to demand the sympathy of her friend under circumstances so pregnant with interest. But though she hardly knew where she was, nor what she did, she still retained sufficient presence of mind to mark how the obedient envoy addressed himself (and, alas! in vain) first to one lounger, and then to another, who all replied by a shake of the head, which said with terrible distinctness, "I don't know."

"Gracious heaven, how provoking!" murmured Mrs. Barnaby, as she pressed her delicately-gloved hand upon her heart to still its beating.... "He will leave the room without finding out my name!"... Had she been only a few hours longer acquainted with Mr. Patterson, it is highly probable she would have desired him, if asked by the little gentleman in black, so actively making his way through the crowd, what her name was, just to have the kindness to mention that it was Barnaby. But though very civil, Mr. Patterson was rather ceremonious; and the unsuccessful messenger had returned to his lord, and delivered all the shakes of the head which he had received condensed into one, before she could resolve on so frank a mode of proceeding. For a few moments longer, however, the amused nobleman continued his fascinating gaze; and then, giving a signal with his eye to Singleton that it was his pleasure to move, that active personage cleared the way before him; and the fat viscount, with his hands in his waistcoat-pockets, stalked out of the room, but not without turning his head, and giving one bold, final, open-eyed, steady look at the agitated widow.

"That man is my fate!" she softly whispered to her soul, as the last frog on the hinder part of his coat has passed from her eye; ... and then, like the tender convolvolus when the sunbeam that reached it has passed away, she drooped and faded till she looked more like a sleeping picture of Mrs. Barnaby than Mrs. Barnaby herself.

"Do you not find the room very close, Miss Morrison?" said she, after enduring for a minute or two the sort of vacuum that seemed to weigh upon her senses.

"Poing do too," replied Miss Morrison, speaking through her nose, which was one method by which she was wont to convey the true Parisian accent, when she desired that it should be particularly perfect.... "Poing do too, Mrs. Barnaby, ... however, I am quite ready to go if you like it, for I don't think I shall buy anything this morning, and I don't see many acquaintance here."

Mrs. Barnaby immediately rose; the two civil gentlemen made way for them, and the widow, followed by her friend, walked out a more pensive, though not, perhaps, a less happy woman, than when she walked in.

CHAPTER XIV

A CHELTENHAM BALL—AN INTRODUCTION—A CONQUEST

A great deal of profound meditation was bestowed by Mrs. Barnaby on the occurrences of that morning before the time arrived for the toilet, preparatory to the ball of the succeeding night. All these will shew themselves in their results as they arise; and for the present it will be only necessary to mention, that, in providing for this toilet, everything approaching to the sordid cares dictated by economy was banished. The time was too short to admit of her ordering a new dress for this occasion; though the powerful feeling at work within her caused a white satin, decorated in every possible way with the richest blonde, to be bespoken for the next. Every other article that Cheltenham could furnish, (and it being the height of the season, Paris itself could hardly do more for her,) every other species of expensive decoration, short of diamonds and pearls, was purchased for this important ball, at which something within her—speaking with the authority of an oracle—declared that she should become acquainted with Lord Mucklebury. Busy as were the afternoon and morning which intervened, she found time for the very necessary business of ordering her broker (he had been her father's broker too) to sell out five hundred pounds stock for her; and this done, and her letter safely deposited in the boarding-house letter-bag, she turned her thoughts towards Agnes.

She had certainly, to use her own language when reasoning the point with herself, the very greatest mind in the world not to take her to the ball at all. But this mind, great as it was, was not a settled mind, and was presently shaken by a sort of instinctive consciousness that there was in Agnes, independent of her beauty, a something that might help to give consequence to her entrée. "As to her dress," thought she, "I am perfectly determined that it shall be the same she wore at Clifton, ... not so much on account of the expense ... at the present moment it would be madness to permit such a consideration to have any effect; ... but because it gives her an air more distinguished, more remarkable than any one else; ... and besides ... who knows but that the contrast of style, beautiful as she is, may be favourable to me?... I have not forgotten our fellow-traveller from Silverton ... she seemed to freeze him. And let her freeze my adorable viscount too, so that I".... But here her thoughts came too rapidly to dress themselves in words, and for a few minutes her reverie was rather a tumult than a meditation.

"Yes, she shall go!" she exclaimed at last, rising from the sofa, and collecting a variety of precious parcels, the result of her shopping; "Yes, she shall go to the ball; and should any mischief be likely to follow, I will make her go out to service before the end of the week."

Having thus at last come to a determination, and upon reasonings which she felt were not likely to be shaken, she mounted to her sleeping apartment, and after indulging herself by spreading forth various articles of newly-purchased finery upon the bed, she turned to the corner in which Agnes, her tiny table, her books, and writing apparatus, were all packed away together in the smallest possible space, and said, "Come here, Agnes ... you must have done lessons enough for to-day, and I have great news for you. Where do you think I mean to take you to-night?"

Agnes cast her eyes upon the bed, and immediately anticipating some public display of which she was doomed to be a witness, replied in a tone that was anything but joyful,—

"I don't know, aunt."

"I don't know, aunt!" retorted Mrs. Barnaby indignantly, mimicking her tone. "What an owl of a girl you are, Agnes!... Oh! how unlike what I was at the same age.... You don't know?... I suppose you don't, indeed. There is not another woman under the sun besides myself who would do for a dependant, penniless girl, all I am doing for you. I sacrifice everything for you ... my feelings, my health, my money, and yet you look exactly as if I was going to take you to school again, instead of to a ball!"

Agnes sighed; she thought of her last ball, of all its pains and all its pleasures; and feeling but too sure that it was as impossible she should escape the former, as improbable that she should find the latter, she replied mournfully enough, "I would rather not go, if you please, aunt ... I do not like balls.'"

"Upon my honour, Agnes, if I had not a temper that was proof against everything, I should be tempted to box your ears.... Is it possible to see anything more disgustingly hypocritical, than a girl of seventeen screwing herself up, and saying, 'I do not like balls'.... I wonder what you do like, Miss Prim? But, I promise you, I do not intend to ask your leave for what I do; and as long as you eat my bread, you will do as I bid you ... or else, turn out, and provide for yourself at once. Let me hear no more such stuff, if you please; but take care to make yourself decent, and be ready to get into the carriage exactly at nine o'clock.... Do you hear?"

Agnes meekly turned to her travelling magazine of sable suits, and was considerably surprised by being told that she must instantly get ready to go out for the purpose of buying satin shoes, white gloves, and one or two other trifles, which the newly-enlarged views of her aunt now rendered necessary. All this was done. Miss Morrison engaged to join their party, the labours of the hair-dresser were completed, and a toilet of two hours' duration was brought to a most satisfactory conclusion within ten minutes of the early hour she had named, and to the ball-room they repaired considerably before any other person entered it.

"I told you it would be so, my dear Mrs. Barnaby," said Miss Morrison, looking rather disconsolately round her: "noo sum tro toe; ... but never mind: let us sit down comfortably on this sofa, and I dare say I shall be able to tell you the names of most of the principal people. Cheltenham is so very delightful, that almost everybody comes over and over again: say too ta fey law mode."

A few straggling strangers began to enter almost immediately, and in about half an hour, the well-pleased Miss Morrison was enabled to redeem her promise by pointing out some scores of well-dressed individuals by name. But still Lord Mucklebury came not, and the widow's heart grew sad, till, happily, she heard a young partnerless lady say as she swept by,—"What a bore it is that all the best men come so late!" In a moment hope was rekindled in Mrs. Barnaby's eye, and with renewed interest she listened to the catalogue of names which her friend poured into her ear.

"Oh! here comes the bride, Lady Stephenson.... What a handsome man her husband is!... I have seen her here often with her aunt, Lady Elizabeth Norris, before she was married.... The old lady dotes upon Cheltenham, they say.... I wish you knew some more people ... but, name port, it will all come by and by, I dare say, and I will introduce you to Lady Elizabeth if I can; ... but I must ask her first, or she may take miff.... Ell hay ung pew fear."

"Stephenson?..." said Mrs. Barnaby,—"is it Sir Edward Stephenson?"

"Yes, Sir Edward, that's his name: do you know him, Mrs. Barnaby?"

"We were most intimately acquainted with his brother at Clifton, ... and with Colonel Hubert too; that's her brother, you know. Pray, is he here too?"

How Agnes trembled as she waited for the answer!

"I don't know ... I have not seen him yet," replied Miss Morrison, "and it is impossible to overlook him—set hun um seuperb!... but comb heel hay fear!... Perhaps he will come in presently: he is always ung pew tar at the balls, for he never dances."

"Oh! I know that," said Mrs. Barnaby.... "I know him perfectly well, I assure you ... he is a most elegant person; but I suspect he is rather of a violent and jealous temper.... However, I'm sure I wish he was here, and his friend Frederick Stephenson too.... He's a charming young man, and used to walk to Bristol with us, and dance three times a night with Agnes."

"Dear me! you don't say so!" exclaimed Miss Morrison, to whom the intelligence was extremely agreeable, as it removed at once all doubts and fears respecting Mrs. Barnaby's real station in society.... "Well, then, I'm sure you ought to know Lady Elizabeth Norris; and I really must, somehow or other, contrive to let her hear of your acquaintance with her nephew Colonel Hubert. They say she dotes upon him, and that he is to be her heir ... and that's almost a pity, for he has a noble fortune of his own already. Do you happen to know how much his sister had, Mrs. Barnaby?... Some say twenty, some thirty, some fifty thousand."

"Young Stephenson never happened to say anything about it that I recollect," replied the widow.... "But, look! Lady Elizabeth is coming this way.... You had better step forward, Miss Morrison, that she may see you."

But there was no occasion for any contrivance on the part of Miss Morrison in order to obtain the notice of Lady Elizabeth; for that lady having descried and recognised the party, she immediately decided that Miss Morrison, whose acquaintance she had cultivated for several successive seasons on account of her admirable French, should be for her the medium of introduction to the pompous widow, who was clever enough to make her niece drink the waters instead of herself.

It was, therefore, by a straight and direct line that, supported by the arm of Sir Edward Stephenson, and followed by his lady, she crossed the room from her own place to that occupied by those whom (in her own particular manner) she delighted to honour.

Miss Morrison's surprise was as great as her satisfaction when she perceived this to be the case; and she felt her triumph doubled by her fine new acquaintance being the witness of it.

"Bon jour, Miss Morrison," said the old lady, holding out her hand; "toujours en bonne santé j'espere?"

Amidst smiles and bows, and blushes and courtesies, Miss Morrison replied in her favourite jargon,—

"Mey we, me ladee ... and I hope your ladyship is the same."

"A good many old faces here, Miss Morrison, and a good many new ones too. You have friends with you whom I do not remember to have seen before.... You must introduce me."

This request threw the good-natured spinster into a twitter of delight which almost deprived her of the power of obeying it: first she made a little movement with one hand, and then with the other; while the ample Mrs. Barnaby stood in happy smiling expectation, and the tall, stiff-looking old lady continued gazing at the group through her half-closed eyes, and determined on no account to hasten a process from which she derived so great amusement.

At length the respective names were pronounced in their proper order, that of the blushing Agnes being included. The old lady gave her a look in which something of surprise was mingled with curiosity, and suddenly turning round to Lady Stephenson who stood behind her, she said,—

"Come, Emily, you must be introduced too.... Miss Willoughby ... Lady Stephenson."

Mrs. Barnaby had prepared another smile, and another majestic bend for the presentation of herself to the fair bride; but it did not follow; a disappointment for which she was soon consoled by Lady Elizabeth's sitting down, and graciously intimating, by an action of her hand, that the widow might sit beside her.

Agnes meanwhile stood trembling from head to foot with her eyes timidly fixed on the beautiful countenance of Colonel Hubert's sister. As it was quite impossible her ladyship could understand the cause of the agitation she inspired, so neither was she at all aware of its strength; but she saw that the beautiful girl before her, notwithstanding the quiet, unstudied grace of her appearance, was not at her ease, and could only account for it by supposing that she was suffering from extreme shyness. Lady Stephenson had not yet forgotten the time when she, too, had hardly dared to look up unless her paternal brother, as she was wont to call him, stood very near to sustain her carriage, and sympathising with a weakness that was in some degree constitutional in herself, she felt disposed to take more notice of the fair stranger than she usually bestowed upon persons introduced to her by the whimsical caprices of her aunt.

Lady Stephenson was, however, altogether mistaken.... Agnes was not at that moment suffering from shyness; there was timidity certainly in the pleasure with which she listened to the voice and gazed at the features of Colonel Hubert's sister; but still it was pleasure, and very nearly the most lively she had ever experienced.

"You are at Cheltenham for the first time, Miss Willoughby?" said the bride.

"Yes," replied Agnes; "we only arrived two days ago."

There was not much opportunity of indicating feeling of any kind by these words; nevertheless, the manner in which they were spoken, and the sweet expression of the beautiful eyes that were raised to hers, convinced Lady Stephenson that however shy her new acquaintance might be, she greatly liked to be spoken to, and accordingly continued the conversation, which, to her own surprise, warmed so much as it proceeded, that at length her aunt being evidently settled down for an elaborate development of the absurdities, whatever they might be, of her new acquaintance, she offered her arm, inviting her to take a turn round the room.

Could this be real?... Was it possible that she was walking round the Cheltenham ball-room on the arm of Colonel Hubert's sister? But though the happy Agnes asked herself this question again and again, neither the asking nor the answering it prevented her bearing her part in a conversation that made her so exquisitely happy with all the pretty earnestness of one interested in every word that was said to her, and too young and fresh-minded to conceal the pleasure she felt.

Lady Stephenson was unexpectedly pleased with her young companion; there was no mixture of niaiserie in the simplicity of Agnes; and though her ladyship in no degree shared her aunt's extravagant passion for originals, she had in her own quiet way a reasonably strong liking for whatever appeared to her untainted by affectation. The beauty of Agnes might perhaps have had some share in the pleasure she gave; but certain it is, that, after taking two or three turns together instead of one, and perceiving Lady Elizabeth about to move her quarters in search of fresh amusement, she shook hands with Agnes before parting with her so cordially, that she felt called upon to offer some reason for it to her husband, who had quitted her during her promenade, but was now returned.

"That is by far the most enchanting girl, Edward, in person, mind, and manners, that I ever remember to have met with.... How very strange that she should belong to one of my aunt's collection."

"She is vastly beautiful, Emily," replied Sir Edward, "and I suspect that covers a multitude of sins in your eyes; for I observe you never fail to pick out the beauties, go where you will: I declare I think your eyes are infinitely sharper than mine in this way.... Having once found out the fairest of the fair, I do not feel so much interest as I used to do in looking about me."

"A very pretty speech, Sir Edward," returned the lady, laughing; "but that sweet girl's beauty is not her greatest fascination. I must ask Lady Elizabeth whether she found the magnificent lady to whom she has been devoting herself answer her expectations."

When this question was put to the old lady, however, she bluntly answered, "No, not at all.... She is as dull as a prize-ox decorated with ribbons at a fair."

"I am sorry to hear it," observed Lady Stephenson, "for I have lost my heart to the fair girl in black whom she seems to lead about as a contrast to her radiant self.... I marvel what the connexion can be.... It is plain they are not related, from the deep mourning of the one and the rainbow brilliance of the other."

"Your inference is altogether wrong, my Lady Stephenson; ... one of this Madam Barnaby's long stories was about this melancholy miss, who is her niece, and who will wear mourning in spite of her.... I must watch them at the pump, just to see if the girl makes up for her disobedience in this respect by swallowing the waters which Pringle says the aunt is determined she shall take, ... and after that I shall trouble myself no more about them.... The great woman does not answer; she is a vulgar, pompous, everyday bore."

"Pray do not give her quite up, aunt, for my sake," said Lady Stephenson; "for I have set my fancy upon seeing a great deal more of her niece ... who, by the way, for so pertinacious a mourner, is wonderfully sprightly; ... but I must flatter myself she found consolation in my society. I must beg you to cultivate the acquaintance a little farther."

"This is something quite new, Emily," replied the old lady. "It is the first time, I believe, that you ever condescended to take any interest in my menagerie.... Far be it from me, my dear, to check so happy a symptom of an improving intellect.... I have already asked the expansive widow and her delicate shadow for Wednesday; and if your fever for cementing a friendship with the latter should happen to continue, yield to it by all means.... You know, Emily, I never wish to control anybody's set of favourites, provided always that nobody interferes with my own."

The only pleasure which the rest of the evening afforded Agnes arose from studying the features, and still more the countenance, of Lady Stephenson, whenever she was fortunate enough to be within sight of her. No one asked her to dance, and no word was uttered within her hearing that gave her the least amusement. One single circumstance cheered the tedious hours during which she was doomed to sit, with her aunt Barnaby before her eyes, in a terror which increased every moment lest she should draw the eyes of every one else in the room upon her. This single circumstance was, that the sister of Colonel Hubert, when standing at three feet of distance from her, turned her head and said, with a smile of strong family affinity to his own,—

"I find that I am to have the pleasure of seeing you on Wednesday at my aunt's, Miss Willoughby ... I am very glad of it.... Good night!"... and soon afterwards the party left the room.

Far different was the fate of Mrs. Barnaby. The evening began for her very gloriously, for she had been spoken to by a Lady Elizabeth; but it ended in rapture, ... for, before its close, Lord Mucklebury made his appearance, stared at her again with the most marked impertinence, inquired and learned her name from Mr. Pringle, by whom he was at his express desire presented, and finally he placed himself beside her on the sofa, where he remained for at least twenty minutes, talking to her in a style that might be said without the slightest exaggeration to have thrown her into a state of temporary delirium.

Nor had it failed to produce some emotion in the noble lord; nay, it is probable it might have lasted longer, had it amused him less; for when he look his leave of the widow, expressing his hope that he should be happy enough to meet her again, he moved with a step rather quicker than ordinary to ensconce himself among a knot of men who were amusing themselves by communicating to each other the most ludicrous remarks on the company, in a distant corner of the room.

"Have you really torn yourself away from that magnificent specimen of womanhood, Mucklebury?" said one of the group as he approached them.... "She is evidently magnetic, by the manner in which you have been revolving round her for some time; and if magnetic, and the power at all proportioned to the volume, it is a miracle that you ever left her side again."

"I never would leave her side again," replied Lord Mucklebury, laughing immoderately, "did I not fear that I should fall at her feet in a fit.... Oh! she is glorious!"

"Who and what is she, in God's name?" said another.

"Who is she?... Barnaby!... Bless her!—Mistress Barnaby!... What is she?... A widow.... Darling creature!... a widow, fair, fat, and forty ... most fat!—most fair!... and, oh! a pigeon, a dove,—a very turtle-dove for kindness!"

"She is really handsome, though ... isn't she, Mucklebury?" said one.

"Yes, upon my soul she is!" replied the Viscount more seriously, "and bears looking at too remarkably well, notwithstanding the pot-full of coarse rouge that it pleases her to carry about on each of her beautiful cheeks."

"And by what blessed chance has your lordship been favoured with an introduction?... Or did your lordship so far overcome your constitutional timidity as to introduce yourself?"

"Alarm not your spirit on that score, Digby," replied Lord Mucklebury. "The medium of introduction was illustrious, ... but my passion was anterior to it, ... for the history of our loves was in this wise. It is said of me ... I know not how truly ... that my taste in beauty tends somewhat towards the Blowzabella order.... Be this as it may, it is certain that yesterday morning between the hours of two and three, being actively employed for the good of myself and my country in Johnson's sale-room, I felt myself penetrated, perforated, pierced, and transfixed by the very bright eyes of this remarkable lady; ... whereupon, overpowering my constitutional timidity, Digby, I fixed my regards, eye-glass and all, upon her; ... but the result was astonishing.... Did any of you, gentlemen, ever happen to watch the effect of the sun's rays when thrown upon some soft substance (a pound of butter for example) through the medium of a burning-glass?... Such and so great was that produced by the rays of my right eye when sent through my eye-glass upon this charming creature.... She warmed, trembled, yea, visibly melted under it. I inquired her name on the spot, but in vain. This evening I have been more successful, and now I have the inexpressible felicity of being enrolled as an acquaintance of this inimitable widow."

"A very interesting narrative," said one of his auditors; "and may I ask your lordship what it can be that has now induced you to leave her fair side all unguarded?"

"Ecstasy, Tom!... I had not strength to witness the emotions I inspired.... I tell you, I must have fallen at her feet had I continued near her."

The conversation of these merry gentlemen went on for some time longer in the same strain, forming a contrast, perhaps not very uncommon, to the solemn and serious meditations of Mrs. Barnaby on the very same circumstances which caused their mirth. Far, however, from exaggerating the effect he had produced, Lord Mucklebury had little or no idea of its strength and reality. He fancied the lady inflammable, and easily touched by any appearance of admiration; but it never entered his head to suppose that his flourishing speeches and audacious eyes had given birth in her mind to the most sanguine hope, and the most deliberate intention, of becoming Viscountess Mucklebury.

Sudden as the formation of these hopes and intentions may appear, it would be doing injustice to Mrs. Barnaby were the reader suffered to believe that they were permitted to take possession of her heedlessly. She remembered Major Allen ... she remembered the agony of the moment in which she beheld his friend Maintry appear in the character of a thief; and sweet to her ears as was the title of her new conquest, she did not suffer it to charm away her resolution of discovering whether he were poor or rich. Every inquiry tended to prove that she was safe in the direction which her ambition and her love had now taken. Lord Mucklebury was a widower, with an only son very nobly provided for, and as capable of making a good jointure, if he married again, as a widow's heart could wish.

Now then all that remained to be done was to foster the admiration she had inspired into a passion strong enough to induce the noble Viscount to settle that jointure upon her. Nothing could be more just than her reasoning—nothing more resolute than her purpose. She knew she was handsome, she felt it to be advisable that she should appear rich; and with the devoted feeling of a warrior who throws away his scabbard as he rushes to the onslaught, Mrs. Barnaby heroically set herself to win her way to victory—coûte qui coûte.

CHAPTER XV

NEW HOPES BEGET A NEW STYLE OF EXISTENCE—A PARTY—AGNES HAS SOME SUCCESS, WHICH MRS. BARNABY DOES NOT QUITE APPROVE—LORD MUCKLEBURY ENTERS INTO EPISTOLARY CORRESPONDENCE WITH THE WIDOW, BY WHICH HER HOPES ARE RAISED TO THE HIGHEST PITCH—BUT LORD MUCKLEBURY LEAVES CHELTENHAM

Lord Mucklebury was a gay man in every sense of the word. He loved a jest almost as well as a dinner, and would rather have been quoted as the sayer of a good thing than as the doer of a great one. He had enjoyed life with fewer drawbacks from misfortune than most men; and having reached the age of forty, had made up his mind, as soberly as he could do on any subject, that the only privilege of the aristocracy worth valuing was the leisure they enjoyed, or might enjoy if they chose it, for amusing themselves. Nature intended him for a good-tempered man, but fun had spoiled him; having laughed with everybody for the first twenty years of his life, he learned during the second that it was a better joke still to laugh at them; and accordingly the principal material for the wit on which his reputation rested was derived, at the time Mrs. Barnaby made his acquaintance, from an aptitude to perceive the absurdities of his fellow creatures, and a most unshrinking audacity in exposing them.

Having pointed out Mrs. Barnaby to a set of his clever friends as the joke in which he meant to indulge during the three or four weeks of Cheltenham discipline to which he annually submitted, it became necessary to his honour that he should prove her to be ridiculous enough to merit the distinction; and he knew well enough that all she required to make her perfect in this line was as much nonsense from himself as would keep her vanity afloat. The occupation suited him exactly; it threatened little fatigue, and promised much amusement; so that by the time Mrs. Barnaby had made up her mind to win and wear his lordship's coronet, he had decided with equal sincerity of purpose to render her the jest of the season to his Cheltenham acquaintance.

An hour's close examination of Miss Morrison concerning the manière d'être of the beau monde during the season, sufficed to convince the widow that, expensive as the boarding-house had appeared to her, it was far from being all that was necessary for her present purpose. She must have a carriage, she must have a tall footman, she must have a smart lady's-maid; and great was the credit due to the zeal and activity of this invaluable friend for the promptitude and dispatch with which these indispensable articles were supplied. Some idea of this may be gathered from the fact, that the carriage which conveyed them to the house of Lady Elizabeth Norris, was one hired, horses, coachman, and all, for the season; while the first applicant of six feet high who appeared, in consequence of the earnest requisition for such an individual made at half a dozen different shops, followed the widow in a full suit of livery the following Sunday to church.

Agnes looked on at first with wonder, which a little reflection converted into great misery. She knew absolutely nothing as to the amount of her aunt's fortune; but there was a wild heedlessness of expense in her present manner of proceeding that, despite her ignorance, made her tremble for the result. The idea that she might by persevering industry render herself fit to become a governess, was that which most tended to console her; but Agnes's estimate of what was required for this was a very high one; and greatly did she rejoice to find that her aunt permitted her to be wholly mistress of her time, seldom inviting her to go out, and receiving her apologies for declining to do so with a degree of complacency which plainly enough shewed they were not unwelcome.

Lady Elizabeth Norris's party was five days after the ball; and before it arrived Mrs. Barnaby had persuaded herself into the firmest possible conviction of Lord Mucklebury's devoted attachment and honourable intentions. Had his lordship not been one of the invited guests, Mrs. Barnaby would unquestionably have given up the engagement, though but a few short days before it had appeared to her very like a permission to enter the gates of paradise; but her estimate of all things was changed; she was already a viscountess in all her reasonings, and perhaps the only person who held an unchanged value was the poor Agnes, whose helpless dependance could not place her in a position of less consideration than it had done before.

"Pray, Miss Agnes, is it your pleasure to go to Lady Elizabeth Norris's this evening?" said Mrs. Barnaby, while watching her new maid's assiduous preparations for her own toilet.

"Oh! yes, aunt, if you have no objection.... I should like to go very much indeed."

"Nay, child, you may go if you wish it.... I imagine it will prove but a humdrum sort of thing.... Wear the same dress that you did at the ball.... My maid shall arrange your hair for you."

Yet notwithstanding all this increase of dignity, Agnes never for a moment guessed what was going on; she had never seen Lord Mucklebury excepting at the ball, and her imagination had not suggested to her the possibility that so casual an acquaintance could be the cause of all she saw and heard.

Had Agnes been as light-hearted as when she used to sit upon her travelling trunk in her closet at Clifton, listening to the lively gossip of her friend Mary, the party at Lady Elizabeth's would have been pregnant with amusement. But as it was, she sat very sadly alone in a corner; for during the first portion of the evening Sir Edward Stephenson and his lady were not present, having dined out, where they were detained much beyond the hour at which the majority of Lady Elizabeth's guests assembled.

But the lively old woman wanted no one to assist her in the task of entertaining her company, for in truth she was not particularly anxious about their entertainment, her sole object in bringing them all together being to amuse herself, and this she achieved in a way less agreeable, perhaps, to one who, like Agnes, was a mere passive spectator, than to those who were expected to take a more active part. During the early part of the evening, few persons appeared excepting such as she had expressly desired to come early, and there was not one of these undistinguished by some peculiarity from which the whimsical old lady derived amusement.

It was her custom to place herself immoveably in a huge arm-chair, with a small table before her, on which was placed her tea, coffee, ice, biscuits, or anything else she might choose, with quite as little ceremony as if alone. A book or two also, with a pair of wax-lights having a green shade over them, never failed to make part of the preparation for her evening's amusement, and to these she never scrupled to address herself, if "her people" proved less entertaining than she expected.

Every one as they entered approached this throne to pay their compliments, and then seated themselves at some distance, one single chair alone being permitted to stand near her. To this place all those whom she wished to listen to, were called in succession, and dismissed when she had had enough of them, with the same absence of all ordinary civility as she was sure to display to all those who were so ill-advised as to appear at her unceremonious bidding.

Both her nephew and niece had often remonstrated with her on the subject of these strange réunions; but she defended herself from the charge of behaving rudely to those who, in accepting her invitations, had a right to expect civility, by saying, "I am as civil as they deserve. My title is the 'Duc ad me' that calls fools into my circle, and till I cease to be Lady Elizabeth, they get what they come for."

For the most part, the company were rather odd-looking than elegant, and the newly-awakened grandeur of Mrs. Barnaby was a little wounded by observing how few persons there were present whose dress entitled them to the honour of meeting her and her dress. Lady Elizabeth, moreover, received her very coldly, though to Agnes she said, "How d'ye do, my dear? Lady Stephenson will be here presently."

"What vulgar ignorance!" thought the widow, as she retreated to a sofa commanding a perfect view of the door by which the company entered.... "Notwithstanding her title, that woman must have been wretchedly brought up.... Should I in my second marriage be blessed with offspring, I shall make it my first object to teach them manners befitting their rank."

The absurdities of Lady Elizabeth's guests on this evening were not sufficiently piquant to justify a detailed description.... One old gentleman was summoned to THE chair that he might recount how many habitual drunkards, both male and female, he had converted into happy water-drinkers by the simple process of making them take an oath; another amused her ladyship for several minutes by what she called "saying his peerage,"—that is, by repeating a catalogue of noble names, all of which he stated to belong to his most familiar friends. One lady was had up for the purpose of repeating her own poetry; and another that she might, by a little prompting, give vent to some favourite metaphysical doctrine, which it was her forte to envelop in words of her own construction. Miss Morrison, too, was courted into talking of Paris in her own French; but altogether the meeting was not successful, and Lady Elizabeth was in the act of arranging the shade of her lights, so as to permit her reading at her ease, when her eye, as she looked round the room, chanced to fall upon Agnes. She was on the point of calling to her by name; but there was a modest tranquillity in her delicate face, that the imperious old lady felt no inclination to startle, and instead of speaking to her, she addressed her aunt.

"Pray, Mrs. Barnaby, does your young lady play or sing? We are mighty drowsy, I think, to-night, all of us; and if she does, I should be really much obliged if she will favour us. Lady Stephenson's instrument is a very fine one."

Mrs. Barnaby was so little pleased by her reception, and so completely out of sorts at the non-arrival of Lord Mucklebury, that she answered as little graciously as it was well possible, "I don't think there is any chance of her amusing your ladyship."

Great was the widow's surprise when she saw the quiet unpresuming Agnes rise from her distant chair, walk fearlessly across the circle to that of Lady Elizabeth, and heard her say in a low voice, but quite distinctly,—

"I do sing and play a little, Lady Elizabeth; and if it be your ladyship's wish that I should make the attempt now, I shall be happy to obey you."

Perhaps Lady Elizabeth was as much surprised as Mrs. Barnaby; but though she understood not the feeling that had prompted this wish to oblige her, she was pleased by it, and rising for the first time that evening from her chair, she took Agnes by the arm, and led her to the pianoforte.

"Does your ladyship love music?" said Agnes, trembling at her own temerity, but longing irresistibly to be noticed by the aunt of Colonel Hubert.

"Yes, my dear, I do indeed," replied the old lady. "It is one of our family failings,—I believe we all love it too well."

"Which does your ladyship prefer, old songs or new ones?" said Agnes.

"Old ones most decidedly," she replied. "But at your age, my dear, and in the present state of musical science, it is hardly likely you should be able to indulge my old-fashioned whim in this respect."

"My practice has been chiefly from the old masters," replied Agnes, turning over the leaves of a volume of Handel.

"Say you so, my little girl?... Then I will sit by you as you play."

The delighted Agnes, wondering at her own audacious courage, assiduously placed a chair for the old lady, and with a flutter at her heart that seemed almost like happiness, turned to the song that she had seen produce on Colonel Hubert an effect never to be forgotten. It had brought tears to the eyes of the gallant soldier, and given to his features such dangerous softness, that the poor minstrel had never recovered the effects of it. To sing it again to the ear of his aunt was like coming back towards him; and the alleviation this brought to the terrible fear of having lost sight of him for ever, not only gave her the courage necessary to bring her to the place she now occupied, but inspired her with animation, skill, and power, to sing with a perfection she had never reached before.

The pleased attention of Lady Elizabeth had been given in the first instance to reward the ready effort made to comply with her wishes; but long before the song was ended, she had forgotten how she had obtained it, had forgotten everything save her own deep delight, and admiration of the beautiful siren who had caused it. Silent and motionless she waited till the last chord of the concluding symphony had died away; and then rising from her chair she bent down over Agnes, and having gazed earnestly in her face for a moment, kissed her fair forehead once, twice, and again with a cordiality that thanked her better than any words could have done.

Agnes was greatly touched, greatly gratified, and forgetting the inexpediency of giving way to feelings that it was neither possible nor desirable should be understood, she seized the good lady's hand, pressed it to her bosom, and looking up to her with eyes swimming in tears of joy, said in a voice of deep feeling, ... "I am so very glad you like me!"

"Why, what a precious little creature you are!" exclaimed Lady Elizabeth, half aroused and half softened; "as original to the full as any of my queer company here, and quite as remarkable for sweetness and talent as they for the want of it.... Where did you grow, fair lily-flower?... And how came you to be transplanted hither by so.... But never mind all this now; if we get on well together we shall get better acquainted. What shall I call you, pretty one?"

"Agnes, if you please, Lady Elizabeth ... Agnes Willoughby," replied the happy girl, becoming every moment more delighted at the result of the bold measure she had taken.

"You must come to me to-morrow morning, Agnes, while I am at breakfast, at ten o'clock remember, for then I am alone.... And you must come prepared, my child, to talk to me about yourself, ... for I can't understand it at all ... and I never choose to be puzzled longer than I can help it upon any subject.... But listen to my monsters! If they are not presuming to be noisy behind my back!...

Then lull me, lull me, charming air,
My senses wrap in wonder sweet.
Like snow on wool thy footsteps are,
Soft as a spirit's are thy feet,"—

exclaimed the old lady in a whisper close to the ear of Agnes...." Sing to me again, my child, and I will send a message to them in words borrowed from the famous epitaph on Juan Cabeca, ... 'Hold your tongues, ye calves!'"... and turning herself round she beckoned to a servant who had just entered with refreshments, saying to him in a voice which might have been heard by most of those in the apartment, "Set down the tray, Johnstone; nobody wants it; ... and go round the room begging they will all be silent while this lady sings."

It was in the middle of the song which followed that Sir Edward and Lady Stephenson returned. The door opened without Agnes being aware of it; and her rich voice swelling to a note at the top of its compass, and sustaining it with a power given to few, filled the chamber with a glorious volume of sound that held Colonel Hubert's sister transfixed as she was able to enter. Unconscious that there was another of the race near her, whom she would have almost breathed her soul away to please, Agnes warbled on, nor raised her eyes from the page before her till the strain was ended. Then she looked up and perceived Lady Stephenson, who had noiselessly crept round to ascertain whom the gifted minstrel might be, immediately opposite, and looking at her with a most gratifying expression of surprise and pleasure. A very cordial greeting and shaking of hands followed; while Lady Elizabeth, her hand resting on her new favourite's shoulder, said almost in a whisper,—

"Who would have thought, Emily, that I should come at last to take lessons from you as to the selection of my natural curiosities?... But you have made a hit that does you immortal honour ... this little singing bird is worth all the monsters I ever got together.... Your ladyship need not look so grave, however," she added in a voice still lower. "I do not intend to treat her as if she were stolen from the Zoological Gardens.... She is to come to me to-morrow morning, and then we shall know all about her.... I wish your fastidious brother were here!... Do you remember what he said the other day about some miss he had heard at Clifton? I fancy we might have a chance of correcting his outrageous judgment concerning her.... What think you?"

Lady Stephenson answered by expressing the most cordial admiration of Agnes's voice, but added.... "There are many people coming in now, dear aunt.... If Miss Willoughby will have the kindness to come to us to-morrow, we shall enjoy hearing her much more than we can now, ... and I think she would like it better too."

Agnes gave her a very grateful look, and whispering an earnest "Thank you!" as she passed, glided back to the place she had left beside her aunt.

"Upon my word, Miss Agnes, your are improving fast in impudence," said Mrs. Barnaby in her ear.... "I desire, if you please, that next time you will wait till I bid you sing."

Agnes did not reply. Nothing that it was in the power of her aunt to say could in that happy moment have caused her the slightest serious uneasiness. She was blessed beyond the reach of scolding, which was the more fortunate, as the widow had seldom been in a more irritable mood. Quarter after quarter had heavily struck upon her ear from the time-piece on the marble slab behind her; eleven o'clock (the hour at which her carriage was ordered) approached with fearful strides, and yet Lord Mucklebury came not.... Had her toilet upon this occasion been less fearfully expensive she could have endured it better; but that all the charms a milliner could give should have been freely ventured on, and HE not see it, was hard to bear.

It is true that, with the dogged firmness of a resolute purpose, Mrs. Barnaby scorned to shrink or tremble as she played her desperate game; nevertheless she knew that selling out stock three times within a fortnight was a strong measure; and anything that seemed to check her approach to the goal she felt so sure of reaching, did produce a disagreeable sort of spasm about her heart. There was no help for it, however; go she must, as nearly all the rest of the company had gone before her, with nothing to console her but an indifferently civil nod from Lady Elizabeth, and the surprise, less agreeable perhaps than startling, of seeing her dependant niece parted with in a manner that shewed she was considered of infinitely greater importance than herself, notwithstanding her carriage, her tall footman, and her magnificent attire.

Miss Morrison was accommodated with a seat in the carriage she had so actively exerted herself to procure, and the first words spoken after they drove off were hers.

"Nest paw que jay raisong?... Did I not say so, Mrs. Barnaby?... Did I not tell you, my dear madam, that you need do nothing but make this young lady sing in order to become the fashion at Cheltenham?... You have no idea what a number of visits you will have to-morrow.... Noo verong."

"Really, Miss Morrison," replied the widow tartly, "I am surprised to hear a person of your good sense speak so foolishly.... How can you suppose that a person in my station of life could desire the visits of such a set of people as we met to-night?... And as to making this poor penniless girl talked of as a singer, I should be ashamed to think of such a thing. Remember, miss, if you please, that from this time forward I never will permit you to sing again, ... unless, indeed, you mean to get your bread by it, ... and I'm sure I won't undertake to say but what you may want it.... I can answer for nobody but myself; and I don't think it probable that others may be inclined to shew the same devoted generosity that I have done to a girl that never shewed the slightest affection for me in return."

And so she ran on till she fell asleep ... but her words fell like rain on a water-proof umbrella; they made a noise, but they could not reach the head which they seemed destined to deluge. Agnes was wrapped in armour of proof, and nothing could do her harm.

Happily for her, one of the facetious Lord Mucklebury's modes of extracting amusement from the widow was by writing her notes, which elicited answers that often threw him into a perfect ecstasy, and which he carefully preserved in an envelope endorsed "Barnaby Papers," lodging them in a corner of his writing-desk, from whence they were not unfrequently drawn for the delectation of his particular friends. One of these notes, intended to produce an answer that should add a gem to his collection, was delivered to Mrs. Barnaby as she passed from the breakfast-table of the boarding-house to her own sitting-room. The emotions produced by these notes were always very powerful, and on the present occasion more so than ordinary, for there were apologies for not appearing last night, and hopes for an interview that morning, which were to be answered instantly, for the servant waited.

Mrs. Barnaby, panting with haste and gladness, seated herself at her table, opened her writing-desk, seized a pen, and was in the very act of venturing the words "My dear Lord," when Agnes drew near, and said, "May I go out, aunt, to call on Lady Elizabeth?"

"Gracious Heaven!... what a moment to torment me! Go!... go where you will ... plague of my life as you are! Get along at once, can't you?"

Agnes vanished,—a Barnaby paper was written; and while the niece was enjoying three hours of the most flattering and delightful intercourse with the nearest relations of Colonel Hubert, the aunt, with a degree of felicity hardly less perfect, was receiving a tête-à-tête visit from Lord Mucklebury, in which he as carefully studied her looks, attitudes, and words, as if their effect on him were all she believed them to be. Nor did either interview pass without producing some important results. His lordship carried away with him wherewithal to keep half-a-dozen of his friends who dined with him on that day in a continued roar for nearly an hour.... Mrs. Barnaby was left with a sweet assurance that all was going well, which led to the purchase of a richly-laced mantelet and a new bonnet ... while Agnes, inspired by so strong a wish to please as to make her follow the lead of her new friends, and converse with them of all her little history just as they wished to make her, created in them both an interest too strong to be ever forgotten, and she left them with a confidence in their kindness that made her endure much subsequent suffering with firmness; for it was long ere she wholly lost the hope that they might meet again in future years.

During the next fortnight this agreeable intercourse was very frequently repeated; for there were few hours of the day in which Mrs. Barnaby was not in some way or other so occupied by the sentiment that engrossed her, either by the presence of its object, or the anticipation of his presence, or meditation upon it when it was passed, that she was well pleased to have Agnes out of the way; and Lady Elizabeth and her charming niece were, on the contrary, so well pleased to have her, that scarcely a day passed without some hours of it being devoted to them.

Lady Stephenson in particular seemed to study her character with peculiar attention. There was a fond devotion in the gratitude which their kindness had produced that could not be mistaken, and which, from one so artless and so every way interesting, could not fail of producing affection in return. From such a friend it was impossible for Agnes to conceal, even if she had wished it, that her home was a very wretched one; and they often conversed together on the possibility of her releasing herself from it by endeavouring to obtain some sort of independence by her own exertions. Lady Elizabeth was repeatedly a party in these consultations, but uniformly gave it as her opinion that any home was better for such a girl as Agnes, than an attempt to support herself, which must inevitably expose her to a degree of observation more dangerous than any annoyance from her aunt Barnaby. Agnes by no means clearly understood the grounds upon which this sturdy opposition to her wishes was founded; and as Lady Stephenson, who seemed more able to sympathise with her actual sufferings, listened without venturing to answer these mysterious threatenings of something remote, she at length took courage herself and said, ...

"Will you tell me, dear Lady Elizabeth, what it is you think would happen to me if I went into a family as a governess?"

"You are a little fool, Agnes," replied the old lady, unable to repress a smile; "but as I do really believe that your ignorance is genuine, I will tell you.... Don't be frightened, my poor child; but the fact is, that you are a great deal too handsome for any such situation."

Agnes blushed instantly a most celestial rosy red, and felt shocked and ashamed at having drawn forth such an answer; but, though she said nothing in reply, she at once decided that Lady Elizabeth Norris should never have reason to believe that she was capable of neglecting her friendly caution. All hopes from her power of teaching ended for ever, and the next time her aunt Barnaby was particularly cross (which happened that night while they were undressing to go to bed) Agnes very seriously began to revolve in her altered mind the possibility of learning so late in life the profitable mystery of satin-stitch.

Once, and once only, during the many hours Agnes passed with his relations, did she venture to pronounce the name of Colonel Hubert. She had often determined to do it, but had never found courage and opportunity till one morning, after an hour or two passed in singing duets with his sister, Lady Elizabeth again alluded to the Clifton miss that her nephew had so vaunted, and whose voice must, she was sure, be so immeasurably inferior to that of Miss Willoughby.

It was under cover of this observation that Agnes ventured to say, ... "I knew Colonel Hubert a little when I was at Clifton."

"Did you?"... said the old lady briskly; "then I'll bet my life he heard you sing."

"Once or twice he did."

"Oh! hah!... that explains it all.... You need not blush so about it, my dear; why did you not tell me so at once?"

"I do not think it is quite certain," returned Agnes, attempting to smile, "that Colonel Hubert spoke of me."

"Don't you, my dear ... but I do, and I know him best, I suppose.... And what was it you sang to him, Agnes?"

Agnes mentioned the songs; but her voice trembled so, that she grievously repented having brought on herself questions that she found it so difficult to answer.

Her embarrassment was not greatly relieved by perceiving,—when at length she looked up to save herself from the awkwardness of pertinaciously looking down,—that the eyes of Lady Stephenson were earnestly fixed upon her.

"Did you ever see Frederick Stephenson with my brother?" said her ladyship; "they were at Clifton together this summer.... Perhaps you don't know that I was married there, Agnes?... and Sir Edward and I left our two brothers there together."

This change of subject was a considerable relief; and Agnes answered with tolerable composure,—"Oh yes!... I did know you were married there, for I heard it mentioned several times; ... and I saw you too, Lady Stephenson, the evening before you were married, walking up and down Gloucester Row with ... with your brother."

"Did you indeed?—Were you walking there, Agnes?"

"No ... we were at the drawing-room window, and my aunt made me look out to see your brother."

"Why particularly to see my brother?" inquired Lady Stephenson with a smile.

"Because ... because he was so tall, I believe," replied Agnes, looking considerably more silly than she had ever done in her life.

"And so you watched us walking up and down, did you, Agnes?"

"Yes, once or twice," answered Agnes, again blushing violently.

"And did you hear what we said, my dear?"

"No!... but I am sure it was something very interesting, you seemed to be talking so earnestly."

"It was very interesting ... it was about Frederick.... You knew him too, did not you?"

"Oh yes!... very well."

"Really!... I wonder you never told me so before."

It was impossible to look at Agnes at this moment, as Lady Stephenson now looked at her, without perceiving that there must be some cause for the agitation she evinced. It immediately occurred to her that it was likely enough Frederick might have laid his heart at her feet, or perhaps stopped short before he did so from the effect of that very conversation of which Agnes had been an eye, though not an ear, witness.

"Poor little thing!"... thought Lady Stephenson; "if this be so, and if she has given her young heart in return, how greatly is she to be pitied!"

No sooner had this idea struck her, which many trifling circumstances tended to confirm, than Lady Stephenson determined to drop the subject for ever; and much as Agnes secretly but tremblingly wished it, no allusion was ever made to the two gentlemen again.

Days and weeks rolled on till the time fixed by Lord Mucklebury for his departure arrived. His collection of the Barnaby papers was quite as copious as he wished it to be; and having indulged himself and his friends with as many good stories as any one lady could be the heroine of, without being fatiguing, he parted with the widow on Saturday evening, assuring her, with a thousand expressions of passionate admiration, that he should be early on the walks to look for her on the morrow, and by noon on Sunday was on his road to London behind four galloping post-horses.

During the whole of that fatal Sunday Mrs. Barnaby roamed through all the public walks of Cheltenham with the disconsolate air of a pigeon whose mate has been shot.... She was sad, cross, tender, and angry by turns; but never for a moment during that long dismal day did she ever once conceive the terrible idea that her intended mate was flown for ever. Nay, even on the morrow, when in answer to an inquiry at the reading-room, of whether Lord Mucklebury had been there that morning, the man replied,—"I believe his lordship has left the town, ma'am!"—not even then did her mind receive the terrible truth.

It was from the hand of her friend Miss Morrison that the blow came at last.... That lady on Wednesday evening entered her room, bringing a London newspaper with her; she was much irritated.

"Mong Dew, Mrs. Barnaby!" she cried, "look here."

The widow seized the paper with a trembling hand, and before she fainted read as follows:—

"Lord Viscount Mucklebury arrived this morning at Mivart's Hotel from Cheltenham. It is rumoured that his lordship is about to depart in a few days for the Continent, in order to pass the winter at Rome, but rather with the intention of kissing the hands of the beautiful Lady M— S— than the toe of his holiness."

VOLUME III

CHAPTER I

MRS. BARNABY LOSES HER SENSES, AND RECOVERS THEM—SHE TAKES A DESPERATE RESOLUTION—MISS MORRISON PROVES HERSELF A FRIEND IN NEED—AGNES FINDS CONSOLATION IN SORROW

Mrs. Barnaby's horror on recovering her senses (for she really did fall into a swoon) was in very just proportion to the extent of the outlay her noble vision had cost her. To Miss Morrison, who had listened to all her hopes, she scrupled not to manifest her despair, not, however, entering into the financial part of it, but leaving it to be understood by her sympathizing friend, that her agony proceeded wholly from disappointed love.

"What a Lovelace!... what a Lothario!... what a finished deceiver!... Keloreur!..." exclaimed the pitying spinster.... "And how thankful ought I to be that no man can ever again cause me such terrible emotion.... Nong jammy!"

"Gracious Heaven! what is to become of me?" cried Mrs. Barnaby, apparently but little consoled by this assurance of her friend's exemption from a similar misfortune; "what ought I to do, Miss Morrison?... If I set off instantly for London, do you think I could reach it before he leaves it for Rome?"

Miss Morrison, having turned to the newspaper, examined its date, and read the fatal paragraph again, replied, "You certainly could, my dear Mrs. Barnaby, if this statement be correct; but I would not do it, if I were you, without thinking very seriously about it.... It is true I never had a lord for a lover myself, but I believe when they run restive, they are exceedingly difficult to hold; and if you do go after him, and fail at last to touch his cruel heart, you will be only worse off than you are now.... Say clare."

"That may be all very true in one sense, Miss Morrison," replied the unhappy widow; "but there is such a thing as pursuing a man lawfully for breach of promise of marriage, and ... though money is no object to me ... I should glory in getting damages from him, if only to prove to the world that he is a scoundrel!"

"That is quite another thing, indeed," said the confidant, "toot a fay; and, if you mean to bring an action against him, I am pretty sure that I could be very useful to you; for my brother is an attorney in London, and is reckoned particularly clever about everything of the kind. But have you any proof, my dear lady?... that is what my brother will be sure to say to you.... I know you have had lots of letters; and if you have kept them all, it is most likely my brother may find out something like proof.... Eel ay see abeel!"

"Proof?... To be sure I have proof enough, if that's all that's wanted; and I'll go to your brother at once, Miss Morrison, for revenge I'll have ... if nothing else."

"Then of course you'll take all his love letters with you, Mrs. Barnaby; and I think, if you would let me look over them, I should be able to tell you whether they would answer the purpose or not.—Jay me coney ung pew."

"I should have no objection in the world to your seeing them every one," replied the outraged lady; ... "but I am thinking, Miss Morrison, that I have an immense deal of business to do, and that I shall never get through it without your friendly help ... I am thinking...."

And Mrs. Barnaby was thinking, and very much to the purpose too. She was thinking, that though she had squandered about seventy or eighty pounds in trifling purchases, by far the greater part of the expenses her noble lover had induced her to run into, were still in the shape of debts, the money with which she proposed to discharge them being as yet paying her interest in the funds. Could she contrive to leave the heaviest of these debts unpaid till she knew the result of her intended attack upon Lord Mucklebury's purse, it would be very convenient. Perhaps some vague notion that she, too, might visit the continent, and thus escape the necessity of paying them at all, might mix itself with her meditations; but at any rate she very speedily decided upon leaving Cheltenham the following day without mentioning her intention to her milliner, mercer, tailor, shoemaker, hosier, perfumer, livery-stable keeper, librarian, or even to her hair-dresser. If she got damages, she should certainly return and pay them all with great éclat; if not ... circumstances must decide what it would be most advisable for her to do.

Great as was her esteem and affection for Miss Morrison, she did not think it necessary to trouble her with all these trifling details, but resumed the conversation by saying,—

"Yes, my dear Miss Morrison, I am thinking that the best thing I can do will be to go to London for a day or two, see your brother, put all my documents into his hands, and then return to Cheltenham for the remainder of the season, for I am sure I should be more likely to recover my spirits in your friendly society than anywhere else."

"Indeed I approve your resolution altogether," replied Miss Morrison; "and I will write a line by you to my brother, telling him that whatever he does to assist you, I shall take as a personal favour to myself."

"I cannot thank you enough!" said the widow, pressing her hand.... "We shall be able to get everything ready to-night I hope; and when my coachman comes as usual for orders at eleven o'clock to-morrow morning, tell him, my dear friend, to drive you about wherever you like to go.... And you may mention, if you please, that I shall want him to take us a long drive on Saturday to see the Roman Pavement.... I mean to return on Friday night ... for what will be the use, you know, of my staying in town?"

"None in the world ... but I think you had better name Monday for the drive ... for fear you should be too tired on Saturday."

"Well, just as you please about that ... but you had better go and write your letter, and I'll speak to Agnes and my maid about packing."

"Perhaps you will not like to take Miss Willoughby.... I will take the greatest care of her, if you will leave her in my charge."

"How very kind!... But I would rather take her.... I can't do without somebody to lace my stays and fasten my dress, and I want my maid to finish the work she is about.... She is an exquisite darner, and I have set her to mend the rent that hateful Lord Mucklebury made in my India muslin.... So I don't mean to take her."

Nothing of any kind occurred to interfere with the execution of this hastily, but by no means unskilfully, imagined plan. The ready-money expenditure of Mrs. Barnaby had been so lavish, that she had bought golden opinions from master, mistress, men, and maids throughout the establishment; and when she summoned Mr. —, the landlord, to her presence, and informed him that she was going to London for a couple of days on business, but should not give up her rooms, as she should take neither of her servants with her, he received the communication with great satisfaction, and promised that no one but her own people should enter her drawing-room till her return.

This preliminary business happily settled, Mrs. Barnaby mounted the stairs to her bed-room, where, as usual, she found Agnes busily occupied in her corner, the hour for an evening engagement made with Lady Stephenson not having yet arrived.

For some reason or other Mrs. Barnaby never enjoyed any flirtation so much in the presence of Agnes as without her; and it was for this reason that at Cheltenham, as well as at Clifton, she had encouraged her making acquaintance for herself; thus her constant intercourse with Lady Elizabeth Norris and Lady Stephenson had never in any degree been impeded by her aunt.

Mrs. Barnaby was aware that Agnes had engaged to pass this evening with them; and when she looked at her tranquil face as she entered the room she felt greatly disposed to plague her by saying that she must stay at home to pack, and could not go.... But a moment's reflection suggested to her that the less fuss she made about this packing the better, and therefore only told her that she was obliged to set off by seven o'clock the next morning for London, on business that would detain her for a day or two ... that she meant to take her, and leave her maid; and that before she set off upon her gossiping visit, it would be necessary to pack her trunk.

Agnes laid down her book, and looked surprised.

"Don't stare so like a fool, Agnes.... Do what I bid you instantly."

"There will be no occasion for me to pack much, aunt, if we are only to stay a day or two," said Agnes.

"When I tell you to pack your trunk, miss, I mean that your trunk shall be packed, and I won't trouble you to give me any opinion on the subject."

"Am I to put everything into it, aunt?"

"Plague of my life, yes!" replied Mrs. Barnaby, whose vexed spirit seemed to find relief in speaking harshly.

Without further remonstrance Agnes set about obeying her; and the little all that formed her mourning wardrobe was quickly transferred from the two drawers allowed her to the identical trunk which aunt Betsy had provided for her first journey from Silverton to Empton.

"And my books, aunt?..." said Agnes, fixing her eyes on the heated countenance of the widow with some anxiety.

Mrs. Barnaby hesitated, and Agnes saw she did. It was not because the little library of her niece formed the chief happiness of her life that she scrupled at bidding her leave them behind, but because she suspected that they, and their elegant little case, were of some marketable value.... "You may take them if you will," she said at length.... "I don't care a straw what you take, or what you leave ... only don't plague me.... You must know, I suppose, if you are not quite an idiot, that when people go to London on business, it is possible they may stay longer than they expect."

Agnes asked no more questions, but quietly packed up everything that belonged to her; and when the work, no very long one, was completed, she said,—

"Can I be of any use to you, aunt, before I go out?"

"I should like to know what use you are ever likely to be of to anybody," ... was the reply. "Take yourself off, in God's name!—the sooner the better."

The very simple toilet of Agnes was soon arranged; and having left everything in perfect order for departure, she uttered a civil but unanswered "Good-b'ye, aunt," and went away.

It so chanced that a little volume of poems, lent to her by Lady Stephenson, had been left in the drawing-room, and Agnes, wishing to return it before leaving Cheltenham, entered the room to look for it. As a good many circulating-library volumes were lying about, it was some minutes before she found it; and just as she had succeeded, and was leaving the apartment, Miss Morrison appeared at the door. She had a letter in her hand, and a bustling, busy look and manner, which led Agnes to suppose that she had something of consequence to say to her aunt.

"Shall I run up stairs and desire my aunt to come to you, Miss Morrison?" said she.

"No, thank you, my dear ... you are very kind, but I think I had better go up to her; I only stepped in first to see if she was here.... She is very busy packing, I suppose, and perhaps I can help her."

"Then you know, Miss Morrison, that she is going to London to-morrow?" said Agnes.

"Oh! dear, yes: I believe it was I put it into her head first, ... and this is the letter she is to take to my brother. I am sure I hope she'll succeed with all my heart; and I should like to hear that Lord Mucklebury had ten thousand pounds to pay her for damages."

"Damages!" repeated Agnes; "what for?"

"What for, my dear child?.... Why, for having used her so abominably ill, to be sure ... there is nobody that saw them together as I did, but must have supposed he intended to marry her."

"And if he has used her ill, Miss Morrison," said Agnes, looking greatly alarmed, "will it not be exposing herself still more if she goes to law about it? Indeed, Miss Morrison, you should not advise her to do anything so very wrong and disagreeable."

"Don't blame me, my dear, I beg of you ... the idea was quite her own toot a fay, I assure you, and all I have done to further it was just writing this letter to my brother for her. He is a very clever lawyer, and I'm sure she could not do better."

"It would be much better, Miss Morrison, if she did not do anything," said Agnes, while tears started to her eyes at the idea of this fresh exposure.

"I don't think, my dear Miss Agnes, that you can be much of a judge," retorted the adviser. "However, as you do choose to give an opinion upon the subject, and seem to be so very much afraid that she should expose herself, I must just tell you that you owe it to me if she does not go galloping after Lord Mucklebury all the way to Rome.... She had the greatest possible inclination to do so, I assure you.... However, I think that I have put it out of her head by talking to her of damages.... But you are going down stairs, and I am going up ... so, good-bye.... Don't frighten yourself more than is needful; it is as likely as not that you will never be called into court.... O revor!"

Agnes, sick at heart, and trembling for the future, repaired to the house of Lady Elizabeth. Lady Stephenson was at the pianoforte, and the old lady reading near a window; but as soon as her young guest was announced, she closed her volume, and said, "You are late, little girl ... we have been expecting you this hour, and this is the last evening we shall have quietly to ourselves; for Colonel Hubert writes us word that he is coming to-morrow, and he is a much more stay-at-home person than Sir Edward."

Colonel Hubert coming to Cheltenham the very day she was to leave it!... These were not tidings to cheer her spirits, already agitated and depressed, and when she attempted to speak, she burst into tears. Lady Stephenson was at her side in a moment. "Agnes!..." she said, "what ails you?... You are as white as a ghost.... Had you heard any agitating news before you came here?"

Struck by the accent with which this was spoken, and perceiving in a moment that Lady Stephenson thought the mention of Colonel Hubert's arrival had caused her emotion, she hastened to reply, and did so perhaps with more frankness than she might have shewn had she not been particularly anxious to prove that there were other and very sufficient reasons for her discomposure.

"News most painful and most sad to me, Lady Stephenson," she said.... "I believe you have heard my aunt Barnaby's foolish flirtation with Lord Mucklebury spoken of.... Lady Elizabeth was laughing about it the other day."

"And who was not, my dear?... The saucy Viscount has made her, they say, the subject of a ballad.... But is it for this you weep?... Or is it because he is gone away, and that there's an end of it?"

"Alas! Lady Elizabeth, there is not an end of it, and it is for that I weep ... though indeed I ought to beg your pardon for bringing such useless sorrow here; ... but I find that my aunt fancies she has a claim upon him—a legal claim, and that she is going to London to-morrow to bring an action against him."

"Is it possible?" exclaimed the old lady, looking at poor Agnes with very genuine compassion.... "God knows you may well weep, my poor child.... I shall begin to think I gave but sorry advice, Agnes, when I told you to stay with her. It may, after all, be better to run some risk in leaving her, than brave certain disgrace and ridicule by remaining to reside in her family."

"Is she going to take you to town with her, Agnes?" inquired Lady Stephenson with a look of deep concern.

"Yes, Lady Stephenson, I am to go with her."

There was a very painful silence of a minute or two. Both the admiring friends of Agnes would have done much to save her from being a sharer in such an enterprize; but to interfere with the indisputable authority of such a woman as Mrs. Barnaby in her arrangements concerning a niece, who had no dependence but on her, was out of the question, and the conviction that it was so kept them silent.

"How did you hear this strange story, my dear?" said Lady Elizabeth.... "Did your aunt explain to you her ridiculous purpose herself?"

"No, Lady Elizabeth ... she only bade me prepare my trunk for going to London with her.... It was Miss Morrison, whom I met by chance as I came out, who told me the object of the journey; ... and dreadful as this going to law would be, it is not the worst thing I fear."

"What worse can there be, Agnes?" said Lady Stephenson.

"I am almost ashamed to tell you of such fears, ... but when I uttered something like a reproach to Miss Morrison for having advised this journey, and writing a letter about it to her brother, who is a lawyer in London, she told me that I ought to be grateful to her for preventing my aunt's following Lord Mucklebury all the way to Rome, for that such was her first intention ... and" ... continued Agnes, bursting anew into tears, "I greatly, greatly suspect that she has not given up this intention yet."

The two ladies exchanged glances of pity and dismay, and Lady Elizabeth, making her a sign to come close to her, took her kindly by the hand, saying, in accents much more gentle than she usually bestowed on any one, "My poor, dear girl, what makes you think this? Tell me, Agnes, tell me all they have said to you."

Agnes knelt down on the old lady's foot-stool, and gently kissing the venerable hand which held hers, said, "It is very, very kind of you to let me tell you all, ... and your judgment will be more to be trusted than mine as to what it may mean; but my reason for thinking that my aunt is going to do more than she confesses to Miss Morrison is, that she has publicly declared her intended absence will be only for two days; and yet, though she told me this too, she ordered me to pack up everything I had, ... even the little collection of books I told you of, Lady Stephenson, ... and, moreover, instead of letting her maid put up her things, I left her doing it herself, and saw her before I came away putting a vast variety of her most valuable things in a great travelling trunk that she could never think of taking, if it were really her intention to stay in London only two days, and then return to Cheltenham."

"Very suspicious ... very much so indeed," said the old lady; "and all I can say to you in reply, my poor child, is this. You must not go abroad with her! I am not rich enough to charge myself with providing for you, nor must your friend Emily here frighten her new husband by talking of taking possession of you, Agnes, ... but ... you must not go abroad with that woman. Governess you must be, I suppose, if things go on in this way; and instead of opposing it, I will try if I cannot find a situation in which you may at least be safer than with this aunt Barnaby. Whatever happens, you must let us hear from you; and remember, the moment you discover that she really proposes to take you abroad, you are to put yourself into a Cheltenham coach, and come directly to me."

What words were these for Agnes to listen to!... Colonel Hubert was to take up his residence in that house on the morrow; and she was now told in a voice of positive command, that if what she fully expected would happen, did happen, she was at once to seek a shelter there! She dared not trust her voice to say, "I thank you," but she ventured to raise her eyes to the hard-featured but benignant countenance that bent over her, and the kiss she received on her forehead proved that though her silence might not be fully understood, her gratitude was not doubted.

The evening was not, like many others recently passed there, so happy, that Mrs. Barnaby's footman often came to escort her home before she thought the time for parting could be half arrived. They had no music, no scraps of poetry in Italian or in English, as touch-stones of taste and instruction, with which Lady Stephenson loved to test the powers of her young favourite; but the conversation rested almost wholly upon the gloomy and uncertain future. At length the moment came in which she was to bid these valued friends adieu; they embraced and blessed her with tenderness, nay, even with tears; but little did they guess the tumult that swelled the breast of Agnes. It was Hubert's sister to whom she clung ... it was Hubert's aunt—almost his mother—who hung over her, looking as if she were her mother too!... and on the morrow he would be with them, and he would hear her named; for notwithstanding their unmeasured superiority to her in all ways, they could not forget her so soon, ... he would hear of her sorrows, of the dangers that surrounded her; and he would hear too, perhaps, of the shelter offered her in the very house he dwelt in.

All these thoughts were busy in her head as she uttered the last farewell, and turned again in passing through the door to look once more on those who would so soon be looked at by him.

There was certainly a strange pleasure mixed with all this sadness, for though she wept through half the night, she would not have exchanged the consciousness of having been brought nearer to him, even by the act of having mingled tears in parting with his nearest relations, for all the enjoyment that a tranquil spirit and a calm night's rest could offer in exchange for it.

CHAPTER II

MRS. BARNABY EFFECTS HER RETREAT FROM CHELTENHAM—SHE CARRIES WITH HER A LETTER—ITS EFFECT—AN AMIABLE ATTORNEY—SPECIMENS OF A NOBLE STYLE OF LETTER-WRITING—CONSOLATION

Though the baggage of Mrs. Barnaby was strangely disproportionate to the period she had named for her absence, it seemed not to excite suspicion, which might, perhaps, be owing to the well known splendour of her elaborate toilet, which she not unfrequently changed four times in a day, requiring—as all who thought on the subject must be aware—an extent of travelling equipment much exceeding the portion assigned to ordinary ladies.

So she passed forth unchallenged, and unchallenged saw her treasures deposited on roof and in rumble-tumble till all were stowed away; and then, having affectionately squeezed the hand of Miss

Morrison, who accompanied her to the stage, she climbed into it, followed by the pale and melancholy Agnes.

Our widow was now beginning to be an experienced traveller, and her first care on reaching London was to secure rooms in a private lodging-house. Notwithstanding the noble visions with which she had recreated her fancy during the last month, she now with great good sense sent them all to the moon, knowing she could easily call them back again if all went well with her; but determined that they should in no way interfere with her enjoyment of the more substantial goods that were still within her reach; so, she commissioned the maid of the house to procure her three dozen of oysters and a pot of porter, with which, while Agnes wept herself to sleep, she repaid herself for her day's fatigue, and wisely laid in a stock of strength for the morrow.

Her first object, of course, was to hold communication with the brother of her friend, "Magnus Morrison, Esq. attorney-at-law, Red Lion Square." Such was the address the letter entrusted to her bore; and at breakfast the following morning she sat gazing at it for some minutes before she could decide whether it would be better to convey it herself, or prepare the lawyer to receive her by letting it precede her for a few hours. She finally decided to send it before her;—the wisdom of which determination will be evident upon the perusal of the letter, such an introduction being well calculated to ensure all the zealous attention she desired.

Miss Morrison's letter ran thus:—

"MY DEAR BROTHER,

"I never fail, as you well know, to catch all the fish for your net that comes in my way ... crowyee sellaw too jure ... and I now send you a client whom I have little doubt you will find answer in every way. She is a most charming woman, and my most particular friend.... I don't know a more charming person anywhere, not even in my dear Paris, ... so rich, so free in all her expenses, so remarkably obliging, and so very handsome for all those who admire tall, large beauties. But you are too good a lawyer to listen to all this when business is in hand, and so I must come o fay. And now, Magnus, be sure to attend to every word. Mrs. Barnaby—this charming friend of mine—has for the last month been receiving the most marked and the most tender attentions from Lord Mucklebury. He is a viscount, my dear Magnus, and—observe—as rich as a Jew. This nobleman has given her, poor dear lady! every reason in the world to believe that his dearest wish, hope, and intention was to marry her; and she, good, tender-hearted creature! perfectly adored him, devoting every hour of the day to the finding out where he was to be seen, and the going there to see him. She had no secrets whatever from me the whole time, and I knew everything that was going on from the first moment he ever kissed her hand to the most tender interviews that ever passed between them. And how do you think it has all ended?... Oh! Magnus, it is impossible to deny that the male sex—lords and all—are most dreadfully deceitful and false-hearted. All this devoted love, going on, as I tell you, for a whole month, has just ended in nothing. My lord set off in his travelling carriage, with four horses and an out-rider, as we subsequently ascertained, without even taking any leave of the lady at all, or explaining himself the least bit either one way or the other. You may easily guess her feelings.... Her first idea, poor thing, was to follow him to the world's end—for there is no doubt in the world that her attachment was of the most sincere kind; but luckily she confided this romantic thought to me, and it struck me directly, Magnus, that the best thing in the world for her to do would be to put the whole affair into your hands. She has got quantities of his letters ... they are very little letters, to be sure, folded up sometimes not much bigger than a shilling; but still letters are letters, you know; and I can't but think that, with your cleverness, something might be made of an action for damages. Of course, it is natural to suppose that I am a little partial to this sort of measure, because I can't well have forgotten yet that the best part of my snug little fortune came to me in the same way, thanks to the good management of our dear good father, Magnus.... The dear lady listened to reason in a minute, and consented to put herself in your hands, for which reason she is going to set off for London to-morrow morning. She will bring all Lord Mucklebury's letters with her, and it will be for you to judge what use can be made of them;—only it is but right to mention, that there is no doubt in the world but that Mrs. Barnaby is quite rich enough to pay handsomely, whether she gains the cause or loses it.

"I am, my dear Magnus,

"Your affectionate sister,

"SARAH MORRISON."

Mrs. Barnaby enclosed this letter in an envelope, in which she wrote,—

"Mrs. Barnaby presents her compliments to Mr. Magnus Morrison, and will be happy to see him on the business to which the enclosed letter refers at any hour he will name."

"No. 5, Half-moon Street, Piccadilly."

Having consigned her packet to the post, the widow declared to her anxious companion that she did not mean to waste her time as long as she remained in London; but should walk to every part of the town, and should expect her to do the same.

"Will there not be danger of losing ourselves, aunt?" said Agnes. "London, you know, is so much bigger than any place you ever saw."

"And what's the good of that piece of wisdom, Miss Solomon? Perhaps you don't know that I have a tongue in my head, and that the Londoners speak English?... Come, and put on your bonnet, if you please, and I'll promise not to leave you in any of the gutters, but bring you safe home again to No. 5, Half-moon Street, Piccadilly. There, you see, I shall know what place to ask for. Won't that do for you?"

Agnes felt that all remonstrance would be in vain, and submitted; though the idea of being dragged through the streets of London by her aunt Barnaby, dressed in the identical green satin gown and pink feathers which had first attracted Lord Mucklebury's attention, was by no means an agreeable prospect.

The expedition, however, fatiguing and disagreeable as it proved, was achieved without any very disastrous results. Mrs. Barnaby, indeed, was twice very nearly knocked down by a cab, while staring too eagerly about her when crossing the streets; and friendly as was the old black crape veil of poor Agnes, it could not wholly save her from some tolerably obvious efforts to find out whether the face it sheltered was worthy the graceful symmetry of the person who wore it; ... but they nevertheless reached their Half-moon Street without any positive injury to life or limb.

At eight o'clock in the evening, while Mrs. Barnaby and her weary companion were taking tea, the drawing-room door opened, and Mr. Magnus Morrison was announced, and most cordially welcomed by the widow, who not only saw in him the lawyer from whom she hoped to learn how to replenish her waning finances, but also the brother of her dear Miss Morrison, and the only acquaintance she could hope at this trying moment to find or make in London.

But now, as heretofore, the presence of Agnes was inconvenient, which she took care to signify by saying to the lawyer, "I am greatly indebted to you, Mr. Morrison, for your early attention to my note; and I shall be very glad to talk with you on the business that brings me to London ... but not quite yet ... we really must be quite by ourselves, for it will be necessary that I should have your whole attention. Will you, in the mean time, permit me to offer you tea?"

Before Mr. Morrison could reply Agnes was on her feet, and asking her aunt in a whisper if she would give her leave to go to bed. "Yes, if you like it, my darling!..." replied Mrs. Barnaby, whose tenderness for her niece was always awakened by the presence of strangers. "I am sure you look tired to death.... But bring down first, my dear, my writing-desk; and remember, my love, to take care that I have warm water when I come up; ... and don't forget, Agnes, to put my bonnet and shawl, and all that, nicely away ... and see that I have paper for curling my hair ready on the dressing-table; ... and don't go to bed till you have put out my lilac silk for to-morrow; and just put a stitch in the blonde of my bonnet-cap, for I pulled it almost off."

All this was said by the widow in a coaxing sort of half whisper, with an arm round her victim's waist, and a smile of the most fascinating kindness on her own lips.

The desk was brought, and the consulting parties left alone; while Agnes, as she performed the different tasks imposed on her, and which her great fatigue rendered heavy, could not for an instant banish from her mind the question that had incessantly haunted her from the hour she left the drawing-room of Lady Elizabeth.... "Will she go abroad?... Shall I be obliged to return to Cheltenham without her?... Shall I be obliged to go to the house where he is living?"

Mr. Magnus Morrison was by no means an ill-looking man, and though a bachelor of thirty-five, had as little of quizzical peculiarity about him as a careful attorney of that age, unpolished by a wife, can be expected to have. Mrs. Barnaby, though a little his senior, was still, as we know, a lady à prétention, and never permitted any gentleman to approach her without making an experiment upon him with her fine eyes. Their success in the present instance was neither so violent as in the case of Major Allen, nor so instantaneous as in that of the false-hearted peer; nevertheless enough was achieved to throw an agreeable sort of extraneous interest into the business before them, and the widow disdained not as it proceeded to decorate her narrative and herself with such graces as none but a Mrs. Barnaby can display.

Having given her own version, and with such flourishes as her nature loved, of Lord Mucklebury's violent passion for her, she asked her attentive and somewhat captivated auditor what species of testimony was required to prove a promise of marriage in such a manner as to secure large damages, "for without being quite certain of obtaining such, you must be aware, my dear sir, that a woman of my station, connexions, and fortune, could not think of appearing in court."

"Assuredly not," replied Mr. Magnus Morrison fervently. "Such a measure is never to be resorted to unless the evidence is of a nature that no cross-examination can set aside. My sister tells me, madam, that you have letters...."

"Yes, Mr. Morrison, I have many ... though I am sorry to say that many more have been destroyed. (This was a figure of poetry, and of a kind that the widow often adopted to give strength to the narrative portion of her conversation.)

"That is greatly to be regretted, Mrs. Barnaby ... though we must hope that among those which remain sufficient proof of this very atrocious case will be found to answer the purposes of justice.

Was there any principle of selection in the manner in which some were preserved and others destroyed?"

"I can hardly say," replied the lady, "that it was done on any principle, unless the feeling can be so called which leads a woman of delicacy to blush and shrink from preserving the effusions of a passion so vehement as that expressed in some of the letters of Lord Mucklebury."

"They were, then, the most ardent declarations of his attachment that you destroyed, Mrs. Barnaby?"

"Most certainly," said the widow, throwing her eyes upon the carpet.

"It is unfortunate, very unfortunate," observed the lawyer, "though it shews a delicacy of mind that it is impossible not to admire. Will you give me leave, madam, to peruse such of the letters as you have preserved?"

"Undoubtedly," replied Mrs. Barnaby, unlocking her writing-desk, "and though I know not how to regret the existence of such feelings, Mr. Morrison, I will not deny that, for the sake of honour and justice, I am sorry now that what I have to shew you is so much the least explicit part of the correspondence."

She then drew forth the packet which contained (be it spoken in confidence) every syllable ever addressed to her by the laughter-loving Viscount; and greatly as Mr. Magnus Morrison began to feel interested in the case, and much as he would have liked to bring so charming a client into court, he very soon perceived that there was nothing in these highly-scented, but diminutive feuilles volantes, at all likely to produce any effect on a jury approaching to that elicited by the evidence of the learned and celebrated Sergeant Buzfuz on an occasion somewhat similar. He continued to read them all, however, and they were numerous, with the most earnest attention and unwearied industry, permitting little or no emotion of any kind to appear on his countenance as he proceeded, and determined to utter no word approaching to an opinion till he had carefully perused them all. Important as Mrs. Barnaby flattered herself these little letters might eventually prove, and interesting as her lawyer found every word of them, the whole collection might perhaps be considered as somewhat wearisome, full of repetition, and even trifling, by the general reader, for which reason a few only shall be selected as specimens, taken at hazard, and without any attention either to their dates or the particular events which led to them.

No. 1.

"PRIMA DONNA DEL MUNDO![1]

"Walk you to-day?... At three be it ... at which hour my station will be the library.

"M."

[Footnote 1: Lord Mucklebury had been assured, on the authority of Mrs. Barnaby herself, that her favourite language was the Italian.]

No. 2.

"BELLISSIMA!

"Should I appear to-day (you may guess where) with a friend on my arm, let it not change the sweet demeanour of my charming widow. He is an excellent fellow, but one whom I always treat as if he were not in existence;—for in truth, being almost as dreadfully in love as myself, he neither sees nor hears.

"M."

No. 3.

"BELLA DONNA!

"It is three days since I have received a line from the fairest lady in Cheltenham! Write me a whole page, I beseech you, ... and let it be such a one as shall console me under the necessity of dining and passing the whole evening with half a dozen he-fellows, when the champagne will but ill atone for the sparkling eyes whose light I shall lose by being among them. But if I have one of your exquisite billets in my waistcoat-pocket, I shall bear the loss better.

"M."

No. 4.

"VEDOVA MARAVIGLIOSA!

"Should I find the Barnaby disengaged in her saloon, were my audacious feet to bear me across its threshold this evening?

"M."

Such, and such like, were the manuscripts submitted by Mrs. Barnaby to the inspection of her lawyer. When he had carefully and deliberately gone through the whole collection, he tied them all up again with a bit of rose-coloured ribbon, as he had found them, and pushing them back to her across the table, said with something like a sigh,—

"It is greatly to be lamented, madam, that some of these little notes had not been consigned to the flames instead of the letters you have described to me, ... for my judgment decidedly is, that although every one of these documents tends to prove the admiration of their author for the lady to whom they are addressed, there is not one of them which can be said to contain a positive promise of marriage, or even, I fear, any implied intention of making a proposal ... so that I am afraid we should not get a verdict against my Lord Mucklebury on the strength of any evidence contained therein; nevertheless, if you have witnesses to prove that such proposal and such promise have been actually made to you by his lordship, I think these letters might help us to make out a very pretty case, and one which, if it did not eventually bring you a large sum of money, would at least be exceedingly vexatious to his lordship—a circumstance which might in some degree tend to soothe the naturally outraged feelings of so charming a lady, so villanously treated."

Mr. Morrison said this with his eyes fixed steadily on the widow's face, intending to ascertain what chance there might be of her wishing to spend a few hundred pounds for the pleasure of plaguing her perfidious deluder; but he could make out nothing from this scrutiny. Nevertheless, the mind of Mrs. Barnaby was busily at work; so many schemes, however, were battling together in her brain, that the not being able to discover which preponderated, shewed no want of skill in the lawyer.

First, she had a very strong inclination for a personal interview with Lord Mucklebury, in order to see how a little passionate grief might affect him. Secondly, she greatly desired to profit by the present occasion for seeing some of those London sights which country ladies and gentlemen so love to talk about. Thirdly, she very ardently wished to avoid the necessity of paying the debts which his lordship's base delusions had induced her to contract at Cheltenham. Fourthly, and lastly, the project of a journey to Rome was beginning to take a very decided shape in her fancy; but amidst all this there remained not the smallest wish or intention of trying to revenge her wrongs by the assistance of the law.... She was beginning to be too well aware of the melting nature of money in the funds, to wish that the villanous Viscount should lead her to expend another shilling upon him.

After the silence of a few minutes, Mrs. Barnaby raised her eyes from the ground, and fixing them with a soft, gentle, resigned smile upon Mr. Morrison, said,—

"I thank you gratefully, Mr. Morrison, for your frank opinion, given too in so gentleman-like a manner as to make me feel that I am indeed rather in the hands of a friend than a lawyer; ... and in return I will use the same frankness with you. I have loved Lord Mucklebury most sincerely!... loved him with all the pure disinterested ardour of my character; but the same warm heart, Mr. Morrison, which thus surrenders itself without suspicion or restraint, is precisely of the nature most prompt to reject and forget a being proved to be unworthy of it.... Therefore I may now truly say, that this poor bosom (pressing her two hands upon it) suffers more from the void within it, than from tender regret; and I am greatly inclined, since I cannot benefit by your able services as a lawyer, to urge my friendship with your dear sister as a claim upon your kindness as a gentleman. Will you assist to cure the painful void I speak of by giving me your help in my endeavours to see all that is best worth looking at in London?... I am sure it would do me good; not to mention that it might give pleasure to the dear child whom you saw with me when you entered. She is quite my idol, and I should delight in procuring her an amusement which I know she would so particularly enjoy."

Mr. Morrison, who was a shrewd, quick-sighted man, thought there was considerable food for speculation in this speech, and, had leisure served him, he might have reasoned upon it in a spirit not much unlike that of Benedict.... "Will you assist to cure the painful void?... which is as much as to say..." and so on.... He waited not, however, to give this all the attention it merited, but remembering clearly his sister's statement respecting the widow's fortune, replied with most obliging readiness,—

"There is nothing, my dear madam, that I would not joyfully do to prove my wish of serving a lady so highly esteemed by my sister; and one also, permit me to add, so deserving the admiration of all the world," replied the gallant attorney.

"Well, then, my dear sir," rejoined the widow, in accents of renewed cheerfulness, "I throw myself entirely upon you, and shall be quite ready to begin to-morrow to go here, there, and everywhere, exactly as you command."

A scheme for St. Paul's and the Tower in the morning, and one of the theatres at night, was then sketched out; and the gentleman departed, by no means certain that this adventure might not terminate by being one of the most important of his life.

CHAPTER III

Mr. Morrison, who really had a little business, though not very much, had named two o'clock as the earliest hour at which he should be able to come to Half-moon Street for the purpose of escorting the ladies in a hackney-coach to the city; and it was during the hours that intervened between her breakfast and this time, that the active-minded Mrs. Barnaby determined upon making a private visit to Mivart's Hotel, in the hope of seeing Lord Mucklebury.

She had quite made up her mind to the worst, as may be seen from the projects already maturing themselves in her brain, as the consequence; nevertheless she thought it was just possible that his lordship might be unable to resist the expression of sorrow in eyes he had so vehemently admired; and, at any rate, there was something so ... so touching in the idea of this final interview, that she could not refuse herself the satisfaction of making the experiment.

Telling Agnes that she had a little shopping to do before their sight-seeing began, and that she would not take her, for fear she should be as stupidly fatigued as on the night before, she mounted to her bed-room, adorned herself in the most becoming costume she could devise, and with somewhat less rouge than usual, that the traitor might see how sorrow worked, set forth on her expedition.

Having reached Piccadilly, she called a coach, and in a few minutes was safely deposited before Mivart's door.

"Is Lord Mucklebury here?..." she inquired in a voice of authority of the first official she encountered.

"Yes, ma'am," was the answer. "His lordship is at breakfast."

"I must see him, if you please, directly!"

"Is it by appointment, ma'am?" questioned the discreet waiter, looking at her keenly.... "His lordship is just going to set off, and is too busy, I believe, to see anybody."

"He is not too busy to see me—I must see him directly!"

"Is it an appointment?" repeated the man, in an accent not the most respectful.

"Yes, it is," ... replied the unblushing widow.

"Better call his own man, Joe," said another napkined functionary, attracted by the appearance of the lady.

"You had better take this sovereign," said Mrs. Barnaby in a whisper.

Apparently the man thought this advice the best; for taking the coin with such practised dexterity as hardly to make the action perceptible, he gave the lady a look with his knowing eye that said, "Follow me!..." and slid away among passages and stairs till he had marshalled her to the door of Lord Mucklebury's apartments. Being probably somewhat doubtful whether the office he had performed would be as gratefully requited by the gentleman as by the lady, he waited not to open the door, but saying, "There's his room," disappeared, leaving Mrs. Barnaby to announce her ill-used self.

She was a little frightened, but still resolute; and, after pausing for one moment to recover breath, threw open the door and entered.

The waiter's account was strictly true, for his lordship was at breakfast, and his lordship was packing. En robe de chambre, with a cup of coffee in one hand, and a bunch of keys in the other, he was standing beside his valet, who knelt before a carriage-seat he was endeavouring to close. Lord Mucklebury was facing the door, and raised his eyes as it opened. The sight that greeted them was assuredly unexpected, but the nerve with which he bore it did honour to his practised philosophy.

"Mrs. Barnaby!" he exclaimed, with a smile, in which his valet seemed to take a share, for the fellow turned his head away to conceal its effect upon him.... "Mrs. Barnaby!... How very kind this is.... But I grieve such obliging benevolence should be shewn at a moment when I have so little leisure to express my gratitude.... My dear lady, I am this instant starting for the continent."

"I know it, sir.... I know it but too well!" replied the widow, considerably embarrassed by his easy tone.... "Permit me, however, to speak to you for one moment before you set out."

"Assuredly!... Place yourself on this sofa, Mrs. Barnaby.... How deeply I regret that moments so delightful.... Confound you, Rawlins, you'll break those hinges to pieces if you force them so.... My dear lady!... I am shocked to death; ... but, upon my soul, I have not a moment to spare!"

"I wish to speak to you, my lord, without the presence of your servant."

"My dearest Mrs. Barnaby, you need not mind Rawlins any more than the coffee-pot!... You have no idea what a capital fellow he is!... true as steel ... silent as the grave.... That's it, Rawlins!... I'll set my foot upon it while you turn the key ... here! it is this crooked one."

"Lord Mucklebury!... you must be aware," ... began the widow.

"Aware!... Good Heaven, yes!... To be sure, I am! But what can I do, my dearest Mrs. Barnaby?... I must catch the packet, you see.... How is dear, good Miss Morrison?... Now for the dressing-case, Rawlins!... don't forget the soap—I've done with it!... For goodness' sake, don't tell my excellent friend, Miss Morrison, how very untidy you have found everything about me.... She is so very neat, you know!... I'm sure she'd.... Mind the stoppers, Rawlins—put a bit of cotton upon each of them!"

"Is it thus, Lord Mucklebury, that you receive one who...."

"I know what you would say, my charming friend!" interrupted his lordship, handing her a plate of buttered toast, ... "that I am the greatest bear in existence!... No! you will not eat with me?... But you must excuse me, dear friend, for I have a long drive before me." And, so saying, Lord Mucklebury seated himself at the table, replenished his coffee-cup, broke the shell of an egg, and seriously set about eating an excellent breakfast.

The widow was at a loss what to do or say next. Had he been rude or angry, or even silent and sullen, or in any other mood in the world but one of such very easy good humour, she could have managed better. But a painful sort of conviction began to creep over her that Lord Mucklebury's present conduct, as well as all that had passed before, was merely the result of high-breeding and fashionable manners, and that lords and ladies always did so to one another. If this were so, rather than betray such rustic ignorance as to appear surprised at it, she would have consented to live without a lover for weeks and weeks to come; ... and the terrible idea followed, that by having ignorantly hoped for too much she might have lost a most delightful opportunity of forming an intimate friendship with a peer of the realm, that might have been creditable and useful to her, either abroad or at home.

Fortunately Lord Mucklebury was really hungry, and he ate so heartily for a minute or two, that the puzzled lady had time to settle her purpose, and take the new tone that her ambition suggested to her, which she did with a readiness that his lordship really admired.

"Well!... I see how it is, my lord," said she; "I come here to ask you to do a commission for me at Rome, where the papers told me you were going; but you are too busy and too hungry to spare a moment to an old acquaintance."

"No! upon my soul!..." said Lord Mucklebury, throwing some of his former homage into his eyes as he bowed to her. "There is no commission in the world you could give me, from New York to Jerusalem, that I would not execute with the fidelity of a western or an eastern slave. What are your commands, bewitching Mrs. Barnaby?"

"Merely, my lord, that you would buy a set of shells for me—as nearly like Lady Stephenson's as possible; and I dare say," she added, very cleverly drawing out her purse, to avoid any misconception respecting the object,—"I dare say your lordship, who has travelled so much, may be able to tell me pretty nearly what the price will be.... About ten pounds, I think."

And ten golden sovereigns were immediately thrown from the purse upon the table.

Lord Mucklebury, perfectly delighted by this brilliant proof of the versatility of her powers, gaily took her purse from her hand, and replacing the money in it, said—

"It is not so that I execute the commissions of my fair friends, Mrs. Barnaby.... I will note your orders in my pocket-book, thus.... 'A set of the handsomest shells in Rome for the charming Mrs. Barnaby. See!... I can hardly overlook it; and when I have the pleasure of presenting them, we will settle about the price."

He replaced her purse in her hand, which he kissed with his best air of Cheltenham gallantry; upon which she wisely rose, and saying, with every appearance of being perfectly satisfied with her reception, "Adieu, my lord! forgive my intrusion, and let me hope to have the pleasure of seeing you when you return," she took her departure, perfectly convinced that her new-born conjecture was right, and that lords had privileges not accorded to other men.

This persuasion, however, as well as the interview which gave rise to it, she determined to keep to her own breast; not sorry, perhaps, that some of her friends might go to their graves with the persuasion that, though deserted by him, she once had a nobleman for her lover, and vastly well satisfied with herself for having found out her plebeian blunder in time to prevent the loss of so very valuable a friend as she still thought Lord Mucklebury might be.

She returned in good time to rest and refresh herself with a draught of her favourite beverage (porter) before Mr. Morrison arrived.

If she had thought this gentleman worthy of some little agaceries before her definitive interview with her noble friend, she certainly did not think him less so afterwards, and the morning and the evening passed away with great appearance of enjoyment to both the gentleman and lady. Mrs.

Barnaby began to think, as upon former occasions of the same kind, that it would be vastly more agreeable if Agnes were not of the party.

The same idea had occurred to the suffering girl herself more than once in the course of the day. Whether her own wish was father to the thought, or that her aunt had purposely permitted her feelings to be seen, it matters not to inquire; but when, on the following morning, Agnes complained of head-ache, and expressed a timid wish to be left at home, Mrs. Barnaby, without hesitation, replied,—

"I think you are right, Agnes.... You have no strength for that sort of thing ... so it is very lucky you brought your books, and you may unpack them, if you will, and set to work."

This release was hailed with thankfulness.... Lady Stephenson and Miss Peters were both written to during the leisure it afforded, and though she could give no very satisfactory intelligence to either, there was a pleasure in writing to them that no other occupation could give her.

After this time several days elapsed, during which Mrs. Barnaby was scarcely at home at all, except for the purpose of eating her dinner, which meal Mr. Morrison regularly partook with them.

More than a week passed in this manner; Mrs. Barnaby becoming every day more convinced that, although every sensible woman ought to marry a lord, if she can get one, yet, nevertheless, that an active, intelligent, obliging friend, full of admiration, and obedient to command, was an excellent substitute for everything else during an interregnum between the more violent attachments by which the career of all distinguished women must necessarily be marked. And Mr. Morrison, as he on his side remarked how freely the lady hired her flies and her hackney chariots,—how little she thought of the price of tickets for plays, operas, and that realization of all her dreams of elegant festivity, Vauxhall,—how liberally wine and even brandy flowed at the savoury little dinners in her drawing-room,—as he remarked on all this, he could not but reason with himself on the greatly superior felicity of being the husband of such a lady, and living without any trouble at all upon her fortune, to the remaining a bachelor in Red Lion Square, under the necessity of working whenever work could be had in order to pay his rent, settle his tailor's bill, and find wherewithal to furnish commons for himself and his one domestic.

It is certain, however, that up to this time no serious idea of marrying Mr. Magnus Morrison had entered the widow's head; on the contrary, she was fully determined that, as soon as she had seen London "well," she would see Paris too, and was not without a vague notion that there might be something very elegant and desirable in becoming the wife of a French grandee. But these ruminations interfered not at all with the amiable amenity of her demeanour to her assiduous attendant.... Agnes was as little in their way as it was possible she could be ... the weather was remarkably fine ... and, on the whole, it may be doubted if any lady of thirty-seven ever made her first debut in the metropolis of the united kingdoms with more perfect satisfaction to herself.

Mrs. Barnaby reached London on a Thursday evening; the first Sunday shewed her the Foundling, all the little children, and a popular preacher, which together constituted one of Mr. Morrison's favourite lions. The Sunday following, being the last, according to her own secret determination, that she would pass in England, she was left during the early part of the day to her own devices, Mr. Morrison having a deed to draw, which could no longer be safely postponed; and she therefore obligingly asked Agnes if she should not like to go to church with her. Agnes willingly assented, and they went to the morning service at St. James's. In returning thence our gaily-dressed widow, full of animation, and the hope of finding Mr. Morrison ready to take luncheon with her previous to their projected walk in Kensington Gardens, remarked, as she gracefully paced along the crowded pavement, that one individual among the many who eyed her appeared to follow her movements with particular attention. Mrs. Barnaby was never stared at without feeling delighted by the compliment she thought it implied, and simpered and frolicked with her parasol in her best manner, till at length, having no one else to whom she could point out the flattering circumstance, she said to Agnes, as they turned down Half-moon Street ... into which the admiring individual turned too.... "Do look at that man, Agnes.... He has never ceased to follow and stare at me since we left the church.... There, now, he is going to pass us again.... Is he not an impudent fellow?"

"Perhaps he knows you, aunt," said Agnes, raising her eyes as the man passed them.... "I think I have seen him at Cheltenham."

This suggestion heightened Mrs. Barnaby's colour so considerably that it was perceptible through all her rouge.

"You have seen him at Cheltenham?... Where, pray?"

"I do not well remember; in a shop, I think."

Mrs. Barnaby asked no more questions, but knocked rather hastily at the door of her lodgings; but though the person had crossed the street, and in doing so passed close to her, he made no attempt to speak to her, but passed on his way, not, however, before he had so refreshed her memory respecting her Cheltenham debts as to make her suddenly decide upon leaving London on the morrow.

She found Mr. Magnus Morrison waiting for her, as well-looking and as devoted as ever; so she did all but quite forget her recent alarm, its only effect being, when Agnes, as usual, declined her invitation to go out with them, to say in a whisper to her in the window recess farthest removed from her waiting gentleman, "I think I shall leave London to-morrow night, so you may employ yourself in getting everything ready for packing, Agnes...." She then turned gaily to her escort, and they set off together.

During the whole of this tedious week Agnes had used every means within her very limited power to ascertain what her aunt's plans were for the future; and this not only to satisfy her own natural curiosity on the subject, but also that she might have sufficient information to justify her writing another letter to Lady Stephenson. But all her inquiries had been so vaguely answered, that she was quite as ignorant of what her next movement might be as when she arrived, and was living in a very torturing sort of suspense, between hope that fate by some means or other would oblige her to return to Cheltenham, and fear lest the mystery that veiled the future might only be elucidated when too late for her to obey the command which, in case of the worst, was to send her there.

So weary was she both of her present position and of the doubt which concealed the termination of it, that she joyfully set herself to obey the parting injunction of her aunt; and having rapidly gone through this task, began her second letter to her Cheltenham friends, stating exactly all she knew, and all she did not know, and at length leaving her letter unfinished, that her postscript, as she said, might contain, according to the imputed custom of all ladies, the essential part of her letter.

The fine bonnets and smart waistcoats of Kensington Gardens, together with a bag-ful of queen-cakes, with which she had provided herself for her own refreshment and that of her companion during a promised hour of repose in one of the alcoves, so pleasantly beguiled the hours, that it was near seven before they returned to dinner; when the widow confessed herself too tired for anything more that day; and at an hour much earlier than usual Mr. Morrison took his departure, well informed, as it seemed, of the lady's intentions for the morrow, for Agnes heard him say,—

"Well, then, Mrs. Barnaby ... one more delightful excursion to-morrow—the Surrey Gardens will delight you!... and at two o'clock I will be here.... Sorry am I to think for the last time ... at least for the present." A cordial hand-shaking followed, and the door closed after him.

"I have done what you bid me, aunt," said Agnes; "all your things are got ready for you to place them as you like, and one of the boxes half filled, just as you did before.... Shall I write the directions, aunt?"

"We can do that to-morrow.... I am tired to death. Ring the bell.... No—run down yourself, for the girl looks as cross as two sticks ... run down, Agnes, and tell her to get my porter directly; and I think you must bring it to me in bed, for I can't keep my eyes open."

"Will you tell me, aunt, where we are going?" said Agnes timidly, as she took up one of the candles to light her steps down two flights of stairs.

"Don't plague me now, Agnes," was the reply; "I have told you that I am tired to death, and nobody but you would think of teazing one with such a question now. You know well enough, though you have not had the grace to thank me for it, that I never take you anywhere that it is not most delightful to go to.... What other country-girl in the world is there at your age that has had the advantages you have.... Exeter.... Clifton.... Cheltenham.... London; and if you don't provoke me too much, and make me turn you out of house and home, I'll take you now ... but it's no matter where—you'll know soon enough to be grateful, if there's such a thing as gratitude in your heart.... But I am a fool to expect it, and see you standing there when I've begged, as if my life depended upon it, that you would please to order me a little beer."

Agnes said no more; but went to bed that night with her fears most reasonably strengthened that she should not learn Mrs. Barnaby's destination till it was too late to avoid sharing it, let it be in what direction it might.

CHAPTER IV

AN ADVENTURE—ANOTHER LETTER FROM MISS MORRISON PRODUCTIVE OF A POWERFUL EFFECT UPON HER BROTHER—HE FORSAKES HIS CLIENT AND HIS FRIEND—AGNES IS LEFT ALONE, AND EMPLOYS SOME OF HER LEISURE IN WRITING A LETTER TO MISS COMPTON

The following day was an eventful one. For the first time since they had been in London, Agnes, on seeing her aunt preparing to go out, asked permission to go with her, and "You may go if you will," was the answer; but before her bonnet was tied on, Mrs. Barnaby changed her mind, saying, "Put down your bonnet, Agnes ... upon second thoughts I don't choose to take you.... Look at all these things of mine lying about here!... I have told you that it is likely enough we may set off by a night coach, and I have got, as you know, to go out with Mr. Morrison; so I should be much obliged if you would please to tell me how all my packing is to get done?"

"If you would let me go with you now, aunt, I shall have plenty of time to do all that remains while you are out with Mr. Morrison," replied Agnes.

"Agnes, you are, without exception, the most impertinent and the most plaguing girl that ever a widowed aunt half ruined herself to provide for.... But I won't be bullied in this way either.... Stay at home, if you please, and do what I bid you, or before this time to-morrow you may be crying in the streets of London for a breakfast.... I should like to know who there is besides me in the wide world who would undertake the charge of you?... Do you happen to know any such people, miss?... If you do, be off to them if you please—the sooner the better; ... but if not, stay at home for once without grumbling, and do what you're bid."

There was just sufficient truth mixed with the injustice of these harsh words to go to the heart of poor Agnes. Her aunt Compton, in reply to a letter of Mrs. Barnaby, written in a spirit of wanton impertinence, and in which she made a formal demand of one hundred pounds a-year for the expenses of Agnes, answered in great wrath, that she and Agnes both had better take care not to change their residence so often as to lose a parish settlement, for they might live to find that a much better dependence than anything they would obtain from her. This pettish epistle, received the day before they left Silverton, was carefully treasured by Mrs. Barnaby, and often referred to when she was anxious to impress on her niece a sense of her forlorn condition and helpless dependence. So all hope from that quarter seemed to be for ever shut out.... And could she forget that even at the moment when the dangers of her situation had so forcibly struck Lady Elizabeth Norris, as to make her approve what she had before declared to be worse than any home,—that even at that moment she had explicitly declared that neither herself nor her niece could take charge of her?

These were mournful thoughts; and it was no great proof of Agnes's wisdom, perhaps, that, instead of immediately proceeding to the performance of her prescribed task, she sat down expressly to ruminate upon them. But the meditation was not permitted to be long; for hardly had she rested her elbow upon the table, and her cheek upon her hand, in the manner which ladies under such circumstances always do, than she was startled by a violent knocking and simultaneous ringing at the street-door, followed, as soon as it was opened, by a mixture of two or three loud and angry voices, amidst which she clearly distinguished that of her aunt; and the moment after she burst into the room, accompanied by the gentleman who had appeared to admire her so greatly in the street the day before, together with two other much less well-looking personages, who stuck close upon the heels of Mrs. Barnaby, with more appearance of authority than respect.

"You shall live to repent this treatment of a lady," cried Mrs. Barnaby, addressing the hero of her yesterday's adventure, who was no other than the keeper of the livery-stable from whom she had hired the carriage and horses which had dignified her existence for the last month. "You shall be taught to know what is due from a trumpery country tradesman like you, to a person of my fortune and station. What put it into your head, you vile fellow, instead of waiting my return to Cheltenham, to follow me to London in this abominable manner, and to arrest me in the public streets?"

"It is no difficult matter to tell you that, Mrs. Barnaby, if that's your name," replied the man; "and you'll find that I am not the only vile fellow holding himself ready to pay you the same compliment; though I, knowing the old saying 'first come, first served,' took some trouble to be the first."

"And do you really pretend to fancy, you pitiful creature," cried Mrs. Barnaby, in a voice in which terror and rage were struggling,—"do you really pretend to believe that I am not able to pay your twopenny-halfpenny bill a thousand times over?"

"Can't say indeed, ma'am," replied the man; "I shall not stand upon sending you to prison if you will discharge the account as here we stand, paying fees and expenses of course, as is fitting... Here are the items, neither many nor high.—

£. s. d.

	£	s.	d.
Carriage and horses one month, twenty-five shillings per diem	37	0	0
Coachman's livery, board, and wages	20	0	0
Footman's ditto, hired to order	25	0	0
——			
	£82	0	0
	——		
Deduct liveries, if returned	12	0	0
	——		
Remains	£70	0	0

And all our expenses and fees added won't make it above 77l. or 78l. altogether; so, ma'am, if you are the great lady you say, you won't find no great difficulty in giving me a write-off for the sum, and my good friends here shall stay while I run and get it cashed, after which I will be ready to make you my bow, and say good morning."

The anger of Mrs. Barnaby was not the less excited because what Mr. Simmons, the livery-stable keeper, said was true; and she seized with considerable quickness the feature of the case which appeared the most against him.

"Your vulgar mode of proceeding at Cheltenham, Mr. Simmons, is, I am happy to say, quite peculiar to yourselves; for though, for my age, I have lived a good deal in the world, I certainly never saw anything like it. Here have I, like a woman of fortune as I am, paid nobly, since I have been in your trumpery town, for every single thing for which it is customary to pay ready money; and when a job like yours, which never since the creation of the world was paid except from quarter to quarter, has run up for one month, down comes the stable-man post haste after me with a writ and arrest. I wonder you are not ashamed of yourself."

"I dare say I should, ma'am, you talking so fine as you do, if I hadn't nothing to put forward in return. I don't believe, Mrs. Barnaby, but what you, or any other rich-seeming lady like you,... I don't believe but what any such might have come to Cheltenham, and have run up debts to the tune of a thousand pounds, and not one of us taken fright at it, provided the lady had stayed quiet and steady in the town, where one had one's eyes upon her, and was able to see what she was about. But just do now look at the difference. 'The season's pretty fullish,' says one, 'and trade's brisk!...' 'That's true,' says another, 'only some's going off, and that's never a good sign, specially if they go without paying....' 'And who's after that shabby trick?' says another:... 'Neither more nor less than the gay widow Barnaby!' is the answer.... 'The devil she is!' says one; 'she owes me twenty pounds....'—'I hope you are out there neighbour,' says another, 'for she owes me thirty.... 'And me ten'—'and me fifty'—'and me nineteen'—'and me forty,' and so on for more than I'll number. And what, pray, is the wisest among them likely to do in such a case? Why, just what your humble servant has done, neither more nor less."

"And what right have you, audacious man! to suppose that I have any intention of not returning, and paying all I owe, as I have ever and always done before?"

"Nothing particular, except your just saying, ma'am, that you should be back in two days, and nevertheless not making yourself be heard of in ten, and your rooms kept, and your poor maid kept in 'em all the time too."

"This man talks like one who knows not what a lady is," said Mrs. Barnaby, her eyes flashing, and her face crimson; "but I must beg to ask of you, sir," turning to one of the Bow-street officials, "whether I am not to have time allowed for sending to my lawyer, and giving him instructions to settle with this fellow here?"

"Why, by rights, ma'am, you should go to a sponging-house without loss of time, that we might get the committal made out, and all regular; but if you be so inclined as to make it worth while to my companion and me, I don't think we shall object to keeping guard over you here instead, while you send off for any friends you choose to let into the secret."

"The friends I shall send to are my men of business, fellow!" replied Mrs. Barnaby, with the strongest expression of disdain that she could throw into her countenance. "You don't, I hope, presume to imagine that I would send for any one of rank to affront them with the presence of such as you?"

"Fair words butter no parsnips, is a good saying and a true one;... but I'll add to it, that saucy ones unlock no bolts; and if you expect to get out of this scrape by talking big, it's likely you may find yourself mistaken."

"A bill must be a good deal longer than this is, man, before the paying it will be much of a scrape to me," said the widow, affecting to laugh. "What a fool you are, Agnes," she continued, turning to the corner of the room into which the terrified girl had crept, "what a prodigious fool, to be sure, you must be, to sit there looking as white as a sheet, because an insolent tradesman chooses to bring in a bill of a month's standing, with a posse of thief-takers to back it.... Get up, pray, and bring my desk here... I wish to write to my attorney."

In obedience to this command, Agnes rose from her chair, and attempted to cross the room to fetch the desk, which was at the other extremity of it; but not all her efforts to arouse her strength sufficed to overcome the sick faintness which oppressed her. "Do, for God's sake, move a little faster, child," said Mrs. Barnaby; but Agnes failed in her habitual and meek obedience, not by falling into a chair, but by sitting down in one, conscious that her fainting at such a moment must greatly increase her aunt's embarrassment.

"I'll get the desk, miss," said one of the terrible men, in a voice so nearly expressive of pity, that tears started to her own eyes in pity of herself, as she thought how wretched must be the state of one who could inspire such a feeling in such a being; but she thanked him, and he placed the lady's desk before her—that pretty little rosewood desk that had been and indeed still was the receptacle of my Lord Mucklebury's flattering if not binding effusions; and as the thought crossed the brain of Mrs. Barnaby that she had hoped to make her fortune by these same idle papers, she felt for the very first time in her life, that perhaps, after all, she had not managed her affairs quite so cleverly as she might have done. It was a disagreeable idea; but even as she conceived it her spirit rose to counteract any salutary effect such a notion might produce; and with a toss of the head that indicated defiance to her own common sense, she opened her desk with a jerk, and began editing an epistle to Mr. Magnus Morrison.

But this epistle, though it reached the lawyer in a reasonably short time after it was written, was not the first he received that day, ... for the Cheltenham post had brought him the following:

"DEAR BROTHER,

"Don't blame me if the gay widow I introduced to you the week before last, should prove to be a flam, as my dear father used to call it.... I am sorry to say there are great suspicions of it going about here. She left us telling everybody that she should be back in two days; and it is now more than ten since she started, and no soul has heard a word about her since. This looks odd, and bad enough, you will think; but it is not the worst part of the story, I'm sorry to say, paw de too, as you shall hear. When she first came to Cheltenham she took very good rooms ... a separate drawing-room, which always looks well ... and dress, and all that, quite corresponding, but no servants nor carriage, nor anything of the high-flying kind.... Now observe, Magnus, what follows, and then I think that you will come to a right notion of what sort of person you have got to deal with. No sooner did Mrs. Barnaby get acquainted with Lord Mucklebury then she set off living at the rate of some thousands a-year; and the worst is, as far as I am concerned, that she coaxed me to go round bespeaking and ordering everything for her. I know you will tell me, Magnus, that my father's daughter ought to have known better, and so I ought; but, upon my word, she took me in so completely that I never felt a single moment's doubt about the truth of all she said.... And I believe, too, that the superior sort of elegant look of that beautiful Miss Willoughby went for something with me. Having told you all this, it won't be necessary, I fancy, to say much more in respect to putting you on your guard.... Of course, you will take care to do nothing in the way of standing bail, or anything of that sort ... paw see bate, you will say. All Cheltenham is talking about it; and I was told at breakfast this morning that Simmons, who furnished the carriage, horses, and servants, is gone to London to look after her; and that Wright the mercer, and several others, talk of doing the same. Too sell aw man we; but it can't be helped.... So many people, too, come to me for information, just as if I knew any more about her than anybody else at the boarding table.... That queer Lady Elizabeth Norris sent for me yesterday, begging I would call upon her; and when I got there I found it was for nothing in the world but to ask me questions about this Mrs. Barnaby. And there was that noble-looking Colonel Hubert, who sat and listened to every word I uttered just as if he had been as curious an old woman as his aunt: maize eel foe dear, Magnus, that men are sometimes quite as curious as women.... However, they neither of them got much worth hearing out of me; and yet I almost thought at one time that the high and mighty Colonel was writing down what I said, for he had got his gold pencil-case in his hand; and though it was on the page of a book that he seemed to be scribbling, I saw plain enough by his eye that he was listening to me. You know, brother, I am pretty sharp, and I have got a few presents out of this fly-away lady, let what will come of it. But I could not help thinking, Magnus,—and if it was in a printed book it would be called a fine observation,—I could not help thinking how such a vulgar feeling as curiosity spoils the elegance of the manners. Lady Elizabeth, who has often told me that I speak the most exquisite French she ever heard, and who always before yesterday seemed delighted to have the opportunity of conversing with me in this very genteel language, never said one word in it all the time I stayed; and once when, as usual, I spoke a few words, she looked as cross as a bear, and said, 'Be so good as to speak English just now, Miss Morrison.' Very impertinent, I thought, may set eh gal. Don't think the worse of me for this unfortunate blunder.... Let me hear how you are going on, and believe me

"Your affectionate sister,

"SARAH MORRISON."

Mr. Magnus Morrison had by no means recovered the blow given him by this most unpleasing news, when a note from Mrs. Barnaby to the following effect was put into his hands.

"MY DEAR SIR,

"A most ridiculous, but also disagreeable circumstance, has happened to me this morning. A paltry little tradesman of Cheltenham, to whom I owe a few pounds, has taken fright because I did not return to my apartments there at the moment he expected me ... the cause of which delay you must be aware has been the great pleasure I have received from seeing London so agreeably.... However, he has had the incredible insolence to follow me with a writ, and I must beg you to come to me with as little delay as possible, as your bail, I understand, will prevent my submitting to the indignity of being lodged in a prison during the interval necessary for my broker (who acts as my banker) to take the proper measures for supplying me with the trifling sum I want. In the hope of immediately seeing you,

"I remain, dear Sir,

"Most truly yours,

"MARTHA BARNABY."

Mr. Magnus Morrison was not "so quick," as it is called, as his sister Sarah, and in the present emergency felt totally unable to fabricate an epistle, or even to invent a plausible excuse for an absence, which he nevertheless finally determined should be eternal. He was ill-inspired when he took this resolution, for had he attended the lady's summons, he might, with little trouble, have made a more profitable client of her yet than often fell to his lot. But he was terror-struck at the word BAIL; and forgetting all the beef-steaks, cheesecakes, porter, and black wine that he had swallowed at the widow's cost, he very cavalierly sent word by the sheriff's officer, who had brought her note, that he was very sorry, but that it was totally out of his power to come.

On receiving this message, delivered, too, with the commentary of a broad grin, even Mrs. Barnaby turned a little pale; but she speedily recovered herself on recollecting how very easy and rapid an operation the selling out stock was; so, once more raising her dauntless eye, she said, with an assumption of dignity but little mitigated by this rebuff,... "I presume you will let me wait in my own apartments till I can send to my broker?"

"Why, 'tis possible, ma'am, you see, that it may be totally out of his power too, like this t'other gentleman ... and we can't be kept waiting all day.... You'll have a trifle to pay already for the obligingness we have shewn, and so you must be pleased to get ready without more ado."

"You don't mean to take me to prison, fellow, for this trumpery debt!"

"'Tis where ladies always do go when they keep carriages without paying for them, unless indeed they have got husbands as can go for them; and as that don't seem to be your case, ma'am, we must really trouble you to make haste."

"Gracious Heaven!... It is incredible!..." cried the widow, now really in an agony. "Why, fellow, I tell you I have thousands in the funds that I can sell out at an hour's warning!"

"So much the better, ma'am—so much the better for us all, as, in that case, we shall be sure to get our own at last; and if the thing can be settled so easily, it is quite beneath such a clever lady as you to make a fuss about lodging at the king's charge for a night or so.... Pray, miss, can you help the gentlewoman to put up a night-cap, and such like little comforts, ... not forgetting a small provision of ready money, if I might advise, for that's what makes the difference between a bad lodging and a good one where we are going.... Dick ... run out and call a coach, will you?"

All further remonstrance proved useless; and Mrs. Barnaby, alternately scolding and entreating, was forced at last to submit to the degradation of being watched by a bailiff's officer as she went to her chamber to prepare herself for this terrible change of residence. The most bitter moment of all, perhaps, was that in which she was told that she must go alone, for that they had no orders to permit the attendance of any one. It was only then that she felt, in some degree, the value of the gentle observant kindness which had marked every word and look of Agnes from the moment when—her first feeling of faintness over—she assiduously drew near her, put needle-work into her hands, set herself to the same employment, and, with equal ingenuity and sweet temper, contrived to make the long interval during which they had to endure the presence of two of the men, while the third was dispatched to Mr. Morrison, infinitely more tolerable than could have been hoped for. But on this point the officials were as peremptory as in the commands they reiterated that she should get ready, promising, however, that application should be made for leave to let the young lady be with her, if she liked it.

"You may save yourselves the trouble, brutes as you are," cried Mrs. Barnaby, as, with something very like a sob, she returned the kiss of Agnes. "I'll defy you to keep me in your vile clutches beyond this time to-morrow.... Take care that this letter is put into the post directly, Agnes; but I will give it to the maid myself.... It will reach my broker by four or five o'clock, I should think; and I'll answer for his not neglecting the business; but it may, however, be near dinner-time before I get back—so don't be frightened, my dear, if it is; and here is the key of the money-drawer, you know, if you want to pay anything."

"Better divide the money drawer with the young lady, at any rate," said one of the men, laughing.

"That you may pick my pockets, perhaps?" replied the vexed prisoner.

"Have you enough money with you, aunt?" whispered Agnes in her ear.

"Plenty, my dear; and more than I'll spend upon them, depend upon it," she replied aloud.... This drew on a fresh and not very gentle declaration that they must be gone directly; and the unlucky Mrs. Barnaby, preceded by one and followed by two attendants, descended the stairs, and mounted the hackney-coach.

It was then that Agnes for the first time began to understand and feel the nature of her own situation. Alone, utterly alone in lodgings in the midst of London, totally ignorant of the real state of her aunt's affairs, and, unhappily, so accustomed to hear her utter the most decided falsehoods upon all subjects, that nothing she had said on this gave her any confidence in the certainty either of her speedy return, or of her being immediately able to settle all claims upon her. What, then, was it her duty to do? During the first few moments of meditation on her desolate condition, she thought that the danger of being taken abroad could not have been greater than that which had now fallen upon her, and consequently that Lady Elizabeth would be ready to extend to her the temporary shelter she had told her to claim, in case of what then appeared the worst necessity. But a very little calmer reflection made her shrink from this; and the fact that Colonel Hubert was now with her, which, under other circumstances, would have made such an abode, if enjoyed only for a day or two, the dearest boon that Providence could grant her, now caused her to decide, with a swelling heart, that she would not accept it.

The nature and degree of the disgrace which her aunt had now brought upon her was so much worse than all that either her vanity or her coquetry had hitherto achieved, that she felt herself incalculably more beneath him than ever, and felt during these dreadful moments that she would rather have begged her bread back to Empton, than have met the doubtful welcome of his eye upon seeing her under such circumstances.

This thought of Empton recalled the idea of the person whose liberal kindness had for years bestowed on her this only home that she had ever loved. Was it possible, that if made acquainted with her present deplorable situation, she could refuse to extend some sort of protection to one whose claim upon her she had formerly acknowledged so freely, and who had never forfeited it by any act of her own?... "I will write to her!" said Agnes, suddenly rousing herself, as it occurred to her that she was now called upon to act for herself. "God knows," thought she, "what my unfortunate and most unwise aunt Barnaby may have written or said to provoke her; but now, at least, without either rebellion or deceit, I may myself address her."

This idea generated a hope that seemed to give her new life, and with a rapid pen she wrote as follows:

"I can hardly dare to expect that a letter from one whom you have declared you never would see again should be very favourably received; and yet, my dear aunt Betsy (permit me once more to call you so), how can I believe that the same person who took such generous pity on my miserable ignorance six years ago would, without any fault on my part, permit me to fail in my hope of turning the education she bestowed into a means of honourable existence, and that solely from the want of her protection? Alas! aunt Compton, I am most miserably in want of protection now. My aunt Barnaby, of whose pecuniary affairs I, in truth, know nothing, was this morning arrested and taken away to prison for debt. Her style of expense has been very greatly increased during the last few weeks, and I have reason to believe that she entertained a hope of being married to a nobleman, with whom she made acquaintance at Cheltenham, but who left it, about a fortnight ago, without taking any leave of her. I am not much in her confidence; but she has so repeatedly mentioned before me her determination to be revenged on this Lord Mucklebury, as well as her certainty of recovering damages from him, that I have no doubt her coming to London was with a view to bringing an action for breach of promise of marriage. What confirms this is, that the only person we have seen is a lawyer; and the same spirit of conjecture, which has made me guess what I have told you, leads me to suspect also, that this lawyer has persuaded her to give the project up; for not only do I hear no more of it, but she has seemed for the last week to be devoted wholly to seeing the sights of London in company with this lawyer. I have not accompanied them, not being very well, nor very happy in a mode of life so much less tranquil than what I have been used to at Empton.

"I tell you all these particulars, aunt Compton, that you may know exactly what my situation is. I am, at this moment, alone in a London lodging; my aunt Barnaby in prison; and with no little danger, as far as I am able to judge, that when she has settled this claim for her carriage and horses, many others may come upon her.

"My petition to you, therefore, is, that you would have the great, great goodness to permit my travelling back into Devonshire to put myself under your protection; not idly to become a burden to you, but that I might be so happy as to feel myself in a place of respectability and safety till such time as my kind friend, Mrs. Wilmot, may hear of some situation as governess, or teacher at a school, such as she might think me fit for. I have very diligently kept up my reading and writing in French and Italian, with the hope of one day teaching both. They tell me, too, that I have a good voice for singing, as my poor mother had ... perhaps I might be able to teach that.

"I shall remain here (unless removed by my aunt Barnaby, of which I would give you notice) till such time as the Silverton post can bring me an answer. Have pity upon me, dear aunt Betsy!... Indeed I want it as much now as when you found I could not read a line of English in your pretty bower at Compton Basett.

"How often I have thought of your flowers and your bees, aunt Betsy, and wished I could be there to wait upon them and upon you!

"Your dutiful and grateful niece,

"AGNES WILLOUGHBY."

"5, Half-Moon Street, Piccadilly, London."

Having finished this letter, Agnes completed one she had before been writing to Lady Stephenson, and then took her solitary way to a letter-box, of which she had learned the situation, at no great distance. She heard her important dispatch to Compton Basett drop into the box, with a conviction that her fate wholly depended on the manner in which it was received; and having walked back as slowly as possible, that she might benefit by the mild western breeze that blew upon her feverish cheek, she remounted the dark stairs to the solitary drawing-room, totally incapable of enjoying that solitude, though it had so often appeared to her the one thing needful for happiness.

Happy was it for her that she had turned her thoughts to her aunt Compton; for, uncertain as was the result of her application, there was enough of hope attached to it to save her from that feeling of utter desolation that must at this moment have been her portion without it. The more she thought of receiving aid from the pity of Colonel Hubert's family, the less could she feel comfort from the idea. When it had been offered as a protection against the notice which they had imagined her likely to excite, it was soothing to all her feelings; but, required or accorded as mere ordinary charity, it was intolerable. A melancholy attempt at dining occupied a few minutes, and then hour after hour passed over her, slowly and sadly, till the light faded. But she had not energy for employment; not one of all her best-loved volumes could have fixed her attention for a moment. She called for no candles, but lying on the sofa, her aching head pillowed by her arm, she suffered herself to dwell on all the circumstances of her situation, which weighed most heavily upon her heart; and assuredly the one which brought the greatest pang with it was the recollection of having won the affection of Colonel Hubert's family, just at the moment when disgrace so terrible had fallen on her own, as to make her rather dread than wish to see him again.

CHAPTER V

AGNES RECEIVES AN UNEXPECTED VISITER, AND AN IMPORTANT COMMUNICATION—SHE ALSO RECEIVES A LETTER FROM CHELTENHAM, AND FROM HER AUNT BARNABY

Agnes was roused from this state of melancholy musing by a double knock at the door.

"Is it possible," she said, starting up, "that she spoke truly, and that she is already released?"

The street-door was opened, but the voice of Mrs. Barnaby did not make its way up the stairs before her—a circumstance so inevitable upon her approach,—that, after listening for it in vain for a moment, the desolate girl resumed her attitude, and endeavoured to recover the train of thought that had been broken. But she was not destined to do so, at least for the present, for the maid threw open the drawing-room door, and announced "A gentleman."

Agnes, as we have said, was sitting in darkness, and the girl very judiciously placed her slender tallow-candle in its tin receptacle on the table, saying, as she set a chair for "the gentleman," "I will bring candles in a minute, miss," and then departed.

Agnes raised her eyes as the visiter approached, and had the light been feebler still she would have found no difficulty in discovering that it was Colonel Hubert who stood before her. He bowed to the angle of the most profound respect, and though he ventured to extend his hand in friendly greeting, he took hers with the air of a courtier permitted to offer homage to a sovereign princess.

Agnes stood up, she received his offered hand, and raised her eyes to his face, but uttered no word either of surprise or joy. Her face was colourless, and traces of very recent tears were plainly visible; she trembled from head to foot, and Colonel Hubert, frightened, as a brave man always is when he sees a woman really sinking under her sex's weakness, replaced her on the sofa almost as incapable of speaking as herself.

"Do not appear distressed at seeing me, dearest Miss Willoughby," said he, "or I shall be obliged to repent having ventured to wait on you. I should not have presumed to do this, had not your friends, your truly attached friends, my aunt and sister, authorized my doing so."

"Oh! what kindness!" exclaimed poor Agnes, bursting into a flood of most salutary tears. "Do not think me ungrateful, Colonel Hubert, if I could not say ... if I did not speak to you.... Do you, indeed, come to me from Lady Elizabeth?"

"Here are my credentials," he replied, smiling, and presenting a letter to her. "We learned that your foolish aunt ... forgive me, Miss Willoughby; but the step I have taken can only be excused by explaining it with the most frank sincerity ... we learned that Mrs. Barnaby, having quitted Cheltenham suddenly, (the ostensible reason for doing which was bad enough), had left a variety of debts unpaid; and that her creditors, alarmed at her not returning, were taking active measures to secure her person.... Is this true?... Is your aunt arrested?"

"She is," replied Agnes faintly.

"Good God!... You are here, then, entirely alone?"

"I am quite alone," was the answer, though it was almost lost in the sob that accompanied it.

"Oh! dearest Agnes!" cried Colonel Hubert, in a burst of uncontrolable emotion, "I cannot see you thus, and longer retain the secret that has been hidden in my heart almost from the first hour I saw you!... I love you, Agnes, beyond all else on earth!... Consent to be my wife, and danger and desertion shall never come near you more!"

What a moment was this to hear such an avowal!... Human life can scarcely offer extremes more strongly marked of weal and woe than those presented by the actual position of Agnes, and that proposed to her by the man she idolized. But let De la Rochefoucault say what he will, there are natures capable of feeling something nobler than the love of self; ... and after one moment of happy triumphant swelling of the heart that left no breath to speak, she heaved a long deep sigh that seemed to bring her back from her momentary glimpse of an earthly paradise to things as they are, and said slowly, but with great distinctness, "No! never will I be your wife!... never, by my consent, shall Colonel Hubert ally himself to disgrace!"

Had this been said to a younger man, it is probable that he would not have found in it anything calculated to give a mortal wound to his hopes and wishes; but it fell with appalling coldness on the heart of the brave soldier, who had long kept Cupid at defiance by the shield of Mars, and who had just made the first proposal of marriage that had ever passed his lips. It was her age and his own that rose before him as she uttered her melancholy "No, never!..." and Agnes became almost the first object to whom he had ever, even for a moment, been unjust. He gave her no credit ... no, not the least, for the noble struggle that was breaking her heart, and meant most sincerely what he said, when he replied,—

"Forgive me, Miss Willoughby.... Had I been a younger man, the offer of my hand, my heart, my life, would not have appeared to you, as it doubtless must do now,—the result of sober, staid benevolence, desirous of preserving youthful innocence from unmerited sorrow.... Such must my love seem.... So let it seem; ... but it shall never cost one hour's pain to you."... He was silent for a moment, and had to struggle, brave man as he was, against feelings whose strength, perhaps, only shewed his weakness.... "But even so," he added, making a strong effort to speak steadily, "even so; let me not be here in vain: listen to me as a friend and father."

Poor Agnes!... this was a hard trial. To save him, worshipped as he was, from a marriage that must be considered as degrading, she could have sacrificed herself with the triumphant courage of a proud martyr; but to leave him with the idea that she was too young to love him!... to let that glowing, generous heart sink back upon itself, because it found no answering warmth in her!... in her! who would have died only to purchase the light of owning that she never did, and never could, love any man but him!... It was too terrible, and the words "Hubert! beloved Hubert!" were on her lips; but they came no farther, for she had not strength to speak them. Another effort might have been more successful, and they, or something like them, might have found way, had not the gentleman recovered his voice first, and resumed the conversation in a tone so chillingly reserved, that the timid, broken-spirited girl, had no strength left "to prick the sides of her intent," and lay her innocent heart open before him.

"In the name of Lady Elizabeth Norris let me entreat you, Miss Willoughby, not to remain in a situation so every way objectionable," he said. "My aunt and sister both are full of painful anxiety on your account, and the letter I have brought contains their earnest entreaties that you should immediately take up your residence with my aunt. Do not refuse this from any fear of embarrassment ... of persecution from me.... I shall probably go abroad.... I shall probably join my friend Frederick at Paris. He did you great justice, Miss Willoughby; ... and, but for me, perhaps.... Forgive me!... I will no longer intrude on you!—forgive me!—tell me you forgive me, for all the pain I have caused you, and for more injury, perhaps, than you will ever know! I never knew how weak—I fear I should say how unworthy—my character might become, till I knew you; ... and to complete the hateful retrospect," he added, with bitterness, and rising to go, "to complete the picture of myself that I have henceforth to contemplate, I was coxcomb enough to fancy.... But I am acting in a way that I should scorn a youth for who numbered half my years.... Answer my aunt's letter, Miss Willoughby ... answer it as if her contemptible nephew did not exist ... he shall exist no longer where he can mar your fortune or disturb your peace!"

Agnes looked at him as if her heart would break at hearing words so harsh and angry, when, losing at once all sense of his own suffering, Colonel Hubert reseated himself, and, in the gentlest accent of friendship, alluded to the propriety of her immediately leaving London, and to the anxiety of her friends at Cheltenham to receive her.

"They are very, very good to me," said Agnes meekly; "and I shall be most thankful, Colonel Hubert, to avail myself of such precious kindness, if the old aunt, to whom I have written, in Devonshire, should refuse to save me from the necessity of being a burden on their benevolence."

"But shall you wait for this decision here, Miss Willoughby?"

"I have promised to do so," replied Agnes; "and as I may have an answer here on Thursday, I think, at latest, I would not risk the danger of offending her by putting it out of my power immediately to obey her commands, if she should be so kind as to give me any."

The eyes of Agnes were fixed for a moment on his as she concluded this speech, and there was something in the expression of that look that shook the sternness of his belief in her indifference. He rose again, and making a step towards her, said, with a violence of emotion that entirely changed the tone of his voice,—

"Agnes!... Miss Willoughby!... answer me one question.... Should my aunt herself plead for me ... could you, would you, be my wife?"

Agnes, equally terrified lest she should say too little or too much, faltered as she replied, "If it were possible, Colonel Hubert ... could I indeed believe that your aunt, your sister, would not hate and scorn me...."

"You might!... You will let me believe it possible you could be brought to love me?... To love me, Agnes?... No! do not answer me ... do not commit yourself by a single word!... Stay, then, here; ... but do not leave the house!... Stay till.... Yet, alas! I dare not promise it!... But you will not leave this house, Miss Willoughby, with any aunt, without letting me ... my family, know where you may be found?"

"Oh no!..." said Agnes with a reviving hope, that if they must be parted, which this reference to her aunt and his own doubtful words made it but too probable would be the end of all, at least it would not be because he thought she was too young to love him.... "Oh no!" she repeated; "this letter will not be left without an answer."

"And you will not stir from these rooms alone?" he replied, once more taking her hand.

"Not if you think it best," she answered, frankly giving hers, and with a smile, moreover, that ought to have set his heart at ease about her thinking him too old to love. And for the moment perhaps it did so, for he ventured to press a kiss upon that hand, and uttering a fervent "Heaven bless and guard you!" disappeared.

And Agnes then sat down to muse again. But what a change had now come o'er the spirit of her dream!... Where was her abject misery? Where the desolation that had made her almost fear to look around and see how frightfully alone she was? Her bell was rung, her candles brought her, tea was served; and though there was a fulness and palpitation at the heart which prevented her taking it, or eating the bread and butter good-naturedly intended to atone for her untasted dinner, quite in the tranquil, satisfactory, and persevering manner that might have been wished, everything seemed to dance before her eyes en coleur de rose, till at last, giving up the attempt to sit soberly at the tea-table, she rose from her chair, clasped her hands with a look of grateful ecstasy to heaven, and exclaimed aloud, "He loves me! Hubert loves me!... Oh, happy, happy Agnes!"

"Did you call, miss?" said the maid entering, from having heard her voice as she passed up the stairs.

Agnes looked at her and laughed. "No, Susan," she replied; "I believe I was talking to myself."

"Well, that is funny," said the girl; "and I'm sure it is a pity such a young lady as you should have no one else to talk to. Shall I take the things away, miss?"

Once more left to herself, Agnes set about reading the letter, which hitherto had lain untouched upon the table, blushing as she opened it now, because it had not been opened before.

The first page was from Lady Elizabeth, and only expressed her commands, given in her usual peremptory tone, but nevertheless mixed with much kindness, that Agnes should leave London with as little delay as possible, and consider her house as her home till such time as an eligible situation could be found, in which her own excellent talents might furnish her with a safer and more desirable manner of existence than any her aunt Barnaby could offer. The remainder of the letter was filled by Lady Stephenson, and expressed the most affectionate anxiety for her welfare; but she too referred to the hope of being able to find some situation that should render her independent; so that it was sufficiently evident that neither of them as yet had any idea that this independence might be the gift of Colonel Hubert.

"It is nonsense to suppose they will ever consent to it," thought Agnes; and this time her spirits were not so exalted as to make her breathe her thoughts aloud; "but I never can be so miserable again as I have been ... it is enough happiness for any one person in this life ... that everybody says is not a happy one ... it is quite enough to know that Hubert loves me ... Oh Hubert!... noble Hubert! how did I dare to fix my fancy on thee?... Presumptuous!... But yet he loves me!"

And with this balm, acting like a gentle opiate upon her exhausted spirits, she slept all night, and dreamed of Hubert.

The four o'clock delivery of the post on the following day brought her this letter from her aunt Barnaby.

"DEAR AGNES,

"The brutality of these Cheltenham people is perfectly inconceivable. Mr. Crayton my broker, and my poor father's broker before me, came to me as early as it was possible last night; and I explained to him fully, and without a shadow of reserve, the foolish scrape I had got into, which would have been no scrape at all if I had not happened to fall into the hands of a parcel of rascals. He undertook to get the sum necessary to release me by eleven o'clock this morning, which he did, good man, with the greatest punctuality ... paid that villanous Simmons, got his receipt, and my discharge, when, just at the very moment when I was stepping into the coach that was to take me from this hateful place, up come the same two identical fellows that insulted us in Half-Moon Street, and arrest me again at the suit of Wright.... Such nonsense!... As if I could not pay them all ten times over, as easy as buy a pot of porter. But they care no more for reason than a pig in a sty; so here I am, shut up again till that dear old man Crayton can come, and get through all the same tedious work again. You can't conceive how miserably dull I am; and what's particularly provoking, I gave over trying to have you in with me as soon as old Crayton told me I should be out by noon to-day; and therefore, Agnes, I want you to set off the very minute you receive this, and come to me for a visit. You may come to me for a visit, though I can't have you in without special leave. Mind not to lose your way; but it's uncommonly easy if you will only go by what I say. Set out the same way that we went to the church, you know, and keep on till you get to the Haymarket, which you will know by its being written up. Then, when you've got down to the bottom of it, turn sharp round to your left, and just ask your way to the Strand; and when you have got there, which you will in a minute, walk on, on, on, till you come to the bottom of a steep hill, and then stop and ask some one to shew you the way to the Fleet Prison. When you get there, any of the turnkeys will be able to shew you to my room; and a comfort I'm sure it will be to see you in such a place as this.... And do, Agnes, buy as you come along half a dozen cheesecakes and half a dozen queen-cakes, and a small jar, for about four or five shillings, of brandy cherries.... And what's a great comfort, I may keep you till it's dark, which is what they call shutting-up time, and then you can easy enough find your way back again by the gaslight, which is ten times more beautiful than day, all along the streets from one end of the town to the other.... Only think of that dirty scoundrel Morrison never coming near me ... after all that passed too, and all the wine he drank, shabby fellow!... There is one very elegant-looking man here that I meet in the passage every time I go to my bed-room. He always bows, but we have not spoken yet. Bring five sovereigns with you, and be sure set off the moment you get this.

"Your affectionate aunt,

"MARTHA BARNABY."

It needs not to say the sort of effect which the tone of this letter produced on a mind in itself delicate and unsunned as the bells of the valley lily, and filled to overflowing with the image of the noble Hubert. Yet there were other feelings that mingled with this deep disgust; she pitied her aunt Barnaby, and could any decent or womanly exertion have done her good, or even pleasure, she would not have shrunk from making it. But what she asked was beyond her power to perform; and, moreover, she had promised Colonel Hubert not to leave the house. How dear to her was the recollection of this injunction!... how delightful the idea that his care and his commands protected her from the horrors of such a progress as that sketched out by her aunt Barnaby. To obey her was therefore altogether out of the question; but she sat down to write to her, and endeavoured to soften her refusal by pleading her terror of the streets at any hour, and her total want of strength and courage to undertake such an expedition; adding, that she supposed by her account there could be no doubt of their meeting in Half-Moon Street on the morrow.

But the morrow and its morrow came, without bringing Mrs. Barnaby. In fact, writ after writ had poured in upon her, but hoping still to evade those yet to come, she only furnished herself with what each one required, and so prolonged her imprisonment to the end of the week. Her indignation at Agnes's refusal to come to her was excessive, and she answered her letter by a vehement declaration that she would never again inhabit the same house with her. This last epistle ended thus:—

"If you don't wish to be turned neck and heels into the street the moment I return, look out for a nursery-maid's or a kitchen-maid's place if you will ... only take care never to let me set eyes upon you again. Ungrateful wretch!... What is Morrison's ingratitude to yours? For nearly seven months you have eaten at my cost, been lodged at my cost, travelled at my cost, ay, and been clothed at my cost too. And what is the return?... I am in prison for debts, which, of course, were incurred as much for you as for myself; and you refuse to come to me!... Never let me see you more—never let me hear your name, and never again turn your thoughts or hopes to your for ever offended aunt,

"MARTHA BARNABY."

Little as Agnes wished to continue under the protection of Mrs. Barnaby, this peremptory dismissal was exceedingly embarrassing. She had declined immediately accepting the invitation of Lady Elizabeth in a manner that made her very averse to throwing herself upon it, till a positive refusal of assistance from her aunt Compton obliged her to do so; and being absolutely penniless (excepting inasmuch as she was entrusted with the key that secured the widow's small stock of ready money), her only mode of not undergoing, to the letter, the sentence which condemned her to wander in the streets, was remaining where she was till she received an answer from Miss Compton.

It is certain that she submitted to thus seizing upon hospitality with the strong hand the more readily, as by doing so she was enabled to obey the parting injunction of Colonel Hubert; and bracing her courage to the meeting that must take place should Mrs. Barnaby's release precede her own, she suffered the heavy interval of doubt to steal away with as little of the feverish restlessness of impatience as possible.

CHAPTER VI

AGNES RECEIVES ANOTHER UNEXPECTED VISIT—MRS. BARNABY RETURNS TO HER LODGINGS AND CATCHES THE VISITER THERE

The seven or eight months elapsed since the reader parted from Miss Compton, passed not over the head of the secluded spinster as lightly as the years which had gone before ... for her conscience was not quite at rest. For some time the vehemence of the indignation and disgust excited by Mrs. Barnaby, during their last interview, sustained her spirits, much as a potent but noxious dram might have done; and during this time the fact of Agnes being her inmate and companion, was quite sufficient to communicate such a degree of contamination to her, as made the choleric old lady turn from all thought of her with most petulant dislike. The letter of Mrs. Barnaby, demanding an allowance for Agnes, reached her just when all this violence was beginning to subside, and acting like turpentine on an expiring flame, made her anger and hatred rage again with greater fury than ever. This demand was refused, as we have seen, in the harshest manner possible, and the writing this insulting negative was a considerable relief to the spinster's feelings. But when this was done, and all intercourse, as it should seem, finally closed between herself and the only human being concerning whom she was capable of feeling any lively interest, her anger drooped and faded, and her health and spirits drooped and faded too. She remembered, when it was too late, that it was not Agnes's fault that she was living with Mrs. Barnaby; and conscience told her, that if she had come forward, as she might and ought to have done, at the time of her brother's death, the poor child might have been saved from the chance of any moral resemblance to the object of her aversion, however much she might unhappily inherit the detestable Wisett beauty. Then, too, came the remembrance of the beautiful vision, whose caresses she had rejected when irritated almost to madness by the tauntings of Mrs. Barnaby; and the idea that the punishment allotted to her in this world for this flagrant act of injustice, was the being doomed never to behold that fair young creature more, lay with a daily increasing weight of melancholy on her spirits.

It was on the afternoon of a fine September day that the letter of Agnes reached her. As usual, she was sitting in her bower, and her flowers bloomed and her bees hummed about her as heretofore, but the sprightly black eye that used to watch them was greatly dimmed. She had almost wholly lost her relish for works of fiction, and reading a daily portion of the Bible, which she had never omitted in her life, was perhaps the only one of all her comfortable habits that remained unchanged.

It would be no easy matter to paint the state into which the perusal of Agnes's letter threw her. Self-reproach was lost in the sort of ecstasy with which she remembered how thriftily she had hoarded her wealth, and how ample were the means she possessed to give protection and welcome to the poor orphan who thus sought a refuge in her bosom. All the strength and energy she had lost seemed to rush back upon her as her need called for them, ... and there was more of courage and enterprize within that diminutive old woman than always falls to the lot of a six-foot-two dragoon.

Her resolution as to what she intended to do was taken in a moment, and without any weakening admixture of doubts and uncertainties as to when and how; but she knew that she should want her strength, and must therefore husband it. Her step was, therefore, neither hurried nor unsteady as she returned to the house, and mounted to her sitting-room. The first thing she did on entering it was to drink a glass of water, the next to endite a note to the postmaster at Silverton, ordering a chaise and four horses to be at Compton Basett by daybreak to take her the first stage towards London. She then rang her bell, gave her note to Peggy Wright, the farmer's youngest daughter, who was her constant attendant, and bade her request that her father, if in the house, would come to her immediately. There was enough in the unusual circumstances of a letter received, and a note sent, to excite the good farmer's curiosity, and he was in the presence of his landlady as quickly as she could herself have wished.

"Sit down, Farmer Wright," said Miss Compton, and the farmer seated himself.

"I must leave Compton Basett to-morrow morning, Farmer Wright," she resumed. "My niece—my great niece, I mean, Miss Willoughby, has written me a letter, which determines me to go to London immediately for the purpose of taking charge of her myself."

"Sure-ly, Miss Compton, you bean't goen' to set off all by your own self for Lunnun?" exclaimed the farmer.

"Not if I can manage before night to get a couple of servants to attend me."

Farmer Wright stared; there was something quite new in Miss Betsy's manner of talking.

"You are a very active man, farmer, in the haymaking season," continued Miss Compton with a smile; "do you think, that to oblige and serve me, you could be as much on the alert for the next three or four hours as if you had a rick to save from a coming storm of rain?"

"That I wool!" replied Wright heartily. "Do you but bid me do, Miss Betsy, and I'll do it."

"Then go to your sister Appleby's, and inquire if her son William has left Squire Horton's yet."

"I need not go so far for that, Miss Compton; Will is down stairs with my missus at this very minute," said the farmer.

"That is fortunate!... He is not likely to go away directly, is he?"

"No, not he, Miss Betsy; he is come to have a crack with our young 'uns, and it's more likely he'll stay all night than be off in such a hurry."

"Then, in that case, have the kindness, Farmer Wright, to saddle a horse, while I write a line to the bank.... I want you to ride over to Silverton for me, to get some money."

"And I'll do it," replied her faithful assistant, leaving the room.

Fortunately for her present convenience, Miss Compton always kept a deposit of about one hundred pounds in the bank at Silverton in case of need, either for the purpose of making the loans which have been already mentioned as a principal feature in her works of charity, or for any accidental contingency. Beyond this, however, she had no pecuniary transactions there, as her habitual secrecy in all that concerned her money affairs made it desirable that her agent should be more distant. This fund, however, was quite sufficient for the moment, for, as will be easily believed, Miss Compton had no debts.

Farmer Wright speedily re-appeared, equipped for his ride.

"You will receive ninety-seven pounds sixteen and two-pence, Wright," said the spinster, giving her draught.

"Would it suit you best to receive the rent, Miss Betsy, before you set off?" said the farmer. "It will make no difference, you know, ma'am, if I pays it a fortnight beforehand."

"Not an hour, upon any account, Wright," replied his punctilious landlady. "I will leave written instructions with you as to what you are to do with it, and about all my other affairs in which you are concerned. And now send William Appleby to me."

This young man, the nephew of her tenant, and the ex-footman of a neighbouring family, had been favourably known to her from his childhood; and a very few minutes sufficed to enrol him as her servant, with an understanding that his livery was to be ordered as soon as they reached London.

This done, Mrs. Wright was next desired to attend her; and with very little waste of time or words, it was agreed between them, that if "father" made no objection, (which both parties were pretty sure he would not,) Peggy should be immediately converted into a waiting-maid to attend upon herself and Miss Willoughby. This last arrangement produced an effect very likely to be destructive to all Miss Betsy's quiet, well-laid plans for preparation, for the news that Peggy was to set off next morning for London very nearly turned the heads of every individual in the house.

The mother of the family, however, so far recovered her senses as to appear again in Miss Compton's room at the end of an hour, but with a heated face, and every appearance of having been in great activity.

"I ax your pardon, Miss Betsy, a thousand times!" said the good woman, wiping her face; "but Peggy's things, you know, Miss Compton, can't be like yours, all nicely in order in the drawers; and we must all wash and iron too before she can be ready. But here I am now to help you, and I can get your trunk ready in no time."

"I shall take very little with me, Mrs. Wright," replied the old lady, who seemed as much au fait of what she was about as if she had been in the habit of visiting London every year of her life; "nor must Peggy take much," she added gently, but with decision; "and getting her things washed and ironed must be done after we are gone. I shall let you know as soon as I can where the luggage that must follow us, shall be addressed; and instead of washing and ironing, Mrs. Wright, I want you and one of the elder girls to assist me in making an inventory of everything I leave behind ... orders concerning which you will also receive by the post."

Miss Compton, though a very quiet inmate, and one whose regular habits gave little trouble, was nevertheless a person of great importance at Compton Basett; and her commands, thus distinctly expressed, were implicitly obeyed; so that before the usual hour of retiring for the night, everything was arranged both for going and staying exactly as she had determined they should be.

It was singular to see with what unvacillating steadiness this feeble-looking old lady pursued her purpose; no obstacle appeared of consequence sufficient to draw aside a thought from the main object she had in view, but was either removed or passed over by an impulse that seemed as irresistible as the steam that causes the train to rush along the rail-road, making the way clear, if it does not find it so.

At daybreak the Silverton post-chaise, with four good horses and two smart post-boys, were at the door; and within ten minutes afterwards all adieux had been spoken, all luggage stowed, and Miss Compton, who had never yet left her native county, was proceeding full gallop towards the metropolis.

"As you drive, so you will be paid," said William to the boys as they set off; and they did drive as boys so bargained with generally do. Miss Compton had shewn equal quickness and good judgment in having secured the services of this William, for he had repeatedly travelled with his late master and mistress to London, was apt, quick, and intelligent; and fully justified the expectation his new lady had formed, that, with carte blanche in the article of expense, he would manage her journey as expeditiously, and with as little trouble to herself, as if she had been attended with half a dozen outriders.

At Exeter she dined, and reposed herself for a couple of hours, during which William undertook to hire a carriage for the journey, furnished with a dickey behind, and all other conveniences; an arrangement which greatly lessened the fatigue to all parties, and enabled the active-minded old lady to proceed as far as Salisbury that night. Daybreak again found her en route; and by means of William's conditional mode of payment to the postilions, Miss Compton arrived at Ibertson's Hotel by two o'clock in the afternoon.

It might be supposed, from the exertion used to reach the wide city in which she knew poor Agnes stood alone, that Miss Compton would drive directly to Half-Moon Street, and save her, as early as possible, from all farther anxiety; but such was not her plan.... There was something still wanting to prove her repentance and her love, before she could present herself before the forsaken Agnes. All her schemes, all her wishes, were explained to her efficient aide-de-camp; and while she and the wondering Peggy reposed themselves, he was sent in search of handsome private lodgings, which must be such as his master the member for Silverton might have approved for his own family.... And then he was to proceed to livery-stables where he was known, and hire for her, by the week, a carriage and horses fit for ladies to use. Such were Miss Compton's vague, but very judicious orders; and the result was, that by the time she had dined and taken an hour's nap upon the sofa, a very respectable equipage was at the door awaiting her orders. In and about this the light luggage she had brought with her was arranged, and ten minutes' drive brought her to handsome, airy lodgings, near the top of Wimpole Street, where William thought he should be able to breathe himself, and where his mistress and Peggy, new as they were to the smoke and dust, might have as good a chance of doing so too as in any other street he could think of.

Miss Compton was pleased, greatly pleased, with her new confidant's promptitude and ability. The carriage pleased her, the horses, the coachman, the house, the furniture, and the obsequious landlady too, all pleased her; and she felt a degree of happiness as she set her Peggy to make arrangements for the especial comfort and accommodation of Agnes, such as she had never known before. It cured all fatigue, it overpowered every feeling of strangeness in her new and most unwonted abode, and gave a gaiety to her spirits, and lightness to her heart, that made her look, as she stepped from room to room, like one of the little benignant old fairies of which we read in French story books.

By eight o'clock all her preparations were complete, the tea-things placed on the drawing-room table, Peggy given to understand that she was to consider herself more as Miss Willoughby's personal attendant than her own, and the carriage again at the door to convey her to the longed-for yet almost dreaded meeting in Half-Moon Street.

Agnes had written to Miss Compton on Monday, and calculated that she might receive an answer to her letter on Thursday morning. But Thursday morning was past, and no letter arrived; and when about half-past eight on that same evening she heard a carriage stop, and the knocker thunder, the only idea that suggested itself was, that her aunt Barnaby was returned, and that she should have to plead for a night's lodging under her roof.

Her spirits were weakened by disappointment ... she had heard nothing from Cheltenham since Colonel Hubert's visit; and this, together with the non-arrival of any Devonshire letter, had caused a degree of depression to which she very rarely gave way.

"What shall I say to her?... How shall I dare to meet her?" she exclaimed. "Oh! if she keeps her word, what, what will become of me?"

She heard steps approaching, and feeling convinced it was her aunt Barnaby, attempted in her terror to open the door that communicated with the other room, but found it locked; and trembling like a hunted fawn, obliged to turn to bay, she cast her eyes towards the dreaded door, and saw Miss Compton gently and timidly entering by it.

"Aunt Betsy!" she cried, springing towards her, and falling involuntarily upon her knees, "Oh! dear, dear aunt Betsy!... Is it indeed possible that you are come for me?"

The poor old lady's high-wrought energies almost failed her now; and had not a chair stood near, she would hardly have saved herself from falling on the floor beside her niece. "Agnes!... poor child!" she said, "you thought I was too hard and too cruel to come near you?... I have been much to blame ... oh! frightfully to blame!... Will you forgive me, dear one?... My poor pale girl!... You look ill, Agnes, very, very ill.... And is it not a fitting torment for me to see this fair bloodless cheek?... for did I not hate you for your rosy health?"

Agnes was indeed pale; and though not fainting, was so near it, that while her aunt uttered this passionate address, she had no power to articulate a word. But she laid her cheek on the old lady's hands; and there was something so caressing and so helpless in her attitude as she did this, that poor Miss Compton was entirely overcome and wept aloud.

No sooner, however, had this first violent burst of emotion passed away, than the happiness such a meeting was calculated to afford to both of them, was most keenly and delightfully felt. Miss Compton looked at Agnes, as the blood beautifully tinged her delicate cheek again, with such admiration and delight, that it seemed likely enough, notwithstanding her strong good sense on many points, that she might now fall into another extreme, and idolize the being she had so harshly thrust from her ... while the object of this new and unhoped-for affection seemed to feel it at her very heart, and to be cheered and warmed by it, like a tender plant receiving the first beams of the morning sun after the chilling coldness of the night.

At length Miss Compton remembered that she was not come there only to look at Agnes; and withdrawing her arms, which she had thrown around her, she said.... "Come, my own child ... this is no roof for either of us. Have you much to remove? Is there more than a carriage can take, Agnes?"

"And will you take me with you now, aunt Betsy?" cried the delighted girl, springing up. "Wait but one moment, and all I have shall be ready ... it is not much.... My books are packed, and my trunk too ... the maid will help me."

"Ring the bell then, love, and let my servant take your packages down." Agnes obeyed ... her trunk ... aunt Betsy's original trunk, and the dear Empton book-box, were lodged on the driving-seat and the dickey of the carriage; and William was just mounting the stairs to say that all was ready, when another carriage was heard to stop, and another knocking resounded against the open street-door.

"Oh! it is aunt Barnaby!" cried Agnes in a voice of terror.

"Is it?" replied Miss Compton, in the lively tone of former days. "I shall be exceedingly glad to see her."

"Can you be in earnest, aunt Betsy?" said Agnes, looking very pale.

"Perfectly in earnest, my dear child," answered the old lady. "It will be greatly more satisfactory that she should be an eye-witness of your departure with me, than that you should go without giving her notice.... Perhaps she would say you had eloped and robbed the premises."

"Hush!..." cried Agnes ... "she is here!"

Mrs. Barnaby's voice, at least, was already with them. It was, indeed, the return of this lady which they had heard; and no sooner had she dismissed her hackney-coachman than she began questioning the servant of the house, who was stationed at the open door, expecting Miss Compton and her niece to come down.

"What carriage is that?... Whose servant is that upon the stairs?... You have not been letting the lodgings, I hope?" were the first words of the widow.

"Oh! dear no, ma'am!" replied the maid; "everything is just as you left it."

"Then who is that carriage waiting for?"

"For a lady, ma'am, who is come to call on your young lady."

"MY young lady!... unnatural hussy!... And what fine friends has she found out here, I wonder, to visit her?... Be they who they will, they shall hear my opinion of her." And with these words, Mrs. Barnaby mounted the last stair, and entered the room.

The two unsnuffed tallow candles which stood on the table did not enable her at the first glance to recognize her aunt, who was wrapped in a long silk cloak, much unlike any garment she had ever seen her wear; but the sable figure of Agnes immediately caught her eye, and she stepped towards her with her arm extended, very much as if about to box her ears. But it seemed that the action was only intended to intimate that she was instantly to depart, for, with raised voice and rapid utterance, she said, "How comes it, girl, that I find you still here?... Begone!... Never will I pass another night under the same roof with one who could so basely desert a benefactress in distress!... And who may this be that you have got to come and make merry with you, while I ... and for your expenses too.... Whoever it is, they had better shew no kindness to you, ... or they will be sure to repent of it."

Mrs. Barnaby then turned suddenly round to reconnoitre the unknown visiter. "Do you not know me, Mrs. Barnaby?" said Miss Compton demurely.

"My aunt Betsy!... Good God! ma'am, what brought you here?"

"I came to take this troublesome girl off your hands, Mrs. Barnaby: is not that kind of me?"

"That's the plan, is it?" retorted the widow bitterly. "Now I understand it all. Instead of coming to comfort me in my misery, she was employing herself in coaxing another aunt to make a sacrifice of herself to her convenience. Take her; and when you are sick and sorry, she will turn her back upon you, as she has done upon me!"

"Oh! do not speak so cruelly, aunt Barnaby!" cried Agnes, greatly shocked at having her conduct thus described to one whose love she so ardently wished to gain.... "Tell my aunt Compton what it was you asked of me, and let her judge between us."

"Shut the door, Agnes!..." said Miss Compton sternly; and then, re-seating herself, she addressed Mrs. Barnaby with an air of much anxiety and interest: "Niece Martha, I must indeed beg of you to tell me in what manner this young girl has conducted herself since she has been with you, for, I can assure you, much depends upon the opinion I shall now form of her. I have no longer any reason to conceal from you that my circumstances are considerably more affluent than anybody but myself and my man of business is aware of.... Nearly forty years of strict economy, niece Martha, have enabled me to realize a very respectable little fortune. It was I, and not my tenant, who purchased your poor father's moiety of Compton Basett; and as I have scarcely ever touched the rents, a little study of the theory of interest and compound interest will prevent your being surprised, when I tell you that my present income is fifteen hundred per annum, clear of all outgoings whatever."

"Is it possible!" exclaimed Mrs. Barnaby, with an accent and a look of reverence, which very nearly destroyed the gravity of her old aunt.

"Yes, Mrs. Barnaby," she resumed, "such is my income. With less than this, a gentlewoman of a good old family, desirous of bringing forward a niece into the world in such a manner as to do her credit, could not venture to take her place in society; and I have therefore waited till my increasing revenues should amount to this sum before I declared my intentions, and proclaimed my heiress. Such being the case, you will not be surprised that I should be anxious to ascertain which of my two nieces best deserves my favour. I do not mean to charge myself with both.... Let that be clearly understood.... The doing so would entirely defeat my object, which is to leave one representative of the Compton Basett family with a fortune sufficient to restore its former respectability."

"And everybody must admire such an intention," replied Mrs. Barnaby, in an accent of inexpressible gentleness; "and I, for one, most truly hope, that whoever you decide to leave it to, may deserve such generosity, and have a grateful heart to requite it with."

"That is just what I should wish to find," returned the spinster; "and before you came in, I had quite made up my mind that Agnes Willoughby should be the person; but I confess, Mrs. Barnaby, that what you have said alarms me, and I shall be very much obliged if you will immediately let me know what Agnes has done to merit the accusation of having deserted her benefactress?"

"It is but too easy to answer that, aunt Compton," replied the widow, "and I am sorry to speak against my own sister's child; ... but truth is truth, and since you command me to tell you what I meant when I said she had deserted me, I will.... I have been arrested, aunt Compton, and that for no reason on the earth but because I was tempted to stay three or four days longer in London than I intended. Of course, I meant to go back to that paltry place, Cheltenham, and pay every farthing I owed there, the proof of which is that I have paid every farthing, though it would have served them right to have kept them a year out of their money, instead of a month; ... but that's neither here nor there ... though there was no danger of my staying in prison, I WAS there for three days, and Agnes could not tell but I might have been there for ever; ... yet, when I wrote her a most affectionate letter, begging her only to call upon me in my miserable solitude, she answered my petition, which might have moved a heart of stone, with a flat refusal.... Ask her if she can deny this?"

"What say you, Agnes?... Is this so?" said the old lady, turning to the party accused.

"Aunt Betsy!..." said Agnes, and then stopped, as if unwilling, for some reason or other, to say more.

"YES or NO?" demanded Mrs. Barnaby, vehemently. "Did you refuse to come to me, or not?"

"I did," replied Agnes.

"I hope you are satisfied, aunt Compton?" cried the widow triumphantly.... "By her own confession, you perceive that I have told you nothing but the truth."

Agnes said nothing in reply to this, but loosening the strings of a silk bag which hung upon her arm, she took from it a small packet, and placed it in the hands of Miss Compton. "What have we got here?" said the spinster sharply.... "What do you give me this for, child?"

"I wish you to read what is there, if you please, aunt," said Agnes. Miss Compton laid it on the table before her, while she sought for her spectacles and adjusted them on her nose; but, while doing this, she kept her eyes keenly fixed upon the little packet, and not without reason, for, had she turned from it for a single instant, Mrs. Barnaby, who shrewdly suspected its contents, would infallibly have taken possession of it.

"My coachman and horses will get tired of all this, I think," said Miss Compton; "however, as you say, niece Martha, truth is truth, and must be sought after, even if it lies at the bottom of a well.... This is a letter, and directed to you, Miss Agnes; ... and this is the back of another, with some young-lady-like scrawling upon it.... Which am I to read first, pray?"

"The letter, aunt Betsy," replied Agnes.

"So be it," said the spinster with an air of great indifference; and drawing one of the candles towards her, and carefully snuffing it, she began clearly and deliberately reading aloud the letter already given, in which Mrs. Barnaby desired the presence of Agnes, and gave her instructions for her finding her way to the Fleet Prison. Having finished this, she replaced it quietly in its cover without saying a word, or even raising her eyes towards either of her companions; and taking the other paper, containing Agnes's reasons for non-compliance, read that through likewise, exactly in the same distinct tone, and replaced it with an equal absence of all commentary, in the cover. She then rose, and walking close up to her elder niece, who proffered not a word, looking in her face with a smile that must have been infinitely more provoking than the most violent indignation, said, "Niece Martha!... the last time I saw you, if I remember rightly, you offered me some of your old clothes; but now you offer me none, which I consider as the more unkind, because, if you dressed as smart as you are now while in prison, you must most certainly wear very fine things when you are free.... And so, as you are no longer the kind niece you used to be, I don't think I shall come to see you any more. As for this young lady here, it appears to me that you have not been severe enough with her, Mrs. Barnaby.... I'll see if I can't teach her to behave better.... In prison or out of prison ... if I bid her come, we shall see if she dare look about her for such plausible reasons for refusing as she has given you. If she does, I'll certainly send her back to you, Mrs. Barnaby. Ring the bell, naughty Agnes!"

The maid seemed to have been very near the door, for it instantly opened. "Tell my servants that I am coming," said the whimsical spinster, enacting the fine lady with excellent effect; and making a low, slow, and most ceremonious courtesy to the irritated, but perfectly overpowered Mrs. Barnaby, she made a sign to Agnes to precede her to the carriage, and left the room.

CHAPTER VII

AGNES ELOPES WITH HER AUNT BETSY

"Is it possible!" cried Agnes, the moment that the door of the carriage was closed upon them, "is it possible that I am really under your protection, and going to your home, aunt Betsy?"

"To my temporary home, dear child, you are certainly going," said the old lady, taking her hand; "but I hope soon to have one more comfortable for you, my Agnes!"

"Where I shall find the bower and the bees? Is it not so, aunt?"

"Not exactly ... at least not at present.... But tell me, Agnes, don't you think I was very gentle and civil to Mrs. Barnaby?"

"It was certainly very wise not to reproach her, poor woman, more directly.... But, oh! dearest aunt Betsy, how well you know her!... If you had studied for a twelvemonth to find out how you might best have tormented her, you could have discovered no method so effectual as the making her first believe that you had a great fortune, and then that her own conduct had robbed her of your favour. Poor aunt Barnaby!... I cannot help pitying her!"

"You are tender-hearted, my dear, ... and a flatterer too.... You give me credit, I assure you, for a vast deal more cleverness than I possess: excepting on the subject of the old clothes which she offered me when we met in the cottage of dame Sims, I attempted no jestings with her.... But tell me, Agnes, have you not suffered dreadfully from the tyranny and vulgar ignorance of this detestable woman? Has she not almost broken your young heart?"

"I have not been very happy with her, aunt Betsy," replied Agnes gently; ... "but she speaks only truth when she says I have lived at her cost, and this ought to close my lips against speaking more against her than may be necessary to clear my own conduct in your eyes."

Perhaps the old lady was a little disappointed at finding that she was to have no good stories concerning the absurdities of the apothecary's high-flying widow, as she called her; but, despite all the oddities of Miss Compton, there was quite enough of the innate feeling of a gentlewoman within her to make her value Agnes the more for her promised forbearance. She threw her arm round her, and pressing her to her bosom, said,—

"Let this feeling of Christian gentleness be extended to me also, Agnes, ... for I have great need of it. This Martha Wisett the second, poor soul, was the first-born of her mother, and seems to have taken as her birth-right all the qualities, bodily and mental, of her vulgar and illiterate dam.... But I have no such excuse, my child, for the obstinate prejudice with which my heart has been filled, and my judgment absolutely confounded. All you have suffered with this woman, Agnes, ought, in truth, to be laid to my charge.... I knew what she was, and yet I suffered you.... Let us try to forget it; and only remember, if you can, that I turned away from you for no other reason upon earth than because I feared you were not ... exactly what I now find you. But here we are at home. How greatly must you want the healing feeling that home should bring! Poor dear!... When have you ever felt it?"

"At Empton, aunt!" answered Agnes eagerly; and even though the carriage door was open, and the step let down, she added, "The only home I ever loved I owed to you."

Hastily as this word was said, it sunk with very healing effect into the heart of the self-reproaching old lady ... it was answered by a cordial "God bless you!" and hand in hand the very happy pair walked up the staircase together. The accomplished William had preceded them, and thrown open the door of aunt Betsy's handsome drawing-room; and no apartment could offer an aspect of more comfort. The evening had all the chilliness of September when its sun is gone; and the small bright fire, with a sofa placed cosily near it, looked cheerily. Wax-lights on the chimney and tea-table, gave light sufficient to shew a large, exceedingly well-fitted up room; and a pretty young woman, neatly dressed, came forward to offer her services in the removal of cloaks and shawls.

Agnes looked round the room, and then turned to her aunt, as if tacitly demanding an explanation of what she saw. Miss Compton smiled, and answered the appeal by saying, "Did you expect, dearest, that I should be able to bring my farm-house and my bees with me?"

"No, aunt Compton," replied Agnes, very gravely, "I did not expect that; ... but...."

"Aunt BETSY—you must always call me aunt Betsy, Agnes. That was the appellation that your dear voice uttered so joyously when I entered the dark den in which I found you, and I shall never like any other as well.... But don't be frightened because I have somewhat changed my mode of living, my dear child. I will not invite you to ramble through the streets of London, in order to visit me when I am in prison for debt. I know what my means are, Agnes—few ladies better—and I will never exceed them."

This was said very gravely, and the assurance was by no means unimportant to the tranquillity of the young heiress. The scenes she had recently passed through would have reconciled her to a farm-house, a cottage, a hut; so that the air of heaven blew untainted round it, and no livery-stable keepers, or bailiff's followers, could find entrance there. But Miss Compton's words and manner set her heart at rest on that score, though they could not remove her astonishment, the involuntary expression of which, on her beautiful face, was by no means disagreeable to the novel-read aunt Betsy. It was just as it should be ... beauty, goodness, misery, ill-usage, and all; and she felt most happily convinced that, if there were but a lover in the case, and such a one as, despite all obstacles, she could approve, she should to her dying day have the comfort of thinking that the moment which she had chosen for ceasing to accumulate, and beginning to spend, was the very best possible.

And this lover in the clouds.... Would Agnes open her heart to her on such a subject?... Had she any right to hope it?... Not yet, certainly not yet, thought Miss Compton as, the services of William over, and the tea-things removed, they drew nearer the fire; and she fixed her eyes anew on the beautiful face she so greatly loved to contemplate, partly because it was so beautiful, and partly because she could not trace in it the slightest resemblance to any member of the Wisett race.

But soft and peaceful as was now the expression of that face, there might occasionally be seen by an accurate observer that indescribable look of thoughtfulness in the eyes which never arises till the mind has been awakened, upon some subject or other, to emotions of deep interest. Miss Compton was a very accurate observer, and saw, as plainly as Lavater himself could have done, that Agnes had learned to feel.

The romantic old lady would have given her right hand to possess her confidence, but she was determined not to ask for it.

"Do you think we shall be happy together, Agnes?" said she, in a voice which, when its cheerful tone was not exaggerated into the ironical levity in which she sometimes indulged, was singularly pleasing. "Do you think that you shall like to be my darling?"

"Yes, I do," replied Agnes, with the sudden bluntness of sincerity; "but I think I shall plague you sometimes, aunt Betsy."

"You have made up your mind to that already, have you?" returned Miss Compton, delighted at the playful tone in which she spoke; "then, in that case, I must make up my mind too, and contrive to make a pleasure of what you call a plague. How do you mean to begin, Agnes?... What will you do first?... Will you cry for the moon?"

"Will you try to get it for me if I do, aunt Betsy?" said Agnes, laughing.

"Yes, I will ... that is, if you will let me know what sort of moon it is, and to what part of the heavens I must turn to find it. Jupiter, you know, has...."

"Oh! my moon is the highest and brightest of them all!..." said Agnes, with a sigh; and, after remaining silent for a moment, she added, ... "Aunt Betsy, may I tell you everything that has happened to me?"

"If you love me well enough to do this, my child," said the delighted old lady, while, nevertheless, a tear glistened in her clear black eye,—"if you love me well enough, I shall feel that I have not given up my bees and my flowers for nothing."

Agnes drew nearer, and, after a moment's hesitation, began.

"I believe that all young ladies' histories have something about a gentleman in them, and so has mine...."

"A young gentleman, I hope, Agnes?" interrupted the aunt, with a smile.

Agnes coloured a little, but replied, "He is not so very young, aunt Betsy, as to make his youth his most remarkable quality."

"Very well, that is all quite right; he ought to be older than you, my dear.... Go on."

"When I was at Clifton, aunt Betsy, I was often in company with Colonel Hubert...."

"A colonel?... That sounds very respectable; he was the father, I suppose, of THE gentleman?"

"No, indeed," replied Agnes, with some vexation; "he is himself the only gentleman that I have anything to say about, ... and his sister says that he will be a general next month."

"Indeed!... A general?... General Hubert!... a very eligible acquaintance, I have no doubt.... I should hardly have hoped you could have had the good luck to meet with such among the friends of your aunt Barnaby."

"An eligible acquaintance!... Oh! aunt, you don't understand me at all!... But I will tell you everything. Colonel Hubert is ... I can't describe him.... I hope you will see him, aunt Betsy, and then you will not wonder, perhaps, that I should have thought him, from the very first moment I saw him, the only person in the world...."

Agnes stopped short; but Miss Compton seemed to think she had finished her phrase very properly.

"And what did he think of you, my dear?... this young colonel?"

"Colonel Hubert never said anything about it at Clifton," replied Agnes, blushing; "but yet I thought—I hoped he liked me, though I knew it did not signify whether he did or not, for he is one of a very distinguished family, ... who could never, I imagined, think seriously of any one living with ... with my aunt Barnaby. But at Cheltenham I became acquainted with his aunt, Lady Elizabeth Norris, and his sister, Lady Stephenson, and they were very, very kind to me; and when I came to London with my aunt Barnaby in this wild manner, they were very anxious about me, and made me promise to write to them.... But before I thought they could know anything about her being taken to prison ... the very day indeed that she went there, in the evening, while I was sitting in that dismal room, just as you found me to-night ... Colonel Hubert.... Oh! aunt Betsy ... the sight of you did not surprise me more.... Colonel Hubert walked in."

"That was hardly right, though, Agnes, if he knew you were alone."

"He brought a letter from his aunt and sister, most kindly asking me to take shelter with them immediately; ... and I am quite sure that when he came he had no intention of speaking of anything but that.... But I believe I looked very miserable, and his generous heart could not bear it, so he told me that he loved me, and asked me to be his wife."

"It was generous of him at such a dreadful moment," said the spinster, her eyes again twinkling through tears.... "And how did you answer him, my love?"

"I told him," replied Agnes, trembling and turning pale as she spoke, "I told him that I could never be his wife!"

"Why, my dear, I thought you said," ... cried the old lady, looking much disappointed, ... "I thought you said you admired him of all things, and I am sure he seems to have deserved it; but I suppose you thought he was too old for you?"

"No! no! no!" replied Agnes vehemently.... "He is young enough for me to love him, oh! so dearly!... It was because I could not bear that he should marry so beneath himself ... it was because I thought his aunt and sister would resent it...."

"Humph!... That was very generous on your part too; but I suppose he knows best.... And what did he say then, Agnes?"

"Oh! aunt Betsy!... he said exactly as you did ... he said that he was too old for me to love him; ..." and, remembering the agony of that moment, she hid her face in her hands and wept.

Miss Compton looked at her with pitying eyes; and, after a moment, said, "And so you parted, Agnes?"

"Yes!" she replied, removing her hands. "It was almost so, and yet not quite.... I could not tell him, you know, how dearly, how very dearly I loved him!... that was impossible!... but I said something about his sister and his aunt; and then ... oh! I shall never forget him!... something like hope ... pray, do not think me vain, aunt Betsy,—but it was hope that shot into his eye again, and changed the whole expression of his face; ... yet he said no more about his love, and only asked me to promise never to leave the shelter of that roof till I heard from his aunt again.... And I did promise him.... But could I keep it, aunt?... It would have been obeying him in words, and not in spirit.... And now I'm coming to my reason for telling you all this so very soon.... What shall I say to them now? How shall I write to them?"

It seemed that Miss Compton did not find this a very easy question to answer, for she took many minutes to consider of it. At length she said, ... "As to setting right the love part of the affair, you need not alarm yourself, my dear ... there will be no great difficulty in that.... If you know your own mind, and really are in love with a general, instead of an ensign, I don't see why you should be contradicted, though it is a little out of the common way.... He is a gentleman, and that is the only point upon which I could have been very strict with you.... But there is another thing, Agnes, in which you must please to let me have my own way.... Will you promise me?"

"How can there be any way but yours in what concerns me, dear aunt Betsy?"

"Bless you, my dear!... I will not be a tyrant ... at least not a very cruel tyrant; but my happiness will be injured for the rest of my life, Agnes, if the next time you see this gentleman and his family, it is not in such a manner as to make them perceive, without the necessity of their listening to an old woman's long story about it, that you are not an unworthy match for him in any way.... Let this be managed, and everything will end well.... There will be no risk of your witnessing, either in the words or looks of these noble ladies whom you call your friends, any struggle between their partiality for you and their higher hopes for him. HE will ever remember with pleasure that he waited not for this to offer you his hand and heart; and trust me YOU will never remember with sorrow that you did wait for it before you accepted him. Do you agree with me?"

"Indeed I do!" fervently replied Agnes. "But could they see me at this moment, would not your wish be answered? Could they doubt for a moment, while seeing you, and seeing the style of all about you, that I am something more than the poor hopeless dependant of Mrs. Barnaby?"

"That is not it.... That would not do at all, child," replied the old lady, sharply. "It shall not be the poor dependant of anybody that this noble-hearted Colonel Hubert shall come to woo. Love him as much as you will, the world may say, and his family may think too, that his rank and station led you to accept him. I will save you both from this danger. Colonel Hubert shall not try his chance with you again till you are the independent possessor of fifteen hundred pounds a-year. When I die, Agnes, if you behave well in the interim, I will bequeath my bees to you, and all the furniture of my two pretty rooms at Compton Basett, as well as all the reserved rents in the shape of allowances, coals, wood, attendance, and the like, which will be mine while I live. This, my dear, shall come to you in the way of legacy, in case I continue to be pleased with your behaviour; but there is no way for me to atone for the injury I have done to the representative of my family by suffering her to remain six months with Mrs. Barnaby, but making her at once the independent possessor of the Compton property."

"My dear, dear aunt!" said Agnes, most unfeignedly distressed, "there can be no occasion at this moment to talk of your doing what, in my poor judgment, would be so very wrong.... Should I be so happy as to make Colonel Hubert known to you, I would trust to him to discuss such subjects.... Oh! what delight, aunt Betsy, for you to have such a man for your friend!... and all owing to me!"

There was something so ingenuous, so young, so unquestionably sincere in this burst of feeling, that the old lady was greatly touched by it. "You are a sweet creature, Agnes," she replied, "and quite right in telling me not to discuss any matters of business with you.... I shall touch on no such subjects again, for I see they are totally beyond your comprehension. Nevertheless, I must have my way about not introducing myself to Colonel Hubert's family, or himself either, in lodgings. Write to your kind friends, my dear; tell them that your old aunt Compton has left her retirement to take care of you, and tell them also that she feels as she ought to do.... But, no; you write your own feelings, and I will write mine.... But this must be to-morrow, Agnes; ... it is past twelve o'clock, love. See! that gay thing on the chimney-piece attests it.... I must shew you to your room, my guest; hereafter I shall be yours, perhaps."

Peggy being summoned, the two ladies were lighted to the rooms above.... These were in a style of great comfort, and even elegance; but one being somewhat larger than the other, and furnished with a dressing-room, it was in this that Agnes found her trunk and book-box; and it was here that, after seeing that her fire burned brightly, and that Peggy was standing ready to assist in undressing her, the happy Miss Compton embraced, blessed, and left her to repose.

It was a long time, however, before Agnes would believe that anything like sleep could visit her eyes that night. What a change, what an almost incredible transition, had she passed through since her last sleep! It was more like the operation of a magician's wand than the consequence of human events. From being a reprobated outcast, banished from the roof that sheltered her, she had become the sole object of love and care to one who seemed to have it in her power to make life a paradise to her. How many blissful visions floated through her brain before all blended together in one general consciousness of happy security, that at last lulled her to delicious sleep! She was hardly less sensible than her somewhat proud aunt of the pleasure which a reunion with her Cheltenham friends, under circumstances, so changed, would bring; and her dreams were of receiving Lady Elizabeth Norris and her niece in a beautiful palace on the shores of a lovely lake, while Colonel Hubert stood smiling by to watch the meeting.

CHAPTER VIII

AGNES APPEARS LIKELY TO PROFIT BY THE CHANGE OF AUNTS

The first waking under the consciousness of new, and not yet familiar happiness, is perhaps one of the most delightful sensations of which we are susceptible. Agnes had closed her eyes late, and it was late when she opened them, for Peggy had already drawn her window curtains; and the gay hangings and large looking-glasses of the apartment met her eyes at the first glance with such brilliant effect, that she fancied for an instant she must still be dreaming. But by degrees all the delightful truth returned upon her mind. Where was the blank, cold isolation of the heart, with which her days were used to rise and set? Where were the terrors amidst which she lived, lest her protectress should expose herself by some monstrous, new absurdity? Where was the hopeless future, before which she had so often wept and trembled? Was it possible that she was the same Agnes Willoughby who had awoke with such an aching heart, but four-and-twenty hours ago?... All these questions were asked, and gaily answered, before she had resolution to spring from her bed, and change her delightful speculations for a more delightful reality.

Notwithstanding the various fatigues of the preceding day, Miss Compton was not only in the drawing-room, but her letter to Lady Elizabeth Norris was already written on the third side of a sheet of letter paper, thus giving Agnes an opportunity of explaining everything before her own lines should meet her ladyship's eye.

The meal which has been slandered as "lazy, lounging, and most unsocial," was far otherwise on the present occasion. The aunt and niece sat down together, each regaling the eyes of the other with a countenance speaking the most heart-felt happiness; and while the old lady indulged herself with sketching plans for the future, the young one listened as if her voice were that of fate, declaring that she should never taste of sorrow more.

"The carriage will be here at twelve, Agnes," said Miss Compton, to "take us into what our books tell us is called THE CITY, as if it were the city of cities, and about which I suppose you and I are equally ignorant, seeing that you never did take that pleasant little walk the dowager Mrs. Barnaby so considerately sketched out for you. So now we shall look at it together. But don't fancy, my dear, that any such idle project as looking at its wonders is what takes me there now.... I have got a broker, Agnes, as well as the widow, and it is quite as necessary to my proceedings as to hers that I should see him. But we must not go till our partnership letter is ready for the post. Here is my share of it Agnes ... read it to me, and if it meets your approbation, sit down and let your own precede it."

The lines written by Miss Compton were as follow:—

"MADAM,

"Permit a stranger, closely connected by the ties of blood to Agnes Willoughby, to return her grateful thanks for kindness extended to her at a moment when she greatly needed it. That she should so have needed it, will ever be a cause of self-reproach to me; nor will it avail me much either in my own opinion, or in that of others, that the same qualities in our common kinswoman, Mrs. Barnaby, which produced the distress of Agnes, produced in me the aversion which kept me too distant to perceive their effects on her respectability and happiness.

"I am, Madam,

"Your grateful and obedient servant,

"ELIZABETH COMPTON."

Agnes wrote:—

"MY KIND AND GENEROUS FRIENDS!

"Lady Elizabeth!... Lady Stephenson! I write to you, as I never dared hope to do, from under the eye and the protection of my dear aunt Compton. It is to her I owe all the education I ever received, and, I might add, all the happiness too, ... for I have never known any happy home but that which her liberal kindness procured for me during five years spent in the family of my beloved instructress Mrs. Wilmot. For the seven months that have elapsed since I quitted Mrs. Wilmot, my situation, as you, my kind friends, know but too well, has been one of very doubtful respectability, but very certain misery. My aunt Compton blames herself for this, but you, if I should ever be so happy as to make you know my aunt Compton, will blame me. Her former kindness ought to have given me courage to address her before, even though circumstances had placed me so entirely in the hands of Mrs. Barnaby as to make the separation between us fearfully wide. But, thank God! all this unhappiness is now over. I did apply to her at last, and the result has been the converting me from a very hopeless, friendless, and miserable girl (as I was when you first saw me) into one of the very happiest persons in the whole world. I have passed through some scenes, from the remembrance of which I shall always shrink with pain; but there have been others ... there have been points in my little history, which have left an impression a thousand times deeper, and dearer too, than could ever have been produced on any heart unsoftened by calamity. And must it not ever be accounted among my best sources of happiness, that the regard which can never cease to be the most precious, as well as the proudest boast of my life, was expressed under circumstances which to most persons would have appeared so strongly against me?

"My generous friends!... May I hope that the affection shewn to me in sorrow will not be withdrawn now that sorrow is past?... May I hope that we shall meet again, and that I may have the great happiness of making my dear aunt known to you? She is all kindness, and would take me to Cheltenham, that I might thank you in person for the aid so generously offered in my hour of need, but I fear poor Mrs. Barnaby's adventures will for some time be too freshly remembered there for me to wish to revisit it...."

When Agnes had written thus far, she stopped. "Where shall I tell them, aunt Betsy, that we are going to remain?" she said.... "If ... if Colonel Hubert" ... and she stopped again.

"If Colonel Hubert ... and what then, Agnes?"

"Why, if Colonel Hubert were to pay us a visit, aunt Betsy, I cannot help thinking that he would understand me better now, than when I was so dreadfully overpowered by the feeling of my desolate condition.... Don't you think so?"

"I think it very probable he might, my dear; ... and as to your sensible question, Agnes, of where we are going to be, I think you must decide it yourself. We have both declared against Cheltenham, and for reasons good.... Where then should you best like to go?"

"To Clifton, aunt Betsy!... It was there I saw him first, and there, too, I was most kindly treated by friends who, I believe, pitied me because ... because I did not seem happy, I suppose.... Oh! I would rather go to Clifton than any place in the world ... excepting Empton."

"And to Empton we cannot go just at present, Agnes ... it would be too much like running out of the world again, which I have no wish at all to do. To Clifton, therefore, we will go, dear child, and so you may tell your good friends."

Agnes gave no other answer than walking round the table and imprinting a kiss upon the forehead of her happy aunt.... Then resuming her writing, she thus concluded her letter:—

"My aunt Compton, as soon as she has concluded some business which she has to settle in London, will go to Clifton, where, I believe, we shall stay for some months; and should any of your family happen again to be there, I may perhaps be happy enough to see them. With gratitude to all, I remain ever your attached and devoted

"AGNES WILLOUGHBY."

Poor Agnes!... She was terribly dissatisfied with her letter when she had written it. Not all her generalizations could suffice to tell him, THE him, the only mortal him she remembered in the world,—not all her innocent little devices to make it understood that he was included in all her gratitude and love, as well as in her invitation to Clifton,—made it at all clear that she wanted Colonel Hubert to come and offer to her again.

Yet what could she say more?... She sat with her eye fixed on the paper, and a face full of meaning, though what that meaning was, it might not be very easy to decide.

"What is my girl thinking of?" said Miss Compton.

"I am thinking," replied Agnes, and she shook her head, "I am thinking that Colonel Hubert will never understand from this letter, aunt Betsy, how very much I want to see him again."

"That is very true, my dear."

"Is there anything else I could say to make him know how greatly he mistook me when he fancied I said NO from my want of love?"

"Oh yes! my dear, certainly."

"Tell me then, my dear, dear, aunt!... I feel as if I had no power to find a word.... Tell me what I shall say to him."

"You may say many things ... for instance, ... you may say, Tell my beloved Colonel Hubert...."

"Oh! aunt Betsy!... aunt Betsy! you are laughing at me," cried Agnes, looking at her very gravely, and with an air of melancholy reproach.

"So I am, my dear: an old spinster of three score is but a poor confidant in matters of this sort.... But if you seriously ask for my advice, I will give it, such as it is. Let our letter go just as it is, without any addition or alteration whatever. If Colonel Hubert sees this letter, as you seem to expect, and if he loves you as you deserve to be loved, he will find food enough for hope therein to carry him further than from one end of Gloucestershire to the other.... If he does not see it, put what you will in it, he would learn nothing thereby.... But if, seeing it, he determines to sit quietly down under your refusal ... then let him; I, for one, should feel no wish to become better acquainted with the gentleman."

Agnes said no more, but folded the letter, and directed it to Lady Elizabeth Norris, Cheltenham.

"Now, aunt, I have folded up Colonel Hubert, and put him out of sight till he shall choose to bring himself forward again.... I will tease you no more about him.... Shall I put my bonnet on?... The carriage has been waiting for some time."

"My darling Agnes!..." said the old lady, looking fondly at her, "how little I deserve to find you so exactly what I wished you should be!... You are right; we will talk no more of this Colonel Hubert till he has himself declared what part he means to play in the drama before us. We shall be at no loss for subjects.... Remember how much we have to settle between us!... our establishment, our equipage, our wardrobes, all to be decided upon, modelled, and provided. Get ready, dearest; the sooner we get through our business, the earlier we shall be at Clifton; ... and who knows which part of our dramatis personæ may arrive there first?"

A happy smile dimpled the cheek of Agnes as she ran out of the room to equip herself, and in a few minutes the two ladies were en route towards the city.

"What makes you wear such very deep mourning, my dear?" said Miss Compton, fixing her eyes on the perennial black crape bonnet of her companion. "Is it all for the worthy apothecary of

Silverton?... But that can't be either, for now I think of it, his charming widow had half the colours of the rainbow about her.... What does it mean, Agnes?"

Agnes looked out of the window to conceal a smile, but recovering her composure answered,... "I have never been out of mourning, aunt, since Mr. Barnaby died.... There was a great deal of black not worn out, ... and as it made no difference to me...."

"Oh! monstrous!..." interrupted Miss Compton. "I see it all: ... while she wantons about like a painted butterfly, she has thrown her chrysalis-case upon you, my pretty Agnes, in the hope of making you look like a grub beside her.... Is it not so?"

"Oh no!... my aunt Barnaby loves dress certainly, ... and greatly dislikes black, and so...."

"And so you are to wear it for her?... Well, Agnes, you shan't abuse her, if you think it a sin.... God forbid!... But do not refuse to let me into a few of her ways.... Did she ever ask you to put on her widow's cap, my dear? It might have saved the expense of night-caps at least."

It was almost a cruelty in Agnes to conceal the many characteristic traits of selfish littleness which she had witnessed in her widowed aunt, from the caustic contemplation of her spinster one, for she would have enjoyed it. But it was so much in her nature to do so, that dearly as she would have loved to amuse aunt Betsy, and give scope to her biting humour on any other theme, she gave her no encouragement on this; so, by degrees, all allusion to Mrs. Barnaby dropped out of their discourse; and if, from time to time, some little sample of her peculiarities peeped forth involuntarily in speaking of the past, the well-schooled old lady learned to enjoy them in silence, and certainly did not love her niece the less for the restraint thus put upon her.

Considering how complete a novice our spinster practically was as to everything concerning the vast Babylon called London, she contrived to go where she wished and where she willed with wonderfully few blunders. It was all managed between William and herself, and Agnes marvelled at the ease with which much seemingly important business was transacted.

The carriage was stopped before a very dusky-looking mansion at no great distance from the Exchange, within the dark passage of which William disappeared for some moments, and then returning, opened the carriage door, and, without uttering a word, gave his arm to assist Miss Compton to descend.

"I will not keep you waiting long, my dear," she said, and, without further explanation, followed her confidential attendant into the house. In about half an hour she returned, accompanied by a bald-headed, yellow-faced personage, who, somewhat to the surprise of Agnes, mounted the carriage after her, and placed himself as bodkin between them. "To the Bank," was the word of command then given, and in a moment they again stopped, and Agnes was once more left alone.

The interval during which she was thus left was this time considerably longer than the last, and she had long been tired of watching the goers and comers, all bearing, however varied their physiognomy, the same general stamp of busy, anxious interest upon their brows, before the active old lady and her bald-headed acquaintance re-appeared.

The old gentleman handed her into the carriage, and then took his leave amidst a multitude of obsequious bows, and assurances that her commands should always be obeyed at the shortest notice, et cetera, et cetera, et cetera.

"Agnes!..." said the old lady, as soon as she had exchanged a few words with William as to where she next wished to go, "Agnes! I look to you to supply the place of my bees and my flowers, and I do not much fear that I shall lament the exchange; but you must not continue to be dight in this grim fashion; it might be soothing to the feelings of Mr. Barnaby's fond widow, but to me it is very sad and disagreeable.... And so, my dear, here is wherewithal to change it."

During the whole of this speech Miss Compton had been employed in extracting a pocket-book of very masculine dimensions from her pocket; and having at length succeeded, she opened it, drew forth two bank-notes of twenty-five pounds each, and laid them in the lap of her niece.

Agnes took them up, and looked at them with unfeigned astonishment. "My dear aunt," she said, "I am afraid you will find me a much younger and more ignorant sort of girl than you expected.... I shall no more know what to do with all this money than a child of five years old. You forget, aunt Betsy, that I never have had any money of my own since I was born, and I really do not understand anything about it."

"This is a trouble of a new and peculiar kind, my dear, and I really don't remember, in all my reading, to have found a precedent for it.... What shall we do, Agnes?... Must you always wear this rusty-looking black gown, because you don't know how to buy another?"

"Why, no, aunt.... I don't think that will be necessary either; but don't you think it would be better for you to buy what you like for me?... It won't be the first time, aunt Betsy. I have not forgotten when my pretty trunk was opened by Mrs. Wilmot, ... or how very nicely everything was provided for the poor ragged little girl who never before, as long as she could remember, had possessed anything beside thread-bare relics, cobbled up to suit her dimensions.... It was you who thought of everything for me then ... and I'm quite sure you love me a great deal better now;" and Agnes placed the notes in Miss Compton's hands as she spoke.

"I had prepared myself for a variety of new occupations," replied the spinster, "but choosing the wardrobe of an elegant young lady was certainly not one of them.... However, my dear, I have no objection to shew you that my studies have prepared me for this too.... Nothing like novel-reading, depend upon it, for teaching a solitary recluse the ways of the world. You shall see how ably I will expend this money, Agnes; but do not turn your head away, and be thinking of something else all the time, because it is absolutely necessary, I do assure you, that a young lady in possession of fifteen hundred a year should know how to buy herself a new bonnet and gown."

The value of Miss Compton's literary researches was by no means lowered in the estimation of Agnes by the results of the three hours which followed; for though there were moments in which her thoughts would spring away, in spite of all she could do to prevent it, from discussions on silks and satins to a meditation on her next interview with Colonel Hubert, she was nevertheless sufficiently present to what was passing before her eyes to be aware that an old lady, who has herself lived in a "grogram gown" for half a century, may be capable of making a mighty pretty collection of finery for her niece, provided that she has paid proper attention to fashionable novels, and knows how to ask counsel, as to what artistes to drive to, from so intelligent an aide-de-camp as William.

In short, by the united power of the money and the erudition she had hoarded, Miss Compton contrived, in the course of a fortnight, to make as complete a change in the equipments of Agnes as that performed of yore upon Cinderella by her godmother. Nor was her own wardrobe neglected; she had no intention that the rusticity of her spinster aunt should draw as many eyes on Agnes as the gaudiness of her widowed one, and proved herself as judicious in the selection of sable satins and velvets for herself, as in the choice of all that was most becoming and elegant for the decoration of her lovely niece.

Never, certainly, was an old lady more completely happy than the eccentric, proud, warm-hearted aunt Betsy, as, with a well-filled purse, she drove about London, and found everything she deemed suitable to the proper setting forth of her heiress ready to her hand or her order. She could not, indeed, have a carriage built for her ... she could not afford time for it; ... but William, the indefatigable William, ransacked Long Acre from one end to the other, till he had discovered an equipage as perfect in all its points as any order could have made it; and on this the well-instructed Miss Compton, whose heraldic lore was quite sufficient to enable her with perfect accuracy to blazon her own arms, had her lozenge painted in miniature; which being all that was required to render the neat equipage complete, this portion of their preparation did not cause any delay.

To Miss Peters Agnes wrote of all the unexpected good which had befallen her, with much freer confidence than she could indulge in when addressing the relations of Colonel Hubert. Her friend Mary already knew the name of "Miss Compton, of Compton Basett," and no fear of appearing boastful rendered it necessary for her to conceal how strangely the aspect of her worldly affairs was changed.

To her, and her good-natured mother, was confided the task of choosing lodgings for them; and so ably was this performed, that exactly in one fortnight and three days from the time Colonel Hubert had left Agnes so miserably alone in Mrs. Barnaby's melancholy lodgings in Half-Moon Street, she was established in airy and handsome apartments in the Mall of Clifton, with every comfort and elegance about her that thoughtful and ingenious affection could suggest to make the contrast more striking.

The happiness of this meeting with the kind friends who had conceived so warm an affection for her, even when presented by Mrs. Barnaby, was in just proportion to the hopeless sadness with which she had bid them farewell; and the reception of her munificent aunt among them, with the cordial good understanding which mutually ensued, did all that fate and fortune could do to atone for the suffering endured since they had parted.

CHAPTER IX

BRINGS US BACK, AS IT OUGHT, TO MRS. BARNABY

It may be thought, perhaps, that the vexed, and, as she thought herself, the persecuted Mrs. Barnaby, had sufficiently tried what a prison was, to prevent her ever desiring to find herself within the walls of such an edifice again; but such an opinion, however likely to be right, was nevertheless wrong; for no sooner had the widow recovered from the fit of rage into which the triumphant exit of Miss Compton had thrown her, and settled herself on her solitary sofa, with no better comforter or companion than a cup of tea modified with sky-blue milk, than the following soliloquy (though she gave it not breath) passed through her brain.

"Soh!... Here I am then, after six months' trial of the travelling system, and a multitude of experiments in fashionable society, just seven hundred pounds poorer than when I set out, and without having advanced a single inch towards a second marriage.... This will never do!... My youth, my beauty, and my fortune will all melt away together before the object is obtained, unless I change my plans, and find out some better mode of proceeding."

Here Mrs. Barnaby sipped her vile tea, opened her work-box that she had been constrained to leave so hastily, ascertained that the exquisite collar she was working had received no injury during her absence, and then resumed her meditations.

"Heigh ho!... It is most horribly dull, sitting in this way all by one's-self ... even that good-for-nothing, stupid, ungrateful Agnes was better to look at than nothing; ... and even in that horrid Fleet there was some pleasure in knowing that there was an elegant, interesting man, to be met in a passage now and then ... whose eyes spoke plainly enough what he thought of me.... Poor fellow!... His being in misfortune ought not to produce ill-will to him in a generous mind!... How he looked as he said 'Adieu, then, madam!... With you vanishes the last ray of light that will ever reach my heart!'... And I am sure he said exactly what he felt, and no more.... Poor O'Donagough!... My heart aches for him!"

And here she fell into a very piteous and sentimental mood, indeed. Had her soliloquy been spoken out as loud as words could utter it, nobody would have heard a syllable about love, marriage, or any such nonsense; her heart was at this time altogether given up to pity, compassion, and a deep sense of the duties of a Christian; and before she went to bed she had reasoned herself very satisfactorily into the conviction that, as a tender-hearted woman and a believer, it was her bounden duty, now that she had got out of trouble herself, to return to the Fleet for the purpose of once more seeing Mr. O'Donagough, and inquiring whether it was in her power to do anything to serve him before she left London.

Nothing more surely tends to soothe the spirits and calm the agitated nerves than an amiable and pious resolution, taken, as this was done, during the last waning hours of the day, and just before the languid body lays itself down to rest. Mrs. Barnaby slept like a top after coming to the determination that, let the turnkeys think what they would of it, she would call at the Fleet Prison, and ask to see Mr. O'Donagough, the following morning.

The following morning came, and found the benevolent widow stedfast in her purpose; and yet, to her honour be it spoken, it was not without some struggles with a feeling which many might have called shame, but which she conscientiously condemned as pride, that she set forth at length upon her adventurous expedition.

"Nothing, I am sure," ... it was thus she reasoned with herself, ... "nothing in the whole world could induce me to take such a step, but a feeling that it was my duty. Heaven knows I have had many follies in my day—I don't deny it; I am no hardened sinner, and that blessed book that he lent me has not been a pearl thrown to swine. 'The Sinner's Reward!' ... what a comforting title!... I don't hope ever to be the saint that the pious author describes, but I'm sure I shall be a better woman all my life for reading it; ... and the visiting this poor O'Donagough is the first act by which I can prove the good it has done me!"

Then came some doubts and difficulties respecting the style of toilet which she ought to adopt on so peculiar an occasion. "It won't do for a person looking like a woman of fashion to drive up to the Fleet Prison, and ask to see such a man as O'Donagough.... He is too young and handsome to make it respectable.... But, after all, what does it signify what people say?... And as for my bonnet, I'll just put my Brussels lace veil on my black and pink; that will hide my ringlets, and make me look more matronly."

In her deep lace veil then, and with a large silk cloak which concealed the becoming gaiety of her morning dress, Mrs. Barnaby presented herself before the gates she had so lately passed, and in a very demure voice said to the keeper of it, "I wish to be permitted to see Mr. O'Donagough."

The fellow looked at her and smiled. "Well, madam," he replied, "I believe there will be no difficulty about that. Walk on, if you please.... You'll find them as can send you forward."

A few more barriers passed, and a few more well-amused turnkeys propitiated, and Mrs. Barnaby stood before a door which she knew as well as any of them opened upon the solitary abode of the broken-hearted but elegant Mr. O'Donagough. The door was thrown open for her to enter; but she paused, desiring her usher to deliver her card first, with an intimation that she wished to speak to the gentleman on business. She was not kept long in suspense, for the voice of the solitary inmate was heard from within, saying in soft and melancholy accents, "It is very heavenly kindness! Beg her to walk in." And in she walked, the room-door being immediately closed behind her.

Mr. O'Donagough was a very handsome man of about thirty years of age, with a physiognomy and cerebral developement which might have puzzled Dr. Combe himself; for impressions left by the past, were so evidently fading away before the active operation of the present, that to say distinctly from the examining eye, or the examining finger, what manner of man he was, would have been exceedingly difficult. But the powers of the historian and biographer are less limited, and their record shall be given.

Mr. Patrick O'Donagough was but a half-breed, and that a mongrel half, of the noble species which his names announce. He was the natural son of an Englishman of wealth and consequence by a poor Irish girl called Nora O'Donagough; and though his father did what was considered by many as very much for him, he never permitted him to assume his name. The young O'Donagough was placed as a clerk to one of the police magistrates of the metropolis, and shewed great ability in the readiness with which he soon executed the business that passed through his hands. He not only learned to know by sight every rogue and roguess that appeared at the office, but shewed a very uncommon degree of sagacity as to their innocence or guilt upon every new occasion that enforced their appearance there. His noble father never entirely lost sight of him; and finding his abilities so remarkable, he was induced again to use his interest in those quarters where influence abides, and to get him promoted to a lucrative situation in a custom-house on the coast, where he made money rapidly, while his handsome person and good address gave him access to the society of many people greatly his superiors in station, who most of them were frequenting a fashionable watering-place at no great distance from the station where he was employed.

This lasted for a few years, much to the satisfaction of his illustrious parent; and it might have continued till an easy fortune was assured to him, had he not unluckily formed too great an intimacy with one or two vastly gentleman-like but decidedly sporting characters. From this point his star began to descend, till, step by step, he had lost his money, his appointment, his father's favour, and his own freedom. Having lain in prison for debt during some weeks, he found means again to touch the heart of his father so effectually, as to induce him to pay his debts, and restore him to freedom, upon condition, however, of his immediately setting off for Australia with five hundred pounds in his pocket, and with the understanding that he was never more to return. The promise was given, and the five hundred pounds received; but the young man was not proof against temptation; he met some old acquaintance, lost half his money at ecartè, and permitted the vessel in which he was to sail to depart without him. This was a moment of low spirits and great discouragement; but he felt, nevertheless, that a stedfast heart and bold spirit might bring a man out of as bad a scrape even as that into which he had fallen.

Some people told him to apply again to his father, but he thought he had better not, and he applied to a gentleman with whom he had made acquaintance in prison instead. This person had, like himself, been reduced to great distress by the turf; but having fortunately found means of satisfying the creditor at whose suit he was detained, he was now doing exceedingly well as preacher to an independent congregation of ranting fanatics. He bestowed on his old associate some excellent advice as to his future principles and conduct, giving him to understand that the turf, even to those who were the most fortunate, never answered so well as the line of business he now followed; and assured him, moreover, that if he would forthwith commence an assiduous study of the principles and practice of the profession, he would himself lend him a helping hand to turn it to account. O'Donagough loved change, novelty, and excitement, and again manifested great talent in the facility with which he mastered the mysteries of this new business. He was soon seen rapidly advancing towards lasting wealth and independence: one of the wealthiest merchants in London had offered him the place of domestic prayer and preacher at his beautiful residence at Castaway-Saved Park, when an almost forgotten creditor, who had lost sight of him for many years, unluckily recognised him as he was delivering a most awakening evening lecture in a large ware-room, converted into a chapel near Moor Fields. Eager to take advantage of this unexpected piece of good fortune, the tailor (for such was his profession) arrested the inspired orator in the first place, and then asked him if he were able to settle his account in the next. Had the manner of transacting the business been reversed, it is probable that the affair would have been settled without any arrest at all; for Sir Miles Morice, of Castaway-Saved Park, was one of the most pious individuals of the age, and would hardly have permitted his chaplain elect (elect in every sense) to have gone to prison for thirty-seven pounds, nine shillings, and eight pence; but being in prison, O'Donagough was shy of mentioning the circumstance to his distinguished patron, and was employed, at the time Mrs. Barnaby first made acquaintance with him, in composing discourses "on the preternatural powers over the human mind, accorded to the chosen vessels called upon to pour out the doctrine of the new birth to the people." There is little doubt that these really eloquent compositions would have sold rapidly, and perfectly have answered the object of their clever author. But accident prevented the trial from being made, for before the projected volume was more than half finished, success of another kind overtook Mr. O'Donagough.

Mrs. Barnaby, on entering, found the poor prisoner she had so charitably come to visit seated at a writing-desk, with many sheets of closely-written manuscript about it. He rose as she entered, and approached her with a judicious mixture of respectful deference and ardent gratitude.

"May Heaven reward you, madam, for this blessed proof of christian feeling.... How can I suitably speak my gratitude?"

"I do assure you, Mr. O'Donagough, that you are quite right in thinking that I come wholly and solely from a christian spirit, and a wish to do my duty," said Mrs. Barnaby.

Mr. O'Donagough looked extremely handsome as he answered with a melancholy smile, "Alas! madam ... what other motive could the whole world offer, excepting obedience to the will of Heaven, sufficiently strong to bring such a person as I now look upon voluntarily within these fearful walls?"

"That is very true indeed!... There is nothing else that could make one do it. Heaven knows I suffered too much when I was here myself, to feel any inclination for returning; ... but I thought, Mr.

O'Donagough, that it would be very unfeeling in me, who witnessed your distress, to turn my back upon you when my own troubles are past and over; and so I am come, Mr. O'Donagough, to ask if I can be of any use to you in any way before I set off upon my travels, ... for I intend to make a tour to France, and perhaps to Rome."

The widow looked at Mr. O'Donagough's eyes, to see how he took this news; for, somehow or other, she could not help fancying that the poor young man would feel more forlorn and miserable still, when he heard that not only the walls of the Fleet Prison, but the English Channel, was to divide them: nor did the expression of the eyes she thus examined, lessen this idea. A settled, gentle melancholy seemed to rise from his heart, and peep out upon her through these "windows of the soul."

"To France!... To Rome!..." A deep sigh followed, and for a minute or two the young man remained with his eyes mournfully fixed on her face. He then rose up, and stepping across the narrow space occupied by the table that stood between them, he took her hand, and in a deep, sweet voice, that almost seemed breaking into a sob, he said,—"May you be happy whithersoever you go!... My prayers shall follow you.... My ardent prayers shall be unceasingly breathed to heaven for your safety; ... and my blessing ... my fervent, tender blessing, shall hover round you as you go!"

Mrs. Barnaby was exceedingly affected. "Don't speak so!... Pray, don't speak so, Mr. O'Donagough!" she said, in a voice which gave her very good reason to believe that tears were coming. "I am sure I would pray for you too, when I am far away, if it would do you any good," and here one of her worked pocket-handkerchiefs was really drawn out and applied to her eyes.

"IF, Mrs. Barnaby!" exclaimed the young man fervently, "IF ... oh! do not doubt it ... do not for a moment doubt that I should feel the influence of it in every nerve. Let me teach you to understand me, Mrs. Barnaby, ... for I have made an examination into the effects of spiritual sympathies the subject of much study.... Lay your hand upon my heart ... nay, let it rest there for a moment, and you will be able to comprehend what I would explain to you. Does not that poor heart beat and throb, Mrs. Barnaby?... and think you that it would have fluttered thus, had you not said that you would pray for me?... Then can you doubt that if, indeed, you should still remember the unhappy O'Donagough as you pursue your jocund course o'er hill and vale ... if, indeed, you should breathe a prayer to Heaven for his welfare, can you doubt that it will fall upon him like the soft fanning of a seraph's wing, and heal the tumult of his soul, e'en in this dungeon?"

There was so much apparent sincerity, as well as tenderness, in what the young man uttered, that a feeling of conviction at once found its way to the understanding of Mrs. Barnaby; and little doubt, if any, remained on her mind as to the efficacy of her prayers.... "Indeed, Mr. O'Donagough, I will pray for you then, ... and I'm sure I should be a very wicked wretch if I did not.... But is there nothing else I could do to comfort you?"

Mr. O'Donagough had often found his handsome and expressive countenance of great service to him, and so he did now. No answer he could have given in words to this kind question, could have produced so great effect as the look with which he received it. Mrs. Barnaby was fluttered, agitated, and did not quite know what to do or say next: but Mr. O'Donagough did. He rose from his chair, and raising his arms above his head to their utmost length, he passionately clasped his hands, and stood thus,—his fine eyes communing with the ceiling,—just long enough to give the widow time to be aware that he certainly was the very handsomest young man in the world; ... and then ... he drew his chair close beside her, took her hand, and fixed those fine eyes very particularly upon hers.

"Comfort me!..." he murmured in a soft whisper, which, had it not been breathed very close to her ear, would probably have been lost.... "Comfort me!... you ask if you could comfort me?... Oh! earth, Oh! heaven, bear witness as I swear, that to trace one single movement of pity on that lovely face, would go farther towards healing every sorrow of my soul, than all the wealth that Plutus could pour on me, though it should come in ingots of gold heavy enough to break the chains that hold me!"

"Oh! Mr. O'Donagough!..." was all Mrs. Barnaby could utter; but she turned her face away, nor was the fascinating prisoner again indulged with a full view of it, though he endeavoured to make his eyes follow the way hers led, till he dropped down on his knees before her, and by taking possession of both her hands, enabled himself to pursue his interesting speculations upon its expression, in spite of all she could do to prevent it. This brought the business for which Mrs. Barnaby came, ... namely, the inquiry into what she could do to be serviceable to Mr. O'Donagough, before she left London, ... to a very speedy termination; for with this fair index of what he MIGHT say before his eyes, the enterprising prisoner ventured to hint, that nothing would so effectually soothe his sorrows as the love of the charming being who had already expressed such melting pity for him. He moreover made it manifest that if she would, with the noble confidence which he was sure made a part of her admirable character, lend him wherewithal to liquidate the paltry debt for which he had been so treacherously arrested, he could find means again to interest his noble father in his behalf, and by giving him such a guarantee for his future steadiness as an honourable attachment was always sure to offer, he should easily induce him to renew his intention of fitting him out handsomely for an expedition to Australia, to which, as he confessed, he was more strongly inclined than even to persevere in listening to the call he had received to the ministry.

Notwithstanding the tender agitation into which such a conversation must inevitably throw every lady who would listen to it, Mrs. Barnaby did not so completely lose her presence of mind, as not to remember that it would be better to look about her a little before she positively promised to marry and accompany to Australia the captivating young man who knelt at her feet. But this praiseworthy degree of caution did not prevent her from immediately deciding upon granting him the loan he desired; nay, with thoughtful kindness, she herself suggested that it might be more convenient to make the sum lent 40l. instead of 37l. 9s. 8d.; and having said this with a look and manner the most touching, she at length induced Mr. O'Donagough to rise; and after a few such expressions of tender gratitude as the occasion called for, they parted, the widow promising to deliver to him with her own fair hands on the morrow the sum necessary for his release; while he, as he fervently kissed her hand, declared, that deeply as he felt this generous kindness, he should wish it had never been extended to him, unless the freedom thus regained were rendered dear to his soul by her sharing it with him.

"Give me time, dear O'Donagough!... Give me time to think of this startling proposal, ... and to-morrow we will meet again," were the words in which she replied to him; and then, permitting herself for one moment to return the tender glances he threw after her, she opened the room-door and passed through it, too much engrossed by her own thoughts, hopes, wishes, and speculations, to heed the variety of amusing grimaces by which the various turnkeys hailed her regress through them.

It would be unreasonable for any one to "desire better sympathy" than that which existed between my heroine and Mr. O'Donagough when they thus tore themselves asunder; he remaining in durance vile till such time as fate or love should release him, and she to throw herself into a hackney coach, there to meditate on the pleasures and the pains either promised or threatened by the proposal she had just received.

The sympathy lay in this, ... that both parties were determined to inform themselves very particularly of the worldly condition of the other, before they advanced one step farther towards matrimony, for which state, though the gentleman had spoken with rapture, and the lady had listened with softness, both had too proper a respect to think of entering upon it unadvisedly.

CHAPTER X

GIVES SOME ACCOUNT OF COLONEL HUBERT'S RETURN TO CHELTENHAM

We must now follow Colonel Hubert to Cheltenham, to which place he returned in a state of mind not particularly easy to be described. The barrier he had placed before his heart, the heavy pressure of which he had sometimes felt to be intolerable, was now broken down; and it was a relief to him to remember that Agnes knew of his love. But, excepting this relief, there was little that could be felt as consolatory, and much that was decidedly painful in his state of mind. He knew but too well that not all the partial affection, esteem, and admiration entertained for him by his aunt, would prevent her feeling and expressing the most violent aversion to his marrying the niece of Mrs. Barnaby; he knew, too, what sort of reception the avowal of such an intention was likely to meet from his amiable but proud brother-in-law, and remembered, with feelings not very closely allied to satisfaction, the charge he had commissioned Lady Stephenson to give him, that he should keep watch over his thoughtless younger brother, in order to guard him, if possible, from bringing upon them the greatest misfortune that could befall a family such as theirs—namely, the introducing an inferior connexion into it.... Neither could he forget the influence he had used, in consequence of this injunction, to crush the ardent, generous, uncalculating attachment of his confiding friend Frederick for her whom, in defiance of the wishes of his whole family, he was now fully determined to make his wife. All this gave materials for very painful meditation; and when, in addition to it, he recalled those fearful words of Agnes, "I will never be your wife!" it required all the power of that master passion which had seized upon his heart to keep him steady to his resolution of communicating his wishes and intentions to Lady Elizabeth, and to sustain his hopes of engaging her actively to assist him in obtaining what he felt very sure she would earnestly desire that he should never possess.

With all these heavy thoughts working within him, he entered the drawing-room of his aunt, and rejoiced to find her tête-à-tête with his sister, Sir Edward being absent at a dinner-party of gentlemen. They both welcomed him with eager inquiries concerning their young favourite, the tone of which at once determined him to enter immediately upon the tremendous subject of his hopes and wishes; and the affectionate interest expressed for her, warmed him into a degree of confidence which he was far from feeling when he entered the room.

"Pretty creature!" exclaimed Lady Elizabeth; "and that wretched woman has actually left her alone in London lodgings?... Why did you not make her return with you, Montague?... It was surely no time to stand upon etiquette."

"I dared not even ask it," replied Colonel Hubert, his voice faltering, and his manner such as to make the two ladies exchange a hasty glance with each other.

"You dared not ask Agnes Willoughby, poor little thing, to come down with you to my house, Colonel Hubert?" said the old lady. "You surely forget that you went up to London with an invitation for her in your pocket?"

"My dear aunt," replied Colonel Hubert, hesitating in his speech, as neither of his auditors had ever before heard him hesitate, "I have much to tell you respecting both Agnes Willoughby ... and myself...."

"Then tell it, in Heaven's name!" said Lady Elizabeth sharply. "Let it be what it may, I would rather hear it than be kept hanging thus by the ears between the possible and impossible."

Colonel Hubert moved his chair; and seating himself beside Lady Stephenson, took her hand, as if to shew that she too was to listen to what he was about to say, though it was their aunt to whom he addressed himself. "From suspense, at least, I can relieve you, Lady Elizabeth, and you too, my dear Emily, who look at me so anxiously without saying a word ... at least I can relieve you from suspense.... I love Miss Willoughby; and I hope, with as little delay as possible, to make her my wife."

Lady Stephenson pressed his hand, and said nothing; but a deep sigh escaped her. Lady Elizabeth, who was not accustomed to manifest her feelings so gently, rose from her seat on the sofa, and placing herself immediately before him, said, with great vehemence, "Montague Hubert, son of my dead sister, you are come to years of discretion, and a trifle beyond.... Your magnificent estate of thirteen hundred a year, and ... I beg your pardon ... some odd pounds, shillings, and pence over, is all your own, and you may marry Mrs. Barnaby herself, if you please, and settle it upon her. No one living that I know of has any power to prevent it.... But, sir, if you expect that Lady Elizabeth Norris will ever receive as her niece a girl artful enough to conceal from me and from your sister the fact that she was engaged to you, and that, too, while receiving from both of us the most flattering attention ... nay, such affection as might have opened any heart not made of brass and steel ... if you expect this, you will find yourself altogether mistaken."

This harangue, which her ladyship intended to be overpoweringly severe, was, in fact, very nearly the most agreeable one that Colonel Hubert could have listened to, for it touched only on a subject of offence that he was perfectly able to remove. All embarrassment immediately disappeared from his manner; and springing up to place himself between his aunt and the door, to which she was approaching with stately steps, he said, in a voice almost of exultation, "My dearest aunt!... How like your noble self it is to have made this objection before every other!... And this objection, which would indeed have been fatal to every hope of happiness, I can remove by a single word.... Agnes was as ignorant of my love for her as you and Emily could be till last night ... I have loved her ... longer, it may be, than I have known it myself ... perhaps I might date it from the first hour I saw her, but she knew nothing of it.... Last night, for the first time, I confessed to her my love.... And what think you, Lady Elizabeth, was her answer?"

"Nay, Mr. Benedict, I know not.... 'I thank you, sir,' and a low courtesy, I suppose."

"I was less happy, Lady Elizabeth," he replied, half smiling; adding a moment after, however, with a countenance from which all trace of gaiety had passed away, "The answer of Miss Willoughby to my offer of marriage was ... Colonel Hubert, I can never be your wife."

"Indeed!... Then how comes it, Montague, that you still talk of making her so?"

"Because, before I left her, I thought I saw some ground for hope that her refusal was not caused by any personal dislike to me."

"Really!..." interrupted Lady Elizabeth.

"Nay, my dear aunt!" resumed Hubert, "you may in your kind and long-enduring partiality fancy this impossible; but, unhappily for my peace at that moment, I remembered that I was more than five-and-thirty, and she not quite eighteen."

"But she told you I suppose that you were still a very handsome fellow.... Only she had some other objection,—and pray, what was it, sir?"

"She feared the connexion would be displeasing to you and Lady Stephenson."

"And you assured her most earnestly, perhaps that she was mistaken?"

"No, Lady Elizabeth, I did not. There are circumstances in her position that MUST make my marrying her appear objectionable to my family; and though my little independence is, as your ladyship observes, my own, I would not wish to share it with any woman who would be indifferent to their reception of her. All my hope, therefore, rests in the confidence I feel that, when the first unpleasing surprise of this avowal shall have passed away, you ... both of you ... for there is no one else whose approbation I should wait for ... you will suffer your hearts and heads to strike a fair and reasonable balance between all that my sweet Agnes has in her favour and all she has against her. Do this, Lady Elizabeth, but do it as kindly as you can.... Emily will help you ... to-morrow morning you shall tell me your decision.... I can resolve on nothing till I hear it."

Colonel Hubert, as soon as he had said this left the room, nor did they see him again that night.

The morning came, and he met Lady Stephenson at the breakfast table, but Lady Elizabeth did not appear, sending down word, as was not unusual with her, that she should take her chocolate in her own room. Sir Edward was not in the room when he entered, and he seized the opportunity to utter a hasty and abrupt inquiry as to the answer he might expect from herself and their aunt.

"From me, Montague," she replied, "you cannot fear to hear anything very harshly disagreeable. In truth, I have been so long accustomed to believe that whatever my brother did, or wished to do, was wisest—best, that it would be very difficult for me to think otherwise now; besides, I cannot deny, though perhaps it hardly ought to be taken into the account, that I too am very much in love with Agnes Willoughby, and that ... though I would give my little finger she had no aunt Barnaby belonging to her ... I never saw any woman in any rank whom I could so cordially love and welcome as a sister."

In reply to this, Colonel Hubert clasped the lovely speaker to his heart; and before he had released her from his embrace, or repeated his inquiry concerning Lady Elizabeth, Sir Edward Stephenson entered, and the conversation became general.

For many hours of that irksome morning Colonel Hubert was kept in the most tantalizing state of suspense by the prolonged absence of the old lady from the drawing-room. But at length, after Sir Edward and his lady had set off for their second morning ramble without him, he was cheered by the appearance of the ancient maiden, who was his aunt's tirewoman, bringing in her lap-dog, and the velvet cushion that was its appendage; which having placed reverently before the fire, she moved the favourite fauteuil an inch one way, and the little table that ever stood beside it an inch the other, and was retiring, when Colonel Hubert said, ... "Is my aunt coming immediately, Mitchel?"

"My lady will not be long, Colonel.... But her ladyship is very poorly this morning," and with a graceful swinging courtesy she withdrew.

The Colonel trembled all over, "very poorly," as applied to Lady Elizabeth Norris, having from his earliest recollection always been considered as synonymous to "very cross."

"She will refuse to see her!" thought he, pacing the room in violent agitation.... "and in that case she will keep her word.... She will never be my wife!"

"Bless me!... How you do shake the room, Colonel Hubert," said a very crabbed voice behind him, just after he had passed the door in his perturbed promenade. "If you took such a fancy early in the morning, when the house maid might sweep up the dust you had raised, I should not object to it, for it is very like having one's carpet beat;... but just as I am coming to sit down here, it is very disagreeable indeed."

This grumble lasted just long enough to allow the old lady (who looked as if she had been eating crab apples, and walked as if she had suddenly been seized with the gout in all her joints,) to place herself in her easy chair as she concluded it, during which time the Colonel stood still upon the hearth-rug with his eyes anxiously fixed upon the venerable but very hostile features that were approaching him. A moment's silence followed, during which the old Lady looked up in his face with the most provoking expression imaginable; for cross as it was, there was a glance of playful malice in it that seemed to say,—

"You look as if you were going to cry, Colonel."

He felt provoked with her, and this gave him courage.—"May I beg of you, Lady Elizabeth, to tell me what I may hope from your kindness on the subject I mentioned to you last night?" said he.

"Pray, sir, do you remember your grandfather?" was her reply.

"The Earl of Archdale?... Yes, madam, perfectly."

"You do.... Humph!... And your paternal grandfather, with his pedigree from Duke Nigel of Normandy; did you ever hear of him?"

"Yes, Lady Elizabeth," replied the Colonel in a tone of indifference; "I have heard of him; but he died, you know, when I was very young."

There was a minute's silence, which was broken by another question from Lady Elizabeth.

"And pray, sir, will you do me the favour to tell me who was the grandfather of Miss Willoughby?"

"I have little, or indeed no doubt, Lady Elizabeth, that Miss Willoughby is the granddaughter of that Mr. Willoughby, of Greatfield Park, in Warwickshire, who lost the tremendous stake at piquet that you have heard of, and two of whose daughters married the twin sons of Lord Eastcombe.... I think you cannot have forgotten the circumstances."

Lady Elizabeth drew herself forward in her chair, and fixing her eyes stedfastly on the face of her nephew, said, in a voice of great severity, "Do you mean to assert to me, Colonel Montague Hubert, that Agnes Willoughby is niece to Lady Eastcombe and the Honourable Mrs. Nivett?"

"I mean to assert to you, madam, that it is my firm persuasion that such will prove to be the fact. But I have not considered it necessary, Lady Elizabeth Norris, for the son of my father to withhold his affections from the chosen of his heart, till he was assured he should gain all the honour by the selection which a union with Lady Eastcombe's niece could bestow;... nor should I have mentioned my belief in this connexion, by way of a set-off to the equally near claim of Mrs. Barnaby, had you not questioned me so particularly."

Had Colonel Hubert studied his answer for a twelvemonth, he could not have composed a more judicious one: there was a spice of hauteur in it by no means uncongenial to the old lady's feelings, and there was, too, enough of defiance to make her take counsel with herself as to whether it would be wise to vex him further. It was, therefore, less with the accent of mockery, and more with that of curiosity, that she recommenced her interrogatory.

"Will you tell me, Montague, from what source you derived this knowledge of Miss Willoughby's family?... Was it from herself?"

"Certainly not. If the facts be as I have stated, and as I hope and believe they will be found, Miss Willoughby will be as much surprised by the discovery as your ladyship."

"From whom, then, did you hear it?"

"From no one, Lady Elizabeth, as a matter of fact connected with Agnes. But something, I know not what, introduced the mention of old Willoughby's wild stake at piquet at the club the other day.... The name struck me, and I led old Major Barnes to talk to me of the family. He told me that a younger son, a gay harum-scarum sort of youth, married some girl, when he was in country quarters, whom his family would not receive; that, ruined and broken-hearted by this desertion, he went abroad almost immediately after his marriage, and has never been heard of since."

"And this is the foundation upon which you build your hope, that Mrs. Barnaby's niece is also the niece of Lady Eastcombe?... Ingenious certainly, Colonel, as a theory, but somewhat slight as an edifice on which to hang any weighty matter.... Don't you think so?"

"I hang nothing on it, Lady Elizabeth. If I did not feel that Miss Willoughby was calculated to make me happy without this supposed relationship, I certainly should not think her so with it. However, that your ladyship may not fancy my imagination more fertile than it really is, I must add, that when at Clifton, I did hear from the Misses Peters, whom I have before mentioned to you, that the father of Agnes went abroad after his marriage, and moreover that no news of him in any way ever reached his wife's family afterwards."

Lady Elizabeth for some time made no reply, but seemed to ponder upon this statement very earnestly. At length she said, in a tone from which irony and harshness, levity and severity, were equally banished,—"Montague!... there are some of the feelings which you have just expressed, in which I cannot sympathise; but a very little reflection will teach you that there is no ground of offence to you in this ... for it would be unnatural that I should do so. You tell me that your father's son need not deem the honour of a relationship to Viscountess Eastcombe necessary to his happiness in life. So far I am able to comprehend you, although Lady Eastcombe is an honourable and excellent personage, whose near connexion with a young lady would be no contemptible advantage (at least in my mind) upon her introduction into life. But we will pass this.... When, however, you proceed to tell me that your choice in marriage could in nowise be affected by the rank and station of those with whom it might bring you in contact, and that, too, when the question is, whether a Mrs. Barnaby, or a Lady Eastcombe, should be in the foreground of the group, you must excuse me if I cannot follow you."

Nothing is so distressing in an argument as to have a burst of grandiloquent sentiment set aside by a few words of common sense. Colonel Hubert walked the length of the drawing-room, and back again, before he answered; he felt that, as his aunt put the case, he was as far from following his assertion by his judgment as herself; but ere his walk was finished, the image of the desolate Agnes, as he had seen her the night before, arose before him, and resumed its unconquerable influence on his heart. He took a hint from her ladyship, threw aside all mixture of heat and anger, and replied.—

"Heaven forbid, Lady Elizabeth, that I should attempt to defend any such doctrine:... believe me, it is not mine. BUT, in one word, I love Miss Willoughby; and if I can arrive at the happiness of believing that I am loved in return, nothing but her own refusal will prevent me from marrying her. This is my statement of facts; I will attempt no other, and throw myself wholly upon your judgment to smooth, or render more rugged, the path which lies before me."

The old lady looked at him and smiled very kindly. "Montague," said she, "resolve my doubts. Is it the mention of your pleasant suspicions respecting Miss Willoughby's paternal ancestry,... or your present unvarnished frankness, that has won upon me?... Upon my honour, I could not answer this question myself;... but certain it is that I do feel more inclined to remember what a very sweet creature Agnes is at this moment, than I ever thought I should again when our conversation began."

Colonel Hubert kneeled down upon her foot-stool, and kissing her hand, said, in a voice that spoke his happiness, "It matters not to me what the cause is, my dearest aunt.... I thank Heaven for the effect!... and now ... do not think that I am taking an unfair advantage of this kindness, if I ask you to remember the position of Miss Willoughby at this moment. With such views for the future as I have explained to you, is it not my duty to remove her from it?"

"What then do you propose to do?" demanded Lady Elizabeth.

"I can do nothing,"... he replied;... "whatever aid or protection can be extended to her, must come from you ... or Lady Stephenson;... and that I should rather it came from you, who have long been to me as a mother, can hardly surprise you. Sir Edward is an excellent young man,... but he has prejudices that I should not like to battle with on this occasion. It is from you, and you only, Lady Elizabeth, that I either hope or wish to find protection for my future wife."

Again Lady Elizabeth pondered. "Did not Agnes tell us," she said at length, "did she not say in her letter to Lady Stephenson, that she had applied to some aged relation in Devonshire, by whom she hoped to be extricated from her present terrible embarrassment?"

"It is very likely," replied Colonel Hubert, "for she spoke to me of such a one, and hoped that Thursday ... that is to-morrow, is it not?... would bring an answer to her application."

"Then, Montague, we must wait to hear what this Thursday brings forth before we interfere to repeat the offer of protection which it is possible she may not want.... And Heaven grant it may be so,... for if she is to be your wife, Colonel Hubert, and it is pretty plain she will be, will it not be better that you should follow her with your addresses to the lowliest roof in Devonshire, than that she should take refuge here, where every gossip's finger will be pointed at her?"

It was impossible to deny the truth of this, and Colonel Hubert cared not to avow that all the favour she had bid him hope for was but conditional, and that till the avowal of his love should be sanctioned by his aunt and sister, he was still to hold himself as a rejected man. He dared not tell her this, lest the feelings he had conquered with so much difficulty should return, upon learning that it was not yet too late to encourage them.

As patiently as he could, therefore, he awaited the expected letter from Agnes, and well was he rewarded for doing so. The letter itself, modest and unboastful as it was, gave a sufficiently improved picture of her condition to remove all present anxiety on her account; and though he certainly had no idea of the transformation she had undergone, from a heart-broken, penniless dependant, into a petted, cherished heiress, he was soothed into the belief that it would now cost his aunt and sister infinitely less pain than he had anticipated, to extend such a degree of favour to his Agnes as might lead her to confirm the hope on which he lived.

But it was not the letter of Agnes that produced the most favourable impression upon Lady Elizabeth; the postscript of Miss Compton was infinitely more powerful in its effect upon her mind. Of Agnes, personally, she never thought without a degree of partial admiration, that nearly approached to affection; and vague as the hope was respecting the family of her father, it clung very pertinaciously to the old lady's memory, while a certain resemblance which she felt sure that she could trace between the nose of Agnes and that of the honourable Miss Nivett, Lord Eastcombe's eldest daughter, was doing wonders in her mind by way of a balance-weight against the rouge and ringlets of Mrs. Barnaby; yet, nevertheless, the notion that not "horrid Mrs. Barnaby" only, but a host of aunts and cousins of the same breed, might come down upon her in the event of this ill-assorted marriage, kept her in a sort of feverish wavering state, something between good and ill humour, that was exceedingly annoying to her nephew.

The keen-sighted old lady at once perceived that the postscript to Agnes's letter was not written by a second Mrs. Barnaby, and from that moment she determined, much more decisively than she chose to express, that she would torment Colonel Hubert with no farther opposition.

After a short consultation between the aunt and niece, that letter was despatched, the receipt of which was mentioned before Miss Compton and Agnes left London for Clifton. Had Colonel Hubert been consulted upon it, he would perhaps have suggested, as an improvement, that the proposed meeting should take place the following week in London; but, on the whole, the composition was too satisfactory for him to venture upon any alteration of it, and again he called patience to his aid, while many miserably long days were wasted by the very slow and deliberate style in which the man and maid servant who managed all Lady Elizabeth's worldly concerns, set about preparing themselves and her for this removal. It was with a degree of pleasure which almost atoned for the vexation of this delay that he learned Sir Edward's good-natured compliance with his beautiful bride's capricious-seeming wish of revisiting Clifton. Colonel Hubert pertinaciously refused to let his gay brother-in-law into his confidence, till the time arrived for presenting him to Miss Willoughby, as to his future wife. Did this reserve arise from some unacknowledged doubt whether Agnes, when the pressure of misfortune was withdrawn, would voluntarily bestow herself on a man of his advanced age? Perhaps so. That Agnes was less than eighteen, and himself more than thirty-five, were facts repeated to himself too often for his tranquillity.

CHAPTER XI

AGNES APPEARS AT CLIFTON IN A NEW CHARACTER

At as early an hour, on the morning after her arrival at Clifton, as Agnes could hope to find her friend Mary awake, she set off for Rodney Place. It was a short walk, but a happy one, even though she had yet to learn whether Lady Elizabeth Norris and her party were or were not arrived.

But there was something at the bottom of her heart that made her very tolerably easy ... more so perhaps than she confessed to herself ... on this point. Every day made the mysterious fact of Miss Compton's being a woman of handsome fortune more familiar to her, and every hour made it more clear that she had no other object in life than to make that fortune contribute to the happiness of her niece. It followed, therefore, that, not having altogether forgotten the fact of Colonel Hubert's declaration at a moment when all things, but his own heart, must have pleaded against her, some very comfortable ground for hope to rest upon, was discoverable in the circumstances of her present position.... "There will be no danger," thought she, "that when he speaks again, my answer should be such as to make him fancy himself too old for me."

The servant at Rodney Place who opened the door to Agnes, was the same who had done her the like service some dozen of times during her last visit at Clifton, but he betrayed no sign of recognition when she presented herself. In fact, the general appearance of Agnes was so greatly changed from what he had been accustomed to see it when she was clothed in the residuum of the Widow Barnaby's weeds, that till she smiled, and spoke her inquiry for Miss Peters, he had no recollection of her.

As soon, however, as he discovered that it was the Miss Willoughby who had left all his ladies crying when she went away, he took care to make her perceive that she was not forgotten by the manner in which he said, "Miss Peters, ma'am, is not come down stairs yet; but she will be very happy to see YOU, ma'am, if you will please to walk up."

As the early visitor was of the same opinion, she scrupled not to find her way to the well-known door, and without even the ceremony of a tap, presented herself to her friend. It is probable that Mary looked more at the face and less at the dress of the visitor than the servant had done, for, uttering a cry of joy, she sprang towards her, and most affectionately folded her in a cordial embrace.

"My sweet Agnes!... This is so like you! At the very instant you entered, I was calculating the probabilities between to-day and to-morrow for your arrival. Ah, little girl!... Did I not tell you to address yourself to Miss Compton, of Compton Basett, long ago? What say you to my wisdom now?"

"That you were inspired, Mary, and that I deserved to suffer a good deal for not listening to such an oracle.... But had I done so, I should have never known...."

"The difference between the extreme of Barnaby misery and Compton comfort?" said Mary, finishing the sentence for her.

Agnes blushed, but said with a happy smile, "Yes ... assuredly I may say so."

Miss Peters looked at her, and laughed. "There is something else you would not have known, I am very sure, Agnes, by that conscious face, ... and it must be something very well worth knowing by that look of radiant happiness which I never saw on your fair face before ... no, not even when for the first time you looked down upon Avon's dun stream; for then, if I remember rightly, your joy shewed itself in tears; but now, my dear, you are dimpling with smiles, though I really believe you are doing all you can to hide them from me. Say why is this?... wherefore ... what should it mean?"

"Mary!... There is not an event of my life, nor a thought of my heart, that I would wish to hide from you.... But how can I begin telling you such very long and incredible stories as I have got to tell, just as you have finished dressing, and are ready to go down to breakfast?" said Agnes.

"Breakfast?" replied her friend.... "I would rather go without breakfast for a month than not hear the beginning, middle, and end of all your adventures from the moment you left this house in crape and bombasin, with your cheeks as white as marble, and your eyes full of tears, up to this present now, that you have entered it again in as elegant a morning toilet as London can furnish, with your cheeks full of dimples, and your eyes dancing in your head with happiness, notwithstanding all your efforts to look demure.... Come, sit down again, Agnes, and tell me all."

"Tell you all I will, depend upon it, but not now, dear Mary.... Think of all your mother's kindness to me.... Shall I sit here indulging in confidential gossip with you, instead of paying my compliments to her and the rest of the family in the breakfast-room?... No, positively no. So come down stairs with me directly, or I will go by myself."

"Aunt Compton is spoiling you, child; that is quite clear.... You used to be obedient to command, and ever ready to do as I desired, but now you lay down the law like a Lord Chancellor. Come along, then, Miss Agnes; but remember that, as soon as breakfast is over, I expect, first to be taken to the Mall (have I not got nice lodgings for you?) and introduced to Miss Compton, of Compton Basett, and then taken to our old seat on the rock, then and there to hear all that has befallen you."

To this Agnes agreed, and they descended together. The interest and the pleasure that her entrance excited among the family group already assembled round the breakfast-table, was very gratifying to her. Mrs. Peters seemed hardly less delighted than Mary; the two girls kissed her affectionately, and gazed at her with as much admiration as astonishment, which is tantamount to saying that they admired her much; good Mr. Peters welcomed her very cordially, and inquired with the most scrupulous politeness for the health of Mrs. Barnaby; and James told her very frankly that he was delighted to see her, and that she was fifty times handsomer than ever.

The conversation that followed was perfectly frank, on the part of Agnes, in all that related to the kindness of her aunt Compton, and the happiness she enjoyed from being under her care; but, from delicacy to them, she said as little as possible about Mrs. Barnaby; and from delicacy to herself, made no mention whatever either of Colonel Hubert or his family.

As soon as the breakfast was over Mrs. Peters declared her intention of immediately waiting on Miss Compton; an attention to her aunt which Agnes welcomed with pleasure, though it still farther postponed the much-wished for conversation with her friend Mary. The whole family declared their eagerness to be introduced to the old lady, of whom Miss Willoughby spoke with such enthusiasm; but as the discreet Mrs. Peters declared that at this first visit her eldest daughter only must accompany her; the rest yielded of necessity, and the three ladies set out together.

"I expect to find this new aunt a much more agreeable personage, my dear Agnes, than your former chaperon, though she was my dear sister.... But on one point I flatter myself I shall find them alike."

"I hope this point of resemblance is not of much importance to your happiness, my dear Mrs. Peters," replied Agnes, "for if it be, you are in a bad way; since night and day are infinitely less unlike than my two aunts in all things."

"Yes, but it is of great importance to my happiness, particularly for this evening, Agnes," replied Mrs. Peters. "The point of resemblance I want to find is in the trusting you to my care. We are going to a party this evening where I should particularly like to take you, ... and it will be impossible, you know, to arrange exchange of visits, and manage that an invitation shall be sent and accepted by aunt Compton, on such very short notice. Do you think she will let you go with us?"

"Ask her, my dear Mrs. Peters," replied Agnes with a very happy smile, "and see what she will say to it."

"I will, if I do not find her too awful," was the answer.

The manner in which Miss Compton received and entertained her visitors, was a fresh source of surprise to Agnes. Though thinking very highly of her intellect, and even of her conversational powers, she had anticipated some symptoms of reserve and shyness on the introduction of so perfect a recluse to strangers. But nothing of the kind appeared. Miss Compton was pleased by the appearance and manner of both mother and daughter, and permitted them to perceive that she was so, rather with the easy flattering sort of courtesy with which a superior treats those whom he wishes should be pleased with him, than with any appearance of the mauvaise honte which might have been expected. Nor must this be condemned as unnatural, for it was, in fact, the inevitable result of the state of mind in which she had lived. With keen intellect, elastic animal spirits, and a position that places the owner of it fairly above the reach of annoyance from any one, (an elevation, by the by, that few of the great ones of the earth can boast,) it is not an introduction to any ordinary society that can discompose the mind, or agitate the manners.

Mrs. Peters did not find aunt Compton too awful, and therefore prefered her request, which, like every other that could have been made likely to promote the pleasure of Agnes, was not only graciously but gratefully complied with. A question being started as to the order in which the party should go, Mr. Peters's carriage not being able to take them all at once, Miss Compton settled it by saying,—"Agnes has her own carriage and servants here, but she must not go alone; and perhaps, if she calls at your house, Mrs. Peters, you will have the kindness to let her friend Mary accompany her, and permit her carriage to follow yours."

This being settled, Mrs. Peters and her daughter rose to take leave; and Mary then hoped that Agnes, by returning with them, would at length give her the opportunity she so earnestly desired of hearing all she had to tell. But she was again disappointed, for when the young heiress asked her indulgent aunt whether she would not take advantage of the lovely morning to see some of the beauties of Clifton, she replied,—"I should like nothing so well, Agnes, as to take a drive with you over the beautiful downs you talk of. Will you spare her to me for so long, Miss Peters?"

"I think you deserve a little of her, Miss Compton," answered the young lady; "and with the hope of the evening before me, I will enter no protest against the morning drive."

The mother and daughter then took leave, and as they left the house, they exchanged a glance that seemed to express mutual congratulation on the altered condition of their favourite.

"Well, mamma, you will be rewarded this time for obeying my commands like a dutiful mother, and permitting me to make a pet of this sweet Agnes.... There is nothing in the Barnaby style here.... I was sure Miss Compton, of Compton Basett, must be good for something," said Mary.

"If I may venture to hope, as I think I may," replied her mother, "that she will never be the means of bringing me in contact with my incomparable sister-in-law again, I may really thank you, saucy girl as you are, for having so taken the reins into your own hands. I delight in this Miss Compton. There is a racy originality about her that is very awakening. And as for your Agnes, what with her new young happiness, her graceful loveliness, now first seen to some advantage, her proud and pretty fondness for her aunt, and her natural joy at seeing us all again under circumstances so delightfully altered, I really do think she is the most enchanting creature I ever beheld."

CHAPTER XII

A PARTY—A MEETING—GOOD SOMETIMES PRODUCTIVE OF EVIL

The superintending the toilet of Agnes for the party of that evening was a new and very delightful page in the history of the spinster of Compton Basett. The fondest mother dressing a fair daughter for her first presentation, never watched the operations of the toilet more anxiously; and in her case there was a sort of personal triumph attending its success, that combined the joy of the accomplished artist, who sees the finished loveliness himself has made with the fond approval of affection.

Partly from her own native good taste, and partly from the wisdom of listening with a very discriminating judgment to the practical counsels of an experienced modiste, the dress of Agnes was exactly what it ought to have been; and the proud old lady herself could not have desired an appearance more distinguée than that of her adopted child when, turning from Peggy and her mirror, she made her a sportive courtesy and exclaimed,—

"Have you not made a fine lady of me, aunt Betsy?"

When Miss Compton's carriage stopped at Rodney Place, it was Mrs. Peters, instead of her daughter, who took a place in it.

"Mary is excessively angry with me," said she, as they drove off, "for not letting her be your companion; but I think it more comme il faut, Agnes, that I should present you to Mrs. Pemberton myself. She is a vastly fine lady; ... not one of us humble Bristolian Cliftonites, who pique ourselves rather upon the elevation of our lime-stone rock above the level of the stream that laves our merchants' quays, than on any other species of superiority that we can lay claim to. Mrs. Pemberton is none of us.... She has a house in London and a park in Buckinghamshire, and flies over the Continent every now and then with first-rate aristocratical velocity; but she has one feeling, sometimes shared by more ordinary mortals, which is a prodigious love of music. This, and a sort of besoin, to which she pleads guilty, of holding a salon every evening that she is not from home, forces upon her, as I take it, the necessity of visiting many of us who might elsewhere scarcely be deemed worthy to approach her foot-stool. We met her at the Parslowes, where the girls' performances elicited a very gracious degree of approbation. An introduction followed; she has honoured me by attending a concert at my own house, and this is the fourth evening we have passed with her. Now you have the carte du pays, and I think you will agree with me, that it is much better I should make my entrée with you on my arm, than permit you to follow with the damsels in my train."

Agnes confessed that she thought the arrangement much more conducive to the dignity of her approach, and thanked her companion for her thoughtful attention.

"Perhaps it is not quite disinterested, Agnes.... I am rather proud of having such an exotic to produce.... What a delightful aunt Compton it is!... Carriage perfect ... servants evidently town-made ... white satin and blonde fit for an incipient duchess! If your little head be not turned, Agnes, you will deserve to be chronicled as a miracle."

"I have had enough to steady the giddiest craft that ever was launched, my dear Mrs. Peters," replied Agnes; "and it would be silly, indeed, to throw my ballast overboard, because I am sailing before the wind."

"Then your head is not turned; ... that is what you mean to say, is it not?"

"No," replied Agnes, laughing, "my head is not turned,—I feel almost sure of it.... But why do you make such particular inquiries respecting the state of my head at present, Mrs. Peters? Shall I be called upon to give some illustrious proof of its healthy condition to-night?"

"Yes, my dear.... You will assuredly be called upon to sing, and you must prove to my satisfaction that you are not grown too fine to oblige your friends."

"Is that all?... Depend upon it I will do whatever you wish me."

Mrs. Pemberton's drawing-room was full of company when they entered it, but that lady espied them the moment they arrived, and stepped forward with so much eagerness to receive them, that Agnes thought Mrs. Peters had, in her account of the acquaintance between them, hardly done justice to the degree of favour she had risen to. But a few minutes more convinced her, that even she, unknown as she was, might flatter herself that some portion of this distinguished reception was intended for her; for Mrs. Pemberton took her hand and led her to a seat at the upper end of the room with an air of such marked distinction, as, spite of the philosophy of which she had just been boasting, brought a very bright flush to her cheeks, if it did not turn her head. A few words, however, spoken by that lady to one of those beside whom she placed her, explained the mystery, and proved that Mrs. Peters had deemed it prudent to intimate her intention of bringing a young friend with her beforehand.

"Miss Eversham, you must permit me to introduce this young lady to you—Miss Willoughby.... Miss Eversham.... From a little word in Mrs. Peters' note this morning, I flatter myself that I shall have the gratification of hearing you sing together. This lady's voice is a contralto, Miss Willoughby, and from what I have heard of your performance at Mrs. Peters', before I had the pleasure of being acquainted with her, your voices will be delightful together."

This most unexpected address was not calculated to restore the composure of Agnes, and it was not without some effort that she summoned courage enough to answer the numerous questions of Miss Eversham, (an elderly young lady too much inured to exhibition to have any mercy upon her,) when, as an excuse for withdrawing her attention for a moment, from the ceaseless catechism that tormented her, she turned away her eyes to look upon the company, and beheld the profile of Colonel Hubert, as he bent to speak to a lady seated on a sofa near which he stood. This was not an occurrence very likely to restore her composure, but at least it spared her any farther anxiety respecting the effort necessary for receiving the attentions of her neighbour properly, for she altogether forgot her vicinity, and became as completely incapable of hearing her farther questions, as of answering them.

"Had he seen her?... Did he know she was at Clifton?... Was his aunt,—was Lady Stephenson there?... How would he address her?... Would their intercourse begin from the point at which it had broken off, or would her altered circumstances, by placing each in a new position, lead to a renewed proposal, and an answer?... Oh how different from her former one!"

These were the questions that now addressed themselves to her, making her utterly incapable of hearing the continued string of musical interrogatories which went on beside her. The short interval during which Colonel Hubert retained his attitude, and continued his conversation seemed an age, and expectation was growing sick, and almost merging in despair, when at last the lady turned to answer a question from her neighbour, and Colonel Hubert stood upright and cast his eyes upon the company.

Her emotion was too powerful to permit bashfulness to take any part in it; she sought his eye, and met it. In a moment all suffering was over, and all anxiety a thousand fold overpaid, for the look she encountered was all her heart could wish. At the first glance, indeed, he evidently did not know her; it was that of a wandering speculative eye that seemed looking out for occupation, and had she quite understood it aright, she might have perceived that it was arrested by a sort of sudden suspicion that it had found something worth pausing upon. But this lasted not above the tenth part of an instant, and then he darted forward; his fine proud countenance expressive of uncontrollable agitation, and the rapidity with which he approached her was such as to show pretty plainly that he forgot it was a crowded drawing-room he was traversing.

By the time he reached her, however, short as the interval was, the glow that had lighted up her face when it first arrested his eye had faded into extreme paleness, and when he spoke to her, she trembled so violently as to be quite unable to articulate. Colonel Hubert perceived her agitation, and felt that it approached in some degree to his own. Had he been twenty-five, this would have probably been all he wished to see; as it was, he felt a dreadful spasm at the heart, as the hateful thought occurred that after what had passed there might be two ways in which it might be interpreted. But it was a passing pang; and longing to present her to his aunt and sister, and at the same time release her from the embarrassing curiosity so conspicuous in the manner of her neighbour, he held the hand she extended to him while he said—

"Let me lead you to Lady Elizabeth, Miss Willoughby; both she and Lady Stephenson are in the next room, and will be delighted to see you."

Agnes rose, and though really hardly able to stand, replied, with all the voice she had, that she should be greatly obliged if he would lead her to them, taking his offered arm as she spoke. At this moment Sir Edward Stephenson crossed the room with his eyes fixed upon her, and with evident curiosity to find out who it was his stately brother-in-law was escorting so obsequiously. The extreme beauty of Agnes, and the remarkable elegance of her dress and appearance had, in truth, already drawn all eyes upon her, and the whispered enquiries of many had been answered by Mrs. Pemberton, with the information that she was an heiress, and the first amateur singer in England. The foundation of these assertions had reached her by the note of the judicious Mrs. Peters, who, while asking permission to bring a young friend, took the opportunity of hinting the two interesting facts above mentioned, and the effect of their repetition among her guests doubtless added not a little to the interest with which Agnes was looked at.

Sir Edward Stephenson was among those who had heard of the heiress-ship and the voice, but the name had not reached him; and while looking at the elegant girl in white satin, who lent upon Colonel Hubert's arm, not the slightest resemblance between her and the fair girl in deep mourning that he had once or twice seen at Cheltenham occurred to him.

There was a stoppage in the door-way between the two rooms, and it was at this moment Sir Edward said in the ear of the colonel, "Who is your fair friend?"

"Do you not know her, Sir Edward?... It is Miss Willoughby."

"What the girl ... the person we saw at.... Nonsense, Montague! Who is it?"

Colonel Hubert shrugged his shoulders at the incredulity of his brother-in-law, and quietly replying, "I have told you all I know," took advantage of a movement among the crowd in the door-way, and led his fair companion through it.

In the short interval occasioned by this stoppage, Agnes so far recovered her composure as to become very keenly alive to the importance of the next few moments to her happiness.... Should Lady Elizabeth look harshly, or Lady Stephenson coldly upon her, of what avail would be all the blessings that fate and affection had showered upon her favoured head?... And then it was that for the first time she felt the full extent of all she owed to Miss Compton; for the consciousness that she was no longer a penniless, desolate dependant came to her mind at that moment with a feeling ten thousand times more welcome than any display of her aunt's hoarded wealth had ever brought; and the recollection that, in speaking of her to Mrs. Peters, Miss Compton had almost pompously called her "my heiress," and "the inheritor of my paternal acres, and some twenty thousand pounds beside," which at the time had in some sort been painful for her to listen to, was at that agitating moment recalled with a degree of satisfaction that might have been strangely misinterpreted had those around been aware of it.... Some might have traced the feeling to pride, and some to vain self-consequence; but, in truth, it arose from a deep-seated sense of humility that blessed anything likely to lessen the awful distance she felt between herself and Hubert in the eyes of his relations.

But with all the aid she could draw from such considerations her cheek was colourless, and her eyes full of tears when she found herself standing almost like a culprit before the dignified old lady, whose favour she had once gained in a manner so unhoped for, whom she feared she had deeply offended since, and on whose present feelings towards her hung all her hopes of happiness in life.

It was not at the first glance that her timid but enquiring eye could learn her sentence, for the expressive countenance of the old lady underwent more than one change before she spoke. At first it very unequivocally indicated astonishment ... then came a smile that as plainly told of admiration (at which moment, by the way, her ladyship became impressed with the firmest conviction that the nose of the honourable Miss Nivett, and that of Miss Willoughby, were formed on the same model), and at last, whatever intention of reserve might have possessed her, it all melted away, and she held out both her hands with both aspect and words of very cordial welcome.

The heart of Agnes gave a bound as these words reached her; and the look of animated happiness which succeeded to the pale melancholy that sat upon her features when she first approached, touched the old lady so sensibly, that nothing but the presence of the crowd around prevented her throwing her arms around her in a fond embrace.

Lady Stephenson was from the first instant all affectionate kindness, and even Sir Edward, who had hitherto never appeared to think it necessary that his lady's singing favourite should occupy much of his attention, now put himself forward to claim her acquaintance, apologizing for not having known her at first by saying,—

"The change of dress, Miss Willoughby, must be my excuse; you have left off mourning since I saw you last."

Agnes smiled and bowed, and appeared not to have been in the least degree affronted; in fact, she was at that moment too happy to be otherwise than pleased with everybody in the world.

Meanwhile, Colonel Hubert stood looking at her with love, admiration, and astonishment, that fully equalled that of his aunt; but the contemplation did not bring him happiness. Without settling the balance very accurately in his own mind, perhaps, he had hitherto felt conscious that his station and fortune (independent at least, if not large) might be set against her youth ... that constant stumbling-block of his felicity ... and her surpassing beauty. But there was something in the change from simplicity of dress, that almost approached to homeliness, to the costly elegance of costume that was now before him, which seemed to indicate a position to which his own no longer presented so very favourable a contrast. She no longer appeared to be the Agnes to obtain whom he must make a sacrifice that would prove beyond all doubt the vastness of his love, and he trembled as he beheld her the principal object of attention, and the theme of avowed admiration throughout the room.

Lady Elizabeth very unceremoniously made room for her next herself, by desiring a gentleman who occupied the seat beside her, which was on a small sofa filling the recess by the chimney, to leave it.

"I beg a thousand pardons, sir, but I see no other place in the room where we could hope for space to sit thus tête-à-tête together, and did you know how near and dear she was to me, you would, I am sure, excuse me."

The gentleman, though not a young one, assured her with the appearance of much sincerity that to yield a seat to such a young lady could be considered only as honour and happiness by every man. Having thus established her restored favourite at her side, Lady Elizabeth began to whisper innumerable questions about Miss Compton.

"How came it, my dear," said she, "that when opening your heart to Emily and me upon the subject of your unfortunate situation with Mrs. Barnaby, you never referred to the possibility of placing yourself under the protection of Miss Compton?"

"Because my aunt Compton having quarrelled with my aunt Barnaby had refused to take any further notice of me,—Mrs. Barnaby at least led me to believe during the six or seven months I passed with her, that every application on my part to Miss Compton would be vain, ... and it was only the dreadful predicament into which Mrs. Barnaby's arrest threw me, that gave me the desperate courage which I thought necessary for applying to her. But I have since learned, Lady Elizabeth, that at any time, one word from me would have sufficed to make her leave her retirement, as she now has done, and remove me from my dreadful situation."

"But it appears that she is not only a kind aunt, but a wealthy one, my dear child.... Excuse the observation, Agnes, ... situated as we now are together, you cannot deem it impertinent, ... but your dress indicates as great and as favourable a change in pecuniary matters, as your letter, and your happy countenance, announces in all others.... Miss Compton, I presume, is a woman of fortune?"

"Her fortune is larger than I imagined it to be," replied Agnes. "She lived with great economy before she adopted me."

"And do you know what her intentions are, Agnes?" rejoined the persevering old lady. "It is only as the aunt of Colonel Hubert ... remember this, my dear ... it is only as Colonel Hubert's aunt that I ask the question."

Agnes blushed with most happy consciousness as she replied. "The interest you so kindly take in me confers both honour and happiness, and however averse to boast of the kindness bestowed, and promised by my dear aunt, I can have no wish to hide from you, Lady Elizabeth, all she has said to me. She knows the honour that has been done me by Colonel Hubert, and knows too, that nothing but the fear of your displeasure could have made me hesitate to accept it; ... and she says, that should no such displeasure interfere, she would bestow a fortune on me."

"Well, my dear, ... I don't believe that any such displeasure is likely to interfere. When will you introduce us to her?"

"To-morrow, Lady Elizabeth!..." Agnes eagerly replied, "if you will give us leave to wait upon you."

"Yes, that is right, my dear, quite right.... She must call on me first, ... and yet I am not quite sure of that either.... I rather think the friends of the gentleman should wait upon the friends of the lady, ... and so I will call upon her to-morrow morning, and remember, when you have introduced us to each other, you may go away; we must talk on business. What is her address?"

Agnes gave the address very distinctly, which was repeated in the same manner by Lady Elizabeth, just as Mrs. Pemberton approached to entreat her permission to lead her to the pianoforte. "You are going to sing, my dear child! Very good.... I shall be delighted to hear you.... And you must get me a place where I can both look at, and listen to her, Mrs. Pemberton," said Lady Elizabeth.

Considerably surprised, but much pleased to find that the acquaintance she had condescended to make with Mrs. Peters had led to her having the honour of receiving so intimate a friend and favourite of her most illustrious guest, Mrs. Pemberton rather ostentatiously performed the service required of her, and Agnes once more stood up to sing with Lady Elizabeth's arm-chair almost as near to her as on the happy night when she first won the old lady's heart at Cheltenham.

But where was Colonel Hubert?... He had stood anxiously watching the first few words that passed between his aunt and Agnes; and when he saw her cavalier dismission of her neighbour, and the cordial style of amity with which she pursued her conversation with the beautiful interloper, he almost forgot his doubts and fears in the happiness of seeing one obstacle so decidedly removed, and prudently denying himself the pleasure of being near them, lest his presence might render the conversation less confidential, he withdrew to the other room, and only appeared again before the eyes of Agnes when he took his place beside her to turn over the pages of her song.

For the first few moments Agnes feared that she was too happy to sing; ... but she tried, and found that her voice was clear, and was determined that it should soon be steady, for she wished ... let youthful ladies judge how ardently ... to renew the impression which she had made on Colonel Hubert on that never-to-be-forgotten morning when she first dared to fancy he loved her.

Nor were her wishes vain. She sang as well, and he felt as strongly as before. Her pleasure as she watched this was perfect, but his was very far from being so; he saw that she was the centre of attraction, and not only, as before, the admired of every eye, and the enchanter of every ear, but also the most distinguished, fashionable, and important young lady present.

There was not, however, a shadow of the paltry feeling called jealousy in this; the pang that smote his heart arose from memory, and not from imagination. Could he, as he now saw this elegant girl the centre of fashion, and the petted favourite of his own proud aunt, forget the generous devoted passion of the unfortunate Frederick? Could he forget that he had used all the influence which the young man's affection to himself had lent him, to make him abandon an attachment so every way calculated to ensure his happiness?... Could he forget that Frederick was now living an exile from his country, the victim of unhappy love, while he, his trusted confidant, but most pernicious adviser, remained to profit by the absence he himself had caused, and to drain the cup of happiness which his hand had dashed from the lips of his wretched friend?

As long as Mrs. Barnaby continued to hang about her, and in some degree to overshadow her with the disgrace of her vulgar levity, Agnes could not be loved without a sacrifice, and the youth and splendid fortune of Frederick Stephenson, as well as the peculiarly strong feelings of his family on the subject, might have stood as reasons why another, less fettered by circumstances, might have married her, though he could not. But how stood the matter now? Agnes had been snatched from Mrs. Barnaby, and borne completely beyond the sphere of her influence; Stephenson's proud brother seemed to bow before her, while his wife selected her as a chosen friend; and worse, a thousand times worse than all the rest, he had learnt, while he wandered among the company before the music commenced, that Agnes was the proclaimed heiress of fifteen hundred a-year. This last, however, for his comfort, he did not believe; but there was enough without it, to make him feel that, should he even be so blessed as to teach her to forget the difference of their age, and make her young heart his own, he must, by becoming her husband, appear to the friend who had trusted him, as one of the veriest traitors under heaven.

Such thoughts were enough to jar the sweetest harmony; and the evening was altogether productive of more pain than pleasure to the unfortunate Colonel Hubert, who having staked his happiness on a marriage, only to be obtained by the consent of his aunt, was now suffering martyrdom from a plethora of success, and would have gladly changed his condition back to what it had been when, regardless of consequences, he had laid his heart at the feet of Agnes by the light of her one tallow-candle in Half-moon Street, while her sole protectress lay imprisoned in the Fleet.

When the party broke up, Colonel Hubert, leaving his aunt to the care of Sir Edward, escorted Mrs. Peters and the four young ladies down stairs, where another shock awaited him on hearing her servant enquire which carriage should be called up first, for before answering, Mrs. Peters turned to Agnes, and said,—

"To which name are your servants accustomed to answer, my dear? Miss Compton told me you would have your own carriage here, but perhaps this might only be another mode of saying you would have hers. Shall they call Miss Compton's carriage, or Miss Willoughby's, Agnes?"

"They will answer to either, I believe," replied Agnes, carelessly, for she was waiting for Colonel Hubert to finish something he was saying to her.

"Call Miss Willoughby's carriage, then," said Mrs. Peters to the servants in waiting.... And "Miss Willoughby's carriage! Miss Willoughby's carriage!" resounded along the hall, and through the street.

CHAPTER XIII

DEMONSTRATING THE HEAVY SORROW WHICH MAY BE PRODUCED BY A YOUNG LADY'S HAVING A LARGER FORTUNE THAN HER LOVER EXPECTED

Miss Compton was not long kept waiting for the appearance of her promised visitor on the following morning, for before twelve o'clock Lady Elizabeth Norris arrived. Agnes very punctually obeyed the commands that had been given her, and having properly introduced the two old ladies to each other, left them together, and hastened at length to satisfy the anxious curiosity of her friend Mary, by giving her a full account of all the circumstances that had led to the happy change in her prospects.

Her tale was listened to with unbroken attention, and when it was ended Miss Peters exclaimed—

"Now then, I forgive you, Agnes, and only now, for not returning the love of that very pleasant person Frederick Stephenson; ... for I do believe it is nearly impossible for a young lady to be in love with two gentlemen at once, and I now perceive beyond the shadow of a doubt, that the superb colonel turned your head from the very first moment that you looked ... not up on, but up to him. How very strange it is," she continued, "that I should never have suspected the cause of that remarkable refusal!... I imagine my dulness arose from my humility; I was conscious myself that I should quite as soon have taken the liberty of falling in love with the autocrat of all the Russias, as with Colonel Hubert, and it therefore never occurred to me that you could be guilty of such audacity; nevertheless, I will not deny that he is a husband to be proud of ... and so I wish you joy heartily.... But do tell me," she added after a moment's meditation, "how you mean to manage about Mr. Stephenson?... Your first meeting will be rather awkward, will it not?"

"I fear so," replied Agnes, gravely. "But there is no help for it, and I must get over it as well as I can ... fortunately none of the family have the slightest idea of any such thing, and I hope they never will."

"I hope so, too, dear. But it would be very unpleasant, would it not? if, upon hearing what is going on, he were to burst in among you, and insist upon shooting Colonel Hubert."

This was said playfully, and without a shadow of serious meaning; but it rendered Agnes extremely uneasy, and it required some skill and perseverance on the part of Miss Peters to remove the effect of what she had said. There were, however, too many pleasant points of discourse among the multitude of subjects before them, for her young spirits to cling long to the only one that seemed capable of giving her pain, and on the whole their long and uninterrupted conference was highly gratifying to them both.

While this was going on in Rodney Place, something of the same kind, but without any drawback at all, was proceeding in the Mall, between the two old ladies, the result of which may be given more shortly by relating what passed between Lady Elizabeth and her nephew afterwards, than by following them through the whole of their very interesting, but somewhat desultory conversation.

Colonel Hubert was awaiting the return of his aunt with much anxiety; an anxiety, by the way, which proceeded wholly from the fear that what she might have to report should prove his Agnes to be un meilleur parti than he wished to find her. This singular species of uneasiness was in no degree lessened by the aspect of the old lady as she entered the drawing-room in which he was waiting to receive her.

"This is a very singular romance, Montague, as ever I remember to have heard of," she began. "Here is this pretty creature, who was introduced to us as niece and adopted child, as I fancied, of the vulgarest and most atrociously absurd woman in England, without money or wit enough to keep her out of jail, and now she turns out to be a young lady of large fortune, perfectly well educated, and well descended on both sides of her house ... and all this, too, without any legerdemain, denouements, or discoveries.... I wish you joy heartily, Montague.... Her fortune is exactly what was wanted to make yours comfortable ... she has fifteen hundred a year, part of which is, by Miss Compton's account, a very improvable estate in Devonshire;—but I suspect the old lady will like to give a name to your second son, or should you have no second son, to a daughter. Nor can I blame her for this. By her account, Compton of Compton Basett has endured long enough in the land to render the wish that it should not pass away a very reasonable one; especially for the person who holds, and has to bequeath the estate, to which it has for centuries been annexed; so that point, I presume, you will not cavil at. You must take care, however, that the liberal-minded old gentlewoman, in making this noble settlement on her niece, does not leave herself too bare.... She talked of the trifle that would follow at her death.... This ought not to be a trifle, and were I you,

Montague, I would insist that the amount settled on Agnes at your marriage should not exceed one thousand a-year.... This, with the next step in your profession, will make your income a very sufficient one, even without the regiment which you have such fair reason to hope for."

During the whole of this harangue, Colonel Hubert was suffering very severely; till by the time her ladyship had concluded, his imagination became so morbidly alive, that he almost fancied himself already in the presence of his injured friend ... he fancied him hastening home to be a witness at his marriage, and gazing with a cold reproachful eye as the beauty, the wealth, the connexions of Agnes were all shewn to be exactly what his friends would have approved for him, had not a false, a base, an interested adviser, contrived to render vain his generous and honourable love, that he might win the precious prize himself.

What a picture was this for such a mind as Hubert's to contemplate!... Had not Lady Elizabeth been exceedingly occupied by the curious and unexpected discoveries she had made concerning the race and the rents of the Comptons, she must have perceived how greatly the effect of her statement was the reverse of pleasurable to her auditor; but in truth her attention was not fixed upon him, but upon Miss Compton, whom she considered as one of the most remarkable originals she had ever met with, and ceased not to congratulate herself upon the happy chance which had turned her yielding kindness to her nephew into a source of so much interesting speculation to herself.... Receiving no answer to the speech she had made, she added very good-humouredly,—

"That's all, Mr. Benedict.... Now you may depart to look for the young lady, and you may tell her, if you please, that upon the whole I very much doubt if the united kingdoms might not be ransacked through, without finding any one I should more completely approve in all ways as the wife of Montague Hubert.... Poor Sir Edward!... How he will wish that all his anxieties respecting his hare-brained brother had been brought to a termination by the young man's having had the wit to fall in love with this sweet girl instead of you; ... but I doubt if Frederick Stephenson has sufficient taste and refinement of mind to appreciate such a girl as Agnes.... He probably overlooked her altogether, or perhaps amused himself more by quizzing the absurdities of the aunt, than by paying any particular attention to her delicate and unobtrusive niece. It required such a mind as yours, Montague, to overcome all the apparent obstacles and objections with which she was surrounded.... I honour you for it, and so, perhaps, will your giddy-headed friend too, when he comes to know her. She is a gem that we shall all have reason to be proud of."

Colonel Hubert could bear no more, but muttering something about wishing immediately to write letters, he hurried out of the room, and shut himself into the parlour which had been appropriated to his morning use. Without giving himself time to think very deliberately of the comparative good and evil that might ensue, he seized a pen, and wrote the following letter to Mr. Stephenson.

"DEAR FREDERICK,

"We parted painfully, and my regard for you is too sincere for me to endure the idea of meeting again with equal pain. I have had reason since you left England, to believe, that notwithstanding the very objectionable manners and conduct of Mrs. Barnaby, her niece, Miss Willoughby, is in every way worthy of the attachment, you conceived for her; nay, that her family and fortune are such as even your brother and sisters would approve. I will not conceal from you that there are others who have discovered (though not so early as yourself) the attractions and the merits of Miss Willoughby; but who can say, Frederick, that if your early and generous devotion were made known to her, she might not give you the preference over those who were less prompt in surrendering their affections than yourself? If, then, your feelings towards her continue to be the same as when we parted at our breakfast table at Clifton ... and this I cannot doubt, for Agnes is not formed to be loved once, and then forgotten ... if you still love her, Frederick, hasten home, and take the advantage which your early conceived and unhesitating affection gives you over those who saw her more than once, before they discovered how important she was to their happiness.

"Notwithstanding the impatience with which you listened to my remonstrances on the subject of a connexion with Mrs. Barnaby, I believe that they were in truth the cause of your abandoning a pursuit in which your heart was deeply interested; and so believing, I cannot rest till I have told you that a marriage with Miss Willoughby no longer involves the necessity of any personal intercourse with Mrs. Barnaby. They are separated, and probably for ever.

"Believe me, now and for ever,

"Very faithfully your friend,

"MONTAGUE HUBERT."

The effort necessary for writing and dispatching this letter by the post, was of service to him; it tended to make him feel more reconciled to himself, and less impatient under the infliction of hearing the favoured position of Miss Willoughby descanted upon. But much anxiety, much suffering, still remained.... How should he again meet Agnes?... Despite a thousand dear suspicions to the contrary, he could not wholly conquer the belief that it was her indifference, or some feeling connected with the disparity of their age, which dictated the too-well-remembered words.... "I never will be your wife;" and his best consolation under the terrible idea that he had recalled a rival to compete with him, arose from feeling that if, when his own proposals and those of Frederick were both before her, she should bestow herself on him, he might and must believe that, spite of his thirty-five years, she loved him; ... but though he hailed such comfort as might be got from this, it could not enable him to see Agnes, while this uncertainty remained, without such a degree of restraint as must convert all intercourse with her into misery.

Agnes meanwhile was indulging herself with all the happy confidence of youthful friendship in relating to her friend everything that had happened since they parted, and returned to the Mall soon after Lady Elizabeth had left it, with a heart glowing with love, gratitude, hope, and joy. The narrative with which Miss Compton welcomed her, was just all she wished and expected; and when told that the evening was to be passed at the lodgings of Lady Elizabeth Norris, she thanked the delighted old lady for the intelligence with a kiss that spoke her gladness better than any words could have done.

The evening came, and found the aunt and niece ready to keep their engagement, with such an equality of happiness expressed in the countenance of each, as might leave it doubtful which enjoyed the prospect of it the most. The pretty dress of Agnes, with all its simplicity, was rather more studied than usual; and it was the consciousness of this, perhaps, which occasioned her to blush so beautifully when Miss Compton made her a laughing compliment upon the delicate style of it....

"You look like a lily, my Agnes!" said the old lady, gazing at her with fond admiration. "You have certainly got very tired of black, my dear child, for I perceive that whenever you wish to look very nice, you select unmixed white for your decoration."

"I think it best expresses the change in my condition," replied Agnes. "Oh! my dear aunt, ... how very, very happy you have made me!"

Nothing could be more gratifying than the manner in which they were received by Lady Elizabeth, Lady Stephenson, and Sir Edward; ... but Colonel Hubert was not in the drawing-room when they entered. For a short time, however, his absence was not regretted, even by Agnes, as she was not sorry for the opportunity it gave her of receiving the affectionate congratulations of her future sister, and it was with a feeling likely to produce much lasting love between them, that the one related, and the other listened to, the history of Colonel Hubert's return from London, of his first bold avowal of his love to his aunt, and of the comfort he had found in the reception given to this avowal by Lady Stephenson herself; ... but still Colonel Hubert came not; and at length Lady Elizabeth exclaimed, with a spice of her usual vivacity,...

"Upon my word, I believe that Montague is writing an account of his felicity to every officer in the British army.... He darted out of the room this morning before I had half finished what I had to say to him.... He hardly spoke three words while dinner lasted, and off he was again as soon as the cloth was removed, and each time something about writing letters was the only intelligible words I got from him.... I wish you would go, Sir Edward, and see if he is writing letters now, ... and I will ring for tea.... I mean to make Montague sing to-night with Agnes. Emily has taken care that you should have a good piano, my dear ... and you must take care that, while I stay here, I have music enough to make up for the loss of my menagerie, ... for I don't think I shall begin collecting again just yet."

Sir Edward obeyed the old lady's wishes, and when the tea was half over, returned with his brother-in-law. This was the first time that Colonel Hubert had been seen by Miss Compton, and the moment was not a favourable one for removing the idea which she had originally conceived, of his being too old for the lover and husband of her beautiful niece. He was looking pale, harassed, and fatigued; but while Agnes feared only that he might be unwell, her aunt, though she could not deny that he was a gentleman of a most noble presence, (it was thus she expressed herself in speaking of him to Mrs. Peters,) thought that it was strange so young a girl should have fixed her fancy upon him, in preference to all the world beside. In fact, Miss Compton's notions of a lover being drawn solely from the imaginary models she had made acquaintance with among her bees and flowers, she would have been better pleased to see a bright-eyed youth of twenty-one as the hero of her own romance, than the dignified but melancholy man who now stood before her. Having received his salutation, and returned it with that tone and look of intelligent cheerfulness which redeemed all she said from any imputation of want of polish, or deficiency of high-bred elegance, she turned her eyes on the face of Agnes, and there she read such speaking testimony of love and admiration, that all her romantic wishes for her perfect bliss were satisfied; and following the direction of those speaking eyes, and once more examining the features and person of Hubert, she satisfied herself by the conviction, that if not young, he was supremely elegant; and that if his complexion had lost its bloom, his manners had attained a degree of dignity superior, as she thought, to anything described among the young gentlemen whose images were familiar to her imagination.

It was slowly that Colonel Hubert approached Agnes, and mournfully that he gazed upon her; but there was to her feelings a pleasure in his presence, which for a long time prevented her being fully conscious that he, on his part, was not so happy as she had hoped it was in her power to make him. By degrees, however, the conviction of this sad truth made its way to her heart, and from that moment her joy and gladness faded, drooped, and died away, like a flower into which a gnawing worm has found its way, and nestled in the very core. This did not happen on this first evening of their meeting under the roof of Lady Elizabeth, for Agnes indulged her with every song she desired to hear. Lady Stephenson sang too, nor could Colonel Hubert refuse to join them, so that to the unsuspicious Agnes that evening seemed delightful; but a silent, melancholy walk on the following morning, made her ask herself where was the ardent love for which he had pleaded in Half-Moon Street?... Had she mistaken him when he said that his happiness depended wholly on her?... And if not, what was it had turned him thus to stone?

Poor Agnes!... she could have no confident in this new sorrow. Her aunt Compton and her friend Mary had both spoken of him as too old to be a lover; and did she breathe to either a fear that his affection had already grown cold, might they not tell her that it was but natural?... Such words she thought would break her heart, for every hour he became dearer to her than before, as she saw he was unhappy; and, thinking more of him than of herself, mourned more for his sorrow, of which she knew nothing, than for her own, though it was rapidly undermining her health and destroying her bloom.

CHAPTER XIV

RETURNS TO MRS. BARNABY, AND RELATES SOME OF THE MOST INTERESTING AND INSTRUCTIVE SCENES OF HER LIFE, TOGETHER WITH SEVERAL CIRCUMSTANCES RELATIVE TO ONE DEARER TO HER THAN HERSELF

The real heroine of this love story has been left too long, and it is necessary we should return to see in what way her generous friendship for Mr. O'Donagough was likely to end. Having kept her promise, and paid the debt for which he had been detained, as well as comforted him by the farther loan of 2l. 10s. 4d., she stated to him her intention of remaining for a month longer at her lodgings in Half Moon-street, adding, with a degree of naïveté that O'Donagough felt to be extremely touching—

"Let this be a month of probation, my dear friend, for us both. We met under circumstances too much calculated to soften the heart for either of us, perhaps, to be able fairly to judge how we may feel when those circumstances are past. Let me see as much of you as your occupations will permit.... I shall dine at five o'clock, because the evenings are drawing in, and I don't love candle-light before dinner.... You will always find a steak or a chop, and a little brandy and water, or something of that sort.... And now adieu!... This is a disagreeable place to pay or receive visits in, and I flatter myself that I now leave it for ever."

Let the most glowing gratitude that heart can feel be set forth in words of fluent eloquence such as befit the class to which Mr. O'Donagough belonged, and the answer which he gave to this speech will be the product.

Nevertheless, Mr. O'Donagough knew what it meant perfectly well. It meant that the Widow Barnaby, although she had made up her mind to give herself and whatever she might happen to possess to a husband, and although she was exceedingly well inclined to let that husband be Mr. Patrick O'Donagough, she did not intend to go thus far in manifesting her favour towards him, without knowing a little more than she did at present respecting the state of his affairs. In a word, he perceived, as he repeated to himself, with an approving smile—

That though on marriage she was bent,
She had a prudent mind.

Nor was he, notwithstanding the little irregularities into which he had heretofore fallen, unworthy of becoming an object of tender attention to Mrs. Barnaby. Much as he admired her, he had steeled his soul to the virtuous resolution of putting a sudden stop to all farther intercourse between them, should he find upon inquiry that prudence did not justify its continuance.

Whatever deficiency of wisdom, therefore, the conduct of either had before shown, it was evident that both were now actuated by a praiseworthy spirit of forethought that ought to have ensured the felicity of their future years.

It will be evident to all who study the state of the widow's mind at this period, that she had considerably lowered the tone of her hopes and expectations from the moment she became aware of the defection of Lord Mucklebury. The shock which her hopes had received by the disagreeable denouement of her engagement with Major Allen had been perfectly cured, at least for a time, by the devotion of the noble Viscount; and so well satisfied was she herself at an escape which had left her free to aim at a quarry so infinitely higher, that what had been a mortification turned to a triumph, and she enjoyed the idea, that when "she seemed to slip," she had so gloriously recovered herself as to leave Mrs. Peters, and other envious wonderers, cause to exclaim, "She rises higher half her length!"... But from the time this coroneted bubble burst, her courage fell. Her arrest was another blow.... Mr. Morrison's desertion one heavier still; and, little as she cared for Agnes, or, in truth, for anybody living but herself, the manner of her departure vexed and humbled her.

"That crooked hag," thinks she, "has made me truckle to her!" she exclaimed, as her aunt and her niece drove off, on the night that Agnes first took up her abode with Miss Compton.... "She thinks that because she spent some of her beggar's money to hire a carriage in order to bully me, I shall count myself despised and forsaken. But the spiteful old maid shall hear of my being married again, and that will be wormwood, I'll answer for it."

It was in this spirit that she set about inquiring into the private character and prospects of young Mr. O'Donagough, and her first step in the business showed at once her judgment and her zeal.

In the history he had given of himself, he had spoken of a certain most respectable book-seller, who, (as he modestly hinted,) knowing his worth, and the exemplary manner in which he had turned from horse-racing to preaching, had exerted himself in the kindest manner to obtain some situation for him that should atone for the severity of his father. It was to him he had owed the engagement as domestic chaplain in the family of the nobleman formerly mentioned, and it was to him Mrs. Barnaby addressed herself for information that might lead to an engagement of still greater importance.

It was not, however, her purpose that her real object should be known, and she, therefore, framed her inquiries in such a manner as to lead Mr. Newbirth to suppose that her object was to obtain either a teacher or a preacher for her family circle.

Having made it known that she wished a few minutes private conversation with the principal, she was shown into a parlour by one of the clerks, and civilly requested to sit down for a few minutes till Mr. Newbirth could wait upon her. It must be the fault of every individual so placed, if such few minutes have not turned to good account; for the table of this exemplary publisher was covered elbow-deep in tracts, sermons, missionary reports, mystical magazines, and the like; but as Mrs. Barnaby was not habitually a reader, she did not profit so much as she might have done by her situation, and, before Mr. Newbirth's arrival, had begun to think the "few minutes" mentioned by his clerk were unusually long ones.

At length, however, he appeared, and then it was impossible to think she had waited too long for him, for the gentle suavity of his demeanour made even a moment of his presence invaluable.

"You have business with me, madam?" he said, with his heels gracefully fixed together, and his person bent forward in humble salutation, as far as was consistent with the safety of his nose....

"Pray do not rise. I have now five minutes that I can spare, without neglecting any serious duty;" and so saying, he placed himself opposite to the lady in act to listen.

"I have taken the liberty of waiting upon you, sir," replied Mrs. Barnaby, a little alarmed at the hint that her business must be completed in the space of five minutes, "in order to make some inquiries respecting a Mr. O'Donagough, who is, I believe, known to you."

"Mr. O'Donagough? The Reverend Mr. O'Donagough, madam?"

The widow, though well disposed to enlarge her knowledge, and extend the limits of her principles, was not yet fully initiated into the mysteries of regenerated ordinations, and therefore replied, as the daughter of an English clergyman might well be excused for doing—"No, sir ... the gentleman I mean is Mr. Patrick O'Donagough; he was not brought up to the church."

But there was something in the phrase, "brought up to the church," that grated against the feelings of Mr. Newbirth, and his brow contracted, and his voice became exceedingly solemn, as he said, "I know Mr. Patrick O'Donagough, who, like many other shining lights, was not brought up to the church; but has, nevertheless, received the title of reverend from the congregation which has the best right to bestow it, even that to which he has been called to preach."

Mrs. Barnaby was not slow in perceiving her mistake, and proceeded with her inquiries in such a manner as to prove that she was not unworthy to intercommune either with Mr. Newbirth himself, or any of those to whom he extended his patronage. The result of the interview was highly satisfactory; for though it seemed clear that Mr. Newbirth was aware of the vexatious accident which had for some months checked the young preacher's career, it was equally evident, that the circumstance made no unfavourable impression, and Mrs. Barnaby returned to her lodgings with the pleasing conviction that now, at least, there could be no danger in giving way to the tender feeling which had so repeatedly beguiled her. "The reverend Mr. O'Donagough" would look very well in the paragraph which she was determined should record her marriage in the Exeter paper; and being quite determined that the three hundred and twenty-seven pounds per annum, which still remained of her income, should be firmly settled on herself, she received her handsome friend, when he arrived at the hour of dinner, in a manner which showed he had lost nothing in her esteem since they parted.

It had so happened, that within half an hour of the widow's quitting the shop of Mr. Newbirth, Mr. O'Donagough entered it. His patron received him very graciously, and failed not to mention the visit he had received, which, though not elucidated by the lady's leaving any name, was perfectly well understood by the person principally concerned.

There are some men who might have felt offended by learning that such a means of improving acquaintance had been resorted to; but its effect on Mr. O'Donagough was exactly the reverse. His respect and estimation for the widow were infinitely increased thereby; for though still a young man, he had considerable experience, and he felt assured, that if Mrs. Barnaby had not something to bestow besides her fair fat hand, she would have been less cautious in letting it follow where it was so certain her heart had gone before.

The conviction thus logically obtained, assisted the progress of the affair very essentially. Having learnt from Mr. Newbirth that the place he had lost by the ill-timed arrest was filled by another who was not likely to give it up again, he once more contrived to make his way to the presence of his father, and gave him very clearly to understand, that the very best thing he could do would be once more to furnish the means for his departure from Europe.

"That you may spend it again at the gaming-table, you audacious scamp!" responded his noble but incensed progenitor.

"Not so, sir," replied the soft-voiced young preacher; "you are not yet aware of the change in my principles, or you would have no such injurious suspicion."

"As to your principles, Pat," replied his lordship, beguiled into a smile by the sanctified solemnity of his versatile son, "I do not comprehend how you could change them, seeing that you never had any."

"Then, instead of principles, sir, let me speak of practice: it is now several months since I exchanged the race-course, the billiard-table, and the dice-box, for the course of an extemporary preacher. I am afraid, my lord, that your taste rather leads you to performances of a different kind, or I would ask you to attend the meeting at which I am to expound next Wednesday evening, after which you could hardly doubt, I imagine, the sincerity of my conversion."

"It would be putting your eloquence to rather a severe test, Master Patrick. But if you have really got a church to preach in at home, why, in the devil's name, should you bother me again about going abroad?"

"Because, my lord, I have no fixed stipend, or any other honest and safe means of getting my bread, and also because there are many other reasons which make it desirable that I should leave this country."

"That at least is likely enough, to be sure, Mr. O'Donagough. But have the kindness to tell me what security you would give me for taking yourself off, if I were again to furnish the means for it."

This was exactly the point to which the reformed son wished to bring the yielding father; for it was not difficult to show many reasons for believing that he was in earnest in his intention to depart with as little delay as possible. It was with great caution, however, that he hinted at the possibility of his taking a lady with him as his wife, whose fortune was sufficient to prevent the necessity of his returning again to beg for bread, even at the risk of liberty or life; for he feared that if he confessed the prosperous state of his matrimonial hopes, they might be held sufficient for his necessities. But here he was mistaken; for no sooner did his father discover that his case was not quite desperate, than he manifested a considerable softening, and before a fortnight had expired, Mr. O'Donagough was able to convince the enamoured widow that, in uniting her destiny to his, she would be yielding to no sinful weakness, but securing both her temporal and eternal felicity on the firmest footing possible. And now every thing went on in so prosperous a manner, as almost to disprove the truth of the oft-quoted assertion of the poet,

"The course of true love never did run smooth;"

for the loves of Mr. O'Donagough and Mrs. Barnaby met with not even a pebble of opposition as they ran evenly on towards matrimony.

This peaceful and pleasant progress was not a little assisted by a visit which the prudent peer deemed it advisable to make to the intended bride. Nothing could be more agreeable to the feelings of the lady than this attention, nothing more advantageous to the interests of both parties than the result. His lordship ascertained to a certainty that the widow had wherewithal to feed his son, and most obligingly took care that it should be so secured as to place her fortune beyond the reach of any relapse on his part, while the fair lady herself, amidst all the gentle sweetness with which she seemed to let his lordship manage every thing, took excellent care of herself.

One thing only now remained to be settled before the marriage took place, and this was the obtaining an appointment as missionary to a congregation newly established in a beautiful part of Australia, where there was every reason to suppose that a large and brilliant society would soon give as much éclat to the successful efforts of an eloquent preacher as could be hoped for in the most fashionable réunion of saints in the mother country. The appointment was, in effect, left in the hands of one or two, whose constant exertions, and never-let-any-thing-escape-them habits, made them of personal importance in every decision of the kind. This little committee agreed to meet at Mr. Newbirth's on a certain evening, for the purpose of being introduced to Mrs. Barnaby, and it was understood among them, that if they found reason to be satisfied with her principles, and probable usefulness in a new congregation, the appointment should be given to Mr. O'Donagough, whose approaching marriage with her was well known to them all.

Mrs. Newbirth, who was quite a model of a wife, and who, therefore, shared all her husband's peculiar notions respecting things in heaven and earth, very obligingly lent her assistance at this important session, both to prevent Mrs. Barnaby's feeling herself awkward, as being the only lady present, and because it was reasonably supposed that she might be useful in giving the conversation such a turn as should elicit some of the more hidden, but not, therefore, the least important traits of female character.

It was not intended that either Mr. O'Donogough or his intended bride should be aware of the importance attached to this tea-drinking in Mr. Newbirth's drawing-room; but the expectant missionary had not lived thirty years in this wicked world for nothing; and though the invitation was given in the most impromptu style possible, he instantly suspected that the leaders of the congregation, who were about to send out the mission, intended to make this an opportunity for discovering what manner of woman the future Mrs. O'Donagough might be. Considerable anxiety was the consequence of this idea in the mind of Mr. O'Donagough. He liked the thoughts of preaching and lecturing to the ladies and gentlemen of Modeltown, and therefore determined to spare no pains in preparing the widow for the trial that awaited her. He found her by no means unapt at receiving the hints he gave respecting several important articles of faith, which, although new to her, she seemed willing enough to adopt without much inquiry, but he had a hard struggle before he could obtain the straightening of a single ringlet, or the paling, in the slightest degree, the tint of her glowing rouge. At length, however, the contest ended by his declaring that, without her compliance on this point, he should feel it his duty, passionately as he adored her, to delay their marriage till she could be induced, for his sake, to conform herself a little more to the customs and manners of the sect to which he belonged. Mrs. Barnaby's heart was not proof against such a remonstrance as this; her resolution melted into tears, and she promised that if he never would utter such cruel words again, he should dress her hair himself in any manner he would choose. "As to my rouge," she added, "I have only worn it, my dear O'Donagough, because I consider it as the appendage of a woman of fashion ... but I will wear much less, that is to say, almost none at all, for the fashion, if such shall be your wish."

"Thank you my dear, ... that's all right, and I'll never plague you about it, after I once get the appointment; only do what I bid you to-night, and we'll snap our fingers at them afterwards."

The party assembled at Mr. Newbirth's consisted of himself and his lady, and four gentlemen belonging to "the congregation" which was to be propitiated. After the tea and coffee had disappeared, Mr. Newbirth, who was the only gentleman in the company (except her own O'Donagough) with whom Mrs. Barnaby was personally acquainted, opened the conversation, by asking if the change of residence which she contemplated, from one side of the world to the other, was an agreeable prospect to her.

"Very much so indeed!" was the reply.

"I suppose you are aware, ma'am," observed Mr. Littleton, who was senior clerk in a banking house, and the principal lay orator of the congregation—"I suppose you are aware that you are going among a set of people who, though decidedly the most interesting portion of the human race in the eyes of all true Christians, are nevertheless persons accustomed heretofore to habits of irregular, not to say licentious living.... How do you think, ma'am, that you shall like to fall into habits of friendship and intimacy with such?"

Mr. O'Donagough listened with a good deal of anxiety for the answer: but it was a point on which he had given his affianced bride very ample instructions, and she did not disgrace her teacher.

"My notions upon that point, sir," she replied, "are rather particular, I believe; for so far from thinking the worse of my fellow creatures because they have done wrong, I always think that is the very reason why I should seek their company, and exert myself in all ways to do them good, and to make them take their place among the first and greatest in the kingdom of heaven."

A murmur of applause ran round the little circle as Mrs. Barnaby concluded her speech, and Mr. Littleton, in particular, expressed his approbation of her sentiments in a manner that inspired the happy O'Donagough with the most sanguine hopes of success.

"I never heard better sense, or sounder principles, or more christian feelings, in the whole course of my life, than what this lady has now expressed; and I will take upon me to say, gentlemen, without making any new difficulty about the matter, that any minister going out to Sydney in the holy and reverend character of a missionary, sent by an independent congregation of devotional men, with such a wife in his hand as this good lady will be sure to make, will do more good in his generation, than all the bishops and archbishops that ever were consecrated after the manner of the worn-out superstitions of by-gone ages. Gentlemen!..." he continued, rising from his chair, "I do, therefore, forthwith propose the immediate election of the reverend Patrick O'Donagough to the office of missionary from the independent congregation of Anti-work Christians of London, to the independent congregation of Anti-work Christians at Sydney, with the privilege and undivided monopoly of tract and hymn selling to the said congregation, together with a patent right (not royal patent, my brethren, but holy patent,) to all fees, donations, contributions, and payments of whatsoever kind, made by the said independent congregation of Anti-work Christians at Sydney, for and on account of the salvation of their souls.... This, gentlemen, is the resolution I would propose, and I trust that some among you will readily be found to second it."

"That, sir, will I, and most joyfully," said Mr. Dellant, rising; "for I neither do nor can feel the shadow of a doubt, that our beneficent objects in despatching this mission will be more forwarded by this appointment than by any other, it is probable—gentlemen, I might say POSSIBLE—we could make—for where, I would ask, shall we find another Mrs Barnaby? May we not say, in the language of scripture, that she is a help meet for him, even for the Reverend Patrick O'Donagough, whom we have chosen."

Mr. Newbirth followed on the same side, giving many unanswerable reasons for believing that nothing which the stiff-necked, unconverted, obsolete ministers of the Church of England could do for the predestined army of saints at present located at Sidney, could approach in utility and saving efficacy of absolving grace, to what might be hoped from the ministry of Mr. O'Donagough, assisted by the lady he was so happy as to have engaged to be his wife.

"It gives me the most heart-felt pleasure, gentlemen," he continued, "that my little humble drawing-room should have been made the scene of this happy election. How many souls, now most probably grovelling in the lowest depths of vice, will have places secured them upon the highest seats of heaven, by your work, gentlemen; begun, continued, and ended within this one propitious hour!... I would now propose that we do all stand up and sing a hymn to the glory of sinners made perfect.... Next, that we do all kneel down to hear and join in an awakening prayer from our new missionary; and, finally, that we walk into Mrs. Newbirth's back drawing-room, there to partake of such creature comforts as she in her care shall have provided."

This speech was also received with great applause. Some few pleasant and holy remarks and observations were made by the other gentlemen present, and all things proceeded to the happy finale suggested by their host, in the most amicable and satisfactory manner, so that before Mr. O'Donagough rose to escort Mrs. Barnaby to the coach which was to convey her to Half Moon Street, he was given to understand, on the indefeasible authority of Mr. Littleton, that he might consider himself already as the anti-work missionary elect, and might set about the preparations for his marriage and subsequent departure without farther uncertainty or delay.

Mrs. Barnaby's troubles now seemed really at an end; nothing could move onward with a smoother, surer pace, than did the business which she and her chosen companion had before them. The bridegroom's noble father became liberal and kind, under the certainty of his clever son's certain departure.... The lawyers behaved exceedingly well about the settlements; influenced, perhaps, in some degree, by the wishes of the peer, who, as it seemed, was almost nervously anxious for the departure of the happy pair.... The dressmakers worked briskly, and a very respectable subscription was raised among the ladies of the independent congregation for the purchase of several elegant little presents for the bride, which they thought might prove useful during her voyage.

In this happy state we will leave our heroine, in order to see how matters were proceeding at Clifton.

CHAPTER XV

AGNES GROWS MISERABLE—AN EXPLANATORY CONVERSATION WITH COLONEL HUBERT LEAVES HER MORE IN THE DARK THAN EVER—A LETTER ARRIVES FROM FREDERIC STEPHENSON

At this period of their history the star of Agnes appeared much less propitious than that of her aunt Barnaby. Not all her inclination to construe every look and word of Colonel Hubert into something wiser and better, more noble and more kind than the looks and words of any other mortal man, could long prevent her from feeling that he was profoundly unhappy, and that, despite some occasional flashes of an emotion which her own heart taught her to know proceeded from love, he evidently avoided being with her, as much as it was possible for him to do without attracting the attention of others.

Her aunt and his aunt went steadily on arranging between themselves a variety of preliminaries to the happy union they contemplated, while no hint that such an union was possible ever passed the lips of the intended bridegroom during any moment that circumstances placed him near his promised bride. More than once she saw him change colour when he approached her; and sometimes, but not often, she had caught his melancholy eyes fixed earnestly upon her, and it was at such moments that she felt persuaded he still loved her ... but wherefore he, who had boldly wooed her when so many things conspired to make his doing it objectionable, should seem to shun her now that everything was made so smooth and easy for him, she vainly laboured to understand.

"For time nor place," she exclaimed with something like bitterness, "did then adhere, and yet he would make both....

'They have made themselves, and that their fitness now
Doth unmake him!'"

By melancholy degrees everything that had most contributed to her happiness, became her torment. The conversation of Miss Peters was inexpressibly irksome to her, particularly when they found themselves in confidential tête-à-tête, for then she could not help suspecting that her friend was longing to ask her some questions respecting the singularity of her lover's manner ... the flattering notice of the well-pleased Lady Elizabeth, the sisterly affection manifested by the amiable Lady Stephenson, and, more than all the rest, the happy, bustling, business-like manner of her aunt Compton, who never for a moment seemed to forget that they were all preparing for a wedding.

So complete was this pre-occupation, that it was many days before the old lady perceived that her Agnes, in the midst of all this joyful preparation, looked neither well nor happy; nay, even when at last the sad eye and pale cheek of her darling attracted her attention, she persuaded herself for many days more that love-making was too sentimental a process to permit those engaged in it to be gay. She knew that the sighing of lovers was proverbial, and though she did not remember to have read any thing upon the subject exactly resembling what she remarked in Agnes, and, to say truth, in Colonel Hubert also, she did not, for she could not, doubt that everything was going on just as it should do, though her own want of practical experience rendered her incapable of fully understanding it.

But if Agnes was wretched, Colonel Hubert was infinitely more so; for all the misery that she darkly feared, without knowing either its nature or for how long it was likely to continue, came to him with the tremendous certainty of a misfortune that had already fallen upon him, and from which escape seemed less possible from day to day. She knew not what to think of him, and great, no doubt, was the unhappiness produced by such uncertainty, but greater still was the suffering produced by looking in her innocent face, and knowing, as well as Colonel Hubert did, why it grew daily paler. Not seldom, indeed, was he tortured by the apprehension that the line of conduct he had pursued in recalling Frederick Stephenson, was by no means so unquestionably right in its self-sacrificing severity as he had intended it should be. Had he not endangered the tranquillity of Agnes, while guarding with jealous care his own proud sense of honour? If an unhappy concurrence of circumstances had involved him in difficulties that rendered his conduct liable to suspicion, ought he not to have endured the worst degree of contempt that this could bring upon him, rather than have suffered her peace to be the sacrifice?

Night and day these doubts tormented him. For hours he wandered through the roads on the opposite side of the river, where, comparatively speaking, he was sure no Clifton idlers could encounter him, and reviewing his own conduct in a thousand ways, found none that would make him satisfied with himself. At length, in the mere restlessness of misery, he determined to tell Agnes all.

"She shall know his love—his generous uncalculating love, while I stood by, and reasoned on the inconvenience her aunt Barnaby's vulgarity might bring. She shall know all ... though it will make her hate me!"

Such was the resolution with which he crossed the ferry after wandering a whole morning in Leigh Wood; and climbing the step-path too rapidly to give himself leisure to meditate temperately on the measure he had determined to pursue, he hurried forward to the dwelling of Miss Compton, and was already in her drawing-room before he had at all decided in what manner he should contrive to get Agnes alone.

In this, however, fortune favoured him; for Miss Compton having some point on which she desired to communicate with Lady Elizabeth, had ordered the carriage, and invited Agnes to pay a visit to Lady Stephenson; but the poor girl had no heart to sustain a conversation with a friend from whom she most earnestly desired to conceal all her thoughts—so she declined the invitation, alleging her wish to write a letter to Empton.

As much alone, and, if possible, more melancholy still, than when, a few short weeks before, he made his memorable visit in Half Moon Street, Colonel Hubert found Agnes listlessly lying upon a sofa, her eyes closed, but their lashes too recently wetted by tears to make him fancy her asleep. She was in an inner room, to which he entered through the open door that led from the larger drawing-room, and he was close beside her before she was aware of his approach.

It was with a dreadful pang that he contemplated the change anxiety had wrought on her delicate features since the evening she first appeared to him in all the bright light-hearted joy of her new happiness under the protection of her aunt. Love, honour, gratitude, tenderness, and remorse, all rushed to his bosom, and so completely overpowered the philosophy by which he had hitherto restrained his feelings, that he dropped on his knees beside her, and seizing the hand that languidly hung by her side, covered it with passionate kisses.

An iron chain is not a stronger restraint than timid delicacy to such a nature as that of Agnes, and therefore she did NOT throw herself on the bosom of Colonel Hubert, and thus obliterate by one moment of unrestrained feeling all the doubts and fears that had so long tormented them both ... she only opened her beautiful eyes upon him, which seemed to say, "Is then the dark cloud passed that has divided us?... Hubert, may I be happy again?"

The unhappy Hubert, however, dared not answer this appeal, though he read it, and felt it at the very bottom of his heart; and what under happier circumstances would have tempted him to kneel beside her for ever, now made him spring to his feet as if terrified at the danger that he ran.

"Agnes!" he said, "you must no longer be left ignorant of my misery ... you may, you must have seen something of it, but not all ... you have not seen, you have not guessed what, the struggle has been between a passion as fervent as ever warmed the heart of man and a sense of honour ... too late awakened perhaps ... which has made it a duty to suspend all pleadings for an avowed return till ... till...."

"Till!..." repeated Agnes, agitated but full of hope, that the moment was indeed come when the dark and mysterious cloud which had dimmed all her prospects should be dispelled.

"Hear my confession, Agnes, and pity me at least, if you find it impossible to excuse me.... Do you remember the first time that I ever saw you?... It was at a shop at Clifton."

Agnes bowed.

"Do you remember the friend who was with me?"

Agnes bowed again, and this time she coloured too. Colonel Hubert sighed profoundly, but presently went on with the confession he had braced his nerves to make.

"That friend, Agnes, the generous, noble-hearted Frederick Stephenson, saw, even in that brief interview, the beauty, the grace, the delicacy which it took me days to develop ... in short, he loved you, Agnes, before, almost before I had ever looked at you.... I was his dearest friend. He hid no thought from me, and with all the frankness of his delightful character he confessed his honourable attachment.... And how was it, think you, that I answered him?"

Agnes raised her eyes to his face with a very anxious look, but spoke not a word, and Colonel Hubert, with a heightened colour that mounted to his temples, went on.

"I told him, Miss Willoughby, that a young lady chaperoned by a person with the manners and appearance of your aunt Barnaby was not a fitting wife for him...."

The eyes of Agnes fell, and her cheeks too were now dyed with crimson. Colonel Hubert saw it and felt it all, but he went on.

"The subject was repeatedly revived between us, and as his attachment increased, so did also my opposition to it. I placed before him, in the strongest manner I was capable of doing, all the objections to the connexion as they then appeared to me, and I did it, as I thought, purely from a sense of duty to himself and his family, which had recently become so closely connected with my own. But alas! Agnes ... my peace has been and is destroyed by the dreadful doubt whether some selfish feelings, unknown to myself, might not at length have mingled with these strong remonstrances. Knowing as I do the character of Sir Edward and his two sisters, no remorse was awakened in my mind so long as you remained with Mrs. Barnaby ... and the last time I conversed with my poor friend, I used language so strong upon the subject, that he left me in great anger. But it appears that, notwithstanding his just resentment, these remonstrances had weight, for he immediately left the kingdom, and has, I believe, remained in Paris ever since. Think then, Miss Willoughby ... judge for me if you can, with what feelings I contemplate the unlooked-for change in your position.... Oh! Agnes ... would that your excellent Miss Compton had preserved her coldness to you till you had been my wife.... Even then, I might have felt a pang for Stephenson—but the knowledge that his friends would not, like mine, have forgotten Mrs. Barnaby in their admiration for her niece, would have furnished a justification of the events which followed his departure, too reasonable to be set aside. But what must I feel now when I think of the banished Frederick?... Banished by me, that I might take his place."

Excepting to Mary Peters, who had been aware of the attachment of Frederick Stephenson long before herself, Agnes had never breathed a hint to any human being of the proposal she had received from him, and it had not most assuredly been her intention ever to have named it to Colonel Hubert. She had, indeed, but rarely remembered it herself, and hoped and believed that, before they met again, the gay young man would quite have forgotten it; but now she could preserve his secret no longer, and, eager to speak what she thought would entirely relieve his self-reproaches to hear, she said, with glowing cheeks and an averted eye,

"Let me, then, confess to you, Colonel Hubert...."

These unlucky words, however, intended as a preface to the only intelligence that could effectively have soothed his agitation, unfortunately increased it tenfold, and raising his hand to arrest what she was about to say, he replied with an impetuosity with which she could not at that moment contend—"Confess nothing, Miss Willoughby, to me.... I see that I have awakened feelings which I ought to have foreseen would inevitably be called into existence by such a disclosure.... Suffer me to say a few words more, and I have done.... A week ago, I did what I ought to have done, as soon as your present position was known to me.... I wrote to Mr. Stephenson, and told him that every obstacle was removed ... and that"...

"You wrote to him, Colonel Hubert!" exclaimed Agnes, greatly disturbed.... "Oh! why did you not tell me all this before?"

"It is not yet too late, Miss Willoughby," he replied, bitterly; "another letter shall follow my first ... more explicit, more strongly urging his return."

"But you will not hear me, Colonel Hubert," said Agnes, bursting into tears. "Have patience for a moment, and you will understand it all."

At this moment a carriage stopped at the door, and the knocker and the bell together gave notice of Miss Compton's return.

"It is my aunt!" cried Agnes. "Indeed she must not see me thus, for how could I explain to her what must appear so strange as her finding me in tears, and you beside me. Let me see you again, Colonel Hubert—I pray you to let me see you again, when I may be able to speak to you ... but now I must go;" and so saying, she escaped from the room just in time to avoid meeting Miss Compton at the door.

From a very early period of their short acquaintance, Miss Compton had made up her mind to consider Colonel Hubert as a very superior personage, but of a remarkably grave and silent character; so much so, indeed, that while she admired and approved her Agnes the more for loving and being loved by so dignified an individual, she could not help wondering a little, occasionally, that so it should be. But this feeling she carefully concealed, and made it a point, whenever a shade of gravity more profound than usual was perceptible on his features, (a circumstance not unfrequent,) to avoid interfering with his reserve by any loquacious civility. This line of conduct had often been a great relief to him, but never more so than on the present occasion, when, if any lengthened greetings had occurred to stop his retreat, it would have been impossible for him to have preserved the outward semblance of cold composure in which he had hitherto found shelter from observation.

"You are going, Colonel Hubert?" she said. "Well, I will not detain you, for I am going to be busy myself—good morning." And so he escaped.

On reaching home, he found a letter waiting for him, which by no means tended to calm his spirits. It was from Frederick Stephenson, and ran thus:—

"MY DEAR HUBERT,

"Your letter puzzles me; but not many hours after this reaches you, I hope we shall mutually understand each other better than we do at present. I am on my road to England, and as all explanation must be impossible till we meet, I will only add, that I am yours ever,

"FREDERICK STEPHENSON."

A few hours, then, and all doubt, all uncertainty, would be over! A full explanation must take place; and rather than endure a continuance of what he had lately suffered, Colonel Hubert felt inclined to welcome the result, be it what it might.

CHAPTER XVI

A DISCOVERY SCENE—PRODUCTIVE OF MANY NEW RELATIONS, AND VARIOUS OTHER CONSEQUENCES

The day next but one after this letter reached him, Miss Compton and Agnes were engaged to dine with Lady Elizabeth. Colonel Hubert had not ventured to present himself in the Mall during the interval, for though, on cooler meditation, he did not believe that the unfortunate words, "Let me, then, confess to you, Colonel Hubert," were meant to usher a confession of love to his rival, he doubted not that they would have been followed by an avowal of her agreeing with himself in deeming his own conduct most reprehensible; and just then, he felt he could not receive this, notwithstanding its justice, in such a manner as to assist in obtaining pardon for the fault. To Sir Edward he had mentioned the probability of his brother's early return, but without hinting at the chance of their seeing him at Clifton on his arrival in England.

The ladies of the party, namely, Lady Elizabeth, Lady Stephenson, Miss Compton, and Agnes, were assembled in the drawing-room, the two gentlemen not having yet quitted the dining-parlour, when a knock at the door announced company.

"Who can that be?" said Lady Stephenson. "Have you invited evening company?"

"Not a soul, my dear," replied her aunt; "I mean to have a treat again.... I think I am growing sick of curiosities."

"Tant mieux, dear aunt!" replied Lady Stephenson. "But invited or not, you have visiters coming now: I hear them on the stairs."

Lady Stephenson was right; the old butler opened the drawing-room door almost as she spoke, and announced "Mr. Stephenson!"

"Frederick!" exclaimed his fair sister-in-law, looking as if she meant to receive him very kindly.

"Young Stephenson!" said Lady Elizabeth, "I did not know that he was coming to Clifton."

"Sir Edward's brother, I suppose?..." said Miss Compton, ... but Agnes said nothing, though had any one laid a hand upon her heart, they would have discovered that his arrival was not a matter of indifference. To receive him with the appearance of it was, however, absolutely necessary, and she very resolutely assumed an aspect of tranquillity; it was not necessary that she should look towards the door to greet him as he entered, and therefore she did not do it; but, notwithstanding the attention she devoted to the pattern of the hearth-rug, she became aware, within a moment after this electrifying name had been announced, that not one only but three people were in the room, and that one of them was a lady.

Agnes then looked up, and the first figure which distinctly met her eye was not that of Frederick Stephenson, but of a gentleman bearing the stamp of some forty years, perhaps, upon his handsome but delicate features. He was not tall, but slightly and elegantly formed, which was perceptible, though wrapped in a travelling frock trimmed with fur, and his whole appearance was decidedly that of a gentleman.

But who these might be who were with him, or how they were received by Lady Elizabeth, the eye of Agnes had no power to inquire, for it was fascinated, as it were, by the earnest gaze of this stranger, who, having already stepped forward a pace or two nearer to her than the rest, stood looking at her with very evident emotion.

The first words she heard spoken were in the voice of young Stephenson, which she immediately recognised, though the purport of them was unintelligible.

"Yes, my dear sir, ... you are quite right," he said; "that is our Agnes."

But though these words were somewhat startling, they drew her attention less than the expression of the large blue eyes that were fixed upon her; there was admiration, tenderness, and a strange sort of embarrassment, all legibly mingled in that earnest look ... but why was it fixed on her?

What effect this mute scene produced on the other persons present, Agnes could not know, for she did not withdraw her eyes from those of the mysterious stranger, till at length he turned from her, and stepping back, took the hand of a very young, but very beautiful girl, whom he led towards the sofa she occupied, and placing her on it, said,

"Agnes Willoughby!... receive your sister ... and let her plead for her father and yours.... You have been long, long neglected, my poor child, but there has been some excuse for it.... Can you forgive me, Agnes?"

"Good God!... My father!" she exclaimed, starting up, and stretching out her hands towards him. "Is it possible, sir, that you are indeed my father?"

"You speak as if you wished it were so, Agnes," he replied, taking her in his arms, and impressing a kiss upon her forehead, "and I will echo your words.... Is it possible?"

"Possible!... O! yes, sir, it is possible.... I have so longed to know that I had a father!... And is this sweet creature my sister?" she continued, turning her tearful eyes upon the beautiful girl, who upon this appeal sprang forward, and enclosing both her father and Agnes in her arms, replied to it by saying,

"Yes, dearest Agnes, I am your sister, indeed I am, and I know you very well, and all about you, though you know so little about me ... but you will not refuse to own me, will you?"

For all reply Agnes bent forward and kissed her fondly.

Miss Compton who, as may be supposed, had watched this discovery scene with no little interest, now stepped towards them, while young Stephenson was engaged in explaining it to Lady Elizabeth and his sister-in-law; and looking from one sister to the other, and from them both to their father, she said—"You will, perhaps, hardly remember that we ever met, Mr. Willoughby ... but my name is Compton, and I recal your features perfectly. You once passed an hour at my brother's house when I was there ... and that these girls are sisters, no one that sees them together will be likely to deny.... God bless them both, pretty creatures!... I hope they will each be a blessing to the other.... But, to be sure, it seems to be a most romantic story ... and wonderfully like those I used to read in my bower, Agnes."

"There is a good deal that is very sad in my part of it, Miss Compton," replied Mr. Willoughby, "but at this moment I can hardly regret it, as herein I hope to show some excuse for my long negligence respecting my poor girl. Take this on trust, my good lady, will you?" he added, holding out his hand to her, "that no displeasure towards me may destroy the happiness of this meeting."

Miss Compton gave him her hand very frankly, saying,

"I have no right to be very severe upon you, Mr. Willoughby, for, without any misfortunes at all to plead as an excuse for it, our dear Agnes might tell you some naughty stories about me.... But she does not look as if she were much inclined to complain of anybody.... What a pair of happy, lovely looking creatures!... And how very strong the likeness to each other, and of both to you!"

Willoughby retired a step or two, and leaning against the chimney-piece, seemed disposed to enjoy the contemplation of the picture she pointed out, in silence. Lady Elizabeth claimed the attention of Miss Compton, that she might express her interest, satisfaction, surprise, and so forth. Lady Stephenson slipped out of the room to communicate the news to her husband and brother, and prepare them for the company they had to receive ... and then Frederick Stephenson approached the sisters, and drawing a chair towards them, very freely took a hand of each.

That of Agnes trembled. She felt that the happiness of her life would be for ever destroyed, if this young man was come back in consequence of Colonel Hubert's letter, with the persuasion that it was her purpose to accept him; and favourable as was the moment for a sort of universal philanthropy and unrestrained épanchement de coeur, she could not resist the impulse which led her to withdraw her hand, and return his affectionate smile with a look of coldness and reserve.

Perfectly undaunted, however, the gay Frederick continued to look at her with an air of the most happy confidence; but suddenly, as it seemed, recollecting that it was possible, though they had all of them been at least ten minutes in the room together, no explanation might have yet reached her, he said, in a manner to show that he was too happy to be very grave, though quite sufficiently in earnest to deserve belief—"If you accept my Nora for a sister, Agnes, you must accept me for a brother too. She knows that till I saw her I thought you the most charming person in the world; and as she forgives me for this, I hope you will show as much resemblance to her in mind as in person, and forgive me for thinking, when I did see her, that she was still more charming than you?"

And then it was that Agnes for the first time in her life felt wholly, perfectly, and altogether happy. She saw in an instant, with the rapid glance of love, that all the misty cloud that had hung between her and Hubert was withdrawn for ever ... and then she felt how very delightful it was to have a father, and such an elegant, interesting-looking father ... and then she became fully aware what a blessing it was to have a sister, and that sister so beautiful, and so capable of inspiring love in every heart ... save one, guarded as Hubert's was guarded. Her joy, her new-born gladness of spirit, danced in her eyes, as she now freely returned the young man's laughing glance, and restoring to him the hand she had withdrawn, she exclaimed, "Oh! Frederick ... why did you not answer Hubert's letter, and tell him this?"

"It is so, then?... it is as I hoped, my sweet Agnes?... and you will be doubly our sister?... Why did I not answer Hubert's letter? Because it was the most mystical, unintelligible, dark, and diplomatic performance that ever was put forth. Did you see it, Agnes?"

"No, I did not," she replied, with a smile; "but I can imagine that it might have been a little in that style. Yet still you should have answered it."

"I did answer it—that is, I replied to it by a line or two written in a prodigious hurry; but you must perceive that I could not enclose Nora in a cover; and as she is, to all intents and purposes, my answer, I was obliged to let him wait till I could convey her properly, and place her before his eyes and his understanding."

"And so convince him," replied Agnes, with another smile, full of her new-born gaiety, "that the moment she is seen all other ladies must be forgotten ... prove that to Colonel Hubert, Mr. Stephenson, and I will prove to you" ...

"What?—you tremendous-looking sibyl, what?"

"A very fatal sister!" she replied; and then the door opened, and Lady Stephenson preceded the two gentlemen she had brought from the dining-parlour, into the room.

Agnes, no longer the fearful, shrinking Agnes, sprang forward to meet them, and taking Colonel Hubert by the hand, led him to her father, saying in an altered accent, that at once entered his heart, and told him that all was right—"Let me present you to my father, Hubert—to my dear father, Colonel Hubert; he will indeed be doubly dear to us, for he has brought with him a sister for both of us, whom I feel sure we shall for ever love."

But hardly did Agnes, who seemed newly awakened from some heavy spell that had benumbed her heart—hardly did she give time for a courteous greeting between the gentlemen, ere she passed her arm beneath that of Colonel Hubert, and led him to the sofa. Frederick started forward to meet him, and laying a hand on each shoulder, said in his ear, yet not so low but that Agnes heard him too—"It was lucky I did not take you to France with me, Hubert, or I should certainly never have got a wife at all; as it is, however, permit me"—he added aloud—"to present you, Colonel Hubert, to Miss Nora Willoughby. Nora, dearest, this gentleman is the best friend I have in the world—my brother's wife is his sister, and your sister, my fair bride elect, will very soon be his wife, or I cannot read the stars ... so, as you may perceive, our catastrophe is exceedingly like that great model of all catastrophes, in which the happy hero says ... 'And these are all my near relations—ecce signum, here is my own elder brother. Sir Edward Stephenson, Miss Nora Willoughby. Is she not charming, Edward? I hope I have pleased you at last, and their ladyships, my sisters, too, for I assure you everything is very elegant, well-born, and so forth.... But you are not to sit down by her though, for all that, unless you make room for me between you, for she has already given away more smiles than I can at all afford to spare; and, besides, I have a hundred things to say to her ... I want to ask her how she likes you all."

Colonel Hubert, as soon as his gay friend had reseated himself, gave one speaking look to Agnes, and then devoted himself entirely to Mr. Willoughby.

By degrees, the party began to talk together with less of agitation and more of comfort; but Frederick was not permitted wholly to engross his young fianceé, for all the ladies crowded round her, and vied with each other in giving a cordial welcome to this young foreigner on the land of her fathers. She was in truth a very sweet young creature, and soon converted the kindness which circumstances called for, into very cordially liking. Distant hopes were talked of without reserve, and immediate arrangements canvassed. Miss Compton kindly invited the young stranger to share her sister's apartment, a servant was despatched to secure rooms for Mr. Willoughby and Frederick at the hotel, and the happiness their unexpected arrival had brought to two harassed hearts of the party seemed to diffuse itself very delightfully among them all.

At length, Miss Compton's carriage was announced, and while the cloaks of the fair sisters were wrapped round them by their vowed servants, Mr. Willoughby performed the same office for her, and took that opportunity of asking leave to wait upon her on the following morning, in order to relate to her such passages of the history of his long exile as might, in some degree, account for his having left her adopted child for so many years without a father.

While this appointment was making with the aunt, the niece contrived, unheard by all, to whisper a word or two which led to an appointment for her also.

Colonel Hubert had more than once that evening taught her to understand, by the eloquence of looks, the delightful change that had been wrought within him; but it was Agnes who first found the opportunity of giving expression to it in words. He stood behind her as he arranged her cloak, and when this was done, she turned suddenly round to him, and said, in an accent of playful reproach, "Hubert!... may I be happy now?"

His answer was, "Will you see me to-morrow?... and alone?" She blushed—perhaps at remembering how often she had before wished to converse with him in the manner he now for the first time proposed, but she nodded her assent; he handed her to the carriage, pressed her hand, and whispered "eleven o'clock" as he put her into it, and then mounted to his chamber without exchanging a word more with any living soul, that he might enjoy, for the first time since he had yielded up his heart, the luxury of meditating on Agnes and her promised love, without any mixture of self-reproach to poison the enjoyment.

CHAPTER XVII

GREAT CONTENTMENT

Had not Nora Willoughby been an interesting and amiable creature, her introduction at this moment to all the freedom of a sister's rights would certainly have been less agreeable than surprising to Agnes; and perhaps, notwithstanding the sweet expression of her lovely face, the pretty tenderness of her manner, and the lively interest which one so near in blood could not fail to awaken, Agnes, as she entered her bed-room on that eventful night, would rather have entered it alone. Her heart seemed too full to permit her conversing freely with any one; and it was by an effort not made altogether without pain, that she turned her thoughts from Hubert and all that vast world of happiness which appeared opening before them, to welcome her fair sister to her bower, and to begin such a conversation with her, as sisters so placed might be expected to hold. But she was soon rewarded for the exertion, for it was quite impossible to pass an hour of intimate intercourse with Nora without loving her, for she was made up of frankness, warm affection, light-heartedness, and sweet temper.

As soon as Peggy had performed all the services required of her, and that the door was fairly closed behind her, Nora threw her arms round the neck of Agnes, and pressed her in a long and fond embrace.

"Dear, dear Agnes!" she exclaimed, "I wish you could share the pleasure that I enjoy at this moment—but it is impossible ... I come upon you suddenly, unexpectedly, unintelligibly, and must rather startle and astound, than give you the delight that you give me. For I have been preparing to love you for many weeks past, and have been longing till I was almost sick to get to you. And after such eager and sanguine expectations as mine, it is so delightful to find oneself not disappointed!"

"And is such the case with my sweet sister?" replied Agnes caressingly.

"Indeed, indeed it is!—Frederick told me you were very beautiful—but I did not expect to find you half so ... so elegant, so finished, so every way superior."

"I shall quarrel with you, Nora, if you say such very fine things to me.... Perhaps I think you very pretty, too, dear; but if I do, I must not say so, because they tell us that we are so much alike, it would be like admiring myself."

"Well!... and you cannot help admiring yourself, it is impossible.... But, sister Agnes, what a blessing it was that you did not happen to fall in love with Frederick! What would have become of me if you had?... for do you know, I loved almost as soon as I saw him. It was all so odd! It was at the Italian opera that we first met; and I could not help observing, that the handsomest man I had ever seen was looking at me almost incessantly. Papa never saw a bit about it, for when he is listening to music he never cares for anything. However, I do assure you, I tried to behave properly, though, if I had done quite the contrary, papa would never have found it out. I never looked at him at all above three or four times, and that was accidentally from happening to turn round my head. But whether I thought about it or not, there were his beautiful large eyes always sure to be fixed upon me; and when the opera was over, he must have run out of his box the moment we left ours, for I saw him as we got into the fiacre, standing close beside it. Well, I hardly know how it happened, but from that time I never stirred out without meeting him; he never spoke of course, but that did not prevent our knowing one another just as well as if we had been the oldest acquaintance. At last, however, he managed very cleverly to find out that papa was acquainted with M. Dupont, who gives such beautiful concerts, and receives all the English so hospitably, and he asked as a great favour to be invited to meet us; and so he was, and then we were introduced, and then everything went on beautifully, for he knew you, and the name of Willoughby, and the likeness, and all that, convinced him that we must be the same family; so he and papa very soon made it all out, and then he came to call upon us every day; and very, very, very soon afterwards I was engaged to be his wife as soon as possible, after we all got back to England."

"Thank you, dearest Nora!" replied Agnes, who, notwithstanding all her pre-occupation, had found no difficulty in listening very attentively to this narrative; "I cannot tell you all the pleasure your little history has given me.... There is nobody in the world I should like so well for a brother as Frederick Stephenson, and there is nobody in the world I should like so well for a sister as Frederick Stephenson's wife."

"That is delightful!" cried Nora, joyfully, "and we certainly are two of the luckiest girls in the world to have everything just as we would wish.... But, Agnes, there is one thing I shall never understand.... How could you help falling in love with Frederick when he fell in love with you?"

"Because I happened just then," replied Agnes, laughing, "to be falling in love with some one else."

"Well! certainly that was the most fortunate thing in the world ... and Frederick himself thinks so now. He told me that he had a great mind to shoot himself when you refused him, but that the very first moment he saw me, he felt certain that I should suit him a great deal better than you would have done."

"That I am sure is quite true, Nora," replied Agnes, very earnestly, "for I too feel certain that I never could have suited anybody but Colonel Hubert.... And now, my sweet sister, let us go to sleep, or we shall hardly be up early enough to meet the friends who, I think, will be wishing to see us again.... Good night, dearest!"

"Good night, darling Agnes!... Is not it pleasant to have a sister, Agnes?... It is so nice to be able to tell you everything.... I am sure I could never be able to do it to anybody else. Goodnight!"

"Bless you, sweet Nora!" replied Agnes; and then, each nestling upon her pillow, and giving some few happy dreamy thoughts to the object they loved best, they closed their fair young eyes, and slept till morning.

The waking was to both of them, perhaps, somewhat like the continuance of a dream; but Peggy came and threw the light of day upon them, while each fair girl seemed to look at her own picture as she contemplated her pretty bedfellow, and appeared to be exceedingly well pleased by the survey.

It was already late, and Agnes, rapidly as she was learning to love her companion, did not linger at her toilet, but leaving Nora, with a hasty kiss, to the care of Peggy, she hastened to the breakfast-table, and made aunt Betsy's heart glad, by telling her at last, that she expected Colonel Hubert would call about eleven o'clock, and that if she did not think it wrong, she should like to speak to him for a few minutes alone.

"Wrong, my child!" exclaimed Miss Compton; "why, I never in my life read a work painting the manners of the age, in which I did not find interviews, sometimes occurring three or four times in a day, entirely tête-à-tête, between the parties."

"Then I may go into the back drawing-room presently ... may I, aunt Betsy?... And perhaps you would tell William...."

"Yes, yes, my dear, I'll tell him everything.... But eat some breakfast, Agnes, or I am sure you will not be able to talk.... I suppose it is about your new sister, and your father, and all that, that you want to speak to him."

"There are many things, aunt Betsy.... But, good heavens! there is a knock.... Will it not look very odd for you to send him in to me?"

Without waiting to give an answer, the agile old lady intercepted William's approach to the door in time to give the order she wished; and in two minutes more Colonel Hubert was ushered into a room where the happy but blushing Agnes was alone.

His first few steps towards her were made at the pace at which drawing-room floors are usually traversed, but the last part of the distance was cleared by a movement considerably more rapid, for she had risen in nervous agitation as he approached, and for the first time that he had ever ventured a caress, he threw his arms around her, and pressed her to his heart. Agnes struggled not to disengage herself, but wept without restraint upon his bosom.

"You do then love me, Agnes?... At last, at last our hearts have met, and never can be severed more! But still you must tell me very often that you have forgiven me, dearest, for is it not difficult to believe? And does it not require frequent vouching?"

"What is it, Montague, that you would have forgiven?" said Agnes, looking up at him, and smiling through her tears.

This was the first time that her lips had pronounced his christian name to any ears but her own, and she blushed as she uttered it.

"Agnes! my own Agnes!" he exclaimed, "you have forgiven me, or you would not call me Montague!... How is it possible," he continued, looking fondly at her, "that a word so hackneyed and familiar from infancy as our own name can be made to thrill through the whole frame like a touch of electricity?"

He drew her to the sofa from which she had risen, and placing himself by her, said, "Now, then, Agnes, let us sit down soberly together, and take an unvarnished retrospect of all that has passed since we first met.... Yet why should I ask for this?... I hate to think of it ... for it is a fact, Agnes, which his subsequent attachment to your sister must not make you doubt, Frederick and his seven thousand a year would have been at your disposal, had not my dissuasions prevented it.... And had this been so, who knows...."

A shade of melancholy seemed once again settling on the noble countenance of Colonel Hubert; Agnes could not bear it, and looking earnestly at him, she said,

"Montague! answer me sincerely this one question, which is the strongest feeling in your mind at this moment—the pleasure derived from believing that your influence on Frederick was so great, or the pain of doubting how the offer you speak of would have been received?"

"I have no pleasure in believing I have influence on any one, save yourself," he answered gravely.

"I am glad of that, Montague," she said, "because you somewhat overrated your influence with my brother elect. Save for your foolish doubts, infidel!... you never should have known it, but ... Frederick Stephenson did propose to me, Hubert, before he went abroad."

"And you refused him, Agnes!"

"And I refused him, Hubert."

"Oh! had I known this earlier, what misery should I have been spared!" cried Colonel Hubert. "You know not, you could not know all I have suffered, Agnes ... yet surely, dearest! when last we spoke together, it was but yesterday, in this very room, you must then have guessed the cause of the dreadful restraint that kept us asunder."

"There was no need of guessing then," replied Agnes, smiling, "for you told me so distinctly."

"Then why not on the instant remove the load from my heart?... were you quite incapable of feeling how galling it must have been to me?"

"I'll tell you how that came to pass," said Agnes, rising.... "Do you sit still there, as I did yesterday, and say, 'Let me then confess to you, Colonel Hubert,' ... and then I will answer thus," ... and raising her hand, as if to stop his speech, she added, mimicking his impatient tone,

"'Confess nothing, Miss Willoughby, to me!'... And then you told me you had written to him, and when I exclaimed, with some degree of dismay at the idea of your having written to recall him, you again interrupted me by saying that you would do it again ... and then my aunt came, and so we parted.... Then whose fault was it that I did not tell you?"

"My own, Agnes, it was my own; and alas!... I did not suffer for it alone.... How wretched you must have been made by my vehemence!... But you have forgiven me, and all this must be forgotten for ever.... There is, however, one subject on which I would willingly ask a few more questions—these, I hope, you will answer, Agnes?"

"Yes!" she replied, gaily, "you may hope for an answer to all your questions ... provided, that just when I am about to speak, you do not raise your arm thus, in order to prevent me."

"I will do my utmost to avoid it," he replied, "and for the greater security will place the offending arm thus," ... throwing it round her; "and now tell me, Agnes, why it was that you would not accept Frederick Stephenson?"

"And will you be pleased to tell me, Colonel Hubert, why it was that you did not propose to ... to anybody else, but me?"

"Because I loved you, and you only."

"Because I loved you, and you only," repeated Agnes.

"Is that an echo?" said Colonel Hubert.

"No!" replied Agnes ... "it is only the answer to your question."

"Then, exactly when I was occupied in finding reasons incontrovertible why the niece of Mrs. Barnaby should never be loved by mortal man, the young, the lovely Agnes Willoughby was loving me?"

"Even so," said Agnes, somewhat mournfully; "false impressions have worked us so much woe, that it would not be wise to let a little feminine punctilio prevent you seeing things as they are.... Yet it is hardly fair, Hubert, to make me tell you this...."

"Oh, say not so!" he replied; "mistake not the source of this questioning, for, Agnes, be secure

'That Hubert, for the wealth of all the world,
Would not offend thee!'

But can you wonder that, after all I have suffered, my heart and soul thirsts for an assurance of your love? What might well suffice another, Agnes, ought not to suffice me.... I am so much older...."

"I cannot help it, Montague ... nor could I help it when you took me out of the clutches of Major Allen, upon the Windmill-hill, nor when you were pleased to be so gracious as to approve my singing ... nor upon a great many other occasions, when it would have been wise for me to remember it, perhaps. But if I love you, and you love me, I cannot see how your age or mine either need interfere to prevent it."

Perhaps at last Colonel Hubert arrived at the same satisfactory conclusion, for the conversation was a long one; and before it was ended, some little sketchings of his feelings during the early part of their acquaintance brought to Agnes' mind the soothing belief, that after the evening of the Clifton ball her image had never forsaken his fancy more, though it was by slow degrees that it had grown into what he called such "terrible strength" there, as to conquer every other feeling.

Agnes listened to him as he stated this with most humble-minded and unfeigned astonishment, but also with most willing belief, and then, following his example, he quoted Shakspeare, exclaiming—

"And if an angel should have come to me
And told me thus,
I would have believed no tongue but Hubert's."

CHAPTER XVIII

A RETROSPECT AND CONCLUSION

Mr. Willoughby was little less punctual to his appointment than Colonel Hubert; and as the young Nora, weary with her journey, and exhausted from the excitement of the scenes which followed it, had not yet left her bed, he too, had the advantage of a tête-à-tête.

It is needless to enter upon any minute repetition of a narrative which had, in fact, little or no connexion with the personages of our drama. It was evident that Mr. Willoughby had suffered much, both from the early loss of his fair young wife, and the continued hostility, or, more properly speaking, the continued neglect of his family. He had exchanged into a regiment sent on a dangerous and, disagreeable service, and with broken spirits and failing health, might very likely have perished before it was ended, had not his "good gifts" very suddenly made captive the affections of a young girl almost as pretty as poor Sophia Compton, and quite as rich as she was the contrary.

This marriage converted him into the only son and heir of a wealthy merchant; all his new family required of him, in exchange for their daughter and their wealth, was, that he should live amongst them. This he consented to do, but his life was not a happy one. With the prospect of great possessions before him, he was kept in almost penniless dependence upon his father-in-law; all his wants, indeed, profusely supplied, but with no more power to assist in the maintenance of the child he had left in England, than if he had been a slave chained to the oar.

For sixteen years he had led this painful life of penniless splendour, in the course of which he was again left a widower with one little girl; but though his existence in his father-in-law's family had lost its only charm by this event, he was prevented from making any effort to change it, as much by his total inability to support himself elsewhere, as by consideration for the interest of his child. As she grew up, he began once more to feel that life was not altogether a bore and a burden, and at length his passive submission to years of wearying annoyance was rewarded by finding himself, at the death of the generous but tyrannical Mr. Grafton, the possessor of a handsome life income, and the sole guardian of the young heiress his daughter.

It was then that, for the first time, he felt disposed to recall himself to the memory of those he had left behind him in England; and the desire to do so became so strong, that he lost no time in finally arranging his affairs in the country of his exile, and taking his departure for Europe. For the sake of having a friend as commander of the ship in which he sailed, he took his passage for Havre, and, once landed on the coast of France, he yielded to Nora's entreaties that they should pass a few weeks at Paris before they left it. His accidental meeting with Mr. Stephenson there was then related, and its consequences as it respected his daughter, and their journey home together, concluded his narration.

"Your romance, Mr. Willoughby," replied Miss Compton, "appears likely to come to a very happy conclusion ... but I confess I wonder that never during your sixteen years of what appears to have been very perfect leisure, you could never have found time to make any single inquiry about your little Agnes."

"And I wonder at it too, Miss Compton ... but it is more easy to recal the feelings that led to this, than to explain them. I believe that the total impossibility of my transmitting any share of the wealth amidst which I lived to a child whom I had great reason to fear might want it, was the primary cause of it ... and then came the hope that at no very distant day my inquiries for her might be made in a manner less torturing to my feelings than by acknowledging myself to be alive, in circumstances of high-fed pauperism, without the power of relieving any wants, however pressing, with which my inquiries might happen to make me acquainted. Had I known that you, Miss Compton, had adopted my little girl, I should not so long have suffered her to believe me dead, because I had not the power of making my being alive a source of joy to her."

Whether Miss Compton thought this apology a good one, or the reverse, does not appear; for all the branches of the party who so unexpectedly met together at the house of Lady Elizabeth Norris, continued from that time forward to live on terms of the most agreeable amity together; and perhaps the only symptom by which some little feeling of disapprobation might have been perceived, was Miss Compton's begging to decline, on the part of all interested, Mr. Willoughby's proposal of insuring his life for ten thousand pounds, as a portion for his eldest daughter.

"I do assure you, sir, there is no occasion for it," said the little spinster, with great good-humour, but also with a very evident intention of having her own way.... "I believe that if you will mention the subject to Colonel Hubert, or to Lady Elizabeth Norris, his aunt, you will find that they both agree with me in thinking such a sacrifice of income on your part quite unnecessary, and decidedly unwise. Your sisters have not behaved to you kindly, but they have connected themselves well, and I believe we all think it would be more advantageous to both your daughters that their favour should be propitiated by your appearing before them in a style which may show you have no need of their assistance, than by anything else you can do for them. The young ladies are both about to marry well, and with fortunes very fairly proportioned to those of their respective husbands, and any family coolness with such near relations as Lady Eastcombe and the honourable Mrs. Nivett would be both disadvantageous and disagreeable."

"My noble sisters will be vastly well disposed to welcome me now, Miss Compton, I have little doubt," replied Mr. Willoughby, with as much asperity as he was capable of feeling for any offence committed against him; "and I confess to you that the reconciliation would be particularly agreeable to me, from the power your generous adoption of my poor girl gives me now of proving to them that my marriage with Sophia Compton was not such a connexion as to merit the severity with which they have treated it."

"I have no sort of objection to your proving this to them in any manner that you please," replied Miss Compton; "and I rather think the most effectual mode of doing so will be, by permitting the portion of Agnes to be furnished by Sophia Compton's aunt."

"Five thousand, then, let it be, Miss Compton; five thousand settled upon younger children," said Mr. Willoughby.

"No, sir," persisted the old lady, "it must not be, if you please. The property of Compton Basett, with the name, and a sum of money withal sufficient considerably to add to and improve the estate, will be settled by me on the second son of your daughter Agnes. Lady Elizabeth, on the part of her nephew, adds ten thousand pounds to the settlement on younger children, which, together with my property, will of course belong to Agnes for her life. I hope, sir, this statement will satisfy you repsecting the provision to be made for Miss Willoughby, and prevent your feeling any further anxiety on the subject."

It was impossible Mr. Willoughby could declare himself dissatisfied, and from this time he ventured no further allusion to the scheme of insuring his life.

Preparations for the two marriages now immediately began; and the interval necessary to the completion of settlements, and the building of carriages and dresses, was, at the earnest request of Agnes, to be spent at Clifton. She loved the place, for it was identified in her memory with the first sight of Hubert, and she often declared that there was no spot on the earth's surface she should ever love so well as that little esplanade behind the windmill on which Colonel Hubert first offered her his arm, without deeming it necessary to utter a word of explanation for doing so. The vicinity of Mary Peters, too, was another reason, and no trifling one, for this partiality; and as not one of the party had any point of reunion to plead for in preference, it was there that several weeks of present enjoyment and happy anticipation were passed.

It was about midway between the time at which everything was settled between the lovers, their beloveds, and all parents, friends, and guardians interested therein, and the happy day on which the double espousals were celebrated, that Mr. and Mrs. Peters invited the whole party to dinner. No strangers were permitted to disturb the freedom of the society thus assembled at dinner, though, to gratify Lady Elizabeth's love of music, one or two proficients in that science were invited for the evening. The gentlemen, who probably thought the society in the drawing-room more agreeable than that of good Mr. Peters, even though backed by his excellent wine, were already partaking coffee with the ladies, when a reduplicated knocking announced the arrival of visiters.

"The Chamberlains, I suppose," said Mrs. Peters. "How very early they are!"

But she was mistaken, it was not the Chamberlains; for a footman threw wide the drawing-room door, and announced "Mr. and Mrs. O'Donagough!"

"Mr. and Mrs. who?" said Mrs. Peters to Mary.

"Mr. and Mrs. what?" said Elizabeth to Lucy.

But before the parties thus questioned could have found time to answer, even had they been possessed of the information required, a lady in sober coloured silk, with little rouge and no ringlets, followed by a handsome young man in black, entered the room, and considerably before many who had seen that lady before could recall the name by which they had known her, or reconcile her much changed appearance to their puzzled recollections, Mrs. Peters was enfolded in her arms.

"My dear sister Peters!" said Mrs. O'Donagough, "you are surrounded by so large a party, that I fear these last moments which I meant to dedicate to the affection of my kinsfolk, may be more inconvenient than pleasurable to you. But you cannot, I am sure, refuse me some portion of your society this evening, as it is probably the last one we shall ever pass together. Give me leave, sister Peters, to introduce you to my husband, the Reverend Mr. O'Donagough. Mr. Peters, Mr. O'Donagough; Mr. James Peters, Mr. O'Donagough; Mr. O'Donagough, my dear Mary; my husband, young ladies; Mr. O'Donagough, my dear Elizabeth and Lucy! Good Heaven! Agnes here? and my aunt Compton, too!... Well, so much the better, my dear Patrick; I shall now have the pleasure of presenting you to more relations, and as I should be proud to introduce you to all the world, this can only be an increase of pleasure to me. Agnes Willoughby, my dear, I can't say you behaved very well to me when the cheerful sort of life I indulged in, solely on your account, was changed for sorrow and imprisonment; but, nevertheless, my religious principles, which are stronger, my dear, than even when you knew me, lead me to forgive you, and, better still, they lead me to introduce you to your excellent and exemplary uncle, the Reverend Mr. O'Donagough."

During the whole course of these speeches not a single voice had been heard to pronounce a syllable in reply, excepting that of Mr. Peters, who put his heels together and made a bow when she paused, husband in hand, before him, and said, "Your servant, sir!"

But Agnes, when her turn came, though colouring most painfully at being so addressed, and with her heart sinking under the unexampled annoyance of this intrusion, contrived to say, "I hope I see you well, aunt."

"Yes, Miss Agnes; well, and happy too, I promise you; and I wish you were likely to be as well settled, child, as I am. But I should like to know who it is has come forward with money to dress you up so?... You have not been singing on the stage, I hope?... Your uncle would be dreadfully shocked at such a thing; for he says that stage-plays are an abomination.... And upon my word, aunt Compton, you are grown mighty smart too in your old age. Mercy on me!... Vanity of vanities!... all is vanity!"... And then looking into the inner room, and perceiving that she had several more acquaintances there, she again took her husband by the hand and led him into it, presenting him to Lady Elizabeth, her niece, Colonel Hubert, and the two Stephensons. But when she came to Mr. Willoughby, who was standing with his youngest daughter at a window, she stopped, and looking at him very earnestly, seemed puzzled.

He bowed, though evidently without knowing her, and then, turning from her unpleasantly curious scrutiny, resumed his conversation with Nora.

"I beg your pardon, sir," said Mrs. O'Donagough ... "but I should really be very much obliged if you would tell me your name."

"My name, madam, is Willoughby."

"Gracious heaven!" exclaimed the bride, "O'Donagough, dearest, this is an eventful day indeed.... Behold your brother!"

The two gentlemen stared at each other with an expression of countenance more indicative of surprise than of fraternal affection ... Mr. Willoughby, indeed, looked very much as if he suspected that the poor lady, be she who she would, was decidedly not in her right mind; while her husband, rather weary, perhaps, of such a continuity of introductions, escaped from her side, and stationed himself at another window.

"Willoughby!... dearest Willoughby!... Is it possible that you can have forgotten me?... Can you, indeed, have forgotten the sister of your wife?"

"Miss Martha?... Is it possible?... I beg your pardon, Mrs. Donagough ... I certainly did not recollect you. I hope that I have the pleasure of seeing you well?"

"My dearest Willoughby!... You have no idea how exceedingly delighted I am to see you.... What has become of you all this time?... I always supposed that you had been sold for a slave on the coast of Barbary ... and I thank God, and my excellent husband ... where is he?... I am sure the Reverend Mr. O'Donagough will thank God for your escape.... And who is that pretty young lady?... Dear me, she looks very much as if she was the daughter of your cruel master, and had fallen in love with you, and set you at liberty.... Poor Sophy!... one could not expect you should remember her for ever ... even I, you see, have forced myself to forget my poor dear Mr. Barnaby.... But now I think of it, you can't know anything about Mr. Barnaby.... Do, my dear Willoughby, sit down with me on this sofa, and let us have a talk."

It was impossible for Mr. Willoughby to refuse, even had he wished it, which he really did not; and the perfect security of being welcome, which Mrs. O'Donagough displayed in her manner of establishing herself, in some sort obliged Mrs. Peters to act as if she were so.... The different groups which had been deranged by her entrance, resumed their conversation; coffee and tea included the intruders in its round, and everybody excepting Miss Compton seemed once more tolerably at their ease. She could not affect to recover her equanimity like the rest, but placing a low chair immediately behind the sofa on which Lady Elizabeth's tall figure was placed, she sat down so as to be completely concealed by her, saying, "Will your ladyship have the great kindness to let me hide myself here?... That horrible woman is, I confess it, my own brother's daughter, but she is ... no matter what she is.... I am much to blame, no doubt, ... but I hate to look upon her."

"Put yourself quite at your ease, Miss Compton," replied Lady Elizabeth, laughing; "I have not the least difficulty in the world in comprehending your feelings. In you she has conquered the feeling of relationship; in me, an instinct stronger still perhaps, namely, that of finding amusement in absurdity. But I almost think she has cured me of my menagerie caprice for ever. Yet it is difficult, too, not to enjoy the spectacle she offers with her young husband in her hand. But I don't mean to lose my music for her.... Miss Peters, my dear—pray set your pianoforte going."

This hint was immediately obeyed, and proved extremely conducive to the general ease. Good-natured Mr. Peters entered into conversation with the reverend missionary, and soon learnt both his destination, and the interesting fact that he and his bride were to sail from the port of Bristol the day but one following. This he judiciously took an opportunity of speedily communicating to his lady, who took care that it should not long remain a secret to any individual present, excepting Mr. Willoughby, who continued in too close conversation with his sister-in-law to permit his being made a sharer in the general feeling of satisfaction which this information produced. Even Miss Compton, on hearing it, declared, that if the bride were really going to set off immediately for Botany Bay, there to remain for the term of her natural life, she thought she should be able to look at her for the rest of the evening with great philosophy. And, in proof of her sincerity, she moved her place, and seated herself beside her friend Lady Elizabeth, more than half inclined to share in the amusement, which, notwithstanding her good resolutions, that facetious lady seemed inclined to take in contemplating the newly-married pair.

The conversation, meanwhile, between the two old acquaintances, went on with considerable interest on both sides. Mr. Willoughby again related his adventures, and introduced his pretty daughter, and then, recurring once more to Silverton, Mrs. O'Donagough said, in an accent that betokened considerable interest in the question—"Willoughby!—can you tell me anything about your old friend Tate?"

"I have heard nothing of him of late years; but of course you know that he married his cousin, Miss Temple, very soon after we left Silverton."

"Very soon?" said Mrs. O'Donagough, with a sigh.

"Yes, my dear sister," replied Willoughby, with a melancholy smile; "it is not often that hearts, lost in country quarters, fail to return to the losers as they march out of the town. Happily both for the boys and girls concerned, but few such adventures end as mine did."

"Happily, indeed, for me!" replied the bride, with a toss of her head: "for aught I know, Tate may be alive now ... and the happy wife of O'Donagough may well rejoice that no such thraldom was the consequence of Captain Tate's presumptuous attachment!"

Though Mr. Peters was really very civil, and though Mr. James joined for several minutes in the conversation, it is probable that the reverend missionary did not enjoy it so much as his lady did listening to Mr. Willoughby; for at an early hour he told her it was time to take leave. She instantly obeyed, and began making her circular farewell—a ceremony of rather an embarrassing nature to many of the party, for out of the fifteen persons she left in the room, she kissed eight; Lady Elizabeth, Sir Edward and Lady Stephenson, Colonel Hubert, and Frederick, being permitted to escape without even an attempt at joining them in this valedictory greeting, and Miss Compton, rising at her approach, making her by far the lowest courtesy her knees ever performed, in a manner which effectually averted it from herself.

Mrs. O'Donagough's departure from England was a great blessing to all the connexions she left behind, for, had she continued within reach of them, it is hardly possible but some annoyance would have been the consequence. As it was, however, sorrow seemed to depart with her; for seldom does so large a portion of happiness as fell to the lot of those she had formerly tormented, attend the career of any.

Colonel Hubert, although he actually did very soon become a general, never again felt any alarm on the score of his age, but had the happiness of knowing that he was beloved with all the devoted tenderness that his heart desired, and his noble character deserved. Agnes never ceased to glory in her choice, and loved nothing better than to make Aunt Betsy confess that her great nephew, notwithstanding his being a general, was more like a hero than any other man she had ever seen. Miss Compton lived to see an extremely fine lad, called Compton Hubert Compton, becoming so fond of the fields and the pheasants of Compton Basett, as to leave her no rest till she had persuaded the trustees of the settlement she had made to expend the money in their hands upon the purchase of some neighbouring lands,—including the manor in which they were situated, and the converting of the old roomy farm-house into a residence which she confessed to be worthy of the representative of the ancient Compton race. This alteration, indeed, took place several years before the old lady died, and it was at Compton Basett, thus metamorphosed, that she had the pleasure of observing to Mrs. Wilmot, that the conversation they had held on that spot together, had not been altogether without effect.

Mr. Willoughby and his elegant sisters become perfectly reconciled, a circumstance extremely agreeable to Lady Elizabeth Norris, as it gave her repeated opportunities of convincing herself that the nose of her niece, Mrs. General Hubert, was decidedly an improvement upon that of the honourable Miss Nivett, though the family resemblance was sufficiently remarkable. Frederick and Nora were as gay and happy a couple as ever enjoyed ten thousand a year together. Occasionally, of course, they were in debt, as all people of ten thousand a year must be; but, on the whole, they contrived to bring matters round wonderfully well, and as their property was fortunately settled, and Sir Edward happened to die without children, their family of six sons and six daughters were left at last very tolerably provided for.

Mrs. O'Donagough's voyage to New England was quite as agreeable as such a voyage generally is; and on arriving, she was greatly consoled for any little inequalities in her young husband's temper by the great success of his preaching. For at least six months after their arrival, he was more in the fashion than any gentleman of any profession had ever been before; but at the end of that time, the reverend preacher unfortunately was present at a horse-race, upon which the recondite wisdom of the fable, which treats of a cat turned into a woman, must have become manifest to every reflecting mind acquainted with the circumstances of Mr. O'Donagough's early life; for no sooner did the race begin, than almost unconsciously he offered a bet to one of his congregation who stood near him; and before the end of the day, he was seen mounted in a blue and yellow jacket, riding for a jockey who had broken his leg in a hurdle race.

It was then that Mrs. O'Donagough became sensible of the blessing of having a settlement; and thankful was she to the noble father of her spouse for all the care bestowed to prevent his bringing himself again to penury, when he was brought home dead to her one fine afternoon, having lost his seat and his life together in a leap upon which he had betted considerably more than he possessed.

She mourned for him as he deserved; but not being upon this occasion very nice upon whom she could devolve the task of wearing black, she announced to all her Sidney friends that it was not the fashion in the old world for ladies of distinction to wear that dismal colour for more than a month for any husband who died by accident; and it was, therefore, once more, in all the splendour of her favourite rainbow colouring that she met a few months afterwards her old friend Major Allen.

He entered into no very tedious or particular details respecting the reasons for, or the manner of, his voyage out, but testified much cordial satisfaction at the meeting; while, on the other hand, Mrs. O'Donagough was as remarkably communicative as he was the reverse, dilating largely on my Lord —'s careful attention to her interest on her marriage with his son, who had insisted upon coming out in a fit of religious enthusiasm, which, as she sensibly observed, was not at all likely to last.

It was not very long after this meeting that Mrs. O'Donagough became aware of the truth of the song, which says,

"Mais on retourne toujours
A ses premières amours."

For it was evident that the sentiment which circumstances had so rudely shaken at Clifton a year or two before, was again putting forth its leaves and flowers, and that it depended upon herself alone whether she should not yet become the wife of the accomplished Major Allen.

For a few weeks she struggled with her remaining affection, but at the end of that time it overpowered all her doubts and fears, and only stipulating that, as before, all she had should be firmly settled upon herself, she once more entered the holy state of matrimony. In justice to the peerage, it ought to be stated, that on this her third wedding-day she wore around her neck a very handsome necklace of shell, carefully sent out to her by the confidential agent of my Lord Mucklebury.

Frances Milton Trollope – A Short Biography

Frances Milton Trollope was born on March 10th, 1779 at Stapleton in Bristol.

She was the third daughter of the Reverend William Milton and Mary, née Gresley. Her mother died after the birth of a son, and her father was now left with three children to raise. It was a difficult and traumatic time.

As a young girl Frances was widely read and was able to read English, French, and Italian literature.

In 1803, her brother Henry Milton was employed in the War Office and moved to Bloomsbury in London.
Her father remarried to Sarah Partington, who Frances didn't like and so, together with her sister Mary, moved in with her brother Henry.

She married, at age 30, Thomas A Trollope, a barrister, at Heckfield in Hampshire on May 23rd, 1809. Frances had seven children but the marriage was to prove difficult due to Thomas' financial misfortunes, and, it was said, to his ill temper.

In 1827 Frances decided that a new life should be found and the family travelled to Fanny Wright's Utopian Community, the Nashoba Commune, in the United States. Unfortunately, the community was not much more than a malaria infested swamp near the Mississippi. The venture quickly failed and she was soon in Cincinnati, Ohio looking for ways to support them all.

This too was to end in failure and necessitated a return to England.

It was now that Frances decided that writing would provide the income and career to move the family on to a more stable footing, an ambition that to her seemed realistic despite nearing fifty years of age.

It was, of course, the beginnings of not only her own prolific and respected career, but also a literary dynasty. Her sons Anthony and Thomas Adolphus, together with his second wife, Frances, would become much lauded as writers.

Her first book, in 1832, Domestic Manners of the Americans, gained her immediate notice. Although it was a one sided view of the failings of Americans, as was a common prejudice among the English elite at the time, it was also witty and acerbic. A good piece of writing that now established her with a willing audience to whom she could now address further works.

More of the same, in all respects came with The Refugee in America and with, The Abbess, in 1833, she moved her view on social standing to social justice and anti-Catholicism, which was also the theme of Father Eustace in 1847.

Together with her son, Thomas Adolphus, she wrote works on travel, such as Belgium and Western Germany in 1833, Paris and the Parisians in 1835, and Vienna and the Austrians, this last one published in 1838.

But much of the attention she received was for her strong novels of social protest. Jonathan Jefferson Whitlaw, published in 1836, was the first anti-slavery novel, and was a great influence on the American writer Harriet Beecher Stowe and her more famous Uncle Tom's Cabin in 1852. Michael Armstrong: Factory Boy began publication in 1840 and was the first industrial novel to be published in Britain.

These were followed by three volumes of The Vicar of Wrexhill, which examined the corruption in the Church of England and evangelical circles.

However her greatest work is more often considered to be the Widow Barnaby trilogy (published between 1839–1843). This set a pattern of sequels which her son Anthony Trollope also used in his career.

In later years Frances Milton Trollope continued to write novels and books on wide, varied and miscellaneous subjects, writing in all in excess of a quite incredible 100 volumes.

In her time she was considered to have great powers of observation, together with a sharp and caustic wit. Her large output though somewhat diminished the impact of much of her work as did a more modern style of writing that was gaining traction and with it a more public criticism of books and arts by the rising mass of critics. Frances was unfairly scorned by some of them with the patronizing moniker of 'Fanny' Trollope.

Her novels were to rouse public conscience and incite social reforms that could help protect the various downtrodden groups, usually women and children and were influential in shaping subsequent women's writing.

In the modern age few of her works receive the readership they deserve. Gradually others are coming to the realization that she was an important author who wrote well, wrote much and brought many social causes to public attention.

Frances Milton Trollope died on October 6th, 1863.

She is buried nearby to four other members of the Trollope household in the English Cemetery of Florence.

Frances Milton Trollope – A Concise Bibliography

Major Works
Domestic Manners of the Americans (1832)
The Refugee in America (1832)
The Abbess (1833)
Belgium and Western Germany in 1833 (1834)
Paris and the Parisians in 1835 (1836)
The Life and Adventures of Jonathan Jefferson Whitlaw; or Scenes on the Mississippi (1836)
The Vicar of Wrexhill (1837)

Frances Trollope (1838),
Vienna and the Austrians (1838)
The Widow Barnaby (1839)
The Widow Married; A Sequel to the Widow Barnaby (1840)
Michael Armstrong: Factory Boy (published in 1840)
The Widow Wedded; or The Adventures of the Barnabys in America (1843)
Jessie Phillips: A Tale of the Present Day (1844)
Father Eustace (1847)
The Lottery of Marriage (1849)

CPSIA information can be obtained
at www.ICGtesting.com
Printed in the USA
LVHW072248110623
749486LV00008B/398